Dear Reader,

The period during and immediately after World War II was a very important time in my life. My husband and I had not been married very long when he was shipped out to serve in the South Pacific theater of war. I never imagined that it would be three lonely years before I would see him again. While he was away, I worked, like so many other wives, in an airplane factory. Then that glorious day came: The war was over. The men returned from the service to take up their lives with their families.

Although the song "Will You Still Be Mine" gave voice to the doubts and fears caused by long separations between couples, my husband and I started our family with less difficulty than Johnny and Kathleen, who meet in the novel WITH HEART. They are two people with such differences in upbringing and education that only love could bring them together. Kathleen, the new reporter for the *Rawlings Gazette,* and Johnny, the rancher who has rescued her from hijackers, are drawn to each other despite the odds. When AFTER THE PARADE takes place, Johnny has returned from the war and they need to face the misunderstandings that have grown up between them.

As I wrote these novels, memories came flooding back, as I hope they will to those of you who lived through those times. To those of you for whom World War II is history, I hope you will discover what life was like in those bitter years . . . and, as always, how important love is.

Dorothy Garlock

Praise for WITH HEART and AFTER THE PARADE

"Another winner! . . . Unique touches and continuous surprises that keep the reader enthralled and turning the pages . . . *With Heart* is a testament to the human spirit."
— BookbugOntheWeb.com

"[A] touching story of two people at cross purposes who struggle to save their marriage and get on with their lives after the Second World War."
— *Romantic Times BOOKclub Magazine*

"The story oozes with danger and intrigue. Ms. Garlock keeps the reader rooting for the lovers . . . A wonderful ending to a terrific series."
— *Rendezvous*

"Fast-paced, poignant . . . No one brings home small-town America in a more picturesque manner than bestselling author Dorothy Garlock."
— *Under the Covers Book Reviews*

Books by Dorothy Garlock

After the Parade
Almost Eden
Annie Lash
Dreamkeepers
Dream River
The Edge of Town
Forever Victoria
A Gentle Giving
Glorious Dawn
High on a Hill
Homeplace
Hope's Highway
Larkspur
The Listening Sky
Lonesome River
Love and Cherish
Loveseekers
Midnight Blue
More than Memory
Mother Road
Nightrose

On Tall Pine Lake
A Place Called Rainwater
Restless Wind
Ribbon in the Sky
River Rising
River of Tomorrow
The Searching Hearts
Sins of Summer
Song of the Road
Sweetwater
Tenderness
This Loving Land
Train from Marietta
Wayward Wind
Wild Sweet Wilderness
Wind of Promise
Wishmakers
With Heart
With Hope
With Song
Yesteryear

DOROTHY GARLOCK

Will You Still Be Mine?

WARNER BOOKS

NEW YORK   BOSTON

With Heart copyright © 1999 by Dorothy Garlock
After the Parade copyright © 2000 by Dorothy Garlock
Compilation copyright © 2007 by Dorothy Garlock
All rights reserved. Except as permitted under the U.S. Copyright Act of 1976, no part of this publication may be reproduced, distributed, or transmitted in any form or by any means, or stored in a database or retrieval system, without the prior written permission of the publisher.

Warner Books
Hachette Book Group USA
237 Park Avenue
New York, NY 10017

Visit our Web site at www.HachetteBookGroupUSA.com.

Printed in the United States of America

First Edition: June 2007
10 9 8 7 6 5 4 3 2 1

Warner Books and the "W" logo are trademarks of Time Warner Inc. or an affiliated company. Used under license by Hachette Book Group USA, which is not affiliated with Time Warner Inc.

ISBN: 9780446178518
LCCN: 2007920769

Contents

With Heart

INSIDE STORY

Extra! Extra! Read about it!
Murder Solved! Black headlines shout it.
Find details you want to get
On page one, *Rawlings Gazette*.

New reporter's Kathleen Dolan,
She will keep the presses rollin'.
Brains inside that head of bright red curly hair.
She's a lady, folks will find, is hard to scare.

Nearly victim of hijackin'
Till Johnny Henry sent thieves packin'.
She very kindly thanked him, never cried.
Got inside her little car and continued on her ride.

Now the girl who knew no fear
Trembles, with love, when Johnny's near.
But Johnny thinks her far above him,
Is sure that she can't love him.

Take a chance with her, John-boy.
.Don't let false fears deny your joy.
You rode a steer on rodeo day.
Grab life's horns! See what she'll say.

—F.S.I.

Chapter One

Tillison County, Oklahoma—1938

"Bury me not on the lone prair . . . ie
    where the coyotes howl and the wind blows free.
In a narrow grave—just six by three,
    Oh, bury me not—"

KATHLEEN STOPPED SINGING abruptly when she rounded a bend in the lonely stretch of Oklahoma highway and saw a dilapidated old car sitting crossways in the road. Her hands gripped the wheel of her old Nash as her feet hit the clutch and the brake at the same time.

"Oh Lord! Hijackers!"

She had read about them, had even written about them while working for a year at a small paper in Liberal, Kansas. Now a hijacking was happening to her! She put the car in reverse and started backing up. Out of the brush beside the road a man sprang up and ran toward the car. Afraid to look away from him and watch where she was going, she began to zigzag. Then, to her horror, the back wheels of the car sank into the ditch beside the road.

Quickly shifting gear into drive, she gunned the motor in an attempt to go forward. The wheels spun, digging deeper into the sandy soil.

The door beside her was flung open, and a big hairy hand gripped her wrist.

"Stop it! You'll strip the gears."

"Let go!" Kathleen jerked on her arm and tramped hard on the gas pedal. The engine roared.

"Stop or I'll break your goddamn arm!"

She looked into a flabby, whiskered face. The man's lips were drawn back showing tobacco-stained teeth. He twisted her arm cruelly.

"All right! All right!" she shouted.

"Get out!"

She took her foot off the clutch. The car jerked and the motor sputtered and died. When she was pulled from under the steering wheel, she fell to her knees next to two pairs of run-down boots planted in the red dirt beside her.

"What she got in there?" The second man peered into the back window of the car. "Jesus! It's loaded with stuff."

"We gotta get this thin' outta the goddamn ditch. You stupid-ass woman! I never met one a ya that had the brains of a suck-egg mule." He reached into the car and snatched Kathleen's purse off the seat. "Got any money?"

"No."

"Liar." He pulled two ten-dollar bills out of her purse. "This all you got?"

"No! I've got a dozen gold bars in the bottom!" Anger was replacing her fear. She had lost one of her shoes when she was pulled from the car. She reached down to get it.

"Watch her!" The first man snarled and gave her a push that sent her reeling backward. He poked the two ten-dollar bills into his shirt pocket, tossed aside the thick pillow

Kathleen used on the back of the seat so that her feet could reach the pedals, and slid under the wheel. "Get back there and push. Both of you."

"If you think I'm going to help you steal my car . . . you're crazy as a cross-eyed mule!"

"And if ya know what's good fer ya, you'll shut yore mouth and do what yo're told."

"Lippy, ain't she?" The second man was shorter and had a big belly. He wasn't much taller than Kathleen, who was five feet and four inches. He leered at her. "She ain't hardly got no titties a'tall, but she shore does have pretty red hair." When he reached out to touch her breasts, Kathleen's temper boiled over. She balled her fist and swung, hitting him square in the mouth.

"Ouch! You . . . bitch!" He dabbed at the blood on his mouth with the sleeve of his shirt and lifted his hand to hit her back. She drew back her fist; too angry to notice her sore knuckles, she prepared to fight.

"Touch me again and I'll . . . knock your head off!"

"Whapsy-do! If I had time, I'd take the fight outta ya."

"Goddammit, Webb." The man in the car turned the key, and the motor responded. "Stop messin' with 'er and help me get this thin' outta the ditch. Push, goddamn it! We've got to get out of here 'fore somebody comes."

The gears were shifted into drive and then into reverse to rock the car. The spinning wheels sent sand and dirt flying out behind. The wheels almost reached solid ground, then rolled back into the hole.

"*She's* not pushin'," Webb shouted, his face splotchy with anger and exertion.

Kathleen moved up onto the road and searched the horizon for something or somebody. The only movement in all that vast landscape was a few white clouds drifting lazily. A dozen scattered steers grazed on the sparse dry grass. There wasn't a car in sight.

Then she saw something coming over a small rise. At first she thought it was another steer; seconds later, she recognized a man on horseback riding across the prairie toward the steers. After a quick glance back at the two men arguing beside her car, she lifted both arms and waved wildly to the horseman and pointed toward the car. The rider gigged the horse and was less than two hundred feet away when Webb came back to the rear of the car.

"Shit!" he shouted. "Somebody's comin'."

The other man got out and looked over the top of the car. The cowboy's horse jumped the ditch and trotted toward Kathleen. She hurriedly got between it and the hijackers.

"They're stealing my car!" she exclaimed, without even looking at the man's face. Anger made her voice shrill.

In the brief silence that followed, the man who had jerked Kathleen from the car eyed the rifle that lay across the rider's thighs.

"Ah . . . naw. We is just a helpin' the lady get her car outta the ditch."

"You . . . lyin' son of a jackass!" Kathleen yelled. "You're stealing it. Make him give back my twenty dollars." She looked up at the rider and almost groaned. He looked to be not much more than a boy.

"Give it back." Young he might be, but he spoke with quiet authority.

"I don't have her damn money."

"It's in his shirt pocket." The rifle, more than the boy, gave Kathleen courage. "Two ten-dollar bills. I was trying to get away from them when I went into the ditch. See. Their car is blocking the road."

The end of the rifle moved. "Toss the money on the seat."

"She gave it to me. It's pay for getting her out of the ditch."

"Liar! You took it out of my purse."

"I'm not telling you again," the cowboy warned.

"Good thing you got that gun, boy." The hijacker threw the bills on the seat.

"Both of you move out and stand in back of the car."

"Make them help me get my car out of the ditch. It's their fault I'm stuck."

"Get under the wheel." The end of the rifle stayed on the two hijackers. Before Kathleen started the motor, she heard the boy say, "Take off your shirts and put them under that right wheel, then lift and push when she guns the motor."

"I'm not puttin' my good shirt under that wheel."

"No? Would you rather I put it under there with you in it?"

"It'll be ruint."

"Don't look like it would be much of a loss to me."

"Don't I know you?"

"Maybe. Are you going to help the lady, or am I going to see if I can shoot the button off the top of that cap you've got on that bump on your shoulders?"

A few minutes later the Nash was up on the road, and the hijackers were putting their shirts back on.

"Which way are you going, lady?" the cowboy asked.

"Rawlings." Kathleen left the motor idling and stood beside the car.

"You two stupid clods get in your car and head back up the road."

"Are you letting them go? I want them arrested."

The cowboy glanced at the girl. Her fiery red hair, thick and curly, was a halo around her head. It was what had drawn his eyes when he first came over the hill to see about his steers. There were not many redheaded women here in Indian country. Her blue eyes sparkled angrily. He noticed the heavy sprinkling of freckles across her nose. Lord! It had been a long time since he'd seen a girl with freckles on her nose.

Ignoring her question, he walked his horse behind the men until they reached their car.

"We got a flat tire," Webb complained.

"Don't you have a tire patch, you lazy son of a bitch? It's easier to steal the lady's car than sweat a little. Is that it?"

One of them muttered something about a blanket-ass. Any other time the cowboy would have made him eat the words. Now he just wanted to get rid of the two of them. He glanced in the car to make sure that no guns were on the seats, then motioned for them to get in. He waited while they got it started and watched as the car bounced along the road on the flat tire. When it passed the Nash and headed away from Rawlings, he went back to Kathleen and spoke as if there had not been a ten-minute interruption in their conversation.

"How do you suggest we get them to the sheriff? I know who they are. I'll see that he knows about this." He slid his rifle into the scabbard attached to the saddle and tilted his hat back.

He was considerably older than Kathleen had at first thought. Inky black hair, dark eyes, and high cheekbones spoke of Indian heritage. He was tall, judging by the length of his stirrups, and lean. She could picture him on the cover of a dime Western novel: horse rearing, guns blazing.

"I really appreciate your help. They would have taken my car and left me stranded here."

"Maybe not. They might have taken you with them."

"They'd a had a fight on their hands," she said spiritedly.

"I reckon they would've."

Her eyes were the color of denim britches after they've been washed a hundred times.

He smiled, and she realized that he was very attractive in a dark and mysterious sort of way. The thought entered her mind that she was out here on this lonely stretch of road with this cowboy, and he had a gun. It hadn't occurred to her to be afraid of *him*.

"Well . . . thank you."

"You're very welcome." He tipped his hat.

Kathleen got in the car, waved, and drove away. She glanced in the rearview mirror and saw the cowboy still sitting on his horse in the middle of the road.

Johnny Henry watched the car until it was out of sight. Why hadn't she told him who she was? Probably she saw no need to introduce herself to a cowboy out here in the middle of the prairie, even if he had saved her pretty little hide from a couple of no-good hijackers. He had known the minute he saw that red hair and the Nash car that she was Kathleen Dolan and that she was on her way to Rawlings to work at the *Gazette*.

A week earlier Johnny had gone over to Red Rock to visit his sister, Henry Ann, and her family. Her husband, Tom, had had a letter from his brother, Hod, in Kansas telling him that their niece, Kathleen, would be coming down to Rawlings. She had been working for a year in Liberal, and for some reason known only to her, had decided to use some of the money left to her by her grand-parents to buy into the paper at Rawlings.

"She wants to see and do a lot of things before she settles down," Hod had written. "She's twenty-six years old. Guess she's old enough to do as she pleases."

She didn't look to be that old, Johnny thought now. That would make her a year older than he was. She had looked to be about twenty-one or -two.

Tom had told Johnny that Duncan Dolan, the eldest of the Dolan boys, had gone to Montana when he was a youth and married a widow from Iowa. He'd had a fierce love for the woman and their child. Many of his letters were lovingly centered on his little girl whose red hair had been inherited from her mother. After Duncan was killed in an accident, his daughter and wife had gone back to Iowa to live with her parents, and for a while the Dolans had lost track of Kathleen. Several years ago she had written that her mother and grandparents were gone and she wanted to know her father's family.

Johnny had not given her more than a thought or two . . . until today. Now he wondered if he could ever get her out of his mind. He chuckled as he watched the car disappear. Not many women would set out alone to drive more than two hundred miles across country. Miss Kathleen Dolan had spunk to go along with that red hair.

A sudden burst of happiness sent his heart galloping like a runaway horse.

Rawlings, Oklahoma, was like most other towns in 1938. Jobs were scarce, farm prices had risen only a little since the bottom price for wheat had been twenty-five cents a bushel, oats ten cents and cotton five cents a pound back in 1932. Most of the cotton farmers were allowing their fields to go to grass to keep the soil from blowing away in the dust storms and were trying to make a living raising cattle. Some of them were packing up and following Highway 66 to the "promised land" in California where fertile fields provided a better prospect of jobs.

A steady stream of hobos looking for work or a hand-out came through Rawlings daily, seeking the community soup kitchen. The town had survived partly because a hide-tanning plant had opened several years ago and now employed more than fifty people. Hides were shipped from the meatpacking plants in Oklahoma City and Wichita Falls.

There was dissatisfaction among some in town, how-ever, because white men who needed jobs believed that too many Indians were working at the plant. Miss Vernon had written that the tanning plant was owned by an oil-rich Cherokee Indian, who was not only wealthy, but smart, and wouldn't stand for any interference in the way he handed out jobs.

During the past two months, Kathleen had learned quite a bit about Rawlings, Oklahoma. Miss Vernon had sent her every issue of the *Gazette* since she had answered the advertisement for a business partner in the Oklahoma City paper. The first *Gazette* had been published in 1910, just three years after Oklahoma became a state. The family had held on to the paper during the worst years of the Great Depression. Now, without an heir to take over, it was in danger of being put to rest.

As Kathleen drove slowly along the street, her heart pounded with excitement. The town was quiet beneath the hot September sun. A dust devil danced down the middle of Main Street, where only a few cars were parked along the curb, and only a few people strolled along the walks.

She stopped at an intersection and sat there viewing the buildings that made up the business part of town. A number of them were vacant, but no more than in other towns she had passed through. The sidewalks on both sides of the street were new, no doubt paid for by President Roosevelt's recovery program. The new school she had passed was another WPA project. Even the water tower had a fresh coat of paint. The district evidently had a hardworking congressman.

Most of the three thousand residents of Tillison County resided there in Rawlings, the county seat. The two-story, solid redbrick courthouse building sat in the middle of a square. An arch made of deer antlers and steer horns spanned the walk leading to the entrance. Kathleen smiled at that.

Her bright interested eyes took in everything. Rawlings was not as big as Liberal, but then she had been aware of that. It did have a good-sized business district because it was the only town of any size for fifty miles around. The Hughes department store was on the corner. Next to it was the Piggly-Wiggly grocery and at the end of the block the Tillison County Bank and Trust. "Bank and trust" she thought was kind of ironic when most folks had little trust in banks since so many had gone broke.

She passed the Rialto Theatre and saw that the movie *Hell's Angels* with Jean Harlow would be shown on Wednesday and Saturday nights. Claude's Hamburger Shack was across the street. Wilson's Family Market had a choice location on the corner across from the bank, and next to it was Woolworth's five-and-dime. Two grocery stores meant advertising money for the paper. Then, there it was near the end of the block between Corner Drugstore and Leroy's Men's Wear—the *Gazette* building, two-story redbrick, narrow, with one large window and two recessed doors; the second door led to a flight of stairs. RAWLINGS GAZETTE was painted in gold letters on the window.

Kathleen was not disappointed. Here she would invest her five hundred dollars and be part owner of a real live newspaper. Her duties would be gathering news and writing editorials for the weekly paper. Miss Vernon would take care of the society news, obituaries, and bookkeeping. Both would work on advertising. Kathleen's only concern was that she might not have time for her *other* writing, the writing that didn't bring in enough money for her to live on . . . yet.

She angle-parked the Nash in front of the building and sat for a few minutes to allow her heartbeat to slow. *Thank you, Grandma and Grandpa Hansen, for making this possible for me.* Several people passed while she sat there. An Indian woman with two black braids hanging over her ample bosom and moccasins on her feet came out of the *Gazette* office. The screen door banged shut behind her and she shuffled down the street.

Kathleen climbed out of her car. The late-September wind blew her hair across her face and wrapped her full skirt around her legs. She looked through the window before she entered and saw a heavy oak desk littered with papers. A typewriter sat on a pullout shelf at one end of the desk. The swivel chair was empty. Coming out of the bright sunlight, she waited beside the door to allow her eyes to adjust. The familiar clanking of a linotype machine came from the back room. No one was in sight.

The newspaper office had an odor she knew well: a combination of melting lead, ink, and paper. The clutter was also typical. As she wasn't being observed, Kathleen let her eyes wander over the office. A few framed front pages of the *Gazette* hung on the wall; Armistice Day, November 11, 1918, the stock market crash in 1929, Roosevelt's election in 1932.

The *Gazette* might be a weekly, she thought with owner's pride, but it had style.

Between the well-scarred desks were two four-drawer filing cabinets. Along the opposite wall on a waist-high counter, a thick book of advertising illustrations lay open. Suspended on long rods from the high ceiling, two fans turned gently.

Then she noticed a leg and a foot jutting out from behind one of the desks. Shock kept her still for a second; then she rushed over to the woman who lay on the floor between the desk and the wall.

"What . . . in the world—?" Kathleen knelt down for a closer look. *This must be Miss Vernon!* There was blood on her forehead. "Help!" Kathleen yelled as she ran toward the back room and the clattering linotype machine. "Help! Come quick!"

The man who sat at the machine continued to type, then dropped the line of lead and started another. He appeared not to hear Kathleen's call for help. She ran to him and put her hand on his shoulder. He jumped and turned. She backed away.

"Help me!" She took a few steps toward the front, then looked back. The big, shaggy-haired man was still standing beside the machine with a stupefied look on his face. "Can't you understand? I need your help!" she screamed. *Oh, dear Lord! He's either deaf or he can't hear me over the racket of that damn machine.*

Kathleen turned, ran back to the office and grabbed the phone. She flipped the receiver holder several times when the operator didn't answer immediately.

WITH HEART 19

"Hold your horses, Adelaide." The voice came at last.

"Operator, we need help at the *Gazette* office," Kathleen said breathlessly. "Miss Vernon's had an accident."

"Adelaide? What's the matter with her?"

"She's unconscious and has blood on her head."

"Is she there in the office?"

"Yes, yes. Get a doctor."

"I'll see if I can find him."

By the time she had hung up the telephone, the man from the back room, still wearing his heavy leather apron to protect him from the hot lead, was kneeling beside Miss Vernon. Kathleen hurried to a large tin sink she had seen in the printing area of the building. When she returned with a wet towel, he had lifted the woman out from behind the desk and was holding her head and shoulders off the floor. Kathleen pressed the towel into his hand. As he dabbed at the blood on the woman's forehead, Kathleen got her first good look at her new partner.

In her letters to Kathleen, Miss Vernon had not mentioned her age. Her dark hair was streaked with gray at the temples, and the creases fanned out from the corners of her eyes. She was slender; almost fragile. Kathleen judged her to be in her middle or late forties.

Little moaning noises came from the man holding her. He was in anguish. He wasn't her husband; Miss Vernon had said she had never married. Kathleen couldn't see his face, but her first impression when she had seen him in the back room, was of a big, strong man, considerably younger than Miss Vernon.

The screen door slammed behind a large woman in a white nurse's uniform. A starched white cap was perched on top of her head. She was six feet tall or more and she looked to be a no-nonsense person who would be able to handle almost any situation. The nurse dropped a bag on the floor and knelt.

"What the hell has Adelaide done to herself now?" Her voice was loud and brisk. "Move over, Paul. Let me have a look."

The man lowered Adelaide gently to the floor and stepped back. As he looked up from the woman on the floor, Kathleen was startled by beautiful amber-colored eyes deeply set in his worried, homely face. His dark lashes were thick and long, his brows smooth and straight. The large nose looked as if it had been flattened in a hundred barroom brawls. A deep scar in his upper lip extended almost to his right nostril. He was broad-shouldered and thick-necked. His arms were heavily muscled. He reminded her of a gentle gorilla, if there was such a thing.

"Wake up, Adelaide." The nurse waved an open vial of smelling salts beneath Miss Vernon's nose. Adelaide sputtered and rolled her head. "Wake up," the nurse commanded briskly. "You're all right. You've just had a little crack on the head."

"Maybe not," Kathleen said. "She may have had a stroke . . . or something." The quelling glance the nurse gave her would have sent a more timid person running. Not Kathleen. She looked the nurse in the eye and said, "Shouldn't she be examined by a doctor?"

"Who are you? Her long-lost daughter?"

"No, but—"

"She's awake," the nurse said, ignoring Kathleen. "Help her into the chair, Paul."

With his hands beneath Adelaide's armpits, Paul easily lifted her into the chair. Her eyes were glazed as she tried to focus on the man kneeling beside her. She flinched when the nurse dabbed at the cut on her forehead with a pad saturated in alcohol.

"You'll not need any stitches if I put a tight tape on it. What happened, Adelaide? Did you drink a little too much of that rotgut whiskey and fall out of the chair?"

Kathleen could tell by the snort that came from Paul that he didn't like the nurse's comment. Kathleen didn't like it either. She thought it very unprofessional. Adelaide continued to try to focus on Paul and said nothing.

"Don't get so huffy, big fellow," the nurse continued. "You know as well as I do that Adelaide is fond of the bottle."

"I didn't smell anything," Kathleen said.

"Who are you?" the nurse demanded again.

She was a very intimidating figure when she stood up, almost a foot taller than Kathleen and *big*, rangy big, like a roustabout who handled heavy machinery. Bangs, cut straight across, hung to the middle of her forehead and straight, henna-colored hair formed loose swirls, Clara Bow style, on her cheeks. Arched high above lashes, heavy with mascara, her brows were a thin line drawn by a reddish brown pencil. She had applied lipstick to her small mouth to make her lips appear fuller. It was smeared at the corners.

"Kathleen Dolan."

"You're new in town." Strong, quick fingers pressed the tape in place on Adelaide's forehead.

"You might say that."

"How long are you staying?"

"A long time."

"I see. Then you're the one who is taking over the paper."

"No. I'll be working with Miss Vernon on *our* paper."

"Here in Rawlings we don't butt into other people's

business. You've got a lot to learn, girl." The nurse picked up her bag. "And for your sake, I hope you learn it fast." With that, she left the office, letting the screen door slam behind her.

Watching her leave, Kathleen had the feeling that she had just met an enemy. She was certain of it when she looked down to see the scowl on Paul's face.

"What put a bee in her bonnet?"

"She doesn't like Adelaide."

"Why not?"

"She thinks that Adelaide may know too much." Paul spoke very softly and smoothed the hair back from Adelaide's face with ink-stained fingers.

"Too much about what?"

" 'Bout that clinic she and Doc run."

"Paul!" Adelaide tried to look up without turning her head. "Shhh . . ."

"It's all right," he said soothingly. "She's the one from Kansas."

"You sure?" she whispered.

"Looks like the picture she sent."

"Kathleen Dolan?" Adelaide turned her head slowly and painfully so that she could see Kathleen.

"Yes, I'm Kathleen. I just got here."

"Oh, Kathleen, I've been thinking that . . . that bringing you here may be the biggest mistake of my life."

"Why is that, Miss Vernon? Are you doubting my ability to help you run the paper?"

"No! No, it isn't that. It's just that—"

"—You can tell her later," Paul said. "Come on upstairs and lie down. You've got a partner now. She'll handle things down here for a while."

Chapter Two

KATHLEEN WAS SURE that she would never forget this day for as long as she lived. Being hijacked was frightening enough without being thrust into the position of having to take over the office. She had no more than said hello and good-bye to her new partner when Paul took Adelaide up the back stairs to her rooms, leaving Kathleen with the explanation that *maybe* Adelaide had fallen out of her chair and with an apology for needing to leave her to cope alone.

Within an hour she had answered a dozen questions from curious townspeople about why the nurse had been there, taken a classified ad and several items for Adelaide's "Back Fence" column.

"Miss Jeraldine Smothers of Randlett spent Sunday afternoon with her aunt, Miss Earlene Smothers. They attended church and had dinner at the home of Miss Earlene Smothers's sister-in-law, Mrs. Willard F. Smothers." Kathleen read aloud the item she had written, based on the information given to her by the woman who had come panting into the office.

"Be sure you spell Jeraldine with a *J*. Jeraldine hates it when her name is spelled with a *G*. Oh, my!" She fanned herself with her handkerchief. "I had to hurry. I was afraid the office would be closed."

"I'll be sure to spell Jeraldine with a *J*."

"You're new here. Where is Adelaide?"

"She's upstairs resting."

"I heard that Louise Munday was here this afternoon."

"The nurse? She didn't mention her name."

"Why should she? Everyone knows Louise. Anything serious?"

"No, I don't think so. I'll give the item to Adelaide for her column."

"Did she hurt herself?"

"She got a little bump on the head."

"Bullfoot. Must have been more than a little *bump* if Louise was needed."

"I wouldn't know."

"You sure do have red hair."

"I can't argue with you about that."

"Well—" The woman waited for Kathleen to say more. When she didn't, she said, "That boy better bring my paper before four-thirty. If not, he'll hear from me. I pay extra for delivery, you know."

"Yes, I know."

"Last week it was almost five o'clock."

"The sign on the window says that the papers are available at four on Wednesdays. That doesn't give him much time."

"P'shaw! That boy dawdles around and don't pay attention to what he's hired to do. He's lucky he's got a job when men are walking the streets every day, looking for work."

"I'll ask him to get it to you as soon as he can."

When the woman left, Kathleen pressed her fingertips to

her temples. A few more like that one and she would have a splitting headache.

The next person to come into the office was the owner of the men's store. He was quite proper and introduced himself as Leroy Grandon, president of the Chamber of Commerce. He was aware that she was Adelaide's partner and invited her to a Chamber meeting. Kathleen sold him a two-column-by-three-inch display ad. She quickly sketched the ad for his shoe sale. At the top she printed, WALK IN MY SHOES. He was pleased and decided to run it in the next two editions. He lingered in the office until a woman came in with another item for the "Back Fence" column.

By six o'clock Kathleen was tired and hungry. She still had to find a place to spend the night. In her correspondence, Miss Vernon had said that there were several good boardinghouses in town. Paul was still at the linotype machine. If she could get him to turn it off, she'd ask him to direct her to one.

The screen door opened as she was on her way to lock up the office for the day. A tall, lanky man came in. *The cowboy.* He lifted a hand and pushed his hat back off his forehead.

"I was just about to close," Kathleen said.

"Adelaide didn't waste time putting you to work. I came by to see if you'd made it here all right."

"I made it. Did you tell the sheriff about the two crooks who tried to steal my car?"

"Yup. He knows about 'em."

"How did you know that I was coming here?"

"You might say that a tumbleweed told me."

"I might, but I won't."

"I saw your car out front. You've not unpacked it."

"I haven't had time. Miss Vernon had an accident—

fainted, I guess. Anyway she got a bump on the head that knocked her out."

"Is she all right?"

"I think so. Paul took her upstairs to rest."

Johnny's eyes roamed Kathleen's face. He liked the way she looked and talked. She was a woman, yet she was a girl, too.

"Where are you staying? Can I give you a hand unpacking your car?"

"Thank you, no. I'm not sure where I'll be staying. I need to talk to Paul, or Miss Vernon if she's able." She looked at him with wide, clear eyes—waiting for him to leave so that she could lock the door.

"I should have introduced myself. My brother-in-law, Tom Dolan, would skin me alive if I didn't help his niece settle in. I'm Johnny Henry." He held out his hand, and she put hers into it.

"Glad to meet you. I'm Kathleen Dolan, but I guess you know that." *So this is the Johnny Molly told me about.*

"Yes. I also know your Uncle Hod and Aunt Molly. I was just at the post office and picked up a letter from Hod. He said that you were on your way and for me to look out for you. 'Course, I'd already had instruction from Tom."

"It was good of them to be concerned for me. You more than did your duty today by helping me with the hijackers." Kathleen pulled her hand from his.

"It wasn't a duty, it was a pleasure. The sheriff may ask you to sign a complaint."

"I'll do that gladly. Now if you'll excuse me. Paul has turned off the linotype, and I've got to talk to him."

"Hi, Johnny." Paul came out of the back room and placed a sheet of newsprint on the counter. "Adelaide proofs this before I lock the type into the frame."

Kathleen glanced at the headline: Lead stories were, BRITAIN IS PLEDGED TO FIGHT and AMERICANS TOLD TO RETURN HOME. Despite her being so tired, Kathleen's interest was piqued. This was heavy stuff for a small-town paper out here on the edge of nowhere.

"Does it have to be done tonight?"

"In the morning. The press starts rolling at noon."

"Is Adelaide all right?"

"Seems to be." He said it in a way to cut off any other inquiry.

"I was going to ask her to recommend a place to stay. I'll stay at the hotel tonight and talk to her tomorrow."

"Mrs. Ramsey has a room for you. Adelaide spoke to her this morning." The big man's amber eyes went from Kathleen to Johnny.

"I'll take her there, Paul."

"I'd be obliged, Johnny. Adelaide's worried about her—"

"There's no need for her to worry. Tell her I'll be here in the morning."

Kathleen glanced at Johnny. When she had time she would try to remember everything Hod and Molly had said about him. For now she welcomed his help.

Paul pulled the shade and closed the door behind them. Out on the sidewalk, Johnny's hand gripped her elbow.

"Have you eaten?"

"Did you hear my stomach growling?"

"Is that what I heard? I thought it was thunder." He smiled down at her, and both of them were suddenly embarrassed. His hand dropped from her arm and he stepped back. "How about one of Claude's hamburgers?"

"Sounds heavenly."

They walked the block to the well-lighted diner that had been converted from an old streetcar. Kathleen was thankful for the tall, broad-shouldered presence beside her in this un-familiar town. She cast a glance up at him; and into her fer-tile mind sprang the image of a perfect male hero from one of her stories: strong, handsome, a champion of the under-dog, yet gentle with his woman.

Music from the jukebox blared through the open win-dows of Claude's diner. Kathleen recognized the familiar voice of Gene Autry, the Oklahoma cowboy, singing a song he had made popular. *"In a vine-covered shack in the moun-tains, bravely fighting the battle of time, is a dear one who's weathered life's sorrows, that silver-haired daddy of mine."*

Several people sat on the stools at the counter that ran the length of the eatery. Behind the counter was the grill, a stove, shelves of dishes and tin Coca-Cola and Red Man chewing tobacco posters. A man in a white apron, a striped shirt, and a black bow tie yelled out as they entered.

"Hi, Johnny. Come right on in and set yourself down." The man's voice reached them over the sound of Autry's singing.

"Hi, Claude." Johnny placed his hat on a shelf above the row of windows, ran his fingers through his hair to smooth it, and ushered Kathleen to one end of the counter. He waited until she was seated on a stool beneath the overhead fan before straddling a stool beside her.

Claude, wiping his hands on his apron, came down the counter. His round face was flushed and his bright blue eyes twinkled. Long strands of dark hair were combed over the near-bald spot on his head.

"Howdy, ma'am."

"Hello."

"This is Miss Dolan, Claude. She'll be working with Adelaide over at the *Gazette*. Claude White, the chief cook and bottle washer at this greasy spoon."

"Glad to meet ya, miss. Adelaide's been needin' somebody to give her a hand over there. Paul's good at printin', but ain't never heard that he was worth a tinker's dam at writin' up a story. Well, now, that's said, what'll ya have?"

Kathleen looked at the menu board above a shelf of crockery, then at Claude, and smiled.

"I'm hungry enough to eat everything up there, but I'll have a hamburger and a piece of raisin pie."

"What will you have on your hamburger?"

"Everything but onions."

"I'll have two hamburgers and a bowl of chili," Johnny said.

"Onions, Johnny?" Claude lifted his bushy brows.

"No."

"You usually have extra onions. Guess that tells me what I wanted to know." Claude winked at Kathleen and turned back to his grill.

Kathleen glanced at Johnny and saw his eyes narrow, his lips press into a firm line, and knew that had the deep suntan not bronzed his face, it would be flushed with embarrassment. A muscle jumped in his clenched jaw. He looked even younger without his hat. Hair as black as midnight sprang back from his forehead and hung almost to the collar of his shirt.

"Claude's quite a joker," Johnny murmured.

"Does he always wear a bow tie when he cooks?"

"Always. I don't think I've ever seen him without it."

Claude brought a bowl of thick, fragrant chili and placed it in front of Johnny.

"Sure you don't want one, miss?"

"It smells good, but I'll wait for my hamburger and pie."

Claude dashed back to the grill, flipped over meat patties with a long-handled spatula, while placing open buns on the grill with the other hand. No wasted motion there. He kept his eye on the door and greeted each customer who came in by name.

"Hi ya, Allen. You're late tonight. How ya doin', Herb? Take a seat. Be with ya in two shakes. You want anythin' else, Jake?" Claude rolled a nickel down the counter. "Put this in the jukebox, Allen. Play 'Frankie and Johnny' for my friend Johnny who has brought me a new customer to brighten up the place. Once she's eaten a Claude hamburger, she'll be back."

"He'd make a good politician," Kathleen murmured.

"That's what I've been tellin' him." Johnny grinned at her. "He takes a backseat to no one once his mouth gets goin'. He's got his fingers in most every pie in town." Johnny said the last loud enough for Claude to hear as he put the hamburgers on the counter in front of them.

"Here ya are, miss." Claude winked at her again. "Don't pay no mind to what this long drink of water tells you. He only comes to town when he gets tired a talkin' to hisself."

"I knew I shouldn't have brought her here. After hearing you spout off she'll probably head right back to Kansas."

"Not on your life." Kathleen chewed and swallowed her first bite of her hamburger. "I'll hang around just for this."

"Smart lady you got here, buster—"

"Hey, Claude. Stop flirting with the pretty redhead and get me some catsup."

"Hold your horses, Jake. I'm making sure she knows that this kid ain't the only single man 'round these parts."

By the time Kathleen finished her meal, Johnny was done with his. When she reached into her purse to pay, he put his hand on her arm to stop her. Not wanting to embarrass him, she waited until they were back out on the walk in front of the diner before she spoke.

"I never intended for you to pay for my supper. Please—" She opened her purse.

"No," he said, his tone so firm that it stopped her protest.

"Well . . . thank you."

"My truck is across the street from your car. I'll lead you to Mrs. Ramsey's. It's only a few blocks."

"Thank goodness for that. I'm about out of gas. I got so excited coming into town that I forgot to stop and get some."

They walked down the darkened street to her car without speaking; then she followed a truck as dilapidated as the car the hijackers had used to block the road. The bed of the truck, without sides, held a piece of machinery lashed down with ropes. A block off Main Street, they left the paving and drove onto a hard-packed road of red clay. Kathleen followed Johnny's lead and dodged the potholes. He stopped in front of a one-story bungalow with a porch that stretched across the front. A dim light glowed from a lightbulb between the two front doors. Johnny came to her car as she was getting out.

"Do you want to meet Mrs. Ramsey before we unload the car?"

"Are you thinking that I may not want to stay here after I meet her?"

"It isn't a fancy place."

"I'm not used to a fancy place. I'm used to a clean place, but I need to know—about Mrs. Ramsey."

"She's decent, if that's what you mean. Adelaide Vernon wouldn't have recommended her if she wasn't. She's a good hardworking lady who hasn't had an easy time of it."

Kathleen was keenly aware of the cowboy who stood close beside her on the darkened road. He looked confident and dangerous . . . yet she felt perfectly safe with him.

"I'll take your word for it." She walked beside him to the porch. As they stepped upon it, one of the doors was flung open and a small girl rushed out.

"Hi, Johnny? Is that her?"

"Hi, Emily."

"Emily, for goodness sake!" The woman who came out to take the girl's hand had snow-white hair and a sun-browned, weathered face. She was short and very plump. "Excuse Emily, miss. She's excited."

"She's pretty, Granny, and she ain't fat. You said she'd—"

"—Well, aren't you smart to see that she's pretty." The woman pulled the little girl's head to her side, hugged her to shut her up, and smiled at Kathleen. "Adelaide sent word this morning that you'd be here sometime today."

"Thank you for the compliment, Emily." Kathleen smiled at the child, who had suddenly turned shy and hid her face against her grandmother.

"Come in. I'll show you the room."

"Mr. Henry was kind enough to show me the way here."

"Go on into the front room, Johnny." The top of the woman's head came to Johnny's armpit. She indicated the door that she and the girl had come through.

"Thanks, but I'll wait out here and help Miss Dolan with her things before I go."

Mrs. Ramsey opened the door and led Kathleen into a room that had the smell of recent cleaning: lye soap, vinegar, and linseed oil. The only furniture was a bed, a dresser, and a wardrobe. The bedcover was a white sheet with a spray of appliquéd flowers in the middle. A colorful rag rug lay beside the bed on the scrubbed wooden floor. Curtains that Kathleen recognized as having been made from white flour sacks and embroidered with yellow-and-green cross-stitch along the hems hung at the windows.

Kathleen glanced around the room, then at the small woman who clutched her granddaughter's hand. There was an anxious look in her eyes. She hurried to open a door revealing a bathroom with a clawfoot tub, a sink, a toilet with the waterbox near the ceiling, and a door leading to another room.

"The water is . . . a little rusty, but I catch rainwater—" Her words trailed.

"I love to wash my hair in rainwater," Kathleen said to fill the void. "Do you rent by the week, or by the month?"

"By the week, if that's all right. Two dollars . . . or four if you want breakfast and supper. Ah . . . nothing fancy, but plain eatin'. We have meat on Wednesdays and Sundays."

"That'll be fine."

"You're takin' it?"

"Oh, yes. This is just the kind of place I like." Kathleen opened her purse and took out one of the ten-dollar bills Johnny had made the hijackers return. "I'll pay for two weeks."

The woman's hand was shaking when she reached for the bill, and Kathleen was sure she saw mist in her eyes.

"But . . . I don't have change."

"That's all right. I'll owe you two dollars for the third week."

"I'll do my best to make you as comfortable as I can."

"Is she stayin', Granny?"

"I plan on it, if you want me, Emily." Kathleen patted the little girl on the head. "Will you help me bring in my things?"

"Uh-huh."

"You can park your car behind the house if you want to get it out of the road." Her new landlady's voice was raspy.

"Thank you, I will."

Kathleen, Johnny, and Emily made several trips to the car before Johnny carried in her heavy typewriter. He looked around for a place to put it.

"Just set it on the floor. My trunk is coming down on the train. I can use it as a table."

"I thought a reporter did her writing at the newspaper office." Johnny divided his glance between her and the near-new machine.

"I do . . . most of it," she said, not wanting to tell him that she used the typewriter almost every night and most always on Sunday afternoon.

"I have a small table out at my place. I'll bring it in, if you like."

"Oh, would you? I'll buy it from you."

"I'd have to have fifty or sixty bucks for it."

"Fifty or sixty—" Her eyes questioned. Then, "Oh, you!" she exclaimed when she saw him trying to keep the grin off his face. "Johnny Henry, you're a tease." His smile would give a charging bull pause for reflection, Kathleen thought, and wondered why it was that he was so "at home" here.

"That's everything out of the car. Do you want me to move it around back?"

"I would appreciate it. I probably won't use it much. Rawlings is about half the size of Liberal."

"Be right back."

When she was alone, Kathleen looked around the room that would be her home for a while. The door leading to the front porch had new screen on the bottom. The one going into the opposite room stood open, and she could see a couch and a library table. The third door led into the bathroom. The rooming house where she'd stayed in Liberal had six boarders, all on the second and third floors, and they shared one bathroom. This was almost like having one all to herself.

She heard Johnny when he came in the back door and paused to talk for a while with Mrs. Ramsey and Emily. She could hear the murmur of their voices but not what they said. She was taking things out of her suitcase and placing them in the drawers when he appeared in the doorway of the connecting room.

"Here are your keys."

"Thank you." Her gaze was drawn to his like iron to a magnet. Occasionally, Kathleen was attracted to men, mostly professionals or businessmen who wore suits and ties and were well versed on world affairs. She never expected to be attracted to a cowboy, a young one at that. The dark eyes that looked into hers were deep-set, and even though they gleamed with a friendly light, they looked to be as old as the ages.

"Welcome," he said after the long silence between them. "I'll bring in the table the next time I come to town."

"I feel that I'm imposing. You've already done so much."

"My pleasure." He slapped his battered hat down on his head. "Good night."

" 'Night, Mr. Henry."

Kathleen heard the squeak of the screen door and went to the porch. He was going down the walk to his truck.

"Thanks again," she called.

"Don't mention it." His voice came out of the darkness.

He ground the starter several times on the old truck before it started. The lights came on, and it moved on down the street. Kathleen watched until it turned the corner and was out of sight.

Damn, but she was pretty.

Johnny hadn't been especially interested in meeting Tom's niece from up north after Tom had told him that she was a newspaper reporter who had written stories that had been sent out on the wire to the big papers, that she was investing money she had inherited in the Rawlings paper, and that she was bold enough to drive across country by herself. He couldn't imagine a woman like that needing any help from him.

Well, she had needed him today with the hijackers. He had done what any decent man would have done under the circumstances.

When he had seen her car sitting, still loaded, in front of the *Gazette,* he had stopped before he had given it much thought. If he hadn't stopped, Paul would have seen to it that she got to Mrs. Ramsey's. But no, old dumbbell that he was, he had to stick his bill in, take her to Claude's, help her unload and then further complicate matters by offering her a table for her typewriter. She had been nice, but she probably was uneasy with the feeling that she owed him.

He wasn't usually uncomfortable around city women, but when he'd first seen Kathleen Dolan he'd been stunned. She was lovely and warm, with a smile that would melt the coldest of hearts. Her hair, and there was plenty of it, was the color of a sunset, her skin creamy white, and those damn freckles— Her looks hadn't matched the image he'd had of her. He'd thought she'd be more hoity-toity with her education and ability to *buy* into a newspaper. He couldn't imagine being able to write down things that hundreds, maybe thousands, of people would read.

She was far beyond his reach, and he'd best stop this silly thinking about her and keep his distance. Everyone in town knew he came from Mud Creek trash and they wouldn't let him forget it. Almost all of them knew him as the offspring of a whore and a redskin. It was true. He had grown up knowing that and also knowing there was nothing he could do about it.

Johnny had made a niche for himself out on the Circle H. In addition, during off-seasons, he made a little money working for the Feds on special jobs. No one around here knew about that, and that's the way he wanted it. He had been content until two o'clock this afternoon when he had come over the rise and seen the sun shining on a head of bright red hair. The damn woman had disturbed him, had made him want to be with her and want to try to interest and impress her.

"Horse hockey!" Johnny pounded the steering wheel with his fist.

The presence of Kathleen Dolan angered him because suddenly his niche no longer seemed enough for him.

Chapter Three

"COME EAT, Miss Dolan. Granny's made chocolate gravy." Emily, dressed for school, stood anxiously beside the kitchen door.

"Chocolate gravy?" The thought made Kathleen's stomach queazy.

"You girls sit down." Hazel Ramsey opened the oven door and took out a pan of golden brown biscuits. "Do you drink coffee, Miss Dolan?"

"If you have it made. Don't make it especially for me. I usually drink tea, a taste I acquired from my grandparents in Iowa. I'll get a box while I'm in town today. I'll leave some at the office and bring the rest home. I like tea hot when it's cold and cold when it's hot."

"Can I have some?" Emily asked.

"Sure."

"You don't drink tea, sugar."

"I will if Kathleen does."

"You don't call grown-ups by their first names," Mrs. Ramsey chided gently.

Kathleen buttered a biscuit and helped herself to the peach jam. Mrs. Ramsey split a biscuit, placed it on Emily's plate, and covered it generously with the light brown gravy.

"Don't you want some?" Emily asked.

"Well . . . I've never had chocolate gravy."

"It's good."

"Then I'd better try it. I may be missing something." Kathleen placed a spoonful of the gravy on a biscuit half and tentatively took a bite. "Humm, it is good. I can't taste the chocolate at all."

"Told ya." Emily glanced at her grandmother and beamed, showing a missing tooth.

Kathleen walked part of the way to town with Emily, who was in the second grade. The little girl cast proud glances up at Kathleen when they met her curious schoolmates and, at one time, reached up and took her hand. She chattered happily about her school activities, making sure the children walking ahead of them were aware that Kathleen was her special friend.

" 'Bye, Miss Dolan. See ya tonight," Emily shouted when they parted.

" 'Bye, Emily." She watched the little girl go slowly down the walk, making no attempt to catch up with the other children.

It was five blocks from Mrs. Ramsey's to the downtown area. Many heads turned to watch the pretty redhead, not only because she was a stranger in town, but because Kathleen walked with the confident grace of a woman who knew who she was and where she was going. She approached the *Gazette* right at eight o'clock, wishing with all her heart for a cup of tea to help fortify herself for the first day at the *Gazette*.

"Good morning." Adelaide rose from behind the desk as soon as Kathleen walked in.

"Hello. Are you feeling better?"

"Oh, yes. I'm sorry you had such a poor welcome yesterday."

"I'm glad I was here to carry on. Did I make too big a mess of things?"

"Not at all. By the way that was a clever ad you laid out for the men's store. How did you get Leroy Grandon to buy *two* ads? He's usually as tight as the skin on an onion."

Kathleen laughed. "I don't know."

"I do." Adelaide looked pointedly up and down Kathleen's trim figure.

Adelaide Vernon was a sweet-looking woman: small-boned and thin. Beneath thick brown hair, gray at the temples, her face was pale, and her expression conveyed her anxiety as she met her new partner. Her fragile looks belied her toughness, a legacy from her father that had allowed her to run this weekly paper alone since his death. She wore a blue print dress with a white collar, a white belt, and large white buttons down the front to the hem.

"Did you find the 'Back Fence' items I put on your spindle?" Kathleen went to the other large desk in the office where she had worked the day before.

"I found them. Too bad you had to be introduced to Earlene Smothers on your first day."

"I knew right away that she was a pain. I assured her that you would spell Jeraldine with a *J*. It was very important to her. She was extremely curious as to why the nurse was here."

"She would be. She's next to the paper when it comes to spreading the news. Did you take the room at Hazel Ramsey's?"

"Yes. Thanks for arranging for me to go there. She's very nice, and the room is comfortable."

"I was hoping you'd stay there. Hazel is having a hard

time. She takes in ironing and anything else she can do to support herself and Emily."

"Where are the child's parents?"

"Emily is one of those unfortunate children without a father. I doubt that even Clara, her mother, knows who he is. Clara comes and goes. Hazel and Emily are better off when she stays away." Adelaide put a sheet of paper in her typewriter. "The press starts rolling at noon. Paul proofed the front page and made up the ad you took from Leroy. We're in pretty good shape for press day."

"What's the press run?"

"We're down to twelve hundred. Five hundred are delivered to the towns around. We have correspondents in Deval, Grandview, Loveland, and Davidson. They send in news. Most people like to see their names in the paper. A hundred and fifty go out in the mail. A hundred and fifty are delivered here in town, and the rest go to the stores and are sold here at the office."

"The paper in Liberal didn't do much better than that."

"We need new ideas, Kathleen. It's what we must talk about. But first let's get this edition out."

"Sounds logical. What shall I do first?"

Kathleen was amazed at the amount of work Paul was able to do. She noticed that he was surprisingly fast on his feet for a big man. She had found very few mistakes when she proofed the stories he had set on the linotype machine.

The press was old and printed only four pages at one time. This week's paper would be eight pages, which would require two runs. The front of the paper would be printed last. When it came off the press the first run would be inserted.

At noon Paul locked the columns of type into the page frame and the frame to the press. After inking the type with a roller, he turned the big iron wheel by hand to print sheets for Adelaide to look over before he started the press.

Kathleen was familiar with the procedure even though the press was much older than the one in Liberal. Every available hand was needed once the press began to roll. She wished she had thought to bring a smock to protect her dress from the wet ink while she helped insert the first run into the second one when Adelaide came to her, with a big loose shirt to put on over her dress.

"Thanks. I'll bring something next week."

"Hello, Woody."

When Adelaide spoke, Kathleen turned to see the man who had come in through the back door. He wore a cap and overalls. She couldn't see his face clearly, but from the way he hurried forward to help Paul lift a large roll of newsprint to the press, she realized he was young and strong.

"Woody helps us on press day," Adelaide said. "He'll take the papers from the press and stack them on the table, then help insert them in the final run. He delivers the papers to the stores. I start addressing for the mail as soon as we start the second run. We have to have the papers at the post office by five o'clock if we want them to go out tonight."

Kathleen nodded and glanced at Paul. He had not said one word to her all morning, and very few words to Adelaide. The two of them worked together as if speech were not necessary. The next few hours flew by for Kathleen. She loved the clank, clank of the press, the smell of the ink, and the rush to get the papers stuffed and out.

Paul left his position by the press, where he watched continuously for a tear in the paper that would clog the flow and cause the press to be shut down, to tell Adelaide quite firmly that she should go sit down.

Kathleen heard her say in a low voice, "I'm all right, Paul. Don't worry."

Kathleen added to the suggestion by saying, "I can handle this back here, Adelaide."

"All right. I'll go up front and start addressing the mailing. Usually a dozen or so people stop in to get papers hot off the press." Adelaide went to the office with a stack of papers, then returned to speak to Kathleen over the clatter of the press. "Hazel came by to find out what time you'd be there for supper. I took the liberty of telling her that I'd like for you to have supper with me tonight so that we could talk. I hope you don't mind."

Kathleen smiled, nodded, and continued to stuff papers.

When the press was shut off at last, Kathleen washed the ink from her hands at the sink, using the harsh Lava soap, then went to the front office where Adelaide was busy with a tray of subscriber plates, stamping the papers, making them ready for the post office.

Three paper boys came in. Each picked up his bundle of papers.

"I have two 'stops' on your route, Gordon." She gave the boy a slip of paper. "If either of these flags you down for a paper, tell them to come see me. I have three for you, Donny, and one for you, Ellis. Get going now and, Gordon, try to get to Mrs. Smothers as soon as you can. She's been complaining again."

"But . . . Miss Vernon, I deliver to her . . . almost first."

"I believe you. Just try to get along with her."

"I hate to stop papers," Adelaide said when the boys were out the door. "But those six subscribers haven't paid for several months."

While they were stamping papers, the nurse, Louise

Munday, came into the office. Her starched uniform and cap were immaculate. She carried a small black bag.

"Well, well. I see you're up and about. Of course, you'd have to be dead not to be down here on the day your little gossip sheet comes out." She marched over to the counter where Adelaide was working as if she was going into battle, took her chin between her fingers, and turned her head toward her so she could look at the cut on her forehead.

"I'm all right." Adelaide jerked her chin to free it.

"You don't look all right. You looked washed-out."

"Thanks for the compliment, Louise." Adelaide took the tray of address plates to her desk. "Have you met my partner, Kathleen Dolan?"

" 'Fraid so. How did you get that bump on the head?"

"Dammit, Louise. It's none of your business."

"She said you fell out of your chair." The big woman turned accusing eyes on Kathleen.

"I didn't say that," Kathleen said sharply, and wondered how long it took the nurse to put all that mascara and paint on her face.

Louise ignored Kathleen's retort and fixed her eyes on Adelaide.

"Where's that big ugly galoot that's always hovering over you? He knows you fell out of your chair." Louise looked toward the back room. "Isn't he a little young for you, dear?"

"Why don't you ask him, *dear*?"

"It isn't any of my business if you make a fool of yourself and set the tongues to wagging."

"That's right. It isn't any of your business."

"Better go slow on that rotgut whiskey, Adelaide. You might fall down out in the street and get run over." She picked up the bag she had set on the desk and headed for the door.

"And you'd cry at my funeral."

"Don't count on it." Louise turned, her eyes narrowed and her small red mouth puckered as if she were going to throw a kiss. "Doc told me to come by and see about you. Guess I can tell him you're still full of piss and vinegar."

"You do that. Don't bother to make another house call."

"I'll be back if Doc tells me to."

She walked out and let the screen door slam behind her.

"What a disagreeable woman," Kathleen said into the silence that followed. "Does she carry so much weight in this town that she can come in here and be rude to the editor of the paper?"

"She thinks she does."

"I could see that. I'm glad you stood up to her."

"Dr. Herman is county commissioner, medical officer, on every board in the county, besides being mayor of Rawlings. He runs things to a certain extent here in Tillison County."

"So when his nurse comes around threatening people, she is speaking for him?"

"I guess you could say that. She's not rude around him. Butter wouldn't melt in her mouth," Adelaide said with a sniff.

"If she's afraid that you'll print something she won't like, it isn't very smart of her to antagonize you." It was an opening for Adelaide to explain the animosity between the two, but the older woman failed to step into it.

Instead she said, "I wasn't drinking, Kathleen." Adelaide waited to speak until after a small boy put a nickel in the cup and took a paper. "Paul and I have a drink sometimes in the evenings, but I never take a drink during the day. My father was a fall-down drunk. Louise likes to think that I inherited his weakness."

"Have you known her long?"

"She came here about fifteen years ago to work for Doc. She was mouthy even then. Doc's wife died soon after that. I think she thought she was going to be Mrs. Doc. It didn't happen, but they're still as tight as eight in a bed."

"He sleeps with her?"

Adelaide rolled her eyes and said drily, "Who knows?" Then she laughed and her eyes lit up, showing a hidden sense of humor. "He'd have to be careful or she'd crush him. She's a head taller and must outweigh him by a hundred pounds."

"Maybe she's interested in Paul and sees you as her competition."

"He's one of the few men in town who's her size." Adelaide continued to smile. "About a year ago, she started flirting with him. A fat lot of good it did her. He dislikes her as much as I do."

"Is she disagreeable to everyone in town?"

"I don't know. You'll find out that folks here know when to keep their mouths shut. One of them might need a doctor for one of their kids one night and would be told that he's out of town."

Kathleen wanted to ask about the "what she knew" that Paul had referred to last night as causing Louise to dislike her, but decided that Adelaide would tell her when she was ready.

"I'm the one who called her," Kathleen said. "I was so scared when I came in and found you on the floor that I called the operator for the doctor. She came."

"I bet that she thought, 'Oh, boy. I've got her this time,' and trotted right over here."

Kathleen laughed. "It didn't take long, but at the time it seemed like hours. By the way, when I drove up and parked out front, an Indian woman came out of the office and walked off down the street. I would have thought that she'd have seen you lying on the floor."

Kathleen was waiting for Adelaide's comment about the Indian woman when Paul and Woody came from the back room.

Paul had taken off his ink-stained apron, had washed, and had combed his hair. He had a terribly homely face, but nevertheless, was such a large, well-built man that he made an impressive figure.

Woody politely removed his cap and tucked it under his arm when he came into the office. While working with him at the press, Kathleen had become aware that he was a light-colored Negro. Now, looking him full in the face, she saw how nice-looking he was. His dark eyes were large, his features fine. It was hard to tell his exact age.

Both men avoided looking directly at Kathleen.

"We're almost finished," Adelaide said. "My, it goes faster with two working. It's just now four-fifteen."

Woody was pulling a big red coaster wagon loaded with bundled papers. He stacked them beside the door.

"They're for the bus," Adelaide said. "The driver drops off bundles at Deval, Loveland, Grandview, and Davidson."

"Do you get any advertising from those towns?"

"Some."

When the mail subscribers' papers were all stamped, tied, and loaded in the wagon, Adelaide gave Woody the necessary papers for the post office and held the door open for him. He eased the wagon over the threshold and took off down the street.

"That's done." She sighed.

"I'll take care of things down here. Why don't you and Miss Dolan go on upstairs? I know you've got things to talk about."

Out of the corner of her eye, Kathleen saw Paul's hand sliding up and down Adelaide's back. *They are more than friends. He's very protective of her. If they are lovers, they must have more of a reason for hiding it other than because he's younger than she is.*

"You'll come up after you close?"

"I hadn't planned on it. You two need—"

"—I'll have supper ready. Like always." Adelaide placed her hand on his arm and kept her eyes on his face.

Kathleen felt like an intruder and busied herself clearing off her desk.

"You're tired and you don't need to cook. I'll go over to the store and bring up some meat for sandwiches." He spoke softly just to her.

"I invited Kathleen for supper. I'm going to fix salmon patties and fry some potatoes. Nothing fancy."

"Don't go to any trouble for me," Kathleen protested. "I can go to Claude's for a hamburger."

"We usually have a sandwich or eggs on press day. Sometimes we're almost too tired to eat."

"I don't see how you two got this paper out all by yourselves. There were six people working at the paper in Liberal."

"Paul does as much work as a dozen people," Adelaide said proudly. "There's nothing he can't do from writing editorials—he'll be mad at me for telling this—to fixing those two monstrous machines we have in the back room. He tunes in to Eastern radio and takes down the news . . . like the headlines we had today: 'Chamberlain Off by Plane to See Hitler.' "

"I wondered how you got that. Pretty clever."

Kathleen watched color flood the big man's face and heard Adelaide's soothing words to him.

"She had to know, Paul, that I couldn't write this entire paper by myself." With her hand on the big man's arm, she turned to Kathleen. "Most of the people here have no idea what it takes to get out a paper. They think that because a man gets greasy working on the press and isn't constantly blowing his own horn, he doesn't have anything up here." She tapped her forehead with her finger. "Paul is smarter than half the town put together," she said defensively. "For several years he's taken care of the national and state news, and I've handled the local stuff and the advertising. He's a better writer than I am, by far."

"Addie—hush," Paul said gently.

"I won't hush. If Kathleen is going to buy into this paper and be working here, she has the right to know that it's mostly due to you that we've kept our heads above water."

"*If* I'm going to buy into the paper? I was under the impression that you had accepted my offer. Don't tell me that you've changed your mind," Kathleen said.

"I've not changed my mind. I thought it only fair that you know what's been going on before we go into a partnership."

"Will my being here make a difference in how you run the paper?"

"Not if you don't object to Paul's being your partner as well."

"Why should I object?"

"We're lovers," Adelaide blurted.

"That's your business and . . . Paul's." Paul had turned his back to the two women and was looking out the window. "I told you in my letters that I wanted to invest my inheritance in something that would help to keep me out of the poorhouse in my old age. You agreed that for five hundred dollars I would own half the *Gazette,* the building it's in, and be a full partner in running it."

"None of that has changed."

"Well, then I don't see that we have a problem."

"You'll hear talk—"

"I probably won't be here a week until you'll be hearing talk about me. I'm not a woman who knuckles under. I stand up for myself, which rubs some the wrong way."

"There are other problems. Things are going on in this town that I mean to uncover if I can. It could be . . . dangerous, and you'd be involved."

"I'd like to hear more about it, but I doubt it would change my mind about my investment here."

"Oh, Kathleen, I knew that I was going to like you."

Kathleen laughed. "Tell me that a couple months from now when I've clashed with your biggest advertiser, written a story that offends the mayor, exposed the Baptist preacher's love affair with a high-school girl, and caused Mrs. Smothers to cancel her subscription."

"Are you really capable of all that? I'm going to love it. Paul, you were right. When you read her letters, you said that she was a woman with guts."

Paul turned and spoke to Kathleen. "There are people here who would want to tar and feather me if they thought I had as much as touched Addie's hand. I am nothing here but a linotype operator and a pressman. I want it to stay that way."

Kathleen shrugged. "Your choice."

"Before I came here four years ago, I spent time in Huntsville, Texas, penitentiary for—"

"—Oh, Paul . . . don't—"

"—For murder."

"Oh, Kathleen, please don't let that information leave this room!"

"I want all the cards on the table, Addie," Paul said, then looked directly at Kathleen. "I came through here on a freight train on Christmas Eve, hungry and cold. She let me in into the back room after I had been turned away all over town. She treated me like a human being instead of a dog to be kicked around. She brought down blankets and let me sleep there in the back room on a cot. I was warm for the first time in weeks. The next morning she invited me to come up for dinner." He paused, looked at Addie, his eyes soft and full of love, but there was nothing soft about his words when he spoke again. "Being with Addie is the nearest I'll ever be to heaven. I'll kill anyone who hurts her or tries to take her from me."

There was a long, deep silence. Kathleen glanced at Adelaide and saw that her eyes were shiny with tears as she gazed into the big man's homely face.

"Paul, dear. What would I do without you?"

"You don't have to do without me, Addie." He spoke in a low voice, a quiet, intimate tone that struck a chord of longing inside Kathleen.

She felt a yearning for someone of her own, a feeling she'd not had for a long time. What would it be like to have a man love her so much that he would be willing to kill to keep her safe? Kathleen shook her head in order to rid her mind of the thought.

"Adelaide is very, very lucky," she said, her voice shaky and barely above a whisper.

"Paul, doggone it, you're going to make me . . . cry."

"No, sweet girl, I don't want to do that. I just wanted

Miss Dolan to know where I stand and that I don't have a life away from you . . . outside this building."

"But . . . it isn't enough for you. You're such a wonderful man. You should have a family . . . children—"

"Shhh— We've been over that before, and it isn't something we should discuss in front of Miss Dolan. Here's the bus. I'll take out the papers."

As soon as he was out the door, Adelaide spoke with a sad shake of her head.

"I didn't intend for all of this to come out before you even got to know us. Paul is an astute judge of character. He made a decision about you, or he'd never have said what he did about his past."

"I'll not betray his trust. I suspected yesterday, when he found you on the floor, that he was in love with you. He was beside himself with worry."

"His affection for me is largely due to the fact that he hasn't had much kindness in his life."

"Oh, I'm sure that's not the case. He adores you."

"He's a dear man, kind and gentle."

"You love him, don't you?"

"Yes, I love him. But . . . I'm ten years older than he is."

"So what? Martha was older than George Washington. I've not heard anyone complaining about that."

Chapter Four

DURING THE WEEK THAT FOLLOWED, Kathleen learned very little more about Paul Leahy's background and a lot more about the merchants in Rawlings, the most important of which was that they were very tightfisted with their advertising dollar. The two grocery stores were competitive as the stores in Liberal had been. If one ran an ad, the other one did too. Each tried to worm out of Kathleen the specials the other store would be featuring the following week.

Legal notices were a sure source of revenue for the paper. Rawlings, being the seat of Tillison County, had a column of "Legals" each week. Adelaide explained that at times the county was a couple months behind in payment, but it was a sure source of income for the paper. Kathleen made a mental note to discuss the delay with the county treasurer.

The sheriff's office and county jail were in a low, flat building attached to the back of the courthouse. With a round-brimmed straw hat on her head to protect her sensitive skin from the hot Oklahoma sun, Kathleen opened the screen door and went into the sheriff's office.

She removed her hat and stood for a moment under the cooling breeze of the ceiling fan as she waited for the man

sitting at a desk to turn and acknowledge her. She waited a
full minute or two, then rapped sharply on the counter with
her knuckles. The man turned with a scowl that slowly disappeared from his face as he stood.

"Well . . . hello." He was a blocky man in his late thirties
or early forties, with watery blue eyes and very noticeable
false teeth. The uppers dropped slightly when he smiled.

"I'm Kathleen Dolan from the *Gazette*."

"Now this's a real treat. I heard that a pretty redhead was
takin' over the *Gazette*."

"Correction. I'm *not* taking over the *Gazette*. Miss
Vernon and I are partners."

"Partners? Now don't that jist frost ya? Adelaide finally
got someone to come in and bail her out. Partners." He repeated the word in a tone of disbelief. "Is she goin' to share
that mud-ugly bum she took in off the street? 'Pears to me
three in a bed'll be a mite crowded. Huh?" He raised his
brows several times causing wrinkles to form on his forehead.

Does he mean what his words implied?

In the silence that followed, she realized that he meant
exactly what he had said after he raised his brows again in a
gesture that irritated her. Her mouth drew down in a thin
angry line and her eyes gleamed with temper.

"Are you the sheriff?" she snapped impatiently.

"Noooo— I'm Deputy Mitchell P. Thatcher, but my
friends call me Ell." He lowered his voice and murmured the
last in a confidential tone. He appeared to be totally oblivious to her sudden testiness.

Kathleen pulled in a hard, deep breath and tried to hang
on to her temper. There was a nastiness and an arrogance
about the man that rubbed her the wrong way. She had

taken an instant dislike to the deputy and chided herself for letting it show.

"Is the sheriff in, Mr. Thatcher?"

"Name's Ell, honey. Ell to my friends." He leaned toward her with his elbow on the counter. The heavy smell of brilliantine came from his slicked-down bushy hair.

"I'm not your friend, Mr. Thatcher. I'm not even an acquaintance. I'm here to see the sheriff."

"He's not in. I take care of thin's 'round here when he's out. What can I do for you?" He wiggled his brows again in that irritating gesture.

Kathleen bit back a hundred answers to his question and looked at the coat of dust on the counter, the wads of paper on the floor, the overflowing ashtrays. Then her eyes met his head-on.

"From the looks of this place you haven't been overworking while the boss was away. Or does this place always look like a hog pen?"

The grin left the deputy's face. He leaned back and crossed his arms over his chest.

"Honey," he drawled, "you may've got by with that smart mouth up in Kansas, but it won't work down here in Oklahoma. We won't put up with it."

"Now that's just too damn bad, *Deputy do-nothing*." A pointed finger stabbed at him. "What are you going to do about it? Lynch me or just tar and feather me and run me out of town?" Her voice was razor-sharp, her face a rigid mask of indignation. She turned to leave, knowing she had made an enemy of the deputy, but too angry to care.

"Naw. Down here we got better uses for . . . a pretty woman." The deputy's words followed her out the door. "On . . . her backside."

Out on the sidewalk, Kathleen slapped her straw hat

down on her head and walked swiftly to the corner, turned and headed for the heart of town, too angry to remember she had planned to stop at the office of the county treasurer. She fumed over the words of the stupid redneck deputy.

How did such a man keep his job? Except for the hijackers, only two of the people she had met during the past week had been less than friendly. Kathleen prided herself on breaking through people's reserve and making them like her. But the nurse and the deputy weren't worth the effort.

She had even won over the owner of the theater, who had wanted her to list the coming movies in a news story so that he wouldn't have to pay for an ad. By the time she left the theater he had agreed to take a two-inch ad each week, and she had promised to write a feature about a drawing for a ten-dollar bill he planned to have every Saturday night.

Her temper had dropped from a boil to a simmer and then petered out as she approached the shoe-repair shop and turned in.

"Howdy." The cobbler looked up as she entered.

"Hello. I need new leather on my heels. I've worn them almost to the wood." Kathleen removed first one high-heeled pump and then the other and handed them to him. She stood in her stockinged feet while he looked at them. "Can you do the job while I wait?"

"You bet. Have a seat. It'll take about fifteen minutes."

"I do a lot of walking. This is the second time I've had to have them fixed."

"It'll cost you thirty-five cents."

"Sounds reasonable to me."

Kathleen sat down on the bench next to the wall and put her hat and purse down beside her. There wasn't a fan in the small shop, but the front and back doors were open, allowing a slight breeze to pass through. She looked up and caught the cobbler glancing at her. He had a head of thick white hair, rounded shoulders and a bent back.

"I'm Kathleen Dolan. I'll be working with Miss Vernon at the *Gazette.*"

"Figured you was her. There ain't many redheaded women 'round here."

"This red hair has gotten me into trouble more than once. I sure can't go around pretending to be someone else unless I put a sack over my head."

"Women can't even get hair like that outta a bottle. Seen some that tried. Some'll try anythin'."

"I don't know why they would want it. It isn't all that great to be different."

"Young folks nowadays is wantin' what they ain't got and figurin' on how they can get it without work. All they want to do is go to picture shows and honky-tonks and loll 'round on the grass in the shade."

"They're no different here than anywhere else. Hard times have brought out the best in some and the worst in others."

"Workin' hard ain't never hurt nobody. Young folk don't want to put in a day's work. They want ever'thin' give to 'em."

"Most of them would work if they could find a job."

"In a few more years they'll be in charge of the country, then watch out. It'll go to the dogs fast. There'll be a saloon and a dance hall on ever' corner and a whorehouse between. Ya won't be able to tell the women from the men. Women is already wearin' men's pants, struttin' 'round smokin' cigarettes. Some even smokin' cigars. Old folks'll be kicked out into the street. It's the end of times, just like it says in the Bible."

If it wasn't for men who used the whore, there wouldn't be a need for whorehouses. Kathleen kept her thoughts to herself, hoping that he would get the hint and stop the tirade. But it didn't happen.

"Roosevelt's atryin' to give us all a number. Social Security, he calls it. Baa! It's the mark of the beast like it says in the last days. Folks won't have no names no more, just numbers. Mark my words, next they'll be putting that number on our foreheads."

"President Roosevelt only wants everyone to have a little income when they can no longer work." Kathleen tried to put some reason into the conversation, but she could have just as well saved her breath. The man was so full of what he wanted to say that he didn't hear a word she said, and continued his ranting as he worked.

"Women is like mares in heat these days. They get in the family way, go off, have a youngun and give it away like it was a sack a potatoes. I tell you, a old dog will fight to keep its young, but not some of these young fillies. They get hung up cause they're out flippin' up their skirts and showin' themselves. Can't blame a man for takin' what's offered."

Of course not. Poor weak men! Big strong women force them to get in bed with them.

It wasn't hard for Kathleen to realize that the cobbler disliked women. He blamed all the woes of the world on the females. She looked out the door and wished that he would finish putting the heels on her shoes so that she could leave. She dug into her purse for a quarter and a dime and held it in her hand so that the minute he finished she could get out of there.

"The Lord says that in the last days there would be fornicatin' in the streets."

"I never heard *that* before." Kathleen was getting impatient.

"The good Lord didn't say it in just them words, but 'twas what he meant."

"Are you about finished? I've got lots to do this morning."

"Ya ort to get ya some sensible shoes. I got a pair hardly wore a'tall I'll sell ya for fifty cents. It's what I got in 'em for puttin' on half soles." He indicated a pair of black tie oxfords.

" 'Fraid they're not my size."

"Don't matter. Ya can stick a little cotton in the toes. Forty cents, and it's as low as I'll go."

Kathleen took one of her shoes from the counter, slipped it on, and waited for him to trim the leather around the heel of the other. As soon as he finished she put it on and placed her money on the counter.

"Thank you," she called as she passed through the door, thinking that she'd not had a very good morning.

Out on the brick sidewalk she paused to put on her hat. At that moment she saw Johnny Henry's old black truck pass with a small table resting on its top in the truck bed.

Kathleen waved, but there was no way he would have seen her unless he had been looking in the rearview mirror. She hurried down the street thinking that he would stop at the *Gazette,* but he passed it by and turned on the street where Mrs. Ramsey lived. He was delivering the table he had promised.

Adelaide was typing when Kathleen entered the office. She stood beneath the fan for a moment. Her dress was stuck to her back, and she could feel rivulets of perspiration running down the valley between her breasts. She fanned her face with the brim of her hat.

"You're getting a sunburn." Adelaide yanked a sheet of paper out of the typewriter.

"It's more windburn. It blows more here than in Kansas,

and it's hotter. My freckles are having a coming-out party. I'm serving them a daily dose of buttermilk, but it doesn't seem to help much." Kathleen placed her hat on the counter and took papers from the folder she carried. "I got a couple of new ads. One from Ginny at Cut and Curl. She's got a special on permanent waves, a dollar and a half, down from a dollar ninety-eight."

"You don't need one of those, that's for sure."

"No, but I had to promise to come back for a cut." She lifted the thick curls off her neck. "I may have her shave my head."

"That would be a sight."

"I do get tired of being referred to as that *redheaded woman.* What do you know about Mitchell Thatcher, the deputy?"

"He's a horse's patoot."

"That's an insult to the horse."

"Yeah, but he's the deputy supported by Sheriff Carroll."

Kathleen snorted. "You can put lipstick on a pig all day long, and he's still a pig."

"That bad?"

"We got into a little tiff, and he didn't like my smart mouth. I asked him if he was going to tar and feather me, and he said that they had better uses for women down here. Was that a threat?"

Adelaide didn't answer right away. Kathleen sat down at her desk and glanced over to see her partner staring off into space and tapping the rubber end of her pencil on the desk. Finally, when she spoke it was thoughtfully.

"Be careful of him, Kathleen."

"Why? Why should I have to take his insinuations without talking back?"

"What was he insinuating?"

"Oh, that he ran things when the sheriff was gone and . . . that women who had smart mouths didn't get along down here." *And that you were sleeping with Paul, and now that I'm a partner you'll share him.*

"He isn't a very nice man."

Kathleen rolled her eyes. "Say it again."

"I mean it, Kathleen. He and the sheriff may be involved in something here that isn't very pleasant."

Kathleen became very still. "Something that has to do with Louise Munday?"

"Why do you say that?"

"Because of something Paul said the day I arrived. He said Louise was afraid that you knew too much. Adelaide, what's going on?"

"Maybe something. Maybe nothing." Adelaide looked over her shoulder to be sure that they were alone. "Paul and I have wondered about the doctor's office. He calls it a clinic. But if someone gets really sick, he sends them to Altus or Lawton. About all he does is deliver babies. A lot of women come to Doc Herman."

"Is Louise the only nurse?"

"As far as I know. There are several other women who work there, and I've seen a couple of them in white uniforms, but without the cap. It just seems strange that someone from out of town would come here to have a baby."

"How do you know they *come here?*"

"Before I was cut off from seeing the records at the court-house, I found registered birth certificates from couples giving their addresses as Colorado, Texas, and even as far away as Missouri. When I asked questions, I got a rebuke from Dr. Herman. He said that he had been recommended by family and friends. He acted as if I were questioning his qualifications. Shortly after that, Louise began to spread it around that I was a heavy drinker and had hallucinations. The story is all over town. When you came, it gave some legitimacy to her story that I'm not capable of running the paper."

"Good heavens! And I called her when you fell out of the chair."

"I didn't fall out of the chair, Kathleen. I was pushed, lost my balance, and fell."

Kathleen looked at her, her eyes full of questions. Finally, she voiced one of them.

"By the Indian woman who came out of the office as I drove up?"

"Yes. Her name is Hannah. She is a pitiful creature, drunk most of the time. I'm afraid that she's used by anyone who will buy her a bottle of rotgut whiskey. She's been pregnant twice during the past few years. Any man who takes advantage of her is not a man but a rutting animal, in my estimation."

"Who takes care of her children?"

"I never see them. They're probably being cared for. The Cherokee are very protective of their children, even the half-breed children of a woman who has been cast out."

"Why did she push you?"

"She wanted money. I've bought a few things for her at the grocery now and then. That day I asked her where her baby was because I could see that her breasts were leaking milk. She didn't say anything, so I asked again where it was. When she didn't answer, I asked her if she had *lost* it. She got mad and shoved me."

"You didn't want Louise to know Hannah had pushed you."

"Hannah is a drunk. A pitiful drunk." Adelaide rubbed the back of her neck.

"There's a social service woman in Oklahoma City. I

think her name is Mable Bassett. She would know what to do about her."

"I've thought about calling her," Adelaide said, and reached for the telephone when it rang. "*Gazette*. Oh, hello, Johnny. Yes, she's here. Just a moment. For you, Kathleen."

Kathleen moved her chair back so she could reach the phone. "Hello."

"Miss Dolan, Johnny Henry. I took the table for your typewriter down to Mrs. Ramsey's."

"Thank you. I want to pay you—"

"Forget it. I wasn't using it."

"At least let me buy you a hamburger at Claude's."

"Yes, well, sometime. See you around. 'Bye."

"Good-bye."

Kathleen hung up the phone and turned back to face the window, feeling that she had been given the brush-off. She had been thinking that Johnny Henry was a man she would like to know. Evidently he didn't feel the same about her. She had thought about him often since the day she came to Rawlings and now was embarrassed to recall those thoughts. She had even thought about asking him to drive with her over to Red Rock to see her uncle, Tom Dolan, and Henry Ann Dolan. Lordy, she was glad the opportunity hadn't come up. She would have made a fool of herself.

"Got a date with Johnny?" Adelaide asked.

"Heavens, no! He called to say he had delivered a table he said he'd lend me."

"Oh, shoot! I was hoping you two could get together. Paul and I like Johnny Henry."

"Does he have a steady girl?" Kathleen hated herself for asking. She had given Adelaide a play-by-play description of what happened when she was hijacked.

"Not that I know of. He stays pretty much to himself. He

goes away every so often for several weeks. When he does, he has someone look after his ranch. No one seems to know where he goes."

Kathleen knew where he went. Her uncle, Hod, had told her that Johnny Henry worked occasionally for the federal government. He and Hod had tracked the movements of Clyde Barrow and Bonnie Parker, and the information they passed on to Marshal Frank Hamer had resulted in their demise. Johnny evidently kept that part of his life from the people in this town. Kathleen was reluctant to reveal it even to Adelaide.

"We got acquainted with him a few years ago after the rodeo. Paul was having a little trouble with some toughs. He can be pushed just so far before he starts swinging. It was four against one. Johnny stepped in. Since that time he and Paul have been friends. Johnny is about the only friend Paul has, I might add."

"I was sure glad he came along when I was being hijacked. He said he turned the names in to the sheriff, but I've heard nothing about signing a complaint."

"And you won't."

"How often do they have a city council meeting here?" Kathleen asked.

"Whenever the mayor calls one. It's usually on short notice. Over and done with before I'm aware of it."

"Do they allow you to see the minutes?"

Adelaide snorted. "Sure. It's the law. They give me the bare bones. The meeting was opened, roll called, minutes read and approved. Usually they have a little discussion about a chuckhole in the street or a crack in the sidewalk, then adjourn. Nothing there you can report on. It's been that way for the past five years."

"Since the doctor became mayor?"

"Right."

"There isn't anyone who stands up against him?"

"He's an icon, a hero around here. If you criticize him, it's like criticizing Jesus Christ, motherhood, or baseball. The man and his cronies have a stranglehold on this town. Folks love him, and woe to the one who exposes the good guy as a bad guy. That kind of truth turns the people against the messenger every time."

"Has he tried to win you over to his side?"

"He asked me out to dinner a few times after his wife died. He was diplomatic about it; but he insinuated that, being an old maid, I think he said maiden lady, he, as my doctor, could teach me the pleasures of the flesh . . . my words, not his. I was so shocked I couldn't remember exactly what he said, but his meaning was clear. He was willing to give the old maid a treat." Adelaide shivered. "What little respect I had for him went right out the window."

"He's the only doctor in town isn't he? Do you go to him when you get sick?"

"Paul had been here only a few months when I got really sick. He took me to Altus. Of course, Doc found out about it and sent the sheriff and the deputy in to question Paul. They didn't find out anything. Paul is very clever. He has managed to create a whole new identity for himself. I didn't know about Paul's past at that time. I'm glad I didn't. It wasn't until later that he told me."

"He's the best linotype operator I've ever seen. The operator in Liberal made ten times the mistakes Paul makes. Sometimes I don't find any in column after column, and I think that I've overlooked something."

Adelaide's eyes shone with pride. "He is good, isn't he?"

"He worked on a paper before he came here, didn't he?"

"Yes. A big paper. Paul is an honorable man. He thought

it fair that you knew something about him when you put your money in the paper. He'll tell you more when he's ready. Do you have any objection to his writing the national news?"

"Absolutely not! He does a really great job; as good as the *Oklahoman and Times* or the *Wichita Eagle*. It's outstanding for a town of this size. I hope the readers realize what they're getting." Kathleen picked up her folder and headed for the door. "I'll get the ad from the grocery store, and we'll have the advertising in for this week except for the classifieds. I'll write the rodeo story when I get back so Paul can set it."

"I have two long obits. Both men were old-timers here. I wish I had time to send their pictures to Lawton for engraving. I may send them anyway and run the pictures next week."

"There was an engraver in Liberal, but he was expensive, and the publisher wouldn't let us put in a picture unless it was something important. We had an extensive file of engravings, pictures of all the prominent people for miles around, and local sites. By the way, I brought mine and put it in the file. You can use it in case I get run over by a truck."

"Oh, go on with you. You'd better not get hit by a truck. I'd be mad as a hornet. I hate doing ads," Adelaide called.

Kathleen laughed at her over her shoulder as she went out the door. The heat beaming up from the sidewalk hit her face. She hurried down the street to the store and failed to see the dilapidated old truck parked at the corner.

Chapter Five

Standing beside the grocery counter, Johnny saw Kathleen as she passed the window and again when she entered the store. He had caught a glimpse of her bright red hair earlier when he passed the shoe-repair shop and was relieved to see her there. She would not be at the Ramseys' when he delivered the table.

Hazel had opened the door for him and watched as he set the table against the wall and lifted Kathleen's typewriter from the floor. The room was neat as a pin; books and papers were stacked, the bed made without a single wrinkle in the cover. He was beset by a loneliness deeper than he'd ever felt before as he stood amid the little home spot she had made for herself. Embarrassed by his own feelings, he made a hasty retreat, even refusing the offer of a piece of sweet potato pie.

Later he had called Kathleen from the telephone office, where he had gone to pay for a call he had placed the week before.

Since their first meeting on the highway, he'd had plenty of time to think about her as he rounded up his horses down on Keith McCabe's range. He had bred his mares to Keith's stallion last April and would keep them closer to home during the winter months in case of a severe norther that could trap them for days without food. During that time he had convinced himself that any further contact with Miss Kathleen Dolan would be dangerous to his peace of mind. Therefore, the only thing to do would be to avoid her whenever possible.

Now, it appeared to be impossible. There was no escape.

He had just given a lengthy list of his needs to Mrs. Wilson when Kathleen came into the store, saw him, and smiled. He touched his fingers to his hat brim and set his dark eyes on her, letting nothing at all show beneath their impenetrable surface.

"Howdy, ma'am."

"Hello." Kathleen walked toward him as Mrs. Wilson moved away with his list in her hand. "Thank you for the table."

"You're more than welcome."

He turned away, scooped up coffee beans, poured them into the grinder, and began to turn the large wheel. He knew that she stood there, hesitant, before she walked past him. His thoughts had scattered when she came in the door, but now they were back in his possession. He was more convinced than ever that the two of them had absolutely nothing in common.

She was refined and educated.

He had barely finished the fifth grade.

She was smart enough to write for a newspaper.

It was a chore for him to write a grocery list.

She came from respectable people.

His mother had been Mud Creek trash.

The differences between them went on and on. It was better, he thought now, to have her think that he was uninterested in her as a woman than to have her know that the man who was on the verge of falling in love with her was the bastard son of a whore and a drunken Indian. It was a fact she would find out soon enough.

Johnny was not conceited enough to think that the welcome smile she had given him when she came into the store, was for him . . . personally. It was for the help he had given her the day she arrived and for the table he had just delivered.

Mrs. Wilson returned and bagged the coffee she took from the grinder.

"Our special next week will be soda crackers. You can have them for sale price if you want."

"I'll take a box. I was in a hurry when I scratched off the list. I'm surprised you could read it."

"I made out most of it. You'd better look it over in case I missed something. You've got quite an order."

"I sold one of my mares and decided to lay in a stock of grub."

"We appreciate your business, Johnny."

He could hear the click of heels on the wooden floor and knew that Kathleen was coming back to the front of the store. He busied himself checking over the list but was terribly aware when she stopped beside him. He folded the paper and put it in his shirt pocket.

"I forgot to put cornmeal on the list, Mrs. Wilson. Give me a five-pound bag." The grocer's wife nodded and went down the crowded aisle of the store.

"I hear that you'll be one of the contestants at the rodeo," Kathleen said. "I'll be cheering for you."

"Thanks. I enter every year just for the hell of it."

"Adelaide says that you usually win."

"Only the bronc-riding."

"You're being modest. She says you win the calf-roping and sometimes the steer-wrestling."

"Once in a while I get lucky." His tone was one of disinterest.

He hadn't looked directly at her except the one time when she first came into the store. Color tinged her face and neck as her irritation mounted. *Who the heck does he think he is? He has no right to snub me. I didn't ask for the darn table.*

"Have I stepped on your tail? Is that why you're giving me the cold shoulder?"

His head turned quickly, and he looked down at her. *Good. I got his attention at last.*

"Why do you say that?"

"I'm not so dumb that I don't know when I'm getting the brush-off. I thought that we could be friends as long as we're both connected to my Uncle Tom. Do you have something against being friends with a woman?"

"Of course not." Johnny felt his face tingle with embarrassment.

"Then perhaps I have body odor or bad breath. I'll keep my offensive body at a distance when I see you at the rodeo. Good-bye." She walked away from him with her head held high.

"Here ya are, Johnny." Mrs. Wilson returned with the bag of cornmeal. "Anything else?"

"I don't think so. Tally up the bill."

After he paid, she packed his order in boxes while he carried a five-gallon can of kerosene out to his truck.

"You should set your cap for Miss Dolan, Johnny," Mrs. Wilson teased when he came back for the boxes. "She's nice. Pretty, too. Every single man in town will be beating a path to her door."

"Ah . . . no," he stammered. "She'd not see me for dirt. I'm a poor rancher who's head over heels in debt."

"Who isn't? She works hard and isn't in the least snooty. By the way, I put a hunk of cheese in the box, our thanks for the big order."

"I'm obliged."

"Good luck at the rodeo, Johnny."

"Thanks."

When Kathleen left the store, she was angry at Johnny and angry at herself for having been glad to see him. Embarrassment mingled with her anger. She had been about to make a fool of herself and ask him if he'd like to go to Red Rock to see the Tom Dolans. She should be grateful that he made his feelings perfectly clear.

Damn him! If he thought she was chasing after him, he could just get that thought out of his block head. *But the idea that he could be thinking that cut her to the quick.*

She was so engrossed in her thoughts that she almost ran into the two men coming toward her. She looked up and recognized them immediately. The two toughs who had attempted to steal her car and her money stood there brazenly grinning at her. Temper that had been simmering since Johnny's snub, boiled up. With her hands on her hips, she stopped in front of them, barring their way.

"How come you're not in jail?" she almost yelled.

"Well, looky here. If it ain't that feisty redhead we helped get outta the ditch." The one called Webb grinned inanely, showing stained, broken teeth.

"Helped, my hind leg!" The tone of Kathleen's voice was keeping pace with her temper. "You . . . you piles of horse dung! You were hijacking my car."

"Hijackin' ya? Hear that, Webb? She ain't grateful a'tall

fer what we done. You'd'a thought a uppity-up like her'd have manners and give us a little somethin' more than a jawin' out fer all the help we done a pushin' her car. Like a little kiss maybe."

"Listen to me, you mangy polecats,"—Her eyes glittered with the light of battle—"I don't know why you're not in jail where you belong, but you can bet your filthy hide I'm going to find out."

"Ya go on and do that, baby doll," Webb leered at her. "Say, sugar, how 'bout goin' honky-tonkin' tonight? Otis and his Ring-tail Tooters is playin' out at the Twilight Gardens. There's a gal there what's goin' to show us how to do the jitterbug dance. Ya've seen it done, ain't ya?"

"You're out of your mind if you think I'd be caught dead with warthogs like you." She wrinkled her nose in a contemptuous sneer.

"She ain't goin' to be friendly. It's a pure-dee shame. Guess we better be on our way."

"Not so fast . . . scum! Johnny Henry told the sheriff about you."

"Yeah. Fat lot a good it done him. Now get outta the way. We ain't got no time to stand here jawin' with a . . . high-tone split-tail when we got things to do." He reached out and grasped her upper arms.

Rage gave Kathleen strength to jerk her arm loose and swing her fist. The blow caught Webb on the side of his face. He let out an angry yelp and raised his hand to slap her.

"Hit me, you yellow-bellied buzzard bait, and some dark night you'll get a belly full of lead!" she shouted as she was suddenly pushed aside. Johnny was between her and the two men.

"Touch her, and I'll bury you."

"She started it. She hit me."

"You grabbed her. I saw you."

"Yeah? Well go tell it to the sheriff. She ain't nothin' but a—"

"—Say it, and your nose will be smeared all over your ugly face."

"Why aren't they in jail?" Kathleen demanded.

"I don't know." Johnny glanced at her, then back, as the two men began to edge around him. "But I'll find out. Go on, get off the street. You've given the folks a show. I'll take them down to the sheriff."

"Won't do no good. We been there and told him how it was."

"You can tell him again why you threatened Miss Dolan. Come on," Johnny snarled, and prodded them ahead of him.

"She come on to us," Webb yelled. "She wild as a hare-lipped mule! Redheaded wildcat is what she is."

Kathleen watched as Johnny herded the two men off down the street. He had rescued her again. She looked around and saw that several people had stopped along the street to watch the *show*. With tears of rage and frustration in her eyes, she hurried on down the street to the *Gazette*. Thank goodness Adelaide wasn't in the office when she reached it, and she had time to gather herself together before she had to face her.

This had not been her best day. Not by a long shot! First the randy deputy, then the ranting cobbler, and the embarrassment of being brushed off by Johnny Henry. Finally seeing the miserable jayhawkers who had tried to rob her walking the street as free as air. It was all too much. She desperately wanted to cry, but her pride forbade it.

She heard the linotype machine start up and knew that

Adelaide would be coming back. She hastily put a sheet of paper in her typewriter, dug in the basket on her desk for the information about the rodeo, and began to write. She wrote three lines, Xed them out, then started again.

> *The fifth annual Rawlings rodeo will be held at the Tillison County fair grounds Saturday Sept. 23. Fifteen contestants have signed up to compete in nine different events.*
>
> *Johnny Henry, local rancher, who took home the purse last year for "Best All-Around Cowboy" will enter seven events.*
>
> *The stock for the event will come from the McCabe ranch just south of the river in Dallam County, Texas.*
>
> *Again this year the local churches will be in charge of the concession stands, and a variety of food and drink will be available.*

The screen door was jerked open, and a big man with a star on his chest came in. He looked around the office, then down at her.

"May I help you?"

"You can if you're Miss Dolan, and I think you are. There's not many women—"

"—in town with hair as red as mine." Kathleen finished for him and got to her feet. Looking up at him made her uncomfortable. "I've heard it a million times. You're the sheriff."

"How'd ya guess?" He hooked his thumbs in the pockets of his trousers and looked steadily at her.

Sheriff A. B. Carroll was a heavyset man with a big neck, broad shoulders, and short arms and legs. The hair beneath the brim of his Stetson was brown, the thick mustache on his upper lip brown sprinkled with gray. The bulge in his jaw, Kathleen suspected, was a plug of chewing tobacco. He wore his importance on his chest along with his badge. She decided then and there that she wasn't going to like him.

"It wasn't hard to figure it out. The star means that you're either the sheriff or from the Star Ice Company. We got ice yesterday."

"Smart-mouthed, just like Ell said."

"Speaking of your deputy, are all women treated with such lecherous behavior when they go to the county sheriff's office?"

"Those who ask for it."

"And who is to be the judge of that?"

"I am. When I'm not there, my deputy is."

"I'd like to remind you, Sheriff, that your salary and that of your ill-bred deputy, and the office you occupy are paid for by the taxpayers of this county, and they are entitled to be treated with civility."

"You've not paid taxes here. What are *you* yippin' about?"

"Hello, A. B., I thought I heard your voice out here." Adelaide had come quietly into the office.

"Hello, Adelaide. I think you've got yourself a little hot-tempered chili pepper here. She just got into a fight out on the street. You know that I can't have a woman, man either, brawlin' in public. Doc says it ain't a good image for the town."

"Wait a gosh-darn minute," Kathleen sputtered. "That man grabbed me. I had to defend myself."

"They disagree. It's two against one."

"The two you're referring to are the men who attempted to hijack me out on the highway the day I arrived here.

They also took my money and would have gotten away with it if Johnny Henry hadn't come along when he did. I'll sign a complaint against them."

"Here we've got two sides again," the sheriff said patiently. He turned and addressed his remarks to Adelaide. "Webb and Krome, the men this woman is accusing, told me that they had stopped to help her get her car out of the ditch. She offered to pay them. They took the money, but when Henry came along she accused them of stealing it. Now, I know that Webb and Krome aren't good upstanding citizens; but I know them, and I don't know her from a bale of hay. Why should I put two men in jail on her say-so?"

Kathleen swallowed down the knot of anger in her throat and forced herself to speak calmly.

"This has nothing to do with Adelaide, Sheriff Carroll. I'm the one involved here. I'm the one accusing your friends, Webb and Krome. My name is Miss Dolan, not *her,* not *she,* and not *that woman.* I'll thank you to remember it and address your remarks to me."

The sheriff sighed. "I'm just trying to get along here. I've got to satisfy everyone in this county, not just one newcomer who more than likely won't be here this time next year."

"Oh, I'll be here, Sheriff. I'm not one to tuck tail and run when the going gets rough. I've been told that it's the red hair. I'm not sure about that, but I do know that I'm stubborn, I'm determined, and I know when right is right. I don't back down even when the law in town fails to do its job."

"All right," the sheriff said harshly. "This town is not paradise, miss. It's just like any other town. Folks here are like folks everywhere—some are pretty decent, others so rotten they stink to high heaven. We've got some saints and some snakes. We do what we have to do to put up with 'em. My advice to you is to do the same."

Johnny had opened the screen door and stepped inside while the sheriff was talking. Kathleen's eyes went to him and found him looking at her from the concealing shadow of his hat brim. His dark eyes bore down at her with an intensity entirely different from the only time their eyes had caught while at the store. With reluctance she turned her gaze back to the sheriff.

"You're not going to arrest them." It was a statement that needed no answer, but he gave one.

"No, ma'am, I'm not." His voice was stiletto-sharp.

The flat refusal drew a faint line of displeasure across her brow. It registered in the barest widening of her blue eyes; then, for an instant, her heavy lashes shuttered her gaze. Mentally, Kathleen had slumped. Physically, she stood with her shoulders back, her head up, and looked the man in the eye.

"I've learned a lot about this town today, Sheriff Carroll, but I'm reasonably sure that you're not interested in my assessment."

"You're right about that, miss. This matter is ended, and I'll be going." He turned at the door. "I'll speak to Ell about how you were treated in my office."

After he had gone, Kathleen shifted her gaze to Johnny and away. Color touched her face. She stared down at the papers on the desk. For a short while she was wholly still, fighting down her embarrassment. When her eyes came up, she was again in control of her emotions.

"Well, I guess that's that," she said.

"I told him how it was. I didn't know he was coming here until I saw his car," Johnny told her.

"Do you believe his version of what happened?"

"Lord, no!" Points of light flared in Johnny's dark eyes. "I was there, remember?"

"Not at first—"

"—I understand what's happening. The sheriff is between a rock and a hard place on this. Someone higher up is calling the shots."

"Doc Herman?" Adelaide asked, and turned her eyes to Paul, who had come from the back room with several pages to be proofed. More than likely he had waited until the sheriff left before coming in.

Kathleen spoke in answer to Adelaide's question.

"Why would the mayor of the town have anything to say about how the *county* sheriff's office is run?" She looked from one to the other, waiting for a reply. None was forthcoming until Adelaide sighed deeply and sank down in the chair behind her desk.

"It's long and complicated, Kathleen."

Johnny watched the emotions flick across Kathleen's face. She had an agile brain and a pair of eyes that missed nothing. She also had guts she hadn't used yet. A slow smile drew little wrinkles in the corner of his eyes. That redheaded temper of hers was going to get her in trouble. There was no doubt about it.

What surprised him was why he was here after he had gone to so much trouble to keep his distance. He had sprinted down the street when he saw one of the thugs she was talking to grab her. If the man had hit her, Johnny wasn't sure what he would have done. He might have torn the man apart.

A desire to protect her washed over him. *Christ, John Henry, if you have any sense, you'd say your good-byes and get the hell out of here.*

"Got a minute, Johnny?" Paul asked. "I've got to turn

around one of the cylinders on the press and I've only got two hands."

"Sure. Glad to help."

Kathleen sat down at her desk, turned, and faced her partner.

"Did I embarrass you, Adelaide? I didn't mean to cause you more trouble." Her eyes were clouded with distress.

"You didn't embarrass me," Adelaide said staunchly. "It's hard for people in this town to accept strangers. They're used to folks *leaving* here, not *coming* here."

"Do you think it possible that those two men were sent out to hijack me, carry me off someplace, and frighten me so much that I'd be afraid to come back?"

"If they were, they met their match." A smile tilted the corners of Adelaide's mouth. "No, I don't think they'd go that far. I had let it be known that a very bright young woman was buying into the paper. Doc Herman had offered to buy in and so had several others in town. I knew that if I let that happen, it wouldn't be long before I lost control completely and Paul and I would be out on the street."

"I've been wondering about something. If Doc Herman runs the town, why doesn't he tell the merchants to stop advertising in the paper. Without advertising, you'd be out of business."

"He doesn't want us out of business. He uses us now and then when he wants to make his point about something."

"Like what?"

"Last year he wanted to get the Greyhound bus rerouted so that it would come through here. He used the paper to get up a petition and to persuade the bus company officials that a town this size with its own newspaper would help to provide a steady stream of passengers."

"Did it?"

"Oh, yes. It's a convenience for those who travel, and I think maybe it helped Doc Herman's clinic."

In the back room, Johnny washed his greasy hands.

"Thanks for the help." Paul handed him a towel. "I could have waited for Woody, but it would have made us late starting the run tomorrow."

"Anytime. I am fascinated with machinery. I've been looking for parts so I can fix up an old earth mover I bought for a song."

"What are you planning to use it for?"

"A storm cellar for one thing. I'm not anxious to dig it one spadeful at a time." Johnny waited for Paul to finish washing, then said, "I guess Miss Dolan being here has taken a load off Adelaide?"

"Yes. I was a little leery at first. I wanted Addie to meet the person she was going to bring into her business, but she said that she could tell from the letters and the recommendation from the Liberal paper that Miss Dolan was going to be just what the *Gazette* needed to put some life back into the paper. Addie is seldom wrong."

"Miss Dolan's got spunk all right. I hope it doesn't get her into more trouble."

"She's pretty, and she isn't a dumbbell by a long shot." Paul's homely face broke into a grin. "Why don't you take her to the picture show or for a ride? The girl needs an outing."

"In my old truck? I'm sure she'd like that." Johnny clapped Paul on the shoulder. "You're hog-tied, my friend, that's plain to see. I'm not, and I'm going to stay that way."

"You don't have to marry her. Just take her out a time or two."

"She'd laugh in my face if I asked her."

"Bet ya two bits. It'd pay for the movie."

"Naw. I'd best get on back to the ranch."

Chapter Six

JOHNNY LEFT THE *GAZETTE* and walked quickly down the street toward where he'd left his truck. As he passed the grocery store, Mrs. Wilson called to him.

"Johnny, can you come in a minute?"

"Sure." Inside the store he saw that Mrs. Wilson had an anxious look on her face.

"What's wrong?"

"I'm worried about Miss Dolan. The men who had a set-to with her came in a while ago. I was down behind the counter looking for a dime I'd dropped, and I heard one of them say that before they left town that redheaded bitch was going to get what was coming to her. They're down-right mean, Johnny. They talked nasty about her."

"What else did they say?"

"They said some words I don't want to repeat."

"You don't have to. I can imagine what they were. Did they say anything about the sheriff or the deputy?"

"They said 'Ell' a time or two. It's wasn't 'hell,' Johnny, it was 'Ell,' referring to Deputy Thatcher. While they were here a couple of men came in and bought a box of shotgun shells. They were Cherokee. The one called Webb made a remark about blanket-asses having money to buy shells because they could get work at the tannery and decent white men couldn't."

"Did they get a rise out of the Indians?"

"No. They ignored them."

"Mrs. Wilson, is it all right if I bring my supplies back in and leave them until morning? I've never had anything taken from the truck while it was parked on the street, but I don't trust those two yahoos. I think I'd better stick around, keep an eye on them, and make sure Miss Dolan gets home all right."

After Johnny left the office, Kathleen set her mind on the work at hand and refused to allow it to drift to other things. She finished the rodeo story that would be on the front page, then worked on the classified advertising section that took up three-quarters of a page.

"Adelaide, what do you think about starting a letter to the editor policy? We'll have space on the classified page."

"It's a good idea. Do you think we'd get any letters?"

"We won't know until we try. We can also fill that space with items from the paper files of ten or twenty-five years ago."

"That's a good idea, too. I've heard of doing that, but never had the time to do the research. We don't have time for it this week, but I could write up columns for several weeks ahead and Paul could set them. I think that we have some old engravings in the file we could use."

"After we get that going we could start a 'Cook of the Week' column featuring a lady from each of the church circles, then the clubs. In Liberal they crawled all over each other to get their names on the list. And we—"

She paused when Johnny came barreling into the *Gazette* as if he had only a minute to do something and he was determined to do it. He stopped directly in front of Kathleen's desk as if prepared to do battle.

"Go out to supper with me tonight, then I'll take you home." He blurted out the words as if he was in a hurry to get them out.

Kathleen stared at him with her mouth open. Then she snapped it shut, remembering that she had tried to be friendly with him at the store and that he had practically shunned her.

"Thanks, but Mrs. Ramsey is expecting me. I have to let her know ahead of time if I'll not be there for supper."

"I'll run down there and tell her. How long will it be before you're finished here?"

"I'm . . . not sure, and I don't think—"

"—You won't be finished before I get back. Don't leave. Wait here for me." Johnny spun on his heel and was out the door before Kathleen could open her mouth to protest.

"Well. What's got into him?" she sputtered. "He's got a lot of nerve. I suppose he thinks that he's doing me a great big favor."

"He wanted to take you out and was afraid you'd turn him down. Men are babies about rejection. That's why he got out of here in such a hurry."

"Oh? How about a woman who tries to be friendly with a man because he has done her a favor, and he gives her the cold shoulder? Is she supposed to jump a mile high when he asks her out?"

"When did that happen? I can't imagine Johnny Henry giving any woman the cold shoulder. He's one of the most polite men I've ever met."

"At the store—when I went for the ad. You'd have thought that I had the brand of a scarlet woman on my forehead."

"Are you sure?" Adelaide frowned. "That doesn't sound like Johnny. He's even nice to Clara Ramsey. Lord knows she chased him enough."

"Emily's mother? I wondered why he was so at home there. They welcomed him with open arms."

"They should. He's taken Clara home a few times when she couldn't make it on her own. She was pregnant again a few years ago and spread it around that the baby was Johnny's. He never mentioned it to us. He may have not even known she was spreading it around. Knowing Johnny, I think that if it had been his, he would have done the right thing."

"Where is the baby now?"

"It died right after birth. Clara left town after that. The last I heard she was down in Texas waiting tables in a beer joint."

"That's too bad. Emily is the one left to suffer the stigma of not having a father. She's such a sweet, cheerful little girl."

"That's Hazel's doing. She's had the care of the child since she was born. Sometimes we think that we've got troubles. Clara came home with that baby and left without her. Hazel has done everything she could to keep a roof over that child's head."

"I'm taking her with me to the rodeo. She was so excited about it last night she could hardly eat her supper."

The office door opened and two women scurried in. One was tall and thin. Her hair was scalloped around her face and held with bobby pins. The other one was about as wide as she was tall and wore a small hat with a tiny veil perched atop her henna-colored hair. They cast curious looks at Kathleen while they told Adelaide about the Methodist Church chili supper to be held after the rodeo.

Later a preacher in a black serge suit, sweat running down his ruddy face, arrived with a notice of a Pentecostal revival meeting that would begin on Sunday beneath a brush arbor a mile west of town. Every other phrase the man uttered was either "praise the Lord" or "hallelujah."

"I know there isn't a Lutheran church here, but is there one in one of the nearby towns?" Kathleen asked when the preacher left.

"None that I know of. Most are Pentecostal, Baptist, or Methodist. The churches here worked together creating the soup kitchen. They feed any hungry person who comes through. That's one pie Doc Herman doesn't have his fingers in."

"The churches did that in Liberal, too. There were so many to feed after the dust storms. The people in the area were so kind. Those that had, shared. Ranchers donated beef, hunters went to Colorado and brought back deer or elk. The whole community united to help those in need."

"We don't have as many as some towns do. We're too far from anything. Most of the folks in our soup lines come in on the freight train."

"I thank God every day for my grandparents. If not for them, I don't know where I'd be. They paid for my business school and left me a little money. Without parents, brothers, or sisters, I have only myself to depend on. I could have easily been one of the unfortunate ones without a home or a job."

"You have your uncles."

"Yes, and an aunt in South Dakota that I've never met. I want to take a Saturday afternoon off in a few weeks and drive over to Red Rock to see Uncle Tom and his family. I'll come back on Sunday. I think it's too far to drive all in one day."

"Here comes Leroy Grandon. I think he's smitten with you. He's been in the office more often since you've been here than in the last couple of months."

"Maybe he's going to put in another ad," Kathleen murmured, then, "Hello, Mr. Grandon."

"Hello." He nodded to Adelaide, then turned back to Kathleen. "I was wondering—"

"—About your ad? Do you have a price change?"

"Ah . . . no. I was wondering if you'd—" He glanced again at Adelaide who was busy typing. "I wondered if . . . you'd like to go to dinner and the picture show tomorrow night."

"Well, ah . . ." Kathleen fumbled for words. "That's very nice of you, Mr. Grandon. I'd love to go."

"You . . . will?" His smile stretched his lips and showed missing teeth along his lower jaw. He wasn't a bad-looking man when he kept his mouth shut, even if he was older than Kathleen by a good fifteen years. "I'll stop in tomorrow and we can make plans. 'Bye." He lifted his hand and was out the door. He was smiling as he passed the window.

"Oh, dear. What have I done?"

"Leroy is a nice man," Adelaide said. "And he's president of the Chamber of Commerce, even if it is a token position. He doesn't have much say in running things.

"He's a careful businessman. His store is well stocked, and he keeps it clean and orderly.

"He's lonesome. His wife died about a year ago. They never had children and were devoted to each other. At first, the widows in town found any excuse to go to the men's store. It was too soon, though, for Leroy. I've not heard that he kept company with any of them."

"I couldn't think of a logical reason not to go," Kathleen

confessed. "I saw how nervous he was and didn't want to hurt his feelings."

"You won't have to worry about Leroy. He'll be the perfect gentleman. Boring, but still a gentleman."

"Tomorrow is press day. More than likely, I'll fall asleep at the picture show."

A little later, Adelaide broke the silence. "Pssst, Kathleen, we're about to be honored by a visit from the big man himself."

Kathleen turned to look out the window to see a small man wearing baggy pants and a white shirt with sleeves rolled up to his elbows coming across the street toward the *Gazette*. The wind blew his sparse gray hair back from a high forehead above a small-featured face. He wore round, wire-rimmed glasses.

"You don't mean—?"

"I do mean."

The man came into the office and without a greeting went straight to Adelaide.

"Louise said you'd had a nasty fall."

"That was over a week ago, and it wasn't nasty."

"Have you suffered headaches, dizziness, nausea?"

"No. I'm fine."

"You should have come to see me right away. Blows to the head are not to be taken lightly."

"It wasn't that much of a blow."

"I should be the judge of that. You and this paper are important to this town, Adelaide. Your companion should take better care of you."

"If you mean Paul, he's the one who's important to this paper. I don't know what I'd do without him."

"Important in other areas as well . . . hum?"

"Of course," Adelaide said coolly, and Kathleen let out a silent whoop of laughter.

Dr. Herman looked long and hard at Adelaide. She looked back and, knowing that he was attempting to intimidate her, refused to look away. He finally pulled a handkerchief from his pocket and wiped the lenses of his glasses. He put them carefully back on and turned to Kathleen.

"Introduce me to your partner, Adelaide."

"Kathleen Dolan, Dr. Herman."

The doctor took the few necessary steps to reach Kathleen and held out his hand. His grip was firm.

"Glad to meet you."

"Thank you." *I'm not glad to meet you, you cold fish.*

"What do you think of our little town?"

"Very nice."

"And we want to keep it that way."

"I'm sure you do."

"Do I detect a Yankee accent?"

"It's possible. I was raised in Iowa by my Norwegian grandparents."

"It's been a long time since we've had a lady in jail for brawling on the street. Back in 1908 to be exact. Her name was Flora Eudora and she had flaming red hair."

"What a coincidence," Kathleen murmured drily.

"Yes, isn't it? Flora believed that her husband was fornicating with the town whore."

"Was he?"

"Of course. Flora met the woman on the street and attacked her. She knocked out a tooth and blackened her eyes. It was the wrong thing to do."

"I agree. She should have attacked her husband,

blackened his eyes, and kicked him in a place that would have discouraged his wanderings for a while."

"Rawlings at that time was a mere speck on the prairie," the doctor continued as if Kathleen hadn't spoken. "The founder, a man by the name of Radisson Hoghorn Rawlings, was a man of law and order. Mistress Flora Eudora was hauled off to jail."

Kathleen whistled through her teeth. "Aren't you glad he didn't name the town Hoghorn? I can see it now— HOGHORN WEEKLY *GAZETTE* across the front of this building." She smiled sweetly at the man standing beside her desk. "What happened to the whore?"

"She went back to work."

"I'd have bet you'd say that. Are you the town historian, Doctor? We're looking for some stories from the past for a new column. Perhaps you can help us out."

"Young lady, this town has gone through some good times and some bad times. We're in better shape than any other town our size in Oklahoma. It's due to good planning, law, and order. During the early thirties a bank went under almost every day. Ours, here in Rawlings, remained solid."

"That's good news. Would you like for me to write an editorial on the economy in Rawlings? Of course, I'd need to have access to the city ledgers. By the way, I plan to attend the city council meetings. In Liberal, they were held the first and third Monday of each month. What is the schedule here?"

"We don't have scheduled meetings. No need for it. If something comes up that requires discussion, we have a meeting."

"You'll let me know?"

"You'll be given the minutes of the meeting."

"Not good enough. I want to attend and become acquainted with the members. I'd be able to write a much better report."

"The meetings are spontaneous. But we'll try to oblige you." Only the slight narrowing of the man's eye revealed his irritation.

"Thank you."

"Nice to have met you, Miss Dolan. Take care of yourself, Adelaide." He walked out the door, crossed the street, and went into the bank. Neither woman said a word until he had disappeared.

"So that's the man who runs things around here." The statement hung in the air for a few seconds before Adelaide answered.

"Can you believe it?"

"Not to look at him."

"He's tough as nails. He was warning you, Kathleen. Word had already got to him about the little set-to you had on the street. He knows everything that goes on in this town."

"He and the sheriff remind me of two dogs we had at home on the farm. One was a big, brown shaggy dog with a deep, loud bark. The other one was little, slick-haired, and quick. He looked like a gentle little pussycat. When strangers came, they would watch the big dog with the loud bark, and the little one would slip up and bite them."

Paul came from the back room with a worried frown on his face. His eyes sought Adelaide's. Kathleen had never seen him enter the office without first finding his Addie with his eyes. His devotion to her, and hers to him, was like a tangible thing. It reminded Kathleen of the love between her grandparents. When her grandmother died, the life had gone out of her grandpa, and he had died soon after.

Kathleen turned back to face the window and heard Paul speaking softly to Adelaide, asking her if she was tired. He would be behind her now, rubbing the spot between her shoulders, but with his eye on the door lest someone come in and observe him. Desolation washed over Kathleen. Seldom did she admit even to herself that it would be heavenly to have someone to lean on, to share her joys and her sorrows. Would she ever know the kind of love that Adelaide knew? Right now that seemed to be as remote as the moon.

Johnny drove slowly along the dirt road trying to stir up as little dust as possible when he passed the lines full of freshly washed clothes. On the road ahead he saw a woman in high-heeled shoes struggling along, carrying a heavy suitcase.

Clara Ramsey. No doubt about it. How long had she been gone this time? Six months? A year? How long would she stay? Johnny hoped not for long. She reminded him of his half sister, Isabel. Tramps, both of them. Nothing or nobody would ever change them.

He slowed the truck when he came alongside Clara. The face she turned to him was pale with a bright slash of red lipstick. She had a bruise on one of her cheeks and a swelling on the bridge of her nose.

"Hello, Clara. Need a ride?"

"Oh, Johnny," she squealed, and let the bag drop to the ground.

Johnny got out of the truck and lifted the suitcase up onto the bed of the truck. Clara lifted her tight skirt up past her knees, stepped up on the running board, and slid onto the seat beside him.

"Jesus, you're a lifesaver. I wasn't sure I'd make it carryin' that damned old suitcase."

"Does Hazel know you're coming?" He knew the answer, but he asked anyway.

"No. I wanted to surprise her and Emily. I brought presents for Emily's birthday."

"Isn't Emily's birthday on the Fourth of July?"

"So they're a little late. A kid don't care. It's a hell of a lot more than I got on my birthday. I was lucky to get a piece of corn bread with syrup on it."

"It was worse for a lot of kids. Some were starving. Your folks did the best they could by you."

"Well, dog my cats! There it is. The old dump looks the same." Clara's quick dry laugh spoke of her contempt. She opened the door when the truck stopped, and slid out, her skirt slithering up to mid-thigh.

Johnny lifted the bag off the truck bed and followed her up the walk to the porch. Clara opened the screen door and went inside.

"Mama, I'm home. Put my suitcase in my room, Johnny." She winked at him. "You know where it is."

Johnny set the bag down beside the door just as Hazel came from the back of the house wiping her hands on her apron. When she saw Clara her face lit up like a full moon.

"Clara? Honey, is that you? I thought I heard you call, but I wasn't sure." Hazel folded her daughter in her arms. "Oh, honey, I'm so glad to see you. Here, let me look at you. My, but you're as pretty as ever. Emily will be beside herself. She been asking about you a lot lately." Hazel hugged Clara again. "I've been so worried. Why didn't you write?"

Clara twisted out of her mother's embrace and dropped down onto a chair.

"Don't start in on me, Mama. I just got here."

Hazel drew in a deep breath. Then, "Hello, Johnny. I didn't see you at first. I was so excited to see Clara."

"Hello, Mrs. Ramsey. I met her out on the road. Where do you want me to put the suitcase?"

"Put it in my room," Clara said. "Where else? I see you've got the door shut, Mama. I used to love havin' the door shut, but you'd come along and open it to see if I had a boy in my bed." She rolled her eyes toward the ceiling.

"Clara, honey, I rented out your room. You'll have to sleep on the couch here, or back on my bed with Emily. I'll take Emily's bed."

"You what?" Clara jumped to her feet and stormed across the room to throw open the door. She looked around the room with her hands on her hips. "Well, I swan. You really want me out of here, don't you? You rented out my room so I'd not have a place to come back to."

"It wasn't like that at all. I needed the money. I couldn't make enough by ironing to keep us going."

Clara picked up Kathleen's brush and flipped it over onto the bed. She pecked at the keys on the typewriter, pulled open the drawer in the table, and attempted to lift the lid on the trunk, but it was locked.

"What'd she lock the trunk for? She think you're goin' to steal somethin'?"

"You've no right to meddle with her things, Clara."

Clara ignored the rebuke. "You never kept it like this when I was here. Who is she? It is a *she*. I'd not be lucky enough for it to be a good-looking *he*."

"Her name is Miss Dolan, and she works for the news-paper."

"Now ain't that just a fine kettle of fish?" Clara brushed by her mother as she left the room.

Hazel closed the door and eased herself down onto a chair as if a sudden move might break her in two.

"What was I to do, Clara?"

"Oh, hell, I don't know. Whine, whine. It's all I ever get when I come back here."

"Then why don't you leave?" Johnny said quietly. "I'll take you to the highway."

"Oh, no, Johnny. Not before she sees Emily. It would break the child's heart."

"All you care about is that kid. Isn't that right, Mama?"

"That's not true. I—"

"—Mrs. Ramsey," Johnny interrupted. He had to get out of there before he shook the stuffings out of Clara. "Miss Dolan will not be here for supper. She asked me to tell you."

"You *feed* her, too," Clara spun around and glared at her mother who got to her feet and faced her angry daughter.

"I do what I have to do," she said firmly. "Miss Dolan pays for her meals if she eats here or not."

"She must pay pretty good. I saw a car out back when we drove up."

"It's Miss Dolan's car."

"She must be rollin' in dough."

"She's a nice lady, Clara. I won't allow you to be nasty to her."

"She took my room, for God's sake!"

"How long are you going to stay?"

"Is this my home or not? Should I write and ask if you have room for me before I come home?"

"I've got to be goin'," Johnny said. "But first I'd like a

private word with Clara." He took her arm and propelled her out onto the porch and let the door slam behind them.

"Let go of me. You ain't got no right to be pushin' me around."

"I've always known, from the first time I saw you, that you are nothing but a worthless piece of shit. Until now I didn't know just how rotten you are. You go off and leave your mother to raise your child when that little girl is your responsibility. She's been workin' like a dog to keep food in that child's mouth. Then you have the guts to come back here and treat her like dirt."

"To hell with you." She jerked her arm from his grasp and tried to get back into the house, but his back was to the door. "You're not the boss of me. At least my kid ain't a half-breed. I didn't go out and screw some dirty Indian like your mama did."

"You're pitiful, Clara. You've got a mother who loves you and a little girl who thinks you get up every morning and hang out the sun. What do you do, but go whoring around and come back to them when you're broke. Has it ever occurred to you to come back here, get a job, and help your mother?"

"What kind of a job could I get around here? You think I'd go out to the tannery and work with the blanket-asses? Well, think again, Mr. Johnny Blanket-Ass Henry."

Johnny held his temper even though he ached to slap her.

"It's decent work. If not that, you could help your mother with the ironing."

"You may be surprised to know that I've been singing in a nightclub down in Fort Worth." Clara lifted her head and preened. "Ever'body thought I was really good. I just came home to get ready to go to Nashville and get on the Grand Ole Opry. When I'm a star, I'll come back here and ever'-

body in this shitty one horse town'll sit up and take notice of Miss Clara Ramsey."

Johnny shook his head. "You've got about as much chance of making it to the Grand Ole Opry as you have reaching up and touching the moon." He walked off the porch and headed for his truck. *Like Isabel, she wasn't going to listen to anything he said.*

"If you're so much, Johnny Henry," Clara called, "how come you're drivin' that old rattletrap of a truck?"

Johnny glanced over his shoulder at the girl with her skinny arms wrapped around the porch post. He tried to muster up some sympathy for her, but it just wouldn't jell. He thought of how his half sister, Henry Ann, had tried to reason with Isabel, and had offered her the opportunity to go to school and make something of herself. Isabel's mind, like Clara's, had been only on the pleasure of the moment.

Johnny started his truck and drove away wondering what was going to happen when Kathleen met Clara. One thing was sure. From now on, she'd better lock her valuables in her trunk when she left the house.

Chapter Seven

JOHNNY PARKED HIS TRUCK behind the newspaper building and, with a bundle under his arm, went in through the back door. Paul was breaking down a page from last week's paper and throwing the lead into a bucket to be melted and reused.

"I'm going to leave my truck back here tonight, Paul. I took my groceries back to the store and will pick them up in the morning. The store will be closed by the time I'm ready to go home."

"You could've left them here."

"I never thought about it. I've never had anything taken from the truck, but I don't trust those two yahoos I took down to the sheriff."

"They're trouble all right." Paul dropped a handful of lead in the bucket. "There's a canvas cot over there in the corner if you want to sleep here. Pound on the door tonight, and I'll let you in."

"Thanks. Mind if I wash up here?"

"Go back to my room if you want. There's soap and water back there. There'll be no danger of your lady friend walking in on you while you wash that horse-hockey smell off."

"Thanks, *friend*. By the way, don't forget the two bits you owe me."

Paul's head swung slowly around. "That was for the picture show."

"You crawfishin' out of the bet?"

"The deal was to take her to a show." Paul's smile was smug. "Drag up enough courage to ask her out to a show, and the two bits is yours."

"To hell with you," Johnny snorted, and stomped off toward the partitioned room in the corner.

The room was nicely furnished with a neatly made bed, a bureau, and a long table on which sat a typewriter and two big radios with antenna wires running up along the ceiling and out the single window. Paul's clothes hung on a rod that spanned one corner of the room.

Johnny stripped off his shirt, poured water from a pitcher into a granite washbowl, and washed. He soaped his face and stared at his image in the oval mirror above the washbasin. Thank goodness he had shaved before he came to town this morning, although he hadn't expected to see Kathleen, much less take her out to supper. He borrowed Paul's comb and tried to tame his hair.

He pulled the new shirt out of the sack, shook it out, and put it on. He now regretted buying a white shirt. Kathleen would know that it was new. But, what the hell? Johnny slammed his hat down on his head and left the room. He paused just outside the door when he heard Kathleen's voice. She was showing Paul a two-page article she had written.

"Can we set the first four lines after the headline in ten point?"

"Sure. I'll set it tonight. If it isn't what you want, we can change it in the morning."

Kathleen hung the sheets of paper on the hook beside the linotype machine, turned, and saw Johnny.

"I didn't know you were here," she said, almost in an accusing tone.

"I came in the back door."

"I'll be ready to go as soon as I wash the ink off my hands, that is if you haven't changed your mind."

"I'm ready when you are."

Unaware that Paul was watching him, Johnny watched Kathleen. For days her image had stayed in his mind. Her fiery curly hair and her pretty face were enough to draw a man's eyes to her, but what riveted his attention to her now was her utter unawareness of just how striking she was. She accepted her good looks as being only a part of her, the other part being a woman completely at ease with herself and her abilities.

Johnny Henry, you don't have the brains of a loco steer or you'd get the hell out of here.

"Pretty, isn't she?" Paul murmured after Kathleen went back to the front office.

"You'd better not let Adelaide hear you say that!"

"She knows it. Sometimes beauty is more of a hindrance than an asset. Addie thinks you're just the man for Kathleen."

"Well, thanks for arranging my life. I don't agree. Now tend to your own business."

"She is my business, cowboy. What concerns Addie concerns me. We're afraid that she'll be in deep trouble before she discovers how to get along in this town."

"She's already in trouble. Why do you think I'm sticking around? It was just luck that I found out that Webb and Krome bragged that she'd get what was coming to her before they left town. That could be tonight or tomorrow. I can take care of tonight."

"She's got a date with Leroy Grandon tomorrow night."

"Grandon? From the men's store? How do you know? She tell you?"

"Just because I'm back here doesn't mean I don't know what goes on up front."

"Shee . . . it. He's old enough to be her daddy." A chill held Johnny motionless for a long minute. "Webb or Krone'd chew him up and spit him out."

"Not if they got orders from higher up. They'd not want one of the merchants, the head of the Chamber of Commerce, to know. It might raise a stink."

"That's true." Johnny pushed himself away from the counter where he'd been leaning. "Guess we'll have to take one day at a time and see what happens."

Johnny had not concerned himself with the politics in Rawlings . . . up to now. He came to town a couple of times a month, and that was that. As far as he knew, it was a pretty peaceful town. The doctor ruled it with an iron hand in a soft glove. His friendship with Paul had opened his eyes to that. Adelaide, Paul, Claude, and the Wilsons were his only friends in town. He added Mrs. Ramsey as an afterthought. Other folks in town knew who he was because of the rodeo.

"Better get along, cowboy. It's six-thirty. Addie will shut the door and turn off the light soon."

"Yeah, I guess I better."

"A little advice, son. Don't pick your nose at the table," Paul murmured as Johnny passed him.

"You know what you can do with your advice, *Daddy*," Johnny growled, and Paul laughed.

*   *   *

Kathleen had been surprised to see Johnny in the back room. He had bought a new shirt. His dark skin against the white made him look incredibly handsome. She was still puzzled by the invitation. It was logical to assume that he intended to leave town as soon as he loaded his groceries. What had changed his mind?

Adelaide was busy typing when Johnny came from the back room. She looked up and nodded.

"Ready?" he asked Kathleen.

"I guess so." She got up from her desk. "See you in the morning, Adelaide."

"Have a good time."

Johnny opened the door, and Kathleen went out ahead of him. On the sidewalk, she paused, not knowing which way to go. He gripped her elbow and they started walking. It was almost dark. The time between sunset and nighttime was short this time of year.

"Let's try the Frontier Cafe? Have you been there?"

"I haven't been anywhere except to Claude's. We could go there for a hamburger. It's fast."

"Are you trying to get this *ordeal* over with?"

"I was just trying to be helpful," she said testily, thinking again of their encounter in the store. "I'm sure you're anxious to get home with your groceries."

"I left them at the store. I'll get them in the morning."

Johnny held tightly to her elbow as they stepped down off the curb and crossed the intersection. She had to admit that they walked well together, their steps matching. It was comforting to have him beside her. Her eyes darted back and forth; she half expected to see Webb and Krome lurking in the shadows.

They covered the three blocks to the cafe in almost complete silence. Its neon sign in the shape of a wagon wheel glowed in the twilight. Inside Johnny steered her to a high-backed booth, hung his hat on the hook on the end, and eased his long length onto the bench opposite her. Rather than look at him, Kathleen studied the box on the wall and read the selections available on the jukebox.

"See something you like?" Johnny placed a nickel on the table.

"Not really. It's all cowboy music."

"You're in cowboy country."

"Here's one that's quite appropriate"—she glanced at him to see him eyeing her intently—"Hoagy Carmichael's 'I Get Along Without You Very Well.' " She picked up the nickel, put it in the slot, and punched in her selection.

He ducked his head as if to avoid a blow. "Ouch! You're still mad."

"I'm not mad. It's not that important," she lied, unable to look at him.

"It is to me."

A young waitress with a perky red apron and headband came to the booth with two glasses of water. She eyed Johnny with interest.

"We have hot beef with mashed potatoes or meat loaf with pork and beans."

They both ordered the hot beef. Kathleen asked for iced tea, Johnny for coffee.

The waitress gave Johnny a slant-eyed smile, then flounced away. In the backwash of silence that followed, Kathleen listened to the music. Johnny watched her. The hot Oklahoma sun had brought out a few more freckles. The rapid pulse at the base of her throat told him that she was nervous. That surprised him. To look at her, you'd think that she was as cool as a cucumber.

"I've a few things to tell you," he said softly.

Kathleen's eyes met his. "You had to bring me here to tell me? You could have said whatever you have to say at the office. You needn't have gone to all this trouble."

"It's no trouble."

"I should have said bother."

"It's not a bother either. You'd not understand if I tried to explain what happened at the store. I'll just say at the moment I thought it was the right thing to do."

Kathleen understood that that was the only apology she was going to get. She stared unblinkingly at him.

"I can take care of myself, you know. There's no need for you to feel obligated to look out for me because your sister is married to my uncle." She spoke quietly, but the very unexpectedness of her tone gave the words an abrupt, harsh quality.

"Get the chip off your shoulder, ma'am. You need friends if you're going to stay in this town." Points of light flared in Johnny's dark eyes.

"Why, all of a sudden, are you interested in being my friend?"

"Let's just say that I changed my mind."

"Since I met Webb and Krome on the street? You didn't have to ride to my rescue. I could have handled them."

"Handle them my hind foot!" Air hissed from between his clenched teeth. "I want you to know that—"

He broke off speaking when the waitress came with their meal and placed a plate in front of each of them. The helping of mashed potatoes and the slab of beef on the white bread, both covered with steaming gravy, looked delicious. Kathleen stirred the small green lumps on the side of the plate with her fork.

"What's this?" she asked when the girl had left their booth.

"Fried okra."

"Never heard of it. Is it a vegetable?"

"Yeah. Grows on a bush like a green pepper. We grew a lot of it on the farm over at Red Rock. It's rolled in cornmeal and fried, or put in soup or cooked with tomatoes and onions. Try it."

"Humm—" Kathleen chewed and swallowed. "It's . . . ah . . . edible."

Johnny laughed. "You either like it or you don't. You don't have anything against potatoes, do you?"

"No. My Norwegian grandparents practically lived on potatoes. Have you ever had potato dumplings? Even though they are a Swedish dish, my grandmother made them as well as potato pancakes, potato bread, soup, salad, fritters, boiled potatoes, mashed potatoes, scalloped potatoes. She even made her yeast out of potatoes."

Johnny generously peppered his meal and Kathleen raised an eyebrow. He grinned at her.

"I don't suppose you used a lot of black pepper up there either."

"Not that much. This is good," she said after she had taken a bite, chewed, and swallowed. "I guess I didn't realize that I was so hungry. Up North we call this a hot beef sandwich."

"We call it that down here, too. Do you plan to go back to Iowa?"

"Nothing to go back to except a few acres of land. A neighbor rents it."

"I've heard that it gets pretty cold up there."

"It was thirty below for over a week in 1936. When it gets that cold, the ground freezes so hard and so deep that they have to use blasting powder to dig a grave. I was used to the cold and didn't mind it so much."

"I've not been any farther north than Kansas City. It was plenty cold there."

They ate in silence. Diners came in and occupied the booths on each side of them. Nickels were poured into the jukebox. "I'm an Old Cowhand from the Rio Grande" was a frequent choice. Kathleen gave Johnny a knowing look and smiled.

"I'm in cowboy country," she said.

Johnny found himself staring dumbly at the thick mass of curly red hair that brushed her shoulders. He had an almost irresistible impulse to reach out and bury his fingers in that glossy mane. He forced his gaze to wander away from her and out over the cafe. When she spoke, he turned to find her quizzically staring at him.

"You don't come to town very often, do you?"

"Only when I have to."

"Tell me about your ranch."

"It's just a little speck out there on the prairie," he said, and dismissed the subject. "Ready to go? I'll get the check."

"Are you sure we can't go Dutch? This isn't a date, so you're not obligated to pay for my supper."

A short dry laugh came from him. "I thought it was a date. I'm not so poor that I can't invite a *friend* out to supper."

"Now it's time for you to get off your high horse. I was just trying to make it easy for you in case you'd changed your mind . . . again."

"Let's get out of here. It won't do for me to shake you in front of all these people." He got up and waited for her to slide from the booth. "We can't talk in here."

Johnny paid the check, and they left the cafe. Night had fallen.

"I'll walk you home. I don't imagine you'd be too happy riding in that old truck of mine."

"So now you think I'm a snob."

"I didn't say that. I said . . . oh, forget it."

"I like to walk. It's a nice night, and I want to hear what you have to tell me."

Johnny threw caution to the wind, took her hand, and drew it up into the crook of his arm. He liked touching her, liked having her close to him as they walked. He liked being in the dark with her. He just wished his damn heart would stop beating so fast.

"I want to warn you about Webb and Krome. They were in Wilson's store bragging that they had a score to settle with you. I'd not put anything past them, so be careful. It's dark now when you leave the paper. Maybe you'd better drive your car up and park it in front of the office."

"Is that why you changed your mind and decided we could be friends?"

"No," he said abruptly. "Listen to what I'm telling you. Webb and Krome are out to get even with you. I think there's a connection between them and Deputy Thatcher. I don't know what it is, and I don't know if Sheriff Carroll is a part of it. But it's mighty fishy that he took the word of those two against ours and let them off the hook."

"Are they out to get even with you? You're the one who stopped them from hijacking my car. You're the one who marched them off to the sheriff's office."

Johnny snorted his disgust. "They're not sure how they'd come out in a fight with me. They might attempt to jump me. What they don't know is that . . . they'll get as good or better than they give."

"Webb had the nerve to ask me to go to a honky-tonk with them and learn the jitterbug dance."

"I suppose you told him you'd go," Johnny teased.

"Yeah. Sure. I've seen the jitterbug dance, and it isn't something I want to do. I like slow romantic tunes like 'Bury Me Not on the Lone Prairie' and 'Red River Valley.'"

"I thought you didn't like cowboy music."

"I was just being contrary. I get that way sometimes." Her soft laughter burst out unexpectedly.

Johnny chuckled. "Now, you tell me."

"I had to play 'I Get Along Without You Very Well.' That was too good to pass up. Considering—" She laughed again softly, teasingly.

"I'll remember that—about you being contrary."

They walked along in companionable silence. After a short while Johnny asked her what had happened at the sheriff's office. Kathleen told him about her encounter with the deputy.

"I couldn't believe the nastiness and arrogance of the man. He was insulting to me, to Adelaide, and to Paul."

Unconsciously Johnny pressed the hand in the crook of his arm tighter and tighter to his side as his anger at the deputy escalated.

"Did he threaten you?"

"Not directly. He said that they had better uses here in Rawlings for women like me than to tar and feather them and run them out of town."

"The son of a bitch!" Johnny tried to put a tight leash on his anger.

"After you and the sheriff left the office, we had a visit from Dr. Herman. He warned me about *brawling* on the street. Can you believe that? Brawling? He recited some of the town's history and told me about a woman with red hair like mine who was put in jail for attacking a woman on the street. She was . . . ah . . . well, she was a prostitute who had been with the woman's husband." Kathleen's giggle came out of the darkness and Johnny felt an unexpected surge of happiness within him.

"I told him she should have attacked her husband and kicked him in a place that would've stopped his whoring for a good long while. He didn't think it was funny. The doctor doesn't like me very much. He's not used to people talking back to him."

Johnny's hand came up to press the one tucked in the crook of his arm.

"Poor Adelaide,"—Kathleen continued—"he made some insinuating remarks about her and Paul."

"I don't know why they don't get married and be done with it."

"I think Paul is willing. He adores her. Adelaide worries that he is ten years younger than she is."

"What's the difference? It's their business."

"I'm glad you said that. It's what I think."

"Here's the school. Let's go sit in the swings. I've got more to tell you," he said, as if he needed a reason for prolonging their walk.

"Not more bad news, I hope."

It was a dark night. To Kathleen the stars seemed extra bright as she and the tall man beside her crossed the playground. She took her hand from his arm and sat down in a swing. She pushed with her feet, then lifted them.

"I haven't been in a swing since I left grade school." Moving behind her, Johnny pushed, his hands gentle in the middle of her back. After several minutes, her laugh floated to him on the night breeze. "Oh, Johnny, this is fun!"

She swung back and forth for several more minutes, the only sound being the creaking of the swing. Holding tightly to the chains, she leaned back, and laughed up into his face. His hands went to her shoulders and he gave a gentle shove. Here with her on the playground, Johnny felt as though he was in another world. Aware that he must be vigilant, he tried to return to reality.

"The stars are so close and . . . so bright."

"Do you see the Big Dipper?"

"No. Where?"

Johnny caught her around the waist as she swung back, held her, and moved forward until her feet touched the ground. She stood, her face toward the star-studded sky.

"Where?" she said again.

He moved behind her, placed his hands on her shoulders, and turned her. Her hair brushed his chin. The sudden, delirious rush of joy was so acute his words came out in a breathless whisper.

"Look over the top of the school. See the chimney? Now straight up from there."

"I see it." She turned her head to look back at him. Their faces were inches apart. "Grandpa used to look at the stars. He showed me the Milky Way."

It came to Kathleen at that moment how glad she was that Johnny was with her; she felt so secure, protected, when she was with him. It gave her pleasure just to look at his tall erect body, shiny black hair, and quiet face.

They stood silently for a while, his hands still on her shoulders. It was a temptation not to close her eyes and lean back against him. The pressure of his hands turned her to face him. Her heart gave a choking, little thump, and she raised a tremulous gaze to his face.

"Are you tired walking? Would you rather sit in the swing while we talk?"

"I'm not tired. You said you had something else to tell me."

"Clara Ramsey came home. I saw her on the road when I went to tell her mother you'd not be there for supper." As they started walking, somehow his hand found hers and her fingers wiggled their way in between his.

"Emily's mother is back?"

"Clara's trouble, Kathleen. She had a fit because her mother had rented her room."

"Do you think I'll have to move?"

"Not if you like it there and can stick it out for a few weeks. Clara won't stay. Mrs. Ramsey needs the money you pay her."

"She's an old girlfriend of yours, isn't she?" The words spilled out as a keen disappointment that she didn't understand filled her.

Johnny stopped. The grip on her hand tightened. "What in the world gave you that idea?"

"Oh, little tidbits I picked up here and there." Kathleen would have walked on, but he held her back.

"I've seen that girl a total of a half dozen times. The first time was outside a honky-tonk. She was so drunk she could hardly walk. I put her in the truck and took her home. I think the next time was at a ball game, then at the rodeo. She reminded me of my half sister, Isabel, dumb as a clod of dirt and completely selfish. I felt sorry for her because she was so goddamn stupid."

"You don't have to explain anything to me."

"I think I do because you've probably heard that I was the father of her child. It's not true. I never touched that girl except to lift her into the truck when she was drunk, and another time when I came through town about midnight and found her sitting on the curb in front of the dry goods store. Someone had worked her over with his fists. I took her home. Later when she became pregnant, she told around that it was mine, but it was NOT." There was anger in his voice.

"I didn't mean to . . . pry into your affairs."

"You didn't pry. I realize that you don't know much about me."

"Or you about me. Tell me about your sister, Isabel. Where is she?"

"Oklahoma City, I guess. Be careful of Clara. She's only interested in what she wants and doesn't care who she hurts getting it. She's unreasonable and downright mean to her mother. You'd better put the things you don't want her rummaging through in your trunk and lock it when you leave the house. I don't trust her any farther than I could throw a bull by the tail. Poor Mrs. Ramsey has gone through hell with that girl."

Kathleen loosened her hand from his. He had held it so tightly it was numb. She put her hands on his upper arms.

"Rescuing damsels in distress seems to be a habit with you. I'm glad that I was one of them. I'll get along with Clara if . . . if she doesn't stay too long or push me too hard. That's as much as I can promise."

She looked up at him and smiled. Her eyes shone in the darkness. *Dear God, what has happened to me? A smile and a few soft words from this woman send my heart racing like a runaway train and my mind desperately groping to stay on the right track.*

From the first he had been attracted to her, much as he had been to other women from time to time. Suddenly it was amazingly clear to him that he was falling head over heels in love with this wonderful, magnificent, redheaded woman. Not that he would ever do anything about it. Still, he knew that she would be in his heart for as long as he lived. Some men lived all their lives and never met a woman who crept into their hearts. This one had come barreling into his, and he thanked God for the sweet memories this night would provide.

Chapter Eight

THE MUSIC FROM THE JUKEBOX was loud, blasting into the heated shadows of the dimly lit room. It was not loud enough, however, to drown out the drunken laughter and crude shouts of encouragement to the two couples jitterbugging on the small dance floor. The air was thick with cigarette smoke, the odors of sweat and cheap perfume. The contortions of the two couples became wilder and wilder. Each time a man flipped his partner over his arm, showing her skimpy underpants, the crowd hooted and pounded beer bottles and glasses on the tables.

The dark eyes of the man standing in the doorway swept over the roomful of oil-field riggers and drillers and women with heavily made-up faces and tight dresses. This was a rough section of Oklahoma City. In polished boots, tailor-made fringed jacket and ten-dollar Stetson, the man stood out from the crowd, not only because of his dress, but because he was tall and broad. Well-dressed Indians were not uncommon in Oklahoma City. Oil had made some of them wealthy.

He waited for the dance to end and for the crowd to clear so he could approach the bar where the bartender was openly dispensing the 3.2 beer and filling beer bottles with whiskey under the counter. He had been told the girl worked here. He wouldn't know her if he saw her. He'd have to inquire.

He made his way along the side of the room, receiving plenty of glances from both the males and the females in the booths that lined the walls. As he stood at the end of the bar, the music came on again, and couples filled the small dance floor behind him, giving him a hemmed-in feeling.

"What'll ya have?" The bartender was thick-necked and meaty. He wore a dirty white apron and duck trousers. He had grizzled reddish hair and a thick red mustache. His eyes were small and suspicious as he looked at the tall man. "Got a little somethin' extra under the counter. Can get ya a case if yo're after that."

"I'll think about the case. Do you have a girl working here named Isabel Perry?"

"What's that little shit done now?" The bartender made a swift swipe at the scarred countertop. "Usually she's got one of the women after her for flirtin' with her man. She ain't interested in a man if he ain't tied to another woman. One of these days one of 'em'll split her throat."

"I'd like to talk to her if she's here."

"Oh, she's here. She was out there dancin' her head off. Now she's out back catchin' her breath so she can wait tables. What's she done? You the law?"

"I'm not the law. I'll pay for a half hour of her time if I can go back and talk to her."

"Okey-dokey, friend. Take the half hour, then tell her to get her skinny ass back in here."

The bartender's eyes bugged in surprise when he saw the five-dollar bill on the counter. He scooped it up, and the bill disappeared beneath his apron as he jerked his head toward the back door.

"What does she look like?"

"Blond and skinny."

"Thanks."

The back room was a jungle of beer and pop cases, discarded bar fixtures and litter. He edged his way through the maze to the back door, which stood open. The girl was sitting on the stoop smoking a cigarette. She looked up as he came out the door. In the light coming from the parking area, he recognized one of the dancers; a thin girl in a yellow dress. Her face was hard, her hair straw-colored.

"Are you Isabel Perry?" he asked, not waiting for her to speak.

"Who wants to know?"

"Barker Fleming." He waited to see if the name registered with her. When it didn't, he said, "Was your mother's name Dorene?"

"Yeah. Did someone die and leave her a million dollars? She's dead. Do I get it?"

"No one's left her anything that I know of. Do you have a brother?"

"Ya sure ask a lot of questions." She drew deeply on the cigarette and blew the smoke in his direction, then flipped the cigarette out into the night. She stood, peered up at him, then stepped behind him and turned on a light. "Well, hello, Chief." She made a clicking sound with her tongue. "Are you the blanket-ass that knocked up Dorene a few years before the oil-field rigger screwed me into her, then took off like a scalded cat?"

Barker Fleming held on to his temper, pulled a silver cigarette case out of his pocket, opened it, and offered it to her. She took a cigarette and waited for him to flip the lighter on the end of the case. He lit cigarettes for both of them before he spoke.

"I'm not sure, Isabel. I was only with her a few times. A few months ago I ran into a fellow that told me she'd had a boy, part-Cherokee. Out of curiosity, I wondered if I'd dropped a colt somewhere."

The lie came easily to Barker Fleming. He had sensed immediately that telling this little floozy how long and how desperately he had searched to find his son would get him nowhere. Memories came flooding back. The little baggage before him was a copy of the woman who, almost old enough to be his mother, had flaunted herself before a naive eighteen-year-old Indian boy with a pocketful of money.

He didn't excuse himself. He had wanted what the woman had offered and had been too stupid to realize the consequences of his actions. Shortly after his wild fling with Dorene, his father had come for him and put him in a boarding school. At the time he had hated him for it.

"Henry's my legal name, but I never use it. Old Henry wasn't my pa. God only knows who was. I doubt if Dorene knew. She would've screwed the devil if he'd paid her." Isabel leaned up against the back of the tavern and drew heavily on the cigarette. "I'd probably better get back in, or Bud'll be havin' a cow fit."

"I asked the bartender for thirty minutes of your time."

"Bet ya had to pay him. He don't give nothin' for free. How 'bout payin' me? It's my time yo're takin' up. I could be in there makin' tips."

"I'll pay . . . if you tell me about the boy."

"Oh, I know about the holier-than-God son of a bitch. I could've got a third of Ed Henry's farm, but he sided with Henry Ann. She's Dorene's daughter by old Ed. The old man left the farm to her. The lawyer said that me'n Johnny was legal Henrys if Dorene was still married to Ed Henry when we was born. But Johnny wouldn't help me get what was ours. He honeyed up to Henry Ann. The two was thicker than hair on a dog's back."

Johnny Henry. His name is Johnny Henry.

"Is your brother still on the farm?"

"Naw. He's got a little piss-poor ranch over near Rawlings."

Barker could hardly contain his excitement. It had been difficult to trace a woman named Dorene who had lived in upstairs rooms on Reno Street and a disappointment to discover that she was dead. No one seemed to know what had happened to her son. Her daughter, too, had disappeared after she left an orphan's home at age eighteen.

The detective, who had been looking for her for almost a year, had notified him a week ago that he had found her working in a honky-tonk under the name Isabel Perry. Now in less than thirty minutes Barker had discovered his son's name and where he was.

"Do you ever see Johnny?" Barker asked casually.

"He came up here a couple of years ago and tried to correct my *wayward ways.*" Isabel's laugh was dry and scornful. "He wanted me to come to his ranch and keep house for him. Can you beat that? I'd rather be dead than stuck out there on the prairie. I had enough of the sticks when Henry Ann dragged me back to the farm after Dorene died. 'Cause I demanded my rights, she sent me to the orphan's home. That damn Johnny let her! When I got out, I dropped the Henry name and took Dorene's maiden name."

And that's why it cost me five hundred dollars to find you.

"What'a ya want to find Johnny for? Good-lookin' as ya are, bet ya got by-blows all over Oklahoma. Looks like ya got money, too." Isabel plucked at the fringe on his leather coat. "Half the women out there"—she jerked her head toward the noisy tavern—"includin' me, would drop and spread for ya the minute ya took off yore hat."

Barker laughed, but he wanted to slap her face. "That's very flattering. My time's about up. I don't want to get you in trouble with . . . Bud." He took his wallet out of his inside pocket and gave her a bill.

"Wow! Twenty big ones. Thanks, Chief. That's the most money I ever made in half a hour. Anytime ya want'a talk again . . . or if ya get a itch that needs scratchin', look me up. I could show ya a trick or two that'd even cause old Dorene's eyes to bug out." She winked at him as she pulled down the neck of her dress and tucked the bill in her bra.

Barker Fleming waited until Isabel disappeared inside, then went quickly down the steps and around the building to his car. *Johnny Henry. Johnny Henry. Johnny Henry, Rawlings, Oklahoma.*

Kathleen and Johnny turned down the darkened street leading to Mrs. Ramsey's house. Kathleen wished that they still had miles to go. She had never spent a more pleasant evening. Her hand was snugly in his, their steps matched, as they walked in companionable silence. Johnny's voice broke the silence between them.

"You'll not forget what I told you about driving your car to work in the morning?"

"Do you think it's really necessary? It's only a few blocks."

"It'll be dark when you leave the office. You'll be safer in the car."

"The jugheads may have just been letting off steam."

"I don't think so. They didn't know Mrs. Wilson was listening."

"I'll have to start carrying a long hatpin." Kathleen

laughed softly. "My grandma insisted that I carry one when I went to Des Moines to business school. She said that there was nothing that would get a masher's attention like a good poke with a hatpin."

"I think I'd like your grandma."

"She'd have loved you if you ate a lot. She liked to set what she called a *generous* table, and she liked to see a hearty eater. It's a wonder I wasn't as big as a moose by the time I grew up."

"I wouldn't have disappointed her when it came to eating. Henry Ann always said that she had to put plenty on the table, or I'd start in on the table legs."

A minute or two passed, then Kathleen said, "I don't like being afraid, Johnny."

"You'll be all right during the day. I'll worry about you at night." He drew her hand up into the crook of his arm and covered it with his. "If Webb and Krome had any brains, they'd get out of town and drop the matter."

"They'll not leave if they're getting paid to hang around."

"That's what I don't know . . . yet. I want you to be careful. Tomorrow I have to go down to the McCabe ranch and help drive the stock up for the rodeo. I can't be here tomorrow night."

"You don't have to feel responsible for me, Johnny. I've been taking care of myself for a long time."

"Maybe so. But you were not living in Rawlings, Oklahoma."

When they reached the house, it was completely dark. Johnny stopped near the porch steps.

"Thank you for dinner and for walking me home. I enjoyed it."

"Likewise. I'll be back in town in a—"

"Hi, Johnny." The voice came out of the darkness just as Clara stepped up onto the end of the porch. "Is this the *wonderful* Miss Dolan I've heard so much about? Well, kiss her good night. It's what she's waitin' for. Then we can go honky-tonkin'."

Johnny's throat clogged with anger, making it impossible to speak. Kathleen had no such problem.

"This must be the *wandering* Miss Ramsey. I've heard a lot about you, too, from a sweet little girl who wishes that her mother would stay at home and take care of her like other little girls' mothers do."

"Holy shit! The pussycat has claws."

"Believe it, sister. You scratch me, I'll scratch back."

"Clara?" Hazel Ramsey's quivery voice came from the doorway. "Please—"

"Don't worry, Mama. I'll not run her off. I've been waitin' for Johnny."

"It's all right, Mrs. Ramsey. I've had to deal with immature adults before. I'll not take anything she says seriously."

"Now ain't she just the cat's meow? She thinks that she's somethin'. Don't she?"

"Of course, I think that I'm *something*," Kathleen said. "I try to use common sense and good manners. I'll say good night. Thank you for the supper, Johnny, and for walking me home." She stepped up on the porch. "He's all yours, Clara."

Kathleen went into her room, paused just inside the door, and smiled when she heard Johnny's angry voice.

"Goddammit, Clara," he snarled. "Get in the house before I forget you're female and knock out a few teeth."

"Oh, goody. You're mad! I just love it when you're mad. That Indian face of yores—"

"—You're damn right I'm mad. Stay away from me,

hear? I've done what I could for you, for your mother's and Emily's sake, not for yours. You're rotten, Clara. You don't deserve to have a mother like Hazel and a little girl like Emily. You're nothing but a millstone around their necks."

"John . . . ny." Clara sidled up to him and hugged his arm. "Don't be mad. Let's go to town and have some fun."

"You stupid little twit! You didn't hear a word I said!"

"You can't like *her!* God, Johnny, she must be thirty years old. Sheesh! She's older'n you by a long shot."

"Shut up about her! And leave her alone, or you'll hear from me." He shook his arm free from her grasp and started down the walk toward the street.

"Clara, please," Mrs. Ramsey came out onto the porch. "Leave Johnny alone and come on in."

"You go in, Mama, and stop tellin' me what to do. John . . . ny—wait. John . . . ny—" Clara's voice became fainter as she ran down the street trying to catch up with the angry man.

Kathleen turned on the light, pulled down the window shades, and saw for the first time the table Johnny had lent her for her typewriter. It was perfect. Books and papers that had formerly been on the floor were now stacked neatly on the table beside the typewriter. She sat down on the edge of the bed and pulled off her shoes and stockings. Her feet hurt, and she had a big hole in the toe of her stocking.

In the doorway of the bathroom, she stopped and stared in anger and disbelief. Her bath salts were on the floor beside the tub along with her towel. The bar of scented bath soap she used so sparingly floated in the half-filled sink. A pair of lacy underpants, having evidently been washed with her scented soap, hung on the line Kathleen had strung to dry her hosiery.

"Miss Dolan." Emily's little voice came from the doorway leading to the other bedroom. "I told her not to get in your things. Are ya mad?"

"Not at you, honey."

"I don't want ya to go." Emily had tears in her voice.

"I'm not going. Don't worry about it." Kathleen lifted the soap out of the water and placed it in the soapdish.

"I can't help it. Granny cried. Mama talked mean to her."

"We'll just have to make it up to your granny, won't we?"

"How?"

"We could take her with us to the rodeo."

"You're still goin' to take me?"

" 'Course. I'm looking forward to it. We'll ask your granny to go with us."

"But not Mama?"

"I doubt that she'd want to go."

"She don't like it here. And . . . I don't care!" The little girl's lips trembled, but she held her head erect, determined not to cry. "She told me to get away and leave her stuff alone. I wasn't goin' to touch it."

The door banged and Kathleen heard Clara's angry voice in the other room.

"He ain't nothin' but a goddamn half-breed. He ain't no better'n them dog-eatin' redskins out on the reservation, but he thinks he is 'cause he's got that little old rinky-dink ranch and a beat-up truck. He must be hard up for a woman to take that . . . that freaky thing with the dyed hair."

"Don't talk about Miss Dolan like that. She's a nice woman. You ought to be ashamed, running after Johnny like you did. I'd think that you'd—" The radio suddenly came on so loud it almost shook the rafters. A few seconds passed, and it was switched off.

"Why'd ya do that for? I want to hear it."

"I want you to listen to me, Clara."

"It's all I've been doin' all my life. Listen to me, Clara. Do this, Clara. Do that, Clara," she mocked her mother's voice. "I wish to hell I'd never come back here."

"Why did you?" Mrs. Ramsey asked quietly.

" 'Cause I need money, that's why."

"I don't have any money to give you. Emily and I just barely have enough to get along."

"I know where to get it without having to beg you for it."

"Where, Clara?"

"Wouldn't you like to know?"

"Yes, I would. You'll not bring any more disgrace down on Emily. She's suffered enough."

"What do you think I'm goin' to do, for God's sake? Open a whorehouse in the living room?" Clara let out a shout of laughter. "That'd jar the prissy Miss Dolan clear down to her dried-up old twat."

"I don't know what has happened to you. You were a sweet little girl and . . . pretty as a picture."

"I'm still pretty, Mama. Haven't you noticed? Men like me. Like me a lot. Rich or poor, they all like what I can do to them." Clara laughed at the shocked look on her mother's face. "I've got a rich one comin' up to see me in a few days. His folks has got a whole town named for them. Conroy, Texas. Ain't that somethin'? He don't know it yet, but he's goin' to take me to Nashville."

"You're never going to change, are you, Clara?"

"Why should I change, Mama? I have me a hell of a time when I'm away from this one-horse town."

"I'm going to bed. Keep the radio down. Miss Dolan gets up early."

"And if I don't?"

"I'll come out here and bust the tubes," Hazel said staunchly.

"Why, Mama," Clara said in surprise, then laughed shrilly. "Don't tell me you're gettin' some backbone?"

"You'll find out if you bring any more shame down on Emily."

"She's mine. I might take her with me."

"You won't. I'll not let you."

"Don't worry. You can have her. All she's done since I got here is whine. Where I'm goin' I don't need a kid hangin' around my neck. Did you hear me, Mama?" Clara shouted at her mother who had gone to the kitchen. "You can have her."

During the conversation between Clara and Hazel, Kathleen tried to keep Emily's attention on something else so the little girl wouldn't hear the hurtful words coming from her mother. She told her about Johnny swinging her in the swings at the school playground.

"It was such fun, Emily. You and I will have to go there some Sunday afternoon."

"Did you swing on the giant-strides? Marie Oden got hit in the head with one."

"Really? Hurt her bad?"

"Cut her head. But she's all right now."

"What's that big round tin thing on the side of the school?"

"The fire escape for the upstairs. We have fire practice and get to slide down it. It's dark and scary. We have a carnival and a spook house on Halloween. You can go down the fire escape if ya got a ticket."

"I'll have to think about it. I'm really a coward."

"Bet ya ain't."

"Bet I am." Kathleen heard Hazel in her bedroom and

steered Emily toward the door. "I've got to take a bath, honey. See you in the morning."

"You ain't goin'?" Emily asked over her shoulder.

"Only to work in the morning."

Emily grinned a gap-toothed grin. " 'Night, Miss Dolan."

" 'Night, Miss Sugarpuss."

Chapter Nine

Before Kathleen left her room to go to breakfast, she locked her personal papers, her manuscripts and all her underwear and hosiery in her trunk, and her toilet articles, including her comb and brush, in her suitcase. All that was left in the room were her shoes, dresses, and coats.

Clara was asleep, sprawled on the couch, when Kathleen passed through the living room on her way to the kitchen. Hazel and Emily were at the table. Hazel jumped up.

"Sit down. I made your tea."

"Thank you. Good morning, Miss Sugarpuss. How would you like a ride to school this morning?"

"In the car?" Emily smiled, showing the big gap in her front teeth.

"In the car. I'm driving uptown this morning."

"Hear that, Granny?" The little girl had lowered her voice to a whisper. Without waiting for a response from her grandmother, Emily leaned toward Kathleen. "We whispered so we'd not wake Mama up."

"I wondered if there was something wrong with my ears," Kathleen whispered back and stuck her finger in her ear.

Emily giggled. "I told Granny she could go to the rodeo with us."

"And I told you that I can't go." Hazel poured Kathleen's tea and set a plate of hot biscuits on the table.

"The *Gazette* has three tickets, Hazel."

"Won't Adelaide use one?"

"She said she'd just as soon skip it this year."

Kathleen drank her tea hurriedly and ate a biscuit with jam. She wanted to be gone before Clara got up. Emily was excited about riding in the car to school and was waiting at the back door when Kathleen came back after repairing her lipstick and putting on a light blue turban that matched her dress.

"You look pretty, Miss Dolan," Emily said.

"Thank you, and so do you."

Emily giggled and took Kathleen's hand. " 'Bye, Granny."

" 'Bye, honey. See you at noon."

Hazel stood on the back stoop and watched the car back out into the alleyway. She looked sad standing there. Kathleen had seen a tear on her cheek when they left, but Emily had been too excited about riding to school in the car to notice.

As soon as Kathleen entered the office, Adelaide wanted to know about her *date* with Johnny.

"It wasn't really a date," Kathleen said, taking off her turban and placing it on her desk.

"Looked like a date to me. He went out and bought a new shirt."

"He probably didn't want to go to supper in a shirt he'd worked in all day. You're making too much of it. He'd heard that the two men who tried to hijack me were going to get even because they had to go to the sheriff's office again. That's why he took me home."

"Does he think they might . . . attack you?"

"I don't know what he thinks they'll do, but he wanted me to drive the car up here so I'd have it to go home in."

"Good idea. Paul says he's got a crush on you."

"Paul's . . . crazy!" Kathleen felt heat on her cheeks.

"Why are you blushing?"

"I'm not," Kathleen protested, and rolled a sheet of paper into her typewriter. "I'm probably—Oh, never mind."

Good Lord, she had almost said that she was probably older than Johnny. Being conscious of the age difference between herself and Paul, Adelaide would have been terribly hurt. But Kathleen's age was what Clara had pointed out last night, and the taunt had stuck in her mind like a burr.

"How'd the big date go?"

Kathleen looked up to see Paul grinning at her.

"It wasn't a *big date!* "

"Johnny bought a new shirt."

"Paul, dear, I already mentioned that." Adelaide and Paul exchanged conspiratorial glances.

"All right, you two. Cut out the matchmaking."

Paul passed behind Adelaide and caressed the back of her neck.

He touches her every chance he gets, Kathleen thought as Adelaide smiled up at him. *Will anyone ever love me as much?*

"I told Johnny that you had a date with Leroy tonight. He didn't seem to be too pleased about it. It doesn't hurt to let a fellow know he's got a little competition." Paul winked at Adelaide and hurried into the back room.

"Oh, my gosh. I forgot all about Leroy Grandon. Sometime today I'll have to go home and tell Hazel that I'll not be there for supper."

For press day, the day went fairly well. Paul had two front page stories: one about Japan declaring that they would provide arms for Germany and Italy if it became necessary. The other story was about fifty-five thousand hungry people rioting in Pittsburgh. Kathleen was impressed, but she was not sure how many people in Rawlings were interested in what went on in Japan and in Pittsburgh. But it was good journalism, causing her to wonder once again about the man's life before he came to Rawlings.

"Paul thinks the war in Europe will spill over, and before long we'll be involved," Adelaide said after she had proofed the piece.

"Oh, I hope not. I don't know how the country could fight a war when we're having a hard time feeding our poor."

Hannah, the Indian woman Kathleen had seen the day she arrived, came into the office. She appeared dazed. Ignoring Kathleen, she went to Adelaide's desk.

"Hello, Hannah," Adelaide spoke gently.

"Baby."

"Is your baby with you?"

"Baby."

"Is it sick?"

"Baby."

"Where is your baby, Hannah?"

"Gone. Baby gone." She turned away and shuffled out the door.

Kathleen watched her as she passed the window. The skirt that came to her ankles was torn and dirty. The neck of her overblouse was torn and exposed one shoulder. The moccasins were so large that she had to shuffle in order to keep them on.

"The poor wretched thing." Adelaide shook her head sadly.

"Did her baby die?"

"I don't know. When she came in a month or two ago, she was as big as a barrel. The next time was the day you arrived. Her breasts were leaking and I asked about the baby. That was when she shoved me."

"Is she unbalanced?"

"She wasn't before she had the baby. She was a little strange but not like she is now. Grieving must be making her crazy."

The next person to come in was Earlene Smothers. She was huffing and sweating. The heavy coat of face powder had caked on her hairy upper lip.

"Adelaide," she wheezed, "I just saw that crazy Indian woman who roams around town. She was dirty, as usual, and muttering something. She should be put away. My goodness gracious! What's the world coming to when decent people can't walk the streets without running into trash like that."

"What can I do for you, Earlene? This is press day, and we're real busy."

"Not too busy, I hope," Earlene said, and sniffed peevishly. "I have something to add to the notice about the concession the First Baptist Church is going to have at the rodeo."

"What is it? I'll try to get it in."

"Add orange NeHi pop to the list of drinks. Ice cold, of course. Maude Ferman is in charge of the tubs of ice, and she says that we'll have room. I hope she's right after we've advertised."

"Oh, you want this in a paid ad?" Adelaide asked innocently.

"Heavens, no! Just add ice-cold NeHi pop to the notice. Surely you'll not charge us for that." The fat woman had a horrified look on her face.

"No. I'll see what I can get it in, but I'll have to hurry." Adelaide got up from the desk and headed for the back room. "Good-bye, Earlene."

"She'll *see* if she can get it in?" Mrs. Smothers echoed. "Who's boss around here? I thought she owned the place or is that . . . that person she took up with in charge now?"

Kathleen acted as if she were stone deaf and continued to type. As soon as the fat woman went out the door and passed the window, Adelaide came back into the office.

"She gets my hackles up," she explained as she sat back down at her desk.

"I know how you feel. Clara Ramsey got my hackles up last night."

"Is she back in town?"

"I'm afraid so. She is utterly self-centered and cares not a fig for anyone but herself. Poor Hazel. Clara had made herself at home with my soap, shampoo, bath salts, towels, and even my tooth powder. Little Emily apologized. This morning I locked everything in my trunk and my suitcase before I left."

"I wonder what she's doing back in town."

"She told Hazel she came back for money."

"I'm always afraid that Clara will talk Hazel into selling her house. Sam Ramsey worked like a dog to pay for that house so that Clara and Hazel would have a roof over their heads."

"I don't think that will happen. Hazel takes her responsibility for Emily seriously. She loves that child."

"Where will Clara get money in Rawlings? Everyone in town knows that she's a tramp."

At that moment, Clara Ramsey was leaving the house in a pout. Miss *Uppity-up* Dolan had stripped the bathroom, leaving only one ragged towel and a bar of Lava soap, and Mama had guarded the doors to the hussy's room as if it were a bank vault, giving her no chance to *borrow* a few things.

Clara picked her way carefully along the rutted road. The spike heels on her shoes were fragile. It wouldn't do to break one off before Marty got there. She would have worn her other shoes, but wanted the hicks in Rawlings to see her looking good. Her clinging pongee dress was blue with little black dots in it. She had used the curling iron on her hair, making high curls out of her bangs. Her lashes were heavy with mascara, her thin brows penciled, her lipstick bright red.

When Clara reached the street with a sidewalk, she tripped along making sure that her hips swayed so that the full skirt of her dress danced around her knees. She watched her reflection in the window as she passed the dry goods store. She looked damned good. No one would believe that she had a kid almost seven years old, but hell, she'd had her when she was sixteen. She'd make sure Emily stayed out of sight when Marty came. She had a surprise for him, and it wasn't Emily.

The Rawlings Medical Clinic was six blocks from the center of town. When Dr. Herman built it in 1919 right after the war, it was out in the country. Since then the town had expanded to reach it. Long and low and made of red brick, it sat slightly farther back from the walk than business buildings built later.

Clara was hot, and her feet hurt by the time she reached the clinic. She opened the door and stood for a minute beneath the cool breeze of the ceiling fan. Three of the four doors leading out of the small empty lobby were closed. The other was slightly ajar. Somewhere, far away, Clara heard the sound of a radio.

"May I help you?" A woman in a starched white uniform came silently into the lobby.

"I want to see Louise."

"Miss Munday is busy right now."

"Tell her to get unbusy. Clara Ramsey wants to see her."

"Have a seat. I'll tell her."

Like a shadow, the woman slipped back through the slightly open door. Clara sat down, reached down, and wiped the dust off her patent-leather pumps and picked up a week-old paper. She glanced at the headline, then looked to see what was playing at the Rialto Theatre.

"Wallace Beery in *The Champ*. Whoop-de-doo!" She tossed the paper aside, crossed her legs, and swung her foot back and forth impatiently.

"Come in here, Clara." The tone of Louise Munday's voice would have sent waves of apprehension through most young girls. Clara rose leisurely to her feet and followed the tall, stout figure into an inner office. Louise closed the door, turned, and said, "Sit down."

"Thanks," Clara said drily.

"What are you doing back in town? I thought you hated this place." Louise backed up to the desk, sat down on the edge, and folded her arms across her chest.

"I do hate this place. I came back because I need a hundred dollars."

"Who doesn't?"

"I doubt if ya do. Ya made plenty."

"What do you mean by that?"

"You know what I'm talking about. You told me never to mention it, and I haven't."

"You came to us, Clara."

"I was sick and pregnant."

"We helped you. Gave you money to get out of town. It's what you wanted."

"Well, I need a another hundred to get out of town again."

"You bitch! Six months from now you'd be back for another hundred. Is that the way it'll be from now on?"

"No. I'm goin' to Nashville and get on the Grand Ole Opry."

Louise rolled her eyes toward the ceiling. "I knew you'd be trouble. I told Doc as much."

"But I had somethin' ya wanted. Right?"

"And you had something you wanted to be rid of. It was a two-way street, Clara. You came to us. We didn't come to you. You'll get no more money than was agreed upon."

"I think I will. Do ya know who Mama's new roomer is?"

"Of course I do. Kathleen Dolan, the new partner at the *Gazette*."

"We . . . ll—"

"Are you threatening me?" Louise's breath quickened as she leaned forward and stared into Clara's face.

"No, but I can see headlines that'd shock folks outta their drawers." Clara reached up and fiddled with an earring. "I'm just tellin' ya that . . . I got things on my side."

"You rotten little slut. You're trying to blackmail me! I won't stand for it, and neither will Doc." Louise's heavy jowls turned red and quivered with anger. Her small red mouth was pressed into a thin line.

"So he knows what ya did? I didn't know *that*."

"Of course, he knows, you stupid little twit."

"He's got money. He owns half the town and wouldn't miss it if he gave me some."

"He's in Fort Worth and won't be back until Monday. In the meantime, keep your mouth shut."

"Monday? I can't wait 'round here till Monday." Clara jumped to her feet. "That's four days. I want to leave here tomorrow or the next day."

"That's just too damn bad." Louise went behind the desk. "Come back Monday, and I'll let you know what Doc has to say. Go on. Get out of here. I've got work to do."

A shrill scream came from another part of the building just as Clara opened the door.

"What's that?"

"What do you think you stupid little twit?"

"Someone's havin' a baby, and Doc ain't here. You're in charge."

The scream came again and was cut off abruptly.

"It's amazing how smart you can be . . . at times," Louise said sarcastically. "Get out of here and . . . if you breathe a word about anything, anything at all that happens around here, you'll wish you'd never heard of the town of Rawlings, Oklahoma."

"Ya ort to know, Louise, that I already wish I'd never heard of Rawlings, or you for that matter," Clara said sassily, and flounced out the door.

She walked out into the bright sunshine with the feeling that for once she had given Louise Munday something to think about. She and Doc would find out that Clara Ramsey wasn't a dumbbell like a few others she could name. Oh, well, if they didn't come through with the money, she had another card to play.

Marty, hurry up and get here.

Adelaide had finished stamping the papers to be mailed, and Woody loaded them in the coaster wagon to take them to the post office. The ancient press had cooperated, and they had not had a single clog-up to delay the run. Adelaide gave all the credit to Paul's knowledge of how to get along with the big, *dumb* machine.

"If Paul knew as much about the stock market as he does about that stupid press, we'd be rich." Adelaide placed a stop notice on the last stack of papers to be delivered in town and went to the back room to wash the fresh ink off her hands.

Kathleen sat at her desk, looked out the window and wished she hadn't made the date with Leroy. The paperboy came in, taking her mind off the evening for a moment. When she looked out the window again, a shiny black car pulled up and parked beside her Nash. A man wearing a light-colored Stetson was getting out. He was well dressed and carried himself like a man who knew where he was going.

Entering the office, he held open the door for the paperboy who was leaving with a bundle in his arms. Kathleen was surprised to see that he was an Indian, a very handsome Indian. She judged him to be in his middle or late forties. His dark hair was threaded with silver at the temples.

"Afternoon, ma'am. I'm looking for some information about the rodeo to be held here on Saturday. Do you have a list of participants in this issue?"

"The story is there on the front page."

He took a paper from the counter, placed a coin in the cup, and began to read. Kathleen noticed a large turquoise ring on his finger and, when his soft fringed jacket opened, a silver belt buckle. He was tall and broad-shouldered. While she was studying him, he finished reading, looked up, and smiled as if he were terribly pleased.

"Johnny Henry must be quite a cowboy," he said.

Kathleen had become used to the Oklahoma drawl. His accent told her that he had lived or had been educated in the East.

"I've been told that he's the best around here."

"You're not a rodeo fan?"

"I've not been here long enough."

He smiled. His teeth were white, his chiseled features perfect. In her other writings, Kathleen painted pictures of her characters with words. She hoped she could remember every detail of this man's face.

"You're from the upper Midwest. Let me guess. Minnesota."

"Close. I'm from Iowa."

"When I was young and foolish,"—he smiled—"I spent a couple of winters up on the Chippewa Reservation."

"I've not been that far north. Iowa was cold enough for me."

"I'm Barker Fleming."

"Kathleen Dolan." Kathleen held out her hand, and he clasped it politely.

"Pleased to meet you, Miss Dolan. It is *Miss*, isn't it?" She nodded, and he continued. "I'll be in town until after the rodeo. Perhaps I'll see you again. By the way, do you know Johnny Henry?"

"I know him, but not well because I've been in town only three weeks."

"Would you know where his ranch is?"

"It's west of here, I think. I can find out for you."

"That's all right. I was just curious." He folded the paper into a roll and clutched it in his hand. He smiled with his eyes, and little lines fanned out at the corners. "Would you be outraged at my audacity if I asked you to go to dinner with me. I'm harmless and not looking forward to an evening in a strange town."

Kathleen laughed. "I'm not in the least outraged. My Iowa grandma trained me to carry a hatpin should I have the need to defend myself. Thank you, but I've plans for dinner."

"I should have known. Lucky man." He put his fingers to the brim of his hat. "Nice talking to you, Miss Dolan."

" 'Bye, Mr. Fleming."

Kathleen watched him get into his car. He was an interesting man, obviously well-off, and handsome enough to be a movie star. She was sure that she would've had a far more entertaining evening with him than with Leroy Grandon.

Adelaide came into the office. "Who was that? I was about to come in when I heard him ask you to dinner."

"His name is Barker Fleming. He was interested in the rodeo."

"He came in to buy a paper and ask you out to dinner. Fast worker. Did you say Fleming? That's a well-known name here in Oklahoma. If he's one of the Flemings from up near Elk City, he's not poor by a long shot."

"He was very nice as well as very good-looking."

Adelaide sniffed. "He was too old for you."

"He said something about spending a couple of winters on the Chippewa Reservation in Minnesota."

"If he belongs to the Oklahoma Flemings, he's a

Cherokee. The story goes that Amos Fleming, a second-generation Scot, came out from Maine and married a Cherokee woman. They had a large family and he saw to it that all his children were well educated. A couple of them are doctors; some are teachers. They are very successful in business. I wonder if he's one of them?"

"He's staying for the rodeo. Maybe we'll find out. Oh, shoot! Here comes Leroy."

"He's dressed fit to kill. Maybe he's going to propose."

"Adelaide, I swear!" Kathleen put her turban on and pulled some of her hair around her face.

"Go right ahead, honey. If I had to spend an evening with him, I'd swear too. Hello, Leroy. My, you look nice. New suit?"

"No, no," he stammered, looking everywhere but at Kathleen. "Are you ready, Kathleen?"

"Sure, Leroy, and I'm hungry as a bear." Kathleen put her arm through his, smiled at Adelaide, and said gaily, "See you in the morning."

Walking down the street with Leroy was different from walking with Johnny. Because Leroy was no taller than she, she had none of the feeling of protection she'd had with Johnny. Realizing that the man was nervous, she chattered about this and that on their way to the only alternative to the Frontier and Claude's: the Golden Rule Restaurant.

They were directed to a table in the corner of the room. It was covered with a white-linen cloth, and a vase held a single fresh rose. Leroy held her chair, and after he was seated, he pushed the vase across the table toward her.

"For you."

"For me? Why thank you." Kathleen leaned forward and sniffed the fragrant bloom.

Throughout the evening, Kathleen had to carry the bur-

den of conversation. Leroy was a good listener, too good.
She tried to talk about his duties as head of the Chamber
of Commerce. He answered her questions and that was all.
He perked up only when Barker Fleming came in. He
spoke to Kathleen and was seated a few tables away.

"Who is that?"

"He was in the office today. His name is Barker
Fleming."

"Fleming? What's he doing in Rawlings?"

"I don't know. He was interested in the rodeo. Do you
know him?"

"I know who he is. Are you going?"

"To the rodeo? I'm covering it for the paper."

"Would you like to go out afterward?"

"I'm sorry, Leroy, but I've already made plans."

"Oh, well—"

After that he seemed to sink deeper and deeper into
gloom and spoke only when she dragged a statement out
of him. There were long stretches of silence. Kathleen was
exhausted and wished fervently that the movie they were
going to was short and so that she could go home to bed
soon.

*I'm sorry for you, Leroy. I know you're lonely, but please
find someone else and don't ask me out again.*

The offices in the front of the clinic on the edge of town
were dark, but lights were on in the back and a car was
parked beneath the portico. Louise Munday opened the
door for a couple leaving the clinic and bade them good-
bye. She waited until the taillights of the car disappeared
around the corner of the building before she went back inside and locked the door.

A woman in a white nurse's uniform came from one of

the rooms along the hall. She closed the door softly behind her.

"Everything all right?" Louise asked.

"She's sleeping."

"Good. You can go home."

Louise continued on down the hall to her office, went inside, and locked the door. After turning on the light and making sure the shades were drawn, she placed an envelope in the safe.

Later she sat at her desk and picked up the phone.

"Flossie, get me the Biltmore Hotel in Oklahoma City."

"Isn't that where Doc Herman is staying?"

"Get me the hotel, Flossie, and don't listen in."

"Forevermore, Louise! It makes me mad when you say that. It's against Bell policy to listen in and you know it."

"I know it, and don't you forget it. Get the number."

Louise had been in a state of agitation since Clara Ramsey's visit. How dare that little slut threaten them? Their dealings with her had been a pain in the butt from the start. If she spilled her guts to that smart-mouthed redhead from the *Gazette* they could be in for some real trouble.

While she waited for the connection, Louise fumed about the lack of dial telephones in southwestern Oklahoma.

"Hello. Ring Dr. Herman's room." After three rings the doctor answered.

"It's Louise, Doc. When will you be back here?"

"Why are you calling? Is something wrong?"

"I have someone here who needs your attention, and I want to know when you plan to be back."

"Is it urgent?"

"It could be."

"And you can't take care of it?"

"I could, but I need your advice."

"If it's critical, I could come back tomorrow. You know that this meeting is important to me."

"I don't want you to cut your meeting short." Louise's tone softened. "You've looked forward to the conference."

"It's an important meeting, Louise. I told you that before I left."

"Don't worry about it, Doc. I can handle things here until Sunday."

"Are you sure?"

"I'm sure, Doc."

"I knew that I could depend on you. See you Sunday."

After Louise hung up the phone, she muttered, "Shit, shit, shit!"

If not for the possibility that Flossie was listening in, Louise could have explained the situation more clearly to Doc. One thing was certain—if she had to, she could take care of the little tramp herself.

"Is something wrong, Darrell baby?" The woman sat up in bed and leaned back against the headboard.

After Dr. Herman hung up the phone, he went to sit beside her. It gave him a warm intimate feeling when she called him by his first name. She was one of the few people who did. Almost everyone called him Doc, even his two sisters who lived in Ponca City. He pulled down the sheet and stroked the tops of her full breasts.

"Nothing that will take me away from you, Mommy." He spoke in a little boy voice and bent to her breast, took the nipple into his mouth, and suckled lustfully.

"Then come back to bed, baby." She held out her arms. "Mama will hold you."

With little whimpers, he settled across her lap and took her nipple into his mouth again. She wrapped him in her arms and, while she rocked him, he sank his nose into her soft flesh and closed his eyes contentedly.

"Sing to me, Mama."

The woman sang softly. *"A tiny turned-up nose. Two cheeks just like a rose. So sweet from head to toes—this little boy of mine."* She rocked back and forth, smoothing the hair back from his forehead. "Be a good boy," she whispered. "Be good or mama will spank."

"I be good, Mommy." He spoke around the nipple in his mouth.

After a while he reached for her hand and carried it into the opening of his pajamas.

"Want mama to make you feel good, baby?"

"Uh-huh."

The woman held him, playing the part of his mama and his lover. He was the strangest of all her regular clients. They had been in this room since last night playing the game of mama and baby. Her nipples were sore. She hoped that he would reach completion soon and go to sleep.

Each time he came to the city, which was every month or so, he called her, and she was glad to play the part he required for the money he paid her.

Chapter Ten

KATHLEEN PARKED HER CAR behind the house and went through the kitchen to her room. The radio was on in the living room. Clara sprawled in a chair filing her nails. Hazel sat in the rocking chair with Emily on her lap. The child looked as if she had been crying.

"Ya been workin' all this time?" Clara asked.

Kathleen ignored her and spoke to Hazel. "I think I'll take a bath and go to bed."

"Ya'll have to light the tank." After making that statement, Clara reached over and turned up the volume on the radio.

Smiling her understanding to Hazel, Kathleen went to her room, turned on the light, and closed the door. What a shame that such a sweet, gentle woman had a daughter like Clara! She would get latches to go on the inside of two of her doors of her room and a lock and key for the outside door. It would not surprise her in the least if while she was out, Clara prowled through her belongings.

Kathleen kicked off her shoes and, making sure the shades were drawn, pulled off her dress and went to the bathroom to light the burner beneath the water tank. It would be fifteen minutes before the chill was off the water.

While she waited, she took her manuscript and paper supplies out of the trunk. A letter to her publisher was long overdue. She rolled a sheet of paper into her typewriter and typed rapidly.

Dear Mr. Wilkinson,

STAGECOACH TO HELL, my story for the March edition of <u>Western Story Magazine</u>, will be in the mail the end of October. Since my move to Oklahoma, I have been unable to keep to my former schedule as getting settled into my new situation has taken time.

Let me assure you that GRINGOS DIE EASY, the story contracted for the June edition, will be in your office as scheduled.

> *Sincerely,*
> *Kathleen Dolan*
> *(K. K. Doyle)*

After she signed the letter and addressed it, she took a quick bath, put on her night dress, and began to read the last few pages of her manuscript, despite the distraction of the loud radio in the next room.

"He jumped into the open, and dust spurted from his hat as a bullet slammed through it. His own gun spit fire. Durango yelled in sudden pain, and Frisco heard his body hit the ground. The Mex howled and swore as hot lead drilled a furrow along his ribs.

The blazing guns roared, throwing bullets in every direction.

Frisco aimed squarely at the crooked sheriff's breast

*and heard the hammer fall on an empty cartridge. He
whirled around while he was still sheltered by—"*

The volume of the radio in the next room was suddenly
raised to a level that almost rattled the windows. Concen-
tration was impossible. Kathleen put away her manuscript,
turned out the light, and went to bed.

She would see Johnny on Saturday at the rodeo. Would
he be cold toward her as he had been at the grocery store
or as companionable as he had been on the walk home? At
this time last night they were in the school yard and he was
swinging her. She remembered how his arms had felt when
they circled her waist to stop the swing. For an instant he
had held her tightly against him. She would not have
minded at all if he had kissed her. She had wanted him to.

Heavens! She was acting like a love-starved old maid.
She'd had brief romances from time to time, but none of
them had touched her deeply. The men had kissed her and
held her close, but that was as much as she would allow.
When the episodes were over, she'd not given them a second thought. She would have to be careful this time. A
man like Johnny Henry could break her heart.

Long ago her grandma had said when her daughter and
Kathleen's mother died, "If there were no heartaches, how
would we know when we were happy?"

Kathleen lay for what seemed to be hours with her pillow over her head in an attempt to blot out the blare of the
radio. Her mind refused to let her sleep.

Hazel was apologetic at breakfast.

"She won't stay long, Miss Dolan. She never does."

"Don't worry about it. Let's just wait and see what happens. By the way, I'll not be here for supper tonight. Where is Miss Sugarpuss this morning?"

"She's still sleeping. I'm going to let her skip school today."

"Is she sick?"

"Heartsick," Hazel said, and turned away.

Kathleen drove to work and left her car on the street in front of the *Gazette*. Today she planned to go to the courthouse and ask to see the delinquent tax records so that she could do a story on how many farms had been lost since the start of the Depression.

After she finished her "Yesteryear" column and hung it on the hook beside the linotype machine, she put on her hat and walked quickly up the street to the courthouse. She entered the building, and was surprised to see that every door was closed. Looking at her watch, she discovered it was noon and decided to go to Claude's for lunch while she waited for the offices to open.

Kathleen left the redbrick building, and as she passed through the arch of deer antlers that covered the walk, she came face to face with Deputy Thatcher. Standing beside him were Webb and Krome.

"Well, looky here, Ell. If it ain't the sassy redhead from the *Gazette*. Reckon she'll take our picture and put us in the paper?" Webb leered at her and moved to block her path when she attempted to go around the trio.

"Only if a buzzard flies down and scoops you up," Kathleen said scornfully.

"Ain't she a corker, Ell? Swear to goodness, she's more fun than a two-tailed monkey."

"Get out of my way, you dirty lout. I've nothing to say to you."

"Don't be in such a yank, Katydid. The law has stopped

ya for a little chat. Least ya can do is be mindful of the law."
Ell spit a mouthful of tobacco juice into the grass beside
the walk.

Kathleen shuddered with revulsion. She had forgotten
about his small eyes and receding chin.

"Law?" she said scornfully. "That's a joke. You're a
joke."

"Watch yoreself, girl. Ya could find yoreself back there
in my jail for a week eatin' bread and beans."

"Are you threatening to jail me? On what charge?
Because I refuse to socialize with you? I'll tell you something, you two-bit yokel. Mess with me, and you'll find
yourself in a jail cell."

"Well, golly-bill. Listen to that. What's all them big
words she spoutin' mean?"

"We've had city people come down here crowin' before.
It never got 'em nowhere."

"Have you ever heard of Alfalfa Bill Murray?"

" 'Course I have, honey. Who in Oklahoma ain't? When
he was governor he plowed up the ground 'round that big
old mansion in the city and planted taters." The deputy
grinned cockily and winked at his two friends.

"He did that and gave the crop to the poor. He's a good
man, but he'll be hell on wheels when he finds out his only
granddaughter has been threatened with jail by a two-bit
deputy who doesn't have enough respect for his job to wear
a clean shirt while on duty. If you annoy me again, my
grandpa will be on you like a duck on a june bug."

The laughter went out of the deputy's eyes, and they
turned mean.

"Ya think yore pretty smart."

"Smart enough to know a big blowhard when I meet
one." Kathleen raised her chin in a superior manner,

stepped around them, and proceeded down the walk. Her feeling of triumph faded when Krome and Webb caught up and flanked her.

"Ell wants to be sure ya get on down the street and ain't bothered by nobody."

Kathleen seethed as they crossed the street. When they stepped up onto the walk again she stopped and turned on them.

"Get away from me," she hissed. "Get away now, or I'll scream my head off. There's enough good men in this town to hang you if I say you're threatening to rape me."

"Why'd ya want to do that?" Krome held up his hands as if to ward off a blow. "We're bein' gentlemanly. Ell told us to look after ya, and it's what we're doin'."

"I'm game if'n it's what she wants to do." Webb smirked.

"You're disgusting," Kathleen said angrily and walked away. They followed. One of them touched her arm.

"Now wait, hon—"

Kathleen whirled around and balled her fist. "I'll hit you again if you don't get away from me!"

"Ya do, and ya'll go to jail fer brawlin' on the street." Webb giggled.

"Miss Dolan." Big and solid, Barker Fleming stepped out of a doorway and moved up beside Kathleen. "May I walk with you?"

"I would appreciate it."

"There's not room on the walk for all four of us." Barker faced the men. The difference between them was vast. The two men looked as though they had slept in their clothes for a week; they each needed a bath and a shave. Barker Fleming was well-groomed and confident. "You two run along. I don't want to hurt you."

"And if we don't?" Krome felt brave. He'd glanced down the walk to see the deputy watching.

Barker's hand came out of his jacket pocket. The knife in it suddenly produced a blade.

"If you don't want to be friendly, my friend here and I will have to do a little persuading. Get the picture? I'd mop up the street with your mangy hide, but I don't want to get dirty." Barker spoke as matter-of-factly as if he were talking about the weather.

Webb backed away. "She . . . it. He ain't nothin' but a breed," he said loudly when he was a safe distance from Barker.

"Come on, ya fool!" Krome hissed. They went back down the street where the deputy waited.

Barker looked down at Kathleen. "That takes care of that."

"Thank you."

"I'm on my way to get a bite to eat. Join me?"

"I'd love to."

"I like a woman who makes fast decisions."

At the Golden Rule Restaurant, they took a table at the end of the room. Barker placed his hat on the empty chair. His thick black hair, with gray threads at his temples, sprang back from his forehead and hung to the collar of his jacket. His Indian heritage was very evident.

"I had a good meal here last night," he said, and handed her the menu. She glanced at it and handed it back.

"A sandwich will do for me."

While waiting for their order, Kathleen smiled into the dark eyes observing her.

"I wish you could have seen the deputy's face when I told him I was the granddaughter of Governor Alfalfa Bill

Murray. I was lucky the dumb cluck knew who I was talking about."

"Are you really related to Alfalfa Bill?"

"Heavens no! I was reading about him in the 1932 edition of our paper this morning as I prepared for my 'Yesteryear' column. As governors go, he must have been an unpredictable character. I just threw in about being his granddaughter to see if it would work. It did."

"I'll have to keep that in mind. I wonder whose grandson I could be."

"You'd have any number of good ones to pick from." They laughed together like old friends.

"Now tell me why the men were annoying you."

"It's a long story. I'm not sure we have the time."

"We can start it now and finish at dinner." He watched her, concern pressing two little grooves between his eyebrows.

"I'd be glad for company for dinner. I was going to eat alone." She picked up her fork and made little dents in the tablecloth.

"Good. It's a rare woman who can make up her mind so quickly." They smiled at each other. "Six o'clock all right? I'll pick you up at the *Gazette*."

"Tell me about your family." It was amazing how comfortable they were with each other.

"My business keeps me away from home much of the time, I miss them."

"I'm sure that they miss you, too."

"I have four beautiful daughters and two sons. One daughter is at the university, one in high school, two in grade school, and my boy started school this year." There was pride on his face and in his voice when he talked about his children.

"You said you had two sons."

"My eldest is a rancher. Ah . . . here comes our meal. Are you sure that will hold you until dinner?" he said, looking at the small sandwich on her plate.

"It will be plenty." Kathleen noticed the interested glances the waitress had given Barker. He was an exceedingly attractive man who would radiate confidence if he stood barefoot and ragged. His eyes were as black as the bottom of a well. Deep crinkly grooves marked the corners, put there when the eyes had squinted at the sun. There were other lines, too, that experience had made.

"I was an only child," Kathleen said after the waitress left them. "I think it would be lovely to belong to a big family."

"My mother was Cherokee. Cherokee take great pride in their children. I lost my wife five years ago, so I am both mother and father to my brood."

"Oh, I'm sorry."

"It's a fact we all have to deal with sooner or later."

"I understand that. I've lost my parents and the grandparents who raised me. But I'm grateful that they instilled in me the ability to take care of myself."

"You were doing a fair job of it out there." He nodded toward the street. "Where was that hatpin your grandmother gave you?"

"You remembered that?"

"Of course. Now tell me why the deputy and his cronies picked you out to pester, or do they pester all the pretty women in town."

"It started even before I got to Rawlings." She told him about working in Liberal and driving across country to Rawlings. "About five miles out of town a car was parked across the road. I knew they were hijackers. I tried to back

up and ran into the ditch." Barker was an easy man to talk
to. He gave her his full attention and nodded from time to
time.

"I was too mad to be scared. They took my money, then
had the nerve to want me to help push the car out of the
ditch."

"They robbed you? Why aren't they in jail?"

"They told the sheriff they were helping me get my car
out of the ditch and the twenty dollars they had was the
money that I had paid them. He said it was their word
against mine. I don't know what would have happened if
Johnny Henry hadn't come along. He *persuaded* them to
give my money back and sent them on their way. Johnny
knew who they were and turned them in to the sheriff, but
the sheriff let them go."

"Do you know Johnny Henry?"

"I've met him a few times." Kathleen felt the slight flush
that covered her cheeks at the mention of the man who
had occupied her thoughts of late, and she took a drink of
iced tea before she continued. "He rescued me again the
other day. Johnny said their names are Webb and Krome.
I'd met them for the second time on the street. They were
smart-alecky like they were today, and my temper got away
from me. One of them took hold of me, and I hit him in the
mouth with my fist." Kathleen laughed nervously. "I'd like
to say that I've never done such a thing before, but I have.
My grandma said I didn't get this red hair for nothing. I
hurt my knuckles when I hit him, but it was worth it."

Barker had stopped eating and was watching her. She
was a lovely girl. Her eyes were as blue as the sky. A spat-
tering of freckles spread across her nose. Her face wasn't
covered with a lot of powder and paint. She blushed so
prettily, something women seldom did these days.

"Johnny took them to the sheriff," Kathleen continued, unaware of Barker's intense interest. "The sheriff let them go again and then had the nerve to come down to the *Gazette* and accuse me of brawling on the street because I hit the man."

"Strange action for a sheriff. Could be that someone is pulling his strings."

"Doc Herman, I imagine. He runs the town. Nothing happens around here that he doesn't know about. He came in on the heels of the sheriff and lectured me about *brawling*. Goodness gracious, how I have gone on. I shouldn't be laying out the town's dirty laundry to a visitor."

"Most towns have dirty laundry of some kind or the other."

"This one's got an extra share."

"I'm glad that you've got someone looking out for you."

"Johnny just feels responsible for me. His sister, Henry Ann, over in Red Rock, is married to my Uncle Tom. I don't think Johnny wants to bother with me, but feels obligated."

"Any man, if he's worth his salt, would jump at the chance to *bother* with you. You're a pretty girl. Is Johnny married?"

"No. Not that I know of. He made me promise to drive my car to work so that I'd not have to walk back to my room. It's usually dark by the time I leave the paper."

"Do you like him?"

The blunt question caught Kathleen by surprise, and her cheeks reddened. She found she wasn't offended by the personal question. Barker was different from any man she had ever met. She liked him, just as she knew she would when he first came into the office.

"Of course. I'd be foolish *not* to like him after he res-cued me twice."

Barker glanced at her from beneath heavy eyebrows, and genuine amusement quirked his mouth. His dark eyes warmed.

"He'd be foolish not to like *you*."

"He may like me as a friend, but that is all. I'm proba-bly older than he is."

"I'd guess you to be about twenty-four or five."

"Twenty-six as of a few weeks ago."

"A mere youngster. If Johnny doesn't set his cap for you, he isn't as smart as you think he is. Will you be at the rodeo?"

"I'll cover it for the paper."

"Maybe I'll get a chance to meet Johnny Henry."

"He'll be the star of the rodeo, so I'm told."

"Is there anything serious between you and Mr. Grandon? Oh, yes I found out who he was when I went into his store this morning to buy some handkerchiefs."

"Heavens no!"

"I didn't think so. You looked rather bored last night."

"Did it show? I wouldn't hurt Leroy's feelings for the world."

"I rather think that he realized that the two of you were not compatible."

Kathleen waited while he paid for the meal. "Thank you for the lunch," Kathleen said when they reached the sidewalk. "Tonight we go Dutch."

"Dutch? What's that?"

"We each pay for our own."

"How times have changed. I'm not sure my gentlemanly instincts will allow that."

"You have all afternoon to prepare for it. I'd better get

back to work. I'm going to do a feature on the many farms in Tillison County that have been repossessed since the start of the Great Depression. I'll head on down to the courthouse to see the records."

"I'll walk with you. I have business there, too."

At the courthouse, Kathleen said good-bye to Barker and turned into the county recorder's office, but not before she heard a booming voice call out Barker's name.

"Barker Fleming, you son of a gun. What are you doing in Rawlings?"

"Hello, Judge Fimbres. Got a few minutes?"

"For you, Barker, I've got as much time as you want. Come in. Come in and tell me about the family."

Chapter Eleven

JOHNNY SAT ON THE TOP RAIL of the corral with his friend Keith McCabe and looked over the tired stock feeding on the hay being pitched into the pen from the hay wagon.

"Good-looking bunch, Keith.

"A little weary from that long drive."

"Thirty miles is just a waltz around the block for that bunch. Some of them are wilder than a turpentined cat."

"Yeah." Keith grinned, threw his cigarette butt on the ground, stepped down from the rail, and ground it into the dirt with the toe of his boot. "You better hope ya don't draw that long-legged piebald over there; you'll have your work cut out for you. That sucker'll throw you from here to yonder."

"That'd tickle you plumb to death, wouldn't it?" Johnny moved down from the rail to stand beside him.

"Don't worry, sissy-boy, I'll be riding pickup." Keith, an inch taller than Johnny and quite a few pounds heavier, slapped him hard on the back. Johnny pretended to stagger.

"They're gettin' hard up for pickup riders, if ya ask me."

"What'er ya talkin' about, Johnny-boy? I'm the best

pickup man in the state of Texas. Don't worry. I'll get to you before he stomps your pretty face into the ground."

"I'd be obliged," Johnny said drily.

Keith McCabe, a rancher from just over the line in Texas, was Johnny's best friend and one of the few who knew about his occasional activities with the federal marshals. Keith was also a good friend of Hod Dolan and his wife Molly. Molly and Ruth McCabe had been childhood friends in Kansas.

"When's Ruth coming up?"

"She and Davis will be here tomorrow. She'd not miss the rodeo especially if you're ridin'."

"How old is Davis now?"

"Two and a half years now. His baby sister should be here by Christmas."

"You certainly are a busy man. It's a wonder you've got time for ranchin'."

"Important things come first, boy. You'll find that out when you have your own woman. When are you going to find a pretty little gal and tie the knot?"

"When I get to be as old as you . . . say twenty, thirty years from now."

"Hey, I don't top you over ten years, if that much."

"If you're so young, why'd you quit rodeoin'?"

"I can give you a two-word answer to that question. *My wife.*" Keith was deeply in love with his wife, and his eyes always lit up when he talked about her and his son.

"Henpecked already, huh?"

"You bet! The year we married I entered the bull-riding contest over at Frederick. The crazy bastard I drew was meaner than a longhorn with his tail tied in a knot. After he threw me, he tried to stomp me to death. Ruth was mad at the steer but madder at me. It didn't matter that I was limping around on crutches; she ripped me up one side and down the other. She said that if I got myself killed, she'd be so mad she'd not go to my funeral and, what's more, when our boy was born, she'd name him Horsecock McCabe. That did it. I couldn't have my boy going through life named Horsecock."

Johnny whooped with laughter. "That sounds like Ruth."

"Yeah. She's a ring-tailed tooter when she's riled up," Keith said proudly. "I know which side of my bread is buttered. I quit rodeoing before she took off a patch of my hide."

"I saw your favorite relative on the way up here," Johnny said.

"Who's that?"

"Marty Conroy. Your cousin from Conroy, Texas. The little turd with the big head, the loud mouth, and shit for brains."

"Good Lord! Was he coming here? I haven't seen the little pipsqueak for a year. Every time I see him, he's trying to hang a big get-rich-quick scheme on me."

"We were on the road between the Kimrow and Dryden ranches when he pulled up behind us in his fancy car. He didn't have any more sense than to honk the horn and spook the herd. Old Potter, riding drag, had to go chase a half dozen head. He cussed a blue streak and threatened to horsewhip Marty if he blew that blasted horn again. I know it about killed the little blowhard to have to tag along behind, eating dust, until we made the turn."

"Marty likes to throw around the Conroy name. It doesn't mean squat except in Conroy, Texas. He thinks he's big-time, but lately he's come down a peg or two. The trustees of his granddaddy's estate are tightening the purse strings. It could be that the trust is about to dry up, and he'll have to go to work. Wouldn't it be a cryin' shame if old Marty had to do a day's work?" Keith grinned devilishly.

"Yeah, it would. I'd feel downright bad about it." Johnny beat the dust from his hat by hitting it against his thigh, then slapped it back down on his head. "I should get on out to the ranch and see about my own stock."

"Let's find a place to wash up, and I'll treat you to supper before we head out to your place for the night."

"Sounds good. I didn't want to cook for you anyway."

The instant he and Keith walked into the Golden Rule Restaurant, Johnny saw Kathleen seated at a table in the back of the room. The light above her head turned her hair fiery red. All that registered in his mind was that she was wearing something blue and laughing with the man she was with. He had thick black hair, was wearing a light doeskin jacket, and giving her all of his attention.

Wishing that he could turn around and go back out but knowing that if he did, he'd have to explain to Keith, Johnny led the way to the farside of the room. He unintentionally sat at a table against the wall that gave him a side view of Kathleen and her friend.

Trying not to let it show that his gut had knotted painfully at the sight of her with another man, Johnny pretended to study the menu.

"What do you usually have here?" Keith asked.

"What? Well, I don't usually eat here. This is a little too fancy for me. I grab a hamburger at Claude's when I'm in town," he said gruffly.

"It'll not hurt you to get the manure off your boots once in a while." Keith turned to the waitress who was hovering at his elbow, smiled, and winked. "I want a big, thick steak, honey, some biscuits and gravy. Coffee, too."

"Give me the same." Johnny slapped the menu down on the table.

The overweight waitress glanced at Johnny then fixed her gaze on Keith, as she had been doing since they walked in the door. When Keith spoke to a woman, if she was sixteen or sixty, he gave her his full attention.

"What?" he said to Johnny when he saw him scowling after the departing waitress.

"I was just wondering if that woman was going to sit on your lap or go get our food." Johnny's gaze went again to the waitress, who was still watching them.

"She was nice and doing a good job. I made her feel good. What's wrong with that?"

"Nothing, if Ruth doesn't mind."

"Ruth knows I love her. She'd not mind me flirting a bit with a girl who needs to feel for a minute or two that a man thinks that she's pretty, even if she isn't."

"Who do you think you are? Dorothy Dix?"

"Dorothy Dix? Who's that?"

"The woman in the paper who gives advice."

"Never read it."

"I haven't either, but I've heard about her."

Keith leaned toward Johnny and slanted his eyes toward the corner where Kathleen was sitting.

"There's a pretty redhead over there that's giving you . . . or me the eye. Do you know her?"

"Yeah, I do. She's Hod Dolan's niece. She came down here about a month ago to buy into the newspaper."

"Hod's niece? Who's that big dude with her?"

"Never saw him before."

"Good-looking woman."

"Yeah."

The waitress came back to the table. "We got only two pieces of peach pie left. Want that I save them for ya?"

"Now aren't you just too sweet for words. Of course I do. I'll take them both."

She took her eyes off Keith long enough to ask Johnny, "What will you have?"

"I'm not much for sweets."

"Okey-doke. Be right back."

Minutes later she returned with the food. Johnny had just started to eat when he became aware that Kathleen and the man with her were leaving the restaurant. He kept his eyes on his plate until he was sure that they were out the door. His appetite left him, and every bite he took seemed to stick in his throat.

Kathleen was quiet as she walked beside Barker on the way to her car. She had seen Johnny when he came into the restaurant, and she knew that he had seen her, yet he hadn't as much as given her a nod of recognition. Not once had he looked her way after he and his friend were seated. She would have liked for him to have met Barker. She was sure that he would have liked him.

Dammit! Why was she feeling so down in the dumps?

"You're quiet. You must be tired," Barker remarked when they reached the car.

"I am a little tired. I'm rather put out with you for not letting me pay for my dinner. This was a Dutch-date, you know."

"I'm not sure I understand this Dutch-date business. Me dumb Indian."

Kathleen burst out laughing. "Dumb like a fox!"

"That's better. I was afraid that you regretted wasting your evening with a lonesome old man."

"Absolutely not. I enjoyed it . . . and you're far from being an old man."

"I'm in the middle of my life. My son is twenty-five. Your age."

"I hope he realizes how lucky he is to have a youthful father. I never had a chance to know mine."

"Ah . . . you're an orphan. Maybe I should adopt you."

"I'm a little old for that. Thanks for dinner. Maybe I'll see you tomorrow at the rodeo."

"I'll make sure of it." He leaned down to speak after she got into the car. "Are you sure you'll be all right? I'd feel better if I knew those two shied-pokes weren't about."

"Shied-pokes? What kind of word is that?"

"An Oklahoma word for someone you had just as soon not know."

"Did you learn that word in college?" Kathleen teased.

"No, from my father, who sometimes used very colorful language." His smile crinkled the corners of his eyes. "I plan to be here for a few more days. If you have any trouble with that deputy or those other two, let me know."

"I may not have any more trouble. Not after the news gets around that I'm Alfalfa Bill's granddaughter." Unexpected laughter bubbled up. "Good night, Mr. Fleming."

"Good night, Miss Kathleen." He put his fingers to the brim of his hat.

Kathleen drove away leaving Barker standing at the curb. She liked him. He was easy to talk to, and he could converse on a variety of subjects. It was comforting to know that he was her friend.

She had enjoyed the evening until Johnny showed up.

At times she thought that Johnny liked her; then at other times, like tonight, when he ignored her, she was sure that he had been looking out for her because of his obligation to her Uncle Tom. She wished that she could get him out of her mind. He was dark, quiet and completely controlled and, to her, utterly intriguing. There were unstirred depths in him that she longed to bring to the surface if they were reachable.

Damn you, Johnny Henry!

Clara snuggled close to Marty Conroy's side and waited for him to stop the car on the little-used road outside of town. As soon as he turned off the engine and the lights, his arms were around her, his hand beneath her skirt.

"Baby, baby—" His mouth devoured hers.

"Marty, honey, not so fast," she said as soon as her lips were free. "I was wantin' to go honky-tonkin'. There's a good nightclub right here in Rawlin's." She stroked the inside of his thigh, her hand teasing up higher and higher.

"I'm not sharin' ya, sweetie. I want ya all to myself. Let's get in back. More room." They got out of the car. He opened the back door, pushed her down on the seat, pulled her skirt up, and fell on top of her. "I been thinkin' of this all the way from Conroy." His fingers worked their way into her panties. "Take 'em off, honeypot," he whispered breathlessly. "I can't wait."

"You're randy as a billy goat, Marty. Have ya been down to Del Rio to have that old Doc Brinkley give ya a goat gland?" Clara giggled as she obeyed.

"I don't need help from a billy goat when I've got you." He grabbed her hand and pressed it to the hardness in his britches. "See how I get when I'm with you. Get me out, baby."

"After we do it, can we go honky-tonkin'?"

He plunged into her roughly before he said, "Sure, honey. Sure."

It was over quickly for Marty. He sat up, lit two cigarettes, and gave one to Clara. He stretched out and put his feet up on the back of the front seat. He was a small man, utterly selfish, with an ego the size of a blimp.

"Let me catch my breath, sweetie, and we'll do it again. I'd drive all the way to California to get that. You're the best piece of ass in Oklahoma. Texas, too."

"Ya think so? Do I get ya horny?"

"Ever'time, sweetie. Every damn time."

"We could go to the Twilight Gardens, dance a while, then come back here and do it again," Clara said hopefully. "You're somethin' special, Marty. I want to show ya off."

His hand traveled up her thigh to the junction of her legs. "I couldn't feel ya up at the Twilight Gardens. I want to get as much of you as I can while I'm here."

"You're goin' with me to Nashville, ain't ya?"

"I'm thinkin' about it, sweetie. You'll knock their socks off in Nashville."

"You said that maybe we could get married."

"I haven't forgot."

"When, Marty?"

"As soon as I get my business taken care of, baby doll. I got to make money so I can buy pretties for my sweetie."

"You got money?"

"Yeah. The town of Conroy was named for my granddaddy. Conroys are big-moneyed people in Texas. I always have a few irons in the fire. Come sit astraddle my lap and whisper dirty words in my ear. That always gets me hornier than hell. You do it so good, baby."

Clara did as he asked and tried to act enthusiastic about it. When it was over, she was exhausted.

"Can we go now?"

"Why do you always want to go to cheap roadhouses?" he asked irritably.

"I like fun. Besides, they might want me to sing."

"Fat chance. The singer with the band out there knows you'd show her up. She'll see to it you don't get near the stage."

"We could just dance."

"Come here, honey-baby. This is what you're best at."

Clara held her temper with an effort. All the horny little jackass wanted to do was screw. She was beginning to think that the big promises he'd made her were dry holes and that he had no intention of taking her to Nashville or even to a honky-tonk. She'd just have to get there on her own; and if he thought she was doing all this for nothing, he had a big surprise coming.

"How long ya stayin', lover?"

"Until Saturday. Want to stay at the hotel with me tonight and tomorrow night after the rodeo?"

"Sure, honey. If you have a hotel room, why are we doin' this in the backseat of your car?"

"A relative of mine is in town, and I want to be sure he's not staying at the hotel. I'll know by the time we get back there."

"Anyone I know?"

"Naw, honey. Come here. I'm gettin' horny again."

"Are you sure you haven't been to Del Rio?" Clara asked irritably, but Marty didn't notice.

Chapter Twelve

By MIDMORNING ON SATURDAY the fairground outside of Rawlings was a scene of bustling activity. Concession stands were being set up beneath the grandstand; cowboys were driving stock into the holding pens; and the crowds coming to the rodeo were arriving by car, wagon, horseback, and on foot.

The day was bright and sunny and, for once, the Oklahoma wind had taken a rest. The hard-packed red dirt in the arena had been stirred, dampened, and stirred again to afford a softer landing for those unfortunates who would be thrown from their mounts.

By the time Kathleen drove onto the field near the fairground and parked alongside the other cars, Emily was jumping with excitement. Hazel was quiet, obviously worried. Clara had not come home last night nor sent a word to her mother. This was not unusual behavior for Clara; but Hazel was anxious, always hopeful that her daughter would settle down and accept her responsibilities.

Hazel and Kathleen walked down the road to the fairground, Emily between them. Kathleen gave the tickets to the man at the gate and, holding Emily's hand, went past the array of concession stands toward the bleachers.

"Do you want a soda pop now or later, Emily?" Kathleen asked.

The child looked at her grandmother, waiting until Hazel said, "You decide, honey."

"Now," the little girl whispered.

"All right. We'll get it at the school booth. The band is raising money to buy a new set of drums."

"Yoo-hoo, Miss Dolan," Mrs. Smothers called as they passed the church stand. "Are you taking pictures for the paper?"

"Only of the winners," Kathleen replied, and kept walking.

"Oh, well—" Mrs. Smothers words were lost as the school band began to play.

With the cold bottle of NeHi pop firmly clutched in Emily's hand, they went to the bleachers and found seats on the fourth row near an aisle so that Kathleen could go down to the fence and take pictures. Beneath the shade of her hat brim, Kathleen scanned the working area for a glimpse of Johnny. Finally she spotted him leaning against a pole corral talking to a tall dark-haired man who was holding a small child. A blond woman, obviously pregnant, stood beside him. The man had been with Johnny at the restaurant. As she watched, the woman grasped Johnny's arm and laughed up at him.

Kathleen tore her eyes away from Johnny and looked down at the Kodak in her lap. When she raised her eyes again, they landed on Barker Fleming standing at the end of the bleachers with the judge who had greeted him the day before at the courthouse. His eyes caught her looking at him. He raised his hand acknowledging her and continued his conversation. Her curiosity about him grew. He appeared to be as comfortable talking to a judge as he had been confronting Webb and Krome.

"There's Mama," Emily whispered loudly to her grandmother.

"Don't point, sugar." Hazel took the child's hand in hers.

Kathleen turned her eyes toward the entrance to see Clara, teetering on high heels and clinging to the arm of a dapper little man wearing a large Stetson and a blue shirt elaborately decorated with white braid. The legs of his twill britches were tucked into cowboy boots that had large white stars inlaid on the sides. The man strutted like a turkey gobbler in a henhouse. It was almost laughable.

"Now, ain't he a fine figure of a man?" Hazel said sarcastically.

"Who is he?" Kathleen leaned back away from Emily when she spoke.

"Mr. Conroy from Texas. He stopped in front of the house yesterday. Clara ran out and got in the car. I haven't seen her since." Hazel spoke in a loud whisper.

"Is he the one taking her to Nashville?"

Hazel snorted and rolled her eyes. An answer wasn't necessary.

"His car is big and has a loud horn," Emily said. "But he wouldn't be nice. Not like Johnny."

With raised brows, Kathleen glanced at Hazel over the child's head. The little girl was very observant. She made no attempt to call out to her mother.

The rodeo started with the contestants parading around the arena on horseback. Johnny, wearing a dark shirt and a red bandanna tied about his neck, was in the middle of the pack. His mount was a high-spirited dapple gray who danced sideways. Johnny kept him under control with a tight rein. As he passed the section where Kathleen was sitting, he looked straight ahead.

"Good luck, Johnny!" The shout came from the blond woman who had been talking to him earlier. She was seated on the first row. The child stood on the plank seat beside her and waved a red handkerchief.

"Who is she?" Kathleen asked.

Hazel shook her head. "I've not seen her before."

After the cowboys left the arena, Barker Fleming moved back from the fence and stood alone at the end of the bleachers.

The first event was the steer-riding contest. The first two contestants were unseated before the time whistle blew.

"These steers are mighty feisty today, folks. Give a hand to that boy who hit the dust." The announcer's voice came over the loud speaker. "The next rider is Johnny Henry, number twenty-two. He's drawn Brimstone, a three-year-old from the McCabe ranch. This sucker is mean, folks. You never know if he's goin' to turn right or left. Our Johnny has his work cut out for him if he plans to stay on for a full ride. You pickup men best keep a sharp eye. Old Brimstone has been known to turn and try to gore a fallen rider."

Kathleen drew in a sharp breath. Her eyes were fastened on Johnny mounted on the bull behind the stout wooden gate. He was winding the bull rope around his gloved hand. After anchoring his hat firmly down on his head, he signaled for the gate to open.

The steer with the man on its back shot out of the chute. Johnny held one hand high over his head, the other wrapped in the rope. The enraged animal leaped into the arena the instant the gate was opened, turned and came down on stiff legs. On the next leap the bull turned in midair and Johnny slipped to the side. He stayed astride for another leap, then he crashed into the pulverized dirt with a thud. In an instant he was on his feet scrambling for the fence, hoping to put distance and a solid object between himself and the charging bull.

"Get 'im, boys," the announcer shouted.

Kathleen's hands went to her cheeks when the maddened steer raced to gore Johnny with its long sharp horns. A rider shot between them throwing a blanket over the animal's head, giving it another target to attack. Johnny sprang up behind the rider and the crowd cheered.

"The pickup man is Keith McCabe." The excited voice of the announcer came over the loudspeaker. "He knows ol' Brimstone is meaner than sin. He owns him."

Kathleen's heart was thudding wildly. She was surprised to realize that she was angry at Johnny. Really angry. The idiot! He could have been killed or maimed for life, all for the sake of a few minutes of glory. She sat quietly, looking straight ahead but not seeing, until her heart settled to its regular beating. She became aware of Emily's tugging on her arm and looked down at the child.

"I was scared for Johnny."

"So was I."

"I wish Johnny liked Mama. If they got married, he'd be my daddy, wouldn't he?"

"Yes, honey." Kathleen's body tensed for a moment at the thought, then relaxed. *No. He'd not marry Clara . . . but does he have someone special? Will that account for the sudden changes in his attitude toward me?*

The afternoon wore on. Kathleen watched and waited for the events in which Johnny participated. He won the calf-roping contest easily, lost the barrel-racing event when his stirrup raked a barrel, and then it was time for the bronc-riding contest, the rodeo's main event.

Three of the first four contestants were thrown from their mounts. When it came time for Johnny to ride, Kathleen felt a tightening of dread in her stomach. She watched as two handlers held the head of a dirty gray, long-legged horse with a black mane and tail while Johnny settled himself firmly in the saddle. Johnny's lanky body was tense and ready. He tugged at his hat, wound the reins around his gloved fist, and dug his feet into the stirrups.

He leaned forward and said something to one of the handlers, then sat back into the saddle. The handlers sprang back, one ripping off the cloth that covered the eyes of the grulla, the other swinging open the gate. Both men dived for the fence out of the way of the slashing hooves. Out of the chute, the horse leaped into the air like a spring coming uncoiled. All four feet left the ground at once, and the animal twisted and came down on stiffened legs.

The gray remained still for a space of a few seconds as if surprised that the weight was still on its back. With awareness came a wild scream and an eruption of crazed fury. The grulla's eyes were wild and rolling with rage. He shot into the air again. Dust swirled as the enraged animal sought to rid himself of the hated man on his back who continued to rake his sides with his spurs.

The crowd whooped and shouted encouragement.

"Ride 'em, Johnny. Ride that cork-screwing cayuse!"

"Whoopee!"

"Watch it, Johnny, he's goin' to roll."

The longer Johnny stayed on the animal's back the more frenzied the grulla became. The man and the animal rose in midair, each time coming down with a crash that could snap Johnny's back. With its black tail and mane flying, its nostrils flaring, the horse charged the fence and would have crashed into it, but Johnny yanked the animal's head to the side. Sharp hooves churned the dirt, creating a cloud of dust.

Kathleen stood with the rest of the crowd. Her hand covered her mouth to stifle a shriek of fear as the horse reared. For an instant she thought it would go over backward and Johnny would be crushed.

"Time! Time! Get him off," the announcer shouted.

The crowd was jubilant. The drovers along the fence pounded each other on the back.

Johnny's hat was gone. His hair, black as the horse's mane, shone in the sun. His sinewy form was still anchored firmly in the saddle as riders flanked the bucking horse. Johnny slipped off and flung himself behind the pickup man.

Kathleen took a full breath for the first time since Johnny had mounted the horse.

"Ladies and gentlemen, settle down! Settle down! I wish to make an announcement. Johnny Henry has been named *All-Around Cowboy* of the Rawlings' 1938 rodeo. Let's hear a shout for Johnny!" The crowd yelled and clapped. When the noise died down, the voice came again. "Come on up here, boy, and collect your money."

Someone pushed Johnny up on the platform. He accepted an envelope, shook hands with the announcer and the judges, and made his retreat.

Kathleen looked down and saw the camera in her lap. Only now did she remember that she had come to take pictures.

"I've got to go take pictures, Hazel."

"You go right ahead. Emily and I will tag along behind. Don't worry about us. If we lose you, we'll go to the car."

As Kathleen made her way down the steps of the bleachers, she saw Barker Fleming waiting for her.

"Did you enjoy the rodeo?" she asked.

"I've not seen a better one. Not even at the stockyards in Oklahoma City."

"I'm on my way to take pictures of the *All-Around Cowboy*. Would you like to come along and meet him?"

"Thank you. I'd like that."

"Then let's go get the job done."

With Barker striding beside her, Kathleen made her way through the crowd to the stock pens, where they found Johnny surrounded by a group of people, including the couple that had been with him before the rodeo began. When he saw Kathleen, his dark eyes lit with pleasure.

"Congratulations, Mr. *All-Around Cowboy*. May I have a picture for the paper?"

"If you're sure you want one."

"I do. Stand back against the fence, face the sun, and tilt your hat brim so that it doesn't shade your face."

"You better take my picture, miss." This came from the smiling man holding the child. "This ugly old son of a gun will break your Kodak, sure as shootin'."

"I'll have to chance it 'cause he's the champ." Kathleen smiled at the man then let her gaze slide down to include the small blond woman at his side.

"Come on, let's get this over." Johnny shifted nervously from one foot to the other trying not to stare past Kathleen at the man who hovered at her side.

"Stand still and look at the camera." Kathleen backed away and looked down into the viewfinder of the Kodak. "I'd better take another one," she said after the first shot. "One might not turn out."

"You can always put one in the barn to keep the rats out."

"Keith, stop teasing. You're as proud of him as I am."

"Ruthy, darlin', I am proud. I'm damn proud he didn't break a leg. I need his help getting my stock back home."

"Don't swear in front of our son," she scolded. "He'll be swearing like a trooper by the time he starts to school."

"Miss Dolan, meet Mr. and Mrs. McCabe. They know your aunt and uncle in Kansas." Johnny seemed shy and uncertain about making the introductions, but Kathleen had never been accused of being shy.

"How do you do?" She held out her hand. "I've heard about you from Uncle Hod," she said to Keith. "And about you, Mrs. McCabe, from Aunt Molly. She said that you were best friends growing up. I was at their house in Pearl when Molly got the news about your son."

"We'll not hold it against you for being related to Hod, Miss Dolan," Keith said.

After they shook hands, Kathleen introduced Barker Fleming.

"Mr. Fleming, this is Johnny Henry, our *All-Around Cowboy*."

Barker stepped up to Johnny and held out his hand. The two tall men eyed one another as they shook hands.

"Hello, Johnny."

Johnny nodded, pulled his hand free, and fumbled in his pocket for the makings of a cigarette.

"Mr. and Mrs. McCabe." Kathleen finished the introductions.

Barker reluctantly looked away from Johnny and took Keith's hand.

"I understand that you own the stock used here today," Barker said.

"Not all, but a good part. Never thought Johnny'd be able to stay on that wild-haired mustang."

Barker glanced at Johnny. "That was some ride."

Johnny merely nodded. There was something about Barker that made him uneasy, not the least of it being that he was with Kathleen. Did she go for older, successful men? He was a breed, that was clear, and it didn't seem to bother her.

"I didn't like it," Kathleen said, tilting her chin to look up at Johnny. "That horse hated you and outweighed you by a thousand pounds. Getting on him was the dumbest thing I ever saw. Next time pick on something your own size."

Ruth chortled happily. "Here's a woman who thinks like I do. If Keith ever even thinks about getting on that horse, I'll take the horsewhip to him."

Johnny looked steadily at Kathleen after her outburst. There was a quizzical look on his face. Their eyes held until Kathleen felt the heat coming up from her neck to flood her face. *What in the world caused me to say such a thing?*

Barker sensed her discomfort and asked Keith the location of his ranch.

"Six miles across the river outside Vernon."

"I know about where that is. Good flat country."

"I've heard of the Flemings. Are you from around Duncan?"

"My brother is. I'm from Elk City."

"Now I remember. A Fleming from Elk City owns the tannery here."

"Only part of it. My sister and her husband own the controlling interest." Barker's eyes went to Johnny. "Where's your ranch, Johnny?"

"Eight miles south." Johnny threw his half-smoked cigarette on the ground and stepped on it.

Keith set his son on the ground beside Ruth. "Hold on to Davis, honey. I'm going to head off trouble."

Kathleen looked behind her to see the man who brought Clara coming their way. He had evidently instructed Clara to wait, because she stood with arms crossed, pouting, against the end of the corral.

"Keith, I heard this morning that this was your stock here at the rodeo."

"Are you offering to buy, Marty?"

"I don't deal in cattle. Hey, how is Ruth? She gets prettier all the time. Gonna kick out another kid, huh?" Marty hit Keith on the upper arm. "It must be handy having your own woman on the ranch. Anytime, anyplace. Huh, Keith?"

"Shut up, Marty." A dark scowl covered Keith's face. "What are you up to? What are you doing here?"

"Keeping an eye on my investment. Johnny Henry made me a little money today." He raised his brows. "Lost the bull ride, won the calf rope, lost the barrel race, and won the bronc-riding. Just the way I bet on him."

"What the hell are you saying, Marty?"

"Nothin'. Me 'n Johnny are shirttail relations, Keith. Just like you and me."

Keith snorted. "Your sister was married to the man who later married Johnny's sister. That's your only connection to Johnny unless you're saying that you and Johnny hatched up a scheme for him to throw some on the contests."

Marty smirked. "I've known the boy for a long time. Like him. Don't hold being a breed against him. Any little deal we cook up is strictly between us."

"In the first place, Johnny is NO boy. He's a twenty-five-year-old man. And if you want to keep your teeth, Marty, you'd better not be putting out the story that he threw any of the events so that you could cash in with the big gamblers."

"Trust me, Keith. I'll not give our secret away." Marty looked unruffled and arrogant. "Listen, Keith. I'm willing to let you in on the ground floor of something big. I came up here just to look around, not knowing that you'd be here. But being that you're here and we're kin, I'll cut you in."

Keith folded his arms and rocked back on his heels. "What big things are you planning now? Are you going to dam up the Red River and flood my ranch?"

"Something bigger than that. I'm going to build a toll bridge across it like they did across the Canadian River up at Purcell."

"You go right ahead and do that, Marty."

"Don't you want in on it? All we'd have to do is sit back and collect the tolls."

"That'd be a good job for you, little man." Keith slapped Marty so hard on the back that he staggered. "Get yourself a rocking chair, sit on the bridge, and collect the tolls. I'm taking my family home."

Marty's face turned ugly. "One of these days I'll hit it big, and you'll be sittin' out there on that pig-turd ranch with nothin' but a handful of cows."

"Well, that's how I like it. Here comes your Kewpie doll, Marty. You'd better take her and get the hell out of here before I forget that I'm bigger than you are."

Marty looked over his shoulder and scowled.

"I got tired waitin', sugar." When Clara reached him she clasped his arm possessively, and smiled flirtatiously at

Keith. "I'm Clara Ramsey, good-looking." She held out a hand.

"Howdy." Keith touched the hand briefly. " 'Bye, Marty. I hope you can find your way back to Texas." Keith walked away.

"Oh, there's Johnny," Clara squealed, and began tugging Marty toward where Johnny stood with his back to the fence. "Come meet Johnny, Marty. We're old friends." She ran to Johnny and would have kissed him on the cheek, if he hadn't reared back and turned his head. "I'm so proud of you, Johnny. I was so . . . thrilled! Did ya hear me yellin' for you?"

Johnny's hands shot out to hold her away from him.

"This is Johnny, Marty. The *friend* I told you about." She giggled.

"I know who he is. Long time no see." Marty held out his hand. Johnny ignored it. The snub was obvious.

"All right, be a dumb Indian," Marty said angrily. "I was just trying to be friendly."

Johnny bristled. He was tired and sore. "This *dumb* Indian might shove your rear up between your shoulders if you don't get the hell away from me and take this bangtail with you."

"It's what I would expect from trash. Wasn't your mama a Mud Creek whore and your daddy a drunk Indian?"

Johnny yanked Marty's hat off his head and hit him across the face with it, then threw it at him.

"And yours was a buzzard. Get out of my sight, and if you come near me again, I'll break your stupid head wide open."

Kathleen glanced quickly at Barker. His dark, intense eyes were on Johnny. A thought in the back of her mind began to wiggle its way forward. Johnny would look something like Barker when he was older. His Indian features were not as prominent as Barker's, but he had the same quiet face. Both he and Keith were waiting to see what happened. Keith was tense, but smiling . . . broadly.

Clara, red-faced and angry, picked up Marty's hat and tugged on his arm.

"Let's go, sugar. He's mad 'cause I don't put out for him," she said in a confidential tone, then shrieked at Johnny. "You'll be sorry, Johnny Henry. You're jealous 'cause you'll never 'mount to any more than a rag-tail *breed* livin' in a shack out on the prairie. Marty and me are goin' to Nashville. We'll make it big and come back here and spit all over all of ya."

Kathleen's eyes went quickly to Johnny. He was clenching his teeth in an effort to hold his temper, and she was glad that Clara was able to pull Marty away.

Kathleen turned to the McCabes and began to talk to avert the attention from Johnny.

"I'll write Uncle Hod and Molly and tell them that I met you. Would you mind if I took a picture of the three of you to send to them?"

"I'd like that," Ruth said. "And maybe I could use the negative to make a copy for us."

"Of course. Turn now and face the sun."

Holding his son on one arm, Keith put the other around his wife and drew her close to his side.

Looking through the viewfinder, Kathleen said, "Now, smile." She took the picture and turned to Johnny. "Get in there, Johnny. Uncle Hod will want a picture of you, too." Johnny sauntered over and stood behind Ruth.

After she snapped the picture, Keith set his son on the ground and reached for Kathleen's Kodak.

"Hod and Molly would like a picture of you and Johnny."

"I don't know about that."

"I do. Now stand over there. Come on, cowboy."

Kathleen took off her hat and fluffed her hair with her fingers. She moved over to stand beside Johnny. He flung an arm across her shoulders and pulled her tightly against him. She looked up at him in surprise. He looked down at her. It was then that Keith snapped the picture.

"Try not to pay any attention to what Clara says. You know what she is," Kathleen whispered.

"Uh-huh," he murmured as his arm dropped from around her.

Kathleen put the straw hat back on her head and reached for her Kodak.

"I'd better get back to the paper and develop this film. Hazel and Emily are waiting for me at the car."

"I'll walk along with you." Barker said his good-byes to the McCabes, then held out his hand to Johnny. "You did a hell of a job out there today. I'll see you again."

"Thanks," Johnny murmured grudgingly.

It had been years since Johnny had felt anything like jealousy toward another man. He had that feeling now as he watched Kathleen walk away with a man who appeared to be well educated and was well-off if he owned half the tannery. Usually name-calling didn't bother him all that much, but today he had been embarrassed to be called a breed in front of the man, yet it was what *he* was, too.

Chapter Thirteen

AFTER KATHLEEN TOOK HAZEL AND EMILY HOME, she went back to the *Gazette*. She let herself into the office with her key, then locked the door behind her. She could hear the radio and knew that Paul was in his room. After hesitating for a minute or two, she knocked on his door.

"I'm sorry to bother—"

"It's all right. Come in. Addy and I were going to listen to old Doc Brinkley down in Del Rio."

"How did the rodeo go?" Adelaide didn't seem to be the least bit embarrassed to be caught in Paul's room. She was wearing a lounge robe and sat on the bed with her back against the headboard. "Did Johnny win?"

"He won *All-Around Cowboy*. I took his picture. If we can get the print on the bus tonight, we'll have the engraving back in time for this week's paper."

"I'll develop the film." Paul glanced at the clock on his desk, then reached for the Kodak.

"I wish I knew how to do that," Kathleen said.

"I'll teach you how to develop and make prints, but not tonight. I'll have to speed up the process if I'm to have it ready by the time the bus comes through."

While he spoke he extracted the roll of film from the

Kodak. He left them and went into the little closet he had made into a darkroom.

"Isn't he amazing?" Adelaide asked proudly. "He can do most everything. If he doesn't know how to do something, it drives him crazy until he learns. He set up the darkroom out of scraps of this and that. He takes beautiful pictures, too."

"Why not take pictures for the paper?"

"I wish he would, but he scarcely leaves the building. He insists on staying in the background. He is a dear, sweet man." Adelaide moved her feet and nodded for Kathleen to sit down.

"I think so, too. If he weren't head over heels in love with you, I might try to beat your time."

"I can't believe how lucky I am. Now, tell me about the rodeo. Was there a big crowd?"

"The bleachers were almost full. It seemed to be a good crowd, but I have nothing to compare it to. The concession stands were doing a good business. I managed to avoid Mrs. Smothers, thank goodness."

"I bet she wanted her picture taken."

"She did, but I avoided it. Mr. Fleming was there. Apparently he's on good terms with Judge Fimbres."

"If there's anyone in town Doc Herman is leery of, it's Judge Fimbres."

"I'm glad to know that there's someone who stands up to him. Sheriff Carroll and that lamebrained deputy were walking around." Kathleen slipped off her shoes and sat cross-legged on the bed. "Clara Ramsey showed up with an obnoxious little *jelly bean* who made Johnny really angry." Kathleen told Adelaide about the incident and finished up with, "The man was mean and vicious, calling Johnny's mother a whore, and then Clara called him a breed. I wanted to knock her teeth out."

"I'm surprised that you didn't." Adelaide laughed.

"I came to within an inch. I was embarrassed for Johnny in front of his friends and Mr. Fleming. Clara is nothing but trouble. She didn't come home last night, and Hazel was worried. Clara will come to a bad end. She's heading for it with breakneck speed."

"Who was the man with her? Was he from around here?"

"Hazel said his name was Marty Conroy, and he's from Texas."

"Conroy? Is he a little guy who wears flashy clothes, drives a fancy car, and struts around like a peacock?"

"I didn't see his car, but he wears flashy clothes and struts like a peacock," Kathleen said drily.

"The first year Paul was here, he and I were over to Red Rock to an air show. Conroy was there trying to sell oil leases. People we met there told us to steer clear of him, that he was a shyster."

"Clara thinks that he's going to take her to Nashville. I hope he does and gets her away from here. She's worrying her mother to death."

Kathleen slipped on her shoes. "I think I'll stop by Claude's for a hamburger. I'll come back and get the photo and wait for the bus."

"Go on home. Paul and I will see to it that the picture gets on the bus."

"I think I will, if you don't mind."

Kathleen let herself out of the office and locked the door. Someone was sitting on the curb beside her car. She approached cautiously and discovered that it was Hannah, the Indian woman who had come into the office several times since she had been here.

"Hello, Hannah." The woman looked at her with blurry, unfocused eyes. "Can I give you a ride home?" Kathleen asked.

"Want . . . beer—" she muttered. "Whish-key—"

"Let me take you home, Hannah." The woman was drunk. Kathleen wasn't sure if she could stand.

"Whish-key?"

"No. I'll help you up and take you home." She took hold of the woman's arm, but she wouldn't budge. "You'll have to help me. Come on, stand up."

"Whish-key—"

"No, whiskey," Kathleen said irritably.

While she was standing there wondering what to do, the sheriff's car pulled up beside them and stopped. He got out.

"Don't arrest her," Kathleen said quickly. "I'll take her home."

Sheriff Carroll ignored Kathleen, went to Hannah, and pulled her to her feet. He held on to her to steady her.

"You've had enough for today, Hannah."

"Whish-key."

"No more. I'll take you home. Come on. You can't stay here on the street." He handled her so gently that Kathleen could only watch with amazement.

"No." Hannah tried to pull away. "Whish-key."

"You can't have any more."

Sheriff Carroll got the front door of his car open and pushed her down onto the seat. He stooped and lifted her feet inside, then slammed the door. Without as much as a nod to Kathleen, he rounded the car, got under the wheel, made a U-turn in the middle of the street, and drove away.

Kathleen was puzzled by what she had just seen. The sheriff who had been so short and nasty with her for "brawling" on the street, had treated the drunken Indian woman far differently. He had been compassionate and gentle with her. Kathleen shook her head in wonderment.

People usually came to town on Saturday night, but there were far more than the usual number milling about because of the rodeo. Kathleen drove slowly down the street. All the stools were full at Claude's when she passed. She finally found a place to park in front of the bank. She walked the short distance to the Golden Rule Restaurant, went inside, and sat down at a booth near the door.

The waitress brought her a glass of water and a cardboard menu. She was trying to decide what she wanted to have when she became aware that someone was standing at the end of the booth. She looked up to see Johnny glowering down at her.

"What the hell are you doing roaming around this time of night by yourself?"

"It isn't night, and I drove the car."

"It'll be dark in fifteen minutes. Webb and Krome were sitting on a bench in front of the shoe repair not five minutes ago. They must have seen you park and come in here."

"So what if they did? I'll go to my car and go home. Do you think they'll chase me on foot?"

"Where's your boyfriend?"

"Boyfriend? What are you talking about?"

"The dude. The dressed-up city man."

"Mr. Fleming? He isn't my boyfriend. And my neck is getting tired looking up at you. Either sit down or go away."

"Come sit with me and the McCabes. After we eat I'll take you home."

"Oh, no. I'm not butting in on your—"

Johnny picked up the glass of water that had been left by the fuzzy-haired, overweight waitress. He turned his back to Kathleen and spoke to her as she came to the booth.

"She's moving over to our table."

"Okey-doke. Be right with you."

"Johnny, I don't want to intrude on you and your friends. I'll sit here; and if it'll make you feel better, I'll leave the restaurant when you do."

"Don't you like the McCabes? They're good decent people. Or is it me that you don't want to be seen with?"

"If we weren't in this restaurant," she muttered as she slid out of the booth, "I'd hit you right on that smart mouth."

"Don't let that stop you. I've been hit in the mouth in fancier places than this."

"Don't tempt me."

With his hand in the small of her back he pushed her toward the corner table where the McCabes were sitting. Keith made an effort to get to his feet even though his son was asleep in his lap.

"Don't get up . . . please," Kathleen hastened to say.

"Sit down," Ruth invited. "I need another woman to help me hold down these two wild broncs. They're still all up in the air over the win at the rodeo."

"Thank you. Johnny insisted that I join you. I didn't want to intrude."

"It's a relief to be able to look at someone besides him," Keith said, and reached over and kissed his wife on the cheek. "I can't look at you all the time, sugarfoot. You've got to admit that Kathleen's prettier than Johnny."

"Don't revert back to your wild ways, Romeo. You're going home with me."

"See what a tight rope she keeps on me? I can't have any fun."

"Oh, poor you," Ruth said. Then she turned to Kathleen. "Molly's baby is due anytime, isn't it?"

"Around Halloween. Uncle Hod teases her about looking like she swallowed a pumpkin."

"Does George Andrews still come to the store everyday?"

"Not as often as he used to. Molly said that he's taken a liking to Catherine Wisniewski and her son Wally, and they to him. He spends a lot of time at the restaurant helping her now that Wally is away at college. Molly thinks that George had a lot to do with his going."

"Oh, wouldn't it be grand if they got married? George had a rough time taking care of his mother and then having her murdered and being blamed for it."

"I understand that it was you, Mr. McCabe, who figured out who killed her."

"Hod had a hand in it, too." The waitress came to the table to take their orders. "Choose the most expensive thing on the menu, Kathleen. We've got a rich man at the table."

"Oh, Keith, stop teasing," Ruth said, which seemed to be something she said often.

"I'll have a roast beef sandwich," Kathleen said. "And give me a separate ticket."

Ruth ordered a sandwich, then Keith and Johnny ordered steaks and fried potatoes.

"Put it all on one check," Johnny said in a tone that brooked no argument.

Kathleen grimaced at him and poked him on the leg with the toe of her shoe.

"You can pay our hotel bill if you want to, Johnny." Keith winked at his wife.

"That's generous of you," Johnny growled.

Kathleen liked the McCabes. They were in tune with each other. Keith looked at his wife as if she were the most precious thing in the world. She cut his steak for him because he was holding the sleeping child.

"Ruthy doesn't have much of a lap right now," Keith said to Kathleen by way of explanation.

"I'm sure she noticed," Ruth said, stabbed a piece of his steak with her fork, and put it in her mouth.

They were halfway through the meal when Barker Fleming came into the restaurant and directly to their table. He spoke politely to all, then directed his remarks to Kathleen.

"I saw your car parked down by the bank. It's got a flat tire. I was concerned."

"A flat tire. Oh, no. Uncle Hod put new tires on my car when I left Kansas. I must have picked up something out at the field where I parked today."

"Is your spare in good shape?" Johnny asked.

"It should be. Uncle Hod checked it and said it was."

Johnny got up from the table. "Stay here with Ruth and Keith. I'll change it. Give me your keys."

"I'll give you a hand," Barker said, and followed Johnny out.

Hod had made sure Kathleen had the equipment she needed for an emergency when she left Kansas. The spare tire as well as a jack, air pump, and tire iron were in the sloping trunk of the car. Johnny and Barker didn't speak until the car was jacked up and the tire removed.

"Son of a bitch," Barker said as he pulled the tube from the tire. "It's been slashed. She had trouble with a couple of roughnecks yesterday. I saw them hanging around on the street tonight. I'd not be surprised if they did this."

"What kind of trouble?" Johnny asked sharply.

"They had her hemmed in, giving her some sass. A little knife in my pocket persuaded them to back off."

Johnny cursed softly. "I'm goin' to have to break a couple of heads some dark night."

"Be glad to give you a hand," Barker said.

"I'll not need any help with those two," Johnny snorted. "She'll need a boot to go in that tire if she uses it again." He lifted out the spare tire and took a new tube out of a box. After he stuffed it in the tire, he attached the air pump.

Barker stood by, watching Johnny work. The scene today with the little twit and Conroy had cut him to the quick. Johnny had had to endure slurs like that all his life. He had a right to be bitter, for the circumstances of his birth were no fault of his own. Barker had hoped to get to know him before he approached him with what he had to tell him. Now was not the time.

Barker Fleming was not one bit disappointed in Johnny Henry.

When Johnny disconnected the pump, Barker knelt and lifted the tire. He bounced it to test the amount of air, then fitted it on the axle.

"That's dirty work," Johnny said, with a note of sarcasm he couldn't conceal.

"I've been dirty before," Barker replied evenly, working on the lug nuts. "Let it down."

Johnny worked the jack handle wondering about the man kneeling beside the wheel. Was he in love with

Kathleen? Had he come to Rawlings just to see her? He appeared to be genuinely concerned about her.

After a little more air from the pump, Johnny kicked the tire and grunted his satisfaction. He put the tools away, slammed the trunk lid, and locked it. Without a word to Barker, he took off down the street toward the shoe-repair shop. Uninvited and ignored, Barker walked along beside him. Webb and Krome were lounging on a bench with their legs stretched out in front of them. Johnny kicked Webb's feet.

"Get up, you pile of horse dung, so I can knock you down."

Webb pulled in his feet, but remained seated. "What's the matter with ya?"

Krome snickered. "Did ya bring *Daddy* along to help ya?"

Johnny grabbed his shirtfront and hauled him to his feet. "Shut your mouth, polecat. I'm telling you both to stay away from Miss Dolan. If I find someone who saw you slash her tire, I'll come for you and stomp you into the ground." Johnny shoved Krome from him. The man hit the bench with a crash.

"What's goin' on here?" Sheriff Carroll walked rapidly toward them.

"We were just sittin' here, mindin' our own business, Sheriff—"

"—They jist come up and grabbed me," Krome finished.

"Johnny?"

"Nothing to do with you, Sheriff."

"It is something to do with me. I'm the law here."

"If you're the law, why haven't you stopped these two from harassing Miss Dolan?" Barker asked.

The sheriff turned on him. "Who'er you?"

"Barker Fleming."

"I've not seen you before. You passin' through?"

"No. I have business here."

"Pussy business if ya ask me," Krome said.

"I'll ignore that . . . this time." Barker looked down at the man with hard eyes. "Next time I'll put a fist in your mouth."

"Talks big fer a breed, don't he?" Webb snickered, feeling brave with the sheriff present.

"Keep your mouth shut," Sheriff Carroll snapped at Webb, then to Barker, "What kind of business?"

"I see no reason to explain myself to you. I've broken no law, but if you feel it necessary, Judge Fimbres will vouch for me."

"You might not have, but Johnny has. Brawling on the street is against the law."

"If you arrest me, arrest these two for slashing Miss Dolan's tire."

"You didn't see us do that," Krome said gleefully.

"I saw you do it." Johnny's intent gaze homed in on Webb.

"You were in the restaurant," Webb blurted, and Krome groaned.

"Jesus Christ," Sheriff Carroll said under his breath. "You two get out of town and don't come back for a month. If I see you around here, I'll throw your asses in jail."

"Hold on, Sheriff," Barker said. "They owe Miss Dolan for the tire."

"We ain't got no money," Webb wailed. "You think if we had money, we'd be sittin' here on the street?"

"You've got a pretty good pocket watch." Johnny reached over and jerked it out of Webb's pocket and handed it to the sheriff. "You could get enough out of this at the pawnshop to pay Miss Dolan for a tire."

"That's not the proper way a doin' thin's."

Barker said, "It'd save you feeding these two in jail for a couple of weeks, besides having a spread in the paper about two thugs slashing Miss Dolan's tire and the sheriff not arresting them."

The sheriff looked at Barker for a long while. "Do I know you from somewhere?"

Barker shrugged. "Maybe. I travel over the state some. If you're sure you can handle this, Johnny and I want to get back to our supper."

"I'll handle it."

Johnny and Barker walked back to the restaurant. At the door, Barker stopped.

"I've had supper. So you plan to see Miss Dolan home?"

"What's it to you?" Johnny asked bluntly.

"I like her. She's a lovely girl. I don't want those two catching her alone in the dark."

"She's a twenty-five year old *girl* . . . a little young for you, don't you think?"

"Maybe, but just right for you, is that it?"

"She might be age-wise, but that's all."

"That's something you'll have to figure out. Tell McCabe that if he's short a drover to driving the stock back to his ranch, I'll give a hand, if he's got a mount for me."

"Isn't riding drag a little out of your line?"

"I've done it."

"Christ! You're just an all-'round jack of all trades, aren't you!" Johnny declared rudely.

Barker slapped Johnny on the shoulder. "I'll be at the hotel." He walked away leaving a puzzled Johnny to go into the restaurant.

Johnny asked the waitress if they had a place where he could wash his greasy hands. She directed him to a back room, where he washed before he went to the table where Kathleen and the McCabes waited. He gave them a short rundown about what had happened, reporting the confrontation with Webb and Krome and noting that the sheriff was aware that they were the ones who slashed the tire.

" 'Pears to me like we ought to limber up those old boys a mite some dark night," Keith said.

"Something's not quite right," Johnny said. "I'm not sure if it's the sheriff or the deputy. Hijacking is against the law. They should have put them in jail when I first turned them in."

"There's someone who doesn't want me here. Those two tried to keep me from coming into town. Adelaide said they seldom have hijackings around here. They were kind of dumb about it. I don't think they'd done it before." Kathleen's eyes clung to Johnny's face. He had avoided looking at her since he came back to the table.

"We should get our boy to bed." Keith moved his chair back and stood. "He's all tuckered out. You're tired too, aren't you, honey?" he said to Ruth. "You've carried that girl around all day."

"It could be a boy. Don't get your hopes up," Ruth said wearily.

"I've got to get home, too." Kathleen got to her feet. "Thank you for the supper," she said to Keith.

"Where's the ticket?" Johnny asked.

"It's all taken care of. Don't get in a fret, boy. We'll consider it even if you bring Kathleen down for a visit."

Kathleen's eyes went quickly to Johnny. His expression was unreadable.

"Thank you for fixing the tire, Johnny. I hope to see you again, Ruth."

"You will. I'd bet the ranch on it."

"Hold on." Johnny took Kathleen's arm as she made to leave. "I'll see you home."

"You don't have to bother."

"It's no bother."

On the walk in front of the restaurant, Keith and Ruth turned toward the hotel, Johnny and Kathleen to where her car was parked in front of the bank.

"Where is your truck?"

"Behind the *Gazette* office."

"I'll be all right now. Thanks again."

"I'll see you home."

"How will you get back?"

"I've got two legs, you know." He opened the passenger door of her car and waited for her to get in before he went to the driver's side. He tossed aside the pillow she usually sat on and got under the wheel.

"Is Clara giving you any trouble?" he asked as he turned onto the rutted street.

"I can put up with her . . . for a while. Hazel is worried. She didn't come home last night."

"She shacked up with Marty somewhere. Maybe he'll take her back to Texas. If he does, he'll dump her somewhere."

"Who is he? You and Keith seemed to know him."

"He's a distant cousin of Keith's. Keith isn't proud of it."

"Adelaide said that a few years ago she and Paul went to Red Rock to an air show. He was there selling oil leases."

"I remember that show. I went up for an airplane ride."

"Were you scared?"

"For a few minutes. Then it was great." He looked at her and grinned.

They were silent until Johnny parked the car behind Hazel's house and turned off the lights.

"I hate thinking about you walking back to town. I've always heard that cowboys hate to walk." She liked sitting with him in the dark and wished it didn't have to end so soon.

"You could walk with me."

"Then you would insist on walking me back." She laughed nervously.

"I could bring you back in my truck."

"You'd better be careful. I might take you up on it."

"You mean it? You'll do it?"

"Why not? It's Saturday night."

Chapter Fourteen

M<small>ARTY</small>, get off me. I got to tell ya somethin'."

"You want to go honky-tonkin'," he said with a deep sigh, rolled on to his side, and kicked the sheet down so he could see all of her naked body.

"Ya really want to go?" Clara asked hopefully.

"No. I wanna do this." He grabbed her bare buttocks and pulled her to him.

"We've already done it twice, Marty," she protested.

"We did it five times in one night in Wichita Falls. That's what I like about you, sweetie. You know how to get me up. We could break our record tonight."

"Be serious, honey." Clara propped herself on her elbow, leaned over him, and kissed him long and wetly. "When are we gettin' married, sugar?"

"How about Christmas?"

"While we're in Nashville?"

"Uh-huh." Marty tried to pull her over on top of him, but she resisted, and moved her finger down over his chest to burrow in his navel and then on down to his limp sex organ.

"Can't it be sooner?"

"What's the hurry?"

"We've got to get married, Marty. 'Cause—"

"This wouldn't be any better if we were married." He pressed her hand tightly to him.

"We'd be together all the time and do it when you wanted to."

"Why have you got this bug all of a sudden to get married?"

"Marty, I'm pregnant—" Her hand went to his cheek and turned his face toward her.

He laughed. "You can still screw, can't ya? Don't think I ever screwed a pregnant woman."

"You don't mind?"

"Hell, no."

"Oh, good. I was afraid you'd be mad."

"Why should I be mad? It ain't my kid."

"Yes, it is, Marty. It's yours, and we got to get married."

Marty's arm shot out, knocking her away from him as he sat straight up in the bed.

"My kid? Oh, no. You're not stickin' me with a kid."

"It's yours, Marty. What am I goin' to do?"

"Get rid of it. Shitfire! You've been around long enough to know what to do. Hell, you can get it done in Dallas or in Wichita Falls." Marty turned and sat on the side of the bed.

"It takes money for that. I don't know why you're so mad. You're hornier than a billy goat and had to know what would happen."

"I'm not going to be tied down with a brat. How the damn hell do I know it's mine? You spread your legs for anyone who walks on two feet."

"I do not! I've only been with you since we met."

"Yeah. Tell that to the man in the moon."

"Come back to bed, sugar. Let's see if we can break that record. I really feel like I want to."

"I'm gettin' the hell out of here." He jumped up and started putting on his clothes.

Clara bounced up out of the bed and stood naked in front of the door.

"You're not running out on me, Marty Conroy."

"Oh, yes, I am. I never bargained for no kid."

"I didn't get pregnant all by myself! It happened, and it's as much yours as mine."

"You said you couldn't have any brats, so I never bothered with rubbers."

"The doctor said maybe I'd not get pregnant again."

"Then let the doctor pay for it." Marty was throwing clothes in a small straw bag.

"You never intended to marry me in the first place, did you?"

"You've got it right there. Mama would have a fit if I brought a cheap floozy like you home to Conroy."

"You miserable little rat! You ugly, dirt-cheap, little shit-head! You never took me anywhere except to that dirty old rodeo. I'm surprised you didn't try to screw me there. I begged you to take me honky-tonkin', and you didn't take me, not even one time."

"I didn't want to be seen with you, you stupid bangtail. Didn't you catch on? You're as dumb as a pile of horseshit."

"Why did you tell me down in Wichita Falls that we'd get married and you'd take me to Nashville? I'd have screwed you without the lie."

"And I'd have had to pay you. It worked out better this way."

"You are cheap!"

"It's no big deal to let a woman think you'll marry her. I've told that to more women than I can count. When they hear that I'm the Conroy from Conroy, Texas, they all want to be Mrs. Conroy."

"Godamighty," Clara shrieked. "Why else would they want a struttin' little pissant like you? Certainly not for that peanut-size thing you've got 'tween your legs."

"Shut up!"

"I won't shut up. I'll yell so loud that everybody in this hotel knows about . . . your peanut!"

"Stop yelling, or I'll slap you!"

"You just try it, you horny little turd, and I'll cut your head open with the heel of this shoe." She grabbed the shoe with the sharp spike heel and drew it back threateningly.

"Here, slut!" Marty threw some wadded-up bills on the floor at her feet. When she looked down at them, he swung his straw bag, knocking the shoe out of her hand. He quickly shoved her to the floor. "You're not that good a whore anyway."

"You . . . you shithead." Clara picked up three crumpled one-dollar bills. "You cheap dirt-eatin' son of a bitch," she yelled. "As soon as the courthouse opens Monday I'm goin' to Judge Fimbres and have you declared the father of my child. I'll tell him you raped me. I'll make sure the hotel clerk sees me leave here lookin' all beat-up! Then we'll see how much good it does you to be *Mr. Conroy* from Conroy, Texas."

"You do that and I'll . . . I'll—"

"You'll what, big *little* man?"

"I'll kill you."

"Ha! Ha! You ain't got the guts."

Marty went out, closing the door softly behind him, and hurried down the back hall to the stairs. Clara's anger dissolved into misery, and she began to cry.

*   *   *

The evening was cool.

Before Kathleen and Johnny had walked a block, she had goose bumps on her arms, but she was so happy being with him that she wouldn't have mentioned icicles hanging from her nose. Johnny had put his hand inside her arm, slid it down to clasp her hand, and drawn her close to his side. Their steps matched and they walked across the school yard in companionable silence.

"Johnny—"

"Kath—" They had both spoken at the same time. Johnny chuckled. "You go first."

"No, you, or you'll not tell me what you were going to say."

"Will you?"

"I promise." Kathleen knew that she was acting like a giddy schoolgirl, but she couldn't help herself. It was so wonderful being with him. Unconsciously, she squeezed his hand and hugged his arm closer to her side.

"I was going to ask you if you had used the typewriter since you had the table."

"Almost every night. I am so grateful for it. It sure beats sitting on the floor."

"Every night? You've got that much news to write?"

"I'll tell you a secret if you promise not to tell."

"Cross my heart and hope to die."

"Poke a needle in your eye?" Kathleen laughed happily.

"It'll have to be a pretty good secret for me to go *that* far." He liked the light chatter between them. He liked to hear her laugh. *Does that mean that she is happy to be with me?*

"I'll accept the 'cross my heart.' "

They crossed the street and reached the sidewalk. Johnny moved to the outside and took her hand again.

"What's the big secret?" he asked, wondering how he could keep her from feeling the pounding of his heart.

"I write Western stories," she whispered.

"You what? Write stories?"

"For *Western Story Magazine*. I've had six stories published and contracts for four more. Do you ever read the pulp magazines?"

"No. I don't read much."

"I write under the name of K. K. Doyle. My publisher said it's mostly men who read the magazines, and they'd not want to read a story written by a woman."

"Humm. I wouldn't think that it would matter."

"I see his point. I've never read a love story written by a man. Oh, maybe I have. Shakespeare's *Romeo and Juliet* was a love story. *What light through yonder window breaks? It is the east, and Juliet is the sun!* That's all I know of it, but it's definitely a love story."

"Humm," Johnny said again.

"Doesn't make much sense, does it?"

"Not to me."

"Would you like to read one of my stories? I write about pounding hooves and blazing guns and hard-eyed strangers." She laughed softly. "Everything is exaggerated. It makes for more exciting reading."

"How can you tell if the stranger has hard eyes?"

"He stares, he squints, he scowls. His eyes are dull, flat and black . . . or blue . . . or gray. It's fun making up the stories. I can kill off the bad characters and save the good ones. I make sure that if a girl is in the story, she likes the good cowboy wearing the white hat. The bad cowboys wear black hats."

"Is that what you were going to tell me?" They had reached town and were about to cross the street when a car shot past them. "Marty's going somewhere in a hurry. I hope it's out of town."

"He isn't a very nice man. I wonder how Clara got mixed up with him."

"Birds of a feather," Johnny said drily. "If there's a rotten man in the country, Clara will find him."

"She didn't come home last night. Poor Hazel worried all night that something had happened to her. Today at the rodeo she didn't even come over and speak to her mother and Emily."

"Maybe she'll leave soon. Hazel and Emily are better off without her." He squeezed her hand tightly and looked down at her. "Now what was it that you were going to tell me. I'm not going to let you dillydally out of it."

"I'm not . . . dillydallying." This new freedom to talk nonsense to him caused her eyes to shine when she smiled up at him. "I was going to tell you that next Sunday I plan to drive over to Red Rock to see Uncle Tom and Henry Ann and ask you if you'd like to go along."

She held her breath while waiting for him to speak. Had she been too bold? Johnny wasn't like any man she had ever known.

"You shouldn't drive over there by yourself."

"Does that mean that you'll go?"

"My truck isn't too . . . reliable."

"We can take my car if you'll promise to fix any flat tires. I don't have a spare now."

"You need a boot and a new tube."

"What's a boot?"

"It's a piece of leather that fits over the hole inside the tire. I'll get one and a tube and gas up the car."

"Are those your conditions for going?"

"I've something else in mind, but I'll not tell you now."

"Oh, you! I hate being in suspense!"

There were still quite a few people in town. Some were sitting in cars watching the people on the street. A few of them yelled at Johnny.

"Hiya, cowboy. Ya've lassoed a good-lookin' filly."

"Hey, Johnny. Ya better get on home. We're driving that stock out early in the mornin'."

Johnny lifted a hand to acknowledge the good-natured joshing and they walked on down the street and turned into the alley behind the *Gazette* building.

"Was there anywhere you wanted to go?" It was dark in the alley, and his voice came softly and intimately.

"There's not much of any place to go in Rawlings."

"There's the Twilight Gardens. But it would be crowded with drunks tonight."

"I'm not much for honky-tonks, but I like to dance."

"We'll go over to Frederick sometime. They've got a fairly nice dance hall over there. They've had Bob Wills playing there a couple of times."

Kathleen's heart leaped. Did he mean that he wanted to go out with her on a real date?

"Sounds like fun." She hoped that she didn't sound as eager as she felt.

"The light's on in Paul's room. Want to go in?"

"No," she said quickly. "I don't want to bother them . . . him."

"You . . . know about them?"

"They told me a day or two after I got here. They love each other. Adelaide worries because she's older than he is."

"It doesn't seem to bother Paul."

"Would it bother you?"

"It might if the woman was sixty. I'm twenty-five."

"I'm twenty-six."

"Really? You don't look over twenty-one."

"Thank you . . . I think."

Johnny chuckled, then drew in a shallow breath. His sore muscles were making themselves known. In the enjoyment of being with Kathleen he had almost forgotten about them.

"Will you drive home tonight and come back to the fairground in the morning?"

"I'm going to stay with Paul . . . rather, on a cot in the back room of the *Gazette*. In the morning Ruth will take me and Keith out to the stockyards before she heads home."

"I like the McCabes. They seem to be well suited to each other."

"Keith met her when he went to Kansas on an investigation. He fell for her like a ton of bricks. She's just what he needed. They live with his grandmother on a ranch down near Vernon, Texas."

Johnny opened the door of his truck, pulled out an old blanket and shook it before spreading it on the seat.

"You might get your dress dirty," Johnny said, as she stepped up onto the running board.

"It's been dirty before." She settled herself on the seat as Johnny closed the door and went around to get under the wheel. Kathleen was sorry that the evening was almost over.

Johnny drove slowly out of the alley and down the street, dodging the potholes and the ruts, in an effort to make the ride easier.

"We didn't swing," Kathleen said regretfully as they passed the park. "I'm just a kid at heart," she added laughingly.

"Shall we stop?"

"Do you want to?"

Johnny slowed the truck to a stop beside a big old pecan tree, but made no effort to get out.

"I don't want the evening to end," he admitted suddenly.

Kathleen turned to look at him. He had pushed his hat to the back of his head and was looking at her. He looked without speaking for so long that she became nervous.

"What?" she finally asked. "Is something wrong?"

After a full minute, he sighed. "There sure as hell is. One of those jolts today must have scrambled my brains. I don't know what I'm doing here with you."

"Oh, well—" Kathleen's heart suddenly felt like a rock in her breast. "I'm sorry to have inconvenienced you." She tried to find the door handle so that she could get out.

Johnny grabbed her arm. "Where are you goin'? What do you think I meant?"

"It . . . a . . . seems to me that . . . you meant that you wished you were anywhere but here with me. That if not for me, you could be doing something you really wanted to do." She finished with a rush.

"I didn't mean that!" The grip on her arm pulled her closer to him. "I meant . . . Oh, hell, I meant that this is the start of a hell of a lot of sleepless nights for me."

"I'm sorry—"

The arm he put around her drew her up close against his chest.

"Don't say you're sorry you're here with me," he said in an agonized whisper. A warmth ran over her skin, for he gave his words a sensual meaning.

"I wasn't going to say that. I don't understand—"

"You and I are not right for each other. Not like Keith and Ruth. They fit like a hand to a glove."

"Well . . . I'll understand if you don't want to get *romantically* involved with me. I'll never throw myself at any man." She almost choked on the words. "I had thought we could be . . . friends."

He groaned. "I'll never be just *friends* with *you*. It will be all or nothing. And if it's all, you'll live to regret it. For me it would be like being in heaven and suddenly plunged into hell."

Abruptly he moved and gathered her in his arms. His mouth found hers before she was aware he was going to kiss her. It was not a light kiss. He kissed her as if he were a starving man. She felt his lips, his teeth, his tongue. She opened her lips to his as the intimacy of the kiss increased, and she felt a strange helplessness in her limbs. When he lifted his head his eyes were staring down into hers. She was breathing fast, and so was he.

"I had to do that. I would have done it if I had known I would be killed for it."

"Don't apologize. It's all right."

"I'm not apologizing because I'm not sorry." His strangled voice sounded miles from her ears. He cupped a hand behind her head and pressed hard fingers under the disarray of her hair and drew her flushed face into his shoulder. "I've been alone all my life. I don't want to care for a woman, lose her, and be alone again."

"I've been alone, too, since I lost Grandma and Grandpa." Kathleen burrowed her face in the warmth of his neck.

"It's different for you." He stroked a strand of her hair behind her ear. "There isn't a single man in town, some married ones, too, who wouldn't give their eyeteeth to be here with you."

"I don't want to be with any of them."

"You'll meet someone."

"If you don't want me, don't shove me off on someone else." Impatience with him caused her to straighten up and try to move away from him. His arms tightened.

"I never said I didn't want you. Calm down."

"Why are we even talking about this? I'm not going to fling myself at you like Clara did."

"Whoa. You can sure get worked up fast."

"It isn't very flattering to know that you're with someone who doesn't want to be with you." She moved back from him.

"That isn't it, dammit. You've not been out of my mind since I met you out on the highway." His hands gripped her shoulders, and he shook her gently.

"Then why are you saying these things? Can't you just go along and let nature take its course?"

"I can see where that path is taking me. I've never known a girl like you."

"I'm no different than most other girls."

"Ha!" he snorted. "You're like a thoroughbred running with a herd of wild mustangs."

In spite of herself she smiled. "That's the nicest thing you've said to me."

"Kathleen, you could take my heart and grind it into little pieces. I'm only trying to protect myself."

He pulled her to him again. With a swift look into her face he lifted her chin and fitted his lips to hers. He kissed her as openly and as intimately as a man could kiss a woman. Kathleen's arm moved up around his neck, her hand caressed his nape. She had never felt anything like the sensual enjoyment she was feeling now.

When he lifted his head, he looked down at the pale luminous oval of her face framed in the tumbled, gloriously red hair that was soft and shining in his fingers.

"You're eyes shine in the dark. Did you know that?" The gentle murmured words sent tremors of joy through her. *He isn't sorry that he kissed me. He enjoyed it as much as I did.*

"Like a cat's?"

"Prettier. Much prettier."

"Thank you," she whispered. "Yours are pretty, too. I think about you when I'm describing the hero in my stories." She cupped his cheek with her palm and reached for his lips. This moment was hers; nothing or no one could ever take it away from her.

"I never expected the evening to end like this." The note of awe in Johnny's voice echoed Kathleen's feelings.

The awe was still with her when Johnny started the truck, and moved on down the road to stop in front of Hazel's house. She sat close beside him, although he'd had to remove his arm from around her in order to shift the gears. After he had turned off the motor, he quickly put his arm around her again.

"Tell me something. What about this Fleming fellow? Is he one of your beaus?"

"Heavens no. He came into the office and bought a paper. He was interested in the rodeo. I saw him again after I left the courthouse the next day and ran into the deputy and the hijackers. The hijackers followed me down the street. Mr. Fleming came out of the bank and ran them off. We had supper together and he told me about his four daughters and two sons."

"And his wife?"

"His wife died."

"And he's looking for another one. He's too old for you, even if he does own half of the tannery and an interest in a packinghouse, a thousand-acre ranch, besides stock in the electric company."

"How did you find out all this?"

"Keith is a fountain of information. If he doesn't know, he finds out."

"Mr. Fleming is a nice man. He was lonely for his family. I enjoyed his company."

"I bet." Johnny removed his arm and got out of the truck. He came around and opened the door for her.

"Johnny? Why don't you like him?"

"I don't know. Maybe it's because he's a breed like me and has made something of himself."

"He had help from his family."

"No one can ever accuse me of that."

"Are you still going with me to Red Rock?" Kathleen asked on the way to the porch.

"Do you still want me to go?"

"Of course."

"Then we'll go. I'll come in next week and get your tire fixed."

They stepped up onto the porch. He pulled her close to him. She felt him trembling and wondered at the cause. She moved her hands up to his shoulders. He seemed to hesitate, then lowered his head and kissed her swiftly. His arms dropped and he stepped back.

"Be careful about being out after dark. The sheriff told Webb and Krome to get out of town, but they still may be here. I don't want them catching you alone."

"I'll be careful. Thank you for bringing me home."

"You're welcome." Still he stayed looking down at her.

"I wish you could get into a tub of water and ease your aching muscles."

"How do you know they're aching?"

"I've seen you wince from time to time and even groan a little."

"I didn't know I did that. Well, good night."

"Good night, Johnny."

Kathleen slipped into the house and leaned against the

door until she heard Johnny start the truck and drive away. He was gone. She ran her tongue over her lips as his had done minutes before and her heart gave a joyous leap. Oh, Lord, how could it be that a few soft words, a smile, and a kiss from that cowboy could make her feel like this?

Chapter Fifteen

RIDING BEHIND THE HORSE HERD, Johnny grimaced as the bay he was on turned sharply. The animal had been trained as a cutting horse and knew without the slightest move from the man on his back that his job was to keep the herd bunched. Sore ribs and a crowded mind had kept Johnny awake most of the night.

The stock being driven back to the McCabe ranch was in two groups traveling about a mile apart. Johnny worked the horses and McCabe the steers. It was a warm, still October day. The dark sky in the west promised rain or a dust storm. Johnny hoped that it was rain lurking in the clouds.

Barker Fleming had been at the stockyard when Johnny and Keith arrived at daylight. Johnny had ignored him, but Keith had welcomed the help he offered.

"What's he butterin' you up for?" Johnny asked while saddling his horse.

"He thinks I'm pretty."

"Go to hell."

"Cheer up, son. You've got an extra man to help. You can sleep in the saddle all the way to Vernon."

After Barker had caught and saddled a skittish buckskin, Keith had made the comment that he was a skilled horseman.

"Why wouldn't he be?" Johnny had remarked sarcastically. "He's an Indian, isn't he?"

By midmorning, after Johnny had been in the saddle for more than four hours, he felt as if he had been kicked in the back by a steer. It was not unusual for him to be sore for a week after a rodeo. His aches and pains had not, however, kept his mind off the evening he had spent with Kathleen. He had played over in his mind every word they had exchanged, every touch. That she had returned his kiss and one time had even initiated it, was still a wonder to him. He could close his eyes and smell the lemony scent of her hair as it swept across his face and feel her soft, seeking lips beneath his.

He groaned when he thought of his blundering words, and how she had reacted when she thought that he hadn't wanted to be with her. He had thought of himself as a man who had been around a bit after the work he had done for the Bureau with Hod Dolan, but, compared to her, he was pure backwoods. He felt like a clod when she talked about some feller named Shakespeare who made up silly verses.

Kathleen wrote stories for the newspaper and for a magazine. Hell, he'd never read a book in his life. How would she feel about him if she knew that? They had nothing in common. For all he knew she hated horses, and he loved them. She lived in town and mixed with people who talked stock market and shares and things like that. His bank was in a milk can in the barn. He and Kathleen were as different as daylight and dark. He couldn't allow himself to fall in love with her. If he did, he could look forward to a lifetime of misery.

Is it too late? If a woman was constantly in your

thoughts, he asked himself, if you saw her face while you lay in a sleepless bed, and if every word she said and every look she gave you were of utmost importance, did it mean you loved her?

Oh, Lord. It *was* too late!

Johnny watched Barker ride ahead and block off a road to keep the herd from turning off. The man had been on a drive or two and seemed to be enjoying the work. If he had to do it day after day, Johnny thought, it wouldn't be so much fun. *This was a little outing for a rich man who had some time to kill.*

The McCabe ranch was a sprawling compound. The main house, built before the turn of the century, was weathered, two-story, and had a wraparound porch. Ruth, who had left Rawlings ahead of the drive, stood on the porch and waved as the herds passed on their way to the lower pastures. By the time the stock was penned, it was noon. The drovers, including Johnny and Barker, washed at the bench on the back porch and went into the house for dinner.

Johnny had been to the McCabes' many times. Keith's grandmother greeted him with affection.

"You haven't been to see me for a while, John. Ya got another girl?" Mrs. McCabe was the only person who ever called him John.

"I've not seen a girl yet who could hold a candle to you, Granny," Johnny said, using the name every man on the place affectionately called her. He felt comfortable here. He knew the old lady genuinely liked him because he had seen her reaction to those she didn't like.

"Ruth said you did good at the rodeo, John. Wish I could a seen it."

"If you had been there, Granny, I'd have been so nervous, I'd not have stayed on long enough to get out of the chute."

"Ah, go on with ya. I knew ya was comin' and had Guadalupe make sweet potato pie," she added in a conspiratorial whisper.

"You're a woman to ride the trail with, Granny." He glanced at the smiling face of the Mexican woman who had been born on the ranch the year Granny McCabe, as a nineteen-year-old bride, came here to live.

With an arm across her shoulders, Keith proudly introduced Barker to his grandmother.

"Be careful. She rules the roost with an iron hand."

The frail little woman held out her hand. "Welcome to our home, Mr. Fleming."

"Thank you, ma'am. It's a pleasure to be here."

"You met my wife yesterday," Keith went on with the introductions. "And this is Guadalupe."

"Mrs. McCabe. Ma'am," Barker said smoothly. "Something smells mighty good."

The table took up one side of the large kitchen. Workers on the ranch had always taken their meals with the McCabe family. Guadalupe or Ruth got up to get more biscuits, pour coffee, or refill the platter of roast beef.

The talk around the table was mostly about the stock drive and the rodeo. Then Keith asked Barker if he thought they would soon be in a war.

"I don't know how the United States can stay out of it if Hitler takes over Europe, and it seems that is what he has in mind."

"There's an ocean between us," Keith argued. "I can't see him attacking us."

"The only thing that would prevent it, if he's determined to rule the world, would be that he would be spreading his troops too thin." Barker's eyes caught Johnny's. "I'd rather we fight him over there than on our own territory."

"Unless we are attacked," Keith said. "I hate to see our boys dying on foreign shores."

Johnny had not heard enough about what was going on in Europe to make a comment. He lowered his head and finished his meal.

After the meal, Keith took Johnny, Barker, and another drover back to Rawlings. Barker sat in the front seat with Keith, and they continued their conversation about the possibility of war.

"I think Roosevelt is smart enough to keep us out of it," Keith said.

"Some of the big companies are already gearing up to furnish arms, tanks, and airplanes to the British. Hitler will hop over the channel as soon as he reaches Normandy."

"What about that *Maginot Line*? I thought that was supposed to stop him from taking France."

"It's my understanding that the *Maginot Line* was built to keep the Germans out during World War I. The French have strengthened it, but this is not going to be a war primarily fought by foot soldiers like in the war against the Kaiser. The Germans now have heavy tanks and airplanes. I'm afraid the *Maginot Line* is not going to be the protection the French think it is."

Listening to the conversation, Johnny realized more than ever just how little he knew about what was going on in the world. What the hell was the *Maginot Line*? Keith seemed to know.

"Those factories you're talking about are putting men to work. Roosevelt likes that. He's done a fair job of pulling the country out of the Depression, but there's a lot to be done yet."

"What do you think, Johnny?" Barker half turned in the seat to ask the question.

Johnny's hat was tilted down over his eyes. He feigned sleep and didn't answer.

At the fairground, Keith stopped where Barker and the other drover had left their cars.

"I'll give Johnny a lift into town to get his car and save you the trip," Barker said. "I know you want to get back home."

"That would save me time. Thanks. And thanks for the help today."

"It was my pleasure and a real pleasure to be in your home."

"Anytime you're down our way, drop in. The door is always open and the coffeepot on."

Johnny got out of the car and lifted his saddle off the carrier on top.

"You going into town?" he asked the drover who got out on the other side.

"Naw." He grinned shyly. "I'm headed for Deval to see my lady friend."

"How about you and Kathleen coming down next Sunday, Johnny?" Keith leaned out the window.

"Can't make it, but thanks."

"Come down when you can. You're always welcome."

"Will do."

"Throw your saddle in the back of the car, Johnny," Barker said after Keith left. He regretted that Johnny was not pleased about being left here with him.

"Pretty fancy car for a dirty old saddle."

"It'll clean."

Instead of getting into the car, Barker went to the front of it and leaned against the fender. He pulled out a pack of cigarettes and offered them to Johnny. Johnny shook his head and built his own smoke from a sack of tobacco he took from his shirt pocket. Barker made no move to get into the car.

"I'm ready to go if you are," Johnny said.

"I'd like to talk to you." Barker's voice was not as calm and as sure as it had been. His dark eyes watched Johnny anxiously as he sought the right words to say.

"Yeah? You want to offer me a job? No, thanks. I've got one."

"Do you like ranching?"

"If I didn't, I wouldn't be doing it."

"I can understand that. You lived for a while with your sister on a farm near Red Rock. I thought you might prefer farming."

"How did you know that?" The coldness of Johnny's tone reflected his emotions and alerted Barker that he might have started out on the wrong foot.

"I talked to Isabel Perry last week in Oklahoma City."

"You . . . talked to Isabel?" Johnny said it softly and menacingly.

"Yes. I wanted to know if her mother was Dorene Perry and if she had a brother."

Their eyes met in a long, silent war. Johnny's breath came fiercely.

"You knew Dorene?" Johnny's lips curved in a sneer. "That says a lot about you."

"Yes, it does. I knew her when I was a stupid, head-strong, resentful kid of eighteen. I went to the city to sow my wild oats and prove to my father that I was a man."

"Don't tell me the story of your life. I'm not interested

in a hotheaded kid cuttin' his apron strings." Johnny spat out the words.

"I'm a half-breed. My mother was Cherokee, my father a white man. Back in those days, and even in some places now, you're looked down on as not worthy to associate with white people, even if you do have financial means. I resented that then . . . and I resent it now."

"You're ashamed of your people?"

"Not now. I was when I was a kid of eighteen. I didn't want my mother to be a Cherokee. I wanted her to be white like my father."

"At least you had a mother. Mine was a whore. She liked being a whore."

"You always knew that?"

"From the time I was old enough to know what a whore was. Before that I wondered why I had to sleep in the closet with the door shut while she slept in the bed with a strange man." Johnny dropped his cigarette and ground it in the dirt with his boot.

"I was with Dorene during the summer of 1912. She was young and fresh and pretty. I didn't know that she had a husband and daughter. I was fascinated with her."

"—And screwed her," Johnny said with disgust.

"Yes. At eighteen the sap runs high. I spent all the money I could get on her until Father came to the city and put a stop to it. He sent me back East to school. I hated him for it then. I love him for it now."

"Well now that you've told me your life story, I'd like to get to town and get my truck. I have things to do."

"I'm your father, Johnny." Barker's voice was quiet and anxious.

The words were dropped in the stillness of the afternoon. They were ordinary words, words that had no meaning to him, Johnny thought, until they seeped into his consciousness and he became aware that the man had said that he was *his* father.

Unreasonable anger flared.

"That's a fine thing to drop on a man."

"I didn't know any other way to do it."

"What do you want me to do? Get down on my knees and thank you for screwing a whore and bringin' a breed into the world who had to root-hog or die during his first fourteen years?"

"No . . ."

"You threw your seeds in the wind, mister. You think that one of them stuck in a whore named Dorene, and I'm the result?"

"I don't just think it. I'm sure of it. I've been looking for you for a long time." Barker knew that Johnny was confused and hurt.

"Yeah? I wasn't hiding anywhere." Johnny felt as if an iron band was squeezing his chest.

"I came through Oklahoma City six or seven years ago and wondered what had ever happened to the girl, Dorene. I knew, even at age eighteen, that she would have had a bad end. I think I felt a little responsible for it."

"Lookin' for more of the same?" Johnny said nastily. "I'm surprised if she didn't give you the clap."

"My wife was in the hospital at the time and being with a whore was the last thing on my mind. From the tavern where she had worked I learned that Dorene had a boy who was part-Indian. I couldn't do anything about finding you then. But after my wife died, I sent a detective to find the last man Dorene lived with. He told us that Dorene talked about her life when she knew that she was dying. She told him that the father of her son was an Indian kid. She wanted to see

her boy, but knew that he was better off with her husband."
This being so important to him caused Barker to speak hurriedly and in jerky sentences.

Johnny turned his back and looked off across the
prairie. He wiped a hand across his face. This was something he didn't want to deal with. He had put the circumstances of his birth behind him, and he wanted to know
nothing about the man who had sired him.

"Didn't you ever wonder about your father?"

Johnny turned. His eyes bored into those of the other
man.

"I didn't have to wonder. I was told up until the time I
was big enough to fight that my mother was a whore and
that my father was a drunk Indian, a blanket-ass, a dirty
redskin, a dog eater, or anything else anyone could think
of to make me feel dirty and worthless. No, I never wanted
to lay eyes on the son of a bitch."

Barker winced at the raw hurt in his voice. "Was it so
bad for you?"

Johnny ignored the question. "The best man I ever
knew was Ed Henry, Dorene's husband. He gave me my
name and a roof over my head. He taught me to love
horses, how to fix a car, and how to be responsible for my
actions. He suspected that I was Cherokee and even told
me to be proud of my people. For the short time I was with
him, he taught me a hell of a lot."

"I'd like to meet him."

"He's dead."

"Do you want to know about me, my family—?"

"Hell no! Why should I? You mean nothing to me.
Nothing is changed. I've made my own path up to now and
will make it alone from now on."

"I found your birth certificate in the courthouse in

Oklahoma City. Dorene listed me as the father of a boy born April 15, 1913. I'll get a copy if you want to see it."

"I don't."

"I would like for you to come to Elk City and meet your half sisters, your brother, and your grandfather."

"Listen, mister, let's get something straight. I've gotten along without you for twenty-five years. As far as I'm concerned, you are like a bull that serviced a heifer. There is no more connection between you and me than between that bull and the calf."

"There is, but I'll not intrude in your life if I'm not welcome. I wanted you to know that you have a family, blood ties; and if you ever need us, we are there."

"What I need is to get to town and get my truck. I've got chores to do at home."

"All right. Get in."

They drove into town in silence. Not a word was exchanged until they neared the alley behind the *Gazette*, and Johnny said, "Stop here."

As soon as the car stopped, Johnny got out.

"This has been a shock to you, as it was to me when I first heard about it. I'm leaving for Elk City tomorrow, but I'll keep in touch." Barker spoke while Johnny was getting his saddle out of the backseat.

"Suit yourself." Johnny hoisted the saddle to his shoulder and walked down the alley toward his truck.

Kathleen began work on her story for the magazine after she had washed her hair. She needed to wash all of her underwear, but it wouldn't do to hang it outside on the line on Sunday. She washed a couple pairs of panties and her hose and hung them in the bathroom.

Clara had come home in the middle of the morning.

She was in a foul mood. Kathleen could hear her arguing with her mother and tried not to let their voices distract her as she sat before her typewriter.

With effort she dragged her mind away from the time she had spent with Johnny. For her it had been wonderful. She would treasure the memory of his kisses forever. For just a small moment in time they had been the only people in the world. He had said that he had thought about her since he met her on the highway; yet, when he said it, it was as if she were a thorn in his hide. How would he act when she saw him again? He had promised to go with her to Red Rock. Surely he'd not back out on the promise.

Kathleen forced herself to go back to the story she was writing. After reading the last few pages of the manuscript, she began to type.

Durango wakened with a start. Someone was trying to get into his ranch house. He eased open the barn door and saw a shadowy figure. "Put your hands up, stranger. No funny business or you'll get both barrels." The stranger turned and the moonlight shone on her face. Durango gasped, "Oh, my God. Hallie, little sister. Is it you?" He shoved his gun into his holster. He—

Kathleen yanked the page from the typewriter, turned it over, and tried to start again. But the words wouldn't come. Johnny's face intruded into her mind's eye. She felt the roughness of his cheeks and the softness of his lips when he kissed her. Why had this man become so important to her?

Pressed by the magazine deadline, Kathleen determinedly brought her mind back to Durango and Hallie.

He ran to her and lifted her in his arms when she sagged against him. "Help me, brother. Hide me—"

It was no use. This wasn't the direction she wanted the story to go. Kathleen stood up and walked to the window. It was late afternoon and she had written only two pages. To meet her deadline she had to write eight pages on Sunday and at least eight pages during the week. So far she was behind schedule.

Today Johnny was going to drive the horses and cattle back to Keith McCabe's ranch. Kathleen wondered how he was able to get back into the saddle after the beating his body had taken. He was hurting last night.

Johnny, Johnny, get out of my mind!

Kathleen started to turn from the window when she saw a car pull up in front of the house and stop. Why in the world was Mr. Fleming coming here? Kathleen opened the door and stepped out on the porch. He got out of the car, came up the walk to the porch, and removed his hat before he spoke.

"Miss Dolan, I hope you don't mind that I took the liberty to find out where you lived."

"Is something wrong, Mr. Fleming?"

"No emergency. I'm leaving in the morning, and I wanted to talk to you. Are you free to take a short ride with me? We could have dinner later."

"I'm not dressed to go out for dinner, but I can go for a short ride. I'll get a jacket."

Kathleen opened the door of her wardrobe and reached for a jacket. It was not there. She looked to see if it had dropped on the floor and checked to see if something had been hung over it. She didn't find it, so she put her coat around her shoulders and went back to the porch to find Clara talking to Barker.

"You from around here?"

"No."

"I saw you at the rodeo."

"I saw you, too."

"Ya did?"

"Yes, ma'am. You should be more careful of the company you keep."

"There's nothin' wrong with Marty," Clara said belligerently. "Bet he's got more money than you got, and he's got a town named after his granddaddy."

"Are you ready to go, Miss Dolan?" Barker said.

"I'm ready." Kathleen ignored Clara and stepped off the porch.

"You'll not have no fun with *her*," Clara called.

Barker opened the car door for Kathleen. When she was settled, he went to the driver's side and got under the wheel. Clara was still standing on the porch.

"I would move out of that house, but I don't think that she'll stay long. She comes and goes."

"She sure tore into Johnny yesterday."

"Yes, and he's tried to be a friend to her because he feels sorry for her mother and little girl. The only reason I stay there is because her mother needs the money from renting the room."

Barker turned south. He drove slowly along a dirt road.

"I helped drive McCabe's stock back to his ranch this morning. I got back a little while ago."

"Johnny told me last night they were driving the stock back. It's a long ride."

"Nice folks, the McCabes. I'm glad Johnny has such good friends."

Kathleen didn't know what to say to that, so she remained silent.

After a while Barker said, "I like to drive. I do my best thinking when I'm driving or riding a horse."

"That's funny," said Kathleen, turning to look at him. "So do I."

"See those buildings over there?" Barker pointed in the distance. "That's Johnny's ranch. Have you ever been there?"

"No. How did you know where it was?"

"I asked my friend, Judge Fimbres. He looked it up in the tax book."

"Why were you interested? Oh, I'm sorry. That was a rude question."

"I want to tell you." Barker pulled the car to the side of the road and stopped. He took off his hat and placed it on the seat between them. He looked at her until she met his eyes before he spoke. "I'm Johnny's father."

The silence was loaded with surprise and almost disbelief.

"Johnny doesn't know?" Kathleen asked when she was finally able to speak.

"He does now. I told him a little while ago."

"I don't know much about his background. His sister is married to my Uncle Tom. I knew that they had the same mother but different fathers."

"I met Johnny's mother, Dorene, in Oklahoma City. I was a stupid undisciplined kid of eighteen who thought he knew all that was worth knowing. I'm Johnny's father. My name is on his birth certificate."

"This is the first Johnny knew about you?"

"He didn't want to believe it. He's had a rough time and doesn't want me intruding in his life."

"He's shocked. After he thinks about it, he might change his mind."

"I'm afraid that he won't. The funny thing about it is that I understand how he feels. It's the way I would have felt."

"Johnny is a son you can be proud of. My Uncle Hod Dolan was in the Federal Bureau. He called on Johnny to help him trace the movements of Bonnie Parker and Clyde Barrow that resulted in the ambush that killed them. Uncle Hod thinks the world of Johnny."

"I'm glad to hear that." They didn't talk for a few minutes. Barker looked toward the distant buildings. "Do you care for Johnny?"

"I like him very much," Kathleen said, keeping her face turned away.

"I think he's on the verge of falling in love with you."

Kathleen's head swiveled around. "Why do you say that?"

"He's concerned for you, watches you when you're not looking. He was embarrassed yesterday that you were there when he had the set-to with that couple."

"It wasn't his fault."

"I'll be back down here in a week or two. In the meanwhile, if you should want to contact me, I'll be in Elk City."

"I don't think it will be necessary. I'll probably not see Johnny until next Sunday. We had planned to go over to Red Rock to see his sister and my Uncle Tom."

Barker started the car. "I wanted you to know about my being Johnny's father should there be something you could do to help him come to terms with it."

"He might never mention it to me. He's a very private person."

"It's his Cherokee blood." Barker looked at her and smiled for the first time.

"It's what makes him so handsome, too," Kathleen said, and smiled back.

Barker turned into a crossroad preparing to turn around and head back to town. A string of calves were crossing the road. Coming up out of the gully behind them was Johnny on horseback. He turned his head toward them, looked briefly, then put his heels to his mount. Johnny and the calves he was driving disappeared in a gully.

"Lordy. That put the hair on the cake," Barker explained. "He'll think I'm out here spying on him."

Kathleen couldn't have said anything if her life had depended on it. All she could think of was that at one time Johnny had thought that Barker was her boyfriend. What would he think now after seeing them together on a lonely road near his ranch?

"Let's go back to town." Kathleen's heart felt like a rock in her breast. "He'll think whatever he wants to think."

Barker heard the tears in her voice, and wished there were something he could say to ease her anxiety.

"Surely he won't think that there's . . . anything between you and me."

"I don't know what he thinks. He said that he and I were not right for each other. He doesn't want to get involved with me."

"Then he doesn't have as much sense as I thought he had."

When Johnny came up out of the gully and saw Barker Fleming's car blocking the road, he felt anger; but when he saw who was in it with him, he felt as if he had been kicked in the stomach by a mustang. His whole thought process had shut down. By the time he got the calves penned he was thinking again.

The son of a bitch was making a play for Kathleen!

The thought came to him on the way to the house. And Kathleen was falling for it. Why not? Fleming could give her a hell of a lot more than he'd ever be able to give her. It was a good thing to find out about them now before he made more a fool of himself than he had last night.

Johnny's mind churned while he got out a hunk of cheese and some crackers for his supper. He would have to give some thought as to how to let her know that he wouldn't be going to Red Rock next Sunday without having to go into the *Gazette* to tell her.

It would be hell to be cooped up in the car with her and have to put on an act in front of Henry Ann and Tom. He was not good in such complicated situations and he was not going to subject himself to handling them. From now on, if he wanted any peace of mind at all, he'd better put as much distance as possible between himself and Miss Kathleen Dolan.

And as for Barker Fleming, he was on the bottom of Johnny's list of concerns.

Chapter Sixteen

Dr. HERMAN WAS EATING BREAKFAST when Rita, his housekeeper, let Louise into the house.

"Mornin', Doc. Glad you're back."

"Mornin', pretty lady. Rita, get Louise a cup of coffee."

"How was the conference?"

"Informative, as usual."

Louise waited to speak until Rita had brought the coffee and she heard her in the room off the kitchen loading the washing machine.

"Clara Ramsey is back and demanding money."

"Is that what you called me about?"

"I was afraid to say too much. I never know when Flossie is listening in."

"Did she say how much she wanted, or was she after anything she could get?" Doc split a biscuit and spooned gravy over it.

"She wants a hundred dollars."

"Hummm—"

"She said that she was going to Nashville. The silly twit thinks she can get on the Grand Ole Opry."

"Hummm—"

"She threatened to talk to that Dolan woman at the *Gazette*. She rooms at Hazel's."

Doc's head came up. "She would get herself in a lot of trouble."

"She isn't smart enough to realize that."

"I don't want to give Miss Dolan any excuse to nose around. She has no loyalty to this town. She's a hard, brazen bitch!"

"I think so, too. She has a smart mouth and the guts to go with it." Louise was pleased to hear that he disliked the redheaded reporter.

"We'll fix that if she starts taking too much on herself."

"Clara is trouble, Doc. If she spills her story to the reporter, we could be in for a bad time."

"We've overcome bad times before. I trust you to keep a lid on things at the clinic, dear lady."

Doc knew what strings to pull with Louise. A flattering phrase here and there, and the woman would die for him. He enjoyed her devotion to him and the power he had over her, which he had cultivated carefully through the years. Most of all, he enjoyed the certainty that should the axe fall, he had a place for it to land.

"And I will, Doc. You know that. But Clara worried me. She came to us twice, and we helped her out. I thought the second time would be the end of it and we'd seen the last of her."

"We made a mistake with Clara."

"I know that, Doc. How are we going to fix it?"

"I'll have to think on it. As you well know, I don't make hasty decisions."

"I know that, Doc," she said again. "You're the smartest man I ever knew. I was anxious for you to get back because I knew that you'd know how to handle things."

"We've been a good team, Louise. I couldn't have done the work I have without you."

"You look tired, Doc. You wore yourself out at that conference."

"It was a lot of work, but made easier knowing that back here things were in capable hands. The last transfer go all right?"

"Slick as a whistle. Nothing to worry about. The papers are filled out. I'll take them to the courthouse this morning."

"I'll do it. I should go over and talk to Sheriff Carroll about Hannah. She was in town a couple of times this past week. That's far too often."

"I'd better get back to the clinic. Let me know what you want to do about Clara. I told her that you'd be back today and I'm expecting her to come in."

"Avoid her today. Tell her you haven't had a chance to talk to me. Give me a chance to figure something out."

"Maybe we should give her the money and get rid of her."

"Never give in to a blackmailer, Louise. Once we weaken, she would be back for money on a regular basis."

As Louise got up to leave, Doc reached out, took her hand, and brought it to his lips.

"I don't know what I'd do without you, dear girl."

Louise's face became warm beneath the thick layer of paint and powder. Her eyes shone with love as she looked down on the head bending over her hand. These were the tender moments she lived for. This exceptional man who held life and death in his hands needed *her*.

"Ah . . . Doc, you'd do all right. You'd do all right." She repeated herself because of the sudden lump in her throat, and it was something safe to say.

"Get along, my capable and beautiful assistant. I'll be over to the clinic later on this morning." He squeezed her hand tightly, kissed it again, and let it go.

Louise left the house feeling wonderfully light-headed, basking in the knowledge that she was important to the man she loved. They would stand together, depend on each other, and share the secret that was going to make it possible for them to be together.

No one was going to threaten him. She would see to it.

Kathleen arrived at the office half an hour before they opened for business. She told Adelaide and Paul about Krome or Webb slashing her tire while she was in the restaurant. She described the scene when Barker and Johnny confronted Krome and Webb and the sheriff's ordering them to get out of town. She was careful to avoid speaking about Johnny and Barker Fleming's relationship. If Johnny wanted it known that Barker was his father, it would be up to him to tell people.

"Law," Adelaide declared. "Things are going from bad to worse in this town."

"Something else happened when I left here last night that I thought was unusual." Kathleen told them about finding Hannah sitting on the curb beside her car. "She was really drunk—could hardly stand. When the sheriff stopped, I thought that he was going to arrest her, but he was real gentle with her. He put her in his car and took her home."

"There's a story there. Hannah was a pretty girl about fifteen years ago before she started drinking. I saw her with Pete Carroll a few times. He lived with his mother and, knowing Ruby Carroll, she would never have stood still for her son's marrying an Indian. Maybe he still remembers that young pretty girl."

"His kindness to her raised him a few notches in my estimation."

"Carroll isn't so bad when you get right down to it," Adelaide said.

"Is he married?"

"He was at one time. His wife couldn't stand Ruby and left. I don't know if he got a divorce or not. Ruby died a few years ago."

Kathleen worked steadily all morning. News this week was plentiful. She wrote up the story about the rodeo and told Paul to save room on the front page for the picture of Johnny with the hope that the engraving would come in on the evening bus. When she had caught up on the news stories, she went out to pick up the ads.

"Miss Dolan," Mrs. Wilson said, after giving Kathleen a small grocery ad, "there's a young girl sitting back there by the stove and I don't know what to do about her. She was in the alley this morning when I came to open the store. She had slept in that old truck bed. I let her in and gave her something to eat."

"Is she from around here?"

"She said she came to Rawlings to find her mother."

"Do you know her mother?"

"There's no one that I know of named DeBerry in town, and she doesn't know her mother's maiden name."

"Maybe Adelaide knows."

"Come talk to her. She's a pitiful little thing."

Kathleen walked back to where the young girl sat huddled in a chair beside the stove. Her thin shoulders were hunched, her arms crossed, and her hands in the sleeves of a ragged gray jacket. She looked up at Kathleen with large, sad eyes. Dark hair and eyes, fine features, and golden skin spoke of Indian blood. She wore ankle socks and tie shoes much like those an older woman would wear.

"Hello. I work at the newspaper. Mrs. Wilson says that you came to town to find your mother."

"Yes, ma'am."

"I haven't been here long enough to know many people, but Miss Vernon down at the office may be able to help you."

"She would?" Hope leaped in the girl's eyes, and her hands came out of the sleeves. "I come all the way from Fort Worth to find her."

"Oh, my. That's a long way. Did you come in on the bus?"

"No, ma'am. I got some rides and . . . walked a lot."

"That wouldn't be an easy trip for anyone."

"No, ma'am." One of the girl's hands fluttered to her face as if to cover her mouth. Her eyes became misty, and her lips trembled in spite of an effort to keep them firm. She looked to be about twelve years old.

"My name is Kathleen."

"I'm Judith DeBerry. Most folks call me Judy."

"How old are you, Judy?"

"Sixteen."

"We can go down to the *Gazette* office and talk to Miss Vernon if you like. She's lived in Rawlings all her life."

The girl stood, leaned over, and picked up a canvas suitcase. She was short, thin, and reminded Kathleen of a little lost kitten. At the front counter, she stopped and thanked Mrs. Wilson for the food and for allowing her to sit by the stove.

"You're welcome, child. I hope you find your mother."

"Is that suitcase heavy?" Kathleen asked after they left the store and were out on the sidewalk.

"No, ma'am. It don't have much in it."

When they reached the office, Judy stood hesitantly beside the door while Kathleen put the ads in the ad box, then motioned for her to follow her to the back room. Paul and Adelaide were working at the proof table.

"I have two more ads to be made up, Paul. One grocery and one from the theater."

"Hello." Adelaide left the table when she saw the girl.

"Ma'am," Judy murmured.

"This is Judy DeBerry, Adelaide. She's looking for her mother, and I thought maybe you could help her."

"I will, if I can. What's her name?"

"I . . . don't know. But . . . I was born here. I think. It's what my birth certificate says."

"Well . . ." Adelaide's eyes turned to Kathleen. "Let's go into the office and sit down."

Kathleen placed Judy's suitcase behind the ad counter, then pulled out a chair for the girl.

"Your father's name was DeBerry?"

"Yes, but he ain't my father." Judy kept her eyes on her hands in her lap.

"Do you know your mother's maiden name?"

"No, ma'am. You see, she wasn't my mother." When she looked up she had big quiet tears creeping down her cheeks.

"Judy, you're going to have to explain a little more if we're going to help you." Kathleen exchanged a look with Adelaide and pressed a handkerchief into the girl's hand.

"I have always known that Mama and Daddy didn't like me very much." Judy told her story haltingly. "I heard Mama say to Daddy that it was his fault they had me; and he said it was her fault, and she should have known what she was getting. I didn't understand any of it, then one day Mama got mad at me and told me how they had always wanted a pretty little girl and how disappointed they were in me . . . that . . . I looked like an Indian or a . . . a . . . darky."

Pride kept the girl's head up. "I asked her what she meant. She said . . . that she wasn't my mother . . . that I was . . . ugly and dark. She said for me to keep my mouth shut about what she said, or something bad would happen to me."

Kathleen groaned inwardly, almost feeling the hurt of the young girl who'd had to hear that she wasn't wanted.

"Mama and Daddy fussed all the time. Daddy slapped her one night, and I heard him say that he was going back to Rawlings and get his money back. Mama said he'd go to jail. After that, they hardly ever looked at me."

Judy wiped her eyes with the back of her hand. Kathleen exchanged a glance with Adelaide.

"Daddy was gone when I came home from school one day. Mama said it was my fault and told me to get out. She gave me five dollars and said she never wanted to see my . . . face again. I didn't know what to do, so I came here thinking that if she wasn't my mother, my mother would be here."

"Judy, did you ever ask your mother why they were in Rawlings?" Adelaide asked.

"She said they were passing through Rawlings and . . . and they found me on a dung pile."

Kathleen and Adelaide both shook their heads at the unspeakable cruelty.

The door opened, and Mrs. Smothers came into the office.

"Oh . . . Adelaide, I'm all out of breath. I was afraid I'd be too late to get my story in."

"The deadline is ten o'clock in the morning, Mrs. Smothers." *As you well know, you old busybody.*

"We . . . ll— Who do we have here?" She turned her beady eyes on Judy. "I've not met you before."

"Of course, you haven't met her. She's my cousin from Constantinople." Kathleen stood and moved between the woman and Judy.

"From where? Is that in Oklahoma?"

"Give me the facts about your sale, Mrs. Smothers, and I'll add it to the front-page story."

"You will? That would be sooooo . . . nice of you."

While Kathleen took notes, Adelaide motioned to Judy and they went quietly into the back room. Mrs. Smothers was so excited that the success of her booth at the rodeo would be prominently displayed on the front page of the paper that she didn't even notice when they left.

After Kathleen got rid of the woman, she went to the door and said, "All clear."

Adelaide was laughing when she came back into the office.

"How did you come up with Constantinople?"

"It was the first outlandish place that came to mind. By the time she left she had already forgotten. She asked me if my cousin from *Cincin—mople* would be staying long. I explained that she would be going on to visit another cousin in Winnebago."

Adelaide laughed. "Where is that?"

"It's a river in Iowa."

"Kathleen, you're the limit."

"That nosy old woman irritates me."

"I want to talk to Paul about what Judy told us. We've

had a suspicion for a couple of years that something was going on at the clinic that they didn't want anyone to know about."

"What can we do with Judy? We can't turn her out on the street. I shudder to think of her meeting up with Webb or Krome, or a dozen other undesirables in this town, including that lecherous deputy."

"We can't turn her out to fend for herself."

"I'd take her home with me and let her share my room for a night or two if it weren't for Clara. It would give her a reason to rant and rave—not that she needs one."

"I'll talk to Paul and see what he thinks about her staying upstairs with me for a day or two. I know what he'll say—that we know nothing about her and that she could have escaped from the asylum. He's very suspicious."

"Suspicious? I'd say he's very protective of you." Kathleen pulled a sheet of paper out of her typewriter. "As soon as I have time I'm going down to the courthouse and look up her birth record. But our job at the moment is to get the paper out. After it's wrapped up tomorrow, I'll nose around and see what I can find out."

Judy slept the entire afternoon on the cot that Johnny used when he stayed overnight with Paul. She was so tired that the clanking noise of the linotype machine didn't seem to bother her at all.

At the end of the day it was decided that Judy would spend the night in Adelaide's apartment upstairs. Nothing was said directly, but Kathleen assumed that Adelaide would spend the night in Paul's room.

The days were getting shorter, and it was dark by the time Kathleen left the office to go home. She parked her car behind Hazel's house and went in through the kitchen door.

"Miss Dolan's home," Emily called to her grandmother.

Kathleen noticed that only three places were set at the table, meaning that Clara was not at home.

"Hi, Sugarpuss."

"Supper is ready, but Mama won't be here. She went somewhere."

"After I hang up my coat and wash the ink off my hands, I'll be right back."

"Miss Dolan," Emily whispered, and pulled on Kathleen's hand. "Mama wore your jacket and . . . and Granny's cryin'." The little girl's eyes were anxious.

"Did they quarrel?"

"Hu-huh."

"Well, don't worry about it, honey," Kathleen whispered back. "I'll tell your grandma that it's all right."

"I don't want Granny to cry." Emily's lips trembled.

"I don't either. I'll be right back."

As she washed her hands in the bathroom, Kathleen wished she had Clara's neck between them so she could throttle her. The selfish girl had taken her jacket, not caring a whit about the embarrassment it would cause her mother or the anguish it caused her child.

When she returned to the kitchen, Hazel was putting the supper on the table. Her eyes were swollen from crying, and Emily hovered close to her anxiously.

"Something smells good, Hazel."

"It's brown beans, tomatoes, and onions."

"Granny made corn bread," Emily said.

"I'm so glad. I'm hungry enough to eat you, Sugarpuss."

Before Hazel sat down, she gripped the back of the chair and looked straight across the table at Kathleen.

"I've got to tell you something." Tears clouded her

eyes. "Clara wore your jacket. I feel so bad about it. I'm sorry, really sorry. I told her to leave your things alone. I'd not blame you if you want to find another place to stay."

"It isn't your fault, Hazel. When she comes back, I'll take it and lock it in my trunk. Don't worry about me moving. I like it here. I like you and I *love* this little sugarpuss." She reached out an arm and hugged Emily.

"She'll leave soon. She always does. I always wonder when she goes if I'll ever see her again."

"Maybe she *will* make it in Nashville."

"She won't. I don't know where she ever got it in her head that she can sing."

While they were eating, Hazel seemed to calm a little. "She went somewhere this afternoon, and when she came back she was madder than a wet hen. Someone owes her money and won't pay. I can't imagine who it could be. She swore to get even with them."

"Where is she now?"

"I don't know." Tears filled Hazel's eyes again. "She took the three dollars I had hidden in the baking-powder can. I guess she remembered that I hid things there when she was a little girl."

After the meal Kathleen stayed in the kitchen to dry the dishes as Hazel washed them and dropped them in the hot rinse water. Emily sat at the table drawing pictures on scraps of newsprint that Kathleen had given to her.

"Hazel, do you remember a family named DeBerry being here in Rawlings about sixteen or seventeen years ago?"

"I don't think I ever heard that name. A lot of people have left Oklahoma since the start of the Depression."

"Someone was in the office inquiring about the family. I thought you might know."

"If they had school-age kids, a record would be at the school."

"That's true." A roll of thunder prompted Kathleen to say, "We may be in for a rain."

"I wish Clara hadn't gone out. I told her that cloud bank in the southwest looked like rain."

"She'll be all right. She probably went to the picture show."

"No," Hazel said slowly and sadly. "She went to a honky-tonk. She loves honky-tonks."

Later, in her room, Kathleen stood by the window and looked out at the star-studded sky before she turned on the light. In the back of her mind all day had been the vision of Johnny looking at her as she sat in the car with Barker Fleming, then, without acknowledging either one of them, turning and riding away.

What had he thought? *He had just learned that the man she was with was his father.*

Kathleen wanted to cry.

Chapter Seventeen

IT RAINED DURING THE NIGHT, a typical Oklahoma rainstorm; wind, lightning and a downpour which lasted for only a short time. It was still overcast when morning came. The moment Kathleen entered the kitchen she could tell by the worried look on Hazel's face that Clara had not come home.

"Good morning." Kathleen removed the saucer from the top of the blue crockery pitcher where the tea had been steeping and poured a cup. "How are you this morning, Sugarpuss?" she said to Emily.

"All right."

"I'll give you a ride to school, if you want."

"All right. Mama didn't come home."

"She probably didn't want to get caught in the rain and stayed with a friend." Kathleen glanced at Hazel who kept her face turned away. "I'll have to leave as soon as you finish your breakfast. The paper goes out today."

"I'll be ready."

It wasn't fair that a child Emily's age had to carry the burden of an irresponsible mother. Kathleen fumed all the way to town after she had let Emily off at the school. The child had not said a word after she got into the car and only " 'Bye, Miss Dolan" when she got out.

Kathleen went by the bus stop, picked up the engravings for the paper, then parked her car in front of the office. Paul had already set the front page, leaving a two-column-by-three-inch space for the picture of Johnny above the story Kathleen had written about the rodeo.

In order to be ready for the press by noon, Kathleen and Adelaide worked steadily after only a brief mention of Judy.

"She was still asleep when Paul and I had breakfast. I left a note telling her to help herself to bread, butter, and preserves that I left on the table."

Shortly before noon the phone rang, three short rings and two long ones.

"I wonder what's happened. That's the emergency call," Adelaide said and reached for the phone. "*Gazette*."

"That you, Adelaide?"

"It's me, Flossie. What's going on?"

"Oh, Adelaide . . . oh, Adelaide—a call came to the sheriff that . . . a woman's body is in the ditch out south of town."

"Where, Flossie? Exactly where?" Adelaide motioned frantically to Kathleen.

"Just before you get to the corner that goes to the Kilburn ranch."

"Thanks, Flossie. I owe you, and I'll not forget it." Adelaide hung up. "Kathleen, a woman's body was found in the ditch out south of town. Go straight out Main Street, turn when the pavement ends and go straight south. The sheriff will be there. We'll hold the front page until you get back."

Kathleen was already checking the camera for film while Adelaide spoke. She grabbed her purse and went out to her car. Following Adelaide's instructions, she turned onto the dirt road made soft by last night's rain. She stayed in the ruts made by the other cars, and after a mile, she saw the sheriff's car and another car ahead of it. She stopped behind them and got out.

A growing sense of dread filled her as she walked toward the group standing alongside the road. The sheriff came toward her as she approached.

"This isn't something a lady should see," he said gruffly.

"I'm a reporter, Sheriff. Who is it?"

"Clara Ramsey."

"Oh my goodness! Poor Hazel." Somehow Kathleen had known who the girl was before he spoke. "What happened?"

"She didn't kill herself, that's sure."

"How long ago did it happen?"

"After the rain."

"I'd like to take some pictures . . . not of the body, but of the scene. Would you stand over there by the sheriff's car?"

"Sure." The sheriff made an attempt to pull in his stomach and puff out his chest as he posed beside the car.

Kathleen took pictures from several angles and one quick shot of the body still clothed in the jacket Clara had taken from Kathleen's room. The pitiful heap sprawled in the ditch looked like a rag doll.

"What do you think happened, Sheriff?" Kathleen took out her pad and pencil. "I'd like to quote you to be sure it will be right." She had learned that the best way to get information was flattery.

"It looks like she was hit by a car and thrown over in the ditch." Sheriff Carroll took off his hat and scratched his head. "Someone beat hell out of her first. Being hit by the car wouldn't have cut up her mouth and blackened her eyes. Her legs are broken . . . but that was from being hit by the car."

"Could it have been an accident?"

"What would she be doing out here by herself at three o'clock in the morning? Why didn't the driver stop and help her? Off the top of my head I say she was beat up, thrown out of the car, run over to be sure she was dead, and then tossed in the ditch."

Kathleen wrote quickly. "Who found her?"

"Mr. Kilburn on his way to town."

"What are you waiting for, Sheriff?"

"Doc Herman. I think that's him coming now. He's the coroner."

"The . . . king . . . the mayor . . . the *savior*—" The sarcastic words came out before Kathleen could hold them back. The sheriff didn't seem to notice as he watched a car come slowly toward them.

"I sure hate to have to tell Hazel," he said. "She's had a peck of trouble with Clara since she was twelve or thirteen years old."

"Would you like for me to go with you to tell Hazel, Sheriff?"

"You'd do that?"

"Hazel is a friend. Shouldn't you ask her minister to be there?"

"Good idey. I've not had to do this but a time or two. It ain't something that's easy. Here's Doc."

The car stopped behind Kathleen's, and the doctor got out. As he came toward them, his shiny shoes became coated with mud. Kathleen looked down at her own shoes and wondered if they would ever be the same again.

"What are you doing here?" Dr. Herman barked at her.

His eyes behind the round-rimmed glasses were not friendly.

"Why do reporters go anywhere? To get news," she shot back sharply.

"Did you call her?" Doc asked Sheriff Carroll, jerking his head toward Kathleen.

"No. I only called you after Mr. Kilburn called me."

"Then it was Flossie."

"If it's important for you to know, a man stuck his head in the office door and yelled that he'd heard a body was found out here in the ditch." She hoped that the lie was convincing and would take the blame from Flossie.

"Bullfoot! What happened here?" He turned his back on Kathleen to shut her out of the conversation.

"See for yourself. She's over there in the ditch."

"Drunk?"

"I don't think so."

"Let's take a look."

"I'll be at the office, Sheriff, when you're ready to go to Hazel's," Kathleen said.

Sheriff Carroll nodded, and the two men went down into the ditch. The sheriff knelt beside the body and lifted the cloth he had used to cover Clara's face.

Kathleen went back to her car, drove down to the crossroads, turned around, and headed back to town. As she passed back by the scene, Dr. Herman had come back up onto the road. Later, she remembered that he had not asked *who* was in the ditch.

At the office she gave Paul and Adelaide the news. Adelaide was shocked and saddened that the dead girl was Clara Ramsey.

"Has Hazel been told?"

"I offered to go with the sheriff to tell her."

"I don't envy you."

Paul had already made room on the front page for a headline and short story. Kathleen typed up the story, after getting some background information about Clara from Adelaide, and took it back to be set on the linotype. The headline, in big black letters, was in place.

LOCAL WOMAN FOUND DEAD.

"I wonder if we have an engraving of Clara in a group picture."

"I looked," Paul said. "Nothing in the file."

"We could use one of the sheriff above his quote. I have a feeling we need to butter him up. We may want him to help us find Judy's mother."

"That would push Johnny's picture down under the fold."

"Then let's skip it. We'll butter the sheriff up in another way."

Paul grinned. "You've got newspaper ink in your veins."

On her way back to her desk, she stopped in the office doorway. Her heart began a crazy dance in her chest. Johnny was standing beside the counter talking to Adelaide. From the shocked look on his face, she knew that Adelaide had told him about Clara. Kathleen went on to her desk and sat down.

"You've been out there?" Johnny asked without a greeting.

"Just got back."

"What does Carroll think happened?"

"She was hit by a car after she'd been beaten up."

"It wasn't an accident?"

"He didn't seem to think so." She rolled a sheet of paper into the typewriter just to be doing something.

"I came in to fix your tire." Johnny stood in front of her desk on spread legs, his hands in the back pockets of his jeans.

"Don't bother. I'll get it fixed." Without looking up at him she knew he was gazing down at her. For some reason, unknown even to herself, she was angry with him.

"I said I would fix it, and I will," he said stubbornly. "First I want to go out to where they found Clara."

"Why? The sheriff won't welcome your help."

"I don't give a damn if he does or not. I know a hell of a lot more about tracks than he does."

"You'd better get going then. People by the dozens will be swarming out there out of curiosity."

"I'm going, but I'll be back to fix that tire."

Kathleen wanted to put her head down on the desk and cry. The combination of troubles set her nerves on edge: worry about Johnny and his thoughts about seeing her with Barker, worry about having to tell Hazel that her daughter was dead, and worry about the poor little waif who had come to Rawlings to find her mother.

An hour passed, and Kathleen was beginning to fear Hazel would hear the news before she and the sheriff got there. Then he drove up in front of the office. A gray-haired man was with him. Kathleen went out to the car.

"Sheriff, I've been thinking about Emily, Clara's little girl. Why don't I go to the school, get Emily, and take her home? In the meanwhile you and the Reverend can tell Hazel. I'll . . . try to tell Emily. It will take some of the burden off Hazel."

"I'd forgotten Clara had a girl."

"A few of the ladies from the church are going out to be with Mrs. Ramsey," the preacher said.

"Where did they take Clara, Sheriff?"

"To the funeral parlor. Doc said it was an accident." When he spoke he looked away from Kathleen.

"An accident? She was beaten up, Sheriff. You said so. Doc is full of hot air," Kathleen said angrily.

"It's what he said, and that's final. He's the coroner."

"For Christ's sake! Doesn't anyone in this town have enough backbone to stand up to that little dictator?"

"Watch your mouth, girl!"

"I'll pick up Emily."

Back in the office, Kathleen faced Adelaide and gave vent to her frustration.

"Doc Herman had pronounced Clara's death an accident. She had been beaten around the head, has black eyes, and a cut mouth. I know enough to know that if she had been killed instantly when she was hit by a car, she'd not be bruised like that, especially when the ground is soft. What's going on here? Sheriff Carroll didn't want me to question Doc's decision.

"Another thing was strange, Adelaide. He wanted to know how I knew to go out to the scene. He blamed Flossie. I tried to cover for her by telling him a man came to the door and told us."

"We'll stick to that. He could have Flossie fired."

"I'm disliking that man more and more."

Kathleen's heart was beating with dread when she stopped at the schoolhouse and went to Emily's classroom. She motioned to the teacher to come to the hall and then waited for Emily to come out.

"Hello, Sugarpuss."

"Miss Ryan said I could go home."

"How would you like to go for a little ride first?"

"Did Mama come home?"

The question caused Kathleen to pause. "No, sweetheart, she didn't."

"Then I better go home and see about Granny."

"All right." Kathleen took the child's hand, and they went out to the car.

She told the child about her mother as they sat in the car beneath the pecan tree at the edge of the playground. Emily cried, Kathleen cried. It was one of the hardest things Kathleen had ever had to do. Although Emily was not attached to Clara as a child is normally attached to her mother, she had feelings for her.

"Granny's goin' to feel awful bad," Emily said after she had stopped crying.

"Yes. Your mother was her little girl."

"I'd better go home and see about her."

Kathleen wiped her eyes and started the car.

Kathleen's eyes were red when she returned to the office and heard the sound of the press printing the paper.

"You didn't have to come right back," Adelaide said. "Judy has been helping stuff the papers."

"Three of Hazel's friends are with her and Emily. That child is old for her years. Her concern was for her grandmother."

"The only good thing Clara ever did for Hazel was to give her Emily. She adores the child. Was anything said about services?"

"Not to me. I think Hazel feared that something like this would happen to Clara but didn't expect it here in Rawlings."

Adelaide tilted her head to look out the window. "Johnny's back. I wonder what he found out."

Johnny's dark eyes swept the office when he entered, then moved over to the desks where Kathleen and Adelaide sat and came right to the point.

"I'd bet my life it was no accident."

"At first Sheriff Carroll said it was not an accident. He's changed his mind now that Doc Herman says it was," Kathleen replied.

"Yeah. That's what I was told down at the funeral parlor."

"You've been there?"

"Eldon is sort of a friend of mine."

"He's the undertaker," Adelaide explained to Kathleen.

"Would you be squeamish about taking pictures of the body?" Johnny addressed his words to Kathleen.

"I've never done anything like it, but I can if it's necessary."

"Then get your Kodak. Eldon agrees with me that it wasn't an accident. Pictures may be the only way that we can prove it. I owe it to Hazel to find out the truth if I can."

"You mean there's one man in this town that isn't in Doc Herman's pocket?"

"I know several . . . Paul, Claude, Eldon, and probably more if it came right down to it."

Kathleen checked the Kodak. "There are eight pictures left on this roll. Is that enough?"

"I'd think so. Let's go out the back and walk down the alley. No need to advertise where we're going."

"Johnny, be careful," Adelaide cautioned. "Be careful about going against Doc Herman."

"I'll be careful; but if Clara was murdered, it's only right that her murderer be found."

Kathleen and Johnny walked behind the stores to the funeral parlor in back of the furniture store.

"You must have good cause to do this." Kathleen had to walk fast to keep up with Johnny's long steps.

"After looking at the body and talking to Eldon, I came to the conclusion she was beaten up; and while she lay in the road, the car ran over her, backed up and ran over her again. Then, not sure that she was dead, the murderer put his foot on her throat."

"How do you know he ran over her while she was lying in the road?"

"Tire tracks. When I was a boy in Red Rock, Tom taught me to read tire marks because we were trying to catch rustlers coming into the fields and killing beef. He showed me the marks made by different tires. I used what he taught me once before when I worked with Hod."

"Oh, gosh! I just remembered Hazel said that Clara had gone somewhere yesterday afternoon and when she came home, she was very angry. She told Hazel that someone owed her money and that she would get it or get even."

"Maybe we can find out where she went." At the door of the funeral parlor, he stopped. "Are you sure you're up to this? It's not a pretty sight. I'd not ask you to do it, but I'm a lousy picture taker, and these need to be as good as we can make them."

"I'll be all right. We'll need plenty of light."

"I'll ask Eldon about that. The body is on a cart that can be moved to the window, and if that isn't light enough, we may be able to open the double doors on the back. The danger would be that someone would see us."

"We'll need as much light as we can get in order to get good close-up pictures."

"Come on. We'll give it our best shot."

To Kathleen's surprise, Johnny put an arm protectively around her as they approached the building.

The instant Johnny rapped on the door it was opened. Eldon Radner was a small, thin man with wiry faded brown hair. He never just walked anywhere but scurried or sprinted. Owner of the furniture store and the funeral parlor, he took the business of laying out the dead very seriously.

"Come in, come in. I've rigged up some lights. Hello, Miss Dolan. We haven't met, but I know about you from Johnny. This is a terrible thing for Rawlings. We must hurry, Johnny. I've work to do on the body before Mrs. Ramsey comes down, and you can never tell who else. Folks are curious, especially in a case like this. There hasn't been a woman murdered in Tillison County in a long time. Doc Herman will want it hushed up. Oh, yes, I discovered her jaw is broken and some of her teeth are missing."

Most of this was said without Eldon taking a breath. Kathleen was to learn that was his natural way of speaking. He threw out a hand beckoning them to follow and bustled through another set of doors, a long white duster flapping about his legs.

Clara's body lay on a waist-high cart just as it had come from the ditch where she died. A string of hooded lights hung above the body and when Eldon turned them all on, Kathleen had to blink. To keep from looking directly at the pitiful heap on the cart, Kathleen fiddled with the adjustments on the camera.

"What do you think, Kathleen? Is it light enough?"

"Do you want overall, or just up-close areas?"

"Mostly close-up."

"Can one of the lights be lowered to the area you want?"

"You betcha," Eldon said, and scurried to the other side of the cart. "Show her the tire marks, Johnny. I'll hold the light where you want it, Miss Dolan. This is sorry business, I tell you. I've not had a corpse this tore up in a long time. I don't know if I can make her presentable for the laying away. Oh, poor Mrs. Ramsey. It'll be hard for her, that's sure."

Kathleen tried to tune out the voice of the undertaker. Johnny folded Clara's skirt up over her thighs. Oklahoma red clay was clearly imprinted on the white flesh.

"Take the thighs, Kathleen. These are tire tracks." He pointed to the mud streaks.

Eldon held the hooded light, and Kathleen lowered the camera until only the area of the marks was visible in the viewfinder and snapped the picture. The prints on the lower, broken legs were not as distinct, but she took a photo of them anyway. Johnny folded back the gray jacket to reveal prints from the muddy tire on Clara's white blouse where the wheel of the car had run over her chest. After the picture was taken, Johnny pointed to the flicks of mud on her side.

"This will be rough, Kathleen," Johnny said as he removed the cloth covering Clara's face.

Kathleen steeled herself to think that what she was seeing and photographing was a broken doll. Clara's face was a sight that would long haunt Kathleen's dreams. When the light was lowered, she snapped the picture. Eldon tilted Clara's chin so a picture would be taken of the neck area. Her windpipe had been crushed. By the time Johnny covered the face, Kathleen was swallowing rapidly.

"How many exposures left?" Johnny asked the question in a sharp business like tone.

"Two."

"Let's turn her over, Eldon." After the body was turned, Eldon lifted Clara's dress up over her bare buttocks. "Are you all right, honey?" Johnny asked gently. Kathleen nodded. "See this bruise? It was made before she died because you don't bruise after your heart stops pumping. It's a bootprint. You can see the heel. He stomped on her before he killed her. Take the last two pictures of it."

Eldon was careful to get the light just right, and Kathleen took the two pictures, each from a different angle. When she finished, she stepped back, turned away, and headed for the door. Johnny caught up and put his arm around her.

"Are you all right?" After she nodded, he said, "I'm proud of you, Kathleen. I've seen men faint after seeing such a sight."

"It wasn't . . . easy—"

"Let me know how the prints turn out, Johnny." Eldon unlocked the back door. "I've got work to do. Poor girl. Poor, poor girl. She was worked over all right. Didn't deserve it even if she was ah . . . loose. Hazel and Sam Ramsey were fine folks. I knew Sam back in the twenties. He was in the war and fought in France. Hazel will be here soon. I don't know how she's goin' to pay for a funeral. I'll do the best I can, but I've got expenses, too."

"I'll check back with you, Eldon."

"He would wear me out," Kathleen said after the door closed.

"It took me a while to get used to him. But he's a man of his word, and he doesn't knuckle under to Doc

Herman." Johnny held her arm as they walked back up the alley to the *Gazette* building.

"I hope the pictures are plain enough to do some good. Paul will develop the film and enlarge the pictures."

"I want to show the prints to Keith. He worked on a tracking case once with me, and he's pretty good."

"Can you tell what kind of car ran over her by looking at the tracks?"

"Maybe not the kind of car, but we may be able to match the prints to tires on a car. This was a big heavy car, I know that."

"Who would have done such a terrible thing to Clara? She was just a stupid, terribly irritating girl."

"She was a girl that started her loose ways young. She must have had Emily when she was fourteen or fifteen."

"Does Hazel know who Emily's father is?"

"I doubt if Clara knew."

"What will a funeral cost?"

"There may be room to bury her beside her daddy. If not, I'd say between fifty to a hundred dollars."

"Hazel doesn't have that kind of money."

"I don't imagine she does," Johnny said sadly.

Chapter Eighteen

I DON'T WANT TO EVER HAVE TO DO THAT AGAIN." Kathleen was in the office with Adelaide. "It was just awful. Poor, poor girl. She looked like a broken doll."

"Johnny seems sure that Clara was murdered. Doc Herman won't stand for there being a murder in his simon-pure town."

"Is that why Sheriff Carroll now calls it an accident?"

"He must have his reasons."

"I wonder if the doctor is afraid of the attention it would bring to the town if it becomes known that a woman was murdered here?"

"I can't think of any other reason." Adelaide leaned back in her chair wearily and stretched her arms over her head. Press day was always hard, but this one had been especially difficult.

"You're worn-out. You had to do my share of the work today."

"Judy was a big help. She and Woody stuffed all the papers. Paul helped me get them ready for the post office."

"With all that's happened, I had almost forgotten about Judy."

"She's a quiet girl. She hasn't asked me one time about

finding her mother. She has thanked me a hundred times for letting her stay. When I went upstairs this morning, the bed was made; and you couldn't tell that she'd been in the kitchen."

"Her sorry excuse for a mother must have taught her something."

"I was glad that she was here today. She pitched right in, and I didn't have to explain things to her but one time."

"Tomorrow I'll go to the courthouse and look at the birth records."

"You'll not be greeted with open arms, I'll tell you that. When I insisted on seeing them a year ago, the clerk watched me like I was about to raid the U.S. Mint."

"They have to let me see public records."

"I was surprised at how many babies were born here. Doc must advertise in Dallas, Fort Worth, Waco, and even as far away as Denver. When I came back and told Paul what I had discovered, we both decided that something wasn't quite right about so many out-of-town women coming here to have babies."

"Did you ever mention it to Sheriff Carroll?"

"Heavens no! Pete is a good man . . . or he used to be. But he's cowed where Doc is concerned. He'd tell me to tend to my own business . . . or something like that."

"I've a niggling suspicion in the back of my mind about all this. I'm going to wait until I see the birth records and get it sorted out before I tell you because you're going to think that I've lost my mind."

"I doubt that. I think you've got a pretty good hold on that mind of yours."

Lately Adelaide appeared to be more lighthearted than when Kathleen had first arrived. It was as if a burden had been lifted from her shoulders. An astute student of human nature, Kathleen was sure that Adelaide's change of mood was because she now shared the secret of her love for Paul with someone who didn't disapprove.

"I should go back to Hazel's, but I'm not eager to be in a crowd of women and make small talk. There were six or more ladies there when I left."

"Stay here then. Come upstairs and I'll fix us some sandwiches. Paul mentioned going to Claude's and bringing back hamburgers."

Kathleen and Adelaide went to the back room where Paul and Johnny were looking at the photos spread out on the ad table.

"It was a big tire. It went over her thighs, came back over her legs, and broke them. It then went over her chest. Damn, but I hope that she wasn't conscious at that time." Johnny swore softly under his breath. "That's about all I can tell from these prints. I'd like for Keith McCabe to see them. I'll give him a call, but not from Rawlings. Too many ears on the line."

"You'll be making a couple of powerful enemies if you stick your nose in this," Paul said. "Doc Herman has declared it an accident and so has the sheriff."

"I can't just stand by and do nothing when I think that girl was murdered."

"If they could figure out a way to do it and make it appear to be legal, they could blame it on you."

"Let them try. I don't see how anyone could pass this off as an accident. Clara's ribs and her legs were broken when the car ran over her, but it sure as hell didn't run over her neck and head. Hellfire, Paul, her jaw was broken, her teeth knocked out! I wish I had gotten there before the place was trampled over. I might have found the track he made when he dragged her into the ditch and got a decent footprint."

"Can you tell anything from the one on her back?"

"It was a boot, and not a very big one according to the space between the heel and the sole."

Paul snorted. "Doc Herman will never admit that it's even a bootprint."

"The best track man in the country is Frank Hamer, the former Texas Ranger, now a U.S. Marshal. I'd like for him to see these prints. Doc Herman would sit up and take notice if he came to town."

"Do you know Frank Hamer?"

"I know him, but not as well as Keith McCabe does."

When Kathleen came up beside him, Johnny moved the picture of Clara's tortured face out of sight.

"Where is Judy?" Adelaide asked.

"She's sleeping there on the cot. It's like she hasn't slept in a week," Paul replied.

"If she walked and hitched rides all the way from Fort Worth, she probably hasn't slept much in a week. Johnny, did Paul tell you about Judy?"

"He said she was here looking for her real mother." Johnny's eyes shifted from Adelaide to Kathleen. "Are you going back to Hazel's?"

"Not right away. There's a houseful of people there, or was when I left this afternoon."

"I'm going to call on her after I fix your tire."

"You're determined to fix that blasted tire, aren't you?"

"I said I'd fix it, and I will."

"Then let's get it over with so I can go home," she said irritably.

Johnny followed Kathleen through the office and out onto the street where her car was parked.

"Why are you mad?"

"I'm not mad! Well, I guess I am . . . but I'm not sure why." She got the keys out of her purse and dangled them in front of him. "It's in the trunk, but I'm sure you know that."

He swept the keys from her hand. "Get in."

Later she waited in the car while Johnny carried the slashed tire into the back of the filling station. He was a puzzle to her, always leaving her with a thousand conflicting emotions. It made her angry that her heart fairly jumped out of her chest at the sight of him. How dare he come into her life and make her so miserable?

She watched him come back to the car with the tire. What was it about this man, this cowboy, that, with a look or a word, could bring her so stupidly close to tears.

"How much did it cost?" She began digging into her purse as soon as he got in the car.

"Forget it. It's taken care of."

"I'll not forget it. I'll not have you paying to fix my tires," she said crossly.

"I'm not rich like *your* Mr. Fleming, but I can afford to fix a tire."

"He's not *my* Mr. Fleming."

"No? Then why are you always hangin' around his neck?"

"Hanging around his *neck!* You make me so damn mad! Where are we going?"

"To Hazel's. I've got to pay my respects."

Not another word was said until they stopped in front of the well-lighted house. A number of people were milling about.

"Stay here. I'll be right back." Johnny took the keys

from the car and held them up for her to see before he put them in his pocket. "So that you'll not be tempted."

Kathleen immediately dug into her purse and brought out the extra set of keys her Uncle Hod had insisted that she have made. She was very tempted to drive off and leave him, but she didn't. She waited and when he returned he found the extra set of keys in the ignition.

"You've got to have the last word, haven't you?" It was dark, she couldn't see his face but she knew that he was grinning.

He drove back uptown, turned into the alley behind the *Gazette*, and parked beside his truck. He turned off the lights and reached for her arm to prevent her from getting out of the car. She said the first safe thing that came to mind.

"How are Hazel and Emily?"

"They're hurtin'. The reality of it hasn't soaked in yet. There are plenty of people there, and the table is piled with food." He paused, then said, "Hazel hasn't been to the funeral home yet. Eldon sent word for her not to come until morning."

"It will be a difficult time for her. I was very young when my father was killed, and about Emily's age when I lost my mother. My grandparents, though, lived to be in their sixties. It was terribly hard when I lost first Grandma, and then Papa."

"It's funny, but when you lose someone you care about, you can think of things you wish that you had said to that person, but never did."

"Who have you lost that you cared about?"

"Ed Henry. He was the nearest thing to a father I had. He said things, quietly, that at the time I didn't pay much attention to. Later, after he was gone, I thought about them. I'd not been to a funeral before I went to Ed's. Aunt Dozie ironed one of Ed's white shirts for me to wear. Henry Ann needed me. I'd never been needed before either. Being needed kind of makes a fellow take heed of his responsibilities." Johnny's voice was low as he reminisced about the past. Kathleen hesitated to interrupt him by asking a question, but finally she did.

"I didn't have an aunt when I was growing up. My mother was my grandparents' only surviving child."

"Aunt Dozie is a colored woman who lived with us on the farm. She still lives there with Tom and Henry Ann. She's getting old. I should get over there more often to see her." He turned and looked at Kathleen. "I love that old woman and Henry Ann. They're my family. They cared about me when not another soul in the world cared if I lived or died."

Kathleen was quiet for a long while before she said, "Are you telling me something, Johnny?"

He looked out the window and fiddled with the steering wheel. Long minutes passed before he said anything. When he spoke, it was as if the words were pulled out of him.

"He told you that he thinks he's my father, didn't he?"

"Yes."

"He can think it all he wants. It makes no difference to me. It could have been him or a dozen others who, for two bits, paid for a half hour in her bed. The woman that had me was a whore not because she had to be one, but because she *wanted* to be one."

"Why do you think that you have to tell me this?"

He grabbed her, giving her no chance to resist, and pulled her tightly against him.

"So that you'll know that the son of a whore and a drunk Indian is going to kiss you."

His face came to hers and he kissed her long and hard. At first her lips were compressed with surprise, but then they softened and yielded. Her palms rested on his chest before they moved around to his back and she hugged him to her. He raised his head. They looked into each other's eyes; his had little lights. He kissed her again, softly, sweetly. She was happy, even though she knew it wouldn't last.

"Don't talk like that about yourself to me again." She had not meant to say that at all, and especially not angrily.

"I'm trying to be fair to you."

"I don't care about your mother or your father. She could have been Lizzie Borden, and he could have been Attila the Hun for all I care. You are not responsible for what they did. Why can't you understand that? Are you afraid I'll interfere in your life? I'm not going to *ask* you for anything."

"That, right there, says it all. You'll never *ask* a man for anything, will you? You'll never *need* a man. Fiery, independent, little Miss Dolan can take care of herself, fight her own battles, fix her own tires."

"You've got it right, mister. I've had to take care of myself for the past eight years because there wasn't anyone there to help me. If what you need is some clinging vine who can't wipe her own nose, you've got the wrong woman."

"I've got the *right* woman," he gritted angrily. Even before the words were out, his arms were crushing her to him. She uttered a little grunt of surprise. "Be quiet!" he snarled, but he didn't kiss her. He held her, his lips against her ear. "You smell so good . . . and feel better."

His voice was husky, tender, his lips nuzzled her ear. He knew that he shouldn't be doing this, but damned if he could stop. The feel of her soft body against his and the scent of her filled his head. He swallowed hard, because he wanted her so much. His hand moved up and down her back and over her rounded hips. He moved his head and found her hungry lips. The kiss was long and passionate, his mouth parting, her lips seeking fulfillment. She clung to him, melting into his hard embrace. The kiss seemed to last forever, both reluctant to end it.

"You are an irritating woman. Why can't I stay away from you?" He kissed her quick and hard and moved away from her.

"You're a moody, unpredictable, complicated man. I never know where I stand with you," she retorted. "On rare occasions you can be very nice and then, like now, a complete horse's patoot! There are times when I don't like you at all!"

"You use all kinds of big words. I don't have the slightest idea what they mean."

"Irritating is a big word. You evidently know what that means." She pushed her hair back with shaky fingers.

"Do you like Fleming?" he asked bluntly.

"Of course, I do. He's a nice man."

Johnny let out an angry snort. "Nice? Bullfoot! How the hell do you know? If he's so damn nice, how come he goes around knocking up whores?"

"He did that when he was very young. He's a well-mannered gentleman. You'd know it, too, if you weren't too damn stubborn to let yourself get to know him."

"I'm not sharing a woman with a damn Cherokee half-breed!"

Kathleen opened her mouth, closed it, and gritted her teeth in frustration.

"Look who's talking? That was a rotten thing to say, Johnny Henry."

"Rotten or not, it's what he is, and it's what I am!"

"Does your Indian blood bother you? It certainly doesn't bother me."

"It would . . . after a while, but forget it. I've got to get the photos and get on home."

"Forget it. That's your favorite thing to say when you don't want to face the facts. Now listen to me, you mule-headed dimwit!" She held his arm to keep him from getting out of the car. "Mr. Fleming told me that he'd been looking for his son for a long time. He's had detectives out looking for you. They finally found your sister in Oklahoma City. He was so proud of you at the rodeo. It seems to me the least you could have done was to be decent to him."

"So he came crying to you, did he?"

"He did not! Johnny Henry, I don't know why I even bother with you."

"If he got anything out of Isabel, it was while she was on her back."

"Get out of my car so I can go home."

"Gladly. I'll be back day after tomorrow to go to the funeral. Sunday we'll go to Red Rock."

"I've changed my mind. I'm *not* going. I'll not torture myself by spending a day with a stubborn, addleheaded, idiot with . . . feathers for brains!"

"*We* made plans to go to Red Rock on Sunday, Kathleen. *We* are going. I'll be in for the funeral on Thursday." He got out of the car and waited until she moved over under the wheel before he closed the door. "Go straight home. I've not seen Webb and Krome, but that doesn't mean they're not around." He closed the door, but stood there looking at her for a minute before he moved away.

Kathleen was furious as she drove out of the alley, but by the time she turned onto the street, a warm glow of happiness had replaced her anger.

Why can't I stay away from you?

I'll not share a woman—

Johnny liked her in spite of himself! He might even be a little in love with her.

Kathleen's grin blossomed into a full smile.

Chapter Nineteen

As soon as Kathleen arrived at the office the next morning, she pinned the pictures she had taken at the site where Clara was killed on a bulletin board. Beneath the photo of the crumpled heap in the ditch, she wrote:

A few hours before this picture was taken, Clara Ramsey was a living, breathing human being.

Beneath the picture of the sheriff:

A. B. (Pete) Carroll, Sheriff of Tillison County. At the time this photo was taken he stated: "This untimely death is not an accident." Later he said that it WAS an accident. After viewing the crushed windpipe and the broken jaw it appears to this reporter that Clara Ramsey was beaten, then run over and tossed in the ditch.

Kathleen placed the bulletin board in the office window and soon everyone who passed by the office stopped to view the display. Word spread and at times three or four people at a time were gawking at the pictures.

The display had not been in the window an hour until the sheriff's car stopped out front and he came into the office.

"I never gave you permission to put my picture in the window, and I didn't say that."

"I didn't have to get your permission. You're a public official. You posed willingly for the picture, and you did say that. I wrote it down word for word."

"Hello, Pete." Adelaide came into the office. "That's a good picture of you. You look real official. Haven't you lost a little weight?"

"Ah . . . maybe a little."

"Are you sticking to your story that Clara's death was an accident?" Kathleen asked.

"I've heard nothing to change my mind."

"Did you examine the body?"

"That's not my job, missy."

"Did the car run over her head? Is that the reason her jaw was broken and her windpipe crushed?"

"Now look here. You have no right to question my decision."

"Was it your decision or Doc Herman's to put out the story that Clara's death was an accident?"

"I was mistaken. I suggest, for your own good, that you drop the matter and tend to your own business."

"Reporting the news is my business."

"Then stick to it."

"If I don't, will you have me knocked off?" Kathleen made a clicking sound with her tongue, imitating a rapidly fired machine gun, shaped her hand like a gun, and pointed it at the sheriff. He never cracked a smile. "Not funny, huh?"

"Not a damn bit."

"Sheriff, what does Dr. Herman have on people in this town that makes some of them forget morals, honor, and basic decency? They allow him to rule this town as if he were a king?"

Sheriff Carroll's face turned a fiery red as he choked down his anger. "You're walking on dangerous ground, miss. Adelaide, you'd better put a rein on her. She doesn't know the lay of the land here."

"I'll speak to her, Pete," Adelaide said calmly. Then, "By the way, Pete, have you ever heard of a family here in Rawlings named DeBerry?"

He took off his hat and turned it around and around in his hands. Kathleen noticed that he had a full head of iron gray hair that was neatly cut.

"Why do you ask?"

"I had an inquiry. It's not important."

The sheriff turned his back, and for several minutes he watched a couple of men as they studied the pictures in the window.

"You've got quite a little sideshow going on out there." When he turned, his face seemed to have aged. His shoulders had slumped. He looked directly at Kathleen. "You'd best be careful, Miss Dolan, that it doesn't backfire on you."

"I've taken precautions, Sheriff. I left a letter with my lawyer that if anything happens to me to look in my lock box and to arrest you and Dr. Herman." She grinned at him.

He slapped his hat down on his head. "If there's any-thin' I can't stand it's a smart-aleck woman." He left and got into his car without ever taking a close look at the display in the window.

"Did I embarrass you, Adelaide?"

"Absolutely not. You can go after anyone in this town you want to. I just don't want you to put yourself in jeopardy."

"If I wasn't so angry with him, I'd feel sorry for Sheriff Carroll."

"When we were kids the sheriff was called Pete, I think because his father's name was Pete. After he died, Mrs. Carroll insisted that her son be called A. B. Basically, he's a good, decent man, who loves his job as sheriff. When he was growing up, his mother was constantly telling him that he was fat and dumb. For the first time in his life he's looked up to. He goes along with Doc Herman because he needs that little bit of respect."

"That's a heck of a reason for not doing his duty. There's no excuse for refusing to give a murdered girl justice, even if she was what some of the people here considered a tramp. She was a human being."

"I know, and I'm shocked and disappointed in Pete."

Wearing a light coat because it was a chilly, cloudy day, Kathleen walked down the street toward the courthouse. She reached under the lapel of her coat and felt for her grandma's long wicked hatpin she had put there this morning. From now on she was going to have something handy with which to defend herself.

She entered a high-ceilinged courthouse. It was so quiet that she wondered if she were the only person in the building. The heels of her shoes made tapping sounds as she walked down the long corridor to the records department. Three desks occupied the middle of the office, filing cabinets lined the walls. A man wearing a visor sat at one of the desks. He made no attempt to get up.

"Hello," Kathleen said pleasantly. "I'm Kathleen Dolan from the *Gazette* and—"

"I know who ya are."

"Well, then, I'll get directly to the point. I want to look at the birth records."

"What for?" He pushed back his chair and stood. It was probably as much exercise as he'd had all day. The saying, wide as he is tall, came to Kathleen's mind.

"Are they public records or not?"

"Yes, but—"

"Are they public records or not?" Kathleen repeated.

"Yes, but we can't have just anybody coming in off the street prowling through the records." The man's eyes shifted between Kathleen and the door as if he expected someone to come in.

"I understand that." Kathleen was still trying to be pleasant. "But if you know who I am, you know that I'm from the *Gazette*."

"It don't make any difference where you're *from*."

"Oh, I thought it did. If you're telling me that I can't see the birth records, I'll just run along, see Judge Fimbres, and get a court order."

"What year do you want?" he asked grudgingly.

"All of them," she said with a pleasant smile.

"There's the files." He jerked his head toward three tall files next to the window.

"Are they cross-referenced?"

He walked to a cabinet and flung open a door. Ledgers were stacked on the shelves in alphabetical order.

"Thank you. On which shelf are the birth records?"

"Third."

"Thank you again. You can go on with your work; you've been very helpful."

Kathleen took off her coat and draped it over the back of a chair. After the records clerk moved away, she took out the ledger marked "D" and quickly found DeBerry. Judith DeBerry was born September 30, 1923, to Martha and Donald DeBerry, Fort Worth, Texas. Attending physician, Darrell Herman, M.D. Kathleen jotted the information down on her notepad, closed the ledger, and placed it back on the shelf.

Without looking at the clerk, who was watching her every move, she went to the file cabinets where she found the birth certificates filed by the year. In the 1923 file, she found the DeBerry birth certificate. She quickly thumbed through the documents and discovered that Dr. Herman had delivered twenty-two babies that year, ten of them to out-of-town parents.

More curious than ever now, she quickly wrote down the date of birth, parents' last name, and the place they were from. After she finished with the 1923 file, she went to the 1938 file. So far this year he had delivered thirty babies, sixteen of them had out-of-town parents. The latest birth was last week. The parents were from Tulsa.

An hour later, fingers cramping, feet hurting, Kathleen closed the file. She had listed the last ten years of births in Tillison County. After putting her notebook in her purse, she slipped on her coat.

"Thank you," she said to the man at the desk, and received only a grunt in reply.

As she was going out the door she saw the deputy hurrying down the hallway. She had heard the low murmur of the record clerk's voice, and now it occurred to her that he had called the sheriff's office.

"Well, hello, pretty little lady. Imagine seeing you here." The deputy had a nervous grin on his face. He stood in front of her.

"I'm sure you're surprised."

Kathleen stepped around him and walked down the corridor toward the door. He kept pace with her and when they reached the door, he put his arm out as if to open it. Instead he held it closed.

"What's the hurry?"

"All right, buster. Let's just stop waltzing around. The clerk called you. Why? I was looking at public records. What are you going to do about it? Put me in jail?"

"Maybe. It's against the law to steal public records."

"Are you saying that's what I did?"

"Melvin saw you put them in your purse."

"He couldn't have because I didn't."

"I'll have a look for myself."

"No, you won't!"

"Are you resisting arrest?"

"Damn right." She lifted her hand as if to adjust her coat and pulled the hatpin out of the lapel.

"This can be settled right quick. Give me the handbag." When he reached for it, she viciously jabbed the hatpin in the back of his hand.

"Yeow!" he yelled, and drew his fist back to hit her.

"Hit me, and I'll shove this hatpin all the way to your gizzard."

"What's going on here?" Judge Fimbres had come out of his office and was walking rapidly toward them.

"Look what she did to me, Judge." The deputy held out his hand. Blood was welling from the wound made by the pin. "I was just opening the door for her."

"Judge, he's accusing me of taking public records. I'll be

glad to show you what's in my handbag, but not in front of him!"

"Did you see her take something, Thatcher?"

"Melvin called. He said she put some records in that bag."

"Come into my office, Miss Dolan." The deputy followed them back down the hall. "Stay outside, Thatcher."

"You know my name," Kathleen said when the door was closed.

"Barker Fleming spoke of you. Now let's see what you have in the handbag and get this mess straightened out."

Kathleen put the hatpin back in the lapel of her coat, opened her purse, and dumped the notebook, pencils, compact, lipstick, comb, and several bobby pins onto the desk. From a compartment on the side of the purse, she brought out her coin purse, car keys, and a small folder with the pictures of her grandparents. She extended the empty handbag to the judge. He shook his head. She turned the pockets in her coat inside out.

"Why did Deputy Thatcher think you had taken something?"

"The record clerk called him." Kathleen began putting things back in her bag. "I came to look at the birth records. We had an inquiry from a girl looking for her mother, and I wanted to see if the mother's maiden name was on the girl's birth certificate."

"Was it?"

"Yes." She looked steadily at him. "I wrote it down on a pad and put it in my purse. I poked the deputy with the hatpin when he attempted to grab it."

The judge chuckled and shook his head. When he opened the door, the deputy was standing close to it.

"Did we talk loud enough, Thatcher?" Judge Fimbres asked drily.

"Huh? Look at my hand. I ought to arrest her for attacking an officer." Blood showed through the handkerchief he had wrapped around his hand.

"It's what you get for grabbing a young lady's breast, Thatcher. You should know better."

Kathleen's eyes shot to the judge, then to the gaping deputy.

"Her . . . brr . . . brr—" The startled man couldn't get the word out. "She's a liar."

"You can file charges, but I warn you when the case comes to my court you will be the one to pay the court cost."

"You believe her over me?"

"You have a reputation of being less than respectful to ladies, Thatcher. We both know that." The judge held open the door for Kathleen. "I'm sorry, my dear, that you received such despicable treatment in our courthouse. I'll speak to Sheriff Carroll. Deputy Thatcher should be relieved from duty if such conduct continues."

"Thank you, Judge Fimbres."

Kathleen managed to keep the smile off her face until she reached the sidewalk.

"I like that Judge Fimbres."

Kathleen had just finished telling Adelaide what had occurred at the courthouse.

"Forevermore! That beats all. That jackass was going to take your notebook." Adelaide's eyes brightened in response to her anger.

"Well, he didn't get it." Kathleen flopped the shorthand book down on her desk. "I can't believe how many babies have been born right here in Tillison County, and since 1925. Doc Herman delivered most all of them."

"Of course he delivered them. He's the only doctor in the county. A few babies are delivered by midwives."

"I found a few of those. There is something else interesting here. Hazel told me that a little over a year ago, Clara came home pregnant. Her baby was stillborn, which is no surprise considering how she lives. There wasn't a birth certificate in the file with Clara Ramsey's name on it. Even if the child was stillborn, it was born."

"I remember when that happened. She left town right after that."

"My grandmother used to say, 'There's something rotten in Denmark.' She meant cheese. I'm referring to that clinic."

In the middle of the afternoon Kathleen looked up from the chart on her desk to see Doc Herman standing in front of the window looking at the pictures she had put on the bulletin board. He was wearing a gray overcoat. A gray felt hat sat on his head at a jaunty angle. When he came into the office, she kept her head bent over her desk and continued to write dates on the chart until he spoke.

"Do you like stirring up folks, Miss Dolan?"

Kathleen looked up and smiled. "Why, hello, Dr. Herman." She pointedly slid a sheet of paper over the chart on her desk to cover the figures she was working on. "What do you mean by stirring up folks?"

"I think you know what I mean. You don't appear to be thickheaded."

Kathleen laughed. "Thank you."

She began to feel good about this encounter. Her cheerfulness irritated him. A frown covered his foxlike features.

He stared at her, thinking that his silence would intimidate her. She stared back, not allowing her gaze to waver.

"Is there something you wanted? Have you reconsidered writing a column for us on the history of Rawlings? In Liberal we had an older man who wrote a column for the *Press*. His column was full of little anecdotes of long-ago Liberal. A column about the olden days in Rawlings by you, Doctor, would be very popular."

It was evident that the doctor was having a hard time hiding his anger. His lips were a tight line; his eyes narrowed, and his nostrils flared.

"Young lady, I suggest you get in touch with the paper in Liberal and see if you can get your job back."

"Why would I want to do that? This town is jumping with news. It's a reporter's heaven. Saturday was the rodeo. A big success, by the way. That night my tire was slashed right on Main Street. Can you imagine that? Yesterday a murdered girl was found in a ditch along a rural road. There is more news in this town in a week than in six months in Liberal."

"Where is Adelaide?"

"I think that she and Paul are in the rooms above. The day after paper day is usually slow. It gives them some time to be together," she added in a conspiratorial tone.

The doctor looked at her for a long moment, then turned and walked out the door. Kathleen knew that she had made an enemy, a powerful enemy. But if what she suspected was true, the man was an unscrupulous, money-grabber who took advantage of desperate people. The thing that troubled her was how was she going to prove it.

"Kathleen!" Adelaide exclaimed after being told about the doctor's visit. "He must be madder than a wet hen."

"I don't care how mad he is. There is something here in these records that stinks to high heaven. I need someone with know-how to help me ferret this out." Kathleen tapped her pencil on the desk, then suddenly got to her feet. "I think we should keep Judy here, out of sight, until we find out what's going on. She could be part of this. If she's out on the street asking questions, something could happen to her."

"Paul agrees with you, and so do I."

"Are you and Paul thinking the same thing I am?"

"We think that he's selling babies. But where is he getting them?"

"It has to be from unwed mothers."

"This is dangerous, Kathleen. I'm worried about you."

"They wouldn't dare hurt me if I can get someone with influence on our side. The only one I know that may be able to pull strings is Mr. Fleming, and he's in Elk City."

"Do you know him that well?"

"I know him well enough. He said if I ever needed him, to call Elk City, but with Flossie's loose mouth—" Kathleen paced to the door and back to her desk. "What the heck. I'm going to call anyway. I'll think of something."

"He might not want to come back down here."

"I won't know until I ask him." Kathleen sat down at her desk and pulled the phone toward her. She lifted the receiver from the cradle and waited for Flossie to answer.

"That you, Adelaide?"

"No, it's Kathleen Dolan. I want to place a call to Mr. Barker Fleming in Elk City. I don't know the number, but I'm sure the operator can find him."

"Is this person-to-person?"

"Of course."

"Person-to-person costs more than station-to-station."

"I know that. I want to speak with Mr. Fleming." Kathleen rolled her eyes toward the ceiling, and Adelaide smiled.

Three or four minutes passed before Flossie came back on the line.

"The operator rang Old Mr. Fleming. He said he was at his ranch. She's ringing now. It'll be a minute . . . oh, here he is. Mr. Barker, you have a person-to-person call from Kathleen Dolan in Rawlings."

"Put her on, operator. Kathleen, is everything all right?"

"Yes, yes, I'm sorry if I alarmed you. I left the picnic basket in your car, and I was wondering when you would be coming back down here. The basket belongs to Mrs. Ramsey and she'll be needing it soon."

"I see." During the small silence Kathleen held her breath. "Have you spoken to anyone about that matter we discussed?"

"Not really, but I have seen the party you were interested in. I don't think the situation is hopeless."

"That's encouraging."

"Mr. Fleming, I really do need the picnic basket. Of course, if you're busy, I'll understand."

"As a matter of fact, I'm coming down to the tannery day after tomorrow. Will you need the basket before then?"

"No. Day after tomorrow will be fine. If you'd drop the basket off at the *Gazette* office, I'd appreciate it."

"I'll be glad to. See you on Friday."

"Good-bye and thank you."

Kathleen hung up the receiver. "He's coming down on Friday and will come to the office."

"Kathleen Dolan, that was quick thinking. He caught on right away, didn't he?"

"There was a short silence . . . at first. I feel better already just knowing that we can lay all this out; and if there is something here, which I certainly think there is, he may be able to help us with it."

"You've opened a can of worms, Kathleen."

"I'd appreciate it if you didn't say anything to Johnny about my calling Mr. Fleming. He doesn't like him very much."

"He's jealous. Johnny is falling in love with you. If you have no feelings for him, let him think you like Mr. Fleming. It will be easier for him in the long run."

"Mr. Fleming is a friend, nothing more, and never will be," Kathleen said firmly. Then her tone softened, and she murmured sadly, "Johnny could very well break my heart."

Chapter Twenty

JOHNNY STOPPED BY THE OFFICE shortly before time for the funeral. He wore a dark suit, white shirt, and string tie. He was absolutely handsome. Kathleen couldn't move her eyes away from him.

"I know enough to dress up for a funeral," he said defensively.

"I was just thinking that you clean up pretty well."

"Hazel asked me to be a pallbearer."

"She told me this morning. She's worried there'll not be very many at the funeral."

"Clara's reputation was not the best."

"Adelaide and I will be there . . . for Hazel and Emily."

"I'll go with Eldon." He stopped at the door and looked back. "You clean up good, too." He winked at her.

Kathleen's heart hammered, and a fluttering sensation settled in the pit of her stomach. She had wanted to look nice today because she knew she would see him. She wore a navy blue dress of soft material, its full skirt gathered onto the bodice. A wide sash with small, light blue flowers circled her waist and tied on the side. Her hair, bright from a rainwater washing, curled softly about her face and shoulders. Around her neck was a silver chain and hanging from it a small locket.

The church was half-filled when Kathleen and Adelaide arrived. It was a testimony to Hazel's standing in the community. The service was an opportunity for the preacher to preach a "hellfire and brimstone" sermon, and he took full advantage of it.

When it was finally over, the congregation stood while the casket was wheeled out followed by Hazel and Emily. The mourners quickly left the church to follow the hearse to the cemetery. It was then that Kathleen saw Dr. Herman helping Hazel and Emily into the backseat of a big black car. Louise Munday was with him.

"Look at that . . . that hypocrite," Kathleen exclaimed.

"He plays every angle. That's how he keeps his popularity up."

"He knows damn well that girl was murdered."

"Like I said . . . this is his town, and he'll not have it soiled by a murder."

"It's more likely that he's afraid he'll get a Federal Marshal in here."

At the gravesite Sheriff Carroll and another man stepped forward to help Johnny and the undertaker carry the casket to its final resting place. Kathleen seethed to see Dr. Herman and Louise flanking Hazel and Emily as they stood beside the gaping hole to watch Clara's body being lowered into the ground.

Poor little Emily. Kathleen remembered her own anguish as she stood with her grandparents at her mother's burial. It was a consolation to know that Emily's life would not be as disrupted as hers had been. The child had not been attached to Clara as a child is normally attached to her mother. In time she would forget the bad things about her mother and remember only the times when Clara came home bringing presents.

Dr. Herman and Louise stood by as if they were family while the mourners came to express their sympathy to Hazel then shake hands with the doctor. After hugging Hazel, Kathleen stooped down to whisper to Emily.

"Your grandma is so lucky to have you, Sugarpuss. You'll take care of her, and she'll take care of you. After a while it will not hurt so much. I'll see you tonight."

Kathleen straightened, looked directly into Dr. Herman's eyes, but didn't offer her hand as the others had done. She met the eyes of the smirking woman who stood beside him. Louise was a half head taller than the doctor even with his hat on. She wore a black coat with a huge silver fox collar. Attached to her small black hat was a black-dotted veil that came down to her penciled brows. On her face was the usual heavy coat of makeup.

Kathleen looked at the woman, and needing to do something to show her contempt, rolled her eyes in a derisive gesture. Louise's cheeks became suffused with color, her balled gloved fists evidence of her surprised anger.

Johnny was waiting beside the car when they reached it.

"Are you going to the house?"

"No. I told Hazel this morning that we'd not come."

Johnny held open the passenger-side door, plainly indicating that he was going to drive. Kathleen dug into her purse for the keys. He stilled her hand and, dangling her extra set between his thumb and forefinger, smirked at her.

"The extra set wouldn't do much good if you can't keep track of them."

"You're . . . sneaky!" She slid onto the seat, moved to the middle to make room for Adelaide, removed her hat, and looped her hair behind her ear with trembling fingers. *Lord! Why do I get the trembles when I'm with him?*

Johnny's hand brushed her knee when he grasped the round ball handle on the gearshift. Her shoulder was behind his, her hip tight against him. It was such a wonderful feeling to be sitting close to him that Kathleen had to caution herself not to be giddy.

"Dr. Herman and Louise were acting like family," Kathleen said in order to occupy her mind with something other than the man beside her. "He's got a lot of nerve. I've never heard Hazel even mention him."

"He wasn't there for Hazel. He was there to show the public how much he *cared*." Adelaide's tone was heavily sarcastic.

"I took the pictures down to Vernon yesterday to show Keith. He agrees that Clara was not hit by a car. A car going forty miles an hour would have tossed her into the ditch, but wouldn't have crushed her windpipe and knocked her teeth out."

"The next question," Adelaide said, "is why. She wasn't raped, or was she?"

"Eldon said there was no evidence that she was." Johnny parked the car in front of the *Gazette*, turned, and put his arm across the back of the seat. "Whoever killed her was in a rage. She wasn't just run over. She was beaten up in a car because there was very little blood at the scene. Afterward he pushed her out of the car, then ran over her as she lay in the road. To be sure that she was dead, he stopped the car and got out. She was still alive, probably trying to get up. He pushed her over and stomped on her back. She may have yelled. That's when he stomped on her neck and crushed her windpipe. After that he dragged her into the ditch."

"That makes sense," Kathleen said proudly. "You'd make a good detective, Johnny."

"Yeah? I thought about it, but I don't like living in the city."

"Oh, dear, there's Hannah, and she's drunk again." Adelaide opened the car door.

Johnny's hand slipped from the back of the seat and squeezed Kathleen's shoulder. His arm tightened for just an instant before he withdrew it and got out of the car.

"I'll take her home, Adelaide. Keep her here while I get my truck."

"No need for that, Johnny," Kathleen said quickly. "Take my car."

Johnny went to where Hannah was leaning against the building.

"Come on, Hannah. I'll take you home."

"Baby—" She looked up at Johnny with big sad eyes. "Baby, baby," she babbled.

She had once been a pretty girl. Now her face was ravaged and gray streaked her raven black hair. Her dress was well worn, but clean.

"Where is your baby, Hannah?" Kathleen asked.

"Baby . . . gone . . . gone—" Tears rolled down her cheeks.

"Did your baby die?" Kathleen asked insistently. Then repeated the question. "Did your baby die?"

Hannah continued to babble and tried to pull away from Johnny, who was holding her up.

"Johnny will take you home," Adelaide said soothingly. "He's a nice man, Hannah. He won't hurt you."

"Whis . . . key—"

"I think you've had enough," Johnny said kindly as he tried to steer her toward the car.

"Leave her alone!"

Kathleen jerked her head around at the belligerent tone and saw the sheriff hurrying toward them.

"Don't you dare arrest her and put her in your rotten jail so that . . . that pervert of a deputy can molest her. Don't you dare!"

"Shut her up!" Sheriff Carroll said to Johnny.

"She can say what she wants, and I'll back her up."

"Hannah's drunk, Pete," Adelaide said. "Johnny's going to take her home."

"Hannah, you . . . promised."

Kathleen's sharp ears heard the murmured remark.

"I'll take her home." Pete elbowed Johnny out of the way and put his arm around Hannah to hold her up.

"Where is she getting the whiskey?" Adelaide asked.

"I don't know, but when I find out, somebody's head's goin' to roll." The sheriff guided Hannah across the sidewalk to the car and opened the door.

"No, Pete—"

"Get in, Hannah." Pete eased her down on the seat, lifted her feet to the floor of the car, and closed the door. Without a word, he got under the wheel and drove away.

Paul got up from Adelaide's desk when they entered the office and helped her off with her coat.

"Where's Judy?" Adelaide asked, when she heard a familiar sound coming from the back room.

"At the linotype machine." Paul grinned. "I've been showing her how to use it. She's a smart kid."

"Forevermore! She'll hurt herself with that hot lead."

"No, she won't, mother hen," Paul said affectionately. "She'll be careful."

"I hope so. Landsakes, whatever caused you to let her touch your precious machine?"

"She's at the age to learn things, honey. Her mind is like a sponge. That girl needs to know that someone has confidence in her."

"Paul darlin', you're right as usual."

"Of course, I am. Remember that the next time we get into an argument." He hung her coat on the hall tree. "Were there very many at the funeral?"

"Hazel's friends turned out. Doc and Louise were there being very solicitous of Hazel and Emily. Kathleen, did you see the spray of fresh gladiolas? They must have come in on the bus from a greenhouse and must have cost four or five dollars. Who around here has that kind of money to spend on flowers?"

"Doc Herman."

"But why would he send flowers to Clara Ramsey's funeral?"

"It looked to me like he was trying to throw up a smoke screen. It was overdone. He probably sent the big ham I saw this morning on Hazel's kitchen table. The show-off!"

"Smoke screen? You think he could have killed her? What reason would he have?"

"Maybe they were . . . ah maybe he was . . . you know—"

"I doubt that it was Doc's car that ran over Clara, if that's what you're thinking," Johnny said. "His car was the only big one at the cemetery beside the hearse. The tread on his tires is a different shape. Does Louise Munday have a car?"

Adelaide answered. "An Oldsmobile."

"If I get a chance, I'll take a look at the tires."

"Louise was dressed to kill," Adelaide said.

"She looked like a moose in that big fur collar." Kathleen broke into laughter. "It was really catty of me to say that." Her eyes flashed to Johnny and found him watching her with a sweet and tender smile on his quiet face. She couldn't look away and became lost in depths of his dark eyes. Only Paul's voice talking about Hannah brought her back to the present.

"Hannah came to the door, but she was too drunk to open it. I didn't help her because I was afraid it might cause problems if someone came in and found her in here alone with me."

Adelaide explained that just as Johnny was getting ready to take her home, the sheriff arrived.

"Did you notice how gentle he was with her?" Kathleen asked. "He was that way the other night. She called him Pete. Isn't that what he was called when he was young?"

"They knew each other quite well at one time, but Pete's mother was dead set against him having anything to do with an Indian, even a half-breed Cherokee whose daddy had a large spread and a good herd of cattle at one time. Heck Lawson was well respected in the town, even if he did have an Indian wife. He lost most of his land during the twenties and died shortly after."

"Where does Hannah live?"

"Out on the edge of town with her mother and a brother who works at the tannery."

"She isn't married?"

"Never has been as far as I know."

"Who was the father of the baby she had just before I got here?"

Adelaide lifted her shoulders. "Who knows."

"Last night I asked Hazel about the baby Clara had a year ago. She said Doc Herman told Clara that it was dead when he took it from her and that it was badly deformed. He put it in a box and had it buried on the lot beside

Hazel's husband. Hazel felt bad that it didn't get a proper burial."

"A plank with the word *baby* and the date is there. I saw it while I was helping Eldon," Johnny said.

"And shortly after Clara had that baby she had enough money to leave town."

"I'd like to know what's in the box buried out there by Sam Ramsey," Adelaide said.

"Watch it, Johnny," Paul warned. "These two have something devious on their minds."

"Why are you interested in what's buried on the Ramsey lot?" Johnny asked.

"We've got another mystery on our hands, Johnny. I haven't had a chance to tell you about it."

"You can't tell him now," Adelaide said quickly. "Here comes Leroy."

"Don't make a date for tonight," Johnny said to Kathleen as he and Paul hurried to the back room.

"Afternoon, Leroy," Adelaide said as he came into the office. Kathleen echoed the greeting. She didn't have time to completely digest Johnny's words, but she felt wonderful.

"Hello, Adelaide, Miss Dolan."

"If you're thinking about an ad, Leroy, we've got a new ad book."

"No. I . . . ah . . . well—" Looking only at Adelaide, he stood on first one foot and then the other as he struggled for words.

"What is it?"

"We had a Chamber meeting this morning."

"I didn't know or I'd have been there."

"It was a special meeting, Adelaide. About you . . . the paper."

"For goodness sake. What about me . . . the paper?"

"Some feel that you're taking too much on yourself to question the sheriff's decision about . . . the accident."

"That's what papers do all the time, Leroy. It's our job to question."

"We . . . ah want you to stop it and take that board out of the window."

For a minute or two silence throbbed between them. Leroy rocked back and forth on his heels, Adelaide looking steadily at him. Finally she spoke.

"If I don't do as you wish, what will you do?"

"Stop advertising."

"That's the word that came down from Doc Herman?"

"We all think that it's bad for the town."

"You weak-kneed, spineless jackass!" The words burst from Kathleen as she shot to her feet. "A girl has been brutally murdered in this town. Her reputation was not the best, but she was a living, breathing human being. Would you feel the same if it had been . . . an upstanding citizen like . . . Louise Munday?"

"Sheriff Carroll says that it was an accident. It was night, the driver may not have even known he hit her. She was drunk and staggering down the road."

"The sheriff is so tied in with Doc Herman that he'll say anything Doc tells him to say. I'm disappointed in you, Mr. Grandon. I thought you were one man in this town with a mind of his own."

"I've got a business here. I've got to get along."

"At the price of losing your integrity?"

"You're new here. You don't understand."

"I'm not new, Leroy, and I don't understand how a group of grown men can knuckle under to one-man rule," Adelaide said.

"I'm just carrying the message, Adelaide."

"Here's one you can carry back. You tell that dim-witted bunch, who have no more backbone than jellyfish, that I'll not take that poster out of the window; and if they withhold their advertising, so be it. I carried every one of them, including you, Leroy, until I almost went broke. I'll not let you or them or Doc Herman tell me what to do."

"Hurrah!" Kathleen shouted and clapped her hands. The red-faced man glanced at her and then away.

"I'm sorry you feel that way, Adelaide. We've been friends for a long time."

"Not friends, Leroy, or you'd have stood up with me for what is right."

"I've told you. It's all I can do."

"No, it isn't," Kathleen said. "You can get those merchants together and tell them it's time to take their town back from the tyrant who's had control for so long."

"The town has prospered under his control," Leroy replied bellicosely.

"You're mistaken," Adelaide said quietly. "The prosperity here is due to the tannery, and you know it. Who comes to buy at your store, Leroy? Could you make it without the tannery people?"

"They help," he admitted, "but Doc Herman sees to it that we have law and order. He talks to our congressman to get WPA projects for our city. His clinic brings people to town, and they buy gasoline, food, and lodging."

"The congressman is obligated to spread the projects over the counties in his district. Rawlings is the only town in the county any larger than a wide spot in the road. There are not enough votes in Tillison County for anyone in Washington to pay any attention to a pipsqueak like Doc

Herman. He has you all buffaloed." Disgusted, Kathleen flopped back down on her chair.

"I've told you what the Chamber members think, Adelaide. The rest is up to you." Leroy turned quickly and left the office.

"Adelaide, I'm sorry. This wouldn't have happened if I hadn't come here."

"No, I would've rocked along and lost the paper anyway. I hate to think that you may lose your investment."

"If we lose it, we'll go down fighting, and I intend to do everything I can to take Doc Herman and Louise down with me. If I have to do it all by myself, I'm going out to the cemetry and dig up that box he buried on the Ramsey lot. I'll bet my entire interest in this paper that it will be empty."

"I swear, Kathleen. Doesn't anything get you down?"

"Some things get me lower than a snake's belly, but not him. He just gets me mad." Her blue eyes were hard and shone with rage.

"I'm proud of you, love." Paul's voice came from the doorway before he came on into the office and went to stand behind Adelaide's chair. His hands massaged her shoulders.

"We may lose the paper, Paul."

"It wouldn't be the end of the world, would it? I know it means a lot to you; but if we have to leave, we'll still be together."

Adelaide's hand went up to cover his.

Kathleen felt an ache in her heart. Not at the thought of losing her investment, but with a longing to have the kind of love Adelaide and Paul shared.

"Did Johnny leave?"

"He went home to do chores. He said to tell you to be

ready to go honky-tonking and that he'd come to Hazel's to get you."

"Honky-tonking? For crying out loud. That's the last place I'd've thought he'd want to go."

"Tell Johnny about the birth records and how the deputy tried to get your notebook."

"I also have to tell him that Barker Fleming is coming tomorrow. I kind of dread telling him that."

Chapter Twenty-one

Dr. Herman walked Hazel and Emily to the porch.

"Do you have time to come in, Doctor?"

"No, thank you, Mrs. Ramsey. I've a patient waiting at the clinic. I must get back. I wanted to make sure that you and the child were all right. It was a terrible accident, just terrible. If there's anything I can do, anything at all, send word. If I'm unable to come myself, I'll send someone."

"Thank you, Doctor. Is there a chance they'll find out who . . . who ran over Clara?"

"Not much, dear lady. The driver could be deep in Texas by now. He may have hit her and been too frightened to stop. It happens in and around the cities. It's something new for us here in Tillison County."

"Thank you for the ham."

"You're welcome." He glanced at the street. People were coming by car and on foot. "You're going to have plenty of friends to share the rest of the day with you. I'll run along."

" 'Bye, Doctor, and thanks again."

Dr. Herman made his escape back to his car without having to stop and chat with the mourners. They were well away from the house before he spoke to Louise.

"That little problem is solved."

"It cost you a ham and flowers."

"Cheap compared to what she was going to stick us for."

"Do you think the sheriff will stay in line?"

"He will. He likes the prestige of being sheriff."

"You understand that we have a problem bigger than Clara was."

"I'm not deaf or blind, Louise."

"I didn't mean that you are," she said hastily. "Mitchell said that Dolan woman from the paper was fooling around in the records department at the courthouse."

"And he would have stopped her if not for that old fool Judge Fimbres. You told me that," he added impatiently.

"The excuse she gave for looking at the records is as thin as water."

"It could be that she was doing just what she said she was. It certainly would be the place to go to look up the maiden name of someone's mother."

"The records clerk told Mitchell that she wrote some things down in a notebook."

"Where else would she write down the information, for God's sake? Use your head, Louise."

Louise was becoming irritated at his logical reasoning where that redheaded bitch was concerned. She had devoted her life to Darrell Herman. The least he could do would be to agree with her once in a while. After all the years they had worked together, he was still a mystery to her. She was sure that he was capable of doing whatever needed to be done to rid them of Clara's threat. That was all right with her; it made him even more fascinating. The little man had a steel trap for a mind and the guts to go with it.

"I wonder what really happened to Clara," she said as they neared the clinic.

"Don't play games with me, Louise." Doc's eyes were as cold as a stone. "We both know what happened to Clara. Don't speak of it again."

It was already dark when Kathleen left the office at six. She, Adelaide, and Paul had had a talk with Judy. They explained their suspicions about the number of births at Doc Herman's clinic and why they wanted to keep her reason for being here quiet for a while. Adelaide had spoken to Mrs. Wilson, and she had agreed to *forget* about Judy being in her store.

After a couple of days' rest and good food, Judy was a different girl. She was bright, personable, and had become attached to Paul, drinking in every word he said. Adelaide explained that the girl probably had never had attention from her father other than in a derisive way and was fascinated with Paul because he treated her like a young person with a mind. It confirmed Adelaide's belief that Paul would make a wonderful father.

Kathleen left the car behind the house and went in through the kitchen. Hazel and one of her friends were putting away the leftovers of the food that had been brought in to serve after the funeral.

"Hello, Mrs. Ashley, Hazel." Kathleen put her arm around Hazel. "You doing all right?"

"I guess so. I'm still in shock."

"It was a nice funeral." Kathleen didn't know how any funeral could be *nice*, but it was something people seemed to say at a time like this.

"Even Dr. Herman came," Mrs. Ashley said. "Wasn't it good of him, being so busy and all?"

"Very good." Kathleen dropped a kiss on the top of Emily's head. "Hi, Sugarpuss."

"Grandma saved you some supper."

"Good. I'm starved. Let me get out of this dress, and I'll be right back."

Kathleen hadn't even been aware that she was hungry. Her mind was forging ahead to the date with Johnny and what she would wear. She changed into a soft blue blouse and a black jersey skirt gathered on a wide band. She exchanged the spike heels she had been wearing all day for a pair of pumps with medium heels.

After cleaning her face and applying fresh makeup, she went back to the kitchen.

"My, you look nice." Hazel placed a clean plate at the end of the table so that Kathleen could help herself from the platters and bowls of food.

"You smell good," Emily whispered.

"Thank you," Kathleen whispered back, and helped herself to a slice of smoked ham. She felt guilty being so happy when she looked at Emily's sad little face.

Johnny followed Hazel into the kitchen after she had answered his knock on the door. Kathleen's heart jumped alarmingly when his dark eyes caught and held hers. He was back in his twill pants, white shirt, and boots. She was glad that she hadn't dressed up.

"I was going to take you to Claude's for a hamburger."

"I like Claude's hamburgers, but this ham and potato salad is delicious."

"Sit down, Johnny, and help yourself. There's plenty here, and I don't want any of it to spoil." Hazel placed a plate in front of him.

"Do you have ice in your box?" he asked.

"It's chuck full. Dr. Herman sent the iceman down."

When Kathleen went to her room to get her purse, Emily went with her. Kathleen placed a little dab of *Coty* perfume behind Emily's ears and powdered her nose with the puff from her compact.

"Are ya comin' back?"

"Of course, honey. I'm just going out with Johnny for a while."

"Don't go to one of them old . . . honky-tonks. Mama did, and she didn't come back."

"Don't worry, Sugarpuss. I'll be back. I promise."

Johnny had spread a clean blanket over the seat in the truck. After he started the motor, he reached for her arm and pulled until she moved over into the middle of the seat.

"This is a date. You're not supposed to sit way over there."

"Do all your dates sit this close to you?"

"Only the pretty redheaded ones."

Kathleen's breath suspended. "Where are we going?" She really didn't care. This was all so new, so wonderful.

"To the Twilight Gardens."

"The honky-tonk?"

"You got something against honky-tonks?" He grinned down at her. "You said you liked to dance."

"I do. Emily asked me not to go to one because her mama did, and she didn't come back."

"That's why we're going. If Clara was there, we may be able to find out who she was with."

"Didn't Sheriff Carroll try to find out where she had been that night?"

"No, he closed the case. That's why we're going to nose around."

"And you need me to do that?"

"Of course."

Kathleen wrinkled her nose. "So you're just using me as a prop for your sleuthing?"

"Pretty smart of me, huh?" His lighthearted words and his smile set her heart dancing.

"It'll depend on how successful you are."

Cars were parked in front and alongside the Twilight Gardens when they pulled in and stopped. Traveling neon lights, in a zigzag pattern, ran across the front of the building. A beer sign flashed in one of the windows.

"Here we are," Johnny said, but made no attempt to get out. "This isn't a very fancy place."

"I didn't expect it to be."

"I heard what Grandon said today. Will you lose the paper if the merchants stop advertising?"

"Maybe. But we won't go down without a fight. I'll write a story about the reason for their boycott and spread it all over the front page. Our subscribers buy the paper for news as well as the advertisements. The merchants' boycott could backfire on them."

Johnny reached out to touch her hair. "Come on, my feisty little redhead. Let's see what we can find out."

Even coming in from the outside, Kathleen's eyes took a minute or two to adjust to the dim lights. A row of booths surrounded a small dance floor where couples were swaying to a slow waltz. A big nickelodeon, with a rainbow of lights, stood at one end of the room and a bar at the other.

"Howdy, cowboy. That's Johnny Henry, the *All-Around Cowboy*." The voice came from one of the booths.

"Howdy."

"Hey, Johnny. Good ridin'."

"Thanks."

Johnny steered her along the edge of the dance floor to

an empty booth at the end. Kathleen scooted in, and he slid in beside her. They had a clear view of the entire room.

"You've got friends here."

"Not friends. They saw me at the rodeo."

"Do you come here very often?"

"A couple times a month when I want to get a cold glass of 3.2. Oklahoma only sells beer with 3.2 percent of alcohol. Some people go across the river to get stronger Texas beer. What will you have? Coke or beer?"

"Coke."

Kathleen watched him as he went along the row of booths to the bar. He stopped a couple of times along the way to speak to people who hailed him. He spoke with the man behind the counter for a minute or two then returned with two bottles.

"Like I said, it isn't fancy. No glasses."

"That's all right. I've drunk out of a bottle before." Kathleen placed his hat on the seat beside her to move it away from the water left by the wet bottles. She wiped the neck of the Coke bottle with her handkerchief and took a deep swallow. "Whee . . . the fizz goes up my nose!"

As they watched the couples on the dance floor, Johnny reached for her hand. She folded her fingers over his, pressing her soft palm tightly to his rough one. Kathleen was as certain as she was breathing that this man would forever occupy a place in her heart. She shoved from her mind the knowledge that before the evening was over she must tell him that Barker Fleming would be in Rawlings the next day. He was going to be angry, and she dreaded that.

"Do you want to dance?" The soft inquiry brought her eyes to his. He was watching her with a half smile on his face. "Let your Coke sit a while and it'll not be so fizzy."

"Your beer will get warm."

"You've not been paying attention, Miss Dolan. I finished my beer."

"Oh, my goodness. I must have been daydreaming."

"Come dance with me. 'Springtime in the Rockies' is a good slow one. Just right for an old cowboy like me."

"You really are old, you know," Kathleen teased as she slid out of the booth.

Johnny took her hand, put his arm around her, and drew her close. She allowed him to mold her body to his and gave herself up to his tight embrace. When he moved it was impossible not to move with him. Her hand on his shoulder slipped up until she could feel the hair at the nape of his neck. He pressed his cheek tightly to the side of her head. Her heart throbbed in her throat.

"You're very soft and sweet tonight, Miss Dolan." He tipped his head and his lips tickled her ear when he spoke.

"You're full of blarney, fer sure, me boy," she answered in a breathless whisper.

Kathleen's eyes were half-closed, and for a short while she forgot that anyone else existed except the two of them. Johnny was a wonderful dancer. Their steps fit perfectly. Kathleen floated in a golden haze. He moved his head, and she tilted hers to look at him. His dark eyes were warm and his mouth slightly tilted at the corners. Emotion was there on his face. Was it love? Whatever it was, it had the power to stop her breath. His arms tightened convulsively when her lashes fluttered down. He pressed his cheek to her hair again, and they glided around the small dance floor to the strains of the slow waltz.

Johnny brought them to a halt when the music stopped. He took a step back, then lifted a hand to finger-comb the hair back from her temple.

"I like your hair. It reminds me of a sunset." A slow smile lit his face. "Shall we try it again? You're good at keeping my big old boots from stomping on your feet."

"They didn't even come close. You're a great, I might even say magnificent, dancer."

His arms closed around her and they began to move to the music coming from the jukebox. Bing Crosby was singing: *When the blue of the night meets the gold of the day, someone waits for you*—Johnny didn't understand what he was feeling. He didn't have words to describe it. There might not even be words. All he knew was that holding this woman in his arms was wonderful, different from anything he ever felt before.

The sheen of her fiery red hair, the delicacy of her profile, and the strength of her personality were enough to intimidate any man. To a dumb cowboy like him she was . . . unreachable. Yet here she was, in his arms and enjoying it. He wasn't so dumb, he told himself, that he didn't know that.

The music ended. They stepped back and looked at each other.

"Shall we go see if your Coke has lost some of its fizz?" Johnny's lips felt stiff as he spoke. His hand rested at her waist as they walked back to their booth. He leaned over to speak to her after she was seated. "Will you be all right for a few minutes? Someone just came in that I'd like to speak to."

"About Clara? Go ahead, I'll be fine."

Johnny crossed the room to where two young cowboys leaned against the wall. They worked on a ranch just outside of town, and both had participated in the events at the rodeo.

"Howdy, Buddy. Hi, Mack."

"I've not seen you out here before, Johnny."

"Showing my girlfriend the sights. Twilight Gardens is one of them."

"She's a looker, Johnny. But I guess the *All-Around Cowboy* has the pick of the litter, huh?" Buddy gave Johnny a good-natured slap on the shoulder.

"It helped," Johnny said confidentially out of the side of his mouth. "Listen, fellows, I'm kind of in a pickle. Were you all here Monday night?"

"Yeah, we came by. It was kind of late."

"Was Clara Ramsey here?"

The young men looked at each other. Finally one of them said, "Yeah."

"Was she with someone?"

"If she was, you'd never know it. She was booth-hoppin' all over the place. Even me'n Buddy could've taken her out for a while if we'd a had the price."

"Here's my problem, boys, and I don't want my lady friend to know it. Clara got hold of my *All-Around Cowboy* belt buckle. I won't tell you how."

Buddy snickered. "You don't have to. We've got a idey."

"When they found her in the ditch, it wasn't on her. I've got to think that she gave it to someone she was with, or sold it. I want to find that man and get it back."

"Wish we could help you, Johnny. We met a couple of girls and you know—"

"Did you see her talking to anyone you know?"

"She was talking to everyone."

"She sat in the corner for a while with Gus Webb," Mack said.

"Gus Webb. Someone said the sheriff had run him outta town."

"He might of, but he come back. He was here Monday night and again last night."

"If he's got my buckle, I'll work him over till I get it back. Thanks, fellows. Keep this under your hats will you. I don't want folks to think I was dumb enough to let some woman take it from me."

"Sure, Johnny."

Johnny went back to Kathleen. She moved to make room for him to sit beside her.

"Clara was here Monday night. I guess she was making a show of herself."

"Was she with anyone?"

"Everyone, I guess. The boys said she was in a back booth for a while with Gus Webb."

"Well, for goodness sake! Do you think he killed her?"

"Not with that old car of his. Are you ready to leave? I've talked to the bartender. He won't admit that she was even here. He's afraid it'll hurt business."

Kathleen handed Johnny his hat, then took the hand he offered as she slid out of the booth. They walked along the side of the dance floor toward the door. As they passed the two young cowboys, Johnny winked. One of them snickered.

Gene Autry was singing "Be Nobody's Darling But Mine," as they left the smoke-filled tavern. Kathleen appreciated the clean, cool air. She held tightly to Johnny's arm as they walked across the uneven ground to his truck. Once they were inside, she shivered.

"Are you cold?" Johnny asked.

"I should have worn my coat."

"Come here." She moved close to him. He put his arm around her and pulled her closer. "I'd like for us to sit out here for a while to see if Webb shows up, but I don't want you freezing while we do it."

Kathleen cuddled against his warm body. "You're warm," she whispered, snuggling her cold nose against his neck.

"You're . . . sweet—" His voice was husky. "I may have to kiss you."

"I couldn't stop you. You're bigger than I am."

"In that case—" His fingers tilted her chin. His mouth was warm and gentle. Every bone in her body turned to jelly. His hands moved across her back and hips, tucked her closer to the granite strength of his body and moved his fingers over the soft mound of her breast. He continued to press sweet kisses to her moist parted lips before his mouth trailed to her ear.

Kathleen's mind felt like it was floating. Primitive desire grew inside her, and she became helpless to stop it. She clung to him weakly, giving back kiss for kiss. He lifted his head, his breath warm on her wet lips.

"I've got to stop this while I can." His voice was a shivering whisper that reached all the way to her heart.

They sat quietly. Johnny didn't speak again until after his breathing had returned to normal.

"This is a good place to watch for Webb. We'll see him before he gets to the door . . . that is, if we're paying attention."

Kathleen glanced up to see him smiling down at her. Without hesitation, she reached up and kissed him gently on the lips.

"That'll have to do for a while."

"You're some woman. Why is it that you never married?"

"I never met a man I wanted to spend the rest of my life

with—" *Until I met you, Johnny, my love.* "How about you? Have you ever been in love?"

"Not even close to it."

"You're a good dancer."

"So are you."

"Did you ever know an Irish lass that couldn't dance?" she said sassily.

"Even if my ancestors did do a rain dance around a campfire, I had two left feet until Henry Ann took me in hand. Then after I came back from Kansas, I spent time at the McCabe ranch. Down there you can go to a dance once a week if you want to. The neighbors get together, clear the furniture out of one room, and wind up the Victrola. Ruth, Keith's wife, danced with me and, after a while, I got to where I liked it."

"And the girls lined up, I bet."

"Woop! There's our friend Webb!" Johnny removed his arm and opened the truck door at the same time. "Stay here," he said urgently.

Three men had come around from the back of the building and stopped to pass around a bottle. They didn't see Johnny until the last one had put a cap on it and shoved it in his pocket.

"Wait right here, Webb," Johnny said sharply. "You fellows go on in. I want a word with Webb."

"I ain't got nothin' to say to you. The sheriff knows I'm here." Webb attempted to follow his friends into the tavern. Johnny grabbed his arm and threw him up against the side of the building. "Hey, ya got no call to do that."

"Go on in, boys," Johnny said again. "My beef is with Webb."

"Don't go," Webb whined. "He's gonna beat me up."

The men shrugged and disappeared inside the tavern.

"Gimme my belt buckle," Johnny demanded. "Give it to me or I'll beat the hell out of you."

"What the shit ya talkin' about? I ain't got yore god-damn belt buckle."

"Clara Ramsey had it. It wasn't on her when she was found, so I figure the last man with her has it. I mean to get it back." Johnny held Webb up against the wall and drew back his fist.

"Hell, man. 'Twasn't me. I come outside with her. She was only chargin' four bits."

"You screwed her out here?"

"Didn't even get 'er to the car. We was 'bout to get in when she spied a big fancy car and let out a squeal. I had my whacker out, ready to do business, when she run off and got in the fancy car. Damn bitch took my four bits and I got nothin'."

"Tell me about the car, Webb. So far you're my best bet. If you've sold that buckle, I'm going to choke the life out of you." Johnny fastened a hand around Webb's neck and bounced his head against the wall of the tavern.

"I told ya. I ain't got yore buckle."

"The car? What kind was it?"

"I ain't knowin' what kind. It was big and black . . . had lots . . . of shiny on it. Stop it! Yo're hurtin'—"

"What else . . . out with it. I don't think there was a car," Johnny said angrily.

"I swear it, Johnny. It kind of sloped down in the back. I saw it when it . . . went by and it had a big old thinga-mabob for a radiator cap."

"Had you seen it before?"

"I . . . don't think so. I swear to God, Johnny. I don't have your buckle. If that twister tail had it, she sure didn't give it to me."

"Why didn't you go to the sheriff and tell him Clara was with a man in a big car the night she was killed?"

"I ain't tellin' that sheriff nothin'. The deputy told me 'n Krome to lay low. It's what we been doin'."

Johnny let up on Webb's throat. "Don't tell a soul what you told me, or I'll be back, and there'll not be enough of you left to tell a tale about."

"What'a ya gonna do now?"

"Find that guy in the big car and get my buckle back. Go on in and keep your trap shut."

Johnny waited until Webb was inside the tavern before he went back to the truck.

Chapter Twenty-two

JOHNNY HURRIED BACK TO THE TRUCK. He reached for Kathleen as soon as he closed the door and hugged her tightly.

"You brought me luck, sweet Kathleen," he murmured against her cheek. "You're my lucky charm! I know who Clara was with. I'm almost sure I know who killed her, but I don't know how we're going to prove it." He was clearly elated.

"Oh, Johnny. How in the world did you find that out?" She was being held tightly against him, happy to be sharing this moment with him. "Who was it?"

"Webb told me that she got into a big black car. I'm sure it was Marty Conroy's, the little jelly bean who was with her at the rodeo. She must have really made him mad, or else she was threatening him with something, and he had to get rid of her. He's usually a spineless blowhard."

"Did Webb see him?"

"No, just the car. He told me about coming outside with Clara. They were going to his car when she saw the car sitting back down the road. She ran to it and got in. Webb was—" Johnny began to laugh. "I can't tell you the rest."

"Why not? I'm a big girl."

"He paid for something he didn't get."

"Uh-oh. Say no more."

Johnny then told her the story that he had spun about Clara taking the belt buckle he had won along with the prize money at the rodeo and about him looking for someone she might have given it to.

Kathleen reared back to look at him. "Johnny Henry! You are devious! But . . . that was a brilliant idea. Wait a minute. How did you tell them she got it in the first place?" She framed his face with the palms of her hands.

"I didn't tell them; I let them use their imaginations."

"You didn't! The story will be all over town."

"Webb will be too scared to tell. The cowboys will think that they know something no one else knows and will keep it to themselves."

"Where do we go from here?"

"I'm not sure. I've got to talk to Keith. He knows Marty better than anyone. We're not going to have real proof. We'll have to get him to admit that he did it."

"Does that mean you'll make another trip down to the McCabe ranch?"

"I'll go down tomorrow. I want to stay on this while it's hot. Want to come along?"

"I can't go tomorrow." She sat back and looked at him. *Oh, Lord! How is he going to take this?*

"Okay. I just thought you might want to go."

"I do want to go, but . . . Johnny there is something else going on in this town. Something very wrong. Adelaide and I are trying to get someone to look into it."

"You don't have to give me an excuse."

"I'm not giving you an excuse. It's a matter of conscience. I'm obligated to do this other thing. I haven't told you what Adelaide and I suspect because we had nothing really to go on until Judy DeBerry, a young girl from Fort Worth, came to town looking for her real mother. I went to the courthouse and looked at the birth records. And, Johnny, you won't believe how many babies are born in this town."

Please, darling, don't be mad and ruin this special time I've had with you.

Kathleen talked steadily for five or more minutes, telling about meeting Judy, her reception at the courthouse, the deputy trying to take her notebook, and Judge Fimbres's interference. The more words tumbled from her, the faster they came, and the more she feared that she would never be able to find the right ones to tell him that she had asked the man that he'd turned his back on to help them. She closed her eyes briefly before she told him.

"We decided that we needed someone who had some credibility with not only Judge Fimbres, but with the district attorney's office in Oklahoma City. We decided to ask Barker Fleming to help us. He will be here tomorrow." She finished the last few words in a rush.

Her last words cut into Johnny like a knife. *The son of a bitch is going through Kathleen to get to me. A hell of a lot of good it will do him.* With his eyes on her face, Johnny retreated to the safety of silence. Tension was alive between them.

"Johnny, Paul, and Adelaide agreed that we must do something. Please come and help us." Her lovely blue eyes were clouded with worry. "We think that over the years there could be as many as two hundred babies sold out of that clinic."

He realized that he didn't dare linger in silence for too long or he might lose the will to break it at all. He'd start the truck and take her home without a word. Should that happen, it would be the end of his ever being with her again.

"Did you call him?"

"Yes. We needed someone who is not under Doc Herman's thumb to investigate him." Her hand shook when she pushed hair back from her face.

"Why bring *him* in?"

"Because he owns the tannery. He has an interest in the town. You don't have to like him or have anything to do with him, Johnny. Just tolerate him for the sake of the girls like Judy, who was sold to people who hated her when she began to show her Indian blood and threw her out on the street to fend for herself."

"I thought I made it plain to you that I don't want anything to do with him."

"I need . . . you to . . . be with me on this. Help me. Please, Johnny. I can't do it without you." Her voice came through quivering lips. Her eyes were bright with tears; her hands clutched at his shirt as if she was drowning.

"Don't cry," he said harshly.

"I can't help it. This is terribly important to me."

"Who? Fleming or Dr. Herman?" he asked harshly.

"You! You, idiot!" she said tersely. "I'm twenty-six years old. I'm not a silly girl with a crush, for Christ sake! It's stupid of me to tell you this, but where you're concerned I seem to have lost my pride. You've become very important to me. I . . . might be . . . in love with you."

He was silent. She was beginning to regret her words when he gritted out angrily.

"Don't play with me, Kathleen."

"Don't play with you? Sheesh! Are you so blind that you can't see what's right under your nose? Are you afraid that I'll chase after you like Clara did? I have pride, too. If you don't want me, all you have to do is start up this truck and take me home."

"I *am* afraid . . . but not that you'll chase me."

"You couldn't possibly be afraid of me," she said tiredly.

"If you want to know the God's truth, I'm scared to death of you."

"I don't understand you at all. Why are you warm and wonderful some of the time and at other times as cold as ice?"

He grabbed her forearms and jerked her to him. Tears had run down her cheeks and stopped at the corners of her mouth. The zigzagging neon lights on the front of the tavern were reflected in her eyes.

"I know I can't have you, and it's tearing me up," he snarled. "I'm only trying to protect myself, dammit to hell!"

"From me?"

"And from myself. Oh, Lord! Don't cry."

"I'm trying not to. Are you married? Is that why you—?"

"—Hell, no, I'm not married."

"Are you . . . in love with someone?" Her voice was a mere whisper.

"I *think* I am." He pulled her tight against him. With his face buried in the curve of her neck, he said, "I *know* I am, and it's hell. I wish you were a waitress at the Frontier Cafe, a ticket-seller at the theater, or a girl from one of the ranches around."

Kathleen pulled back from him. She was trembling and wildly flushed. A corner of her mind believed that he was saying he loved her. Then—

"Why do you say that? What's wrong with me?" She put her hand on his chest and held herself away from him.

"Nothing is wrong with you. You're the smartest, prettiest, spunkiest, most wonderful woman I've ever met. There's plenty wrong with me."

"What's wrong with you? You're a man with principles. You're kind and compassionate, proud and independent. You cared about a girl like Clara and tried to help her. Johnny"—she put her hands on his shoulders and spoke earnestly—"you've got all the qualities I ever hoped to find in the man I'd share my life with."

"Aunt Dozie used to say that 'birds of a feather flock together.' You're a beautiful redbird, Kathleen. I'm just a crow."

"I heard what that Marty person said that day about your mother. Mr. Fleming also told me. He made no excuses for himself for what he did. He only wants to make it right now. Do you think that I'm such a shallow person that I'd care who your parents were?"

"It's not only that. I only went to the fifth grade in school," he said, and the words almost choked him. "When I went to live with Henry Ann and Ed, I was ashamed to go to school because I was so far behind. That's one of the reasons why I'm not with the Federal Bureau. I'd never pass a test. Hell, I've never even read a book, and you *write* them."

"—Thomas Edison only had three months of formal schooling."

"I have a rag-tail ranch with a big mortgage," he continued, determined to say it all. "I could lose it lock, stock, and barrel by next year. I've nothing to offer a woman, especially a woman like you."

"You've got yourself, Johnny. We could be a team. What I lack, you make up. What you lack, I make up." In desperation, Kathleen wrapped her arms about his neck and held him tightly. "If you care for me at all, give us a chance. Don't throw it away before we give it a try. We may regret it for the rest of our lives."

He kissed her softly, sweetly, to close her mouth. His lips then roamed over her tear-wet face, and returned to hers again and again, hard, demanding. His fingers forked through her hair to cradle her head, while other fingers grasped her hips, pulled her closer, then moved up to caress her soft, round breasts.

"Please don't break my heart, Johnny," she gasped when his mouth left hers.

"Ah, sweet woman. You'll likely break mine when you realize what an ignorant, rough man I am. But you're a fever in my blood, and I can't stay away from you."

"Oh, I'm glad! Then you do care for me?"

"Care? I'm crazy about you!"

"I love you, too. Love you so much."

"You do? Really—?"

"Yes, yes, yes. You're every hero I've ever written about all rolled up in one."

He laughed joyously against her face.

"Are you as happy as I am?" she asked, and leaned back to look into his face.

"I don't know. How happy are you?"

"Let's see . . . happy as a dog with a tub full of bones. Happy as a fox in a henhouse. Happy as a boy with a new slingshot—"

"Happy as a cowboy kissin' a pretty, sweet little redbird?"

"As happy as that! Johnny? I need to hear you say it."

"Sweet girl, I'm not good with soft words. I've never said those words in my life. I'm crazy about you—"

"Say you love me, but only if you mean it."

"I love you," he said with a touch of desperation. "But

I'm scared! So many things could go wrong. What if, after a while, you change your mind . . . and see me as nothing but an ignorant breed with manure on my boots? Christ, that's why I'm so damned afraid to take that step over the line."

"I love you." She drew back to cradle his face in her hands. "You're afraid since we have the power to hurt each other simply because we love each other. I understand what you mean," she said, and kissed him gently on the lips. "I'm afraid, too, you know."

"I don't want you to ever be afraid of anything."

"But I am . . . at times." She rested her cheek on his shoulder. "I'm afraid of being old and having no one to love me. Now I'll be afraid of losing you."

"The same goes here," Johnny gently reminded her.

It didn't matter that they were sitting in front of a honky-tonk. They could have been sitting on a busy street in the city. The cab of Johnny's old truck was their world. Johnny told her of his dream to have a large cattle and horse ranch. She told him how lonely she had been growing up and that she would like to have lots of children. He hugged her, kissed her, and said that he would do his part to help her get them.

They laughed, hugged, kissed, and talked nonsense. It was past midnight when Johnny stopped the truck in front of Hazel's and walked Kathleen up to the porch.

"I'll not go down to Vernon tomorrow if you'll go with me on Saturday."

"Does that mean that you'll come in tomorrow and sit in on the meeting?"

"Kathleen, sweet girl, don't expect me to accept that . . . man. I simply can't. He means nothing to me."

"He told me that he understands how you feel because he would feel the same. He just wants to know you."

"Kathleen, I don't want him hanging around waitin' for me to call him *Daddy!*"

"Just come help us. If what we suspect is true, it will turn this town upside down."

"Do you still want to go to Red Rock on Sunday to see Tom and Henry Ann? It's about fifty miles over there. We'll have to leave early."

"I wasn't going to let you wiggle out of that." Kathleen wrapped her arms around his waist. "I don't want to go in. I'll not sleep a wink."

"I've got to get home. I've got stock to tend to."

"Tonight?"

"At daylight." He kissed her quick, then with a groan, long and hard. His hand moved down to her hips and for a moment held her tightly against his aching maleness. "Go in while I'm still able to let you go," he whispered.

"You'll not get much sleep."

"More than if you were sleeping with me. 'Night, sweetheart. See you tomorrow."

Kathleen did sleep, so well that she had a bounce in her step and a sparkle in her eyes when she came into the office and went through to the back room.

"Morning," she called out to Adelaide and Paul, who were standing close together beside the table where Paul was tearing down a page and throwing the type in a bucket.

"My, you look bright-eyed this morning." Adelaide's hand lingered on Paul's arm when she turned to speak to Kathleen.

"Must be the date she had last night with that cowboy, huh?" Paul said with a wink.

"We did some great detective work last night. But I'll wait and let that *cowboy* tell you about it when he gets here."

"He's coming back in today? He spends more time here than at the ranch. We ought to charge him rent," Paul said in a complaining tone.

"All right, you two. I am happy this morning. Happy as a dog with two tails to wag."

"Are we invited to the wedding?" Adelaide asked with wide-eyed innocence.

"It hasn't gone that far, but if it does, you'll be at the head of the list." Unable to keep the smile off her face, Kathleen went back to her desk determined to get as much work done as possible.

She worked steadily to catch up on the items for the next week's paper. She wrote the church and school news first, then a story about the local baseball team, who would play their last game of the season next weekend. She had begun to work on an editorial she had started about the need for a benefit for the local Volunteer Firefighters' Association when a husky gray-haired man came into the office.

"I was lookin' at the pictures ya got out there of that girl. I was the one who found her. Name's Kilburn."

"Hello, Mr. Kilburn. I'm Kathleen Dolan. I took the pictures."

"It warn't no accident, miss. I said that when I brung the sheriff out there. That girl was beat up bad and throwed out."

"The car did run over her—"

"Pete Carroll's brains is scrambled," he continued as if

she hadn't spoken. "When he looked at her, he said that she couldn't a got all that done to her gettin' hit by a car. Now he's changed his tune."

"Perhaps someone changed it for him, Mr. Kilburn."

"Why'd anyone go and do that? It's plain as yore nose on yore face. I hit Pete up about it this mornin'. He said Doc Herman looked at her and said she was hit by a car. That's what he said. 'Course, if Doc said black was white, Pete'd take it for gospel."

"I wonder why that is. Do you know?"

"I ain't knowin', miss. I ain't wantin' nothin' to do with that Doc Herman."

"Why is that, Mr. Kilburn?"

"He's got too uppity to lance boils, sew up cuts, or come out to see sick folks. He's got that nurse to do it all, and she ain't no doc."

"He delivers babies," Kathleen said, and watched his face.

"Harrumpt! I heared tell that he'll take in a girl what got ruint and not charge her folks a dime. Folks come from all over bringin' him girls that ain't wed."

"Do you know that for a fact?"

"No, missy, I don't know it fer a fact, but it's been talked about 'round here for years."

"A lot of *married* women come here to have their babies," Kathleen said softly.

"I ain't knowin' 'bout that. When any a my folks get sick, we go down to Vernon."

"Do you mind if I quote you saying that you think Clara Ramsey's death was no accident?"

"In the paper?"

"Yes, I'm writing a story about it for next week's paper."

"Ya can say so if ya want. I'm sayin' what I think."

"I'll see that you get a copy of the paper."

"I ain't sayin' this just to get my name in the paper."

"I know that. You seem to be a man of conscience."

"I ain't been able to think of nothin' but that poor girl since I found her." He anchored his battered hat down on his head. "Got to get back home to Mama. She's all tore up, too, thinkin' what happened out there on the road."

"Thank you for coming in, Mr. Kilburn."

As soon as the man left, Kathleen ripped the paper out of her typewriter, inserted a fresh sheet and began to type rapidly.

The death of Clara Ramsey was not an accident according to the rancher who found her body in a ditch alongside the road last Tuesday morning. Mr. Dale Kilburn, whose ranch is a mile south—

By midmorning she had finished the last page of her story, read it and edited it, and was ready to put it on the hook beside the linotype machine. She looked up. Johnny was lounging in the doorway leading to the back room, watching her. Her heart fluttered with a joyous surge of pleasure, then took off like a runaway horse.

"I didn't know you were here." She stood, her eyes bright with happiness at the sight of him.

"You were writing. I didn't want to bother you."

"I've got a story from Mr. Kilburn, who found Clara's body. Do you want to read it?"

"Tell me about it."

Unable to keep her feet from going to him, she crossed to the doorway. His eyes feasted on her face.

"Tell me I didn't dream last night," she whispered, her hand on his chest.

"What did you dream?" he teased.

"That you and I . . . that we—"

"That we what?"

"Johnny Henry!" she scolded. Both hands were against his chest, now, pushing him back out of sight of the front window. She tilted her face, her eyes smiling as her hands and her arms encircled his waist. "Don't . . . tease me, you nitwit!"

Johnny's face was creased with smiles. *Oh, Lord, he is beautiful, and sweet and dear and thank you, God, for bringing me here!*

He lowered his head and kissed her, softly, gently, and quickly.

"Hey, there, cut that out!" Paul's voice was stern. "We can't be having such as that going on in our pressroom."

"It's been going on in this pressroom for three or four years when you thought I wasn't looking," Johnny retorted. "You kiss Adelaide every chance you get."

"Yeah, but . . . Addie and I are adults."

"I'm not forgettin' that you owe me the price of two tickets to a picture show. And where's that two bits you owe me?"

"What are you two talking about?" Kathleen kept her hand on Johnny's arm as if she was afraid he'd disappear if she wasn't touching him.

"A while back he offered to pay if I'd take you to a picture show. Now he's trying to chicken out."

"Well of all things! You had to be bribed to take me out?"

"I was going to take you anyway; but if he was dumb enough to offer to pay, I wasn't going to turn it down."

The smile in his eyes and on his lips was real.

Chapter Twenty-three

At noon Kathleen and Johnny walked down to Claude's and ordered hamburgers. Seated at the end of the counter they watched Claude at the grill and listened to Gene Autry singing "Red River Valley." Johnny put a nickel in the jukebox and soon Bing Crosby was crooning, *"I don't know why I love you like I do, I don't know why, I just do."* His hand beneath the counter searched and found hers.

"Well, well—" Claude brought the hamburgers and lifted his brows up and down several times. "What's going on here?"

"None of your business, you nosy old goat," Johnny retorted angrily, but he was smiling.

"Knowed it the minute ya brought her here. Ya was lookin' all cow-eyed then." He wiped his hands on his apron and glanced at the other diners before leaning close to say in a confidential tone, "You owe me, son. My burgers draw pretty girls like flies."

"What do you want, Claude? My arm or my leg?"

Claude's face had lost its grin when he spoke to Kathleen. "You've stirred up a hornets' nest, miss, with those pictures in the window. Some of the merchants are wanting to boycott the paper. The sheriff says she was hit by a car."

"Dr. Herman says it was an accident. We think she was murdered—beaten, thrown out of the car, and run over."

"Doc says folks won't come here and buy goods if they think a murderer is running loose."

"If they withhold advertising because we're trying to get to the truth about a poor girl's death, then we'll fight back with a story that will shake up this entire county; and the merchants might find themselves being boycotted by their customers."

Claude's laugh was as dry as corn shucks. "Ya got ya a little fighter here, boy. Hold on to her."

"Pressure was put on the *Gazette* to accept *his* decision that what happened to Clara was an accident. Why? Don't you want to know why he was so anxious to do that? It isn't because people won't come to town. That story won't wash."

"Town's got a clean record compared to some."

"They had a hijacking, but I guess they didn't want it on the *record*," Kathleen said drily. "Johnny will find out what happened to Clara. He worked with my uncle to track Bonnie Parker and Clyde Barrow and the result was—"

"Kath! Hush!" Johnny hissed.

"What's this?" Claude said.

"Nothing. She's been listening to her uncle's tall tales."

"I thought for a minute we had us a hero here."

Kathleen was almost giddy with embarrassment. Her eyes glittered with both anger and despair. A customer came in, and Claude moved away. She couldn't look at Johnny. With fingers that trembled, she picked up a slice of pickle Claude had placed on her plate.

"People around here don't know anything
part of my life."

"Why? Are you ashamed of it?" Kathleen pre
lips tightly together and half turned so that he c
see her face.

"I just don't want my business spread around."

"Do Adelaide and Paul know that you've worked w
the Federal Bureau from time to time?"

"They know that I go away sometimes for a while."

"I'm proud of what you did. I didn't think that I would
offend you by telling Claude. Evidently I was mistaken."

"Let's drop it."

"There is a lot we have to learn about each other."

"Yes," he said dejectedly.

They finished the meal in silence. Kathleen decided
that this man she loved was far more complicated than
she had imagined. It wasn't until they were walking back
toward the *Gazette* that Kathleen spoke.

"I don't understand why it's so important to Doc
Herman to hush up what happened to Clara. Could he
have had anything to do with it?"

"Stranger things have happened."

"I keep thinking about the baby buried out on the
Ramsey plot. It was buried before Hazel knew anything
about it."

"I see the wheels turning in your head right now."

When he grinned down at her with that unfettered
look of love in his eyes, happiness flowed over her. They
would have their ups and downs, but if they loved—

"Do you think we should—?"

"Look in the box? I thought about it."

"Oh, my. It gives me goose bumps to think of it."

"I'm thinking Clara came home pregnant and had her

ɔaby at the clinic. Doc paid her for it and she left town again. Didn't Hazel say that someone owed her money?"

"She did. Do you think Clara went back to the clinic to hit them up for more?"

"She could have."

They were so absorbed in their conversation that they didn't notice the man who got out of a car parked in front of the *Gazette* and stood waiting for them. With her hand tucked into the crook of Johnny's arm she felt his steps slow, looked up, and saw Barker Fleming.

"Hello, Mr. Fleming."

Barker tipped his Stetson. "Hello, Miss Dolan. Johnny."

Kathleen wasn't sure, but she thought Johnny grunted a reply.

Barker stepped over to the car and opened the door. A small dark-haired boy slid off the seat and got out. Two girls several years older than Emily got out of the back-seat. One girl wore a pink-checked gingham dress, the other blue-checked. The boy was dressed in duck pants and scuffed shoes. All had the dark hair and eyes of their Cherokee ancestors.

"These are my three youngest," Barker said proudly. The flickering of his eyes from the children to Johnny betrayed his nervousness. "They're having a holiday from school. This is Lucas." He touched the boy on the head. "The girls are Marie and Janna. This lady," he said to the children, "is Miss Dolan, who works for the newspaper. And this is Johnny Henry, the *All-Around Cowboy*, I told you about. I saw him ride at the rodeo."

"Gol . . . ly!" Lucas took a couple of steps forward and looked up at Johnny with hero worship in his eyes. "Gol . . . ly!" he said again. "Can I see your spurs? Do you have a lasso? Gol . . . ly!"

"Daddy, can't he say anything but Gol . . . ly?" the older girl complained. "He's so . . . dumb."

"Yeah, he's dumb," the younger girl echoed.

"He gets carried away once in a while," Barker explained patiently to the girls, "But he is *not* dumb."

Lucas didn't seem to care if his sisters thought he was dumb. He was still looking expectantly up at Johnny.

"Yeah, I got a lasso," Johnny finally mumbled. He reached out and tousled the boy's hair.

"Can I see it . . . sometime?"

"Sure."

"Daddy! I can see his lasso . . . and his spurs." Lucas grabbed Barker's hand.

"He didn't say anything about spurs," Marie said irritably, and rolled her eyes.

"The girls are tired from the trip. Lucas slept part of the way." Barker opened the car door. "Hop in," he commanded. "I'm taking them out to stay with Mrs. Howland—"

"Daddy, it stinks out there," Marie whined.

Barker ignored his daughter's complaint. "Howland is manager at the tannery. They live about a quarter mile south of the plant. I'll be back in say . . . an hour?"

"Daddy—"

"Girls, we had this settled before we left home. Hush your complaining and get in the car. We'll eat dinner at the restaurant and spend the night at the hotel."

"Oh . . . goody." Janna clapped her hands.

"I want to stay with Mr. Henry," Lucas said.

"Some other time," Barker said patiently.

Kathleen moved away from Johnny and went to the car. She leaned down to speak to the girls.

" 'Bye. Nice to have met you."

"I wanted to see your typewriter," Marie said sulkily.

"You can see it when your daddy brings you back."

" 'Bye, Mr. Henry," Lucas called. "Ya won't forget?"

"No." Johnny shook his head as he spoke. He stood as if his feet were stuck to the sidewalk.

After the car moved away, Kathleen put her arm through Johnny's.

"You can say one thing for Barker Fleming, he has beautiful children." Her eyes laughed up at him. "Let's go tell Adelaide and Paul about our idea."

"What idea?"

"About what's *not* in that box out at the cemetery, my dear and beautiful man."

"Now I know your brains are scrambled." His voice was stern, but his lips were smiling.

If Adelaide and Paul noticed that Johnny didn't address any of his remarks to Barker Fleming during the afternoon session in the pressroom, they attributed it to the fact that he was jealous of the man.

After being introduced to Barker, Judy had gone upstairs to Adelaide's apartment to bake a cake.

"She took homemaking in school and is a good cook," Adelaide explained, and sat down where she could see if anyone came into the office.

Kathleen started from the beginning and told Barker about being hijacked before she reached town and about the sheriff refusing to arrest the men despite the fact that she and Johnny could identify them. She related every encounter she'd had with the sheriff, the doctor, and the record clerk at the courthouse.

"Birth, death, and arrest records have not been made available to the paper," Paul explained. "Time and again

Adelaide has tried to get these records only to be told they are not yet recorded. They haven't been sent over, and at times the records office door has been locked. I think Kathleen took them by surprise when she got in the other morning."

Kathleen's chart showing the names and dates she had copied from the public birth records was placed on the table. The discussion then centered on the unusual number of women who came to Rawlings to have their babies.

"Tulsa, Oklahoma City, Dallas, Fort Worth, Denver, Colorado? All these women came to Rawlings to have their babies? Unbelievable," Barker exclaimed.

"Almost two hundred over a fifteen-year period," Kathleen said. "Mr. Dale Kilburn was in this morning. He's sure that Clara didn't die from being hit by a car. During the conversation he told me that it had been rumored for years that unwed girls came to the clinic to have their babies."

"We need to have more than rumors," Barker said. "It seems to me Dr. Herman has a stranglehold on the whole county. Do you have an extra copy of the names and dates of birth you got from the records department?"

"Judy made a copy for you. Her parents, or rather the people who now say they are not her parents, Mr. and Mrs. DeBerry, live in Fort Worth. They were disappointed in Judy when it became apparent that she had Indian blood. Judy said she heard Mr. DeBerry say something about getting his money back."

"She's a sweet girl. Paul and I have become quite attached to her," Adelaide added.

"They told her that they'd gotten her here?" Johnny asked.

"She had seen her birth certificate and heard Mr. and Mrs. DeBerry discussing the fact.

"Her name is there on the list," Kathleen said, pointing to it. "Baby girl born to Mr. and Mrs. Donald DeBerry, Fort Worth, Texas. Attending physician, Dr. Darrell Herman."

"Darrell Herman and Louise Munday are selling babies out of that clinic," Adelaide said staunchly. "I think that's why he wants Clara's murder declared an accident. He's afraid that the state or Federal Marshals will get wind of it, come here to investigate, and maybe turn up something about what they are doing."

"Doc Herman goes to Oklahoma City quite often for medical meetings. There may be a connection there," Paul said.

"That's right," Adelaide said as she suddenly remembered. "Flossie said he was there last week."

Barker made a few notations in a small pad.

"We'll not get any help from the sheriff, Mr. Fleming." Kathleen folded her notebook. "He's in the doctor's pocket."

"Grant Gifford would be interested in this. He was elected attorney general a year ago. He'll know what to do." Johnny dropped this bit of information into the conversation.

"I heard that he was a crackerjack lawyer and straight as a string," Barker said.

"He is."

"I'll get in touch with him when I go to the city. I know a good man up there who will investigate the doctor's background and look up the parents of some of these babies born here. We could find a few more cases like the DeBerrys."

Kathleen was burning with the urge to ask Johnny if he knew the attorney general and was relieved when Adelaide did it for her.

"Do you know Mr. Gifford, Johnny?"

"Yeah. He taught me how to pick out a tune on a guitar. He's good, too, at lancing boils, milking, and chopping cotton among other things." Johnny was trying not to smile.

"The state attorney general lances boils?" Kathleen asked.

"Among other things." Johnny's lips quirked with a supressed grin. "Don't get in a snit. I knew him when I was a snot-nosed kid who didn't know straight up. He's as good a man as I ever met."

Barker refrained from asking Johnny any questions. The relationship was fragile, and he didn't want to put a strain on it.

Paul went to the front office, where Adelaide was collecting for a subscription.

"My father wants me to take over the running of the tannery here," Barker said when the three of them were alone. He folded the papers Kathleen gave him and put them in his pocket.

"Will you be moving to Rawlings?" Kathleen asked.

"Not until after the first of the year. The children are in school in Elk City, and I don't want to disrupt them."

"They are beautiful children, Mr. Fleming. You must be very proud of them."

"I am. They are usually well behaved. I feel that I should apologize for Marie's and Janna's behavior. They're at the age where everything that Lucas does is dumb and stupid. But Elena, their sister in high school, thinks everything *they* do is dumb and stupid. The one in college

thinks they all are dumb and stupid. So it evens out."
Barker's eyes smiled as he talked of his children.

"I never had a brother or a sister. They don't know
how lucky they are."

Barker threw up his hands. "Try and tell them that."
He stood and reached for his hat. "I'd like to take the two
of you to dinner if you think the bickering between the
girls and Lucas wouldn't ruin your appetite." He looked
directly at Johnny.

"I've got chores out at the ranch."

"And I'm going with him," Kathleen said quickly. "But
thanks anyway."

"I'll leave early in the morning and get the kids back
to Elk City. I'll be back when I have some news. I take it
you don't trust the telephone operator not to listen in."

"You take it right."

"I'll figure out another way to get in touch. Good-bye,
Johnny." Barker held out his hand.

Kathleen held her breath until Johnny accepted it.

"Good-bye, Mr. Fleming." She took his hand when he
offered it. "Thank you for coming and for any help you
can give us."

"There's something not quite right here. It deserves an
investigation."

They heard Barker talking to Adelaide and Paul in the
office before he went out the door. Alone, Kathleen
tugged on Johnny's hand and pulled him behind the
press. She put her arms around his waist and laid her
head on his shoulder.

"I'm tired. I just want to be with you."

He lowered his head and rested his cheek against hers.
He held her gently, but firmly.

"I must go home and do chores," he whispered after a

short while. "Come with me and we'll go on down to Vernon tonight and see Keith."

"Will we stay all night?"

"Not unless you want to."

"We can take my car."

"You don't like riding in my truck?"

"I have a special place in my heart for your truck . . . when it's parked at the Twilight Gardens."

He laughed against her forehead. "Come on. Let's gas up the car and go tell Hazel you won't be home."

It was dusk when Kathleen and Johnny drove into the yard at the McCabe ranch.

"Just can't stay away, can you?" Keith shouted the good-natured greeting as soon as they stepped out of the car. He had come out onto the porch. Ruth stood in the doorway.

"I'm thinking about moving in," Johnny said as they approached.

"Not during my lifetime, boy."

"Come in, Kathleen," Ruth called. "Pay no attention to these two. The feud goes on all the time."

"He's always trying to get my woman," Keith complained. "But now that he's got one of his own—"

"We just finished supper, but there's plenty left."

"We had something at Johnny's."

"It was only pork and beans," Johnny grumbled.

"Poor Johnny. Come sit down. I'll find you some biscuits and beef gravy. But first you'd better say hello to Granny and introduce her to Kathleen."

"See there?" Keith said in a confidential tone to Kathleen. "My women fall all over him 'cause he's little and cute."

Kathleen liked the McCabes immediately and longed

for her and Johnny to be like them, easy and relaxed in the company of their guests. They were being themselves, very happy and secure in their love for each other.

She also saw a side of Johnny she had not seen before. With genuine affection he had carefully hugged the fragile old lady and played with Davis, and he was obviously fond of Ruth.

While Kathleen helped Ruth finish the cleaning in the kitchen, Keith and Johnny went to a front room lit by several big glass lamps.

"How's Gertie getting along?" Johnny asked when the women joined them. Kathleen went to sit beside Johnny on the sofa. Keith sat in a big leather chair.

"Getting more rambunctious every day."

"She kicked me last night 'cause I was gettin' too close to Mama." Keith pulled Ruth down and cuddled her on his lap.

"Johnny has called this poor little baby Gertie so often that even I'm getting to where I think of her as that." Ruth rolled her eyes. Keith rubbed her protruding stomach. They were completely at ease talking about their unborn child.

This, too, was new to Kathleen. Pregnant women she had known had not talked about their pregnancy in mixed company. Keith McCabe adored his wife. Would Johnny be that loving when she was round and clumsy with their child?

Johnny told Keith and Ruth that he suspected Marty Conroy had killed Clara, or if he hadn't, he knew something about what had happened to her out on that lonely road.

"I talked to someone who saw her get in a big fancy black car. The car was sitting off down the road from the

Twilight Gardens as if the driver was waiting for someone and didn't want to be seen. There was a fancy doodad on the radiator cap."

"Sounds like our Marty. He loves big doodads."

"I'll be surprised if Marty did that," Ruth said. "He's obnoxious, but I never thought he was the type to kill a girl."

"You can't tell what a little bugger like Marty will do, honey, if he's backed into a corner. Especially if he thinks somebody's goin' to take away his doodads."

"We've got two problems," Johnny said seriously. "We'll not be able to prove he killed Clara with the pictures of the tire tracks. There are too many big cars with big tires. We have to get him across the line into Oklahoma, and we have to get him to confess."

"Uh-oh," Kathleen said. "I hadn't thought of that."

"I'll get him across the river, Johnny; you get him to confess." Keith's big hand was massaging Ruth's back.

"How are you going to get him to cross the river?" With her fingers on his chin, Ruth turned her husband's face toward her.

"Sweetheart, have you no faith in your husband?" Keith chided gently and punctuated each word with a kiss. "Remember when I told you his latest hare-brained scheme was to build a toll bridge across the river? He said we could just sit back and collect tolls. I'll call and tell him that I changed my mind and that I want to look over the spot where he wants to put the bridge. He'll come running with a grin on his face like the wave on a slop bucket."

"I'd like to figure out a way to give Sheriff Carroll the credit for the arrest, that is if there is an arrest," Johnny said seriously. "I think he's a decent sort, but under Doc Herman's thumb for some reason."

"He owes him for his job," Kathleen murmured.

"Yeah, but if we can get him to go over Doc's head and do something on his own, it might give him the confidence to help us on another matter that's cookin' up in Tillison County."

"That's a perfectly brilliant idea," Kathleen explained. "Johnny, I'm so glad you thought of it."

"She's in love," Keith whispered loudly to his wife. "I think it's a dumb idea. Old Marty will be a hard nut to crack."

"Maybe not. If he beat her up in the car, there was blood. Blood is hard to clean up. Chances are he waited until he got back over the line, and it would have been dried by then. If he's our man, there will be bloodstains in that car."

"All right, cowboy, deal me in. Where do you want him and when?"

"How about Wednesday at noon? Be sure you get him on the Oklahoma side."

"Leave it to Cousin Keith, son. He's been after me for years to go in on some deal or the other. He'll be there."

Chapter Twenty-four

THE HEADLIGHTS OF THE NASH forged a path into the darkness. Johnny maneuvered the car with his left hand on the wheel, his right arm around Kathleen. Snuggled close to his side, Kathleen glanced at his sharply etched profile. Not only was Johnny Henry handsome, but he was a moral, decent man and, she suspected, an utterly ruthless one if the occasion demanded it.

"How long have you known the McCabes?"

"A few years. I met them when I went up to Pearl to help Hod, when he was working on the Pascoe and Norton case."

"They were the Kansas City gangsters who killed Molly's parents. I remember."

Kathleen was extremely happy. She looked out onto the dark Oklahoma plains. The car lights were the only ones she could see in any direction. She felt comfortable and safe here in this small spot on earth with Johnny. A few short months ago she had not known the man behind the name Johnny Henry. It was strange, she thought, that she hadn't realized she had been lonely. Would she ever be satisfied again to spend long evenings alone with only the creaking of the house and the sound of her typewriter to break the stillness?

"Johnny," she snuggled closer against him pressing her lips to the side of his neck, "I love you."

"Hummm, what brought that on?"

"I was thinking how lonely I'd be without you."

"We've not been together all that much."

"I may sound silly, but since I met you, you seem to be a part of me." Her hand slid across his chest to hug him closer.

"Better stop that, or I'll have to stop and kiss you."

"Right here in the middle of the road? You wouldn't dare!" Her lips moved over his neck, while her hand caressed his lean midsection.

The car came to a sudden stop in the middle of the road. He wrapped her in his arms and kissed her soundly. He lifted his head to look at her, then settled his mouth against hers again. The lips that touched hers were warm and sweet as they tingled across her mouth. A longing to love and be loved washed over her. The kiss became more possessive, deepened, her lips parted, his tongue touched hers, and his hand slid beneath her jacket to cup her breast. She unbuttoned her blouse and his fingers moved inside to stroke soft flesh.

"I want to hold you, love you." His voice was choked with the harsh sound of desire.

Johnny's arms were the only arms in the world, his lips the only lips. His tongue circled her mouth, coaxing it to open. Her skin tingled; the tiny hairs on her body seemed to be standing on end.

"You . . . taste so good—" He took his lips away and buried his face in her throat.

"Are we very far from your house?"

"Not far."

"Let's go there."

For a moment he was still. Then, "Are you sure?" he asked in a hoarse whisper.

"I was never more sure in my life." Her fingers inside his shirt moved lightly over his chest. His body answered the movement of her hand with a violent trembling.

The car moved down the road. They didn't talk. She wanted to tell him what she was feeling, but she felt certain he knew. A minute or two later he turned the car off the main road, and after another minute he stopped in front of his house. He turned off the motor and the lights and looked down at her.

"This is a big step. Once I get you in there, I'll not be able to let you leave."

"I won't want to go." She cupped his cheek with her hand. "I've waited all my life for a man like you and for a moment like this."

He kissed her. His mouth tender on hers, reverent. They got out of the car and, with his arm around her, they went to the house.

Kathleen stood inside the door while Johnny lit a lamp in the kitchen. Only a faint ribbon of light came through the doorway. He came to her and to her surprise lifted her in his arms, carried her to the bed, and sank down on it with her still in his arms.

"I'd love you on a feather bed in a fancy room . . . if I could." He laid her down and leaned over her.

"I don't need a feather bed or a fancy room. I need you." Her arms encircled his neck and drew his face down to hers.

It was all so sweet, so right, so natural. He was unhurried and tender when he undressed her. She was terribly conscious of the part of him that throbbed so aggressively against her. His lips and his hands sent waves of weakening pleasure up and down her spine.

His callused palm lightly stroked the curve of her hip, then slid up to her breasts. His fingers squeezed her nipple and she hurt deep, deep inside of her. So many sensations crashed through her body and mind that she was unable to distinguish one from another. It was all too pleasurable, too wonderful.

If this is the coupling men and women do together, dear God, how beautiful!

Her body arched, seeking, wanting. She became aware of a hard pressure against her, a slow, gradual filling of that aching emptiness. A sudden movement brought a pain-pleasure so intense that she cried out.

"Sweetheart . . . I had to!" he whispered in her ear and lay still for a long moment.

"It's all right . . . all right!" She kissed his face with quick, passionate kisses and clutched at him to keep the throbbing warmth inside her.

Later she heard him cry out, as if from a distance, "Kath . . . Kath, sweetheart—"

She couldn't speak, aware of only that thrusting, pulsating rhythm that was pushing her toward a bursting, shivering height.

When she came back into reality, Johnny's weight was pressing her into the bed. She moved her mouth against his shoulder. He lowered his head to kiss her lips. She wrapped her arms around him in a wave of protective love. He buried his face in the curve of her breast like a child seeking comfort, and she held him there.

He rolled away, taking her with him. They lay side by side. His mouth teased her lips, her lashes.

"It was wonderful," she breathed.

"I didn't use anything. You could be . . . pregnant."

"I hope so. Oh, Johnny, I hope so."

They loved each other deep into the night, until sheer exhaustion sent them into a deep sleep where she lay molded to his naked body, her cheek nestled in the warm hollow of his shoulder.

It was the middle of the morning when they drove into Red Rock, Oklahoma. At daylight, Johnny had heated water on the kerosene stove for Kathleen to wash while he did chores. Then, as they passed through town they had stopped at Hazel's so that Kathleen could change clothes. Since Hazel and Emily were not awake, Kathleen left a note saying that she and Johnny were going to Red Rock and would not be back until late.

Red Rock was not nearly as large a town as Rawlings. Only the main street was paved. They passed through, and a mile out of town, Johnny turned into the yard of a neat farmhouse surrounded by huge pecan trees.

"Johnny!" As soon as Johnny got out of the car, a young boy came running from the house. "Mama, Daddy, Johnny's here."

"Is that you, Jay? Lordy! I thought your daddy had a new hired man. You've grown a foot."

"You haven't. You're gettin' shorter, Johnny."

The two clasped hands, then wrestled a bit. It was clear that they were happy to see each other. By the time Kathleen had slid out of the car a slim woman and a man who looked amazingly like Hod had come out onto the porch.

Henry Ann Dolan, her face laced with smiles of welcome,

hurried across the yard. Johnny went to meet her, put his arms around her, and hugged her tightly.

"Johnny! It's so good to see you."

"Hello, sis. I've brought someone to meet you."

"I see you have, and I'm guessing it's Kathleen Dolan."

"You guessed right. Kath, come meet my sister, Henry Ann."

"Hello." Kathleen held out her hand. "I've heard a lot about you from Johnny."

"Johnny and I had to grow up suddenly and fast when we had this farm to run. Meet your Uncle Tom, Kathleen. He's been champing at the bit to get over to Rawlings to see you."

Kathleen was suddenly enveloped in strong arms. "Welcome, Kathleen."

"I'm glad to meet you, Uncle Tom. Oh, my, you look so much like Uncle Hod."

Tom laughed. "I've heard that a lot. That red hair of yours reminds me of Aunt Biddy, our mother's sister."

"My mother had red hair. I always thought that was where I got it."

"Your daddy's hair wasn't black like mine and Hod's. It was a sandy color."

"I don't remember him at all. I was about two years old when Mama and I went back to Iowa to live with her parents."

"Git yo'self on up here, boy, if'n yo ain't wantin' me ta tan yo hide." A large colored woman, a blue handkerchief tied about her head, stood on the porch. Johnny strode quickly to the porch and put his arms around her.

"Hello, Aunt Dozie. You're gettin' prettier every day."

"Hee, hee, hee! Yo is still jist a runnin' off at the mouth, ain't ya?"

"Kathleen, come meet the first girl I ever had a crush on."

"Lawsy, ain't ya jist as pretty as a redbird." Dozie's round face was split with a big smile.

"Thank you." Kathleen held out her hand.

"I ain't a handshakin' woman. I a huggin' woman, if it be a gal my boy here brung to see me," Aunt Dozie said.

"In that case—" Kathleen's laugh rang out. She put her arms around Dozie's ample waist and hugged her.

"Ya like my Johnny, gal?" Dozie asked bluntly.

"He's all right," Kathleen's twinkling eyes sought Johnny's.

"Hee, hee, hee. Lawdy mercy. I gots ta show ya how to make tater pie. It keep him happy an' like dough in yo hands."

A little girl came out onto the porch and threw herself at Johnny, who caught her up in his arms. His hat fell to the floor of the porch as he nuzzled her neck.

"You tickle," she yelled. Her fingers searched his shirt pocket and found a stick of chewing gum.

"Did you think I'd forget, punkin?" Johnny's eyes caught Kathleen's over the child's head.

"Let's go in," Henry Ann urged. "Aunt Dozie is getting cold."

Kathleen would remember this as one of the most enjoyable days of her life. At noon they gathered around the big kitchen table. Kathleen couldn't keep her eyes off Johnny. He smiled continually. This was his family. He adored the children; nine-year-old Jay, six-year-old Rose, and baby Eddie. It was apparent that they adored him.

Later in the afternoon, while the older children were out playing and Aunt Dozie sat in the rocking chair with baby Eddie in her lap, Johnny told Henry Ann and Tom about Clara's death and about it being ruled an accident when he was sure it was murder.

"I want to prepare you, Tom. I think it was Marty Conroy who killed the girl, and I'm going to do my best to see that he pays for it."

"We haven't seen him in years. He steers clear of here."

Henry Ann looked at Tom before broaching a new subject. "I had a letter from Isabel."

"I suppose she wanted money."

"She didn't ask for money this time. She said a man who claimed to be your father came to see her at the honky-tonk where she worked. He was part-Indian and according to Isabel well-off. Of course, she would think that anyone with two dollars to rub together was well-off." Henry Ann waited for Johnny to say something, and when he didn't, she said, "Isabel wanted to know if I had heard from you and if I knew the man's name. I'm sure she wants to get in touch with him."

"Sheesh!" Johnny snorted. "Why?"

"Only one reason that I know of. Money."

"He came to see me. Told me he was my father. I want nothing to do with him and told him so. Ed was the only man I'll ever think of as being anywhere near a father to me." Johnny got up and stood looking out the back door, his hands in his back pockets. When he turned around, he had the saddest look on his face Kathleen had ever seen. "How did you escape the Perry curse, Henry Ann? All that inbreeding down on Mud Creek made Dorene what she is and Isabel what she is."

"Being from Mud Creek had nothing to do with it, Johnny. Look at yourself. I couldn't be prouder of my brother. Our mother was what she was because it was what she wanted to be. It's the same with Isabel. Blood has nothing to do with it."

Johnny's eyes caught and held Kathleen's. She knew what he was thinking and longed to reach out and hold him and reassure him. He came to stand behind her chair. She felt his fingers brush through her hair before they settled on her shoulders.

"We'd better get on down the road. It'll be dark by the time we get back to Rawlings."

Tom arose, gathered the sleeping child out of Aunt Dozie's lap, and carried him into a bedroom. Henry Ann took the old lady's arm and helped her up out of the chair.

"I sits ta long, I gets stiff," Dozie explained.

After saying good-bye to Aunt Dozie, Kathleen and Henry Ann walked out to the car. Johnny and Tom had disappeared into the barn.

"Did you meet the man who says he's Johnny's father?" Henry Ann asked as soon as they were away from the house.

"Yes, and he is very nice. He had been looking for Johnny for a long time. He was just eighteen when he . . . had his fling with Dorene. Five years ago he learned she'd had a son who was part-Cherokee. He looked up the birth certificate and, sure enough, she had listed him as Johnny's father."

"Johnny seemed bitter."

"He is. We don't talk about Mr. Fleming. He came to Rawlings the other day and brought three of his children to meet Johnny. He wants to claim him as his son, but he'll keep his distance as long as Johnny feels the way he does."

"I used to get so mad when Isabel would throw it up to Johnny that his daddy was a dirty, drunken Indian."

"Mr. Fleming came to see Johnny ride in the rodeo. He was so proud when Johnny won *All-Around Cowboy.*"

"I saw him ride one time. The bull tried to gore him. It scared me to death." Tom and Johnny came from the barn and stood by the well. "Thank you for telling me about Mr. Fleming. I'll not tell Isabel, but don't be surprised if she shows up in Rawlings someday."

"Johnny has me now. I love him, Henry Ann."

"I'm glad. I love him, too. Johnny came to us an angry boy of fourteen. He hadn't had a happy childhood. But after Daddy died, I couldn't have made it without him. He worked like a beaver. Half of this farm belongs to him because without him I'd never have been able to keep it."

Later, after they had said their good-byes and were on the road to Rawlings, Kathleen snuggled close to Johnny's side.

"This has been a wonderful day. Thank you for bringing me."

"You liked Henry Ann?"

"Oh, yes. She loves you. They all love you. You're lucky to have such a family."

"She and Ed took me in. I probably wouldn't have amounted to a hill of beans without them."

Kathleen tucked her shoulder behind his and hugged his arm. He took his hand from the wheel and held hers. She wished they could ride on like this forever through the dark vast prairie land. She had enjoyed the day, but . . . last night. There would never be another night compared to it. The only cloud on her horizon was the fact that Johnny hadn't said anything about their getting married.

Johnny had a lot on his mind. Monday morning, he was up at daylight, did his daily chores and went to the shed where he worked on the stock tank that had sprung a leak. After he tarred the hole in the tank, he turned on the windmill to fill it and went to the house to fix a bite of breakfast.

His eyes were drawn to the sagging bed with the dingy covers as soon as he entered the door. Here he had made love to the only woman he would ever love. Thank God, the lamplight had been dim. And they had left before daylight. In the unforgiving glare of the sun the place looked like what it was . . . a shack.

Lord, she is sweet, loving, giving. How can I ever ask a woman like her to share my home?

At midmorning Johnny headed to town to talk to Sheriff Carroll. He parked his truck on the street beside the courthouse and went into the sheriff's office. Deputy Thatcher looked up when he entered.

"Whatta *you* want?"

"I want to see Sheriff Carroll."

"What for?"

"None of your goddamn business."

"Now see here. Ya better keep a civil tongue in yore head when talkin' to the law."

"Bullshit! Is the sheriff here or not?" Johnny raised his voice and slapped his palm down on the counter with a sharp crack to emphasize his words.

"Ya don't have to get all shitty about it."

The door of the inner office was flung open. Sheriff Carroll stood there with his hands on his hips, a scowl on his face.

"Who'n hell's makin' all that racket out here?"

"Wasn't me." Thatcher jerked his thumb in Johnny's direction. "Was him."

"Got a few minutes, Sheriff? I'd like to talk to you."

"Go ahead."

"Not in front of him." Johnny imitated Thatcher's gesture and jerked his thumb toward the deputy.

"Come in." The sheriff went back through the door of his office. Johnny's voice stopped him.

"Not here. Outside." He glared at the deputy.

"Jesus Christ!" Sheriff Carroll stomped to the door. "This goddamn job is killin' me."

"Ya can always quit," Thatcher said to the sheriff's back, as he and Johnny went out and down the sidewalk.

"Why do you put up with him?" Johnny asked when they reached the curb where his truck was parked.

" 'Cause I ain't boss, that's why," Sheriff Carroll snarled.

"That's what I want to talk to you about and why I didn't want to say it where Doc's stool pigeon could eavesdrop." Johnny watched the sheriff closely before he continued. "I'd be obliged if what I tell you goes no farther."

"I ain't no blabbermouth."

"I'll take your word because Adelaide says that you're a decent man who got his tail in a crack. That's why I'm trusting you." Johnny leaned against the side of his truck and folded his arms over his chest. "For the last four years I've worked on and off with the Federal Bureau on special cases. I've worked with Hod Dolan, Frank Hamer, and others."

"Hamer, the Texas Ranger, who caught Bonnie and Clyde Barrow?"

"Hod Dolan and I tracked the Barrow gang's movements. Hod and I found the farmhouse where Charles Urschel, the oil man, was kept when he was kidnapped by Machine Gun Kelly and his gang."

Sheriff Carroll looked at Johnny with new interest.

Johnny was silent for a minute or two, letting what he'd said soak in before he spoke again.

"Something's going to happen here soon that'll break Doc Herman's hold on this town. Adelaide hates to see you go down with him."

"That's a pile of horseshit. He's in here tighter than a miser's purse."

"I want to know if you're with us or if you're ears and a mouth for Doc."

"If I cross him, I'll lose my job. It's plain as that."

"At times a man has to do what's right regardless. You'll lose it for sure unless he's in jail."

"Jail? Shit! I was afraid it would come to this. It's the clinic, ain't it?"

"I'm not saying. Why did he want Clara Ramsey's death declared an accident?"

"I swear I don't know. He insisted and threatened my job if I didn't go along."

"Clara Ramsey was murdered. I think I know who did it, and it had nothing to do with Doc Herman. He's scared about something, and I'd like to know what it is."

"I don't know, and that's the God's truth."

"Are you willing to stick your neck out and arrest the man who killed Clara if I can get him to confess?"

"Hell, yes. Somebody beat the shit out of that girl before he threw her out and ran over her."

"Doc may think he knows who killed her and is protecting that person. The man I think did it is from Texas and has no connection with Doc Herman."

Johnny spent the next ten minutes telling Sheriff Carroll about Marty Conroy and the meeting he and Keith had set up for Wednesday morning.

"Keith McCabe will get him across the river into

Tillison County. Will you come with me and arrest him if I can get him to confess?"

"Damn right. Hell, Johnny, I hated seeing that girl go to her grave with folks thinking she's just wandered out there on the road and got hit by a car."

"All right. Come down to my place Wednesday morning, and we'll go down to the border." Johnny turned his back and leaned on the truck. "Thatcher is watching us from the doorway."

"Bastard! He's probably already called Doc." Carroll let out a stream of obscenities. "Tell you one thing, Johnny. Doc is all het up about Miss Dolan being in the records office. Tell her to watch her step."

"If Doc or one of his thugs lays a hand on her, he'll answer to me." Johnny's face had never looked more Indian than it did when he turned to the sheriff.

"I knew that things would come to a head around here sooner or later. Doc thought they could go on forever."

"You mean the selling of babies born to unwed mothers at the clinic?" Johnny spoke matter-of-factly as if it were common news. It caught the sheriff by surprise.

"Hell and damnation! You . . . you know about that?"

"A girl came to town a week or two ago. She was looking for her *real* mother. Adelaide is keeping her out of sight down at the *Gazette*. She's not much more than a kid. You should go talk to her. Her folks, the DeBerrys, got her here sixteen years ago. They don't want her now and threw her out. She says DeBerry wants his money back because he wasn't told she had Indian blood."

Johnny was taken aback by the stunned look on the sheriff's face. He went as still as a stone. Seconds passed before he swallowed, coughed, and muttered something under his breath before he spoke.

"Doc . . . know about this?"

"No. Miss Dolan went to the records office to check Judy's birth certificate. What she found surprised the hell out of her."

"For God's sake, don't let Doc find out about the girl!" Carroll blurted.

"We're doing our best. We'd appreciate your help."

"You got it." He wiped his brow with a handkerchief he pulled from his back pocket.

"Sheriff," Thatcher called from the door of the office. "Phone."

"See you Wednesday." He turned away as if he had the weight of the world on his shoulders.

When Sheriff Carroll walked into the office, Thatcher handed him the telephone receiver.

"Carroll, what's going on down there?"

"Whatta you mean, Doc?" Sheriff Carroll glared at his deputy, who grinned brazenly back at him.

"What business does Johnny Henry have with the sheriff that he doesn't want your deputy to know about? Thatcher seemed to think you're hatching up something behind his back."

"Horsecock! Johnny Henry wouldn't talk to Thatcher if he was the last man on earth. He hates his guts. As for what we're *hatching up,* somebody rustled a couple of Johnny's steers, and he's mad as hell about it."

"Explain that to Thatcher. He's a good man and we need good men, Carroll." The call was abruptly cut off.

At the door of his office, Sheriff Carroll turned his head to stare at Deputy Thatcher.

"You son of a bitch," he said, and slammed the door.

Chapter Twenty-five

SHERIFF CARROLL SAT AT THE SCARRED TABLE that served as his desk, adjusting his weight to take pressure off the broken spring in the seat of the chair. It was an unconscious action. He had been sitting in this chair for twelve years . . . a lifetime. Each year the weight of the guilt he carried became heavier. In a small corner of his mind he was glad it was coming to an end.

The door was pushed open, and Thatcher leaned against the doorjamb.

"Want me to go out ta where the steers were rustled and take a look around?"

"No! And shut the goddamn door!"

"Johnny musta really twisted yore tail." His grin showing his tobacco-stained teeth, the deputy stepped from the room and gently closed the door.

"Son of a bitchin' bastard sneak!" Sheriff Carroll muttered. A few minutes later he reached for his hat and slammed it down on his head. Thatcher was leaning on the counter, a cigarette hanging from his lips when he opened the door. "Clean this place up!"

"You're gettin' mighty bossy, Sheriff. Somethin' eatin' on ya?"

"Yeah. You're eatin' on my nerves. I'm going out to where those steers were rustled. Be gone a couple of hours."

"A half dozen bums built a fire in the gulley back down the tracks. Want me to run 'em off?"

"Hell, no. Leave 'em alone."

"You're the boss," Thatcher said with a snicker as Sheriff Carroll went out the door.

Goddamn him. He's been a millstone around my neck long enough.

The sheriff drove south out of town toward Johnny's ranch but turned off at the first crossroad he came to, slowed the speed of the car until it was crawling along, then stopped. *No use burning up gas even if the county does pay for it.*

He placed his hat on the seat beside him, mopped his face with the palms of his hands, and let his mind wander back to when he was a nineteen-year-old kid and had just graduated from high school. The previous year had been the happiest of his life. He'd found a girl who loved him, a girl who didn't laugh at his blunders and didn't make fun of him because he was overweight. A girl he didn't dare let his mother know about.

Hannah had been so pretty, so sweet. She had been a happy, smiling girl then. It broke his heart to see her now. She was what she was because he'd not had the guts to face down his mother and take her for his wife. Dr. Herman had made their problem so easy to fix, and Hannah had loved him enough to let him make the decision; but afterward, grief for the loss of her child had broken her spirit and driven her to whiskey for forgetfulness.

She'd had two more babies since she had given birth sixteen years ago. He doubted that Hannah even knew who had fathered them while she was in a drunken stupor. The disgrace of her pregnancies had caused her family to take her to the clinic where her first child was delivered. Both babies had been declared stillborn by Dr. Herman, but Pete knew better than that.

Doc had arranged for him to get the job as deputy and later helped him get elected sheriff. From that day on, he'd been firmly under Herman's thumb, paying the price to keep the doctor from talking about his affair with Hannah, the town whore. After his mother died, he would have been free to marry Hannah, but it was too late.

He enjoyed the respect he received as sheriff. For the first time in his life he was an official and not merely Pete and Ruby Carroll's fat kid. Through the years he had thought of the baby he and Hannah had had. He'd even made it his business to find a birth certificate that had listed the date and time Hannah had given birth. Someday, he had told himself, he would go to Fort Worth, look up the DeBerrys, and see his and Hannah's child, if only from a distance.

He tilted the rearview mirror and looked at himself. The years had not been kind. He was thirty-six years old and looked ten years older. His hair was gray; his jowls sagged. He had bags beneath his eyes. It was time to face up. Maybe he could make up . . . a little, for the damage he'd done to the only person who had ever loved him.

The sheriff parked behind the *Gazette* and went in the back door. The first thing he saw was a small, dark-haired girl picking type from a rack with a long pair of tweezers. Without conscious thought, he took off his hat.

"Hello, Sheriff." Paul positioned himself protectively

between the sheriff and the girl. "Adelaide is up front. Go on through."

Pete Carroll felt a heavy lump in his chest. On stiff legs he went through to the front office. Both Adelaide and the redheaded reporter were busy at their typewriters. Alarm showed on Adelaide's face when she looked up and saw him. Her eyes darted to the door leading to the back room.

"Hello, Pete. I didn't know you were here."

"I need to talk to you, Adelaide. Can we go somewhere . . . private?"

"Well . . . ah, yes, but wait here until I talk to Paul."

"I've seen her. You don't need to tell him to hide her."

"For gosh sake, Pete—"

"I'm not here to cause trouble. I just had a long talk with Johnny Henry."

"Go on, Adelaide," Kathleen said. "I see Mrs. Smothers and a couple of her cronies across the street. They may be headed this way."

Paul looked askance when Adelaide came into the back room with the sheriff. Under Carroll's intense scrutiny, the young girl moved closer to Paul as if seeking protection. Her dark eyes went from the man with the star on his chest to Adelaide. She put her hand on Paul's arm.

"It's all right, Judy. The sheriff isn't here to arrest you. Pete, this is Judy DeBerry. She's been helping us here for the past couple of weeks."

"How do you do, sir?" Judy's voice was barely above a whisper.

"Hello." Pete's throat was so clogged he could barely speak.

Oh, Jesus. This is my little girl. Hannah and I made this pretty child out of our love for each other. She could almost be

Hannah sixteen years ago. What did I give away . . . so long ago?

"Pete," Adelaide said, then repeated it when he didn't seem to hear. "Pete, we can go into Paul's room, but I want him to hear whatever you have to say. I have no secrets from Paul."

"Honey," Paul said to Judy, "use the type out of this number six tray for the headline and out of number four for the subheading."

"All right." Judy looked anxiously at the sheriff. He was still staring at her with a strange look on his face. Then he turned and followed Adelaide. Paul gave her shoulder a squeeze before he left her.

As soon as the door closed behind them, Sheriff Carroll turned and faced them.

"She's my . . . mine," he blurted. "She's my little girl." Sobs came up out of his throat and threatened to choke him. "Mine and . . . Hannah's."

Tears flooded his eyes and rolled down his cheeks. For a minute he tried to hold back the flow, then in a defiant action threw his hat on the floor. He stood like a swaying oak before sinking down on the edge of the bed. He leaned over, his forearms on his knees, and his thick shoulders shaking with sobs.

Adelaide and Paul looked at each other helplessly. Paul opened a drawer, took out a handkerchief, and pressed it into the sheriff's hands. Paul was the only grown man Adelaide had ever seen cry. He had cried almost silently when he had told her about his life until the time he came to Rawlings. Pete Carroll was not so reserved; he sobbed as if his heart were broken. Adelaide sat down on the bed beside him and put her arm around him.

"Do you want to tell us about it, Pete?" she asked when he had quieted a bit.

He dried his eyes and blew his nose on the handkerchief Paul had given him.

"I'll wash . . . this and give it back."

"Pete, how do you know that Judy is yours and Hannah's?" Adelaide asked.

"Hannah had a baby sixteen years ago. It was mine. Doc said the thing to do would be to find it a good home. We let him have it. I found out he gave her to people named DeBerry."

"We know what Dr. Herman and Louise are doing. They don't care if the baby has a *good* home. They are selling the babies to whoever has the price," Paul declared angrily. "We're trying to get proof so they can be stopped."

"Doc's a dangerous man. Louise Munday is just as bad. I've known it for a while, but didn't know how to get out from under it." Pete Carroll's eyes were still wet, but he held up his head and looked each of them in the eye. "May God forgive me for what I've done to that girl and to Hannah."

"There's nothing I can say that will bring peace to your mind, Pete. I know what pressure you had from your mother. It still is no excuse. But that's in the past. What you do in the future is what is important."

"He'd not think twice about getting Judy out of town if he finds out who she is. He didn't want Miss Dolan to come here; he was afraid an outsider would dig up something."

"He hired Krome and Webb to hijack her?"

"Yeah, they were to take her to Texas and scare hell out of her so she'd not come back. They were not to hurt her. I'd not stand for that."

"Are you willing to help us, Pete?" Adelaide asked.

"I'll do what I can. I'm turning in my badge."

"Don't do that," Paul said hastily. "You've got to carry on as usual until we hear from a fellow who is doing some investigating. We don't want Doc or Louise to get wind that anyone suspects anything."

"Pete, do you think Dr. Herman had anything to do with Clara Ramsey's death?"

"I don't know. Clara gave him that last baby she had. I know he paid her off and she left town. She might have come back and wanted more money. She was out at the clinic while Doc was away in the city." The sheriff stood and ran his fingers through his hair.

"There's a baby buried out on the Ramsey lot. Do you know about that?"

"Harrumph!" Pete snorted, but said nothing.

"Pete? Do you know anything about it?" Adelaide persisted.

"Nothing for sure. Doc uses men passing through to do his dirty work. He might have buried something out there to satisfy Hazel." Pete stooped and picked up his hat and looked at Paul. "Can I talk to the girl, Judy, for a minute?"

"She's a sweet kid, and she's had a hell of a time. Don't put the burden of who you are on her now," Paul said sternly.

"I just want to look at her and hear her talk. I'd not hurt her for the world."

The sheriff stood back from the counter where Judy was setting type while Paul inspected her work.

"You did good, kid, but we've got some white space in that top headline. Instead of saying: *Skating Rink Coming to Town,* why don't we lengthen it to say: *Skating Rink Coming to Rawlings?* Town is five spaces and Rawlings takes up eight."

"Yeah." Judy laughed, forgetting for a minute the sheriff was there and looking at her.

"Have you ever skated?" Paul asked.

"Not on a skating rink. I skated on the sidewalk."

"Same thing. How about you, sheriff. You ever been on a rink?"

"Once or twice when I was young."

"You don't need to worry about the sheriff knowing you're here, Judy," Paul said when he saw anxiety return to her face. "We explained to him why you had run away from home."

Judy looked across the counter at the sheriff. Her eyes were large and deep brown. Her hair, too, was deep brown and not Indian straight like her mother's, but with a bit of natural curl. *She is so pretty.*

"Don't worry," he managed to say. "You'll not have to go back there. No one will make you do anything you don't want to do."

"I'm glad of that. I'm never going back *there*." She smiled at him, and it encouraged him to say,

"You like being here with Adelaide and Paul?"

"Oh, yes! I'm going to hate to leave. But I . . . know I can't stay here forever."

"I don't know about that," Paul said with genuine affection. "You're the best printer's devil I've ever had."

"The printer's devil," Judy said, her eyes twinkling at the sheriff, "is the one who does the dirty work of tearing down the pages. Paul let me think that's a very important job."

"It is, you little twerp." Paul jerked on a strand of her hair.

Pete choked down his jealousy of the friendly affection that was evident between Paul and his daughter. Maybe someday she would feel that way toward him.

After he left the building and got into his car, he could still see in his mind's eye the face of a pretty young girl with soft brown eyes and dark fluffy hair.

We have a daughter and she is beautiful. I wish you could see her, Hannah. You'd be so proud.

A message awaited Sheriff Carroll when he arrived at the office on Wednesday morning.

"Doc wants you down at the city office."

Thatcher had ceased taking orders from the sheriff and made no bones about it. He had not cleaned the office. He went out without saying where he was going and made no pretense of being civil.

"What for?"

"You'll find out when you get there."

Instead of walking the half block to the city office, the sheriff got in his car and headed south out of town. By defying the doctor's orders, he faced losing his job; but, what the hell, he was getting his self-respect back. He had enough money stuffed in the mattress to last a little while, even with a daughter to support.

Judy had been constantly in his mind since he found out about her. Judy Carroll. He wondered how he could go about getting her name changed. Would she be angry when she learned that he had fathered her and given her away? He hoped that he could get Hannah sobered and cleaned up before Judy met her. When that was all over, he would sell his house, take his money and his daughter, and go someplace where they were not known.

Yesterday he had gone to the *Gazette* on the pretense of

paying his subscription. Adelaide and Paul seemed to understand that he just wanted to see Judy. Even the fiery redhead had been friendly. Judy had greeted him when he came in the back door.

"Morning, Sheriff. Paul is showing me how to load the press."

"Foolish move on my part," Paul had growled. "She'll be taking my job."

Sheriff Carroll thought about Paul Leahy. When he had first come to town Doc had insisted that they find out everything they could about the man. They learned that he had been a reporter for a paper in Houston, Texas, and worked his way up to the position of editorial editor. From a family of means himself, he had married into a prominent Houston family.

After an explosion and fire that killed his wife and mother-in-law, his father-in-law had insisted that he be arrested for murder even though he had been badly burned in an attempt to save the two women. Paul had served ten years in Huntsville prison before a man, who had been having a love affair with Paul's wife, confessed to the crime on his deathbed. He had intended to destroy the house, not knowing the women were inside.

Paul Leahy had been given a full pardon by the Texas governor and money from the rather large insurance policy he'd had on his wife, and his home had been restored. He had promptly given it to a hospital that specialized in treating burn victims, then disappeared.

Doc tried hard to find out something to discredit the man. He didn't dare use the fact that Paul had been in prison for murder lest he alienate the Texas governor who had pardoned him. Doc finally had backed off, hoping that Paul would move on. But he had stayed and provided the strength Adelaide needed to keep the paper out of Herman's hands.

Johnny had not been sure the sheriff would show up to go with him to the river to meet Marty and Keith, and was relieved when Carroll drove into the ranch yard. He went out to meet the sheriff when he got out of the car. The man looked as if he hadn't slept in a week.

"Morning, Sheriff."

"Morning. I wasn't sure what time you wanted me to be here. I may be a mite early."

"No, just right. We've got to keep you out of sight down there until I whistle for you. We can go on down and find a place. Things go all right, Sheriff?"

"I talked to Adelaide and saw the girl. It was like a blow in the gut, Johnny. She's mine and . . . Hannah's."

"I figured there was a connection. You looked like a poleaxed steer when I told you about her."

"There's no turning back the clock to make good a mistake."

"No, but you can help us to put a stop to the baby-selling. I might as well tell you, I plan to dig up that box on the Ramsey lot and see what's inside."

"Let me know, and I'll stand watch."

"Thanks, Sheriff."

"I'm turning in this badge as soon as this is over. 'Course, if you don't pin Doc down, I'll be fired and won't get a chance to resign." His laugh was a dry cackle. "I hope they don't give the job to Thatcher."

"You might have to stay sheriff just to keep him from having the job. We'd better get going. I'll fire up the truck, and you can follow me down to the river."

*   *   *

Marty Conroy's cord britches were tucked into the tops of spit-polished boots with white stars on the sides. His Stetson was light tan with a brown band around the crown that matched his string tie. He was all business when he arrived at the McCabe ranch. Keith went out onto the porch to meet him.

"Mornin', Marty. You're right on time."

"Well, I try to be when I'm doing business."

Keith stepped off the porch. "You got a map and all the figures on the deal?"

"I've got the map. I'm still working on the figures." Marty spread the map out on the hood of his car and pointed to a little-used county road that ran east of the McCabe property. "The bridge here is a one-laner."

"How about the bridge over the main road? It would get more traffic. The relic that's there was built in the 1880s."

"Cost a little more money."

"I think we'd better go whole hog or nothing."

"Okey-dokey." Marty folded the map.

"Let's go take a look at it."

Keith opened the door on the passenger side. His eyes swept the light gray upholstery and saw the splotches of stain on the seat and on the back of the seat. *Just as Johnny had suspected; the little shithead had killed that girl!*

Marty was clearly elated to be talking to Keith about the toll bridge. He was surprised that of all the schemes he had proposed to his distant cousin this was the one that he was interested in.

"Ever since I crossed that bridge up at Lexington I've thought of putting a toll bridge across the Red River. There's a lot of traffic between Oklahoma and Texas in this area."

"How much are you going to invest, Marty?"

"I haven't decided. We can get backing; I'm not worried about that. Your name carries weight, Keith." Marty grinned.

"Hummm . . ." was Keith's noncommittal answer.

"I was thinking of a name for our company. How does Conroy and McCabe sound to you? The sign would hang on the bridge just over the toll booth. Twenty-five cents would be a fair price for a car and fifty cents for a truck. Some might want to cross on the riverbed if the river is low. They do that up in Lexington because the Canadian has a good sandy bottom. Highway number 77 crosses there; that makes a difference. No one will cross free under our bridge. If we own the land on the riverbank, they'll have to pay to get to the riverbed. That'll put a stop to that."

Marty talked continuously until they reached the rickety bridge that crossed Red River. He stopped the car on the Texas side. Both men got out.

"We would want to put our bridge just a little east of here so that the old bridge can be used while the new one is being built." Marty walked along the riverbank.

"It's all right on this side of the river, but the other side is overgrown with trees and brush. You can't see what kind of a bank is over there. Let's go take a look."

"Shall we walk?" Marty asked, and stepped out onto the bridge.

"Take the car," Keith said nonchalantly. "We may want to drive down that lane that runs alongside the river."

"Okey-dokey."

"Turn right," Keith said after they had crossed the bridge.

"Looks like a car down there."

"Somebody fishing. There's catfish in the Red a yard long."

Keith got out of the car and walked to the bank. Marty hurried around the car to join him.

"What do you think, Keith? This is—" Marty cut off his words when Johnny came out of the bushes that grew along the bank.

"Hello, Johnny, catchin' any fish?" Keith stepped back behind Marty and nodded as he spoke.

"Not biting today. How are you doin', Marty?" Johnny sneered. "Still blowin' and goin'?"

"No need to be sarcastic," Keith said evenly. "Marty and I are discussing a business deal."

"Why didn't you come to your girlfriend's funeral, Marty? You did know that she was killed."

"Who . . . was killed?"

"Clara Ramsey, a week ago."

"How would Marty know the girl was killed? He was down at Conroy. Isn't that right, Marty?"

"That's right. How would I know?"

"You were outside the Twilight Gardens the night she was killed."

"That's a lie. I was in Conroy."

"Now see here, Johnny, don't be accusing my cousin of something if you don't have proof."

Johnny stepped over and opened the car door. "Explain these bloodstains, Marty?"

"Stay out of my car. You've no right—" He started around the car to the driver's side. Keith moved in place and leaned against the door.

"Tell him, Marty, so we can go."

"I spilled soda pop."

"Liar," Johnny said. "Those are bloodstains. It's almost impossible to get them out once they've dried." Johnny bent over the seat and started looking on the carpeted floorboard and around the seat.

"What're you doing? Stay out of my car!" Marty tugged on Johnny's arm.

"Keep your hands off me, or I'll use you for catfish bait," Johnny snarled and brushed him off. He continued to search, lifting the mat running his hand along the floor beneath the seat.

"Uh-oh!" He straightened and turned to face Marty. Keith was watching over the top of the car. Johnny opened his hand, and lying on his palm was a small white tooth. "Here's my proof, Keith. Eldon Radner, the undertaker told me that Clara had two teeth knocked out. Here's one of them. Explain that, Marty." Johnny closed his fist over the tooth.

"It's . . . it's not hers."

"We can dig her up and find out. Or did you beat up another girl in your car?"

"No, I didn't. Keith . . . ?"

"Tell him, Marty. We'll all stand by you. Johnny, go easy on him. He is my cousin."

"Keith, I . . ."

"The only thing that'll keep him out of the electric chair is a confession, and he's too stupid to realize that. Hell, I'll drag him in and turn him over to the Feds. They got ways of making a man confess he killed his grandma even if she's still alive."

"Do you have to go that far?" Keith asked.

"I'll go as far as I have to. Clara's mother is a friend of mine."

"Keith, I didn't mean . . ."

"Didn't mean what, Marty? Johnny, stay out of this. Marty is my cousin."

"She was going to— Keith, I didn't mean to."

"What was she going to do? Tell me so that I can help you."

"She was going to tell . . . Mother she was pregnant. Jesus, Keith, Mother wouldn't have let me marry a whore like Clara even if she was pregnant."

"She told you she was pregnant? Hell, Marty, that was no reason to kill her."

"She called Mother. She told her we were engaged and that she was coming down to see her. Mother got all worked up and—I had to stop her."

"How'd it happen?" Keith asked gently.

Chapter Twenty-six

I WAITED AT THE HONKY-TONK 'cause I knew she'd go there," Marty said, his voice squeaky. "She came out and got in the car. We drove out and parked on the road. She just wouldn't listen to reason. Then she hit me. I wasn't going to let a whore get away with hitting me. I hit her back. She bit me on my . . . you know where."

"You had your tally-whacker out?"

"Well . . . she wanted to do it. Begged me to. After I hit her she said she was sorry and then she just leaned down and before I knew what she was going to do, she bit me. Hard. It hurt like hell. I lost my temper."

"So you beat her, threw her out, and ran over her with the car. You're a big man, Marty," Johnny sneered. "What did you hit her with?"

Marty ignored Johnny's question so Keith asked it. "What did you hit her with?"

"A soda pop bottle."

"The deed is done," Keith said. "We've got to decide what to do about it."

"Can't we just . . . forget it?"

"Not with Johnny knowing about it. Use your head."

"Well . . . we could . . . could—"

"Kill him? I don't think so. We'd have to kill the sheriff, too."

"What? Where?"

"Right behind you."

"Oh, Jesus! Oh, God, Keith. What'll I do?"

"Let me think. What's the best thing to do?" Keith took
a notebook from his pocket. He placed it on the top of the
car and began to write. "I'll put this down, Marty. You read
it and sign it and go along with the sheriff. I'll hightail over
to Mineral Wells and get the best lawyer I can find. He'll be
up there to see you pronto."

"But . . . I don't want to go to jail."

"Clara didn't want to get killed either, you shithead!"
Johnny growled the words.

" 'Course you don't want to go to jail," Keith assured
Marty, "but this is the best way to get out of this fix. There's
too much evidence. The bloodstains, the tooth, and they've
got pictures of the tire tracks that ran over the girl. You can
explain it all to your lawyer."

Keith finished writing. "This is what I've written. 'I,
Marty Conroy, do freely confess to killing Clara Ramsey in
Tillison County on the night of October 20, 1938.' Read it
and sign it, Marty."

"You didn't say anything about her biting me," Marty
whined.

"You'll have to tell the lawyer and the judge about that."

"Do you think this is the best thing to do?"

"Absolutely. You said that you killed her."

"But I didn't mean to." Marty signed the confession and
gave it back to Keith.

"She's still dead."

"You didn't mean to run over her three times after she
was down and lying in the road?" Johnny taunted.

"You just stay out of this. You always wanted to get something on me." Marty turned on Johnny. "You're nothing but a dirt farmer and the by-blow of a drunk Indian and whore. Your own sister said so."

Johnny hit him squarely in the mouth. Blood spurted from his split lip. Marty took several staggering steps backward, then stretched out on the ground.

"That wasn't for what you said to me. It was for Clara's little girl and her mother. Get up, you son of a bitchin' bastard. Sheriff, put the handcuffs on him and haul his ass off to jail. I hope I'm there when they fry you in the chair."

The sheriff put Marty in the back of his car and handcuffed him to a bar that had been installed along the back of the front seat. By the time they left, Marty was blubbering like a baby.

"I don't feel one bit sorry for him," Johnny said. "You should have seen that girl. Her jaw was broken, her mouth split, and she had bruises all over her face and arms. The bastard stomped her when she was down. Then he ran over her, backed up, and ran over her again."

"You were lucky to find that tooth," Keith said with a grin.

"Yeah, wasn't I? I found it out in the barn where old Becky had her pups. Pups are getting old enough to shed teeth. I was thinking I'd have to pull one."

"Even surprised me when you came up with it. That was a pretty good act we put on. Maybe we ought to go out to Hollywood and get in the movies."

"Hod and I did that a time or two, but Hod was the mean one. He could be meaner than a cornered polecat."

"I'll take Marty's car back to the ranch until they decide

what they want to do with it." Keith slapped Johnny on the back. "You done good, son."

"You're no slouch yourself. I'm going on into town. I don't think Carroll will have any trouble with Marty, but he might with Doc Herman. I told him to put that confession in a safe place."

"Marty's arrest will tear up Conroy, Texas."

"It just might tear up Rawlings, Oklahoma, too."

Marty Conroy had not been locked up in the Tillison County jail ten minutes when word reached Doc Herman at the clinic. He hurried down the hall to where Louise was supervising two aides and told her to come to the office.

"Thatcher called and said Carroll has arrested a man for killing Clara Ramsey."

Louise sat down heavily in the chair. "I thought . . . I thought—"

"That I had killed her. That's rich. I thought you had. That's the reason I insisted that what happened to her was an accident."

Louise began to laugh. "You were protecting me?"

"Of course. I reward loyalty. Speaking of loyalty, I'm going to have to do something about Carroll. He's assuming too much authority. I sent word for him to come in this morning. He didn't. He never said a word to me or to Thatcher about a suspect. I think it's got something to do with Johnny Henry."

"You might have to bring out your ace in the hole, Doc. Threaten to tell that he sold his and Hannah's kid. He'll knuckle under. He loves that job as sheriff."

"I don't want the state marshals coming in here. Carroll knows that."

"You think the state marshals are interested in the murder of a whore down here in Tillison County?"

"They might be. I think we should shut down here for a while."

"The girl from Shawnee will give birth any day now."

"Maybe we should send her packing."

"We can't do that. We've got a couple coming in from Waco for that baby. I told them five hundred dollars."

Doc paced up and down the room. "All right. This will be the last for a while." He placed his hat carefully on his head and tilted it to just the right angle. "I'll go down to the jail and see what's going on."

Louise watched through the window as Doc left the clinic. Her heart was soaring. Doc, her love, had been protecting her at the risk of his own credibility when he believed that she had killed Clara to keep the little bitch from demanding more money.

He loved her. It was clear to her now that he might never tell her, but it was all right. She knew in her heart that he did.

Johnny came into the back door of the *Gazette,* went to the door of the office and beckoned to Kathleen and Adelaide. He had a large grin on his face. After swooping down and kissing Kathleen soundly, he told his news.

"We got a confession out of Marty Conroy. He killed Clara."

"Johnny! That's wonderful!" Kathleen hugged his arm.

Paul turned to Judy. "Start taking out the skating rink headline, Sweet Pea."

"Keith managed to get him across the river. The sheriff and I were waiting for him. We didn't call the sheriff in until after Marty had confessed. We got a signed confession. He said he had to stop Clara from telling his mother that she was pregnant."

"She couldn't have been pregnant. Hazel told me that when she had that last baby, Doc Herman fixed her so that she wouldn't have more children."

"He killed her for that?" Adelaide asked.

"What really set him off was that she bit him after he hit her." Johnny realized he was getting onto a subject unfit for Judy's ears and quickly changed it. He told about the stains in the car and *finding* the tooth.

"I'll write up the story. I'll need quotes from Sheriff Carroll. I don't know if Rawlings can stand this much excitement."

"Honey, this is just a drop in the bucket," Johnny said. Then, "Have you heard anything about the other?"

"Nothing, but it's only been a week. We've got Sheriff Carroll on our side, thanks to you." Kathleen slid her hand down his arm to capture his.

"Adelaide's instincts about him were right. He's a good man who got in over his head and didn't know how to get out." Johnny loosened his hand from hers and put his arm around her. "I wonder what's going on down at the jail. Doc isn't going to like having his decision proven wrong."

Sheriff Carroll looked up when Doc Herman opened the door.

"It didn't take Thatcher long to call you."

"I understand you arrested a man for Clara Ramsey's murder."

"That's right. He's back in the jail."

"Just how did this come about?"

"I have feelers out all the time, Doc. I heard that a Texas Ranger knew that he was the killer and was bringing him across the river. I went down, talked to him, got him to confess, and brought him in. It's that simple." The sheriff glanced at Thatcher and saw the smirk on his face.

"Who is he?"

"Marty Conroy from Conroy, Texas."

"I've heard of him. His family has influence."

"He's still a killer."

"Let me see the confession."

"I don't have it."

"Who has?"

"The ranger."

"You mean to tell me that you put a man in jail and you don't have your hands on his confession?"

"I'm saying it's not in my hands at the moment, but it'll be here in time for the hearing."

"Let him out."

"No. He stays where he is at least until Judge Fimbres gets here."

"I say let him out. We'll be the laughingstock of the state if we try to convict a man on a confession you got out of him after you worked him over."

"I suppose Thatcher told you Conroy had a busted mouth." Sheriff Carroll sneered. "He don't miss much."

"We have the reputation of the town to consider. What's got into you, Carroll? You've been acting strange lately."

"I'm doing my job, the job the people elected me to do."

"Give Thatcher the keys so that he can let that man out. He'll be on his way. Once he's in Texas, he's out of our hands."

"I won't do that. He killed that girl, and he'll stand trial."

"You're going to be sorry for this when this town is overrun with state lawmen. Your skirts are not entirely clean. Mark my word, Carroll. You'll be very sorry."

"I'm already sorry, Doc. I'm sorry that I never had the guts to stand up to you a long time ago. Better late than never. I'm doing it now."

"Speak to you for a minute, Sheriff?" Johnny opened the door, but didn't enter the office.

"What are you doin' back here?" Thatcher said. "You might as well move in."

"Move in with a stinkin', lowdown skunk like you?" Johnny said. "I'm not that crazy."

Doc Herman brushed past Johnny without speaking. His face was red, and he was breathing hard in an attempt to control his anger. He jerked his head, and Thatcher followed him out.

"Doc givin' you trouble?" Johnny asked when they were alone.

"He wants me to let Marty out and forget about this thing."

"What's his reason?"

"He's heard of his family. Says they've got influence. He's afraid state marshals will come in."

"What are you going to do?"

"I'll not turn that son of a bitch loose. They'll have to kill me first. Judge Fimbres is a straight shooter. I don't think he approves of all that Doc does. He might help if I can get word to him. I don't dare leave the jail."

"Want me to get the judge?"

"I'd appreciate it. Give him a rundown about what's going on. I'll not be able to talk freely because of Thatcher. I want the judge to hold the confession. If I turn my back, Thatcher will tear this place apart looking for it."

Later when Johnny was in the back room of the *Gazette,* Kathleen came back with the story she had written about the murder and the arrest for the next day's paper.

"I'll read it to you. I've edited it so many times it's hard

to read." She sat down beside him on the cot he used sometimes when he stayed overnight and read her story. When
she finished she asked, "What do you think?"

"You could mention that Keith is a member of the Texas
Rangers. A former member, but you can forget that. You're
giving me too much credit. Give the credit to Carroll. He
needs it, and I don't."

"I could couple his name with yours when I write about
the pictures and the stains in the car. I didn't think I'd better mention the tooth trick." She laughed and wrinkled her
nose at him.

Kathleen scribbled on the paper. "I'll have to retype
this. Paul will be totally confused when he tries to set it on
the linotype. Are you coming in tonight?"

"Kathleen, phone," Adelaide called.

"Oh, shoot," Kathleen said and stood. "You won't run
off, will you?"

"Not right away. Go on, take your call."

She hesitated, then leaned down and whispered in his
ear. "I'm so proud of you." She kissed his ear, hurried to
the front office, and picked up the receiver. "Hello."

"Miss Dolan, Barker Fleming."

"Hello," she said again, motioning for Adelaide to stop
typing.

"I have a picnic basket for you to replace the one I lost."

"You needn't have gone to the trouble." Kathleen heard
a click on the line, then another.

"I took the liberty of filling it, Miss Dolan. I think you'll
be pleased."

"I'm sure I will. When will you be coming this way?"

"Would Friday afternoon be convenient? I'll be bringing a friend. Gifford is interested in seeing a fellow he used
to work with. And, Miss Dolan, could I impose on you to

deliver a message to Judge Fimbres that I would like to see him sometime Friday afternoon."

"I would be glad to. Shall I tell him that you will come to the courthouse?"

"If you will, please. How are things in Rawlings?"

"Fine, Mr. Fleming. I'll be looking for you on Friday."

Kathleen was smiling when she hung up the receiver.

When the phone rang at the clinic, Louise hurried to answer it. Doc could be calling from the city office.

"Hello."

"This is Flossie. A long-distance call came to the *Gazette* from Oklahoma City, but it was nothing important."

"Who called? You don't have to give me your valuable opinion."

"Barker Fleming talked to Miss Dolan. You know, he's that good-looking Indian with the big car. I think he's got a crush on her. He lost her picnic basket and is bringing her another one. I heard someone talking from the tannery last week. He's going to be running it. His family owns it, you know."

"What else did he say to Miss Dolan?"

"He's bringing a picnic basket and he's filling it for her. Isn't that romantic? I can't help it if they didn't say anything important. You told me to let you know of any out-of-the-area calls." Flossie sounded peeved.

"I know I did. Thanks, Flossie. Let me know if there are any calls between the paper and the sheriff's office."

"Sheriff's office? Why—"

"Just let me know," Louise said impatiently, and hung up the phone.

Chapter Twenty-seven

KATHLEEN AND JOHNNY SAT IN THE TRUCK parked behind the *Gazette*.

"Such beautiful hair." Johnny stroked her curls, then tipped her chin with a finger and kissed her.

"Not everyone likes red hair. I'm stuck with it."

"And stuck with me."

"I'm happy to be stuck with you, Johnny Henry. How come you changed your mind about digging up the box at the cemetery?" Kathleen asked and snuggled her hand into the open collar of his shirt.

"I began to think of it as evidence. If I go out there and dig it up, find nothing in it and put it back, it could be said I removed what was in it. If we wait and dig it up with witnesses, maybe Grant and Judge Fimbres, and find it empty, it'll be credible evidence."

"That makes sense. I hadn't thought of it that way although one of the dates I got at the courthouse corresponds with the date Clara's baby was born. Hazel remembered it because it was her mother's birthday."

"You got the ball rolling, honey."

"Are you eager to see your friend, Mr. Gifford?"

"Yeah, I haven't seen him for a couple of years." He

drew her head to his shoulder. "The paper goes to press tomorrow. Tonight we'd better tell Hazel about Marty being arrested. We don't want her to hear it from someone else."

"You'll go with me?"

"Sure."

She curled her arm around his neck. "I like you a lot, Mr. Henry."

"That's a relief. I was thinkin' you kissed men you didn't like."

His lips touched hers, lightly at first, then with longer and more intense kisses, concentrating his attention on doing this while his palm wandered from one of her breasts to the other.

"Did I tell you that the other night was the most wonderful night of my life?" she murmured.

"Only about a dozen times. It *was* great, wasn't it? I might have to marry you so that we can do it again." He kissed her again and again; his mouth wandering over her nose, her eyes, her cheeks. When he lifted his head, his breath was warm on her wet lips. "I've got to get crackin'. I'll take you around to your car and follow you home."

The first paper to come off the press was displayed in the window of the *Gazette*. Paul had done an excellent job making up the front page. TEXAN ARRESTED FOR MURDER blazed across the top. A picture of Clara Ramsey lying in the ditch and a picture of Sheriff Carroll beside his car were stacked along one side. The subtitle read: SHERIFF CARROLL BRINGS IN CONFESSED KILLER OF LOCAL WOMAN.

In the story, Kathleen had given as much credit as she could to Sheriff Carroll, reported that at first he thought the death was an accident, but after viewing the body in the funeral parlor, he realized that Clara Ramsey had been murdered. Assisting in the arrest, Kathleen wrote, had been Johnny Henry, a local rancher, and Keith McCabe, a Texas Ranger. A paragraph detailed Marty Conroy's background, stating that he was from a prominent Texas family and had been seen with the victim at the rodeo and again at the Twilight Gardens on the night she was killed. The hearing would be held November 3, allowing time for Conroy's Texas lawyer to find representation for him in Oklahoma.

The usual number of papers reserved for sale in the office were gone within an hour. Paul had wisely increased the print run, and more papers were brought from the back room. Adelaide said she couldn't remember when there had been such a demand for the paper.

Johnny came to the office just as Woody was taking the bundles to the post office. He held the door until the wagon cleared, then came in, his eyes on Kathleen and hers on him.

"I've been down to the sheriff's office. He spent the night at the jail since he didn't know how much he could trust Allen Lamb, his extra man."

"So he's hanging in there?"

"You bet. He was afraid Thatcher and Doc Herman would find a way to let Marty out and get him back over the line into Texas."

"Doc is in a panic, or he wouldn't even think of doing anything so foolish," Paul said.

"He came back last night and told Carroll that he was fired and to give his keys to Thatcher. The sheriff is more of a man than I thought he was. He told Doc that he had been elected by the people of the county and, as mayor of Rawlings, Doc had no authority to fire him. Judge Fimbres backed him up."

"Oh, my. If you think Doc is mad now, wait until he finds out he's being investigated." Adelaide's eyes sought Paul as they always did when she was worried.

"He won't find out unless they come up with something that'll stand up in court."

"They've found something, or Grant Gifford wouldn't be coming down. Judge Fimbres has called in a state marshal from Elk City. He'll be here tonight. I told Carroll to keep his gun handy until then. Desperate men do desperate things." Johnny took a paper off the counter and dropped a nickel in the cup.

"You don't have to pay for a paper," Adelaide protested.

"I'm taking this down to Carroll."

"Paul and I are going to talk to Judy tonight. We think we should tell her everything. She took a big risk coming here and has the right to know."

"Even about the sheriff?" Kathleen asked.

"Even that."

Paul rolled his eyes when Kathleen took Johnny's hand and led him to the back room.

"I remember when *you* got *me* in the back room every chance you got." Adelaide cocked a brow.

"I don't have many chances nowadays with so many people around." Paul complained, then came to her, and whispered. "I'd rather get you in *my* bed."

Out of sight of the front office, Johnny put his arms around Kathleen and kissed her.

"I'm going to stay with Carroll until the state marshal gets here. Then I'll go home and get some things done."

"You'll be here tomorrow?"

"I don't figure the others can get to town before noon. I'll be here before then."

*   *   *

At the clinic, Doc Herman paced his office. Louise sat in a chair beside his desk, her rabbitlike front teeth worrying her lower lip. She had chewed the thick coat of lipstick, and it was smeared on her teeth.

"I've got a feeling there's things going on here that I don't know about. Carroll has got his back up. He's getting encouragement from somewhere."

"Johnny Henry. And he's being egged on by that red-headed bitch at the newspaper."

"What could she have found out from the birth records except that there are more births here than in most towns? For obvious reasons, none of the people who send their girls here would talk."

"Maybe we don't have anything to worry about. If the marshals come in, it will be only to work on the Conroy case. They've no proof of anything."

"Call the people in Waco and tell them not to come. Tell them the baby died."

"What'll we do with the baby when it's delivered?"

"Keep it for a while and see what happens. Destroy the file of places we've advertised the clinic as a home for unwed mothers. That will be a start."

"Let's shut down and go away, Doc. You said we would when we got enough money."

"The money wouldn't last any time at all, Louise. I want to show you the world."

Louise hoisted herself up out of the chair. Her dyed hair was stuck to her forehead with sweat, and perspiration stained her uniform beneath her armpits. Revulsion made Doctor Herman close his eyes for a long moment, preparing himself for the ordeal of kissing her. He went to her and kissed her gently on the mouth, forcing himself to take his time.

"Now run along, my dear. I need to think about what's best for us to do."

"You're the best man in the whole world, Doc. Just tell me what to do. I'll stick my head in the fire if it'll help you."

"Thank you, dear, sweet lady. No man has ever had a more faithful lady friend." He patted her cheek.

Christ, but I'll be glad to see the last of you and your rabbitlike teeth, your painted face, and your cowlike devotion.

By Friday morning Kathleen's nerves were standing on end. At breakfast Hazel had been quiet. To lose her daughter by accident had been bad enough, but to know that someone had deliberately killed her was devastating. Kathleen hoped that Marty Conroy's conviction would help ease her pain.

As soon as she reached the office, Kathleen asked Adelaide how Judy had taken the news that Sheriff Carroll was more than likely her father and that her mother was a Cherokee girl who, unable to cope with the loss of her baby, had turned to alcohol.

"She is so mature for her age," Adelaide said. "Her response to that was, 'She must have loved me very much.' "

"What did she say about Sheriff Carroll?"

"Not much. She said he was nice."

"It was a lot for a young girl to swallow all at once."

"Paul explained to her how important she was to the building of a case against Doctor Herman and Louise Munday. He asked her to write down every word she could remember that either of the DeBerrys said to her about when they came here to get her. She was never adopted by them, because their names are on her birth certificate."

"I wish you would marry Paul. He's such a wonderful man."

"I'm thinking about it. He loves children. His wife wouldn't give him any, and I'm too old."

"Adopt one. You and Paul would make wonderful parents."

"We could have *bought* one from Doc," Adelaide said bitterly.

Kathleen cocked her ear toward the back room. "Johnny's here."

"When are you two going to get married?"

"He hasn't asked me, Adelaide."

"He will," Adelaide said confidently, then: "Mr. Fleming is here."

With Barker Fleming was a man dressed in a light tan suit with a Stetson to match and wearing round wire-rimmed glasses. Another car pulled up alongside Barker Fleming's and two men got out. All four came into the office.

After greeting Kathleen and Adelaide, Barker introduced Grant Gifford and two marshals.

"Miss Dolan and Miss Vernon, meet Grant Gifford, Oklahoma State Attorney General, and Marshals Whitney and Putman."

After shaking hands with the two women, Grant Gifford looked past them to where Johnny lounged in the doorway leading into the pressroom. A smile lit his face.

"Johnny Henry, I've a notion to give you a damn good licking for not coming up to see us." Grant threw his hat on the desk, dropped into a crouch, and put up his fists. Johnny did the same.

"You've got so soft you couldn't whip Aunt Dozie," Johnny retorted.

"Think not? Want to take me on, boy?"

The two met, clasped hands, and pounded on each other. "Good to see you, Grant."

"Good to see you, too, Johnny. It's been two years. We're not going to let that much time go by again."

"How's Karen?"

"Sassy. Our Mary Ann is going to be just like her. Margie is more like me, calm and sweet!"

"Has Karen heard you say that?"

"Lord, I hope not! We got down to Red Rock a few months ago. Karen's dad is getting on."

"Aunt Dozie told me you were there."

"Don't yawl be trackin' dat cow-doo on my clean 'noleum. I wearin' de flowers off scrubbin' after yawl." Grant imitated the old woman, and both men laughed. "She was a crackerjack."

"She still is and she's getting on, too," Johnny said.

Barker introduced the two marshals to Johnny and Paul, then stood back and proudly admired the way Johnny presented himself to the marshals. He had not mentioned to Grant Gifford that Johnny was his son, leaving it to Johnny to tell his friend if he wanted him to know.

They went into the pressroom and, after Paul was introduced, Johnny told Grant that Marty Conroy was locked up in the jail.

"Marty Conroy? What's the little jelly bean done now?"

Johnny explained about Clara's death and Dr. Herman's part in wanting the death to be declared an accident. He told how he and Keith had worked together to get a confession.

Grant chuckled. "It's nothing to laugh about, but I can just hear Marty telling the judge that he is the Conroy from Conroy, Texas."

"The doctor ordered the sheriff to let him out, but the sheriff refused. Then he tried to fire the sheriff, but Judge Fimbres interfered."

"What connection would Conroy have with Dr. Herman?" Grant asked, looking from Johnny to Paul.

"We don't think he has a connection," Paul said. "We believe he feared the state marshals coming in and uncovering some of his activities."

"Fleming laid out a good case against the doctor," Grant said. "We went to work right away investigating every aspect of the doctor's life. We contacted Mr. and Mrs. DeBerry in Fort Worth. Mr. DeBerry is bitter and will testify against him. I understand the DeBerry girl is here."

"She is," Paul said. "She doesn't want to go back to the DeBerrys. We are quite sure we know who her father is. She was born to an unwed mother. We don't want her going to the orphans' home. Adelaide and I will take care of her."

"If she's safe and content here, we can decide what to do about her later."

"Clara Ramsey, the girl Marty is charged with killing, had a baby a year ago," Johnny said. "It is supposed to have been stillborn and buried out on the family lot. Kathleen discovered in the records at the courthouse a birth certificate made out to a couple from Weatherford, Texas, just one day later. Kathleen and I believe the box Doc had buried to satisfy Clara's mother is empty."

Kathleen was glad to leave the telling of the details up to Johnny. There was genuine affection between him and Grant Gifford. She wished he would direct some of his remarks to Barker Fleming, but that would have to come when he was ready to acknowledge the relationship.

Grant glanced at the pretty redhead who sat beside

Johnny listening with rapt attention to every word he said, and realized that they were more than friends.

"We should find out what's in that box. I'll take Marshal Putnam and go see Judge Fimbres." Grant stood. "Meanwhile, Fleming, why don't you and Johnny go with Marshal Whitney to the cemetery. There should be two witnesses to what's in it, or not in it. Then come down to the courthouse. If it's empty as you suspect, you'll need to sign an affidavit."

In the middle of the afternoon two cars drove up to the clinic. Barker Fleming and Grant were in one car, the two marshals in the other. Johnny had been invited to come along, but had declined.

The woman at the desk looked up with large frightened eyes when four men came into the reception area. Grant and Barker held back and the marshals took the lead.

"May I help you?" the woman asked timidly.

"Dr. Herman," Putnam said. "Where is his office?"

"I'll get him."

"Is he with a patient?"

"No. I don't think so." She stood and moved toward the door behind her.

Marshal Putman stepped quickly around the desk. "Don't bother. Sit back down, ma'am, and stay here. We'll find him."

Marshal Whitney flung open the door. Dr. Herman was standing in the middle of the room.

"I thought I heard voices out there. Who are you?" Doc's eyes went beyond Marshal Whitney to the other three men. "What do you mean coming into my office without knocking?" The four men said nothing, but looked at the doctor, letting their silence work on his nerves. "Is this a holdup?"

Doc's voice was hoarse when it broke the silence. "I don't keep money here."

Marshal Putman opened his coat, showing a holstered revolver, then reached into his inside coat pocket and flipped out a badge.

"Federal Marshal James Putman. This is Marshal Whitney, Mr. Gifford, Oklahoma State Attorney General, and Mr. Barker Fleming."

"What can I do for you?" Dr. Herman's face was flushed, and his voice trembled slightly.

Grant stepped forward. "Sit down, Doctor, and tell us why you buried an empty box out on the Ramsey plot."

"What are you talking about?" The doctor moved behind the desk but didn't sit down.

"I think you know, but I'll tell you anyway. Clara Ramsey had a baby a year ago. She told her mother it was stillborn. She sold you a live baby, took the money, and left town. You sold that baby to Mr. and Mrs. Carl Sheldon of Weatherford, Texas. You fixed the records to show that Mrs. Sheldon had come here and had had the baby."

"Why . . . why . . . that's the most ridiculous thing I ever heard of! The Sheldons were on their way home when she went into labor. They stopped here, and I delivered their baby."

"Sit down, Doctor." After the doctor was seated, he asked, "Why did you bury an empty box?"

"It had the body of a stillborn child in it when I hired a man to bury it."

"Mr. Fleming and Marshal Whitney just dug up the box and all that was in it was medical waste, bandages, gauze, and several empty bottles. The trash in that box came from this clinic."

"That's a lie!" Doc jumped to his feet. His face was beet red and cords stood out on the sides of his neck.

"Well, never mind that. Sit down, Doctor." Grant said patiently. "Sixteen years ago you sold a baby to a couple named DeBerry for two hundred dollars. You told the father of the baby that you knew a couple who were well-off and would give the baby a good home, something he couldn't do. The DeBerrys threw her out and want their money back. You told them that the girl's mother was blond and blue-eyed. The truth is that the baby's mother was a Cherokee. The girl is here in town looking for her real mother."

"That redheaded hussy at the paper has dug up all this nonsense."

"We have talked to a number of women who supposedly had babies here. Some of them have admitted you furnished them a baby for a fee. We'll have a number of these people at the trial."

"Trial? You can't prove anything. It's their word against mine. I'm a respected doctor. I've looked after this town and kept it going when other towns this size dried up."

"The First National Bank in Oklahoma City released your bank records. It seems that for eighteen years you have sent checks in the amounts of one hundred, two hundred, then three or four hundred dollars. You increased the price to fit the demand."

"My assistant must . . . have . . . could have. I never—" Doc stammered.

"Do you know a woman by the name of Ardith Moore? She visited you each time you stayed at the Biltmore in Oklahoma City. You like the kinky stuff, huh, Doctor?" Grant lifted his brows. "What you do in bed won't have much bearing on the trial, but it'll be good juicy stuff for the newspaper."

"You're out to ruin my good name."

"It's already ruined."

"I've worked for years to help unfortunate girls." Spit ran down the side of Dr. Herman's mouth, and a vein throbbed in his temple.

"Did you ever stop to think that selling a human being is a federal offense? This is big-time stuff, Doc. So big that you'll not have to share a jail cell with Marty Conroy. You'll get a cell all to yourself in the federal prison."

"I've done nothing wrong! My assistant will tell you—"

"We plan to talk to her. She'll turn on you if it means saving her own hide."

On the other side of the door leading into the examination room, Louise Munday listened, and her world fell apart.

They're arresting Doc! My beloved Doc is going to jail. My darling Doc, who kissed me so sweetly just this morning. We'll never be able to leave this dreadful town and go away together.

This can't be happening! They'll use me to send Doc to prison! She looked frantically around. *They'll not use me, if they can't find me.*

Louise grabbed her purse and headed for the door, then went back to her desk, took out a small pistol, and shoved it in the pocket of her uniform. She tore the starched cap from her head, grabbed the blue nurse's cape, and flung it around her shoulders. She ran down the hall past the kitchen and the laundry room to the back door. Just as she reached it, a loud pop came from the front of the clinic. Without giving a thought to what it was, she hurried to her car and drove away.

Chapter Twenty-eight

SHERIFF CARROLL WAS RELIEVED when the state marshal arrived from Elk City. Judge Fimbres had told him that he had the authority to fire Deputy Thatcher; but he knew that there would be trouble, so he waited for the marshal. When he told Thatcher to turn in his badge and leave, the man refused to go quietly. Johnny arrived during the confrontation and when the deputy stated his intention of going to Dr. Herman, Johnny suggested that he be put in a jail cell for a few hours.

"Only until Grant and the Federal Marshals get back," Johnny told the state marshal. "We don't want Thatcher going over to the clinic and gumming up the works."

Down the street at the *Gazette*, Kathleen had tried to write some routine stories while she waited for Johnny to return to tell them what had happened at the cemetery. Finally she gave up and stared out the window.

Judy had come down from the floor above and was helping Paul tear down the pages from this week's paper. The only sound in the office was the *clunk* as lead that was to be melted and reused hit the bucket.

When Johnny returned to the *Gazette* from the courthouse, Sheriff Carroll was with him. They went to the back room so that Paul and Adelaide could hear what Johnny had to tell them.

"The box at the cemetery was full of trash. Fleming and I signed affidavits, and Judge Fimbres issued an arrest order for Dr. Herman. Grant and the marshals are out there now."

Sheriff Carroll looked as if he hadn't slept for a week. His eyes kept darting to Judy. Her head was down, and she didn't look at him. Finally, he spoke to her.

"Ah . . . Judy?" When she didn't answer or look up, he tried again. "Judy, can't you look at me? I know Adelaide told you that I'm . . . I'm—who I am."

When she didn't answer, Paul said, "Honey, this is hard, but it's best if you and Sheriff Carroll talk a bit. We'll go leave you alone—"

"Don't go." She grabbed Paul's arm, her big dark eyes pleading. "Please stay."

Kathleen and Johnny moved away and went into the office.

"Judy, I was a nineteen-year-old scared kid when I gave you away," Pete Carroll began, his voice scratchy. "I had no way of making a living for myself, much less for a wife and child. My mother was the ruling force in my life. I did what I thought was best at the time."

"It's all right."

"No, it isn't. I ruined your mother's life by being so gutless. Thank God, you got away from those folks before yours was ruined."

"I'm all right now."

"That damn doctor told me that he knew people who would give you a good home, treat you like a princess, and provide you with things I'd never be able to afford. I'm sorry. I can't tell you how sorry I am."

"It's all right."

"I talked to Judge Fimbres. You don't have to worry about going back to Fort Worth or anywhere you don't want to go. I've saved up a little money. It's all yours. Every last cent of it."

"I don't want it. I want to see my . . . mother."

"She's ah . . . not well right now."

"Adelaide told me. I don't care if she's a drunk. I want to see her, help her. You should have helped her. It was hard for a mother to give up her baby."

Tears came into Pete Carroll's eyes. He turned away for a moment. When he turned back the tears ran down his face.

"You're right. I should have tried harder to help her. I was a weak-kneed fool."

"Well, you can't put spilt milk back in the bucket. You just have to go on from here," Judy said with maturity far beyond her years.

"I have a house—"

"I don't know you. I'll stay here for a while, if it's all right with Adelaide and Paul."

"Let me know if you need anything. I think I still have a job."

"I don't need anything. Not now. Paul was right. I'm glad I talked to you."

"I'd better get on back down to the jail. Things are happening fast now." Sheriff Carroll addressed his words to Paul. "Thank you for . . . looking out for her."

"It's been no trouble. I've got a lot of free work out of the little twerp. She's learning so fast that I'm afraid I'm going to have to start paying her a wage."

"I'm planning to start my own newspaper. Didn't I tell you?" Judy said with a sassy grin.

*   *   *

"What do you think is happening at the clinic?" Kathleen asked, when she and Johnny were in the office.

"I think they'll arrest him and get him out of town. Marshal Whitney filled the gas tank on the car before they went out there."

"Will Mr. Gifford go with them?"

"I would think so."

"This town is going to be turned upside down."

"It'll recover. There are good people here. They just found themselves under the thumb of Doc Herman and didn't know how to get out. A good talker can make folks think black is white. Look what that fellow Hitler is doing over in Germany."

"You're so calm and reasonable."

"Not all the time." He pulled her back from the window and kissed her.

"I'm glad you're not reasonable all the time."

They were still standing close together when the door opened. Kathleen looked around Johnny's broad shoulders to see that Barker Fleming had come in. He stood just inside the door, his hands buried in his pockets, his face grim.

"What happened?" Kathleen asked.

"He's dead." Barker placed his hat on the counter. "It happened so fast!"

"Doc Herman is . . . dead?" The back of Kathleen's hand went to her mouth, and her eyes went wide with disbelief. She recovered and headed for the back room, calling, "Adelaide and Paul—"

The four of them stood in shocked silence while Barker told them what had happened at the clinic.

"Gifford had been talking to him, telling him that he

was charged with a federal offense. When he told him it was time to go, Herman said he wanted to find his address book so that he could contact another doctor to take over the clinic. He opened a drawer, came up with a pistol in his hand, put it under his chin, and pulled the trigger."

"Oh my goodness!"

"It was a powerful slug. In a fraction of a second, his head seemed to explode. He knew what that gun would do."

"What are they doing now?" Johnny asked.

"The undertaker is there. The only staff out there are a laundress, a cook, and a nurse. The woman in the office is hysterical. They have only four patients, not very many for such a large, well-equipped clinic."

"Louise Munday will be able to take over." Adelaide held tightly to Paul's arm. "They say she's almost as good a doctor as Dr. Herman."

"She's not there. The cook said she left. I don't know if it was before we got there or while we were there. According to the staff, she runs the place."

"She was crazy in love with him and had been for years," Adelaide said. "She'll be out of her mind when she finds out."

"She's as guilty as Dr. Herman. He had to have had help in running that baby-selling business." Johnny voiced his opinion solemnly.

"I agree." Kathleen squeezed Johnny's hand. She looked up at him. He was her anchor in this tilting world of events.

"All right, ladies. Get crackin'," Paul said. "The *Gazette* is about to put out it's first *extra* edition."

"Do you think we should?" Adelaide asked.

"Absolutely. You're a newspaper woman, aren't you? The people of this town are entitled to know what's happened. If we get cracking on it, we can have it on the street by midnight."

"We . . . can't."

"We can. Judy will run the linotype, I'll get the press ready. Kathleen write your story. Adelaide set the headlines."

Excitement put a shine in Kathleen's eyes. "Johnny, while I'm taking down Mr. Fleming's account of what happened, will you go out to the clinic and ask Mr. Gifford if he'll come in when he's finished out there and give a statement?"

"Sure. Sheriff Carroll just left here. Has he been told?" Although his remark was addressed to Barker, Johnny didn't look at him.

"I'm not sure. I only heard Gifford call the undertaker when he found out that Dr. Herman was the coroner. He told the telephone operator in no uncertain terms what would happen if she listened in on his conversation."

"That must have really got Flossie flustered." Adelaide shook her head.

"I'll stop and tell the sheriff to keep his eye out for Louise Munday. I'm sure Grant will want to talk to her."

Kathleen went with Johnny to the back door. "I feel bad about Dr. Herman killing himself. When we started this we never—"

"Are you feeling guilty? He did it rather than face the music for what he had done. It has nothing to do with you. Now go write your story. It might get picked up on the national news. This is your chance to be famous."

"Will you be back?"

"Of course. I'll not let you go home alone. When your paper hits the street, it might be like seven-thirty on Saturday night around here."

"I love you, Johnny Henry."

"I love you, too."

He kissed her quick and went out.

Adelaide and Kathleen divided the task of writing the story. Adelaide wrote about Doc's background and his involvement in the community. Kathleen wrote of the events that caused him to take his life without giving details of the investigation. She mentioned that a young girl who wished to remain anonymous, had come to town looking for her parents. It had started an investigation that was ongoing.

Paul had the headlines set and locked in place. DOCTOR HERMAN IS DEAD. His subtitle read: DOCTOR TAKES HIS LIFE WHILE BEING QUESTIONED BY STATE ATTORNEY GENERAL. From the file a large engraving of the doctor was placed in the middle of the page.

Judy worked at the linotype. Paul watched over her proudly. Adelaide pulled bits and pieces of Dr. Herman's biography from the file and put them on the hook for Judy to set while she and Kathleen worked on the current story.

At eleven-thirty, the press began to roll. Adelaide and Kathleen had pored over the proof page and pronounced it as good as it could be given such short notice.

Adelaide called in her paperboys and told them the paper would sell for a dime and they could have a nickel of it. As soon as the cry was heard lights came on in homes all over town.

"Extra! Extra! Dr. Herman killed." Adelaide had told the boys to say no more than that.

It would be a night to remember, but it was not over yet.

Two hours after the paper hit the street, the excitement began to subside. The paperboys had come in, turned in the paper money, and collected their pay. They were elated over their extra money. Judy had gone up to Adelaide's apartment to go to bed. Adelaide and Paul were in his room.

Kathleen cleared her desk as Johnny watched from where he lounged in a chair. He was waiting to take her home.

"This is a night we'll never forget."

"As important as that other night you said you'd never forget?" Johnny teased.

"This night is like ho-hum compared to that night," Kathleen retorted. "But it has been exciting. Nothing like this ever happened in Liberal."

Kathleen reached under the desk and pulled out her typewriter cover. She straightened to see Louise Munday push open the door. Her hair looked as she had just come through an Oklahoma tornado. Dark lines of mascara streaked her cheeks. The look in her eyes was wild. At first her mouth worked, but nothing came out. Then a flood of words burst from her.

"Bitch! You goddamn bitch! You started it all . . . you did it . . . you're goin' to pay . . . for what you did to . . . him. He helped those sinful whores get rid of their brats and you . . . none of you understood how . . . good he was—"

Kathleen stood frozen. Johnny had risen to his feet.

"You'll pay—" Louise screamed. "Doc is gone!" she sobbed. "You killed him!"

"No!"

Kathleen saw the gun Louise drew from under her cape. She held her palm out against the crazed woman, as if to ward off the bullet she knew was coming.

"No!"

Johnny's shout came a second before she felt something slam into the side of her head. Her eyes blurred, her legs turned to water, and she began to sink to the floor. Her hand clutched at her desk. She was vaguely aware that Louise had turned the gun toward Johnny as he sprang at her.

Kathleen came out of a dream where she was riding a dark horse in the sky above the treetops. She first realized that someone was holding her. They were in a car and going very fast. Her head felt as if a thousand hammers were pounding on it. The pain was so severe that she was afraid to open her eyes. Then, a vision of a gun turned toward Johnny flashed behind her closed lids and wild panic consumed her.

"John . . . ny!" She wanted to scream, but her voice was barely audible to her own ears. "John . . . ny—"

"I'm here, sweetheart." The calm, dear voice reached into her consciousness. "Lie still. We're on our way to the doctor."

"Are you . . . are you . . . ?"

"I'm all right. You'll be all right, too. We're almost . . ."

Johnny's voice faded, an inner darkness leaped at her, and she fell back into the dream.

"Can I give him some scraps, Gran? Please—"

"Sure, if you want to."

"He's so skinny and . . . scared."

"He'll be all right."

"Can I keep him? I can't give him a name if I don't keep him."

"What do you want to call him?"

"I'll have to—" Kathleen opened her eyes to see Johnny

bending over her. "Oh, Johnny. I was dreaming. Where am I?"

"In the doctor's rooms in Frederick. He stitched your head. I'm afraid you're going to have a bald spot for a while. Would you like a drink of water?"

"Oh, yes." She licked her dry lips, and Johnny put a glass straw in her mouth. She sucked up the water greedily. "That was good. What time is it?"

"Ten o'clock."

"Do we have to stay here?"

"For a while. The doctor said if you woke up and could see all right, talk rationally, and weren't sick to your stomach, we could leave this afternoon."

"I can see all right. So far, I'm not sick to my stomach."

"You were talking kind of silly when you first woke up. I thought uh-oh, she's out of her head."

"I was dreaming about a little dog I found a long time ago. Grandma said we had two dogs and didn't need another. Grandpa let me keep it."

"What did you name him?"

"We called him Zack, but he answered to anything. Zachary Taylor was one of Grandpa's favorite men in history."

Barker Fleming's body blocked the doorway. "She's awake," he said, and came to the bedside and held out a small sack to Johnny. "I wasn't sure if you'd had anything to eat."

"You needn't of—"

"It's only a sandwich."

"A lot went on last night that I don't know about," Kathleen said.

"Louise shot you." Johnny placed the paper bag on the bed and took Kathleen's hand. "The bullet grazed the side of your head. I didn't see the gun until it was too late, but I got to her before she could shoot again. Paul heard the shot, came running, and held her so I could get to you."

"Poor Louise—"

"You're too softhearted," Barker said. "She tried to kill you. A half inch to the right, and she would have."

"He brought us here." Johnny glanced at the man on the other side of the bed. "I couldn't have done it alone."

"I wouldn't have wanted to ride with him last night." Barker spoke confidentially to Kathleen. "He hardly knew which end of him was up after you were shot." He laughed at the dark look on Johnny's face. "I'll have the car out front when the doctor says she can go."

After Barker left, Johnny ate the sandwich.

"He had spotted that blue cape and figured it was Louise. He followed her to the *Gazette*. She's a big woman. It took both him and Paul to hold her until the sheriff and one of the marshals got there to take her to jail."

"I like Barker." She chewed on her lower lip and waited for him to say something.

"Not too much, I hope. I'd hate to have to shoot him after he brought us over here last night."

Kathleen sighed with relief when she saw the glint of humor in his eyes. He finished the sandwich, bent over her, and kissed her mouth.

"Do you think that we'd hitch well together, sweetheart? Last night, I almost died when that crazy woman shot you."

"Is this a proposal?"

"Kind of. I've never proposed before. I've never loved a woman before either. I want you so badly that I hurt. But I'm afraid that after a while you may have second thoughts

when you really get to know me and . . . how different we
are."

"I won't have second thoughts. I know you to be gentle
and kind. You face up to your responsibilities. My grandpa
always judged a man by whether he was lazy or not. He'd
love you. I worry that you'll be disappointed in me. I'm
stubborn and fly off the handle. And I'll—have a bald
spot."

"Shhhh . . . You're sweet, and beautiful and smart. I
love you very much, and I wouldn't care if your head was
completely shaved." He kissed her lips lingeringly.

"Does this mean that we're engaged?"

"Hummm. . . . I guess so. I want to do a little work on
the house before I bring you home."

"Can I help?"

"If you come out, I'll not be able to keep my mind on
my work. I'll be thinking about getting you in bed."

"Well . . . what's so bad about that?" She reached up
and pulled his lips down to hers.

The following recipe was sent to me by Mary Patchell, Oklahoma City, Oklahoma. It was a favorite of her family during the Great Depression.

CHOCOLATE GRAVY

4 level Tbs. cornstarch (My grandma used 8 Tbs. flour)
2 level tsp. cocoa
½ c sugar
dash of salt
2 c milk
1 tsp. vanilla
1 Tbs. butter

Into a pan or skillet, sift together first four ingredients. Add milk slowly. Cook over medium heat, stirring until thick. Remove from heat and add vanilla and butter. Serve over hot biscuits.

Mrs. Patchell writes: *Sometimes Grandpa butchered hogs and we had bacon, ham, or sausage with our biscuits. And Grandma cooked the best pinto beans, corn bread, and fried potatoes. Even today that is my favorite meal for supper.*

After the Parade

DEDICATED TO

82ND U.S. NAVAL CONSTRUCTION BATTALION
—THE FIGHTING SEABEES—

AND IN MEMORY OF

MY HUSBAND
HERBERT L. GARLOCK, SR.

WHO SERVED WITH THE 82ND IN THE
SOUTH PACIFIC
1943–1945

TO A HOMECOMING HERO

After the victory and the parade,
After the hometown band has played,
After the cheers and four long years,
Can we, at last, break free of our fears?

After the bombs and cannonade,
After the bravery you displayed,
After the pain and wounds that bled,
Can you face with me what lies ahead?

I stand and I wait and I long for a sign.
The love you once gave, will it still be mine?
Can we recapture the passion mislaid?
Will you come back to me, after the parade?

—F.S.I.

Chapter One

October 15, 1945
Rawlings, Oklahoma

> "Hurrah for the flag of the free.
> May it wave as our standard forever.
> The gem of the land and the sea,
> The banner of the right—"

THE RAWLINGS HIGH-SCHOOL BAND, decked out in full uniform and lined up beside the platform at the depot, played with gusto John Philip Sousa's "Stars and Stripes Forever." A crowd of a hundred or more had gathered to greet a group of the men who had fought to keep them free. When the huge WELCOME HOME banner that stretched across the front of the depot was loosened by the wind, willing hands hurried to hold it in place.

The gigantic engine, belching smoke, whistle blasting, wheels screaming against the rails, slowly passed the station and came to a jerking halt. There was a sudden expectant quiet. The conductor stepped down from the coach and stood with his hands clasped in front of him.

When the first of the weary war veterans, a surprised Marine, came through the door, the music from the band mingled with the cheers of the crowd and the horns of the cars parked along the street. The Marine stood hesitantly before he bounded down the steps, swung the heavy duffel bag from his shoulder to the platform, and was soon surrounded by laughing and crying relatives.

At the back of the crowd, Kathleen Dolan Henry watched six more veterans alight from the train. All were greeted by loved ones. She waited anxiously for her first glimpse of Johnny Henry in more than four years. When someone waved a flag in front of her face, she hurriedly brushed it away just as a tall sailor, his white hat perched low on his forehead, a duffel bag on his shoulder, stepped down and stood hesitantly on the platform. His eyes searched the crowd. There was a sudden hush, then the band began to play the Civil War song they had practiced for a month.

"When Johnny comes marching home again, hurrah, hurrah.
We'll give him a hearty welcome then, hurrah, hurrah,
The men will cheer, the boys will shout,
The ladies, they will all turn out,
And we'll all be gay, when Johnny comes marching home."

The band stopped playing and the crowd took up the chant: "Johnny, Johnny, Johnny—"

The hero of the small Oklahoma town had come home from the war.

Johnny Henry was stunned. At one time the people of this town had blamed him for bringing disgrace and death to one of their own. Now they were cheering him.

Everyone had heard how Johnny Henry, on an island in

the Pacific, had lifted the blade of the bulldozer he was operating and, amid a shower of gunfire from the Japanese en-
trenched on the beach, had driven it straight toward an
enemy machine-gun nest that was preventing his platoon
from building a landing site. The powerful dozer had buried
the men and their guns inside the concrete structure, permit-
ting the large-scale landing that had secured the island.

Johnny grinned at the young girl who dashed up to take
his picture, waved to acknowledge the crowd, then walked
slowly toward a small group at the end of the platform. His
father, Barker Fleming, his black hair streaked with gray,
stood with his arms folded across his chest, his Cherokee
pride preventing him from showing emotion. The lone tear
that rolled from the corner of his eye was seen only by his
daughter, who stood by his side.

Kathleen watched as Johnny shook hands with Barker
and his young half brother, Lucas. He said something that
drew a laugh from his older half sister, and he patted the
younger one on the head. As proud as she was of him and
thankful that he had survived the war, Kathleen couldn't
force her feet to carry her to the platform and greet him
with all the town looking on. Feeling vulnerable, knowing
that some in the crowd were watching her, she hurried off
down the street to watch the parade from the window of
the *Gazette* office.

*Beneath the brim of a brown felt hat a pair of ice-blue eyes
watched Kathleen with keen interest as she watched her husband step off the train. Noting with satisfaction that she didn't
go to meet him, the man, his face darkened by a week's growth
of whiskers, casually moved away from the cluster of people
at the depot and slowly followed her down the street.*

*   *   *

At the war's end, two months earlier, Kathleen had been working at the Douglas Aircraft plant in Oklahoma City. The front page of the August 15, 1945, *Daily Oklahoman* had screamed the news.

JAPS QUIT, WAR IS OVER

TRUMAN TELLS OF COMPLETE SURRENDER.

WASHINGTON, August 14. The Second World War, history's greatest flood of death and destruction, ended Tuesday night with Japan's unconditional surrender. From the moment President Truman announced at 6 A.M., Oklahoma time, that the enemy of the Pacific had agreed to Allied terms, the world put aside for a time woeful thoughts of cost in dead and dollars and celebrated in wild frenzy. Formalities meant nothing to people freed at last of war.

Tears had filled Kathleen's eyes, overflowed, and rolled down her cheeks. Brushing them away, she hurriedly scanned headlines.

DISCHARGE DUE FOR 5 MILLION
IN 18 MONTHS.

Another headline made her smile.

OKLAHOMA CITY CALMLY GOING NUTS!

Johnny would be among the first to come home because of the time he had spent in the combat zone. Kathleen thought of the ranch outside of Rawlings where, for a while, she had been happier than she had ever imagined she would be and where, later, she had sunk into the depths of despair. She had thought that she could never go back there, but she knew that she must . . . one last time.

Kathleen folded the newspaper carefully. This edition she would keep to show to her children someday . . . if she ever had any more. The ache that dwelled in her heart intensified at the thought of the tiny daughter she had held in her arms that night five years ago, while the cold north wind rattled the windows in the clinic and she waited for death to take her child.

The war was over.

Soon she would be free to leave her defense job, go back to Rawlings, tie up some loose ends, and decide what to do with the rest of her life. She was still part-owner of the *Gazette*. Adelaide and Paul had kept it going during the war, but they'd had to cut it from an eight-page paper down to six pages once a week.

On that wondrous day when the war's end was proclaimed, Kathleen had volunteered to work an extra shift in the payroll department of Douglas Aircraft. The pay was double overtime for the day. The money would come in handy when the plant closed.

Tired after the twelve-hour shift and the long bus ride into town, she had stepped down onto the Oklahoma City street thronged with shouting and cheering people. Cowbells, horns, and sirens cut the air. Hundreds of uniformed airmen from Tinker Airforce Base and sailors from the Norman Naval Base mingled with the crowd. Total strangers hugged and kissed one another.

"How 'bout a hug, Red?" A young sailor threw his arm across her shoulders and embraced her briefly. "You got a man comin' home, honey?"

"Thousands of them."

"Bet one of 'em can hardly wait to see ya."

The sailor went on to put his arm around another girl, and Kathleen stood back against a building and watched the jubilant crowd. Her eyes filled with tears, and her heart flooded with thankfulness. This celebration was something she would remember for the rest of her life.

Vaughn Monroe's voice came from the loudspeaker on the corner.

"When the lights come on again, all over the world,
And the boys come home again, all over the world—"

Kathleen stood for a short while and listened to the music. When the next song was "Does Your Heart Beat for Me," she felt a pain so severe that a lump formed in her throat. The last time she had been with Johnny before he went overseas, they had sat in a strained silence in a restaurant. Someone had put a coin in the jukebox, and she had been forced to listen to that song.

Kathleen walked hurriedly on down the street to get away from the music. As she waited on the corner to catch the bus that would take her to the rooming house where she had lived since coming to the city to do her bit for the war effort, she looked around cautiously.

Several times during the past weeks she had seen a man standing in the shadows near the bus stop, and she had been sure he was a man from the plant, the one who had seized every opportunity to talk to her. He had not been persistent with his attentions but had offered several times to take her home.

Not many people were leaving the downtown area, and the bus when it arrived was almost empty. After she was seated, Kathleen caught her reflection in the window and wondered if she had changed much during the war years. Her hair was still the same bright red. She had tried to tame the tight curls into the popular shoulder-length pageboy style but had given up and let it hang or wrapped it in a net snood.

Johnny had teased her about the color of her hair, saying that since he could always spot her in a crowd, so could a bull, so she'd better carry a head scarf when she went to the pasture.

Walking up the dark street to her rooming house, Kathleen felt . . . old. In a few months she would be thirty-three. It didn't seem possible that seven years had passed since Johnny had saved her from the hijackers on that lonely Oklahoma road outside Rawlings. For a few years she had been extremely happy, then her world had fallen apart. Their baby was born with no chance to live, and Johnny's stupid feeling that his "bad blood" was responsible had dug a chasm between them. After this length of time, she doubted it ever could be bridged.

Kathleen had not filed for a divorce even though Johnny had asked her to during that last meeting. As his wife she had received family allotment money sent by the government. Every penny of the money had gone to Johnny's bank in Rawlings. He would have a small nest egg to help him get started again.

When he came home, Johnny would be free to make a new life for himself and with whomever he chose to share it. As for herself, she was sure that she would never be completely happy again, but she could, if she tried hard enough, find a measure of contentment in her work. She had stayed in contact with her editor at the pulp magazine where her stories were published. Now that he had moved on to work for a book publisher, he had suggested that she write a book. It was something she planned to do when her emotions were not so raw.

Johnny had not expected the welcoming party and was embarrassed by it. He wished, in hindsight, that he had stayed on the train until it reached Red Rock to have avoided all this. In the back of his mind had been the hope that Kathleen would be at the station. It was stupid of him. She had probably met and fallen in love with a 4-F'er or a draft dodger while working in that defense plant in Oklahoma City.

He wondered if divorce papers were waiting for him.

During the ceremony at the depot, the mayor welcomed the veterans home, gave each an envelope containing gift certificates to be used at various businesses in town, then escorted them to the hayrack that had been decorated with flags and welcome-home signs. Johnny sat with the other returning veterans and waited patiently for the ordeal of being paraded through town to be over. He searched the crowd that lined the street for a head of bright red hair and chided himself for hoping that she cared enough to be here when he came home.

Two months ago Johnny, with the rest of his battalion, had watched the Japanese plane with the huge green cross painted on its bottom fly over Okinawa on the way to meet with General MacArthur and surrender on the battleship *Missouri*; he realized then that a phase of his life had ended. The siren that in the past signaled an air raid blew triumphantly that day, announcing that the war was over.

The racket was enough to raise the dead! The celebration had begun.

Lying on his cot, trying to read, Johnny grimaced at the

thought because there were plenty of dead on the island to raise.

"Damn fools are going to shoot themselves," he muttered. The other man in the tent couldn't hear his words over the racket going on in the camp.

"The war's over, Geronimo! We're goin' home!" His exuberant shout reached Johnny above the sound of the gunfire.

As the only Native American in the construction battalion of Seabees attached to the 3rd Marine division, Johnny had been dubbed Geronimo.

"Yeah, we're going home."

Four years was a long time to have been away from home, yet he could clearly visualize the clear blue sky and the broad sweep of rolling prairies of southwestern Oklahoma. He longed to get on his horse and ride to a place where there was not another human being within miles and miles.

He had discovered firsthand that war was hell. Would he ever forget the bombings on Guadalcanal while they were trying to build an airstrip for Allied planes to land? Would he forget the steaming Solomon Islands with their coconut plantations and hut villages of ebony-skinned natives, bearded, short, stocky, and superstitious? He knew that he would never forget the stench of burning flesh as flamethrowers drove the enemy out of the caves of Okinawa.

"Ya know what I'm goin' to do when I get home, Geronimo?" The excited voice of Johnny's completely bald tentmate interrupted his thoughts. "I'm going to take my woman and my kid in the house, lock the door, and not come out till spring. Do you think my kid will remember me? Hell, she was only two years old when I left. It's hard to believe that she'll be startin' school."

"Sure, she'll remember you, Curly," Johnny assured him. Then, "Goddammit!" he exclaimed, as a bullet tore through the top of the tent. The celebration was out of control.

What a relief it was when finally a voice came over the loudspeaker. "Cease fire! Cease fire!"

"It's about time," Johnny growled. "Damn officers sitting up there with their heads up their butts while the idiots shoot up the place!"

He had come through the war with five battle stars for major engagements and had only a few minor shrapnel wounds to show for it. He was grateful for that. *But, hell, he had no wife to go home to.* If Kathleen hadn't divorced him yet, she would as soon as she reached the States.

His sister, Henry Ann, had written every week and would be glad to see him, but even she didn't need him anymore. Her life was with Tom and their kids. Barker, working hard at playing the father, had sent him a package once a month. One package had contained a camera and film. He'd used it. Adelaide had sent him the *Gazette* each week. Sometimes the issues were a month old, but he had read every line, looking for news of Kathleen.

Johnny clasped his hands under his head, stared absently at the bullet hole in the tent, and thought of what he'd do when he got home. He still had the land that he'd bought before he and Kathleen were married. As his needs had been few, every month his pay, except for five dollars, had gone back to pay on the mortgage. Keith McCabe had paid to run some cattle on his land. That money, too, had gone toward the mortgage. Considering that he had given almost five years of his life to Uncle Sam, he wasn't in too bad shape financially.

After the first six months he had stopped looking for

mail other than V-mails from Henry Ann and occasional letters from Adelaide and his half sister, Maria.

The first Christmas he was in the Pacific Theater, he had hoped for a card from the only woman he had ever loved. He had made her a bracelet out of aluminum from a downed Japanese aircraft. Many hours of painstaking work had gone into engraving it with her name. From a Guadalcanal native he had stupidly bought her a comb made out of trochus shells, from which pearl buttons are made.

Weeks dragged into months and he began to dread mail call, fully expecting one of the *Dear John* letters that a few of his fellow Seabees had received from wives who had found new lovers.

He had packed away the bracelet and comb and concentrated strictly on trying to stay alive while he raced out of a flatboat onto an enemy-held island and while he drove the big bulldozer to clear the land or the packer that rolled the coral to make the landing strips.

But, dammit to hell! No matter how hard he'd tried to forget, there was still a vacant place in his heart.

Preoccupied with his thoughts and waving automatically to the crowd that lined the street, Johnny was suddenly jolted back to reality when he saw Paul and Adelaide frantically returning his wave. Behind them he could discern a slender figure standing in the window of the *Gazette* office. Was it Kathleen? Hell, no. If she'd been in town, she'd have been at the depot to take a few pictures and get a story for the paper. Now he wished he'd asked Barker if he had heard from her. His father and Kathleen had always been thick as thieves, and at one time he had feared that she was in love with the guy.

When the truck pulling the hayrack stopped in front of

the courthouse, Johnny jumped down and hoisted his duffel bag to his shoulder. Barker was waiting there.

"Your sisters and I would like you to come out to the ranch for dinner. Lucas thinks that you won the war all by yourself."

"Thanks, but I think I'll go on out to the Circle H. It's been a long time since I've seen it."

"It's up to you. You know that you're always welcome. The car is just down the street. The kids are down at Claude's."

"That old coot still fryin' hamburgers?"

"He's still at it."

Barker slid under the wheel of his '41 Dodge, one of the last cars made before the automobile plants shut down and converted to making war materials.

"When Elena graduated from college she got a teaching job in Boston." Barker reported the news of Johnny's half sisters casually as they drove out of town. "Carla and her husband are in New York."

Johnny grunted a reply, looked out the window, and watched the fence posts fly by. Barker had always driven like a bunch of wild Apaches were after him. He did that now, dust trailing behind them like a bushy red tail. Johnny considered asking about Kathleen, then thought better of it. Instead he brought up the town's main industry, a tannery that Barker owned.

"How's the business doing?"

"Good. We're getting summer and fall hides and keeping more of the good stuff for our own factory. The government cut down their orders when the European War ended and then almost stopped completely a few months ago. We're looking for another market."

"I'm sure you'll find one."

Johnny's hungry eyes roamed the flat Oklahoma plains and then lifted to the eagle that soared effortlessly in the clear blue sky. It was good to be home. He noticed along the road things that he had once taken for granted, like the occasional oak or hawthorn tree that was heavy with mistletoe. The white berry parasite was the state flower of Oklahoma. The first Christmas after he and Kathleen married, he had put a clump of mistletoe in each doorway of the house as an excuse to kiss her.

Thank goodness Barker knew when to be quiet. Johnny glanced at his father's stoic profile and the hair that was broadly streaked with gray. That had been a surprise. He'd had only a little gray at the temples four years earlier.

Johnny's mind stumbled back to the present. In a few days he'd buy some kind of car and go over to Red Rock and see Henry Ann and Tom. He wondered if his cousins Pete and Jude Perry had come through the war. The last he'd heard Pete was in the navy. Jude had gone to medical school, then had been thrust into the army. Grant Gifford had written that he was in the 45th Infantry out of Fort Sill. The Thunderbirds had seen heavy action at Anzio and had taken heavy casualties. God, he hoped Jude had come through. He was the best of the Perrys.

Barker stopped the car in front of the small unpainted frame house but kept the motor running. After Johnny got out of the car he lifted his duffel bag from the backseat, bent over, and peered through the window.

"Thanks."

"Don't mention it."

Johnny straightened, and the car moved away. The first thing he noticed after distance had eaten up the sound of the motor, was the quiet it left in its wake. During the years he had been away, there had always been a racket in the background, even on the boat going and coming across the Pacific. He stood still, not wanting to break the silence even with his footsteps.

The small four-room house looked lonely and unloved. Grass stood a foot high in the places where Kathleen had long ago planted flowers. The old washtub he had nailed to a stump to serve as a planter was still there, but dried weeds had replaced the colorful moss rose that once filled it. He eased his duffel bag down onto the porch and walked slowly around the house.

The stock pen was empty. The windmill towered like a still, silent skeleton against the blue sky.

Johnny sat down on the back steps, rested his forearms on his thighs, and clasped his hands tightly together. Coming back was not as he had imagined it would be. In the jungles of Guadalcanal, New Guinea, and Bougainville he had dreamed of this place. After that first Christmas when he had not heard from Kathleen and realized that he had lost her, the desire to get back to his ranch was the force that had kept him sane during the long months of bombings and shelling.

Now that he was here, what was it but one small lonely speck in all the vast universe?

Johnny watched the sun sink slowly beneath the horizon before he made a move to go into the house. The craving for a drink of cold well water stirred him to his feet. He removed the key from a small pouch in his bag, unlocked and pushed open the door.

Oh, Lord! It was so dearly familiar that it brought moisture to his eyes.

The green overstuffed chair and couch he and Kathleen had bought a week after they married were just as he had left them. The table where the battery-powered radio had sat now held a kerosene lamp with a shiny chimney. Electricity still hadn't made its way to the Circle H. A large framed picture of a covered wagon on the trail west hung on the wall over the couch. On the opposite wall was a picture of an Indian on a tired horse. Kathleen said it was called *Trail's End* and, because she liked it so much, had named one of the stories she wrote for the *Western Story Magazine* after the painting.

Johnny eased his duffel bag down to the floor and took off his sailor hat. From the peg on the wall he lifted the battered Stetson and rolled it around in his hands for a long moment before he set it on his head. It felt strange and . . . big. He returned it to the peg.

In the doorway leading into the kitchen, he stood for a long while, letting his eyes take in every familiar detail. The room was spotlessly clean. The windows shiny. The blue-and-white checkered curtains were freshly ironed. On the table was a square cloth with flowers embroidered in the corners. A mason jar with a ribbon tied around the neck was filled with yellow tiger lilies and brown-eyed daisies. A note was propped against it. Johnny's fingers trembled when he picked it up.

Welcome home, Johnny.

I am truly thankful that you came home safe and sound. We will need to meet soon and tie up the loose ends of our lives so we can get on with whatever is ahead. I have an apartment above the Stuart Drugstore.

Your dinner is on the stove. Adelaide made your favorite chocolate cake.

Kathleen

Johnny replaced the note carefully against the jar as if he hadn't touched it. She was in Rawlings and hadn't come to the depot to meet him, nor had she showed her face in the crowd that lined the street.

You are a stupid fool, John Henry. Get her out of your mind. It is over.

He went through the kitchen to stand in the doorway of the tiny room she had fixed up as a place where she could write her stories. It, too, was spotlessly clean. What caught his eye first was the table he had given her for her type-writer when she first came to Rawlings. The typewriter was gone, as was every other trace of her.

He went back through the kitchen to the bedroom. The fluffy white curtains Kathleen had bought were freshly washed. The white chenille spread with a spray of blue and pink flowers in the middle covered the bed without a wrin-kle. The multicolor rag rug was still at his side of the bed. Kathleen had put it there after he had complained about putting his bare feet on the cold floor.

Nothing of Kathleen's remained in the room, not even their wedding picture, which had stood on the bureau. But she had been here, cleaned the house, and taken her things. Had she taken the picture? He went to the bureau and opened the top drawer. There it was, facedown, on the folded flannel shirts. *She hadn't wanted it.*

He gazed at the smiling faces for a long while. He was wearing a dark suit, the first one he had ever owned. Kathleen's dress was blue with short puffed sleeves and a V-neckline. His wedding present, a locket in the form of a book, hung from a chain around her neck. Inside the locket, he remembered, were their faces. Kathleen had cut them out of a photo taken at a rodeo. Her hair, fluffed on top, hung to her shoulders in soft curls. Her eyes were laughing, her lips parted and smiling. He remembered how proud he was that day on a street in Vernon when they met a cowpuncher he knew who worked the rodeos, and he introduced her as his wife. The man couldn't take his eyes off her.

Johnny looked at himself in the photo that had been taken the day after they married; the second happiest day of his life. He had lived two lifetimes since that day.

Had he ever been that young and happy and so crazy in love that he foolishly believed he, with his trashy background, would be a fit mate for a woman like Kathleen?

He looked up at his image in the mirror above the bureau. Crinkly lines fanned out from the corners of his eyes. The skin on his face stretched over his high cheekbones. He had never looked more like his ancestors who roamed the plains hundreds of years ago than he did now. His hair was still thick but shorter than when he left for the service. Some of the men in his battalion had lost their hair in the hot, humid jungle.

Suddenly feeling the pressure of his lonely homecoming bearing down on him, he set the photo on the bureau and took one more glance around. His eyes were drawn to the bed where he and Kathleen had spent endless, wonderful nights making love.

Did she miss the cuddling, the whispers, the slow loving kisses, and the passion they had shared? Did she have it now with someone else? The thought sent shards of pain knifing through him. Shaking his head to rid his mind of the thought, he went quickly to the back door and out of the house.

Chapter Two

Kathleen watched the parade pass, unaware of the tears that wet her cheeks. Her eyes fastened on Johnny until he was out of sight. He looked as if he wanted to be anywhere but sitting on that hayrack being paraded through the town. He appeared older, thinner. Was it the tight, sailor uniform that made him look so thin? He had seen and done unimaginable things in the jungles of the Pacific; they were bound to have taken a toll on him.

She had tried to make his homecoming more pleasant by cleaning his house. When she went to collect her personal things, she had found the house littered with mouse droppings and covered with layer upon layer of red Oklahoma dust.

After packing her car with what she intended to take with her, she had begun scrubbing and cleaning the house, handling with loving care the things she and Johnny had bought the first few weeks after they were married: a tin measuring cup, a mixing bowl, and a set of glasses. She washed the multicolor Fiesta dishes given to them by the McCabes for a wedding present and returned them to the shelves.

The second day she had brought out the washtubs and,

while crying what she was sure was a bucket of tears, washed the clothes he had left behind. She laundered bed linens, towels, and curtains. As soon as she took the dried clothes from the line she sprinkled and ironed them, put them away and rehung the curtains at the windows and on the strings that stretched across the kitchen shelves. The chore brought to mind how Johnny hated her having to use the scrub board and had insisted that they buy a washing machine with a gasoline motor. It was in the barn. She didn't have any gasoline, and, anyhow, she didn't know how to start the motor.

This morning, she had hurried out to the ranch with a block of ice melting in the trunk, a kettle of beef stew with potatoes and carrots on the floor of the sedan, and a chocolate cake that Adelaide had insisted on sending.

She had written the note three times before she finally arrived at what she wanted to say. Now she wished that she had added that living with an uncertain future was driving her insane.

Oh, Lord. As soon as we come to some arrangement about the divorce, I'll leave here. I'll not be able to live here and see him with someone else.

Adelaide and Paul were interested in buying back her share in the *Gazette* if she planned to sell. The paper had been in Adelaide's family for generations. She had sold an interest to Kathleen only because during the lean years she had been about to lose it. The banker had refused to lend her money for the day-to-day operation of the small-town newspaper.

Times were much better now than they had been seven years ago when Kathleen had used the inheritance from her grandparents to buy into the *Gazette*. During the war she had received a little income from the paper after

Adelaide and Paul had taken out their salary, and she had saved money. Her stories were bringing in more money now that the pen name K. K. Doyle was gradually becoming known to Western fiction readers.

"Did you see him?" Adelaide and Paul came back into the office. "I can't believe that he's home. He looks so thin and . . . dark. He was always tan, but that sun over there has baked him as brown as a berry. Oh, honey—" Adelaide exclaimed, when she saw the stricken look on Kathleen's face. She hurried to her and put her arm around her. "He was looking for you. I know he was. Wasn't he, Paul?"

"I can't be sure, honey. He was scanning the crowd, that's sure."

"No. He doesn't even know I'm here. He doesn't know anything about what I've been doing unless you or Barker told him."

"You asked me not to tell him, and I didn't. Barker may have. Anyway, he'll know when he gets out to the ranch. No one else would have gone in there and cleaned like you did." Adelaide and Paul were Kathleen's dearest friends and were sensitive to her emotional hurt and confusion.

"I left him a note."

"He would have known if you *hadn't* left a note. Barker said that he was going to meet him and take him home."

"He'll not have a way to get back to town." Kathleen worried her bottom lip with her teeth.

"That old Nash of yours has about seen its last days, even if it was up on blocks during the war. I'm surprised Eddie could find tires to go on it." Paul stood behind his petite wife, rubbing her back. "Feel good?" he whispered.

"I could stand here all day."

"You're a glutton," he said softly in her ear.

"Eddie told me he could have sold the Nash a dozen

times," Kathleen said. "He wouldn't take a dime for storing it all this time. He did it for Johnny not me."

"I got two rolls of pictures." The dark-haired girl announced as she burst through the door. She was a bundle of energy, small, quick, and pretty. "I got several of Johnny when he got off the train and again while he was on the float. Lord-dee mercy, he's good-looking. I don't think he knew who I was."

"When he left, you were just a kid. You've grown up while he was gone."

"I'd forgotten he was so handsome." Judy rolled her eyes. "Maybe I was too young to notice."

"Want me to develop these? We should decide on the pictures we want for this week's paper." Paul opened the camera and took out the film. Judy was like a daughter to Paul and Adelaide, although she had lived with her father, Sheriff Carroll, since her mother's death three years ago.

"I'll do it." She picked up the film and headed for the darkroom, her skirt swirling around her bare legs.

"I can hardly remember when I was that young. She gets prettier all the time," Kathleen said wistfully. "It's hard to believe she's twenty-three. When she came here looking for her real parents, she was just sixteen."

"And already mighty gutsy," Paul added.

"She was worried that she'd be out of a job when you came back," Adelaide said to Kathleen.

"I hope you told her that I'd rather not come back full-time. I want to take a stab at writing a book."

"She knows that now."

"I'm thinking about moving to Elk City or maybe back to Liberal. Barker said he'd help me find a place in Elk City. He invited me to come stay at the ranch. They have plenty of room. Wouldn't that set the tongues to wagging?"

"You're not moving out there . . . are you?" Adelaide had a worried look in her eyes.

"No. It would only make a deeper rift between Johnny and his father. Just before Johnny left he brought up his old suspicion that I was attracted to Barker because I was spending so much time out at the ranch. He just couldn't understand that I just liked his father."

"I think it was a little more than that. Johnny was jealous and afraid you'd like Barker more than you loved him. To his way of thinking Barker was everything he wasn't: well-off and educated." Adelaide seldom criticized Johnny. She was terribly fond of him. She did so now because Kathleen was so miserable. "Barker was a shoulder for you to lean on when Johnny let you down."

"I've got to see him and tell him that I'll do whatever he wants to do about the divorce. If I divorced Johnny Henry, a hero who spent four years fighting for our country, I'd be the most hated woman in Oklahoma. I'll do it if that's what he wants, but I'd rather he'd do it."

"He might think that you've already filed."

"I haven't, even though the last thing he said to me was: 'Get a lawyer to make out the papers. Tell him that half of the ranch is yours and, if you want your money now, to put it up for sale. Send the papers. I'll sign them and send them back.' He turned and got on the train and didn't even look at me again."

"He loves you, Kathleen. I never knew a man who loved a woman as much."

"Ah . . . hum!" Paul cleared his throat loudly.

Adelaide gazed lovingly at her husband. "Don't get in a snit, love. I was not including you."

"If he loved me, he wouldn't have left me to grieve by

myself. I lost my baby and then my husband," Kathleen said with a sudden spurt of spirit.

"It's a well-known fact that women can handle grief much better than men."

"It was his damn feeling of inferiority that caused the trouble. He firmly believes that our baby was born deformed and without a chance to live because of him. He thinks that the Perrys, his mother's family, are an incestuous clan and that any children he has will be like our little Mary Rose."

"That's nonsense."

"I told him so. The doctor in Frederick told him. Another thing that bothers him is that he feels inferior because he can only read on a very low level. I didn't know that and asked him to read one of my stories. He went through the motions, but when I asked him about it, he threw the magazine down and walked out. I gradually became aware that he could read only the simple words."

"That must be why he'd never take the test to become a Federal Marshal."

"I would have taught him if he had given me the slightest hint that he wanted me to."

"Johnny is a proud man."

"I have pride and feelings, too. Did he ever ask you about me when he wrote to you?"

"He never wrote anything except his name on the V-mail he sent. It was usually a cartoon or a copy of their Thanksgiving or Christmas dinner menu they gave to the men to send home. Barker said all he ever heard from him was 'thanks for pkg' on a V-mail after he had sent him a package."

"He hated to write even a grocery list."

"Most men would have made an effort to keep in touch with their loved ones even if they couldn't write very well."

"He never asked me to write when he left. He didn't want to hear from me. I think he thought it was a good time to cut me loose and forget me."

"If he doesn't make an effort to make up with you, he's a fool."

"I'd better go," Kathleen said, eager to leave because talking about her pain seemed to make it worse.

"Would you like to stay and have supper with me and Paul?"

"Thank you, but I'd not be very good company. I've got some reading to do about the Shoshone Indians. The book I'm going to write will take place up north on the Shoshone Reservation."

"Why don't you write about the Cherokee? You could get the information straight from the horse's mouth and not have to do all that reading."

"Barker would love to know that you called him a horse." Kathleen smiled, but only slightly.

"I'm thinking that he's been called worse."

With her head bowed, she walked down the alley toward the stairs leading to the rooms above the drugstore and slowly trudged up the steps and into the darkened hallway. While fitting her key into the lock, she heard a door farther down the hall close softly. For only a minute she wondered about the occupants of the other two apartments in the building.

The window in Kathleen's one-room efficiency apartment looked down onto the alley. She went there now and stood gazing at the bleak landscape. Her head was pounding. She wanted desperately to cry but refused herself the luxury.

She had come to Rawlings as soon as her job at the plant had been eliminated. It had been a couple of miserable weeks, made more so by living in this dark, dreary place. She could not write here. Her imagination refused to function. She longed for the bright and cheery room she had at the ranch, where she could look out onto the wide stretches of grassland and envision the scene she was writing about.

Where would she go when she left here? Rawlings had become home. Her friends were here. But they were Johnny's friends, too. She hated the thought of leaving, and she hated the thought of staying and seeing him with someone else. Could they meet on the street and give each other a civilized greeting just as if they had not at one time meant the world to each other?

While she was considering her options, there was a light tap on the door. She opened it to see Barker with his hand lifted to rap again.

"Adelaide said that you were here."

"Hello, Barker. Come in."

"I thought you might want to get out of this rathole for a while," he said after he entered and closed the door.

"You're speaking of my home." Kathleen allowed humor to surface briefly.

"Home, my hind leg. I'd not stable a horse in here."

"Of course, you wouldn't. You'd not be able to get him up the stairs."

"I took Johnny out to the ranch. I didn't stay."

"How did he . . . seem?"

"Quiet. But then he's always been quiet around me. He never mentioned . . . anyone."

"Did you expect him to?"

"I thought he might." Barker noticed the tired lines in her face and the circles beneath her eyes.

"He'll not have a way to get back to town or down to the McCabes' to get his horses."

"In the morning I'll drive out in my truck and leave it for him to use until he gets something. Marie will follow and bring me back."

"That's good of you, Barker. I'd offer the Nash, but more than likely he'd not take it."

"He may not accept the truck from me. Do you want to go out with me?"

"No. I'll wait for him to come to me. He will when he is ready."

"Are you sure he wants out of the marriage?"

"I'm sure. Before he left he told me to file for divorce, and I never heard one word from him all the time he was gone. He couldn't have made it plainer than that."

"He's a fool to let you go."

"You're a dear man, Barker. I wish things were different between you and Johnny."

"He thinks that I deserted him even though I didn't know he existed until he was twenty years old. It took me years to find him." Barker folded his arms across his chest as he sometimes did when he was in a serious mood. "He didn't have a pleasant childhood living with that . . . woman."

"You can say it outright, Barker. She was a whore. Johnny said she was one because that was what she wanted to be. I've thought about it a lot. You've done your part to make it right. It's up to Johnny now."

"He tolerates me. It's more than he did at first."

"He wants to like you. His darn pride gets in the way."

"Are you going to stay here in Rawlings, Kathleen?"

"I don't know what I'm going to do."

"I want to show you a house. You can't stay in this place. I won't allow it."

"And I'll not allow you to buy me a house, Barker. You know that."

"The tannery owns the house. One of the men left, and we don't plan to replace him. The house will stand empty or be rented out. I'd rather you rent it."

"How much is the rent?"

"Ten dollars a month. You'll have to pay your gas and electric. That's another five a month. Telephone, and there is one already installed, will be another couple of dollars. But what the hell, you'll be rich as soon as you finish your book."

"Not unless friends like you buy a trainload."

"I just might do that and give one to everyone in the state. Not every man has a daughter-in-law who is an author."

"I may not be your daughter-in-law much longer. Johnny will want this thing settled."

"You'll always be my daughter, little redbird." Barker's hand reached out and stroked her shining hair. He seldom touched her. It was at times like this when he most revealed his Indian heritage. His handsome coppery features looked as if they were chiseled in stone.

"Thank you." Kathleen turned away so that he'd not see the tears that came suddenly to her eyes.

"Get your coat. It's cold when the sun goes down. I want to show you the house."

"We won't be gone that long, will we?"

"We will, if you come home with me for supper."

"All right. I don't think I could face an evening alone tonight."

*   *   *

The watcher in the upstairs window had opened the door a crack after Kathleen and Barker passed it. He saw them walk down the front stairs, then hurried to the window to watch them cross the street to where the Indian had parked his car. He knew that the Indian was her father-in-law and that he owned the tannery. The watcher took the stairs two at a time; and by the time Barker had backed out of his parking space, he was in his own car.

I'll write down in my observation diary that she wore a blue dress today and that for a while I stood close behind her at the depot. I was so close that I could smell the lemon rinse on her hair. I managed to touch her back. She didn't know that it was me, didn't even look my way. All her attention was on that son of a bitch that got off the train.

The small, square, three-room house sat on the edge of town. Kathleen was surprised that it was in such good condition and that it had a large, freshly painted bathroom. The tub, lavatory, and toilet were like new. The hot-water heater was in a closet on the back porch and had a thermostat so that she would have hot water all the time.

"The furnishings were for sale," Barker said. "I bought the lot for twenty-five dollars. You can have them for that. I don't intend to make a profit off my daughter."

"You're kidding!"

"About making a profit?" His dark eyes twinkled at her.

"No. That you paid twenty-five dollars for all this."

"He was in a hurry to leave and couldn't take them with him."

Kathleen's eyes swept over the upright stove, the small icebox, and the kitchen table and chairs. In the bedroom was a brass bed and a dresser with a hinged mirror. The front room had a brown-leather couch, a chair, and a library table. The carpet on the floor was maroon and of good quality.

Barker wasn't looking at her. Kathleen knew immediately that he had paid more than twenty-five dollars for the furnishings. She thought about the fact for a moment and decided to accept the gift graciously and not to question him about it.

"Who do I pay the rent to?"

"The tannery."

"I'll take it, and I thank you for thinking of me. I wish that I could move in tonight, but tomorrow will have to do."

"After we take the truck out to Johnny, Marie and I will come by and help you move."

"You'd better be careful, Barker. I might start thinking that you're about the nicest man I ever met."

"Ah . . . Chief Wonderful. I like the sound of it." He smiled, and his dark eyes shone with pleasure.

Kathleen had been at the Fleming ranch many times, but only once since her return from Oklahoma City. The ranch house and outbuildings were a reflection of the owner, richly furnished without seeming to be so. Orderly and well tended, the one-story house appeared to have no inside walls because one room flowed into another.

The Flemings were proud of their heritage. Indian art covered the walls and Indian-designed rugs, the floors. It was a lived-in house with comfortable leather couches and chairs and a large fieldstone fireplace.

Barker's father had amassed a fortune in oil, cattle, packing plants, and tanneries, making his family one of the richest in the state. The ranch and the tannery were Barker's special responsibility. He ran both with an easy hand, having learned the value of delegating authority to responsible people.

His home was managed by Thelma Fisher, a distant relative who had lived with them for years, and Marie, who had graduated from high school, but had not the desire, as had her two older sisters, to go on to college. Janna, 15, and Lucas, 12, went to school in Rawlings.

Kathleen was greeted warmly by Marie.

"Daddy told us he'd try to get you to come for supper."

"He didn't have to try very hard."

Kathleen was fond of the small girl with the dark hair and coppery skin. Marie was a born homemaker, eager to have a home and children of her own. While waiting for the right man to come along, she was content to live in her father's house and help tend to her siblings.

"Hello, Mrs. Fisher." Kathleen spoke to the woman who came to the dining room with another place setting.

"How ye been doin', Kathleen?"

"All right. You?"

"I be all right." Mrs. Fisher, who came from the Scottish side of the family, adopted the dress of the Cherokee while she was at the ranch. Today her loose brown dress hung from her shoulders to just inches above her beaded moccasins; but when she went to church in town, she dressed as stylishly as any woman there. "Get washed up, Lucas," she called. "Your daddy will be here in a minute."

"Hello, Kathleen." The boy who stuck his head out of the kitchen door to speak could have been Johnny at that age. He was handsome, and his straight black hair framed a serious face.

Barker came to stand behind his chair at the head of the table. He had put on a fresh shirt, and his newly combed hair hung to his collar.

"Where's Janna?"

"She's coming," Marie said.

"I'm coming! I'm coming! I'm . . . here!" Janna dashed into the room, smoothing her hair back with wet palms. She was as tall as Marie, but much thinner. She was an outdoor girl and was happiest when she was astride her horse, riding for pleasure or helping the hands with the cattle. "Hi, Kathleen. I didn't know you were here."

Kathleen loved every member of this family. She had felt at home with them as soon as she met them, which was before she and Johnny were married. Johnny had felt nothing but anger when he learned seven years ago that Barker was his father. Having endured taunts since childhood that his father had been a drunken Indian, Johnny could not accept Barker's explanation of why he had been left all those years with a mother who was a whore. The pain was too deep.

While he and Kathleen were together, he had warmed to the family a little; but when the strain in his marriage occurred, he had begun avoiding being with them.

Johnny, Johnny, you're missing so much. You could be a part of this family, if only you'd forget how you were conceived and let them love you.

Chapter Three

THE TRUCK IS AT JOHNNY'S. Marie and I left it before he could come out and make a fuss." Barker took a heavy box from Kathleen. "Where do you want this?"

"In the backseat."

"What do you have left to bring down?"

"The only heavy thing is my typewriter."

"I'll get it."

Kathleen had carried suitcases and boxes down to the Nash, swearing that never again would she live in a place where she had to carry anything up or down a steep, rickety stairway.

"This is everything," she said later, as Barker placed her typewriter on the front seat of the car. "I'll be glad to see the last of this place. I'll go tell Adelaide I'm moving."

The three of them walked down the alley and went into the back of the *Gazette* building. In the pressroom, Paul and Judy were looking at the pictures she had taken at the depot and during the parade. Kathleen's eyes feasted on the two pictures of Johnny: one as he stepped off the train and the other a close-up of him smiling down at Judy.

"These are good, Judy. You've turned out to be quite a good photographer."

"What did you expect?" Paul said with a smirk. "She had a darn good teacher."

"There's nothing modest about this guy." Judy winked at Kathleen. "I'll make copies of the pictures of Johnny for you. Would you like copies, Mr. Fleming?"

"I sure would. Could you make them about . . . so big?" He held his hands about eight inches apart.

"They should blow up to eight-by-tens and still be clear. If they are grainy, I'll make five by sevens."

"Listen up, you-all. I've got news." Adelaide came from the front office. Her Oklahoma drawl was always pronounced when she was excited. "I just heard that a new doctor is coming to take over the clinic."

"It's about time. Rawlings has been without a doctor for almost three years." Paul continued to trim the photos. "The old man who replaced Dr. Herman died on us."

"This one is a veteran who was injured in Italy. He's fully recovered and is ready to practice. Claude came by and told me."

"Did Claude say why he chose Rawlings?" Barker asked. "Every town around is begging for a doctor."

"All I know is that Claude was contacted by Mr. Gifford, the attorney general. He asked Claude what he planned, as mayor, to do about the clinic and told him about a crackerjack of a young doctor who wanted to start a practice. Claude said that we were eager for the clinic to be reopened and that if Mr. Gifford recommended him, the doctor was bound to be all right."

"Gifford isn't one to make a recommendation lightly."

Barker's remark went unheard by Kathleen as her mind wandered back to when she first arrived to work at the *Gazette*. She remembered Dr. Herman, who had been mayor, a cold-hearted monster with such a hold on the town that no one dared to do anything without his permission.

"Has anyone heard anything about Louise Munday?" Kathleen wondered what had happened to the big blond woman who had been Dr. Herman's nurse.

"She must still be serving her ten-year sentence for helping Dr. Herman with his little scheme. Want me to ask Daddy about her?"

"Don't bother. I really don't care as long as she stays away from me. Adelaide, I came by to tell you I'm moving to one of the houses owned by the tannery. It's the last house on the road going west."

"A small white house with the porch on two sides?"

"That's the one. I've got the Nash loaded. Barker said he'd stop here and get my trunk in a day or two."

"I'm glad you found a better place, although it was nice having you so close. Do you have everything you need?"

"Before I leave, I'll go to the five-and-dime and get a couple of plates, a cup or two, a pan and a skillet. That's about all I need."

"You'll not go to the five-and-dime. Paul and I will be down this evening. I have plenty of extras."

Tears sprang to Kathleen's eyes. Her heart had been pounded to a pulp and her emotions so mangled that tears were always near the surface these days. Her only escape was to force her numb mind to come up with a sassy retort.

"Feed Paul before you bring him. My cupboards are bare."

"I'll pick up a block of ice and follow you down to the house."

"I don't have anything to put in the icebox, Barker."

"It'll be cold when you do."

"But, Barker, you don't have to—"

"You might as well give up and let him have his way." Marie laughed and grasped Kathleen's arm. "Once Daddy gets the bit in his teeth there's no stopping him."

"I'm beginning to find that out."

Barker headed for the door. "Marie and I will help you unload, then I've got to get out to the tannery. See you later, folks."

Before she got into her car, Kathleen said, "I don't want to like that little house too much. I may be moving on."

"Oh, I hope you stay, even if you and Johnny . . . don't work things out." Marie's expressive face creased in a worried frown.

"I've no hope of that, Marie. No hope at all."

Above the drugstore the man watched both cars leave the alley.

She's moving into the house the Indian took her to last night. Having her down the hall has been wonderful for me, but she's too bright and lovely to have to spend time in that dingy place.

I knew the minute I saw her that she was the one. Since that time she's been all that has made my life worth living. I live only to be near her. Someday she will really look at me, see that I love and cherish her, and will love me back . . . I know it.

By noon, Kathleen had put her things away and made her bed. Her mind returned constantly to Johnny. She was unable to get used to the thought that he was so near, yet so far away. He looked like the same flesh-and-blood Johnny she had married, but older, somehow different.

She herself was not the same, she thought, as she drove to the store. She hadn't realized how much until she looked at the wedding picture. She had wanted to take it from the ranch house, wanted badly to take it, but remembered that Johnny had paid the photographer with silver dollars he had won at the rodeo. After the divorce she would ask him to let her have it.

Her mind was so busy that she sat in her car in front of the grocery for a long moment. They had been so in love. At least she had been. Her mind had been his, her heart his, her body his, just as his had been hers. She had been sure that they would be together always. How could the feelings they'd had for each other vanish because the child they had together had been less than perfect? The love he professed to have for her had not been lasting. She just must face that fact and go on. People didn't die of broken hearts . . . or did they?

Suddenly the thought that Johnny could be in town today occurred to her. Anxiety cut through her. She scanned the street for Barker's truck, then dashed into the store. She needed to be calm when she came face-to-face with him, and she certainly didn't want to be wearing this grubby old dress and dirty white sandals.

Fifteen minutes later she carried two sacks of groceries to the car and hurried back to the sanctuary of the little house. Kicking off her shoes, she put the milk, eggs, and butter in the icebox and the rest of her supplies in the cupboard above the sink.

A sudden rap on the door startled her. *Barker was back.* He had promised to come turn on the gas and light the water heater. Kathleen raked her fingers through her hair, looked around for her shoes and didn't see them. Oh, well, he had seen her barefoot before.

She didn't see the tall figure in the cowboy hat until she reached the door. He was standing on the edge of the porch with his back to the house. She gaped, unable to utter a sound, incapable of accepting that Johnny was just a few feet away. Panic struck fresh and sharp. Her heart began to pump like a piston. Her first thought was to turn and run out the back door. She feared it would take more courage than she possessed to face him and hear him say that he wanted to be rid of her. Shaken to the core, she was unaware that a small sound had come from her throat.

Hearing it, he turned. His face seemed frozen. His dark, intense eyes beneath the brim of his old hat were fixed on her face. From somewhere the realization came to her that he was wearing a shirt that she had ironed two days before.

Oh, God! Oh, God! A strange sensation began seeping rapidly through Kathleen's mind, a fuzziness, a distant humming noise sounded in her ears. She sucked in her breath.

"Hello, Kathleen." The pounding in her ears made the words seem to come from far away.

"Hello." Her throat was tight, and she just barely managed the word.

They stared at each other through the screen door. It seemed an eternity before he said, "May I come in?"

Unable to speak for the chaos raging in her brain, she pushed on the door. He pulled it open and stepped into the small room and took off his hat. Kathleen backed up and turned away. Suddenly it was too much for her. She felt the tears and couldn't bear for him to see them.

"Excuse me for a moment."

She stepped into the bedroom then darted into the bathroom, closed the door, and leaned against it. She had mentally rehearsed the meeting with him a thousand times during the past four years, and never had she imagined it would be as devastating as this. She wet her face with her hands and dried it. Not wanting to see how terrible she looked, she avoided the mirror, picked up a brush, and smoothed her hair.

Going back through the bedroom, she paused in the doorway. He was sitting on the edge of the couch. Her eyes clung to him as he flicked a match and put it to the cigarette he held between his lips. The light shone for an instant on his dark face. He drew deeply on the cigarette, and the end flared briefly. Before he blew out the match he raised his lids, and she had a glimpse of steady dark eyes.

"Looking for your shoes?" he asked quietly.

She nodded, came into the room, and sat down on the edge of the chair across from him. She had regained control. Her mouth was taut, and there was an air of unconscious dignity about her poised head. She clasped her hands in her lap and pulled her bare feet back close to the chair as if to hide them.

"You always liked to go barefoot."

"I was raised on a farm. Remember?"

"I remember a lot of things." His eyes held hers while he drew deeply on the cigarette.

"I'm sorry. It was rude to run out. I didn't mean to behave like that. It was the strain of . . . moving . . . the uncertainty of . . . things and seeing you so suddenly."

"How did you plan to behave?"

She lifted her shoulders, trying to encompass a world of explanation with the silent gesture.

"How did you know I was here?"

"I went by the *Gazette*. Adelaide told me."

"I couldn't stand that room above the drugstore. Barker told me about this house being for rent and I grabbed it. I bought the furniture . . . for a song."

"Does Barker own the house?"

"The tannery does."

"Same thing."

"I pay my way. I don't expect you, Barker, or anyone else to feel obligated to help me." Her eyes were wide and dry. She was startled by her own tone of voice and her bluntness.

"You haven't changed. You still don't need anyone."

"I needed you . . . once." The words burst from her. She hadn't meant to say them and tried to soften them, by saying, "You look good. Maybe a little thinner."

"You should have seen me after Guadalcanal. I sweated off so many pounds that I looked like a walking bag of bones."

"I watched the paper for news of your battalion. The only time I saw it mentioned was when you covered the Japs with the bulldozer. I have the clipping if you'd like to see it."

"Hell. That was overblown. The newsboys needed something to stir up the folks back home so they'd buy War Bonds." He looked around for a place to put the ashes from his cigarette. Kathleen hurried to the kitchen and returned with a cracked saucer she had found beneath the sink.

"I don't have an ashtray or dishes yet. Adelaide is going to lend me some."

"Still don't smoke?"

"I never acquired the taste for it."

"Why didn't you take the dishes out at the ranch? They're just as much yours as mine."

"Your friends gave them to us. You should have them."

A long, silent minute went by before he spoke. "How did you like working at Douglas Aircraft?"

"How did you know that?"

"Was it a secret?"

"No. I just didn't think you knew where I was. Adelaide said you didn't ask her, and she didn't tell you."

"She didn't. Were you Rosie the Riveter?"

"I worked in the payroll department. We paid twenty thousand people every Friday. I could work as much over-time as I wanted, so I usually worked ten or twelve hours a day."

"I heard that the defense workers made a pile of money."

"I wanted to do my part to help end the war."

"Commendable of you," he said dryly.

He seemed to be studying her, seldom took his eyes from her face. It made her nervous.

"Did you see your name on the sign on the courthouse lawn? Over four hundred went to the service from this area."

"Some of them didn't come back."

"Thank God, you did. I said a prayer for you every night and hung a banner with a star on it in the window."

"Thanks," he said, and looked away from her.

"I wanted to write."

"No stamps?"

"I didn't know where to send it."

"Henry Ann would have given you my address."

"Would you have read it?"

"A man away from home gets pretty desperate for mail."

I wrote you a thousand letters in my mind. I would have mailed them, but couldn't bear the thought that you might re-turn them unopened.

"I just came from the bank." Johnny's voice broke into her thoughts. "From the size of the account, you didn't use any of the family allotment money the government sent you."

"I didn't need it."

"Didn't want *even* that from me, huh?"

"That wasn't it at all. I was getting along on what I was making and saving a little. I knew you'd need money to get started again."

"Why didn't you send me the divorce papers?"

"I didn't think it was right to divorce you while you were over there fighting for our country."

"Several of the men in my battalion got *Dear John* letters from wives who wanted a divorce."

"I'm sorry if you were disappointed that you didn't get one."

Her words penetrated his cool armor. He was getting angry. Lines around his mouth became deeply etched, and his nostrils flared. She knew the signs.

"Did you find someone else?" The words seemed to be snatched out of him.

She saw that he was waiting for an answer to his question. Her mind was too confused to tell him anything but the truth.

"No. I didn't have time for anything but work."

"You wouldn't have had to do much looking. There must have been plenty of 4F'ers and draft dodgers working at the plant."

"They did their jobs, too. They built the planes that helped end the war."

There was a silence while he lit another cigarette. *He was still wearing his wedding ring!* She could feel her heart beating through her fingertips and spoke before she thought.

"You're wearing your wedding ring."

"I'm still married. Where's yours?" He looked pointedly at her hand.

"I . . . didn't think you'd want me to wear it."

"Horse hockey!" he snorted. "Do you have a lawyer?"

"I'm not filing. You'll have to file to get rid of me."

"Kathleen," he said her name menacingly. "You're trying my patience."

"That's too bad. I don't mean to be contrary. How would it look if I divorced a hero as soon as he came home from the war?"

"You're concerned about what folks in this town will think?" When she didn't answer, he said, "Then you plan to stay here?"

"I haven't decided. I've been selling more and more of my Western stories. My editor is urging me to write a book. One thing about being a writer, you can do it anywhere. I should take that back. I couldn't write a line in that dark apartment above the drugstore."

"I read some of your stories while I was overseas."

Kathleen's mouth dropped open in surprise. "You . . . did? I didn't think that you liked to read."

"We had little breaks between campaigns. When you have nothing else to do, you can learn to like most anything. The Salvation Army brought in boxes of magazines and books. I picked out the ones with stories written by K. K. Doyle."

Was there pride in his voice? Kathleen smiled for the first time since he had come into the house. Their eyes caught and held. It was so wonderful to look at him. It was hard for her to believe that it was Johnny sitting across from her.

"You . . . read my stories over there?" she managed to ask, her heart thumping painfully.

"Yeah. They were pretty good." His lips quirked a little at the corners.

He had felt a surge of pride when some of the men remarked, *"That fellow Doyle writes a damn good story."* After his tentmate had taught him how to sound out words, he had read everything he could get his hands on. Practice makes perfect, Curly had said, and he had been right. During the first year, his reading had been painfully slow, but because he felt closer to her while reading her stories, he'd stuck with it. By the end of his tour of duty, he could get so immersed in a story that he didn't want to go to his foxhole when the air-raid sirens sounded.

Johnny had intended to wait a few days before coming to see her; but when Adelaide told him where she was, he was on his way before he had given it much thought. He wanted to find out if what they once shared was still there. Now he knew that it was for him, and stronger than ever.

"I'm surprised that you got books and magazines over there." Her voice broke into his thoughts.

"Some of the magazines were so old they were held together with tape. You had a story in an old *Western Story Magazine* that was about to fall apart. It was called 'Hot Lead . . .' and something."

"'Hot Lead and Petticoats.' It was the first story I sold. I think now that it was not very good."

Johnny put his cigarette out in the saucer and set it on the floor. Kathleen's eyes followed the movement and for the first time noticed that he wore black shoes.

"I've never seen you in anything but cowboy boots. You even wore them to our wedding."

"You saw me at the depot when I left to go back after my leave."

"That's right I did."

"I put on my boots, but they were so stiff and dried-out, I couldn't wear them." Dead silence followed the remark, then he said, "Thanks for washing my clothes."

She lifted her shoulders in a noncommittal shrug and

tried to think of something to say so that he wouldn't leave. Her love for him was as intense as it had been seven years ago when they met and fell in love. At times, during the past four years, an almost unbearable longing for him had swept over her. It was more than a physical need, as it was now. Only pride kept her from throwing herself in his arms and begging him to stay with her forever.

"Eddie didn't charge me for keeping the Nash." The comment came from some small corner of her mind.

"He said that three of the four tires he put on for you are pretty good. The fourth one will bear watching."

"When did you see him?"

"A little while ago. I bought a car from him. I wanted a truck, but there isn't one to be had around here. He's putting a hitch on behind the car so I can pull a flat rack." He looked at the watch on his wrist. "He should be about done by now."

"You could have had the Nash."

He ignored the remark, stood, and reached for his hat. "The car I got isn't much, but it'll do for a while."

"What do you plan to do?" Kathleen got to her feet. "Besides ranching, I mean."

"I've had a couple of offers. I was discharged at the naval base at Norman. During the week I was there I called Grant Gifford. Remember him? He's still the attorney general. He came out to the base to see me and said that he was sure that there was a place for me with the Oklahoma Highway Patrol or the Marshal's Office, if I wanted it."

"Do you?"

"I've not decided. A representative from a construction company came to the base trying to hire bulldozer operators. The pay is good, but the work is in Central America."

Kathleen's heart gave a sickening leap. She tried to control her sudden shivering and failed.

"Are you going?"

"I'm too glad to be home to leave right away. I'll not have any trouble finding a job driving a bulldozer around here if I decide to do that. It stands to reason that there'll be a building boom now that the war is over."

"You loved the ranch."

"It's hard to make a living on the number of acres I have." He stepped out onto the porch, and she followed. "I'm glad you're doing all right. If you need anything, let me know."

"Thanks." Her voice was shaky.

"Half that bank account is yours and half the ranch when you're ready to take it."

She felt as if he had kicked her in the stomach. The strength seemed to drain out of her, and her usually straight shoulders slumped. Her mouth suddenly went dry, and she felt sick.

"I'll *never* be ready to take it." Her voice was firm and convincing. She looked down to hide the hurt he was sure to read in her eyes.

"Sure you will," he said confidently. "You'll take it because you're entitled to it."

"You'll see." She clamped her lips tightly together to keep from telling him to take the bank account and the ranch and shove it. Not for anything would she let him know that his words had cut her to the quick. "Are you going to see a lawyer here?"

"Why? Do you have someone on the string you're anxious to marry?"

"I told you that I didn't have. But this isn't fair to you. You'll meet someone . . . want a family—"

"I've been through that, Kathleen. Don't be trying to arrange my life." He stepped off the porch and headed for the truck he had parked in the road in front of the house.

"I wouldn't even think of trying to arrange your life," she sputtered, her head tilted proudly, but color draining from her face, a sure sign of her anger.

"No, I guess not." He lifted his shoulders. Kathleen saw for an instant a forlorn expression on his face. It prompted her to say:

"I put a marker on Mary Rose's grave," she called.

He stopped and turned. "I saw it this morning. I'll pay you for half of it."

She was so jolted by the remark that the walls holding her emotions in check suddenly crumbled. Anger at all she had endured came boiling up out of the pit of her stomach. Words when they came, were unguarded and loud. Her voice, shrill and breathless didn't even sound like her voice.

"You don't owe me a blessed thing, you . . . horse's ass," she yelled not caring who heard. "You didn't even like her! You wouldn't even hold her. I'll not take a penny from you for her marker. She was *my* baby. Mine! I was the only one who loved her, grieved for her. The great Johnny Henry, best *All-Around Cowboy*, was ashamed of having a deformed daughter. Get the hell away from here and don't come back or . . . I'll get my gun out and . . . shoot you!"

Her eyes were fiery now. Her head felt tight, and her eyes smarted; and for the first time in her life she wanted to really lash out at someone, to do something violent. She turned and ran back into the house.

Johnny went taut as he listened to her outburst. A muscle twitched in the corner of his mouth as he stood for a minute and looked at the empty porch. Her words had shocked him. He had only offered to help pay for the marker. Why did that make her so angry?

In the house, Kathleen threw herself down on the bed and cried with deep disappointment. She had always held out a tiny hope that when Johnny came home he would tell her how sorry he was for his rejection after their daughter was born and that he had been as hurt when they lost her as she had been. Now, she knew that it wouldn't happen. It was over. The finality of it was crushing.

Why didn't you take the job in Central America? I had reconciled myself to the fact that I had lost you forever and was going to go on with my life. Now . . . I don't know what to do—

Chapter Four

DURING THE WEEK that followed, Kathleen doggedly tried to keep her thoughts from dwelling on Johnny, although twice she woke up in the middle of the night with tears on her cheeks.

She worked on her book and became immersed in the story. She concentrated on the scene she was writing, then the next scene and the next, until she had written the first chapter. She had followed the advice her editor had given her. *You have only a minute or two to catch the interest of the readers. Open with a hook that will keep them reading to see what happens.* Scanning the typed pages, she was pleased with what she had written.

Kathleen had not left the house since Johnny's visit, but Adelaide and Paul had been to see her, as had Barker and Marie. This morning she needed to go to the grocery store and then to the ice dock to pick up a card to put in her window so the iceman would stop. It was still warm in southern Oklahoma and would be for another month.

Her intention had been to walk to town, but noticing that one of the tires on her car was low, she decided to drive it to the station to get air before it became completely flat. She drove slowly down Main Street past the Rialto

Theatre where *Sergeant York* was playing. She and Johnny had seen the film while she was pregnant with Mary Rose. So many memories were here. The town of Rawlings had become home to her. She would hate to leave it.

At Eddie's station she pulled up to the air hose. A man came slouching out of the building, a cigarette dangling from his mouth. He stopped in front of the car, placed his hand on the hood, and looked at her through the windshield. She looked steadily back at him. He wore a battered felt hat and his clothes were so greasy he must have been wearing them for a month. He also needed a shave. Finally he took a last puff of the cigarette, dropped it on the paving, and stepped on it.

"My front left tire is low. Will you check it, please?"

"Sure. You wantin' gas too?"

"A couple of gallons."

She heard the hiss as the air went into the tire, then the gas cap being removed. She reached for her purse when he came to the side of the car.

"How much?"

"Four bits. You're Kathleen Henry, ain't ya? Ya married Johnny Henry, then run off when he went to war. Heard ya was up in the city a raking in the dough at the airplane plant. Back for good?"

She recognized him then as a man who had been around town when she came here seven years ago. He had been one of the toughs who hung around doing as little as possible.

Kathleen ignored his question, handed him a dollar, and waited for her change.

"I ain't blamin' ya for leavin' Johnny. He was a high-handed, know-it-all sonofagun. Still is, if ya ask me. Folks are fallin' all over him 'cause he killed a few Japs."

"What did you do during the war?" Kathleen looked straight at him, her temper overriding her desire to get away from him.

"I didn't have to go." He grinned, showing tobacco-stained teeth. "Draft board gave me a 4F card 'cause I got four toes shot off while I was hunting squirrels back in '40."

"How could you be so lucky?" she said with heavy sarcasm.

"Better'n gettin' my legs blowed off. Cletus Birdsall came home with stumps."

"I'd like my change, if you don't mind."

He pulled a handful of change from his pocket and picked around in it with greasy fingers.

"Need any help out there let me know."

"Why would I need any help from you?"

"You're out there in Chief Big Shot's house, ain't ya? It's right on the end of town, ain't it?"

"I rent the house from the tannery."

"If you say so." He let his eyelid droop in a wink and raised the corner of his mouth. "Ain't much goes on in this town that folks don't know."

The gesture disgusted her. "My change?"

He dropped the change in her palm with one hand and with the other he deftly lifted the windshield wiper, unhooked it and took it off before she could start the motor.

"What are you doing?"

"Washing your windshield." He lifted a mop on the end of a stick out of a bucket of water and slopped it on the windshield. "I danced with ya at the shindig they put on for the Claxtons when their house burned. Guess ya don't remember?"

"No, I don't."

"Gabe Thomas. Does that ring a bell?" He used the squeegee to take the excess water off the windshield.

"Yes. I remember. Your name was on the police log at the city office for bootlegging and stealing gasoline. I'm surprised Eddie lets you work here."

"I'm the best mechanic in Tillison County, that's why." He grinned. He seemed to be terribly pleased that she remembered him. "Ya hadn't been knocked up when we danced."

Kathleen's face reflected shock on hearing his crude words. She sat tight-lipped, staring straight ahead. The instant he snapped her wiper blade back in place, she moved the car ahead so fast that he had to jump out of the way.

"Be seein' ya," he called.

She was so angry that she didn't care if she ran over him when she drove out of the station. *That's what you think, you ignorant horse's patoot.*

Gabe stood in the drive and watched her until the Nash turned the corner. *Yeah, babe, ya'll be seein' me all right. Always did want to get in yore pants. I'm thinkin' it won't be too hard to do. Ole Johnny broke ground, but now he's outta the picture.*

From a car parked next to the vacant lot down the street, the encounter was watched through powerful binoculars by her *Guardian* as the man liked to call himself. This was the first time that she'd left the house in a week. He could tell that she was agitated about something when she drove out of the filling station. He started his car and followed slowly.

Two nights ago he had given himself a treat. He had left his car on a side street, walked across a vacant field, and approached her house from the back. The kitchen window shade was halfway up and he could see her sitting in her nightdress at the table working on her manuscript. The radio was on and Eddie Arnold was singing, "I'm Alone Because I Love You." He had become so excited he could hardly breathe when she lifted her arms, arched her back, and stretched. *The gesture was so familiar it made him doubly sure that she was the one.*

He watched her and daydreamed that someday he would walk into the house and she would greet him as if he belonged there. He would tell her what he had done with his inheritance, and she would be proud that he had invested it in a company selling arms to the British at the time when the world was at war and that he had made a vast amount of money. *My very own dear, he would say, we can afford for you to have whatever you want.*

A dog began to bark, breaking into his dream. She looked toward the window. He hurriedly backed away and went back across a field to where he'd left his car.

Months ago, when he'd discovered that she wrote stories for a Western magazine, he'd had a searcher find every magazine that had a K. K. Doyle story in it. He had read them all, over and over. He kept the magazines locked in a suitcase. They were his treasures.

The nerve of that trashy, whopper-jawed, nasty, dirty polecat, Kathleen fumed as she shifted into second gear and tramped on the gas pedal. She was so angry that the Nash went over the curb and swerved to the wrong side of the street before she realized it. *Johnny would tear him apart if he knew what he had said to me.* A block away, she slowed the car. *Or . . . would he care?*

The Greyhound bus had come into town and was

parked in front of the drugstore. Kathleen passed it on her way to the icehouse, where she picked up a card to put in her window on delivery day. Coming back she stopped at Miller's grocery store and was about to get out of the car when she saw Johnny come out of the store with a sack of groceries. He went to a dark sedan, said something to a woman in the front seat, then put the grocery sack in the back.

With two cars angle-parked between them, Kathleen could see only the back of the woman's head, but she knew that she was young. Old ladies didn't wear bleached, shoulder-length hair. Kathleen felt as if the air had been sucked from her lungs. She turned her head, hoping and praying that he wouldn't see her, and, if he did, he'd not know that she'd seen him and . . . the woman.

Johnny backed the car out and drove down the street. On a sudden impulse Kathleen followed. *He may be taking someone home,* she reasoned, remembering how concerned he had been for her when she first came to town. At the library corner the sedan turned south. Kathleen turned, then stopped. She could see all the way down the street to the flatlands outside of town. The sedan continued on out of town, and it was clear to Kathleen that Johnny was taking the woman out to the ranch.

She put her hands to her head, and her fingers massaged her aching temples. She was grateful that he hadn't seen her and wouldn't know that she had followed him.

She had thought that she would be prepared for the inevitable when it happened, but it had happened far sooner than she had expected.

Kathleen began to shake all over, and it was such a peculiar sensation that it frightened her. Fear ate into her very being. Would she never be free of this power he had to hurt her? Would she ever be able to empty her mind of Johnny and the love they had shared?

Of course not, she chided herself. Heavens! He had been a part of her life for seven years. They had made a child together. There was no way she could ever get him out of her mind. But she hoped someday to get him out of her heart.

Suddenly she was ashamed.

Where and when had she lost her pride? Johnny had made it plain that he didn't want her, and here she was, following after him like a puppy. She stiffened her resolve to do her utmost to hide her love for him. She would never, she vowed silently, allow him to use it as a weapon against her.

The man following Kathleen stopped his car a block behind hers. He waited to see if she was going to get out and go into the library. When she didn't, he picked up from the seat beside him what he called his observation diary and read the entry he'd made earlier.

10:30 A.M. *Kathleen, Kathleen, Kathleen. I love to write her name. It is as beautiful as she is. She wore a skirt today that came to just below her knees. Thank goodness, she no longer wears that awful leg makeup she wore during the war. I hated to see her wear it, and I hated it when she wore her beautiful hair in that ugly net snood.*

At the 66 station, she bought gas, got air in a tire, and talked for a while to a greasy, uncouth individual who made her angry. When I find out what it was he said to upset her, he'll be sorry.

When he finished reading, he took an expensive Sheaffer fountain pen from his pocket and added another entry.

11:00 A.M. My beautiful Kathleen is hurting because the son of a bitch she's married to has another woman. From the looks of the blonde in his car, he scraped the bottom of the barrel. My beautiful girl was faithful to him all during the war, and as soon as he gets home he takes up with a bleached-blonde floozy. He isn't fit for her to wipe her feet on. She's leaving now—going home. I wish I knew what it was that she needed from the store. I'd buy it and leave it on her porch tonight.

In the middle of the week Adelaide came out to tell Kathleen about the reception to be held for the new doctor.

"Please come, Kathleen," she said after they sat down at the kitchen table. "I'm heading the welcoming committee. We'll serve cake and coffee and iced tea. Claude is seeing to the cake."

"He's taking his duties as mayor seriously."

"We've discovered he has talents other than making hamburgers."

"Was this reception your idea or his?"

"Mine. I'm taking care of the decorations. I'm going to use my lace tablecloth, and Paul is polishing my mother's silver service."

"Silver service? This is going to be a fancy affair."

"The service hasn't been used since Mother died fifteen years ago. I'm not sure how it's going to shine up; but Paul says it will, and he's usually right."

"When is this shindig you're so excited about?" Kathleen smiled at the woman she loved like a sister and handed her a glass of iced tea.

"Tomorrow afternoon, two o'clock. We've put posters in all the store windows. Dr. Perry arrived yesterday, and Claude took him out to Doc Herman's house. The arrangement is that if he stays, he can buy the house for what the bank has in it. They took it and the clinic after Doc died."

"I hope he stays after you've gone to all this trouble, but maybe his wife will not like a small town and they'll go back to the city."

"He isn't married."

"Well, unless he's got an eye in the middle of his forehead and all his teeth are missing, every single woman in town will be after him."

"We may be able to use him to make Johnny jealous." Adelaide lifted her brows in question. "That boy needs someone to give him a swift kick. I'd ask Paul to do it, but he likes him too much."

"Don't even think about trying to get us back together, Addie. Johnny wouldn't care if I paraded through downtown Rawlings as naked as a jaybird."

"I think you're wrong."

"We won't argue that now or ever. Tell me about the new doctor," Kathleen said quickly, hoping to change the subject. She didn't want to hear about the woman Johnny was keeping company with.

"Claude said that this is his first civilian practice. He went into the army after medical school."

"He should be pretty good at patching up gunshot wounds. The trouble is that there may not be many of those now that there isn't a draft to dodge."

"What brought that on?"

"I ran into Gabe Thomas today at the filling station, and he was bragging about not being drafted because he'd had four toes shot off squirrel hunting. He got under my skin. I don't know why Eddie hired him."

"It irked a lot of people, including me, that he was here during the war, bragging that he had been too smart to get caught in the draft." Adelaide took the last drink from her glass and set it on the table. "I've got to get back to the paper. I'll come by for you tomorrow."

"You talked me into it. I'll have on my best bib and tucker to meet the new doc, and I promise that I won't pick my nose or tell him dirty jokes."

"Oh . . . you— I'm glad to know that you still have your sense of humor."

Kathleen watched her dearest friend drive away. Adelaide was fifty years old but didn't look or act a year older than thirty-five. Love for her husband, Paul, was keeping her young. They adored each other as much today as they had when she first met them seven years ago.

Lucky, lucky Adelaide.

John J. Wrenn, president of Oklahoma State Bank of Rawlings, tried to conceal his amazement as a cashier's check was placed on his desk by the man who sat across from him.

"Deposit the check in the name of Hidendall, Incorporated. We wish to pay for the property outright. The balance is to be kept in a checking account."

"Of course. The house has historic value. It was built by a cattle baron in 1912."

"I'm not interested in the historic value, Mr. Wrenn. It suits my purpose. I insist on privacy."

"The Clifton place is one of the largest holdings here. Only the BF Ranch is larger. We have been leasing the land to local ranchers for grazing."

"Continue to do so. I'll have a man down here in a few days to look over your books."

"Folks will wonder—"

"You are to tell the curious that I'm a weather observer,

which I am part of the time. My main occupation is that of writer. My books are published under a very well known pen name. I don't want to be bothered by people knocking on my door seeking autographs. I hope you understand that my name is not to be mentioned to anyone at any time nor under any circumstance. Is that clear?"

"It is," the banker hastened to say.

"How long before I can move in?"

"In just a few days. I'll send a crew out tomorrow to clean the house. It's been vacant since old Mrs. Clifton died last year. She left the house and the property to a nephew in New Jersey. He told us to sell it. The furnishings, as you could tell, are old, but good quality. We decided to sell them with the house rather than hold an auction."

The man who stood looked more like a movie star than a writer. A few months short of his thirty-ninth birthday, he was average height, with ice-blue eyes and blond hair turning gray at the temples. He wore a dark shirt, a string tie, and a mohair jacket with dark brown oval patches on the elbows. There was an air of purpose to his movements that was particularly evident when he strode to the door of the bank president's office and turned for a final word.

"I'll be doing other business with this bank if my wishes for complete confidentiality are respected. I'll return day after tomorrow and sign the final papers."

"They'll be ready." The banker began to stand, but before he could get to his feet, the man calling himself Robert Brooks was out the door, so he sat back down.

Will wonders never cease to happen? He had unloaded that old Clifton estate, and he couldn't even brag about it to anyone.

He had been surprised when the man phoned and inquired about the Clifton place. It had been on the market for a year and had been shown only one time. The man who called wanted to see the inside of it, as he had already inspected the grounds and the surrounding property. Wrenn had sent a junior clerk out with a key, and not two hours later he was looking at a cashier's check for *fifty thousand dollars*.

John Wrenn pulled the telephone toward him and told the operator to get him the First National Bank in Oklahoma City. While he waited, he wondered how much longer it would be before Rawlings Telephone Company would install dial telephones.

"Hidendall, Inc., is as solid as the Rock of Gibraltar," the officer of the bank in Oklahoma City assured him. "Theodore Nuding is the sole owner of the corporation. His check is good."

"Mr. Nuding bought a property after seeing it only one time. Does he usually leave a balance of five thousand in a checking account?"

"Nuding is an unusual fellow. However, his needs seem to be few. He does not live high on the hog, even if he is able to."

"He's . . . well-off?"

"To put it mildly. If you want his business, I advise you to follow his instructions to the letter. He's got an uncanny business sense, and he's a man who demands anonymity."

"Thanks for telling me. If that's what he wants, I can assure you that's what he will get."

"Ah . . . I thought you'd agree. He's not hard to get along with unless you try to put something over on him. Then watch out. He can be vicious."

John Wrenn hung up the telephone and leaned back in his chair. Damn. Theodore Nuding, alias Robert Brooks, was well-off. Did that mean he was comfortably rich or a millionaire? The banker regretted that he hadn't added another five thousand to the estate and made himself a nice little profit.

The man who walked into the hotel down the street wore a well-worn suit coat and an old brown felt hat on a head of dark brown hair. He shuffled as he crossed the lobby to the desk. He removed his glasses and massaged the bridge of his nose.

"Any mail?" he asked the desk clerk in a meek voice.

"A couple of letters, Mr. Brooks."

"Thanks." He put his glasses back on and glanced at the letters. Both were from business places back East. He put them in the pocket of his jacket and headed for the stairs.

In his room, Theodore Nuding took a bulky notebook from his inside coat pocket before he hung the coat on a hanger. He adapted easily to any environment. He liked the smallness of Rawlings, although he realized that it would be harder to blend in than it had been in the city. But he could do it. He knew how to make himself into a forgettable fellow or into a man long remembered.

He sat down at a table near the window, looked across at the courthouse, and then down on the street. He recognized the man who was getting out of a car in front of the bank, and reached for his ever-handy binoculars. He studied Johnny Henry as he stood beside the car talking to his father, Barker Fleming. He had made it his business to find out all he could about Kathleen's husband and rather admired him for his attitude toward a father who had abandoned him. Johnny's mother had been a whore and his sister was a slut who worked in a honky-tonk in Oklahoma City.

Nuding was a man with an extraordinary memory for

detail and a knack for picking up information, especially anything pertaining to Kathleen Dolan Henry. His obsession with her was a fact that he readily admitted and reveled in.

Theodore Nuding's own father had died when he was nine years old. It had been God's gift to him and his mother. Thank God he'd had no brothers or sisters. He'd had his darling mother all to himself for almost thirty years.

He took out his fountain pen and began to write.

4:00 P.M. *I'm so glad that I found her, Mother. Her hair is gloriously red like yours, but then you know that because you urged me to take the job in the aircraft plant so that I would meet her. I bought a house for her today. It's a big old house, somewhat like the one you and I lived in when I was taking care of you. It will take a while to get it ready for her. Then I'll look after her and keep her safe just as I did you. And after a while, like you, she will come to depend on me and will love me for my gentle care. So much to be done. I wish I didn't have to waste time sleeping.*

Chapter Five

KATHLEEN DREADED going to the reception for Dr. Perry. She didn't fear that she would run into Johnny because she couldn't think of a reason why he would be there. Her fear was that someone would mention him and the blond woman.

Night after sleepless night, she had pictured Johnny and another woman in the house that had been hers for almost three years and in the bed she had shared with him. Had he been writing to someone here in Rawlings while he was away? Was she from here or from out of town?

Get out of my mind, Johnny Henry, or I'm going to lose it.

Kathleen was ready when Adelaide came by. Forcing herself to show some enthusiasm for her friend's sake, she hurried out to the car with a perky smile on her face.

"You look so pretty I'm surprised Paul will let you out the door without him."

"He knows that no one but he would have me." Adelaide moved her purse to make room on the seat for her friend. "Judy will be at the reception taking pictures. Paul thought that he'd better stick around the office in case the bank was robbed or the schoolhouse caught on fire."

"Every newspaperman's dream."

"We'll be a little early. I want to get things set up before the crowd arrives. It's open house, thank goodness. Everyone won't come at the same time."

"Don't count on it. Mrs. Smothers, our number one complainer about paper delivery, will come early and stay late."

"And try to get free medical advice from the doctor," Adelaide added.

"I'm not much in the mood for small talk. I'll help you get set up, stay a polite length of time, and walk home. I need the exercise."

"I can't afford to stay the entire afternoon either. I've got plenty to do back at the paper," Adelaide said as she parked behind a row of cars in front of the clinic. "We can carry in everything in one load if you help me."

"I wasn't planning on it," Kathleen teased, "but I will."

Claude had set up a table in the reception area of the clinic. It was covered with a lace tablecloth. In the center of the table was a large decorated sheet cake. WELCOME TO RAWLINGS, DR. PERRY was written in green icing. Around the edge of the cake were large red roses with green leaves.

"The cake is beautiful. Did Claude bake it?"

"One of the restaurants made it." Adelaide unwrapped the silver service and set it up at the end of the table. "I'm glad for the chance to use Mother's silver. Oh, hello, Dale. Are the coffee and tea ready?"

The woman who came down the hall and into the reception room was, as Adelaide would describe her, pleasingly plump. From the starched cap perched proudly on top of dark brown hair to her gleaming white oxfords, Dale Cole was the classic nurse and so efficient that most people didn't realize that she was not an RN.

"The coffee is perking. We even chipped the ice for the tea."

"Dale, meet Kathleen Henry."

Dale's smile was beautiful. "Hello. I've heard a lot about the young reporter who came to this town and broke the hold Doc Herman had on it."

"For heaven's sake! I didn't do it all by myself."

"She gave us the push that we needed to get rid of that tyrant." Adelaide fanned the napkins out on the table.

"Have you met Dr. Perry?" Dale asked. "If I weren't already married to the most wonderful man in the world, I'd be after him like a shot."

"That good, huh?" Adelaide winked at Kathleen.

"He's just as sweet as he can be, a crackerjack, and a caring doctor to boot. Every single woman in town and some of the married ones are going to suddenly get a bellyache, a sore throat or palpitations." Dale picked up a clipboard. "Nice to have met you, Kathleen." She tilted her head toward the inner office, where the murmur of masculine voices could be heard. "You're in for a treat," she said brightly, and scurried down the hall.

"She's nice. How long has she—" Kathleen cut the words off in mid-sentence when the office door opened, and her eyes collided with Johnny's. He came into the room followed by a man with a thin, pleasant face and curly blond hair. Kathleen's eyes went from Johnny to the man, and down to the cake.

"Hello, Johnny, we didn't know you were here."

Thank goodness for Adelaide. Kathleen wouldn't have been able to say fire if her clothes were ablaze.

"I came to see if my old friend had time to go squirrel hunting." Johnny's eyes were still on Kathleen. "Have you met Mrs. Leahy, Jude?"

"The publisher of the newspaper? We've not met, but Claude White spoke of you. He warned me not to get on your wrong side." The doctor held out his hand.

"Did he tell you that I charge him too much for his ads and that he wants to pay me in hamburgers?"

"Now that you mention it, he did say that he'd trade me burgers for house calls." The doctor's voice was warm and friendly.

Kathleen was slightly breathless by the time his eyes left Adelaide and turned to her.

"Jude, this is my wife, Kathleen," Johnny said without taking his eyes off her. "Kathleen, do you remember me telling you about my cousins, Jude Perry and his brother Pete?"

Kathleen's eyes flicked to Johnny, then back to the smiling man who was holding out his hand. She put hers in it.

"You mean . . . from down on—"

"—Mud Creek," the doctor said. "A lot of water has gone under the bridge since we were down on Mud Creek, huh, Johnny?" Smile lines fanned out from the corner of large brown eyes. "I knew that you were Kathleen as soon as I opened the door. Karen and Grant Gifford told me about Johnny's pretty redheaded wife." Jude Perry was still holding her hand. He turned and spoke to Johnny. "How did an ugly old cowboy like you manage to talk her into marrying you?"

Kathleen's face flushed at the compliment. Her eyes shot to Johnny. He stood on spread legs, his arms were folded across his chest, his eyes daring her to explain their separation.

"It wasn't easy," he said with a raised brow and a quirk at the corner of his mouth.

You . . . you horse's patoot! Why haven't you told him that we're separated? How will you explain the blonde you took to the ranch?

"How are the Giffords?" She had to say something.

"Fine. They are coming down in a few weeks. I was just telling Johnny that we'd have to get together and catch up on all that's happened since we were last in Red Rock." He released her hand and moved away. When he turned she noticed that he limped. "As much as I'd like to stay and visit, I've got two patients to see to before this shindig gets under way. See you in a day or two, Johnny?"

"I'll give it a try, Jude. Thanks."

"See you in a while, ladies," Dr. Perry said, and limped down the hall.

Johnny waited until the sound of a door closing reached them before he spoke, his direct gaze on Kathleen.

"About ready to leave? I'll give you a ride home."

Kathleen almost choked, and her heart pounded in response to her anger. A hectic flush stained her cheeks, and her eyes, when she glared at Johnny, shone like those of a wildcat he'd once treed.

"When I'm ready to leave, I'll walk."

"When will that be?" He gave her back stare for stare.

"I've not decided yet."

"You came to meet the doctor, didn't you? You met him. Do you need her help, Adelaide?"

"Hey, I'm out of this." Adelaide picked up the silver coffee server and headed for the kitchen.

"I hope you're satisfied." Kathleen's blue eyes sparkled angrily. "You've made Adelaide uncomfortable."

"Adelaide's skin is thicker than that. If she's embarrassed, it's because you've got your back up."

"All I said was that I'd walk."

"I saw you in front of the store the other day." He

dropped the news in a calm, sure voice that unnerved her even more.

"I usually buy my groceries at the store."

"Why didn't you go in?"

"I changed my mind. Is there a law against that?"

"You followed me out of town."

"I went to the library!" Her face was fiery now, her eyes like blue stars. Her head felt tight, and her eyes smarted. She wanted to hit him. It was a ridiculous notion. *He knew that she had seen him with the blonde. But why was he trying to humiliate her?*

"I want to talk to you."

"Well, talk. Dammit!"

"Not here. These walls have ears." A muscle twitched in the corner of his mouth.

"I'm home most nights," she said in a voice wooden with control, but some of the desperation she was feeling made itself known by the quivering of her lips.

"Don't be difficult, Kathleen. I know that you can hardly stand the sight of me, but unbend a little. I need to talk to you."

"Is it safe to come back in?" Adelaide asked from the doorway.

"Of course. I'm sorry you were uncomfortable. I'll be going now if there isn't anything else you want me to do."

"I wasn't bothered in the slightest. Go on. In a few minutes I'll have more help than I'll know how to manage. You're excused." Adelaide made a little shooing motion with her hand.

Kathleen picked up her purse and walked out the door, conscious that Johnny followed close behind her. At the end of the walk, he took her elbow and turned her toward his car. After she was settled in the seat, he went around to the driver's side, opened the door, and got in. It was then she noticed the extra space between the seat and the dash. He had evidently unbolted the front seat and moved it to make room for his long legs.

"It isn't like riding in a Buick, but it's a shade better than my old truck." He glanced at her set profile before he started the car. "Do you want to go someplace and get something cold to drink?"

"No. I've got iced tea at home."

"Will I be invited in, or do you want to talk in the car?"

"You can come in. That is if you can spare the time." She turned to look out the window and failed to see the frown that puckered his brows.

Nothing more was said until they reached her house and he had parked the car behind her Nash. Kathleen got out and led the way into the house.

"I'll fix the tea," she said on her way to the kitchen. Her nerves were a tangled mess, and her hands shook as she threw back the top lid on the small icebox and chipped enough ice from the block to fill the glasses.

He's made arrangements for the divorce. She should be prepared for it, but she wasn't. Oh, Lord, help me not to blubber like a baby when he tells me.

Johnny was sitting on the couch in much the same place he had sat when he was there before. In his hand was a page of her manuscript he had taken from the stack on the end table. Smiling dark eyes met hers. He was grinning as if he were terribly pleased. Kathleen drew in a deep breath and tried to remain calm.

"Pretty good," he said, and replaced the page before reaching for the glass she held out to him.

"That's one of the exciting scenes. There are several pages of dull narrative leading to that. Writing a book is different from writing a short story. It requires much more detail."

"I kind of got hooked on Western stories." When she didn't speak, he said, "What are these things on the glasses?"

"Socks. My landlady in Oklahoma City knitted them. They help to keep the glass from sweating and the ice from melting so fast."

"Socks for tea glasses—what'll they think of next?" He turned the glass around and around in his large hands. Kathleen's eyes were drawn to them. *He was still wearing his wedding ring.*

An uneasy silence hung between them. Johnny clasped his hands 'round his glass and looked at it intently. Kathleen was confused. She had prepared herself for what she was sure he was going to say. What thoughts were going through that handsome head?

"What did you want to talk about? Have you seen a lawyer?" She decided to jump in and get the agony of suspense over with.

"Are you in a hurry to break with me?"

"You left me. Remember?" she said quietly. "I'm sure you want your freedom to—"

"—To what?" His body was still except for the slight flicker of his eyelids.

"Marry someone else." The words almost choked her.

"What gave you that idea?"

"Let's don't beat around the bush. Come right out with what you want to say."

"I don't know if I should even bother to ask you now. You seem in such an all-fired hurry to get me out of your life."

"Under the circumstances, what choice do I have?"

"Have you got someone else?" Looking intently at the glass in his hand, he spoke softly.

"No." Then she added, "Not yet," in order to keep a little of her dignity intact.

"Does that mean that you have someone in mind?"

Kathleen's anger flared. "How dare you sit there and question me about my private life when you . . . when you—"

"All right. Let's forget it." He set his glass on the end table and stood.

Kathleen remained seated. Her voice shook with anger when she spoke. "I can't forget it. Maybe you can, but I can't. You came to say something, so say it."

Johnny sat back down, leaned over, and rested his forearms on his thighs. His hands were clasped together tightly. He seemed to be studying his new boots.

"Tell me this, Kathleen. If you don't have another man, why are you in such a hurry to divorce me?"

Kathleen looked at him. His face was leaner, harder. His hair had grown during the past few weeks, and he looked more like the old Johnny. She thought of herself. Too much time had been wasted. She should have confronted him years ago, instead of taking his repeated rejections in silence. She didn't want to wait any longer for fate to make its play.

"How can you ask . . . under the circumstances? What did I do to you to make you want to humiliate me?"

"I never wanted that." His head came up. "I know how bad you want . . . a family. I can't give you children . . . not the kind that will make you happy."

"So you cut and run. You don't want to risk another Mary Rose, is that it?"

He was silent for a long while, then he said, "You don't understand me at all, do you?"

"I tried to. Are you afraid that I'll demand part of your ranch if we get a divorce? If that's what's holding you back, you can get that thought out of your head."

"Goddammit!" Suddenly his shoulders slumped. "I was going to ask if you would be willing to sign papers at the bank so I could get a loan to rebuild my herd. The government will guarantee a loan to a veteran for a home or business; but since you're my wife and co-owner of the ranch, I needed your signature. But forget it." He went to the door.

"I'll sign the papers." Kathleen followed, but stood back so she could look up at him. "Isn't there enough money in your account to help you get started?"

"I won't use that." It was his tone of voice more than the words that wounded her.

"You don't want even that from me," she said, throwing back at him words that he'd said to her previously. Her control broke like a dam being pushed by flood waters. She balled her fist and pounded him on the chest to emphasize her words. "You make me so damn mad!" Tears of frustration filled her eyes when she realized what she had done.

"Still the fiery redhead. You can't hold your temper any better today than you could seven years ago."

"You, more than anyone else, can cause me to lose it. Why won't you use the money?"

"Pride, I guess. I can't explain it. I don't have a way with words like you do. I only know that I can't take the money you saved when you don't want anything from me."

"It was the allotment money the government sent me as your wife."

"Not all of it. I can add. Think about it; and if it's something you're willing to do, stop by the bank and ask Mr. Wrenn for the papers." He slapped his hat down on his head and stepped out onto the porch. "I'll understand if you don't want to be obligated, because if I can't make the payments, they'll come after you."

"I'll go in tomorrow."

"Thanks." He looked at her for a long while, then headed for the car. Before he got in, he turned. " 'Bye."

" 'Bye, Johnny."

He lingered by the car, Kathleen on the edge of the porch. She was thinking that he might come back to the house when he finally spoke.

"Isabel is out at the ranch. She's sick and didn't have any place to go."

"Your sister?" Kathleen's breath caught in her throat, and she felt the heat come up her neck to her cheeks.

"My half sister. I told you about her."

"I remember. What's the matter with her?"

"I'm not sure. I'm going to try to get her into the clinic to see Jude."

"Does the doctor know her?"

Johnny snorted. "Oh, yes."

"Was she the woman with you . . . the other day?" The words came even as she thought them.

"Yeah. She came in on the bus. She'd called Sheriff Carroll before she left the city. He sent word out to me."

"I'm sorry. If there's anything I can do, let me know."

He snorted again. "You'd not be able to stand her."

"Why didn't she go to Henry Ann?"

"She hates Henry Ann. She hates me, too, but hates Henry Ann more."

"Poor miserable thing."

"She's hard. I'm sorry to say, I've never known a woman

as hard and as selfish. Whatever is wrong with her, she's brought on herself." He got in the car and started the motor. He continued to look at Kathleen standing on the porch as he backed out. On the road he lifted a hand and drove away.

Kathleen could do nothing but smile. A weight had been lifted from her heart. He hadn't been taking a woman out to *her* house. The one in his car had been his sister.

"Where have you been? I've been here all day by myself. You knew I wanted to go to town and you slipped off without me. You're a son of a bitch, Johnny."

Isabel began raving at Johnny the minute he stepped upon the porch carrying a chunk of ice. While Isabel continued to berate him, he slid the block into the icebox and shut the door.

"Did you bring me any cigarettes? This place is so damn quiet I heard a bird fart when it flew over. I don't see how you stand it out here without electricity or an indoor toilet. Talk about backwoods! I thought Mud Creek was back in the sticks, but here there ain't even any sticks, for Godsake."

"You didn't ask for cigarettes."

"I told you last night I only had two packs left. Jesus Christ!"

An ashtray with a dozen butts in it was on the table, the dishes hadn't been washed and the dish towel was on the floor. He picked it up.

"This place is drivin' me crazy." Isabel's breathing was uneven. "I've been stuck here for over a week. I want to go to town. I've not seen a soul but you and that old coot that works for you. I can't understand a word he says. He's not got a tooth in his head."

"Don't take your spite out on Sherm. It isn't his fault that you're here. I told you to listen to the radio all you want. I'll keep the battery charged up."

"All you can get is that old station down at Vernon." She grasped the back of a chair to steady herself.

Johnny was embarrassed to look at her. She wore only a single sleeveless garment, the armholes so big that her flat breasts were visible. Her trembling legs were so thin they looked like sticks.

She was thirty years old and looked fifty.

"You're sick, Isabel. You should see a doctor."

"Hell, I know I'm sick. I've seen a doctor. He told me to rest. Why do you think I came here? There's nothin' to do here, but rest. I've had about all the *rest* I can take."

"You're not in any condition to go anywhere. You couldn't walk fifty feet."

"Ha! Just give me the chance."

Her voice was weak, and she was breathing hard; but there was defiance in her eyes. The skin on her bony face had a yellowish tinge, and dark circles surrounded her deep-set eyes. Her dry, straw-colored hair had come out in patches, revealing her scalp.

"Remember Jude Perry?" Johnny hurried on before she could interrupt. "He's a doctor now. A good one. He just took over the clinic in town. You should go see him."

Isabel hooted. "Jude, Hardy Perry's smart-mouthed, sissy-britches kid? How'd he ever get to be a doctor? Well, never mind. I'd not let that flitter-headed ninny treat my sick cat, if I had one."

"He left medical school at the head of his class and went into the army with a commission. He was wounded at Anzio. He's a long way from being a flitter-headed ninny."

"Anzio? Where's that?"

"Italy. He was shot in the thigh while tending a wounded man."

"If it'd been his head, it wouldn't hurt him. All he wanted to do was read his damn books. He wouldn't even help with the still unless Hardy threatened to beat the tar outta him. God, it was funny seeing him dancing with Hardy."

"When you're young you do things you don't want to do to keep a roof over your head and food in your belly," Johnny said tightly.

"Yeah, well, he'll never be the man Pete was. That man knew how to dance."

"I remember that you lied about your age to be in the dance marathon with Pete and got both of you thrown out of the competition."

"He was madder than a pissed-on snake." Isabel laughed. "It was probably a good thing that the sheriff got me out of there. Pete wanted to kill me."

Johnny went through the living room and paused in the doorway leading to the bedroom. Letters, pictures, and mementos from his rodeo days that Kathleen had saved lay scattered over the unmade bed. A bureau drawer hung open.

"Goddammit," he swore. "I told you to stay out of my things. You were to use the bed and that was all."

"Hell, what'er you riled up about? I was just looking at your old pictures. There's nothin' else to do." Isabel watched as Johnny put the pictures, rodeo clippings, and souvenirs back in the drawer.

"You could do some cleaning around here." Even as he said it, he knew that she hadn't the strength even to keep herself clean. She made him so angry he had to say something.

"Did you go to see your wife while you were in town? Is she a whore? Bet that red hair in the picture came out of a bottle at the five-and-dime."

"You would try the patience of a saint."

"Saint? I ain't no saint. Is the redhead givin' you a little tail now and then?" She laughed nastily. "You didn't go without it while you were gone. I'd bet my life on that! Ain't no man I ever heard of can go without it that long."

"Shut up, Isabel."

"God, I don't blame her for leavin' you. This place is deader than a graveyard."

Johnny picked up the drawer and walked out of the house. Isabel followed him to the porch.

"What'er you goin' to do? You afraid I'll tear up the pictures of your darlin' Kathleen? I want to go to town, Johnny."

On his way to the barn, Johnny turned. "Not until you agree to go to the clinic and see Jude."

"You . . . horsecock!" Isabel yelled, before she went back into the house and slammed the door.

Inside the barn, Johnny looked at his and Kathleen's wedding picture for a long while before he turned it face-down in the drawer, then slipped the drawer into a gunny-sack and tied the end securely. He climbed a ladder and carefully placed his burden on the support beams, where it would be safe from Isabel's prying eyes.

Chapter Six

Dr. Jude Perry sank down in the chair behind his desk and rubbed his aching thigh. The open house had been a success. According to the mayor's count, more than a hundred people had showed up to give him a warm welcome. He was tired, but elated too.

He had Grant Gifford to thank for arranging the purchase of the clinic. This is what he'd always wanted. He'd had no desire for a big-city practice. Being in the same area as Johnny was an extra bonus. It had been good to see him. Grant had told him about Johnny's war record and that he suspected that Johnny's marriage was breaking up. According to Grant and Karen, Johnny and Kathleen had been terribly in love when they wed. Jude wondered what had happened to drive them apart.

Kathleen was a pretty woman. Jude could understand why Johnny was still in love with her. Now how did he know that? he asked himself. Was it the way Johnny's attention had been drawn to voices in the reception room while they had been in the office, and the fact he'd not mentioned a separation? Grant had said they'd lost a child before Johnny went to the service. He wondered if that had anything to do with the rift between them.

Jude hadn't thought of Isabel Perry in years. When she first came to Mud Creek, a fourteen-year-old who didn't have the brains of a flea, he sensed she would come to a bad end, just as her mother had. Johnny had said that she was sick and had come to stay with him because she didn't have anyplace else to go.

Johnny suspected, because of her lifestyle, that she might have a venereal disease. If that were the case, there wouldn't be much he could do if the disease was in the advanced stage. What an ironic turn of events. Isabel had hated him when they were young. He hadn't had much use for her either.

"Doctor?" The nurse had entered the office quietly and broke into his thoughts. "Someone to see you."

"A patient?"

"No. He could be a salesman."

"How are you doing, Theresa? You've been here since six this morning."

"This has been a special day. I'll be leaving soon. I wanted to make sure the night nurse had a handle on things."

"Is Mrs. Cole still here?"

"Her husband came for her a few minutes ago. He apologized for taking her away early. He said something had come up, but didn't say what it was."

"Do you like her?"

"Yes, I do. She's very pleasant, very capable."

"I want you to tell me if you think there should be any changes in the staff. You're in charge."

"It will be a while before I know if there should be changes. So far everyone seems efficient and enthusiastic."

Jude studied the woman. She was an excellent nurse. Saint Anthony Hospital in the city was sorry to lose her.

She was not much over five feet and had a round, full figure. Although she weighed more than she should for her height, she was neat as a pin. Her uniform looked as if she had just put it on. The starched cap with the black stripe sat atop short, dark brown hair that was pulled back and pinned. Soft brown eyes in a pretty face with a flawless complexion looked back at him.

Theresa's husband had been killed on the Normandy beach, leaving her with a son he had never seen.

"Has Ryan settled in?"

"He's glad to be out of that apartment in the city. He's crazy about Mrs. Ramsey and her daughter Emily." Theresa's eyes lit up when talking about her son. She was glad, too, to be away from her in-laws, who were trying to take over the raising of their grandchild.

"Then you're happy here?"

"If my son is happy, I'm happy. I was lucky to find a place to rent just a block from the Ramseys."

"I'm glad you're with me."

Theresa blushed at the compliment and lowered her head to study a chart she was holding.

"I'm glad to be here, Doctor."

"I'm not sure sometimes how to proceed in a private practice," Jude continued. "All I've done lately is work in a veteran's hospital. You've worked with general practitioners. You'll have to help me stay on the right track."

"You took your brush-up courses and have all the right qualities to make a fine small-town doctor."

"I appreciate your confidence."

"I'd better show in your visitor before he seduces our receptionist. He's already got her in a twitter."

"He's probably going to try and sell us some new

equipment. I'll lay out our bank statement. That'll discourage him."

Theresa went out and closed the door, but not before Jude heard a male voice and a woman's nervous titter.

He was lucky to have Theresa. She'd met her husband during her last year of nursing school. They had been married two months when he was drafted into the service. She had given birth to their son without ever seeing him again and had worked for four years in Oklahoma City. Jude wondered what had caused her to accept a job in a small clinic at a third less pay.

When the door opened, all thoughts of Theresa, the clinic, and his aching thigh rushed from Jude's mind. Fourteen years had passed since he had seen the big blond man who filled the doorway. Pete Perry had joined the navy back in 1932 as soon as he was cleared of the murder of Emmajean Dolan. His ship had been sunk in the Battle of the Coral Sea, and Jude had not heard whether his brother had survived. Now here he was!

"Pete? God Almighty! Pete!" Jude got up from behind his desk on numb legs and without taking his eyes off the man, managed to meet him in front of his desk.

"Hello, little brother." Pete's voice was husky with emotion. He grabbed Jude's hand.

The two men stood looking at each other. Pete's eyes were unnaturally bright, and Jude's were misty.

"Lord, Pete, I never was able to find out if you made it after the *Lexington* was sunk."

"Broke my leg is all. While I was in the hospital on New Caledonia, I got word the old man had died; and I didn't know how to get in touch with you."

"It's good to see you. Lord, it's good to see you." Jude gripped his brother's shoulders in his two hands.

"It's good to see you, too. My little brother is a doctor. I was over at Red Rock looking for a trace of you. Henry Ann told me where you were. I hightailed it right over."

"You always had a crush on Henry Ann," Jude said with a nervous laugh.

"Yeah. Reaching for the moon, wasn't I? I realize now that we'd not have suited each other and that I wanted something I knew I couldn't have. I'd have made her miserable with my wild ways." Pete grinned the devilish grin that women loved. "She said that Johnny came through the war and that he lives near here. She's talked to him several times on the phone."

"He was here today. Isabel has come to stay with him."

"I thought sure that someone would have killed that little split-tail by now."

"She's sick. Johnny said that she's very sick and didn't have anywhere else to go. She turned out just like her mother, Dorene."

"A whore, huh? I figured she would."

"Are you going to stay awhile?"

"I didn't re-enlist. I got a hankering to see familiar sights. I gave the navy sixteen years and saved a little money. I'd like to raise horses and dogs."

"Stay with me until you decide what you want to do. I've got plenty of room."

"I'd planned to stay at the hotel for a day or two."

"No need for that. The doctor who built this clinic owned a house just a short distance away. I bought it along with the clinic."

"Lord, but I'm proud of you, Jude." Pete grasped Jude's shoulder. "Never thought I'd see a Perry become a doctor. And you did it all by yourself."

"You helped me once in a while. I know you slipped old

Mrs. Hunting a little money now and then to help me with my studies."

"I should have done more. I should have gotten you away from Mud Creek. All that was on Hardy's mind was women, dancin', and bootleggin'. He was no fit father to you."

"I don't think about it anymore. Our pa lived the way his pa lived. What's important now is what we do with our lives."

"Looks like you're doing pretty good."

"That's yet to be proven. Let me show you around. This is a clinic, but we have bed patients. It's a clinic/hospital because we do minor surgery. It is well equipped thanks to army surplus. Our X-ray rooms and the lab are the first ones on your right. I'm hoping to get a couple of good technicians soon. I've contacted old army buddies who may be interested. The surgery is at the end of the hall."

Jude led Pete through a door and into a long hallway. They met Theresa, who had removed her starched cap and changed her white shoes for black ones with heels that made her appear taller.

"I'm leaving, Doctor. See you in the morning."

"Theresa, I'd like for you to meet my brother, Pete Perry. Pete, this is Mrs. Frank. I was lucky enough to lure her away from a big-city hospital to work with me here."

"Your brother?" Theresa looked up at the tall man. A slow smile started in her eyes and spread to her lips. Pete responded to the smile with one of his own. "We were sure that you were going to try and sell us bandages or bedpans," Theresa said. She was really pretty when she smiled, Jude noticed.

"Now what would give you that idea?" Pete held on to her hand and looked down at her as if she were the only woman in the world. It was his natural response to a pretty woman. "Brother," he said to Jude, "you do have all the luck."

"You'll have to excuse him, Theresa. He's fresh from the navy."

"That accounts for it. Welcome home, sailor." She pulled her hand from Pete's and turned to Jude. "I checked Mr. Case's temperature. It's steady at one degree above normal."

"Good. Did you tell Miss Pauley to call me if it goes up as much as two degrees?"

"I told her, and she will. I'd better get going. It's time to pick up Ryan. Nice to have met you, Mr. Perry."

"Nice to have met you, ma'am."

Jude continued with the tour of the clinic, introduced Pete to the night nurse, Miss Wanda Pauley, a no-nonsense spinster, and to Mr. and Mrs. Tuttle who were employed to do the cleaning and the laundry.

"Is Rawlings big enough to support all this?" Pete asked when they were outside, standing beside his car.

"I hope so. It's the only clinic in the county with a full-time doctor. The next town of any size is Frederick. Anything we can't handle here we'll send over there. We'll be ready for most things. Of course, there's always the unexpected. We're getting an iron lung from the government. I'm hoping we don't need one before it gets here."

"Polio isn't particular who it hits. A couple of young fellows on board ship came down with it. They took them off at Pearl and put them into iron lungs. I don't know if they're still alive."

"So far, there have been only four cases identified in Tillison County. I don't know if the records are correct.

Sounds low to me, considering the number of cases in Oklahoma during the past ten years."

"Do I get free doctoring?" Pete asked with a twinkle in his eyes.

"You'd trust me?"

"Well, now, I'll have to think about it. How long is your memory?"

"Long enough to remember you knocking me on my butt a few times and cussing me out a lot of times."

"That's what I was afraid of. How far did you say it was to Frederick?" Pete laughed and slapped Jude on the back so hard he staggered. "Let's go get those hamburgers. My belly button is rubbing against my backbone."

When Dale Cole was told by the receptionist that her husband was waiting for her in the reception room, she blanched. She turned quickly back to the cabinet and returned the package she had removed. This was the second time Harry had been to the clinic during the four months she had worked here. She trembled at the memory of what had happened that day when they got home.

"Dale, did you hear me? Mr. Cole said something important had come up and wanted to know if you could leave early. Mrs. Frank was there and said for me to come find you."

"Thanks, Millie. Tell him I'll be there in a minute."

Dale needed that minute to compose herself. Her mind raced back, trying to think of something she had done to set him off. She had seen him briefly when he had made an appearance with other members of the Chamber of Commerce. He had been in conversation with John Wrenn, the banker, and appeared to be in a good mood. She had been busy cutting and serving cake and unable to leave the table to speak to him. Had that been her mistake?

Dale picked up her purse and walked down the hall to the reception area on legs that trembled. Before she rounded the corner she took a deep breath and squared her shoulders. Her eyes went directly to her husband. He would notice if she looked frightened of him in public. He got to his feet when he saw her. He was a man of medium height with a head of thick brown hair and heavy brows. He worked as a supervisor for Oklahoma Gas and Electric Company.

"Harry, what has happened? Is Danny all right?" Dale asked with a worried frown.

"He's all right. I had a call from your sister." He said the last loudly enough for it to be heard by Millie Criswell, the receptionist. Then he grasped Dale's elbow and steered her out the door.

"Which one?" Dale hurried to keep pace with him. His grip on her elbow was getting tighter and tighter, and her heart began to thump. *What have I done? Oh, Lord, what have I done now?*

"Get in the car," he said when they reached it. He opened the door. He didn't shove her; he was always careful in public.

Dale's fearful eyes followed him as he rounded the front of the car. He was terribly angry. When he started the motor, he eased the car slowly away from the curb. He said nothing, which was not a good sign.

"Who called, Harry?" Dale asked when they were almost home.

"No one called," he answered calmly.

"Then why did you want me to leave early?"

"I wanted to talk to you before Danny got home. I saw

you rubbing up against that son of a bitch from the furniture store. You really think you're something, don't you, Dale? It was disgusting, is what it was. You must outweigh him by fifty pounds, and you were acting so coy, so *cute*. You were in his face, practically licking it, like a lapdog."

"I wasn't. I was serving cake—"

"—You fat bitch! Are you calling me a liar? You were slobbering all over him. You've been getting out of hand since we moved here. That job has gone to your head. The only reason I let you work was because of the labor shortage. Well, that's almost over. Defense workers are being let go by the thousands. There'll soon be more nurses looking for jobs than you can shake a stick at." He stopped the car in front of the house. He turned and looked at her with pure hatred in his eyes. "Get in there unless you want the neighbors to see me kick your fat ass all the way up the walk."

"Harry, it was my job to cut and serve the cake."

"Your job is to see to the one who feeds you and keeps a roof over your head. All you do is embarrass me, Dale, and talk behind my back. I can hardly look people in the eye anymore."

"I've never, ever said a word about . . . anything." *I've kept the secret, hidden my bruises.*

"I'm tired of your lies. Lie, lie, lie. You're lucky I put up with you. I should have sent you packing years ago. Jesus! You're about as sexy as a fat cow. I'd be better off sticking my pecker in a bucket of lard."

Dale had heard the same demeaning remarks over and over. Last week it was because she had put too much salt in the corn bread. His insults had become so foul she had asked him if Danny could leave the table.

She thought about not getting out of the car. But in the

mood he was in she didn't know what he would do. Why was he like this? Dale answered her own question. He wanted wild, hard sex and accusing her of something helped him get aroused. It was always the same and had been since they married.

Harry had shown a little jealousy while he courted her, and she had been dumb enough to think it was because he loved her. Now she knew that he was incapable of loving even his own child. He wanted to possess her, humiliate her. It was the only way that he could feel superior to her. She felt the same hopelessness that she'd felt a hundred times before

Lord, how can I endure it?

It was best to get it over so that she could get herself composed before Danny came home. She was sure that their five-year-old son would know that something had happened between his parents, but he wouldn't say anything. He was unusually quiet at times like this as though accepting that this was the way life was supposed to be. Someday Dale hoped to make him understand that not all men hit their wives and that she was enduring this so that she could be with him.

When she got out of the car, she looked to see if any of the neighbors were in their yards or on their porches. Harry's fear that one of them would come over was the only thing that might stall for a while what she knew was coming, and even that would only prolong the inevitable.

For the past four months her work at the clinic had given her a new sense of self-worth. For the first time in years Harry was not supervising every move she made. She had enjoyed a freedom that had begun slipping away from her from the day she married him. Now he was going to take it away again.

Inside the house, Dale set her purse down and turned. She was unprepared for the open-handed blow that caught her on the side of the face, and she stumbled. Harry was on her in an instant, pushing her against the wall and holding her with his forearm against her neck.

"Get in there and get your clothes off, you fat slut. You been wantin' a hard pecker, and you're goin' to get one." Harry always talked nasty when he was in a rage. He emphasized his words by pushing his arousal against her.

"All right." Dale had learned that to defy him enraged him more.

He released her and shoved her toward the bedroom. She stumbled into the room as she heard him going toward the bathroom for the razor strop. She knew what was coming. He would whip her bare buttocks until he was about to climax, then he would plunge roughly into her.

I'm afraid, she thought, that someday I will kill him.

Chapter Seven

KATHLEEN PUT ON HER COAT, flipped a scarf over her head, and tied the ends beneath her chin before she left the house to walk to town. The sun was still warm this first part of November, but a brisk wind shook dried leaves from the trees that lined the street, and they crunched beneath her feet.

She'd had a restless night. Once, she had even left her bed to look out a window when a dog barked furiously. Was that a man leaning against her car? She hurried to another window, mistakenly thinking that she would have a better view. When she returned, no one was there. Kathleen stood at the window for a long while, finally deciding that she had seen a shadow, that the man had been a figment of her imagination.

This morning the incident had left her mind as she crossed a street and stepped up on the sidewalk. Coming toward her was a woman wearing white shoes and white stockings. She wore a hip-length coat and a scarf on her head. Kathleen recognized her as Mrs. Cole, whom she had met at the clinic the day before.

"A nice cool morning, isn't it?" Kathleen said.

"Yes, it is," Dale answered. "But the wind isn't doing my

hair any favors." Her jaw hurt when she spoke, and this morning she'd not been able to eat. There was a bruise on her cheekbone that she managed to cover with rouge. She had smeared salve on the welts on her buttocks before she pulled on her underpants, but she could not bear to put on the girdle Harry always insisted she wear. He would be angry when he found out.

"We haven't had a frost yet, but when we do, the leaves will fall like rain."

"My chrysanthemums are still blooming." Kathleen Henry was a person Dale would like to have for a friend, but she knew that Harry would never allow it. "I'd just as soon the cold weather hold off for a while."

"Was the reception as much of a success as expected? I had to leave early."

"Oh, yes. We used all of the first cake that served fifty and most of the second cake. Many people had only coffee or tea. Theresa estimated that over a hundred came during the afternoon. A photographer was there taking pictures for the paper." Dale glanced back to see a car coming slowly down the street toward them.

"I'd better scoot or I'll be late at the clinic. Nice seeing you again." She hurried away.

Kathleen wondered if the woman was not feeling well. She certainly wasn't the friendly person she had met at the clinic. Her eyes had a haunted, or was it a frightened look, especially when she noticed the approaching car. When Kathleen glanced over her shoulder, she saw the car stop and Dale walk over to it. Later when she looked back again, Dale was still walking and the car had gone on.

As Kathleen entered the *Gazette* office, Adelaide looked up from her desk with a broad smile.

"Good morning. Can I interest you in a full-page ad?"

"Do I get a discount?"

"Of course. How's the book coming?"

"Good. I'm really getting into it. I'm on chapter ten."

"How many chapters?"

"I don't know. I've set up the conflict and introduced the characters. That took care of the first third of the book. The last third will be tying up the loose ends and seeing that the villain gets what's coming to him. The hard part is the middle third."

"Interesting." Paul came in from the back room. "What are we talking about?"

"Kathleen's book," Adelaide said. "Have you decided on a title?"

"I may call it *Gone With the Wind*." Kathleen pulled off her scarf and fluffed her hair.

"Hummm. Seems to me I've heard that before."

"A publisher would never allow me to use it even though a title can't be copyrighted. I had thought of calling it *The Heart Rustler*, but my male readers might think it was a love story. So I'm naming it *The Hanging Tree*."

"That should clear up any notion about its being a love story. When do I get to read it?" Paul asked.

"Not for a while. Did Judy get some good pictures at the reception for the doctor?"

"She sure did. I've been trying to get her to set her cap for the doctor, but she's got a cowboy on the string. I don't know what it is about cowboys that dazzles the girls."

"Here, love." Adelaide pulled a sheet of paper from her typewriter and handed it to Paul. "We met the doctor's brother last night. They were having hamburgers at Claude's."

"Johnny told me the doctor had a brother named Pete

who had been in the navy for a long time. Did you know that they are Johnny's cousins?"

"Not until Johnny mentioned it yesterday. The brothers are both blond, but don't look much alike otherwise. The doctor isn't as heavily built as his brother. I wonder if Pete's going to be around here for a while. He is a good-looking man in a rough sort of way."

"I heard that, Addie." Paul paused in the doorway leading to the back room.

"He isn't as good-looking as you are, love." Adelaide's eyes shone when she looked at her husband.

"I'm relieved to know that." Paul pretended to wipe sweat from his brow. "I was about to go mess up that guy's pretty face. I've got a couple of pages ready for a proofer if anyone is interested."

"I'll do them for you, Adelaide." Kathleen took off her coat and hung it on the hall tree. "I can't get into the bank until nine o'clock."

A man in an old felt hat and a shabby coat followed Kathleen into the bank. He was standing behind her when she told the teller that she was there to sign papers regarding Johnny Henry's loan. The man known in Rawlings as Robert Brooks could have reached out and touched her; but it would not have been wise, and he resisted the temptation.

That she didn't recognize him as a coworker whose desk had been less than fifty feet from hers in the office at Douglas Aircraft for two years was a source of satisfaction to him. He was good at changing his appearance. His mother had told him many times that he should have been a movie star or an actor on the stage.

After Kathleen was directed inside the partition that

separated the lobby from the office area, Mr. Brooks produced a bill and asked the teller for change. He put the bills in his pocket and went out to his car to wait for Kathleen to leave the bank. While waiting, he opened his *observation diary* and began to write in a small neat script.

> 9:30 A.M. *Johnny Henry is taking out a GI loan. Kathleen went to the bank to sign the papers. She must have agreed to do that when he took her home from the clinic yesterday, but that does not necessarily mean they are getting back together. If they do, it will make it harder for me to do what I plan.*
>
> *Last night that lowlife from the filling station went by her house a couple of times. Had he stopped, I would have been forced to take action. Using the night glasses I ordered from the Army Surplus store, I saw her standing in her bedroom window in her nightdress. Kathleen, Kathleen, it won't be long until you will be safe. I will take care of you forever.*

It was the middle of the morning.

"We're getting there." Johnny and Sherm, an old man he had known since he first came to the ranch, had been working since dawn on the corral. "In a day or two we'll go down to McCabe's and get my horses. You'll have to go along to drive the car and trailer back. I've already made arrangements to buy a load of hay."

"I ain't never drived no car pullin' a trailer, but reckon I can." Sherm scratched his grizzled head and looked toward the house when the sound of singing reached them.

> "Way down yonder in the Indian Nation
> I rode my pony on the reservation,
> In the Oklahoma hills where I belonged—"

"I don't know why she has to play the radio so damn loud," Johnny grumbled. He was not in a good mood. He wanted his house back. He wanted his wife back and in his bed. He was tired of sleeping on an army cot in the barn.

"Is she goin' to stay long?"

Sherm glanced shyly at Johnny. It wasn't his nature to ask questions, but he was thinking of moving on if Johnny's sister was going to be here from now on. Before she came, he and Johnny had fixed decent meals, talked a while, or listened to the radio for an hour or two before he went back to the shack he lived in behind the barn. Now he dreaded going in to eat.

"I don't know, Sherm. She's sick, awful sick. I'm trying to get her to see a doctor. I'd consider it a favor if you'd overlook some of the things she says."

"I ain't ort to be sayin' it, but she goes outta her way to be mean. It don't seem like you and her could rightly be kin a'tall."

"We had the same mother. That, I'm sure of." Johnny hung the hammer on a strand of wire and squinted at a car that turned up the lane, came alongside the house, and stopped. "Now who can that be?" When a tall man in a light-colored Stetson hat got out of the car, Johnny let out a whoop and hurried forward. "Holy hell! Pete? Pete Perry, where in the world did you come from?"

"Howdy, Johnny. It's been a long time." The two men met and clasped hands.

"Doggone, Pete!" Johnny's broad smile lit his face. "Doggone, I can't believe it's you. Golly-damn, Pete. It's been many a year. It's damn good to see you."

"Same here, Johnny-boy. How ya doin'?" The two tall men continued to clasp hands and smile at each other.

"Good. You?"

"Good. What's it been? Sixteen years? When I left to go to the navy, you and Jude were kids. Now you're men. Hellfire, where did the time go?"

"It didn't go very fast in the Solomons. I heard you were on the *Lexington*. When it went down, I figured you were a goner."

"Only the good die young, Johnny-boy. I was the meanest son of a bitch on Mud Creek. Remember?" Pete laughed. He was the same, just older. His blue eyes twinkled in the old devilish way. His blond hair was still thick and wavy.

"I don't know about being the meanest, but you were working pretty hard to get there."

"Yeah, I was. But I was taken down a notch or two when Grant Gifford beat the tar outta me that Sunday afternoon I crashed Henry Ann's ice cream party."

"I remember that. And I remember accusing you of rustling our beef."

"That I *didn't* do. Not because of you, but because of Henry Ann." Pete clapped Johnny on the shoulder and grinned. "I wonder what ever happened to Chris Austin and Opal after he finally got the guts to leave home and take her to California?"

"Henry Ann said they came back when Mrs. Austin took sick. They have three boys and Rosemary, Opal's daughter. Henry Ann said that she heard Rosemary had turned out real pretty."

"She wasn't mine," Pete said quickly. "I know folks thought she was, and I let them think it. At the time I didn't want to think that it was my pa who forced himself on the girl. I was afraid that if I knew for sure, I'd kill him."

"That's probably why Opal never told who raped her."

"I look back now and wonder how Jude turned out the way he did, considering what we come from."

"You didn't do too bad either, Pete. Considering—"

"Considering what?"

"Well, considering you did everything you could to make folks think you were wild as a hare and horny as a billy goat."

"Yeah, I did, didn't I?" Pete grinned sheepishly.

"Remember Marty Conroy?"

"Tom Dolan's brother-in-law? I remember that I was itching to knock his teeth out. I still think he was the one who set Tom's house on fire."

"He's over at McCalister serving life for murdering a girl right here in Rawlings."

"Well, hallelujah! He was a son of a bitch if there ever was one. Not that I wasn't one, too."

"I'll not argue that." Johnny laughed, and slapped Pete on the shoulder. "Come meet Sherm. He lives here on the place and helps me out. I've got maybe thirty head of horses on a ranch down near Vernon. We're trying to get this corral in shape so that I can go get them."

"Let me give you a hand for a day or two. Your line of work is more up my alley than Jude's. Isn't it something 'bout Jude being a doctor? Little shit knew what he wanted and went after it."

"From what I hear, he's a damn good doctor. The three of us were damn lucky that we came through the war. Eighty-two men from right here in Tillison County didn't come back. A lot of them were in the 45th Infantry out of Fort Sill."

"That was Jude's outfit. We talked last night until we were hoarse. I've decided to settle down around here some-place. Jude's all the family I've got. I've saved a little money these last fifteen years and want to put it into a little place to call home."

"What was your job in the navy?"

"Chief machinist's mate. But that's behind me. I'd like to have a horse ranch, but it takes a wad of money to get started."

"That's what I've got here, but on such a small scale it's darn hard to make a living. I've applied for a GI loan."

"I've been thinking about doing that."

"I'd be glad for your help for a few days, Pete, but I can't offer you bed and board. Isabel is here. She's in bad shape. You'll understand when you see her."

"Jude told me."

"She's about as pleasant as a boil on the butt. I've been trying to talk her into going in to Jude's clinic, but she won't hear of it. She can't walk across a room without stopping to rest, but she'll nag you to take her to a honky-tonk."

"What's wrong with her?"

"Damned if I know. But considering her line of work for the past ten years, it could be most anything. She looks fifty years old."

"Turned out like her ma, huh? I figured she would."

"I get angry with her, but I pity her, too."

"How is your wife making out with her here?"

"My wife lives in town." Johnny turned, picked up the tools, and spoke to the old man. "I'll fix us some grub, Sherm. You come on up to the house for noon. Hear?"

Sherm grunted a reply and shuffled off toward the shed.

"Come on in, Pete. Isabel has probably been looking out the window and wondering who is here. She can smell a man a mile away."

As soon as Johnny opened the door and saw his sister

sitting in a kitchen chair, he knew that she had tried to fix herself up in case the visitor came to the house. She was a pitiful sight. She had dampened her hair, brushed it behind her ears, and rouged her hollow cheeks. Her mouth was a slash of bright red. She wore a low-necked dress that showed her bony neck and a large sore on her collarbone.

"We have company." Johnny walked in, then stood aside for Pete to enter.

"Hello, Isabel."

Isabel attempted to put out her cigarette. With her eyes on Pete, she missed the ashtray completely and jabbed it repeatedly onto the oilcloth that covered the table.

"Pete . . . Perry? S'that you, Pete?" She attempted to stand and then sank back down on the chair. The pain in her lower back caused her lips to tremble and brought tears to her eyes.

"Yeah, it's me. It's been a long time, Isabel."

"I . . . never thought . . . I'd see you again." Her voice was weak and hoarse. "You look just the same."

"I doubt that, Isabel."

"You're heavier, is all."

Johnny went to the living room and turned off the radio, then went to the sink to wash. He felt pity for the half sister who had taunted him all his life about his Indian blood. Yet when she needed help she'd come to him. She had wasted her life, and she had just turned thirty. He was probably the only person in the world who cared if she lived or died . . . and he wondered why he cared. She'd not throw a bucket of water on him if he was on fire.

"Have a chair, Pete. I'll rustle up something to eat."

"I'm so glad to see you." Isabel had eyes only for Pete. "This place is deader than a doornail. Nobody comes here. The only thing that happens around here is that the wind blows. The damn wind blows all the time. It's enough to give a body a duck fit!" Isabel's voice turned into a whine. "Johnny won't take me to town, Pete. He slips off and leaves me with that harelipped old billy goat that hangs around here. I'd give a man anything he wants for a night at a honky-tonk with good music and dancin'."

Embarrassed, Johnny kept his head bent and his shoulders hunched over the frying pan he'd placed on the stove. Pete, however, didn't seem to be uncomfortable with Isabel's proposition.

"You don't look like you're up to a night on the town, Isabel, much less a night in a man's bed. Johnny said you've been sick. What does the doctor say?"

"That crackpot said rest was all I needed. Hell's bells, Pete. People rest when they're old and can't do nothin' else. I'm sick of restin'."

"What doctor told you that rest was all you needed?"

"One I saw in the city."

"I'd not take his word for it. You need something more than rest. Why not go in and see Jude?"

"Jude! You're kiddin'. That smart-mouthed shithead wouldn't know a snotty nose from a dose of clap."

"You're wrong. Jude went in the army after medical school. They had the best equipment, and he learned a hell of a lot from the best doctors. He may be able to help you."

"I ain't turning my ass up . . . to that pussyfooter unless he's payin' *me*. He did ever'thin' he could to turn Hardy against me. He'd do his damnedest . . . to see that I croaked." Isabel had to stop and take a breath.

Pete shrugged. "It's none of my business if you'd rather sit here, dry up, and blow away."

"We could go to town and have . . . some fun," Isabel said hopefully.

"I'm not taking you to town and have you keel over on me. No, sir. I'll take you to see Jude. If he says you're up to it, we'll go honky-tonkin'."

"Shit!" The cigarette between Isabel's fingers shook, dropping ashes on the table. "Jude always thought that he . . . was something on a stick. Bet now he thinks he's Jesus Christ."

"You're wrong about that. Dead wrong. Jude isn't like that at all. He went out onto the battlefield and dragged a wounded man to his foxhole. That's how he got shot. Even with a bone sticking out of one of his legs he managed to get that man to safety." There was pride in Pete's voice. Anger too.

"Well, when I knew him . . . he was a smart-mouthed little bastard."

"No, he wasn't. Hardy married his ma. He didn't marry mine. I'm the bastard in the family." Pete got up from the table and went to the washbasin. A couple strokes from the water pump filled it.

"You . . . didn't act like a bastard."

"How is a bastard supposed to act? I'm not going to argue with you about Jude, Isabel. It's up to you whether or not you want to help yourself." He splashed water on his face. After he dried it on a towel, he turned his back on Isabel and spoke to Johnny. "Fried potatoes and onions. Lord, I haven't had that in a long time."

"It's about all we have around here. I don't know why we can't have something decent to eat," Isabel grumbled. "I'm hungry for spaghetti and tomatoes, but Johnny don't care what I'm hungry for." Both men ignored her.

"Are you planning on raising horses for the rodeo, Johnny?" Pete asked.

"Yeah. Quarter horses mostly. I had a Tennessee Walker

once and got kind of interested in show horses. But, I don't know enough about training and couldn't afford to hire a trainer."

"I remember that little pinto you had. You practically slept with that horse."

"Ed Henry gave him to me when I was fourteen. I brought him over here when I bought the place. He was getting pretty old, so I put him out to pasture. He was struck by lightning the summer before I went into the service. It was like losing a member of the family."

"Pete," Isabel said, breaking into the conversation.

Pete ignored her for a minute, then looked her way. "If you're going to continue to run down Jude, I don't want to hear it."

"I'm not going to say anything . . . about the wonderful *doctor*." Isabel paused. "What I'm saying is, I'll go."

"You'll go? Where?" Pete acted disinterested. He passed behind Johnny and nudged him in the back with his elbow.

"I'll go to the damn clinic if . . . you'll take me honky-tonkin'." Isabel's face was white and her eyes feverish.

"Let's get this straight. We'll go to the clinic, and if Jude says you're able, we'll go honky-tonkin'."

"He'll not want me to go just for . . . spite." Isabel's voice was shrill.

"If that's going to be your attitude, it may be best if you don't go see him. You'll not do what he tells you." Pete turned to Johnny. "When are we going to get your horses?"

"How does day after tomorrow suit you?"

"I said I'd go see the damn doctor and I'll . . . and I'll do what he says," Isabel added irritably.

"All right. I'll take you this afternoon. Want me to slice the bread, Johnny?"

Chapter Eight

"You'll never know just how much I love you.
You'll never know just how much I care—"

KATHLEEN SWITCHED OFF THE RADIO. That song always left her weepy, and she was trying desperately to keep her emotions under control. It was stupid, she told herself, to pine for a man who didn't want you.

After leaving the bank, she had stopped at the grocery store and bought a jar of peanut butter and two packages of strawberry Jell-O. Jell-O, one of her favorite foods, had rarely been seen in the stores during the war. After making up one of the packages and leaving it to cool before putting the bowl in her icebox, she treated herself to two slices of bread and peanut butter before she settled down to work on her book.

Her fingers worked the typewriter keys rapidly, but her thoughts raced ahead of them. By the middle of the afternoon she had written six pages. She rolled her seventh sheet into the machine.

Beulah heard the clink of shod hooves on pebbly
ground and, almost immediately, the thud of booted
feet. A shadow fell in front of her, a shadow with wide
shoulders and large cowboy hat.

"Having trouble?" asked a deep voice she recog-
nized as belonging to a man she knew and feared.

Kathleen paused, read what she had written, and realized it wasn't heading in the direction she wanted her story
to go. She pulled the sheet of paper from the typewriter,
turned it over, and rolled it back in. For five long minutes
she sat staring at the blank page, trying to bring forth a
mental vision of the scene.

After a while, she came to the conclusion that her cre-
ative juices had dried up for the moment. She would wash
her hair and think about the scene while she was doing it.
Fifteen minutes later she squeezed the excess water from
her hair and wrapped a towel around her head. Carrying in
her hand the bottle of vinegar she'd used as a rinse, she left
the bathroom and headed for the kitchen.

"Ohhhh—" The word was scared out of her. A man
holding a tire pump was standing in the middle of her living room. "What . . . are you doing in my house?"

"I knocked." Gabe Thomas, the mechanic from Eddie's
service station, grinned at her.

"Get out!"

"I knew you were here." He was wearing the same old
greasy clothes he'd worn the day she went to the station
and the same battered felt hat.

"Get out of my house."

"Ah . . . don't be that way, Kathy. I've had my eye on ya
for a long time. Since we danced 'fore the war. Ya ain't got
no man now 'n yo're the kind a woman who needs one. Ya

and me'd match up pretty good." He lifted his eyebrows and touched his crotch. "If ya know what I mean."

"I know what you mean, you uncouth piece of horse hockey! I'd rather match up with a warthog. Now . . . leave."

"Ya don't mean that. Ya need a man, Kath—"

"What I need or don't need is no concern of yours. Get out of my house!"

"I told ya I was willin' to give ya a hand. Yore tire's goin' down again. I'll pump it up . . . or pump you, if ya ask me right nice." He took a step toward her.

"Leave now, or I'll call the sheriff." She gripped the neck of the vinegar bottle, determined to hit him with it if he came a step closer.

"Ya ain't gonna call no sheriff. Yo're just actin' hard to get." He stepped sideways, blocking her path to the phone, and she drew her arm back.

"Get out or I'll scream my head off after I bash you over the head with this bottle."

"Sh . . . it! You'll not hit me with that, and ya ain't gonna to yell neither. Who'd hear ya? Ya'd like to have somethin' big—"

A loud knock sounded on the door, then another. Kathleen darted past him and threw open the door before the slow-thinking man could prevent her. A stranger in a brown felt hat and an old worn coat stood there.

"Ma'am, do ya know if some folks named Woodbury live 'round here?" His Southern accent was heavy.

"I believe so. I'll have to think a minute. This man was just leaving." She opened the door wider and jerked her head toward the man still standing in the middle of her living room. "You are leaving!"

"I ain't through here yet."

"Yes, you are. Good-bye."

"Ain't nobody by that name in Rawlings," Gabe said irritably.

"Leave," Kathleen said through clenched teeth, and opened the screen door. When he hestitated, she said angrily, "Leave now!" With a deep scowl on his face, he went through the door, shouldering the other man out of the way.

"I'll be back . . . to fix your tire."

"No! Don't come back here. Ever!"

"Was he givin' ya trouble, ma'am?" the man asked, after Gabe got into his car.

"Nothing I couldn't handle. I don't know of anyone around here by the name of Woodbury. I was just stalling so that awful man would leave. He came here with the excuse of pumping air in my tire."

"I have a tire pump in my car. I'd be glad to pump up your tire. I noticed it was goin' flat."

"That's nice of you, Mr.—"

"Brooks. Robert Brooks."

"You look vaguely familiar, Mr. Brooks. Have I met you before?" She wrapped the towel more snugly around her wet head.

"I doubt that, ma'am. I've not been in town long. But maybe you saw me at the bank or in one of the eating establishments. I'm staying at the hotel for a while."

"At the bank. I saw you this morning at the bank. I hope you find the people you're looking for."

"It was a long shot, thinkin' they were here."

"Well . . . good-bye." Katheen stepped back to close the door, his voice stopped her.

"Ma'am, you should keep your door locked. I don't like the looks of that fellow."

"You're right, and I will. Thank you."

After Kathleen closed the door, a niggling memory caused her to go to the window to get another look at the man. Something about him struck a chord. She watched him go to a mud-splattered car and take out a tire pump. Then for a while he was out of sight behind her car as he pumped air into her tire. She was still at the window when he returned to his car and drove away.

Surprised that she still had the vinegar bottle in her hand, she walked into the kitchen. Just as she was about to set it down, another knock sounded on the door.

"Lord, have mercy!" Thinking Gabe Thomas had returned, she angrily flung the door open. "What now?"

"Does that mean you're glad to see me or not glad to see me?"

"Johnny!" Joy and relief made her gasp his name. "I'm glad to see you. Come in."

"For a minute I thought you were going to hit me with that bottle," he said after he'd stepped inside.

"I would have if you'd been that, that ... disgusting horse's patoot that was here earlier."

"Who's that?" Johnny's brows beetled in a frown.

"Gabe Thomas. He works for Eddie."

"I know who he is. What was he doing here?"

"He said he came to fix my tire. I don't know why a nice guy like Eddie hires scum like him."

"What'd he do?" Johnny asked quietly. If Kathleen hadn't been so giddy at the sight of him, she would have recognized the sign of smoldering anger.

"I was washing my hair and didn't hear him knock. I came out of the bathroom, and he was standing here in the living room. I asked him to leave. He wouldn't until a man came to the door asking directions."

"Are you saying that he came in uninvited and refused to leave?"

"He thought we'd match up, as he put it. He made a few off-color remarks. Nothing worse than some things I'd heard while working in the city."

"The son . . . of . . . a . . . bitch! Did he put his hands on you?"

"If he dared, he'd have had this bottle upside the head."

"I'll take care of it."

"Someone should tell Eddie what kind of man he has working there."

"He'll not bother you again." Johnny followed her to the kitchen. He reached over and took the vinegar bottle from her hand and set it on the table. "You've got water running down the back of your dress." He tossed his hat on a chair, gently pushed her down in another, then unwound the towel from around her head.

"He said he knocked. If he did, I didn't hear him because I was washing my hair." Kathleen's voice was strained, and she wondered why she had stated the obvious. She was breathless from the rapid beating of her heart.

"I just came over to thank you for signing for the loan." Johnny said as he rubbed her hair with the dry end of the towel. She closed her eyes and reveled in the wonderful feeling of his hands on her. When she opened them and glanced up, she was surprised to see his reflection in the small mirror that hung on the wall beside the door. His eyes were closed or very near it. Was he remembering the times he had dried her hair while she sat beside the wood cookstove in the ranch kitchen? *Sit here close to the oven door. I don't want you catching a cold.*

"Your hair isn't as long as it used to be," he said quietly.

"It's easier to take care of . . . this way."

"It's curlier."

"I'm getting too old to let my hair hang down my back."

"Too old? Where did you pick up a dumb idea like that? I like the short curls, but I liked it long, too."

"I'm seven years older than I was . . . back then," she said, hoping he hadn't noticed the squeak in her voice.

"But just as pretty. I'll never forget you standing in the road the day the hijackers stopped you. You looked like a beacon with the sun shining on this bright red hair." The dark eyes that fastened on the top of her head held a familiar hint of sadness.

"You rescued me."

"Yeah. You've got this hair to thank for me even seeing you."

"You're kidding!" Kathleen glanced up at him. "You'd not have ridden to my rescue if I'd a been a blonde?"

"I'd have gotten around to it after a while," he teased as he hung the towel on the back of the chair and forked his fingers through the short tight curls. "You'll be dry soon, but don't go outside. The wind is pretty cool."

"Yes, sir," she said, and saluted.

"You'd better get that bowl of Jell-O in the icebox if you want it to set up."

"Right away, sir!"

"Smart aleck." He grinned, and her heart thumped wildly. "How's the book coming?"

"Pretty good. I wrote six pages today, then suddenly the ideas stopped coming."

"Does that happen often?"

"It depends on how far I am into the book."

"I suppose I'll have to buy a copy when it comes out."

"If you do," she laughed nervously, "it might be one of

the three copies sold in Tillison County: to you, Adelaide, and Barker."

"I suppose Barker comes by now and then," he said, making her wish she hadn't mentioned his father.

"Not a lot. I see more of Marie. Barker comes by and lights my water tank. The pilot goes out at the drop of a hat, and I haven't got the hang of how to light it."

"I'll take a look at it sometime. I tinkered around a bit with that sort of thing while I was in the service."

"Would you? It's handy having hot water when you want it. How about an egg sandwich? My landlady taught me how to make a good one. I'm not sure why, but she called it a Denver."

"I was going to invite you out to eat and meet a cousin of mine. Pete Perry is in town. He's Jude's brother."

"Adelaide told me about him this morning. She and Paul met him and Dr. Perry at Claude's." She sat down after Johnny straddled a chair and folded his arms on the back.

"Pete took Isabel over to the clinic. He had to promise to take her to a honky-tonk if Jude said she was able to go. There isn't much chance of that. She's in bad shape."

"Do you have any idea what's the matter with her?"

"I've got an idea. Every man in the service was lectured on venereal disease."

"Oh, no!"

"I'm boiling everything she's used in the big iron pot."

"Johnny, I'm sorry." Kathleen placed her hand on top of his. He turned his hand over and gripped hers tightly.

"I feel guilty because I don't want her in my house. I have no feeling for her. I'm sorry for her as if she were someone I didn't know, but that's all."

"That's understandable. You don't really know her."

"I knew her when she was very young, and then for a

few months when she was fourteen. I didn't like her even then." Johnny looked down at Kathleen's hand clasped in his. "I don't know what will become of her. I can't keep her at the house much longer. She pays no attention to anything I tell her. Pete can handle her better than I can."

"He's her cousin, too, isn't he?"

Johnny snorted. "Yeah, but he's a man first, and that's all she's interested in."

"Do you think Dr. Perry can help her?"

"I don't know. They do great things now days with penicillin." Johnny looked at his watch. "I'm to meet Pete at the clinic in a little while. Would you like to come along?" His voice had a velvet huskiness to it.

"If you want me to." The normal rhythm of her breathing and heartbeat had flown, and she feared she would not be able to regain them before she made a complete fool of herself.

"I do. I'd like for you to meet Pete. He's very different from Jude." *What I really want is for Pete to see my beautiful wife.* The thought raced joyously through his mind.

"I'll change my dress." She raked her fingers through her hair next to her scalp. "I think my hair is dry enough."

Johnny reached over and ran his hand across the top of her head, fluffing her hair with his fingers.

"You can put a scarf over it until we get to the clinic."

With a fluttering in the pit of her stomach and every cell in her body surging to life, she hurried to the bedroom. *There was a chance that he loved her still.*

Theodore Nuding kept his face expressionless, hiding the emotions that engulfed him until he had stepped off the porch. A messy mixture of feelings swirled through him: elation at being so close to her and talking to her, and cold hatred for the man who had invaded her privacy and caused her discomfort.

He lifted a hand and slapped himself on the cheek. Damn! He should have done something about the man days ago. He had been busy with the house and establishing the image of himself he meant the town to accept.

Thank goodness he had been watching when that disgusting son of a bitch stopped at Kathleen's house. If that mongrel had as much as put a hand on her, he would have killed him then and there. It would still have to happen, but now he had time to decide where and when.

Kathleen was watching when he returned with the tire pump. This was the first of many services he would perform for her. As he attached the rubber tube to the valve on the tire, he felt a warm glow of unqualified delight. He wished that he could stay all day and pump tires for her, but all too soon he was finished and feared he would blow the tire if he continued. He glanced to where she stood in the window and wanted to wave to her, but he didn't want her to know that he knew she was watching.

He drove out of town and parked the car on a rise where he could view Kathleen's house with his binoculars. His response was prepared should anyone be curious about what he was doing there for hours at a time.

The story had been tested two days ago when Sheriff Carroll came by and asked what he was doing. He had explained that he was studying cloud formations for the United States Weather Department because of the number of tornadoes in this part of the country. He had shown the sheriff the notes he'd written and the chart he was keeping. He threw out a few words like *vertical updraft* and *cumulonimbus*.

The lawman had bought the story. Robert Brooks was free to sit here on this rise all day if he wanted to.

When he swept the area with his binoculars, he was surprised to see that another car had stopped at Kathleen's house. The husband's car. He wasn't pleased that Johnny Henry was there, but he knew that he wouldn't hurt her. He hoped that she'd not go back to him, but if she did, it would be only a mild stumbling block in his plan for her. Nuding took his journal from under the seat. He'd filled one notebook and had started on another.

> 3:30 P.M. *Today I helped my Kathleen, maybe saved her from an unpleasant experience. She is so pretty, Mother. Even with a towel wrapped around her head she is the only woman I've ever seen that compares with you. I could believe that you have come back in her body, except she is independent, like the women of today, but not as bad as some. Mother, you would be shocked to know that some try to be like men, working at men's jobs and wearing trousers. I've not seen her in trousers but a time or two, and I didn't like it.*
>
> *The man from Eddie's station went into her house today. He is the one that made her so angry that she pulled out of the 66 station and ran over the curb. I get extremely angry when I think about him going into her house uninvited and refusing to leave. He will not bother her again.*
>
> *The room I'm fixing for her is coming along. I'm determined that she have every comfort, and I'm grateful that I'm handy with a saw and a hammer. I've had to take boards from other parts of the house and I work only at night, so it will be a while. But no hurry. I know where she is, and I know that she is mine. Even if she goes back to that cowboy, she is still mine.*

He closed his notebook and settled down to watch. He liked to think of himself as the *Guardian.* He was good at watching and guarding. Today, however, he had something else on his mind. He had to plot carefully his next move, one that in no way could be connected with him or with Kathleen. Nuding took great pride in the fact that he planned things very precisely. His cunning mind sorted through several scenarios and finally settled on one.

Now all he had to do was wait until the right time.

Chapter Nine

Dr. Perry came to the reception-room door and motioned to Pete to join him in his office.

"Is Johnny coming?" Jude asked after the door closed behind the two men. "As Isabel's next of kin, he's the one I should talk to. Lord, she's got a mean mouth. She was a brat when she was young, and she's worse now. Mrs. Cole and Theresa shouldn't have to put up with her. But they're doing what needs to be done despite her calling them and me every foul name in the book."

"She's got an advanced case of syphilis." Pete's diagnosis brought a nod from his brother. "I've seen it in the islands."

"I hope Johnny has been careful. The disease is most commonly transmitted by sexual contact, however transmission can occur through infected blood or an open wound. Isabel has a number of eruptions on her skin. Syphilis also damages the brain, bones, eyes . . . places not so obvious. It can be treated successfully with penicillin unless there has been extensive damage to the nervous system." The office door opened. Jude said, "Come in, Johnny."

"My wife is with me."

Jude stood. "Do you want to ask her to come in?"

"I did, but she said she'd wait. I want her to meet Pete. Has Isabel been causing trouble?"

"She has the honor of being the most unpleasant patient I've ever had." Jude sank back down in the chair, grateful to be off his aching leg. "I've been telling Pete that Isabel has an advanced case of syphilis for one thing."

"I suspected that. What else?"

"Several other things to be exact. I can't say absolutely, until I can X-ray, but I'm reasonably certain that she has breast cancer. It's lumpy, it's draining, and I believe it has spread to the lymph glands. I wanted to X-ray, but she put up such a fuss, I didn't press the matter further for now."

Johnny shook his head. "If that's the case, what can we do?"

"Keep her as comfortable as possible during the time she has left. She also has an erratic heartbeat, which is not unusual under the circumstances, and it's possible her kidneys are failing."

"Then . . . it's a matter of time. Is that what you're saying?"

"It's my opinion that it's too late for treatment."

"What do you suggest we do?"

"The logical place for her is here. Large doses of morphine will be needed soon."

"I'll pay for it somehow."

"Don't worry about that now. Hope that my nurses will put up with her and not quit on me."

"She's a hard one," Pete said. "She told Jude in front of the nurses that he didn't know his ass from a hole in the ground."

Johnny shook his head again. "She's gone downhill fast this past week."

"She has a number of open skin lesions. Syphilis can be transmitted through infected blood or open wounds."

"I knew about that. This morning I put the towels and the bedding she used in the boiling pot. Sherm is watching them for me. Her clothes are in a pile on the bedroom floor."

"Burn them."

"She's not going to want to stay here. You may have to tie her down."

Jude answered a knock on his inner door. When it opened, Dale Cole stood there with a worried look on her face.

"Doctor, Miss Henry is swearing a blue streak and calling for someone named Pete."

"Has she been given a sedative?"

"Not yet. We'll have to restrain her to do it."

"I'll go see if I can calm her down." Pete went to the door where Dale waited and followed her down the hall.

"She refuses to give us any information about herself," Dale said. "Perhaps you can help us fill in a few blanks."

"I doubt it. This morning is the first time I've seen her in sixteen years."

Dale stopped and looked up at him with a puzzled frown. "Sixteen years? The way she talks . . . well, never mind."

"Yeah. I've been in the navy sixteen years."

"Oh, then it was before . . . that."

"What'a you mean . . . before that? Before that, I knew the little twit for about three or four months. She's a distant cousin . . . of sorts."

"Interesting." Dale started walking again.

"What has she been telling you?"

"Not much about herself. She says plenty about Dr.

Perry and Johnny Henry and about you. I was sure you'd be wearing a halo."

Pete chuckled, and Dale smiled into his eyes. "Wait until I tell her she's got to stay here. She'll be singing another tune. Nurse," Pete put his hand on her arm to stop her before she went into Isabel's room. Dale tensed and looked up at him. "Don't let anything she says get to you. She can't help being what she is; and if the truth were known, she's scared spitless."

"Don't be concerned, Mr. Perry. I've been cussed at, called every unflattering name that can be thought of, even spat upon and knocked off my feet. This poor, sick, miserable woman cannot do more than that." Dale's voice quivered. She hoped that this rough, but kind man would never know the humiliation that she had described had been at the hands of her own husband.

Pete looked at Dale with a new respect. "You've got guts, ma'am. It's a shame that people you try to help are mean to you. I'd like to blame Isabel's meanness on damage to her brain, but she's always been meaner than all get out."

"We need to give her a sedative. Nurse Frank doesn't want to strap her down."

"Let's see if I can charm her into being nice. I used to be pretty good at it, but I'm a bit out of practice at the present time."

Pete's attempt to put a smile on Dale's face succeeded. She even laughed and rolled her eyes to the ceiling. His face was soft with charm; his eyes moved over her warmly. Dale felt suddenly young and almost . . . giddy. She felt free enough to say the first thing that came to her mind.

"Then come on, Romeo. Do your stuff." The hand that

rested lightly on her back was comforting as he ushered her into Isabel's room.

Sitting on the side of the bed, Isabel squealed at the sight of Pete.

"Get me outta here, Pete. You promised we'd go . . . honky-tonkin'."

"I promised to take you if the doctor said you could go. He wants you to stay here a while for treatment."

"I'm not stayin' in this shithole, and that's that!" she yelled, and flung the hospital gown aside until it barely covered her crotch.

"Stay in the bed, Miss Henry," Dale said firmly, and hurried to the bed.

"Don't touch me, you snotty bitch. I don't have to . . . stay here if I don't want to. And I told you my name is Perry. Perry. Can't you get that through your dumb head? My name is Perry, just like Pete's, just . . . like that bastard who calls himself a doctor. Shit fire! I knew him when his pecker was the size of a peanut. Ain't much bigger now if ya was to—"

"That's enough!" Pete's voice was so loud it thundered in the small room. "Goddammit! Get back in that bed! Call yourself any damn thing you want to, but your legal name is Henry. Keep that foul mouth shut, too, Isabel. You straighten up and let these folks take care of you, or I'll see that you're put in the asylum where you belong."

"Asylum? You can't. I won't go," she shouted.

"You won't have anything to say about it. You've got syphilis, did you know that?" When she didn't answer, he said, "That's what I thought. You knew you had syphilis. It drives people so crazy they end up in an asylum."

"That other doctor told me to rest. I don't have . . . be here to do that."

"You're lying, Isabel. If you went to a doctor, he would have put you in the hospital. Now listen to me. I won't put up with you mistreating the people who are trying to help you."

"You ain't my next of kin. Johnny is." She was lying down, but still defiant.

"Johnny has washed his hands of you. He turned you over to me. I'm a hard-ass, Isabel. While I was in the navy I whipped hundreds of whining kids into shape. Some of them worse than you, if that's possible."

"I thought . . . you liked me."

"I like the side of you that's nice and reasonable. I don't like a foul-mouthed, stubborn woman who hasn't got sense enough to take care of herself."

"I've been doin' it all my life."

"You've made a hell of a mess of it, too."

"I don't like . . . her!" Isabel's hate-filled eyes moved over to Dale. "She don't like me. She thinks she's better'n me. She thinks she's so goddamn smart prancin' around in that white dress with that shitty cap on her head. She's a fat—"

"—Shut up!" Pete shouted. "You're rotten, Isabel."

"Maybe, but I ain't never had no trouble gettin' a man. Ask her how many she's had."

Pete stood by the bed and looked down at the wasted body of the girl he'd known so long ago. The only feelings he had for her were revulsion and pity.

"I don't think Jude can help you here," he said quietly. "Your brains are already scrambled." He headed for the door. "I'll tell him to call the asylum—"

"Pete! Nooooo— Please! I don't want to go there."

"It seems we have no choice, Isabel."

"I'll do what they want. I promise," she said in a rush, tears filling her eyes.

"Yeah? As soon as I turn my back you'll be talkin' nasty to the folks who are trying to help you."

"I won't. I swear I won't."

"All right. Prove it. They need to give you a shot."

"What for? Does Jude want to put me out so he can cut off my breast or a foot or screw me?"

"Dammit, Isabel! The shot is for pain."

"I don't hurt nowhere. I could dance all night, if that son of a bitch—"

"Dammit, you forgot already."

"Will you stay a while, Pete? I won't say a word if you'll stay. I don't like bein' here by myself. They won't even let me have a cigarette."

"I'll stay if you'll behave."

"I will. Sit down . . . please—"

"I need to go out for a minute, but I'll be back."

"When?" She raised up in the bed.

"I'll be back before you can count to a hundred."

"Are you goin' out with her?" Isabel's feverish eyes went to Dale.

Pete leaned down and murmured. "Not unless she's going with me to the head." He followed Dale out and closed the door. They moved a short way down the hall. "Damn! She's worse than I thought. I'll go in with you when you give her the shot."

"I'll not be doing it. Nurse Frank will. I'll tell her to get it ready."

"I'm sorry she's given you such a bad time. The last time I saw her she was a pretty young girl of fourteen. She had a mean mouth then, but nothing like now. Will the shot put her out?"

"For about six hours. I don't understand why she isn't in terrible pain."

"She may be, but too stubborn to admit it."

"You did a fine job in there. That's a kind of charm I've not seen used before." Dale's eyes smiled up at him.

"Oh, I've got other kinds of charm I drag out and use once in a while."

"Is her name Perry or Henry? I need it for the records."

"Her legal name is Henry. Her mother was married to Ed Henry when she was born. She took her mother's name later because Ed wasn't her natural father."

"Do you know the date of her birth?"

"No."

"Maybe I can get the information from her brother."

"Pee . . . te! Pee . . . te!"

Pete quirked a brow and glanced toward the room. "I guess she's counted to a hundred."

"Pete, dammit, you said you'd come back. Pee . . . te." Isabel's voice could be heard up and down the hall.

"Kind of nice being wanted, isn't it?" Dale was surprised at how easy it was to tease with him.

"Careful, nurse, I might not go back in there."

"Please, please, don't do that to me." Dale let out a grunt of laughter. Her jaw hurt so bad she could hardly open her mouth.

Pete was reluctant to end the conversation. He kept trying to see if Dale wore a wedding band, but her fingers were wrapped around the chart she held.

"I'll tell Nurse Frank to bring the sedative."

Pete ignored the calls from Isabel and lingered a minute to watch Dale walk down the hall. *If a man held her, he'd know he had a real woman in his arms and not a bag full of bones. She's nice, too, and got plenty of horse sense.* Dale passed out of sight, and there was nothing for him to do but go back into Isabel's room and try to quiet her.

Dale could feel Pete's eyes on her and wished that she were young again. When she married Harry, she had been slim and pretty and trying to finish her nurse's training. Her family had been dirt-poor and pleased that a man with a good job was interested in her. Over the years she had put on weight. Harry reminded her constantly of it and of her poor background. Now she felt . . . big and ugly. Pete Perry probably had known plenty of young, slim girls and was thinking that she looked like a fat cow waddling down the hallway. She didn't know why that mattered to her, but it did.

"Let's go sit in the car. Jude said he would send Pete out," Johnny said to Kathleen when he returned to the reception room. He took her elbow to help her stand up. "Better put that scarf back on. It's windy." He anchored his hat on his head.

Kathleen didn't speak until they were in the car and she had pulled the thin, flowered scarf from her head.

"You look tired."

"I am. I've been sleeping on a canvas cot in the barn and worrying that Isabel was going to burn my house down."

His dark eyes soberly searched her face. If she could believe what she saw in his eyes, it was loneliness. Without thinking about it, she reached for his hand.

"Did Dr. Perry tell you what was wrong with Isabel?"

"There's a lot wrong with her. She has syphilis and breast cancer."

"Can he help her?"

"She's too far gone. It's only a matter of time."

"I'm sorry. Is there anything I can do?"

"No. I don't want you in the same room with her. You've never heard a mouth as dirty as hers. Jude said that syphilis damages the brain. Hers must have been damaged long ago. She's always been mean.

"I remember one time Henry Ann and I were trying to chop weeds so we'd get a cotton crop. When we made Isabel help us, she deliberately chopped out a half a row of cotton plants. She laughed because she had outsmarted us. I wanted to slap her."

"Did you?"

"No. After that she went down to Mud Creek to stay with the Perrys."

"I heard the nurses talking. Isabel isn't a very good patient."

"That's an understatement. Jude said he'd never had one as bad. Pete thought he might be able to calm her down. She offered to go to bed with him if he would take her honky-tonking."

"But . . . she's got— You mean she would—?"

"You don't know Isabel. I wonder how many men she has infected."

"Oh, Johnny." Kathleen hugged his hand to her. "I'm not sorry that I never met her, but I still feel sympathy for her. She's all alone and dying."

"It's her own fault. I'll pay to keep her here. That's my only obligation to her."

"Will you call Henry Ann? She's her sister, too."

"I thought I would. She can decide whether she wants to come. Isabel won't thank her for it."

"Regardless, her kin should be with her. You all had the same mother—"

"You still don't get it do you?" Johnny pulled his hand from hers. "Isabel and I are the unwanted results of a horde of men who slept with Dorene. Her blood was so tainted from years of incest that whoring was the logical thing for her to do. She saw absolutely nothing wrong with it. And Isabel is just like Dorene, a whore because she wants to be."

"Henry Ann—"

"If I've got any decent blood in my body," he continued angrily and turned his head to look out the car window, "I have to thank that Indian who paid Dorene to let him screw her." After a minute or two he turned back and took Kathleen's hand, looked at it intently, and plucked at her fingers. "I never intended to get started on that subject. I'm sorry."

"Don't be." She wanted to say more and would have if this sudden closeness between them were not so fragile.

"Jude told me to burn her clothes," he said after a silence. "I'm going to use Lysol to—scrub down everything she's touched."

"I could help you."

"Pete'll help me. He's going to stay with me for a while. I'll put a bed in the little room off the kitchen."

Disappointment was a lump in Kathleen's throat. *He had no plans for her coming back to the ranch. He couldn't have made it plainer.*

"You'll like Pete. All women do." Johnny didn't notice that she had drawn her lips between her teeth to hold them still. "The navy changed him. Hell, the war changed all of us. Pete used to be a hell-raiser. I've told you some of the things he used to do. He was in love with Henry Ann when they were young. He did dumb stunts trying to impress her. He laughs about it now." Johnny tilted his head so he could look into her face. "I'm rattling on. I guess I've been hungry to talk to you."

"Who did you talk to while you were overseas?"

"I had a tentmate when we had tents. I daydreamed a lot."

"Were you ever scared?"

"Lots and lots of times. I'm scared now."

"I can understand that. Your sister is dying."

"That isn't it. I'm scared every time I'm with you."

"With me? Now I *don't* understand that."

"I can't explain it. I'm not good with words, as you well know."

"Are you afraid that I'm going to demand something from you? I've already told you that I'm not going to. I'm willing to go along with whatever you want to do."

"And what if I don't know what I want to do?"

"Then I guess I'll have to wait until you do."

"You, of all the people in the world, have the power to make me so damn mad, so damn quick. I wanted us to have a nice evening. I wanted to show you off to Pete. We're not alone ten minutes until your temper shows up."

"I'm not in a temper. I stated a fact."

"That you're not going to demand anything from me. You want nothing from me at all." Annoyed, he gripped her hand so tightly it hurt. She knew he was unaware of it.

"There are things I want from you, Johnny, but you're not willing to give them."

"How do you know until you ask?" His dark eyes were boring into hers.

Oh, Johnny. I want your love back. I want to go back to our house and sleep in your arms every night. I want us to make a baby again, and when it comes, I want you to love it. I want us to grow old together. I want to share everything with you . . . the good and the bad.

Knowing that she could not voice any of those desires,

she said instead, "I would like to have our wedding picture, if you don't want it."

His eyes scanned her face for a long while before he spoke.

"What makes you think I don't want it?"

"Well, you . . . seem anxious to get that part of your life behind you. I thought you might not want reminders—"

"—Why didn't you take the picture when you came out to collect your things?"

"I wouldn't do that. You paid for it with your rodeo winnings. Forget it. If the photographer down in Vernon is still in business, he may have kept the negatives."

"You can have it."

"No—"

Suddenly his hand was behind her head jerking her to him. He put his mouth against hers and muttered, "You make me so mad I've either got to kiss you or hit you."

Kathleen was incapable of moving. The lips that touched hers were warm, sweet, and demanding. The kiss became possessive and deepened. Her lips parted, his tongue touched hers, his fingers forked through her hair, and his hand slid over her breast. This was Johnny, her love. Her arm moved up and around his neck, holding him to her.

A rapping on the window brought them to their senses. Johnny lifted his head and frowned at the man grinning at them through the glass.

"Don't you know it ain't nice to neck right out here in public?"

Johnny reached over and jerked open the door.

"You wouldn't know *nice* if it jumped up and bit you. Pete, this is my wife, Kathleen."

Chapter Ten

KATHLEEN DECIDED that she liked Pete Perry. He acted as a buffer between her and Johnny as they ate T-bone steaks at the Frontier Cafe. After a brief conversation about Isabel on the way to the restaurant, she was not mentioned again.

Pete flirted outrageously with Kathleen, and Johnny didn't seem to mind.

"How did a pretty girl like you settle for this ugly old cowboy?"

"He was the only best *All-Around Cowboy* in town," she retorted. "I had to settle for him or nothing. It was an accident that we met." Kathleen glanced at Johnny's relaxed and smiling face. "I was being hijacked out on the highway when this cowboy came charging over the hill on his trusty steed, his six-guns blazing. The bad guys knew when they were outgunned and hightailed it before a shot was fired. I swooned," she said dramatically, "in the arms of *my hero*."

Johnny chuckled. "Horse hockey. You never swooned in your life."

"That explains how you met; but after you were around him for a while, couldn't you tell that he didn't have much between his ears?"

"Well, I did wonder what was holding them apart, but

he was so . . . pretty and . . . he *was* the best *All-Around Cowboy* at the Tillison County rodeo. What's a girl to do?"

"All right, you two. You've had enough fun at my expense. I've got some pretty good stories I can tell about Pete. You see there was this older, married woman who lived over in Ringling and Pete—"

"Whoa, there partner. You start telling that, and I'll have to tell Kathleen about the time you and Jude went to town and swiped a freezer full of ice cream off Mrs. Miller's back porch. Henry Ann was mad as a hornet when she found out about it."

"She was really afraid that someone had seen us and we'd get caught. Mrs. Miller, the old busybody, had been spreading gossip about Henry Ann and Tom, so Jude and I decided to get even." Johnny flashed a grin at Kathleen.

"Poor Henry Ann. I bet she had her hands full with you."

"When will I get to read some of the stories you've written?" Pete winked at the waitress and slipped the check she placed on the table into his shirt pocket.

"How . . . did you know about that?" Kathleen's eyes darted from Johnny to Pete.

"Jude told me. Then Johnny told me that you're writing a book. I've never known anyone who wrote a story, much less a whole book."

"I've not written the whole book yet. I'm just working on it."

"I've not known anyone who was even working on one." Pete placed a generous tip on the table for the waitress and stood. "Where do I buy the magazines?"

"You don't have to buy them. I've got copies I can lend you . . . if you're serious about reading them."

"I've got on my serious face. Didn't you notice? Say,

Johnny, what say we stop off at the town hot spot and have a beer so I can dance with the town celebrity."

"Only if you give me the check. This was my idea." Johnny helped Kathleen on with her coat, then reached to yank the check out of Pete's shirt pocket.

"Keep your cotton-pickin' hands to yourself. You can pay for the beers. Is he always so grabby, Kathleen?"

"Always." Kathleen felt light, airy, giddy, happier than she had been in a long time.

They crowded into the front seat of Johnny's car. Kathleen sat close to him, her shoulder tucked behind his. His hand brushed her knee as he shoved the car into gear and they took off. When he turned to look at her, their faces were only inches apart. Tremors of joy went through her. She wondered if he could feel the beat of her heart through the breast that was pressed tightly against him.

You're happy tonight, my Johnny. Is it because you are with me or your cousin, Pete? Are you remembering how it was between us after we discovered our love and before Mary Rose was born?

"I was discharged in San Diego." Pete's arm lay across the top of the seat behind her. "I could hardly wait to get into civilian clothes and go to a beer joint without keeping an eye out for the MPs. Know what? It wasn't as much fun as I thought it would be. I was lonesome for the red hills of Oklahoma."

"At the Norman Naval Base where I was discharged, they loaded us on a bus and took us straight to the train station."

"He came home to a parade through town." Kathleen glanced at Johnny and saw his teeth clench and a muscle jump in his jaw.

"How do you know?" Johnny asked.

"I was there." Kathleen wished she'd not mentioned his homecoming.

"I didn't see you."

"You were too busy looking at the girls swooning over the returning hero." She turned toward Pete. "The band played, 'When Johnny Comes Marching Home.'"

"Golly-bill, I'm out honky-tonkin' with a real live hero and a celebrity."

"Dry it up," Johnny growled as he turned in and parked in front of the Twilight Gardens, "or I'll leave both of you here and you can walk back to the clinic."

"The place is jumpin' tonight," Pete said dryly, observing that only two other cars were parked at the joint.

"Just the way I like it," Johnny said in a faint faraway voice that only Kathleen could hear.

She wondered if he was remembering the night they sat in front of this place in his old truck? It was strangely the same, even though some of the neon had dimmed from around the windows and the building needed a coat of paint. The parking lot was as full of chuckholes as it had been seven years ago.

Kathleen struggled to keep her breathing even as memories swamped her, making her eyes misty. It was here that she and Johnny said the words that bound her to him forever. Not even their marriage ceremony was as binding to her as the declarations of love they made that night. She had given him her love unconditionally. She was still his, even if he no longer wanted her.

"Let's go in and liven up this place." Pete got out of the car and held out his hand to Kathleen.

Inside, Kathleen paused to allow her eyes to adjust to the darkness. A row of booths lined three sides of the small dance floor. The bar was at the end. Neon beer signs provided the only light except for the dim glow from the juke-box selectors at each booth. None of the booths were occupied.

"This is our lucky night," Johnny said dryly, and Kathleen wondered if he was sorry that they had come here. "We have our choice of booths. Choose one, and I'll get the beers."

Kathleen slid into a booth at the back.

"Don't want anything to happen to my new hat," Pete said, and hung his light-colored Stetson on the peg above the selector before he sat down opposite her. "It cost me three dollars. Imagine paying three dollars for a hat."

"It's a nice one."

"You love him, don't you?" he asked abruptly.

There was no doubt in Kathleen's mind what he was talking about. She looked straight into serious blue eyes that seemed even bluer because of his tanned face and answered honestly.

"I'm crazy about him. Always have been and always will be."

"I thought so."

Johnny returned and set two bottles of beer and a cola on the table. He placed several coins in front of Kathleen and sat down beside her.

"It's a little early for much activity here. Crowd comes late," he explained after a drink from his bottle.

"Are you going to let me dance with Kathleen?"

Johnny took another long drink from his bottle before he answered. "It's up to her."

"How about it, Kathleen?"

"Sure."

"What do you like, fast or slow?" Pete picked up one of the coins from the table and put it in the slot.

"Anything but the 'Beer Barrel Polka,'" she said with a nervous laugh.

"How about, 'I'm in the Mood for Love'?" He punched the correct number and looked over at the jukebox to see if the record had fallen in place.

Without comment, Johnny got up and waited for Kathleen to slide out of the booth. She didn't look at him as she took Pete's hand and let him lead her to the postage-stamp-sized dance floor.

They swayed to the music for a short while before they began to dance. Pete was an inch taller than Johnny. He held her firmly, lowered his head and pressed his cheek to hers.

"Johnny's crazy about you." The words were a soft whisper in her ear.

"Why do you say that?"

"The signs are there."

"I don't think so. Too much time has passed."

"What went wrong?"

"It's a long, long story, very complicated."

"What's complicated about two people who love each other? If I had a woman like you lovin' me, I'd move mountains, dry up rivers, and chop down forests to keep her."

"It's sweet of you—"

"Johnny's glaring at us. He thinks I'm whispering sweet nothings in your ear."

"He wouldn't care—"

"I bet with just a little effort, I could make him jealous as hell." Pete's lips were against the hair at her temple.

"Please don't. Don't jeopardize your friendship. He needs you now."

"Then you think he'd want to bust me up?"

Kathleen pulled back so that she could see his face. "I'm not sure."

"We won't rock the boat . . . yet. But that dumb Indian had better wake up and see what he's got before someone else takes it."

That *dumb Indian* knew what he'd had, and had convinced himself that he could never have it again. But that didn't mean that he'd stand by and see Kathleen hurt by a man like Pete Perry. Pete loved women, any woman that was available. It came as naturally to him as eating and sleeping. Kathleen might not understand that and fall for his line of flattery. To see her in another man's arms was like a knife in his guts.

When the music ended and Kathleen and Pete headed back to the booth, Johnny slipped a coin in the selector and stood.

"My turn," he said, and took Kathleen's hand.

On the dance floor, he put his arm around her and pulled her up close. She turned her head so that her forehead nestled against his cheek. The hand on his shoulder slipped up and up until her fingers could feel the hair at the nape of his neck. When he moved, it was impossible not to move with him. Had he selected this song on purpose, or had he just punched in a number?

> "You'll never know just how much I love you,
> You'll never know just how much I care.
> And if I tried, I still couldn't hide my love for you—"

Kathleen's heart throbbed in her throat. She closed her eyes and for a while forgot that anyone else existed except for her and Johnny. She floated in a haze of happiness as they glided around the floor to the strains of the slow tune.

He moved his head, and she tilted hers to look at him.

"It's been a long time, hasn't it?" His dark eyes were fastened to her face.

"Do you remember the last time we danced together?"

"Of course." His arms tightened convulsively when her lashes fluttered down. "I had four and a half years to remember everything we ever did. I even remember the song we danced to." He pressed his cheek to her hair and sang softly, *"The moon stood still, on Blueberry Hill, on Blueberry Hill where I found you."*

"You remembered that!"

"And a lot more."

Kathleen let him mold her body to his. Her half-closed eyes were filled with a look of intense longing. For a while she wanted to forget that he no longer wanted to live with her as husband and wife. She nestled closer and moved her arm farther around his neck.

The music stopped. Johnny didn't. He continued to dance until the music came on again. The song made Kathleen's heart ache with longing. The Ink Spots were singing,

> "If I didn't care, would I feel this way?
> If I didn't care, more than words can say—"

Johnny became aware that they no longer had the dance floor to themselves when he led her nearly into a collision with another couple. He was also aware that his longing for her was causing his sex to harden. Hoping that she hadn't noticed, he pulled back until their bodies were no longer pressed tightly together from chest to thighs.

When the music ended, he steered her by the hand back to the booth, where two more cold bottles of beer waited. Pete was at the bar talking to the bartender. When he saw them sit down, he came back to the booth.

"The bartender is a navy man, Johnny. He served on the USS *Saratoga*. He asked me to join the VFW here. Have you joined?"

"No. I'm not much of a joiner."

"I think I'll join. We veterans should stick together so that what happened to the World War I vets won't happen to us."

"I'm not interested in pressuring for a handout from the government. I managed before I went to the navy."

Pete grinned. "Still stubborn and independent. How'd you get along in the Seabees? I heard that those guys were tough as boot leather and had a short fuse. Anyone knock you on your ass?"

"A couple tried to. One succeeded, but I got even." Johnny smiled, remembering.

Pete looked at Kathleen. "There's a story here, and if you ask him nicely, he'll tell it."

"Tell it, Johnny," Kathleen urged with her hand on his arm.

"If you insist." He covered her hand briefly, squeezed it, then wrapped both hands around his beer bottle.

"We had a guy in our outfit who had a huge chip on his shoulder. One night we got into a squabble about something or other. He outweighed me by fifty pounds and got in a good punch that knocked me six ways from Sunday. I let it go, knowing that I'd get even.

"This sucker was scared spitless when the Japs came over. We all teased him about it. While we were on Sterling Island, he found himself a little hole in a rock shelf and hung a white cloth over it so that he could dive in when the sirens went off. One night I moved the cloth to the side. When he dived for his hole, he hit his head on the rock and knocked himself out."

"Did he know you did it?" Kathleen asked.

"He suspected. Another time one of the guys tied his shoelaces together while he slept and when the sirens went off, as they did every night, he got up and fell flat on his face. We all hooted and ran for the foxholes."

"We had one of those on our ship." Pete turned the beer bottle around and around with his big hands. "He was so scared he'd wet his pants. I felt sorry for him, but every man had his spot to fill and I had to see to it that he'd fill his. He was finally shipped out to stateside duty. It was a relief to all of us."

Silence stretched between the two men like a taut rubber band. Both were remembering other times.

"We had quite a few close calls," Pete finally began again. "I really never thought I'd make it back."

"I did my damnedest to do my job and stay alive. That's all any of us could do."

"Did you ever listen to Tokyo Rose?"

"Yeah, we heard her when we were secure enough to have a radio. It made us plenty sore when we found out that she was an American citizen who went to visit a relative then turned traitor for the Japs. She had a soft coaxing voice and fed us a bunch of bull about what was going on."

"She's been arrested and is being tried for treason."

"If they don't hang her, I hope that they put her away for life."

"Yeah. The war was an experience I'm glad I had a part in as long as there had to be a war, but I wouldn't want to do it again."

"Me too," Johnny said. "It already seems as if that was another life, or that it happened to someone else." He turned to Kathleen. "Are you ready to go? I doubt this conversation is interesting to you." He stood and held her coat.

"You're wrong about the conversation, but it is getting late."

They drove Pete to the clinic, where he had left his car. When he got out, he told Kathleen that he was going to hold her to her promise to lend him some of the magazines so he could read her stories. She laughingly told him to come by anytime and pick them up.

"I've got a few extra copies at the ranch, if he really wants to read your stories," Johnny said grumpily, while driving Kathleen home. He was quiet after that and didn't speak until he stopped at her house.

"Do you have locks on your doors?"

"I checked them today. I have the telephone, too."

"I'll be in tomorrow. I'll have a talk with Eddie at the garage; and if Thomas isn't there, I'll look him up. If he ever pulls such a stunt again, call the sheriff. If there's anything left of that mechanic after I get through with him, he'll go to jail."

"It's a shame when a person has to lock her doors in broad daylight. I've never had to do that before."

Johnny got out of the car, came around, and opened the car door. They walked to the porch.

"Did you lock the door when you left?"

"Oh, shoot. I didn't even think about it. It was daylight when we left."

Johnny turned the knob, pushed open the door and switched on the lights.

"I'll go through the house."

Kathleen waited in the living room while he made the circle through the kitchen, small back room, the bathroom, then through her bedroom. When he returned to the living room, Kathleen swallowed hard, knowing that he had seen the panties she had washed in the bathroom and left hanging on a line stretched across the bathtub.

"I locked your back door and hooked a chair under the doorknob. Do the same to this front door. These locks are flimsy."

"I'm not afraid, Johnny. I was by myself at the ranch when you were away."

"Times have changed, and you're in town now. I'll take care of Gabe Thomas. But there are others out there just as bad or even worse than he is."

"Don't get into any trouble on my account."

He was concerned for her. Kathleen tried her best not to be thankful that Gabe Thomas had come into her house.

"Your car running all right?" he asked, dismissing the subject.

"Good enough. The tire keeps leaking air. Didn't we used to have a tire pump?"

"It may be out at the ranch. I'll take a look."

"If there's anything I can do to help with Isabel, let me know."

"I'm going to call Henry Ann tomorrow and tell her about Isabel. If she decides to come, would it be all right if she stayed with you?"

"Of course. I'll be glad to have her."

"I'll tell her that when we talk." He pulled open the door. "I'd better get going, I'm going to stop by the clinic."

"Good night, Johnny."

He reached out and placed his hand on her shoulder, squeezed it gently, and nodded. Then he was out the door, his long legs taking him in swift strides across the porch and to his car, as if a mad dog were on his heels.

"Shitfire, shitfire," he cursed.

She looked at me with those big, sad eyes, and I know she wanted me to stay. God, I wanted to stay and love her all night long; but if I did, it would have been the same thing over again. She should be with a man who can give her healthy babies. Tonight Pete watched her like a hawk stalking a chicken. I don't dare let him think she and I are through for good or he'd be after her like a shot, and his blood is as bad as mine.

A light glowed in the three-sided shed behind Eddie's service station. Gabe Thomas lay under the wreck of an old car, removing parts. He was allowed the use of the shed as part compensation for helping out at the station when Eddie had to be away.

The wheels of the wreck had been removed and the frame set upon blocks. With light from a single bulb on the end of a long cord, Gabe was pulling out the bolts that held the engine in place and thinking about Kathleen Henry. Damn, but she was pretty, and with that red hair, she would be hotter than a pistol.

He'd'a had her today if that fool hadn't knocked on the door. But . . . there would be another day. A woman like her, who had had *it*, couldn't go without very long, and he hadn't heard of her being with anyone since she came back to Rawlings. She wasn't going back to Johnny or she wouldn't have moved into that house. He'd give her a little more time . . . let her sweat a little, it would make her all the more eager. Next time, he'd not be so stupid as to try for her in broad daylight.

The wide crack between the boards gave the watcher a full view of the shed. He had studied the wreck sitting on the blocks and now waited patiently for Gabe to position himself beneath it. The shed was a dark, quiet area.

Nothing had moved up or down the adjoining street for half an hour. The man in the dark clothes calculated distance, angles and how much of a bump it would take to move the wreck before he turned away and walked quickly back to where he had left his car.

Minutes later, a car without lights came slowly down the alley, picked up speed when it neared the shed, turned sharply, and rammed the wreck, knocking it off the blocks and into the side of the shed. The light went out. Darkness and quiet prevailed.

Satisfied that he had accomplished what he had intended, the man calmly drove out of the alley and away.

Chapter Eleven

"TELL THAT DOCTOR YOU'RE QUITTING."

Harry dropped the words into the silence while his face was still behind the newspaper.

"What?" Dale was so startled that her hand shook as she returned her cup to the saucer.

"Have you lost your hearing, Dale?" He lowered the paper, frowned at Dale, then smiled pleasantly at his son. "Danny, if you've finished your breakfast, run get your coat, and I'll give you a ride to school."

"You wanted me to have this job, Harry." Dale waited until the child left the room before she spoke. She did her best to keep her voice from quivering.

"That was then. This is now. Your place is here at home taking care of Danny."

"He's in school all day, Harry. He spends an hour after school with Mrs. Ramsey. I'm home and dinner is ready by the time you get here."

"I'm not going to argue with you." Harry gave a deep sigh and shook his head as if talking to a stubborn child. He moved his coffee cup aside, carefully folded the *Gazette*, and placed it on the table beside his plate.

Dale watched the action. During the six years of their

marriage, she had cataloged in her mind every move he made leading up to one of his black moods. First his voice would soften, then he became overly neat and orderly; breaking a matchstick before he dropped it in the ashtray, dusting lint from his coat sleeve, smoothing the hair at his temples.

Next would come the questions. *Don't I provide for you? Don't you have everything you need? Didn't I take you off that dirt farm and put you in a house with a flush toilet?*

Dale began to quake inside, but as usual she stood up against him as long as she could.

"They are short-handed at the clinic, Harry. A terminally ill patient was admitted yesterday. I should give a month's notice so they can hire another nurse."

"Jesus Christ, Dale. We both know that you're not a nurse. Did you graduate from nursing school? Did you get your certificate? You empty bedpans and clean up vomit and shit. It doesn't take brains to do that. Tell him that you'll be gone in two weeks. That's my limit."

"No." Dale stood. "They need me, and I need the job."

"Why do you need the job? Don't I provide for you?" Harry got slowly to his feet, his eyes boring into hers. "What's got into you? You're getting more difficult all the time."

"I won't give the doctor notice, Harry." Dale hoped and prayed that Danny's being in the house would keep Harry's fists from lashing out.

"Then I guess I'll have to do it myself." He walked slowly around the table, then as fast as a striking snake, his hand was at her throat shoving her up against the wall. He knocked her head against it repeatedly until a plate on a plate holder bounced off the shelf and crashed to the floor.

"I'm tired of you defying me when I tell you to do something. Who pays for the roof over your head and food that goes into that fat belly? Huh? Who took you from that dirt farm and set you up in a decent house? Huh?"

Dale clawed at the hand squeezing her neck, closing off her windpipe. Over the ringing in her ears, she heard her son's pleading voice.

"Daddy, Daddy. Stop . . . please stop—"

Dale gasped for breath when the hand left her throat, only vaguely aware that Harry was talking calmly to their son.

"Your mother and I were just having a little fun. She fell against the wall and knocked your grandmother's plate off the shelf. You know how she is . . . not the most graceful mother in the world, huh? We'd better move, son, or both of us will be late." With his hand at the back of Danny's head, Harry urged him toward the door. The child resisted for just a moment, looking back at his mother.

Dale didn't move until she heard the car start and was sure he was leaving. When she did, her foot crunched the broken glass. She stroked her throat gently and swallowed to be sure that she could.

Someday he will kill me.

Johnny was up at dawn after a sleepless night. Last night Sherm had finished boiling the sheets and had hung them on the line to dry. After making up the bed, Johnny had stripped and fallen into it. But sleep had not come as he had expected. He continued to feel Kathleen in his arms, warm and moving, to smell the scent of her hair when he buried his nose in it, and to see the curve of her lips when she smiled.

She had not been outraged, as he had expected, when he kissed her. Lord, how many nights had he crouched down in his foxhole while the Japs strafed and bombed their building site, thinking of kissing her and more . . . burying himself in her soft body? He relived in detail the hours, during the dark of night, that they had spent making love, whispering, teasing, making plans. At other times, dark times, he had remembered her turning away from him after they had buried their baby, refusing to understand his determination never again to father a child.

Five years had dimmed the pain he had felt on seeing the small piece of deformed humanity he and Kathleen had brought into the world. It had not, however, dimmed his resolve never again to put her through the agony of giving birth to a child of his. But would he be able to endure seeing her stomach swell with another man's child. Good Lord! He should have taken that job in Central America when it was offered.

When morning came, Johnny put the coffeepot on, then began clearing the house of Isabel's belongings. He piled her clothes in the yard, poured gasoline on them, and set them ablaze. Thanks to his navy training he had already been careful with the cups, glasses, and eating utensils she had used, washing them separately and letting them sit in the boiling water.

He told Sherm when he came in for breakfast that Isabel wasn't coming back.

"I knowed she warn't well but didn't figure it was so bad."

"I've got to go back to town this morning. When I get back, I'll scrub this place down with lye soap. I don't think she ever went to the outhouse."

"I ain't never seen her go there."

"That's one less thing we have to worry about. I set the chamber pot on the porch. I'll build a fire under the wash pot and scald it good. I never use it, but I don't want it sitting around here with germs on it."

"I can do it while yo're gone. Is that feller comin' back to help drive up the horses?"

"I don't know. Pete seems to be the only one who can do anything with Isabel. She's so ornery, the doctor is afraid his nurses will quit."

"Hit's a pity, is what it is. Her bein' young and all."

Johnny drove slowly into town. After he tended to the business with Gabe, he would go to the telephone office and call Henry Ann to tell her about Isabel. He believed that she would come to Rawlings. She would think it the decent thing to do. He would have to watch Pete when she got here. Johnny wasn't sure whether Pete still had strong feelings for Henry Ann, and he didn't want his sister to have to deal with that on top of everything else.

When he rounded the corner to drive into Eddie's station, Johnny could tell that something out of the ordinary had happened. Several cars were parked in the alley and along the street, one of them a hearse. Jude, wearing his overcoat over his white jacket and holding his black bag, was talking to the undertaker. Johnny parked and crossed the street.

"Morning. Has something happened to Eddie?"

"No, to Gabe Thomas." Douglas Klein, the undertaker and owner of the furniture store, answered. He was a friendly man with a husky body, dark hair, and a small mustache.

"What happened?"

"The old wreck he had up on blocks fell and crushed him flat as a fritter."

"Not quite that flat," Jude said. "But he died instantly."

"Too bad. Where's Eddie?"

"He went to find a jack to lift the wreck so that we can get the body out. He said Gabe was usually pretty careful about blocking up those old wrecks."

"He must have slipped up this time. Are you through here, Jude?" Johnny asked.

"Just about. As coroner, I've got to sign the death certificate. The sheriff and I can't see it as anything but an accident. What are you doing in town so early?"

"I was going to speak to Eddie. Guess I have no reason to do that now." Johnny put a cigarette in his mouth, struck a match on the sole of his boot, and held the flame to the tip. "I plan to call Henry Ann this morning. She has a right to know about Isabel. How was she this morning?"

"About the same. She won't let us check her vitals. We have to do it when she's sedated. We're trying to keep her quiet. She wastes a lot of her strength yelling and thrashing around. Miss Pauley, the night nurse, said she made so much noise she woke everyone in the clinic."

Eddie returned with the jack and several men went with him into the shed to help the undertaker recover the body.

"Jude, I don't have much, but I'll pay for Isabel's keep somehow. Just give me a little time."

"You'll not owe me a thing for my services, Johnny. The clinic is another matter. The board of trustees will give you as much time as you need to pay them. So don't worry about it."

"I'll worry about it. There's just not much I can do about it right now."

"I'll keep her as comfortable as I can until the end. There will be an end, Johnny, and soon."

"Does she know?"

"I'm not sure. I think she has brain damage. That's not

my line, so I can't be absolutely sure. A completely sane person would understand the seriousness of her condition."

The stretcher bearing Gabe Thomas's body was placed on the cart from the hearse, and Mr. Klein came to speak with Jude.

"If you've seen enough, Dr. Perry, I'd better get him on down to the parlor. He's going to take a lot of fixin' before his folks see him."

"I have. I'll finish up at the clinic and give the death certificate to the sheriff." Jude and Johnny crossed the street to their cars. "After you talk to Henry Ann, come by the clinic. We need to get some background information on Isabel."

"You know as much about her as I do. All I know is that she was born in Oklahoma City. Dorene listed the father as unknown. The only reason I know that is when Isabel tried to get part of Ed Henry's farm, the lawyer Henry Ann hired got a copy of the birth certificate."

"I don't suppose it matters all that much," Jude said, getting into his car. "I hope Henry Ann comes. It'll be good to see her."

Jude parked his car at the clinic and went into the side door to his office. He removed his overcoat and sat down in the chair behind his desk to complete his paperwork.

Would his damn leg ever stop aching?

He was a little puzzled as to why a man who had worked on cars for most of his life would crawl under a wreck without making sure it was up on solid blocks. Judging by the congealed blood, he presumed the accident had happened around midnight. The body hadn't been found until early this morning. It wouldn't have mattered if it had been discovered minutes after the accident. The man had died instantly. Jude filled out the death certificate and left it on his desk for delivery to the sheriff.

"You were out early, Doctor." Theresa Frank came in as he was preparing to make his rounds.

"Yes. An accident."

"I heard about it."

"Sheriff Carroll will be by for the death certificate. I was about to make my rounds. Anything you need to tell me?"

"Mr. Case is better. You may want to consider dismissing him. He's worried about the cost of being here." Theresa consulted her chart. "Mrs. Warren has developed large welts on her body and her lips are swollen. We should check and see if she's allergic to some of the medication."

"Check to see if the medication she's been taking has codeine in it."

"I did that, and it does."

"That could be the cause. Take her off it."

"I told Dale to hold off giving it to her until I talked to you." Theresa continued with her report. "Mrs. Smothers is in the reception room, insisting on seeing you right away. She says that her legs are swelling. We have a patient with an infected toenail and a six-year-old girl with tonsillitis. Marie Fleming is here with her brother, who poked a nail in his hand. She thinks he needs a tetanus shot."

"He won't need me for that. You give better shots than I do."

"I don't know about that, but I'll give it."

Theresa was certain that Marie Fleming would be disappointed at not seeing the doctor. She had noticed how the girl had looked at him during the open house. She was young, pretty, and her daddy was rich—surely Jude had been aware.

"How about Miss Henry?"

"She refused to eat the oatmeal, but drank the coffee. She's fussing for a cigarette and calling for your brother to come get her out of here."

"Pete will be along soon. He sat up with her half the night."

"She's taking the oral sedatives, but soon she'll need something stronger. Her breast is swollen and draining. She did let me put a pad over it." Theresa folded her arms over the charts and held them against her. "If we have a few minutes, I'd like to talk to you about something."

Jude saw the concerned look on Theresa's face and backed up to sit down on the edge of the desk. He rubbed his aching thigh.

"What is it? You're not going to quit, are you?"

Theresa smiled. "No, I'm not going to quit."

"That's a relief. You scared me for a minute. How's Ryan? I've not seen him for a while."

"He's fine. He likes going to Mrs. Ramsey's and says he's going to marry Emily when he grows up." Theresa's eyes brightened when she talked about her son.

Theresa Frank had had a hopeless crush on Dr. Jude Perry since the day she met him. He was the kindest, most thoughtful man she had ever known besides being so darn handsome it almost hurt her eyes to look at him. She was realistic enough to know that when he took a wife, it wouldn't be a dumpy nurse with a four-year-old child. But she daydreamed, and went on crash diets trying to look thin and desirable. In the meanwhile, she helped him in the only way she knew, by being the best nurse possible.

"Now, what is it that you wanted to talk about?"

Jude studied the woman who stood a short distance from him. He liked what he saw. She was pretty, quiet, and dependable. He wondered how many hours she spent washing and ironing her uniforms. They were always fresh. The starched cap was carefully perched on top of her soft brown hair, and she had a complexion some women would give five years of their lives for.

Most of all Jude liked who Theresa was: her attitude toward life, her compassion for the ill, her dedication to service, and her love for her child. She was just what he thought a woman should be—far from the sluts he had grown up with down on Mud Creek.

"It's about Dale Cole." Theresa's voice broke into Jude's thoughts. "I'm sure she had been crying when she came in this morning. I asked her what was wrong and she tried to assure me that nothing was wrong, that she just had a headache."

"Maybe that was true. Did she take some medication?"

"She took some because I was watching her. That's not all, Doctor—"

"Can't you call me Jude when we're alone? I call you Theresa."

"Yes, but you're . . . the doctor. I'm only the—"

"—Very important part of my practice. I want us to be friends as well as associates."

"I . . . want that too." Theresa's cheeks turned rosy red.

Jude laughed. "You're blushing, Theresa."

"I am not!" she insisted, but knew that she was. "Sometimes you get me so . . . flustered."

"I do?" He looked surprised. "I thought that you were . . . unfluster . . . able." They both laughed at his difficulty in pronouncing the word. "I'll not interrupt again. Tell me about Mrs. Cole."

"She has bruises on her neck. She tried to keep them covered just as in the past she has tried to keep me from seeing the bruises on her arms."

"We can't draw any conclusions from that," Jude said slowly.

"You may not be able to, but I can. I think that cold-eyed husband of hers is mean to her."

"Has she ever said anything?"

"No. She talks about him as if he was the most wonderful man in the world."

"Humm— What do you think we should do?"

"There probably isn't anything we can do as long as she keeps denying it. There's one more thing that has caused me to come to the conclusion that her husband abuses her."

"All right, Sherlock Holmes, what is it?" Jude enjoyed teasing her.

"Dale's son, Danny, stays with Mrs. Ramsey after school until Dale gets home. He was playing with Ryan and got pretty rough. He put his arm across his neck and held him against the wall. When Mrs. Ramsey got after him, he said he wasn't hurting Ryan, his daddy did it all the time."

"Did Mrs. Ramsey tell you this?"

"Yes, but she assumed Mr. Cole did this while playing with Danny. She didn't think it was the thing for a father to do even in play."

"I agree there. A little too much pressure could crush a windpipe."

"Dale is a natural-born nurse. She's dedicated, efficient, and soaks up knowledge like a sponge. I'm sure that with just a little study she could pass the nurses' exam. She was just a few months from graduation when she married Mr. Cole."

"Does she know that she's got such a good friend?"

"Now, there you go again." Theresa feigned annoyance.

"I like to tease you, Theresa. You're so pretty when you blush."

Theresa opened her mouth, then closed it. Her heart had jumped in her throat, making speech impossible. He was looking at her with warm, smiling eyes. He looked younger and less tired when he smiled. Determined to make light of the situation, she shoved the stack of patient charts in his hands.

"Go tell that to Mrs. Smothers. You may get her out of here in less than two hours."

Chapter Twelve

JOHNNY STARED AT KATHLEEN when she answered his knock on her door. She was wearing the blue-silk negligee he had given her the Christmas before the baby was born. She appeared to be totally unaware of the effect it had on him.

"Johnny. Come in. Have you had breakfast?"

"Hours ago, but I'll take coffee if you have it made."

"It won't take a minute to make it. Meanwhile you can have some toast and Mrs. Ramsey's peach jam."

"I forgot that you drink tea." He followed her into the kitchen.

"Did you talk to Henry Ann?"

"She'll be here in the morning about ten-thirty. Would you mind picking her up?"

"Of course I don't mind. The bus stops at the *Gazette* office. I'll go early. I like Henry Ann and have from the minute I met her. I bet she misses Aunt Dozie."

"Aunty was like a mother to her and to me. I was on Bougainville in the Solomons when I got the letter that she had died. It shook me up. When I was a kid Aunty and Henry Ann were the only two people in the world that gave a hoot about me."

"I wish I had known you then."

"Why? I had a chip on my shoulder the size of a boulder."

"And I would have tried to knock it off. How many pieces of toast?" Kathleen struck a match and lit the waist-high oven on the stove.

"How many do you have?" He grinned when she rolled her eyes to the ceiling.

"We'll start out with four, how's that?" She buttered the bread, arranged it in a flat pan, and slid it beneath the flame. "Coffee will be ready in a minute or two." She stood beside the stove, peeking at the toasting bread every few seconds.

Johnny was terribly conscious that all she had on beneath the negligee was her nightgown. Her feet were bare, and her hair was a mass of curls. He liked looking at her when her face was scrubbed and she wore not a trace of makeup. Lord, how he would like to tumble in bed with her and let her ease the ache as only she could. Thank God, he was sitting down and she couldn't see the lump that had suddenly appeared in his jeans.

"Whoops! I'd better get it out." Kathleen grabbed a potholder and pulled the pan from the stove. "A few seconds more and you'd have had burned toast."

"What are you going to have?"

"A piece of your toast with peanut butter, while more bread is toasting." When the toast was on a plate in front of him, she buttered more slices and slid them under the flame.

"It looks like I'm going to owe you a whole loaf of bread."

"You can pay me back . . . sometime."

When Kathleen sat down across from him, her knees came in contact with his beneath the small table. She moved them to the side and reached for the peanut butter. It seemed so natural to be sitting at the breakfast table with him.

Johnny, Johnny, what happened to the love we once shared?

He waited until they had finished eating before he told her about Gabe.

"You won't have to worry about Gabe Thomas anymore. He was killed last night."

"For goodness sake! What in the world happened?"

"He was taking parts off an old wreck of a car when it fell on him. Jude said it probably happened around midnight."

"I hate to hear it. He wasn't a very nice man, but he was someone's loved one."

"I was going to read the riot act to him this morning and threaten to break his neck if he came near you again. Fate stepped in and took care of it."

"I don't know what possessed the man to walk in here yesterday. It scared the life out of me to come out of the bathroom and find him in my living room."

"Lock your doors. Especially at night."

"We didn't even lock the doors out on the ranch."

"This is different. You're a good-looking woman living here by yourself."

"I don't feel good-looking. I feel like a clock that's running down. I'll soon be thirty-three years old."

"That's not old."

"But . . . I feel old. Where has the time gone? Life is going by so fast." Tears came to her eyes. She blinked to hold them back, but they rolled down her cheeks. "Sorry—" Her eyes shone like stars.

"What's the matter? Why are you crying?"

"I'm . . . crying because . . . I'm just a silly woman."

Johnny was on his feet and reaching to lift her out of the chair. She wrapped her arms around his waist and hugged him to her. He stood for a minute holding her, then moved to the chair, sat down, and pulled her down on his lap. Her arms went up and around his neck. She burrowed her face into a broad shoulder that was soon wet with her tears. It felt so luxurious to be in his arms that she melted against him, loving the familiar feel of his hard body.

"Shhh . . . don't cry. Don't cry, honey—"

Sensitive fingers played lightly with the curls over her ears, then plunged into the soft masses to work gently at the nape of her neck. When her sobs ceased, he tilted her face to his and kissed her tear-wet eyes.

"Are you all right now?"

"No. I'm . . . getting old . . . and I—"

"Hush. You'll never get old. When you're sixty, you'll be as fiery as you are now." The words were murmured against her ear in such a tender voice that she cried again.

"But . . . I'll be alone . . . Johnny."

"No, honey—"

His mouth slid over hers. Kathleen closed her eyes and felt her lashes scrape his face before feathery kisses touched her lids, then moved across her cheek, searched for her mouth, found it and melted her lips to his. After the first deep pressure of his mouth he lifted it.

"Oh, God! Oh, God, honey—"

Then he made tender, adoring love to her mouth with warm lips and exploring tongue. He nibbled, licked, caressed until they both felt they were slipping into oblivion. He pulled on the bow at the neck of her nightdress, his hand burrowed inside to cup her naked breast, his thumb stroking the hard point. Kathleen's blood, suffused with fire, flooded riotously through her body. It suddenly wasn't enough and she wiggled to get closer.

"Be still, honey," he muttered urgently. "Be still or I'll not be able to stop. Dear God. It's been so long. I want to crawl inside you, feel every inch of you." He buried his face in the curve of her neck and took deep, gulping breaths. Their hearts beat together in thunderous pounding.

Kathleen wriggled again on the part of him that throbbed so aggressively beneath her hips.

"Don't stop. Please don't stop. I've dreamed every night of being with you like this. I love you. I'll always love you—"

"We . . . can't—" Desperately Johnny tried to fight down the desire that spiraled crazily inside him. "To hold you, touch you like this drives me crazy," he said in a strange, thickened voice, his mouth at her throat, then sliding up to close over her mouth hard and seeking. The searching movement parted her lips and he drank thirstily.

"Please, Johnny—"

"God help me for being such a weak son of a bitch," he snarled and stood with her in his arms. Long strides took him to the bedroom, where he placed her on the unmade bed and lay down on top of her, his mouth feasting on hers. The weight of him felt so good! She had missed, so much, the way he made her feel. This way, together, they relinquished control, and flew away into the sensuous world where there were only their hands, their lips, the hard strength of his male body and the softness of hers.

He wanted her, ached with the wanting.

"I shouldn't . . . I'll hate myself, but I have to—"

"I'm glad. I've never been anyone's but yours. Love me. Love me like you used to do. Make me forget everything but you."

"You're like a fire in my blood. I only have to think of you and I get like this." He brought her hand down to the hard and throbbing erection that was straining for release.

"I want to feel it. I want it in my hand—"

"I don't have a rubber—"

"It'll be all right—"

Between chopped breaths, he cursed with frustration. His desperation to be with her, inside her, made his hands clumsy. But finally, his jeans lay on the floor and he stretched out beside her, groaned, and rubbed his erection against her belly. She reached down and touched him, made a gentle fist with her hand, caressing, sliding, in the motion he taught her years ago.

He uttered a hoarse cry and burrowed, hard and urgent into the softness of her. He hesitated with momentary surprise at the tightness of the passage, then gave a swift thrust and embedded himself inside her with absolute possession. The pleasure was acute. The heat fierce. With his hands beneath her buttocks, he clutched her desperately, and made a moaning sound.

"I've missed you . . . missed you. Oh, Lord—"

She made a small helpless sound. "Open your eyes. Look at me. I love you—"

Dark eyes stared into blue ones. "Jesus! What am I doing to you?"

"Loving me. Don't stop." She raised her hips to meet his plunging strokes.

"I can't get enough of you," he groaned. "I can't get enough," he repeated.

Then, locked together they clung helplessly and surrendered to the sensuous void. The pleasure rose to intolerable heights, and she lost consciousness of everything but the powerful body that was driving her toward weightlessness. Her stomach clenched in fierce panic. She spun crazily, cried out wildly, and clung to the only solid thing in her tilting world.

Hands gently stroked her taut body. Soothing words calmed and reassured her. Her heart settled in to a quieter pace as the tension left her. Still joined to the man who had taken her heart, she began to cry.

"I'm sorry, honey. I'm sorry. I wanted you so damn bad—"

"Please . . . don't be sorry." She held his face in her hands and kissed him frantically. "I wanted you, too."

He withdrew from her, loosened his arms, and sat up on the side of the bed. "Go on. Go use the bathroom."

Kathleen slid out of the other side of the bed. She knew what he wanted her to do—sit on the toilet and let his sperm slide out of her in the hope that she wouldn't become pregnant. He needn't fear. She wouldn't be so lucky.

They had been married two years before she had conceived. At first Johnny had insisted that they use contraceptives because of their financial situation. But their appetite for each other had been so voracious that they had made love sometimes twice during the day and they didn't always take the necessary precautions.

Kathleen was elated. This was a new beginning. Johnny hadn't said that he still loved her, but his tender loving of her said that he did. She washed, put a touch of toilet water behind her ears, and opened the door . . . to an empty bedroom. She hurried to the window to see Johnny's car going down the street.

She put her hand around her throat to ease the terrible ache there. She must not cry. If once she let herself weep, she would never stop.

"Johnny, Johnny." Her unsteady lips seemed unable to

frame any other words. She felt sick and cold and terribly afraid.

Johnny cursed himself all the way to the clinic. When he got there, he sat in his car feeling nothing but contempt for himself. He had done the very thing that he had vowed not to do. He had exposed her to another heartbreak that could destroy her completely. And he let her think the door was open to the possibility of their having a future together.

She was lonely. She wanted a family. Hadn't she cried because she feared getting old and being alone? Christ on a horse! What had he been thinking of? She needed a clean break from him so that she could find someone who would give her the family she had always wanted. The thought of her with someone else was like a knife in his gut. He wasn't sure about what to do; but whatever it was, it'd have to wait until this thing with Isabel was over. In the meanwhile, he'd be careful not to be alone with her again.

Pete was in the reception room flirting with Millie when Johnny went into the clinic. Johnny was wearing what Pete called his Indian face.

"And good morning to you, too," he said cheerfully when Johnny didn't speak.

"How is Isabel?"

"I've not seen her yet. Reports aren't good."

"Henry Ann will be here tomorrow."

"You'd better prepare her for Isabel's nasty mouth. Even in her sleep last night, she spit out words I hadn't heard during sixteen years in the navy."

"Henry Ann's coming because it's what a decent person would do under the circumstances. If it upsets Isabel for her to be here, Henry Ann will know what to do." Johnny turned back to the door. "It upsets her to see me, too, so

I'll go on back to the ranch and try to get some work done. I'll be back in tonight."

"I'll see how things are going here. If they put her under for a while, I'll come out and give you a hand."

Johnny nodded and left, leaving Pete puzzled as to the reason for his black mood.

"Mr. Perry," a nurse's assistant called from the doorway, "Nurse Frank said you can see Miss Henry now."

"Thanks, honey," Pete said, and winked. He then watched with pleasure the blush that covered the young girl's cheeks.

"Shame on you," Millie said after the girl disappeared down the hall. "She's young enough to be your daughter."

"But you're not . . . honey."

"No, and I'm old enough to know a rogue when I meet one." Millie stabbed at his chest with her pencil. "Flirt with someone your own age."

"And who might that be around here?"

"Theresa and Miss Pauley, the night nurse. Have you met her? I think the two of you would make a handsome pair." Millie pushed her glasses up on her nose, and poked the pencil into the thick gray hair over her ear.

"Flying catfish! That woman is sour as a lemon, cross as a bear, and is about as friendly as a case of the measles."

"Use that famous Perry charm on her. Who knows, with a kiss from the right man, Miss Pauley might turn into Betty Grable or Ginger Rogers."

"More than likely Marie Dressler or ZaSu Pitts," Pete grumbled, then walked away, grinning.

In the hallway he met Nurse Frank. Now, she was a pretty little thing, soft and sweet. Jude had told him that her husband had been killed during the war.

"Go on in, Mr. Perry. She's been sedated, but it hasn't

taken effect yet or else it wasn't a big enough dose. Dr. Perry is afraid to give her too much because of her heart. Mrs. Cole is with her."

"My brother says she's going to die in a few days. Why can't you give her enough to let her sleep until the end?"

"Because it doesn't work that way. As long as there is life we must do what we can to prolong it."

"I guess I'm not quite as civilized as you and my brother."

The odor in the room was stronger this morning. He had smelled it at Johnny's and again in his car coming here. Jude said it was from the cancer that was eating away at Isabel's breast. Mrs. Cole looked over her shoulder when he opened the door, then adjusted a cloth over Isabel's upper body before she moved away.

"Get away from me, you . . . ugly bitch!" Isabel's voice was weak and slurred. "Where's Hardy? He'd take me . . . dancin'. Hardy is a son of a bitch. He screwed ever'thing on Mud Creek that moved. Even a rabbit, if he could catch one." Isabel turned her fevered eyes toward Pete. "You're a bastard, a cocksuckin' bastard. Know that?"

"Would you like a drink of ice water?" Pete asked.

"Hell no. I'll take a . . . cold beer. This broad-ass pussy here won't give me one. I want to . . . I want to go—" The words trailed away, but her mouth still worked as her eyes closed.

Mrs. Cole had turned her back and was putting the soiled bedclothes in a bag. Pete waited until she headed for the door, then stepped in front of her.

"I'm sorry you have to take this abuse." Pete put his hands on her upper arms. "Confound it. You shouldn't have to put up with this."

"Someone's got to. The poor thing doesn't realize what she's saying."

"I think she does." He tilted his head to look at her neck. "Dale! What happened to your neck. Did she grab you?"

"Heavens, no. She hasn't the strength." She attempted to go around him. "I've got to get this down to the laundry."

"If she didn't do this, who did? I've seen bruises like this before." He fitted his hand to the marks on her neck. She angrily knocked it away.

"Tend to your own business, Mr. Perry. What happened to my neck is no concern of yours."

Pete dropped his hand. "I'd like for it to be, Dale." He spoke so sincerely that her eyes caught his and held.

"I have a husband who looks after me, Mr. Perry."

"Did he do this to you?"

"No!"

"Is he out looking for the bastard who did? If you were my wife, I'd hunt him down and take strips of hide off him. I'd make sure he never hurt another woman."

"But I'm not your wife—"

"No. I'd not be so lucky."

"I would appreciate it if you wouldn't make fun of me." Pete was shocked to see tears in her eyes.

"You . . . think that?"

"I know what I am, Mr. Perry. I am plain, overweight, and not a clever conversationalist. I know what you are, a man with a gift of gab. Also a flirt."

"What makes you think you're plain? It's what's on the inside of a woman that comes through and says whether she's plain or not. You may have a few extra pounds, but so what? I'd rather hold a soft woman in my arms than a bag of bones."

"Why are you telling me this?"

Pete ignored the question. "I had men come into the navy with an attitude like yours, and I sometimes found out that a father or a mother had constantly put the man down until he thought he wasn't worth anything. Is that happening to you?" he asked bluntly.

"I don't know what you're talking about. Please let me pass."

"Not until you promise me that you'll let me know if you ever need help. I'm going to stay here so I can be near my brother and my cousin, Johnny Henry."

"Why are you interested in my affairs?"

"Hell, I don't know. I just know I'm damn mad that some son of a bitch hurt you."

"I thank you for your concern." Dale lowered her eyes and then turned her head to look past him at the door as it opened. Jude stood there looking from one to the other. "Excuse me, Doctor. I've got to get these down to the laundry."

Jude stepped aside, then came into the room and closed the door. He walked over to the bed and looked down at Isabel.

"I wish there was something I could do for her. There are so many things wrong with her that I don't know which to treat first." Jude picked up her limp wrist and felt her pulse.

"Johnny was here. He said that Henry Ann will be here tomorrow."

Jude nodded. He had seen death dozens of times, and it always affected him as if it were the first. He placed the thin hand back down at her side.

"She'll sleep now until early afternoon."

"She was talking about Hardy when I came in. Said that he would take her dancing. She talks mean to Mrs. Cole. I wish that she'd not do that."

"Mrs. Cole understands that sometimes a person in her condition is irrational."

"The woman's hurtin', Jude."

"Mrs. Cole?"

"Take a look at the bruises on her neck. Someone tried to squeeze the life out of her."

"I noticed as she passed me just now. Theresa told me about them."

"She denied that her husband hurt her. What do you know about him?"

"Nothing. He was here at the reception. Seems to be very personable. He works at the Gas and Electric Company. Office manager, I think."

"I might go down and have a little talk with him."

"You can't accuse him of anything." Jude looked at his brother searchingly. Pete never could stand by and see a woman abused. He remembered Opal Hastings down on Mud Creek. If Pete had found out who raped her, he would have killed him. "What happens between a man and his wife is their business."

"Not if he's mistreating her."

"Even then, if she won't file charges. It's the law, Pete."

"Well, it's a shitty law."

"Theresa thinks Dale's husband mistreats her. She said Dale was crying this morning when she came to work."

"Did she say anything to Theresa?"

"No. She might sometime. They are good friends. Why are you taking such an interest in Dale? She's married and has a five-year-old boy."

"Hell, I don't know. She seems to be a damn nice woman who has a hell of a problem." Pete shoved his hands down into his pockets and walked out.

Jude watched his brother leave the room. In his youth Pete had been coarse, rude, and undisciplined. Mud Creek had never spawned another hell-raiser as wild as Pete Perry. Back then he would not have cared about Isabel. He would have voiced the view that she had made her bed and she'd have to lie in it. Nor would he have taken an interest in a woman who had a few bruises on her neck.

Pete had changed. War did that to a man.

Chapter Thirteen

THEODORE NUDING CAREFULLY STRIPPED a length of paper from the wall of the room he was preparing for Kathleen. Looking at bright red-and-yellow roses climbing a white trellis day after day was bound to be annoying. Arranging a comfortable, safe room was taking much longer than he had at first believed. It had to be perfect for her to be happy here.

It was daylight now. He removed the pieces of carpet he used to cover the windows so that he could work at night without a light showing from the outside and stood back to admire the stout door he had put in place the night before. It would be necessary to keep Kathleen locked in until she became adjusted to being here. Then, like his mother, she wouldn't want to leave the room.

He washed, ate breakfast cereal, then set his alarm clock and lay down to sleep for a while. By noon he was parked on the rise outside of town with his weather-observing props in place should it be necessary for him to use them.

After scanning Kathleen's house with his binoculars and seeing no movement there, he removed his notebook from the compartment beneath his seat and began to write.

12:15 A.M. The timetable for bringing Kathleen to her new home will have to be moved to after Christmas. I am removing the old wallpaper and preparing the walls of her room for repapering. The room is next to the bathroom so I had only to close off one door and make another going out of her room. The fixtures are adequate. Later when I can have workmen here, I'll modernize the bath and maybe even put in one of those things French women sit on to wash their private parts. The furnishings in the house are of good quality, but for some things I'll have to make a trip to the city. I'll buy a lovely Persian rug, a few lamps, and other doodads that Kathleen will like. While I'm there I'll buy the best typewriter to be had and reams of paper so that when I have to leave her, she can amuse herself by writing her stories. I'll order toilet articles and a new wardrobe for her from Neiman Marcus. Only the best will do for my Kathleen.

Note: I was lucky last night. An opportunity fell in my lap to take care of a matter that could have consumed a lot more time than it did.

"Adelaide! Come in."

"Brought you the latest *Gazette*."

"Thanks." Kathleen closed the door quickly behind her friend. "It's getting cold out there."

"It's that time of year. Thanksgiving will be here before we know it." Adelaide laid the paper on the table, headlines up, then took off her coat and draped it over the back of a chair.

Johnny has been home for a month and I still don't know where I stand with him. What does he want from me? Kathleen's next words were totally unrelated to her thoughts.

"When I was growing up in Iowa we always had snow before Thanksgiving."

"Over the river and through the woods to grandma's house?"

"My grandma always made a big deal out of Thanksgiving and Christmas. Grandpa would bring in a wild turkey for Thanksgiving and a goose for Christmas. They didn't have much cash money, but Grandma always set a good table."

"You're welcome to have Thanksgiving with me and Paul."

"Thanks. Barker and Marie mentioned my going to their place when they were here the other night. I'll let you know."

"Have you heard about Gabe Thomas getting killed?" Adelaide nodded to the headline.

"Johnny was here this morning and told me."

"This morning?" Adelaide raised her brows. "Early this morning? That's interesting—"

"—Don't let your imagination work overtime. Yesterday Gabe Thomas just walked into my house, as bold as brass, while I was washing my hair. I don't know where the man ever got the idea that I was interested in him. Anyway, he left when a fellow came to the door looking for someone. I told Johnny about it, and he was going to give him a talking-to this morning. He came by to tell me what had happened."

"I heard that you were out on the town last night with Johnny and Dr. Perry's brother."

"Oh, my goodness. You can't do anything in this town without it becoming gossip."

"Was it a secret?"

"No. Pete Perry is a nice man. Rough, but nice."

"Good-looking too, if you ask me. Why don't you use him to make Johnny jealous?"

"Adelaide, you'd be the first to flay me alive if I even suggested such a thing."

"I know, but at times I'd like to yank a knot in that guy."

"Johnny or Pete?" Kathleen plowed through her hair with all ten fingers, holding it off her face.

"Johnny. But I didn't come to talk about him. Well, maybe I did, but I want to talk about something else too."

"I'm all ears."

"I'm heading a committee to organize a fund-raiser to furnish a room at the clinic. They have only four rooms for overnight patients. Dr. Perry tells me that through a government program they will soon be getting an iron lung, and they need a room prepared to put it in. A boy from the southern part of the county died last summer before they could get him to a lung in Frederick."

"You don't have to sell me on the project. What do you want me to do?"

"We've come up with the idea of having a Christmas carnival at the school the week after Thanksgiving. We're asking all the church circles to have booths and sell crafts. The VFW will put on a barbecue. We will have a cake walk, a bingo room, a kissing booth."

"Count me out on that one."

"Chicken." Adelaide snorted.

"Paul wouldn't let *you* do it," Kathleen declared.

"Who'd want to kiss an old woman?"

"An old man."

"Want to bet? An old man wants to kiss something young. I wasn't going to ask you to be in the kissing booth. We're turning the gym into a ballroom and charging ten cents a dance."

"Good idea."

"A lot of men will come stag if they know they'll have

someone to dance with. I want six of the prettiest girls in town to entice them to spend their money. If two or more men want to dance with the same girl, she'll go to the highest bidder."

"If you're asking me to be one of the *girls*. I'm not a *girl*, Adelaide. I'm old enough to have a *girl* in high school."

"You're one of the prettiest women in town. Say you'll do it. It's for a good cause."

"You're buttering me up . . ."

"Yeah, I am. I need you."

"What if no one wants to dance with me?"

"Are you dreaming? I'll have Paul keep an eye on you, and he'll see to it that you're not a wallflower. How's that?"

"Fine." Kathleen sighed. "I'll do it, even though I don't want to."

"Thank Jesus, Mary, and Joseph! Now there's just one more thing."

"I figured there would be."

"Don't be a sorehead. You'll be the most popular girl at the dance." Adelaide opened her notebook and scanned a list of names. "I'd appreciate it if you'd be on the committee to collect items for our auction to be held before the Christmas carnival."

"New or used?"

"Preferably new, but used if in good condition."

Kathleen glanced out the window. "Barker is here. You can hit him up for something."

Kathleen opened the door before he could knock. "Hello, Barker. Come in."

"Hello." He stepped inside. "Oh, hello, Adelaide."

"I was going to come out to see you today, Barker. You've saved me a trip."

"Better sit down, Barker. Adelaide is on one of her crusades."

"Marie took Lucas to the clinic this morning for a tetanus shot and heard that Johnny's sister, Isabel, is at the clinic."

"She's been there for a couple of days now. She's terminally ill, I'm afraid."

"I didn't know that she and Johnny had been in touch."

"As far as I know they haven't talked in years. I've never met her. She came to him because she was sick. He and a cousin took her to the clinic hoping Dr. Perry could do something for her. It's too late. She's dying."

"I'm sorry to hear it. What did you want to see me about, Adelaide?"

"Have you heard about our Christmas carnival?"

"Oh, yes. Janna has talked of nothing else."

"The teachers and the students are pitching in. Each room is going to do something to help us raise money. We want the families to have a good time. Will you donate an item from the tannery for our auction?"

"Of course."

"That's what I like to hear. I hate arguing with people to get them to cooperate." She glanced significantly at Kathleen.

"You didn't ask *him* to line up and wait for a lady to ask him to dance."

"I didn't ask you to wait for a lady to ask *you* to dance."

"I swear to goodness, Adelaide." Kathleen's tone was one of exasperation.

"I'm going. I've pushed as far as I can go today, but . . . I'll be back." Adelaide put on her coat. "As much as I'd like to stay and visit with you fine folks, I've got things to do."

"I'll be going, too," Barker said.

"Everyone is deserting me at once."

Adelaide paused at the door. "I just had a thought."

"Move back, Barker, this could be dangerous."

"Smarty. Why don't you write a Western story? Paul would set it on the linotype. We could sell autographed copies at the fair."

"No one would buy a story run off on newsprint."

"I think they would. When you're famous like Sinclair Lewis or John Steinbeck, an item like that would be worth a lot of money."

"Dream on, Adelaide."

"I think it's a good idea. I'd buy one," Barker said.

"You don't have to buy one of my stories, Barker. I get a dozen extra magazines from the publisher."

"Come down to the paper and go through the archives. Find something to write about that took place right here in Rawlings. Remember the story Doc Herman told us about the wife who met the woman on the street who had been sleeping with her husband, knocked her down and landed in jail for assault? That would be a good subject."

"I'll think about it. If I do it, will you let me off the list of dancing girls?"

"No, but I'll take you off the auction committee."

"You are taking advantage of our friendship."

"I sure am, sweetie!" Adelaide patted Kathleen's cheek. "Gotta go. 'Bye, Barker."

Barker lingered by the door after Adelaide left. "Has anything changed between you and Johnny?"

"I don't know. Sometimes I think he loves me and at other times I don't."

"Lucas keeps asking about him. It would be good for Lucas to get to know his brother. He thinks it's because we're Cherokee that Johnny doesn't want anything to do with him."

"That isn't it. It has nothing to do with Lucas. Right now he has Isabel to worry about, and he isn't sure how he's going to make a living on the ranch. He has applied for a GI loan. I'm not sure if he plans to use the money to buy cattle or more land. He won't use the money from the allotment check the government sent me while he was gone."

"I'd offer to help, but it would be like throwing gasoline on a fire." Barker's usually stoic features took on a look of sadness. "Come out anytime, Kathleen. We don't want to lose you, too."

Barker drove away from Kathleen's thinking about the day he told Johnny that he was his father. He hadn't known what reaction to expect, but certainly not the hostility he had received. Over the years his son had become less hostile, but the resentment was still there. Barker knew better than to jeopardize their fragile relationship by offering financial assistance. Johnny had grown up to be an angry man with strong feelings about most things.

When Barker walked into the reception room at the clinic, Millie looked up and smiled.

"Hello, Mr. Fleming."

"Hello, Mrs. Criswell."

"You're the third member of your family to be here today. Did Lucas suffer a reaction from his shot?"

"No. He's fine. I'd like to see Dr. Perry if he has a spare minute."

"I'll call the nurse—"

"—No, this is business."

"I see. I'll go back and see if the doctor can slip away for a few minutes."

Barker looked around as he waited. He remembered another time, seven years ago, when he had come to the
clinic with Grant Gifford and two Federal Marshals to
question Dr. Herman. The atmosphere was much friendlier
now.

Millie returned. "It just so happens that the doctor is in
his office." She went to the connecting door and rapped before she opened it. "Mr. Fleming to see you."

"Ask him to come in."

After shaking hands, the two men assessed each other.
Grant Gifford had told Jude about Barker Fleming, rancher
and owner of the tannery, and about his being Johnny's
father. Jude remembered Johnny's being taunted by folks
down on Mud Creek because of his Indian blood. This dig-
nified, handsome man seemed to be a father any man
should be proud to acknowledge.

"What can I do for you, Mr. Fleming?"

"You've known Johnny for many years." It was a statement. Jude nodded, and Barker continued. "I've known
him for only seven," he said regretfully.

"We were fourteen when Johnny came to Red Rock, to
stay with Ed and Henry Ann Henry. He had a chip on his
shoulder a yard wide, but Ed Henry got around that by getting him interested in horses."

"I wish the man were here so that I could thank him."

"Johnny paid him back. After Ed died, Johnny worked
like a son of a gun helping Henry Ann hold on to the farm."

"How is funding for the clinic going?" Barker asked,
changing the subject abruptly.

"It's tight, but that's not unusual for a clinic in a town
this size. We're getting a little government surplus, which
is a great help, and the community is very supportive."

"My family has made a donation to the clinic each year for the past few. Absolutely anonymous, you understand."

Jude nodded. "It's appreciated."

"We are prepared to increase our donation this year, but with a string attached. I'll have our bank in Oklahoma City send a cashier's check so that the bank here will not know the donor."

"We would have no problem with that, if that's the condition."

"It is, and I'll explain."

Fifteen minutes later Jude walked to the door with Barker Fleming. "It was a pleasure to meet you, Mr. Fleming. You can be sure that your request will be carried out to the letter." He held out his hand.

"It was my pleasure," Barker said, shaking Jude's hand. "We would be honored to have you out to the ranch for dinner sometime soon." He smiled. "We're quite civilized. You'll not have to eat out of a communal bowl with your fingers as my ancestors did."

"I remember a time or two in Italy when I'd have been glad to eat out of a communal bowl." *And at home too, if my Pa had cared for me like you care for Johnny.* "I'll not forget the invitation."

"I'll have Marie or Mrs. Fisher give you a call. We appreciate your being here in Tillison County."

"And I'm glad to be here. Your donation will help us a great deal. All of us connected with the clinic thank you for it."

Jude sat at his desk for a few minutes after Barker left. A load had been lifted from his shoulders. Johnny Henry didn't know how lucky he was.

*　　*　　*

Johnny Henry worked the posthole digger as if he were trying to reach China before suppertime. Sweat dripped from
the end of his nose even though the temperature was only
70 degrees. He dug the holes faster than Pete could set the
posts.

"Slow down, dammit," Pete said gruffly. "Let's take a
breather."

"What's the matter, sailor-boy? Have you gone soft in
your old age?"

"You've been a hard dog to keep under the porch today
and about as pleasant as a bobcat with a belly full of cock-
leburs." Pete sat down with his back to the post he had just
set and pulled his cigarettes from his pocket. "What's eating you?"

"I'm anxious to get this done while I've got cheap help."

"I'll be around for a while. No need to work me to death
today."

"It never occurred to me that you'd have a hard time
keeping up with a youngster like me."

"She . . . it! We've set twenty posts. How many horses
do you have anyway?"

"Keith tells me thirty head. But I owe him every other
foal for taking care of them while I was gone. Hell, I might
have to sell the damn horses anyway." Johnny sank on the
ground and wiped his face with the sleeve of his shirt.
"Keith will buy them."

"I thought you planned to build a herd from that stock."

"I did, but things have changed. I'll have quite a bill at
the clinic, and then there's the burial. I'm thinking about
giving up ranching for the time being and getting a job."

"What kind of jobs are to be had around here?"

"It doesn't have to be here."

"Yeah? I thought it did."

"The government is starting a rural electrification program up around Duncan. Eventually it'll work its way down here. I can operate heavy equipment. You name it, and I've driven it."

"What about Kathleen?"

"What about her?" Johnny looked up, his eyes boring into those of his friend.

"You don't plan to try and work things out with her? If you do, you can't do it while you're up around Duncan."

"Why do you ask?"

Pete shrugged. "Curious, I guess. She's special, and I like her."

A wave of sickness rose into Johnny's throat. He fought it down. Had Pete fallen in love with Kathleen? If so, Pete went after what he wanted and . . . he had a way of getting it. Henry Ann was the only woman Johnny knew that Pete hadn't charmed.

Johnny got to his feet. "I'll dig a couple more holes, then we'll stop for the day."

"Are you going back into town tonight?"

"Haven't decided."

"Before I go to the clinic, I'm going to stop by Kathleen's and pick up the magazines. I betcha I've read some of her stories. We had a load of Western magazines on board ship. They were read and reread until there was nothing left of them."

Watching Johnny, Pete noted that the posthole digger paused for a second or two on its way to the ground. He grinned with satisfaction.

"Okay, slave driver," Pete said, getting slowly to his feet. "You've worked the holy hell out of me today. I'll set three more posts, and then I'm on my way."

"Suit yourself," Johnny growled.

"Why don't you come along. I'm going to ask Kathleen to come over to Jude's for supper. I told him that I'd cook up a batch of corn bread to go along with the navy beans I cooked last night." Pete chuckled to himself when he saw that Johnny was now wearing his Indian face. Not a flicker of expression was on it.

Pete continued to ramble on while he worked.

"I never had a decent piece of corn bread all the time I was in the navy. I asked the chief cook about it one time when we were sitting out from the Marshalls. He said that if I didn't like what he baked, I could throw it overboard for all he cared." Pete snorted. "That bread would've sunk a Jap sub if I'd a been lucky enough to hit it. Hell, I can make better corn bread with my eyes shut than those belly robbers that call themselves cooks."

He watched Johnny attack the hole he was digging as if he were digging for gold.

The darn fool is eating his heart out for her and is too damn stubborn to admit it.

Chapter Fourteen

Y̵OU STAYING AT JUDE'S or coming back out here?" Johnny asked as he finished pouring water into the wash dish and hung a towel over Pete's shoulder.

"Is that an invite?" Pete dipped his hands in the water and splashed his face.

"Yeah, I guess so."

"Are you going to the clinic in the morning?"

"I thought I'd go in about noon. Henry Ann's bus will be pulling in then."

"I'll help string the wire on those posts."

"It won't take more than a couple of hours." Johnny took off his shirt and headed to the bedroom to change his clothes.

"Henry Ann hasn't changed much," Pete remarked on the way to town.

"You still carrying a torch for her?" Johnny turned to look at him sharply.

"Yeah. I'll always have a soft spot in my heart for Henry Ann. She was the driving force that made me want to be more than Mud Creek trash."

"Don't be getting any ideas about Henry Ann."

Pete laughed. "Hell, if I did, she'd slap me down quicker than a goose shittin' apple seeds. Don't worry. I'm still more in awe of her than anything else. When I was young, she was my idea of a queen. I'd act the fool to get her attention. Couldn't stand it when she ignored me."

"She's more than a sister to me. She's—" Johnny stumbled for words, then became quiet as he remembered the hard times on the farm back in '32 when he and Henry Ann were trying to save their cotton crop and Isabel was doing everything she could to make their lives miserable.

They reached town and Pete turned down the street where Kathleen lived. He slowed when he noticed a woman hurrying along the sidewalk.

To Johnny he said, "It's Mrs. Cole. She's the nurse taking care of Isabel." He slowed the car, stuck his hand out, and waved.

Dale managed a slight wave of the hand, kept her eyes straight ahead, and hurried on.

"Know anything about her husband?" Pete asked.

"Only what Paul told me. The guy works for Oklahoma Gas and Electric, and he's a real horse's ass."

"Yeah? In what way?"

"According to Paul, he's not very well liked by the men who work there."

"I think he's mean to his wife. If I find out it's true, I'll catch him out some dark night and beat the shit out of him."

"Christ on a horse, Pete. You've not changed much after all."

"Nothing gets my dander up quicker than a man who beats up a woman or a kid. Far as I'm concerned, they're not fit for buzzard bait."

A pickup truck with a bedstead and a mattress was

parked at Kathleen's house when they reached it. When Johnny snorted on seeing it, Pete glanced very quickly at him, frowned slightly, and looked away, then back again, as if puzzled.

"You don't approve of your wife's company?"

"It's none of my business who she keeps company with." Johnny opened the door and stepped out of the car.

"I'm glad to hear that. I was afraid you'd poke me in the nose if I asked her out on a date."

Johnny, rounding the car, paused. "Don't try to add Kathleen's name to your string of women, Pete."

"String of women? Hell, son, I ain't got no string. I ain't got even one woman."

Pete followed Johnny up onto the porch. The door was open. Johnny could hear Kathleen laughing. He opened the screen door and banged it shut to get her attention. She came through the living room from the kitchen, Barker behind her.

"Johnny, Pete, come in. Barker brought in a bed for me to use while Henry Ann is here. Pete, have you met Barker? Barker Fleming, Pete Perry. Pete is Dr. Perry's brother." Kathleen made the introductions, then stepped back. After the first glance at Johnny, she didn't look at him again.

The men shook hands, then Barker said, "How'er you coming with your corral, Johnny?"

"Good. Pete's given me a couple days' work."

"If you need help driving the horses up from McCabe's, let me know. Lucas and I will lend a hand."

"That's on hold for a while." Johnny looked directly at Kathleen. "Need help setting up that bed?"

"Sure. Barker hasn't brought it in yet. We were moving things around to make room for it."

The men went to the pickup. Pete and Johnny carried

in the springs, Barker the foot- and headboards. Kathleen held open the door. Pete winked at her as he passed. It was more of a conspiratorial wink than a flirtatious one. She smiled.

Barker went back to the truck and brought in the bed rails and the slats while Johnny and Pete set up the bed. Kathleen watched. Pete was one of the most cheerful men she had ever met. His eyes flirted, his smile was continuous. He laughed at himself when Johnny told him that he was putting the side rails on upside down. There was a suggestion that, though he was probably slow to anger, he would make a very dangerous enemy when roused. Kathleen was sure that there was enough strength in his big, well-knit body to support that notion.

When the telephone rang, she hurried to answer it.

"Kathleen, this is Marie. Is Daddy there?"

"He's here. I'll get him. Barker, it's for you."

Kathleen stood in the doorway of the small bedroom while Barker spoke with his daughter.

"I didn't think about you having to get another bed when I asked if Henry Ann could stay with you." Johnny spoke as he tightened the nut on a bolt with the pliers Barker had left on the floor.

"I was talking to Marie on the phone and mentioned that your sister was coming. It was her idea to send over the bed."

Barker finished his conversation and hung up the phone. "I have to go. One of the men has been hurt, and they need the truck to take him to the clinic."

"Not serious, I hope."

"Marie thinks it is, but then she's quite upset. We won't know until the doctor takes a look. The mattress is all that's left in the truck. I'll get it."

"I'll get it." Johnny was already out the door.

"Thanks, Barker," Kathleen called.

"Johnny's daddy, huh?" Pete said from behind her.

"Yes. Johnny has had a hard time accepting him."

"Why? Because he's an Indian?"

"Not that. He feels that he was just a seed sown in the wind, so to speak."

"That's nothing new. My pa had kids scattered all up and down Mud Creek as his pa had done before him."

"Did that make you think less of him?"

"I didn't think of it at the time. It seemed normal for Mud Creek."

"But did you . . . like him?"

"I respected his fists until I got to be as big as he was and learned to fight back. He treated me all right after that." He pinched her chin with his thumb and forefinger. "I'd better go help big, bad John with the mattress."

"He isn't bad," Kathleen protested, and got a grin from Pete.

After the bed was set up, Johnny went to take a look at the water heater.

"I'll come by with some tools and fix the pilot," he said when he returned.

"How about the Western magazines you were going to lend me?" Pete asked. He had noticed that Johnny and Kathleen avoided looking directly at each other. Something had changed since last night.

"I keep three copies of each," Kathleen said, as she placed a stack of magazines on the kitchen table. "Take what you want, but I would like them back."

"K. K. Doyle," Pete said admiringly and smiled his charming smile. "Did you really write these stories? If the boys had known that K. K. Doyle was a beautiful redhead, they would've been writin' for your picture."

"Not true, but it's nice of you to say so." Kathleen's face reddened. She glanced at Johnny.

"I've not read this one." He was gazing intently at the cover of *Western Story Magazine* that displayed her nom de plume in large print.

"That one takes place in the Texas panhandle and is one of the longest stories I've written. I just couldn't seem to end it. I try to move my stories around to different locations. The one I'm working on now is set in Montana."

Kathleen stood beside the table, terribly conscious that Johnny was standing beside her. She could feel the warmth from his body and smell the lotion he had put on his face after shaving.

He's sorry that we made love. He must feel that it was my fault for clinging to him like a cheap floozy. And, I guess it was. I wanted him to love me.

Suddenly she was aware that she was terribly afraid and didn't know why. It was something to do with Johnny. Everything was something to do with Johnny nowadays. When her eyes flicked to him, he was thumbing through the magazine, apparently oblivious to everything except what he was reading. *Look at him read! How did he learn to do that?*

"Get your bonnet and come have supper with us. I'm cookin' tonight." Pete's cheery voice sliced into her thoughts.

"You're cooking? Where?"

"At Jude's. I'll make you the best corn bread you've ever eaten to go along with the navy beans I cooked last night."

"Thank you, but I don't think so."

"Don't think, sugar. Just come. You'll not be sorry."

"I don't know your brother that well."

"You know me, and you sure as hell know Johnny. Come now, grab a coat."

"I can't go anywhere looking like this."

"You look damn good to me."

Kathleen glanced at Johnny and found him looking at her with indescribable sadness in his dark eyes. She took a hesitant step toward him before she could stop herself.

"Johnny?"

"You'll like Jude when you get to know him."

"I'm . . . sure I will."

"We'd better get going. We'll need to stop at the clinic and see about Isabel." Pete picked up several magazines. "I'll take good care of these."

"If someone is needed to sit with her at night, I'll take a turn."

"No," Johnny said quickly and emphatically. "I don't want you anywhere near Isabel."

"He's right," Pete said quickly when he saw the hurt look on Kathleen's face. "If you were my girl, I'd not want you near her either. I doubt that you've met anyone like Isabel."

"That's silly! I've heard bad language—"

"Are you coming to Jude's for supper?" Johnny asked, cutting off the argument.

"Will I be intruding on your time with your friends?" she asked boldly, looking directly at him.

"What gave you that idea?"

"Why do you always answer my questions with a question. It's terribly irritating."

Johnny shrugged, apparently unconcerned that he had angered her.

Kathleen ignored him. She headed for the bedroom,

then turned, "I'd love to have dinner with you, Pete. Be back in a minute."

She sat between the two men in the front seat of the car. This time Pete was driving and it was Johnny's arm that was flung along the top of the seat behind her. His hand had rested on her shoulder briefly, then was quickly removed.

Down the street from Kathleen's a porch light was on and a small boy sat on the steps. Pete slowed the car.

"Is that where Mrs. Cole lives?"

"I think so."

"Do you know her?" Pete asked.

"I've met her a couple of times. She seems to be very nice."

"She's one of the nurses who takes care of Isabel."

Nothing more was said until Pete stopped the car behind Barker's truck parked at the clinic.

"Goin' in, sugar?" Pete asked Kathleen because Johnny had already opened the door.

"Might as well. I'll wait in the reception room."

Johnny waited on the sidewalk and, to Kathleen's surprise, took her elbow. She thought she heard him mumble something that could have been "sugar"?

My gosh! Is he jealous of Pete? Oh, Lord. I hope so. That would prove that he still loves me!

Marie was the only person in the room when they opened the door. She jumped to her feet, went straight to Johnny, and wrapped her arms around his waist before he could even get his hat off. Her face was streaked with tears.

"Oh, Johnny. It's all my fault."

"What's your fault?" he asked gently and, with his hands on her shoulders, held her away from him.

Of all the Flemings, this little half sister had been the

one who crept past his resistance and wiggled her way into his heart. She had written to him faithfully all the time he was overseas, sent him cartoons, newspaper clippings, and funny stories.

"He was on that darned old stallion Daddy bought the other day and . . . and I went out as he was getting him into the pen, the wind blew my skirt, and . . . the horse went wild. He threw Bobby against the fence—"

"—Who?"

"Bobby Harper. His leg is broken, and his face—it's all cut up. He's not been home very long. Daddy gave him a job—"

"A broken leg is something that can be fixed. Dry up, now. Who's back there with him?"

"Daddy and Mr. Boone."

"The foreman?"

"No, his son. Mr. Boone isn't well, and Mack has been doing most of the work. Kathleen, I didn't even speak to you—"

Kathleen was pleased and surprised at how concerned and gentle Johnny was with Marie.

"Don't worry about that. Marie, this is Dr. Perry's brother, Pete. Marie is Johnny's sister," she explained to Pete, without looking at Johnny.

"Hello, I'm sorry for being such a crybaby. Johnny"— Marie was still holding on to him—"go back and see if he's all right. They told me to stay here."

"Stay with Kathleen. I'll see what I can find out." Johnny gently pushed Marie down into a chair and placed his hat on the seat beside her.

Pete followed Johnny down the hall. "Guess I didn't think of you having sisters on your daddy's side. That one is pretty as a picture."

"And way too young for you."

Pete took Johnny's arm and stopped him. "Let's get one thing straight, Bud. I can think a woman is pretty without wanting to hop in bed with her."

"I remember when she didn't even have to be pretty."

"You're not going to let go of that, are you? I admit that I was plenty mouthy when I was going over *fool's hill*, but I didn't do all that I bragged about doing. If I'd had a little sister like Marie, I'd have knocked every man on his ear that looked at her cross-eyed."

"I didn't notice you looking at her cross-eyed or I would've." Johnny grinned and hit Pete on the shoulder. "Let's see what we can find out for her."

Sitting on a couple of chairs at the end of the hall were Barker and Mack Boone. Johnny had never liked Mack. Before the war he had been a hard-drinking, reckless cowboy who had wanted to make it big in the rodeo circuit but had fallen short. Johnny had made it a habit to steer clear of him.

Barker got to his feet as they approached. Mack slouched in the chair, stretched out his legs, and crossed his booted feet.

"How's Harper? Marie's worried about him."

"We don't know yet. The doctor and nurse are with him." Mack got to his feet. "I'll go stay with Marie."

Johnny moved slightly and stood in front of him. "No need. Kathleen is with her."

Mack's expression hardened into anger. It irked him that Johnny Henry stood so close he had to look up at him. He lifted his shoulders, stared at Johnny for a few seconds, and sat down. He was smart enough not to make a fuss in front of the boss.

Everyone in town knew that Johnny was Barker's

bastard. The mystery was why Johnny didn't move into the big house and live high on the hog. That was what Mack was going to do as soon as he married Marie. It was too damn bad Bob Harper hadn't broken his neck instead of a leg. It was what Mack had wished for when he hit that stallion in the rear with his slingshot. It served Bob right for getting cozy with Marie.

Mack was not an ugly man, nor was he handsome. His eyes were too small and deep-set, his brows too heavy. He wore his hair long and combed back in a ducktail, a style he copied from the zoot-suiters he saw while he was stationed in California. He considered himself to be quite attractive to the ladies.

Miss Pauley, the night nurse, came out of Isabel's room. Pete and Johnny went to intercept her.

"How is Miss Henry?" Johnny asked.

"How do you think she is?" Miss Pauley said bluntly. "With all that's wrong with her, I'm surprised that she's still alive."

"Is she going to die tonight?" Johnny asked irritably.

"How do I know? Talk to Dr. Perry."

"Thank you," Johnny said with exaggerated patience and, to her back as she hurried down the hall, "You're a big help."

"She's a sour mouth, but Jude said she's a crackerjack nurse. I bet you a dollar to a doughnut that Isabel has been giving her a bad time." Pete went to the door of Isabel's room and listened, then came back to Johnny. "She's not yelling, so she must be sleeping."

Nurse Frank came out of the surgery and propped open the door.

"The leg has been set, but we'll need help getting him

off the table and onto a gurney so we can move him to a room. The doctor wants to keep him overnight."

Mack got to his feet, but Pete moved smoothly ahead of him and into the room.

"I'll give you a hand. I've done this many times on board ship."

Nurse Frank motioned to Johnny. "It's hard for the doctor to lift because of his leg," she whispered when he came near to her. He followed Pete into the room.

In spite of the cuts on his face and a bandage on his forehead Johnny recognized the man on the table. He had been just a kid from a neighboring ranch when Johnny went to war.

"Hi, Bob."

"Johnny. Haven't seen ya since ya come back." He spoke out of the side of his mouth because of the stitches on his cheek.

"See you had a bout with a barbed-wire fence."

"He's lucky he didn't lose an eye," Jude said, washing his hands at a sink.

The nurse had pulled the gurney up alongside the bed. "If you two will get on the other side of the bed, slip both arms beneath and lift him while I pull on the sheet, we can slide him onto the gurney."

"The plaster isn't dry, so we'll have to be careful." Jude went to the end of the table to lift the foot of the plaster-encased leg. "After we get you into the room, we'll give you something so you can sleep."

"Before you do that would it be all right if Marie come in to see him?" Johnny asked. "She feels bad because she spooked the horse."

"It wasn't her fault," Bobby protested quickly. "I just

wasn't anchored in the saddle. And . . . it's what I get for showin' off."

His face paled, but he didn't let out a sound as he was shifted from the table to the gurney and then to a bed. He lay in a white undershirt stamped US AIR FORCE. A sheet covered all but his broken leg which Jude had placed in a troughlike contraption so that he couldn't move it. The nurse returned with a hypodermic syringe and needle.

"It takes about fifteen minutes for this to take effect," she explained.

"I'll get Marie," Johnny said.

As he went out the door, he passed a scowling Mack Boone, who had stayed in the hall when Barker went into the room.

Marie had calmed when Johnny reached the reception room. Both she and Kathleen got to their feet when he entered.

"He's all right. He'll stay overnight so the plaster on the cast can harden. You can go see him."

"Oh, Johnny, thank you." Impulsively she hugged him, the top of her head a couple of inches beneath his chin. "Where do I go?"

"Go on down the hall. The door is open, and they know that you're coming."

Chapter Fifteen

KATHLEEN THOUGHT that Johnny would go with Marie, but he lingered and finally sat down.

"Did you find out anything about Isabel?"

"Couldn't get anything out of the nurse. I'll have to ask Jude."

Silence settled down in the reception room so that the closing of a door in the back of the clinic sounded aggressively loud in the stillness.

"Marie was telling me about Bobby Harper," Kathleen said when she could stand the silence no longer. "She said that he was a gunner in the air force. He came home about the same time you did."

"He was just a kid when I left."

"Evidently he was old enough for the service. Marie said he enlisted when he got out of high school."

"Are they keeping company?"

"She didn't say. Why? Don't you approve of him?"

"I don't know him and, besides, it isn't any of my business who she keeps company with."

"Oh, Johnny," Kathleen said wearily. "You try so hard to distance yourself from anyone who cares about you."

Before he could reply, Barker and Mack Boone came in, followed by Pete and Marie.

"Daddy, I told Bobby we'd come back for him tomorrow, but I don't know how he can ride in a car with that leg in a cast."

"We'll think of something. Right now I've got to go tell his folks what happened."

"I completely forgot about that. Mrs. Harper should have been told right away."

"Take the truck back, Mack."

"I can take Marie with me, Mr. Fleming."

"Marie will go with me," Barker said, dismissing him. "And thanks for your help."

Mack left. Johnny knew that he was seething. His face was as easy to read as a road map.

"I've talked Theresa into coming and having supper with us," Pete announced. "How about it, Marie? Come have supper with us. We're all going over to Jude's. Johnny and I will take you home before we go back to the ranch."

Johnny looked at Pete and, for once, surprise showed in his expression. No one seemed to notice but Kathleen. Her heart beat high in her throat as she waited for Johnny's reaction.

"Oh, I don't know—" Marie fumbled for words, her dark expressive eyes traveling between her father and Johnny.

"You'll be well chaperoned by big brother here," Pete urged. "What'a ya say?"

Barker waited for his daughter's decision.

"All right. I'd like to go, if it's all right with you, Daddy."

"Johnny?" Barker looked at his tall son.

"I'll see her home," Johnny said, his mouth very grimly set. Again, none of the others seemed to notice.

*   *   *

Dr. Jude Perry's house was one of the finest houses in town. Built back in the prosperous 1920s, its rooms were large, its woodwork gleaming oak. Although the furnishings were the original and some of them needed to be replaced, the gas stove and refrigerator were new. Swinging doors, propped back, separated the kitchen from a formal dining room that would seat twelve.

The house, lacking personal possessions such as pictures, books, or other mementos, seemed cold to Kathleen. She wondered if the doctor noticed. Perhaps this was just a place to eat and sleep after he left the clinic.

Pete took over the cooking chore and made two large pans of corn bread. Kathleen found a head of cabbage in the refrigerator and chopped it with carrots and onions to make coleslaw. Theresa and Marie set the table.

Jude was tired, and his leg ached. That was evident in the lines in his face and in the way he absently rubbed his thigh. Theresa insisted that he sit and visit with Johnny. She had been disappointed to learn that Marie Fleming had been invited. Theresa felt heavy and awkward beside her. But to her surprise, the small dark-haired girl was not just a beauty; she was also nice.

As the evening progressed, Johnny loosened up a bit. He had asked Jude about Isabel and was told that her condition continually worsened and that the only thing they could do for her was to keep her as comfortable as possible.

"The Nuremberg military trials start tomorrow," Jude said after a moment of silence. "We'll probably hear only the verdicts."

"Paul, down at the *Gazette*, was telling me that before long transoceanic radios will be as common as a regular radio, and we'll hear everything that goes on all over the world."

"I'm probably like the ostrich with its head in the sand, but I don't want to hear the gory details of the trial. I've seen what the Nazis were capable of doing."

After that, Johnny and Jude talked about old times and both carefully avoided any mention of their experiences during the war.

"I'm eager to see Henry Ann," Jude said. "I'll never forget the two of you coming down to Mud Creek with blood in your eye because you suspected Hardy of rustling your cattle."

Johnny laughed. "We had more guts than sense. I don't know what I'd have done if your pa had grabbed me out of that car and wiped the ground with me."

"He wouldn't have done that. Hardy was scared of what Pete would do. Pete didn't want you to know it at the time, but the folks on Mud Creek knew that you and Henry Ann were off-limits and not to be bothered."

Johnny chuckled. "Not by anyone but him, huh?"

"All right you two," Kathleen said. "Get yourselves to the table."

Kathleen found the evening one of the most pleasant she had spent in a long time. They ate the corn bread and teased Pete that it wasn't fit for hogs and that the only thing good enough to eat was the coleslaw. He took the ribbing with his usual good humor. When the meal was over, the girls cleared the table and washed up the dishes.

"Now I know why they asked us to come for supper," Kathleen said as she hung up the dish towel she took from Theresa.

"I'll have to be going soon and get my little boy. I called Mrs. Ramsey, and she said that she'd give him his supper.

He plays hard and is usually asleep by the time I get him undressed."

"How old is he?"

"He's four and big for his age."

"I'd like to see him sometime," Kathleen said wistfully. *Mary Rose would have been almost five if she had lived.*

"He's a handful at this age. I measured him when he was two years old. If it is true that he will be twice that height when he is grown, he's going to be six feet tall. Imagine me looking way up there at my little boy." Theresa's smile was beautiful.

"Aren't you through in here yet?" Pete demanded from the doorway. "You're holding up the rest of the program."

"And what is that?"

"Come on. You'll see."

The furniture had been pushed back, and from the radio came the signature tune of President Truman, "The Missouri Waltz."

"I should be going," Theresa protested.

"Not until I've danced with each of you beautiful ladies." Pete grabbed Kathleen's hand. "That's old Harry's favorite song." He swung her around the floor. Their laughter mingled with the music. "Jude, you and Johnny grab a girl. This one's mine for this dance and the next."

Theresa's heart jumped out of rhythm and her breath caught as Jude got to his feet and held his hand out to *her.* She had been sure that he would prefer to dance with young and pretty Marie.

"Nurse Frank, would you honor me with this dance?"

"I'd be delighted, Doctor. But I must warn you, it has been years and years since I danced."

"Then it is time you did."

He pulled her to him and they moved slowly. It would

have been all right with Theresa if they had not moved at all. When he lowered his head and pressed his cheek to hers, she closed her eyes, and her heart settled down into slow heavy thuds.

The music ended. She leaned back and whispered. "Your leg."

"What leg?" he said, and pulled her tighter against him as the music started up again and a female vocalist began to sing, "I'll never smile again, until I smile at you—"

"Do you want to try it, Marie?" Johnny asked when he saw her effort to fade into the background. "Come on. I'll try not to break your toes."

Marie was so small that her head barely reached Johnny's shoulder. He held her lightly and tried to keep his mind on the steps and not on Pete and Kathleen, who were talking and laughing as if they were having the time of their lives. He was sure that Pete was not interested in an affair with Marie, but he wasn't sure about Kathleen or Jude's Nurse Frank.

When the dance ended, Pete reached for Marie and Jude held out his hand out to Kathleen.

"It's the luck of the draw," Johnny said as he put his arm around Theresa and they began to move to the music. "I've never been much of a dancer."

"I've not done it a lot myself, so we'll be well matched. I'll try not to step on your toes if you promise not to step on mine."

"Lady, I can't promise a thing." He smiled down at her. She was a soft, sweet woman and pretty even in that white uniform, white stockings, and heavy shoes.

The dance ended. Kathleen stepped back from Jude, not sure if Johnny would want to dance with her. On the radio the announcer was saying that this was the last number of the evening and to tune in next week for another hour of dance music. She felt a hand on her arm as Jude reached out for Marie.

Johnny pulled her into his arms. She went willingly and leaned against him. It was so good to be held by him. His arms encircling her pulled her so close that her breasts were crushed against his chest. They fit perfectly against each other. She could feel the warmth of his body through her dress, and the wild beating of her heart against his. Was his breath coming faster than usual or was it just wishful thinking on her part?

"Good night, sweetheart, till we meet tomorrow. Good night, sweetheart, sleep will vanish sorrow—"

Johnny pressed his cheek tightly to hers. Kathleen felt as if she was in another world. She closed her eyes and wished the song would never end.

But it did, and he pulled away from her.

"It's late. I don't like the idea of Theresa going to pick up Ryan by herself," Jude was saying.

"Doctor! I do it all the time." Theresa was putting on her coat.

"Not at eleven o'clock at night. I'd go with you, but I shouldn't leave the telephone."

"Don't worry, little brother." Pete picked up his coat and handed Johnny his. "We'll follow Theresa and make sure she gets home."

"You don't need to do that," Theresa protested.

"Yes, he does," Jude insisted. "See you in the morning." Then he said to everyone in general, "This has been great. Come again, all of you."

"How about Thanksgiving?" Pete said. "I'll cook a turkey."

"I couldn't leave the family." Marie's dark eyes went from Johnny to Kathleen.

"Do you have plans, Theresa?" Jude asked.

"Why no. I'd love to come, but only if I can bring part of the dinner."

"That can be decided later. You and Johnny can come, can't you, Kathleen?" Jude stood at the door, waiting for his guests to put on their coats.

"I can, but I can't speak for Johnny." Kathleen was sure that her face was fiery red.

"He'll be here," Pete said confidently. "Wave a drumstick under that boy's nose, and he'll jump fences and wade across raging rivers to get to it."

Kathleen sat in the backseat of Pete's car with Marie as they followed Theresa's small car to Mrs. Ramsey's house. This was where she had boarded when she arrived in Rawlings seven years ago. Johnny had come to the newspaper office and had shown her the way. She wondered if he remembered.

Without a word, Johnny got out of the car and went to the house with Theresa. Soon they emerged, with Johnny carrying the sleeping child. Mrs. Ramsey waved from the doorway. Kathleen wanted to cry. He had never held their child in his arms.

If he married Theresa, he would have a son without having to sire one and risk the deformity he feared. In the back of her aching mind she doubted that she was strong enough to endure the pain. If that should happen, she would never be able to go far enough from this place to forget him. Her heart would be broken.

He didn't come back to the car. He sat in Theresa's car, holding the child, and she drove to her house. Pete followed. Johnny carried the boy inside and came out immediately. He got into the car, turned to her, and said, "Mrs. Ramsey said to tell you hello and to thank you for lending Emily the books."

"It was nothing," Kathleen murmured.

"You'll have to show me the way to the Fleming ranch," Pete said.

Johnny got out again to walk Marie to the door. Johnny thought he smelled cigarette smoke as if someone nearby was smoking.

"This was so much fun. Thank you for telling Daddy you'd bring me home. Johnny . . . if you don't go to the doctor's house for Thanksgiving, will you come here? We were going to ask you and Kathleen."

"I'll have to go to Jude's. My sister, Henry Ann, may still be here, and that would be the logical place for us to go."

"I understand. You'll want to be with her as much as you can. Just don't forget that we want you, too."

"I won't forget."

Marie opened the door and slipped inside. Johnny stood for a second or two. He could feel that someone was near. It was the same sort of feeling he'd had while he was in the jungles of the Pacific. Usually the person had been a native, but a few times it had been a Jap who wanted to surrender but was afraid to show himself for fear of being shot, or a Jap spying on the camp. Johnny's eyes searched the darkness, seeing nothing. He went quickly back to the car.

Mack Boone stood flat against the wall of the house. He hadn't been able to hear what was said, but he knew that it was Johnny Henry with Marie. The old man's bastard was playing his cards close to his chest. The son of a bitch was planning to come out here and take over. Well, he, Mack Boone, was going to do his level best to see that it never happened. He had a few cards up his sleeve that he could play.

Kathleen went through the house one last time to make sure everything was in order before she left for town to pick up Henry Ann. She had seen Johnny's sister just a few times, the last before Mary Rose was born, but she felt that she had known her forever.

Kathleen had had a restless night and had risen early to sit at her kitchen table, drink tea, and think about the night before. Johnny had walked her to the door, held the screen while she put the key in the lock, then said good night and backed off the porch as if to get away from her as soon as possible.

He's afraid that he's made me pregnant, she thought now. He needn't worry. The chance of it happening that one time was one in a hundred, and she had never won anything in her life. One thing was sure. He was going to see to it that he didn't tempt fate again. He had made that clear by his actions.

She went to her car, thankful that the bad tire still had air in it. She would go to Eddie's and see if he could put on another tire or patch the one she had.

From the rise above, Theodore Nuding watched Kathleen leave the house. Last night while she was at the doctor's house, he had taken his tire pump to her house and filled the tire as full of air as he dared because it would lose some before morning. Then, knowing that she was safe, he had gone back to work on her room.

He put down his binoculars, pulled his diary out from under the seat of the car, and began to write.

10:20 A.M. *She is leaving the house. I believe that she is going to have company because the Indian brought a bed last night. It could be a relative coming to see that slutty woman who is in the clinic. I heard from the cleaning people that she was dying. Good riddance, I say. She was a whore who was taking up space and breathing good air that could be used by someone decent.*

The room is coming along, Mother. I wish I knew someone I could trust to help me. This small town isn't like the city. I have to be very careful and not draw attention to myself. The banker, John Wrenn, is the only weak link. He's ignorant, nosy, and likes to talk. If one word about me is leaked, it will be curtains for him.

Mother, I miss you. But soon I'll have Kathleen, and my life will be full of joy again.

Nuding read over what he had written, then quickly shoved the diary under the seat as a car approached, slowed, and stopped. It was Sheriff Carroll. Nuding grabbed his *props*, got out of the car, and stretched.

"Morning, Sheriff."

"Morning. How's it goin'?"

Nuding laughed. "Boring. Tornado season is about over. Another month will wind up my work here unless the bureau calls me in early." He shifted an instrument gauge and a chart clipped to a board to his other hand.

"We don't get much cold weather here until January. Out in the panhandle a northerner blows in once in a while."

"It's getting easier to predict them. Gives a fellow a little time to prepare."

"Where did you say you were from?"

"Louisiana."

"I was thinking you were from Texas. I don't know

where I got that idea." Sheriff Carroll scratched his gray head.

"I may have said that. I guess I thought you meant where did I come from before I came here."

"Well, no matter. Hear that you're out at the old Clifton place."

"Yeah. A friend of my boss bought it. I'm staying there until a crew shows up to work on it."

"Kind of spooky, isn't it?"

Nuding laughed. "I haven't seen a ghost yet."

"I hope your luck holds. They say old lady Clifton is hovering around out there. I'd better get on down the road." The sheriff started his car.

"Thanks for stopping, Sheriff. It can get pretty boring sitting out here."

"See ya." The sheriff put his fingers to the brim of his hat in a gesture of farewell. A cloud of dust followed the car as he drove away.

"And I'll see *you*, if you get too nosy," Nuding muttered on his way back to his car.

At the filling station, Eddie found a pinhole leak in Kathleen's tire, patched it, and put the tire back on the car. He also replaced the valve, which he thought could be another source of the leak.

"Johnny told me to let him know as soon as I got a shipment of new tires and to hold one for him."

"This old car isn't worth a lot. I don't want to put much money in it. By this time next year, new ones will be coming out, and I may be able to get a good used one."

"Used cars will be pretty well worn-out after being used all during the war."

"I'll just have to take a chance. I won't be able to afford a new one."

When she left the station, Kathleen stopped at the grocery store and bought a few things, then parked in front of the *Gazette*. She went into the office to wait for the bus that would be bringing Henry Ann.

Chapter Sixteen

Henry Ann Dolan was a strikingly pretty woman with rich brown hair, heavy brows, and soft brown eyes. But it was her smile, revealing an inner beauty, that drew people to her. Not quite so slender as she had been thirteen years ago when she met and married Tom Dolan, Henry Ann had thickened slightly at the waist, and her breasts had rounded after three children. Still, she looked younger than her thirty-seven years.

Kathleen introduced her to Adelaide and Paul before bringing her home where they would wait for Johnny. She carried Henry Ann's suitcase to the small back room she had made as pleasant as possible on such short notice. Then she headed for the kitchen.

"The towels in the bathroom with the crocheted edges are yours. I'll fix us some tea while you get settled in," Kathleen called. "Would you rather have iced or hot?"

"Iced, if you don't mind."

Kathleen was a little nervous, aware that Henry Ann was curious as to why she was living here instead of out at the ranch with Johnny. Evidently Johnny hadn't told her about the separation.

"Oh, dear. I miss Tom and the kids already. This is the

first time I've been away from them for any length of time."
Henry Ann came in and sat down at the kitchen table.

"I bet they miss you, too." Kathleen dropped the
chipped ice into the glasses and filled them from a pitcher
of tea.

"I'm eager to see Johnny. He has called several times,
but I've not seen him since he came home."

"He looks the same, just thinner and, of course, a little
older. When he first got here, his hair was short, and he
was brown as a berry. His hair has grown out now, and he
looks more like his old self."

"I've not seen Isabel since she was fourteen. My, but she
was a handful. I had no choice but to send her to the or-
phanage in the city. I'm sure she hates me for it."

"She had been out at the ranch for more than a week
before I knew she was there. According to Johnny, Pete
talked her into going to the clinic. She didn't want to be
treated by Dr. Perry, but Pete promised to take her to a
honky-tonk if the doctor gave his permission. Of course,
he knew that wasn't going to happen."

"Have you seen Isabel?"

"I've never met her. Johnny didn't seem to want me to."

Henry Ann's expression showed her concern.
"Kathleen, don't think I'm being nosy, but . . . there seems
to be something wrong between you and Johnny."

Kathleen looked away for a moment, trying to blink the
tears from her eyes before she answered.

"It depends on the viewpoint, I guess. Johnny thinks it
right to be separated from me, and I think it's wrong."

"You love him?"

"I love him . . . and will always love him."

"He loved you when you first married. I've never seen

him so happy. When he gave his heart, I was sure it was for keeps."

"We had two and a half wonderful years. Then he joined the Seabees, and I never heard one word from him while he was gone that four and a half years."

"I can't believe that . . . of him."

Kathleen said quickly, "Please don't mention to him that I said that."

"I won't if you don't want me to. Do you want to tell me what happened?"

"I don't know if I should. You're his sister. He loves you more than anyone in the world." Kathleen picked up the hem of her skirt and dried her eyes.

"Along with you—"

"No. No, I don't think he loves me. Sometimes I'm sure of that. I feel kind of disloyal talking about him to you."

"Then don't. I know he was hurt when you lost your little girl."

"Did he tell you that?"

"Of course. He called and cried like a baby."

"He . . . did?" The puzzled expression on Kathleen's face led Henry Ann to say, "Why are you surprised?"

"He never held Mary Rose. He never looked at her after . . . the first time."

"What . . . are you saying?" Henry sat back with a look of utter disbelief on her face. "Johnny has always loved kids. I looked after Tom's son Jay for a while before Tom and I married, and Johnny was so good with him. I thought at the time that he'd be a wonderful father."

"He was happy when I got pregnant, but after the baby came he changed overnight."

"I'm disappointed in him," Henry Ann said sadly.

"Oh, don't be!" Kathleen spoke in anguish. "He has his reasons, and they are real to him."

"They would have to be pretty darn good reasons."

"I'll have to tell you the rest so you'll understand. Mary Rose was not a pretty baby to look at, but she was my baby." Silent tears crept from her eyes and trickled unheeded down her cheeks. "She . . . had no skull on the top . . . of her little head and . . . her eyes protruded. She lived two days. She had no chance. No chance at all."

"Oh, Kathleen, I'm sorry." Henry Ann clasped both Kathleen's hands. "I'm so sorry."

"Johnny thinks it's his fault. He said the curse was passed down to him because of . . . incest in his family. He swore that he'd never have another child. He left me right after we buried Mary Rose and told me to get a man with better bloodlines if I wanted a family."

"That's not so. The curse of incest, I mean. Dorene was my mother, too. My children are perfect. It has always been rumored that Dorene's father seduced his daughter, and she gave birth to Dorene. I don't know how true it is. The people who lived on Mud Creek were a strange clan."

"Johnny said that his sister Isabel had always been a little . . . odd. He only remarked about it one time. After that he'd walk away when I brought up the subject."

"For goodness sake, look at what Jude has accomplished. He's a Perry. My children are as smart as whips. What happened to your child was one of those unusual things that happen. I'll have to talk to him."

"Please don't, Henry Ann. He will be angry with me. He was so glad you were coming. I don't want anything to spoil it."

"Maybe he'll give me an opening—"

Kathleen jumped to her feet and disappeared into the

back room. "They're here," she called. "I've got to wash my face. Go open the door, Henry Ann."

Henry Ann was waiting in the open doorway when Johnny came bounding up onto the porch, a smile lighting his face.

"Hen Ann," he exclaimed, using her pet name. He grabbed her the second he came through the doorway and hugged her tightly to him. "Lord, I'm glad to see you. Hell's bells, it's been a long time."

"Aunt Dozie would wash your mouth out with soap for swearing, young man." She leaned back to look at him with tear-filled eyes. "Oh, Johnny, I was so afraid for you when you were . . . over there. I prayed every night."

"It must have done some good, sis. I came back all in one piece."

She kissed his cheek again and again. "You rascal. Golly, how I love you."

"How about me, Hen Ann? Don't I get a welcome?" Pete asked from behind Johnny.

"I've seen you since you came home. And yes, you're a rascal too. Always have been." Henry Ann smiled at him. "As a matter of fact, you were a pain in the behind . . . for years!"

"Yeah, I was. But wait till you see Jude. That little pup is smart as all get out. He's a doctor. A real doctor. Can you believe it?"

"Why are you surprised that he's smart? He was smart enough to figure out who killed Emmajean Dolan and get you out of jail." Johnny was still holding on to Henry Ann as if he feared she would disappear.

"Yeah, I owed him for that, and what did I do? I went right out and joined the navy and left him to cope with our old man who was about as worthless as teats on a boar."

"It does us no good to look back. We all did the best that we could during those hard times. I thank God every day that both of you came back from the war."

"Even me, Henry Ann?" Pete asked.

"Of course, you. I was on to your game, Pete Perry. You wanted everyone to think that you were Red Rock's bad boy." Henry Ann reached up and kissed Pete on the cheek. "Don't tell my husband that I did that."

Johnny turned to see Kathleen standing in the doorway leading to the bedroom. She was wearing a green dress with a wide black belt cinched about her small waist. Her hair was its usual unruly mass of bright red curls, but she looked pale to him.

Kathleen had stayed in the background while Johnny met his sister. Now she came out into the room.

"I have sandwiches ready if you would like to eat before you go to the clinic."

"Sounds good to me." Pete sailed his hat into a chair and followed Kathleen to the kitchen. "Tell me how I can help."

"Wash your hands first, then chip ice for the tea."

"Bossy women," he grumbled. "Always tellin' a fellow to wash."

"That'll teach you to ask," Kathleen retorted.

"I'll remember that."

"This isn't much," Kathleen said as she set a plate of ham and egg salad sandwiches on the table, "but it will hold you for a while."

"Did Jude call?" Johnny asked as he sat down.

"Was he planning to?"

"Only if . . . we were needed."

"He didn't call."

"I told him that you'd be here before noon, Henry Ann,

and that we'd come over there about one o'clock. They'll hold off putting her to sleep in case you want to talk to her."

"Oh, my. What can I say after all these years?"

"Henry Ann." Pete had genuine concern on his face. "If Isabel's awake, she's going to be . . . mean-mouthed. She's always been naturally mouthy, and now Jude thinks the syphilis or the cancer has gone to her brain. She has nothing good to say to anyone."

"Don't worry. I know she is sick, and I'll not take to heart anything she says. Even if she is . . . mean, she should have her family with her at a time like this. Johnny and I are all the family she has . . . that we know of."

The sandwiches disappeared from the plate so fast that Kathleen wished that she had made more than three each for the men and one each for herself and Henry Ann.

Henry Ann asked Kathleen to go with them to the clinic; but she refused, saying she would stay and work on her book although she knew that her mind was in such a turmoil that not a word would reach the page.

Johnny did not look directly at her during the meal. His eyes seemed to pass right over her. He did speak to her as he followed Henry Ann out the door when they left to go to the clinic.

"Thanks for the dinner and for picking up Henry Ann."

"You're welcome." Kathleen made sure that there were no tears in her voice. She wanted him to leave before she broke down and bawled. Talking to his sister about their child had stirred up all the misery again.

As soon as the car headed down the street, Kathleen went wearily to the bedroom, lay on the bed, and let the tears flow.

*   *   *

"Hey, beautiful doll, is Jude busy?" Pete asked in his cheery voice when they walked into the reception room.

Millie rolled her eyes to the ceiling. "The *doctor* is in his office, Mr. Perry."

"Mr. Perry? You were callin' me darlin' and sweetheart last night."

"You better be satisfied with Mr. Perry, *darlin'*. 'Cause I know a few other names I could call you."

Pete turned to Henry Ann. "She means it," he said with a mock frown.

Millie smiled at Henry Ann. "Go on in. Doctor knows you're out here." She tilted her head toward Pete and raised an eyebrow. "They probably know it down on Main Street."

Henry Ann moved to the doorway and gazed at the handsome man who rose from the desk and came to meet her. He was tall, slender, and confident. Her mind flashed back to recall the skinny kid from Mud Creek who had been so determined to get an education. He met her in the middle of the office, and Henry Ann wrapped her arms around him.

"Dr. Perry. I'm so proud."

"Hello, Henry Ann."

She hugged him for a long moment, then stepped back to look at him, then at Pete and Johnny. Pete was beaming with pride. Johnny was smiling, too.

"Oh, you boys! I was sure none of you would amount to a hill of beans. Now look—you've turned out just fine."

"You turned out pretty good yourself," Jude said. "You were always the prettiest girl in Red Rock with a bunch of suitors, too."

"Ah, come on," Henry Ann scoffed. "It wasn't me they were after. It was the farm. Enough about me. How is Isabel?"

Jude's smile faded. "Not good, I'm afraid."

"Johnny said there's nothing you can do for her."

"We could have treated the syphilis. The cancer has spread beyond treatment. We're giving her morphine."

"How long?"

Jude shook his head. "I believe that her heart will fail before the cancer gets her. The end could come today, tomorrow, or a week from now. I've not had a lot of experience with cancer, but my nurse, Mrs. Frank, worked in the cancer ward at St. Anthony Hospital in Oklahoma City. She believes, and I concur, that if Isabel lives another week, it will be a miracle."

"Poor, poor thing. Maybe if I had kept her with me, she would have had a different kind of life."

"The world is full of *what if's*, sis. You can't blame yourself for how Isabel chose to live." Johnny's face was grim.

"Can we see her?"

"Sure. Anytime."

"Oh, before I go see her, I want to give you this." Henry Ann opened her purse and pulled out some bills. "Tom and I know that being in the hospital is expensive. We want you to have this, and we will send more from time to time."

"Sis! No!" Johnny reached across and took hold of the hand holding the money. "I've already told Jude that I'll pay for Isabel's care—"

"Hold on, both of you," Jude said sternly. "Isabel Henry is an adult. Neither of you is responsible for her. This clinic has a built-in fund through anonymous donations to take care of patients who can't afford to pay. We either use that fund or we lose it. Isabel's care here will be paid for out of that fund. Put your money back in your purse, Henry Ann."

"No, Jude." Johnny shook his head. "That's charity. I'm

not proud of it, but Isabel is my sister, and I'll pay, in time, for her care."

"Then you'll have to take her out of the clinic and find another place for her because I've already submitted her name as a patient qualified for the anonymous fund."

Johnny looked thunderstruck.

"You've got too much pride for your own good, Johnny," Jude said kindly. "Are you going to throw the generous donations back in the faces of the folks who gave them?"

Johnny didn't answer immediately, then insisted, "It goes against the grain to take charity."

"Then think about it the next time you offer to help someone or give someone a small part of something that you have plenty of."

"But, dammit, Jude—"

"Dammit, Johnny. I may be calling on you in the spring. I've plans to make some changes around here. I'll need all the donated help I can get."

"You'd have had it anyway," Johnny growled.

"I know that. Henry Ann, I'll take you down to see Isabel. Come on, Johnny. Pete won't be far behind. He never misses a chance to flirt with my nurses." Jude glanced over his shoulder at his brother and grinned.

At the door of Isabel's room, Jude said, "Wait just a minute." He opened the door a crack and looked in. Mrs. Cole was giving Isabel a drink of water. When she finished, he went in, motioning for the others to follow.

"Hello, Isabel," Jude said.

"Hello, Isabel," she mimicked. Her voice was raspy and weak, but still full of venom. "What'er you wanting? Cause I'm flat on my back . . . ya thinkin' to crawl on an' screw me? Cost ya two dollars for one time, three dollars for two . . . if you can go two times." She snickered.

Jude ignored what she said to him. "There's someone here to see you."

"A man?" She tried to look beyond him. "Has he come to take me dancin'?"

"Pete and Johnny are here, but someone else is, too." Jude stepped aside, and Henry Ann moved up beside the bed.

"Hello, Isabel."

Henry Ann would not have recognized the sunken-cheeked, bony, hard-faced woman who lay on the bed. Her hair was so thin you could see her scalp, and it stuck out from her head like straw. Her eyes seemed to be slightly out of focus. She said nothing at first, just stared.

"God's pecker and all that's holy!" she swore. "If it ain't Miss Tight-ass Henry Ann come all the way from that piss-poor farm to gloat over my bones."

"I just found out the other day that you were sick, Isabel."

"Hell, I ain't sick. Ain't sick," she tried to yell, but it came out as a weak squawk. "Jesus, I hate your damn guts for sayin' I'm sick. I . . . ain't . . . no . . . way . . . sick! You ugly bitch."

"You're my sister, Isabel. I'd like to stay and visit with you."

"Shit a mile in broad daylight! I suppose that big-peckered, blanket-ass Johnny come, too. Damn turd-eater kept me locked up. Wouldn't let me go nowhere. Wanted to keep me there naked for him to use—"

"Isabel, that's enough!" Pete was beside the bed. "Dammit, shut up tellin' those nasty lies."

"Honey, wanta fuck me? Climb on. I ain't goin' to

charge ya. And I don't care if prissy-tail watches." She chuckled. The sound was dry and scratchy.

Pete looked across the bed at Dale Cole. Her face had turned a rosy red. She glanced at him and then away.

"Henry Ann, don't stay and listen to this," he whispered. "She's not been this bad before."

"I understand that she's out of her head."

"I'm not so sure. She knew who you were."

"Son of a bitch," Isabel muttered in a dry whisper. "Goddamn son of a bitchin' whore. Bastard would screw a knothole if he had nothin' else. Pussy-grabbin' asshole—" Her eyes were completely unfocused.

"The poor miserable thing. I'll sit with her for a while. You and Johnny go on out."

Jude moved up to the bed, holding a hypodermic needle close to his side. Mrs. Cole held back the sheet and he sank the needle into Isabel's buttock. She didn't seem to be aware of it. When he removed it, Mrs. Cole quickly put a pad and a tape over the puncture and covered her with the sheet.

Johnny had already backed out the door of the room. He felt sick to his stomach, to his soul. Jude came out and put a hand on his shoulder.

"How do you stand it, Jude?"

"This is a bad one. On the other side of the fence, when you make people well and they walk out of here, it makes it all worthwhile. A boy in Italy was like this in the end. The things he said were so foul they would turn your stomach. He had been a gentle, quiet boy planning to go to a theological school before he was drafted into the army."

"It's bad blood, is what it is."

"There's no such thing as bad blood that causes behavior problems. I could exchange your blood with a killer on death row, and if his blood was free of disease, you'd still be the same kind of man you were. Sometimes family traits are passed along, but it's all a matter of chance. Look at me and Pete. We're not alike yet we had the same father. You and Henry Ann are not like Isabel even though you had the same mother."

"Bad genes can skip a generation. I've read a bit about it. If I thought that I'd be like her, or had a child that would be like her, I'd shoot myself."

"Sometimes the books you read don't give a complete picture. If you're interested in the subject, I can give you a good medical book to read."

"Henry Ann is one of the best people I know and Isabel is one of the worst. It's strange, isn't it?"

"It is, but I've seen many strange things during the short time I've been a doctor."

"Doctor," Theresa called from down the hallway.

Jude started to go, then turned back to Johnny. "I hope you will come for Thanksgiving. Henry Ann, too, if she's still here. Kathleen has already said that she's coming."

"Henry Ann won't want to be away from Tom and the kids on Thanksgiving."

"Then I'll expect *you*." Jude smiled and walked to where Theresa waited for him.

Johnny went to the reception room to wait for Henry Ann. Jude had made him reconsider some of his ideas. He had some thinking to do.

Chapter Seventeen

Henry Ann sat quietly beside the bed watching Isabel's ravaged face. The vile words that had come out of her mouth had shocked her. She had never heard such vulgarity. It was doubly embarrassing to listen to in the presence of the others. She kept telling herself that no woman would speak like that if she were fully in charge of her reasoning.

Yet Isabel had looked at her with pure hatred in her eyes. She had *reasoned* enough to know that she hated her. So sad. She had wasted her life hating. The poor creature would never know the love of a good man or the love of children. All that could be done was to pity and forgive her.

Henry Ann was conscious that Pete was still in the room. The nurse moved around picking up soiled linens and stuffing them in a pillowcase. She came to stand by Henry Ann and look down at Isabel. She smoothed the stiff dry hair back from her patient's forehead, a gesture Isabel would have sneered at had she been awake.

"The poor thing will have a few hours of peace now," Dale said softly.

"I'll sit beside her for a while."

"Stay as long as you like. Can I get you something? Water, tea, or coffee?"

"No, thank you."

"I've some other things to tend to. I'll be back in a little while."

When Dale Cole left the room, Pete was close behind her.

"Dale, wait a minute."

"Yes? Did you want something?"

"Just to talk to you for a minute. How are you doing?"

"Fine. Why are you interested in how I'm doing?"

"Because I can't get you out of my mind. I keep seeing those big sad eyes and the fingerprints on your throat."

She looked at him doubtfully and he saw a faint hint of color rise on her cheeks.

"Don't add to my problems. Please."

"That's the last thing I want to do. I passed by your house last night and saw a little boy sitting on your step. Yours?"

"Yes." Dale drew in a deep breath. "He . . . he saw you wave at me."

"Your little boy?"

"No. My husband. Please don't do it again." Large brown eyes pleaded with him.

Pete was stunned. Then his face hardened into a scowl.

"Did he hurt you?" The words came out in a husky whisper.

"No. But he . . . thought that . . . we—"

"Christ on a horse! Is the man insane? Can't a man wave at you without him thinking you're having an affair?"

"He thinks that . . . a man wouldn't pay attention to me . . . unless he thought I wanted him to take me to bed. He says no man would pass up an invitation like that . . . even from me." The words were hard for Dale to say.

"Dale!" Pete's fingers closed on her arm. "That's not

true. I'd be honored to have you for a friend, and that's all I intended . . . at first."

"At first?"

"Until I got to know you, saw the bruises on you. Oh, hell! Now I want to take that bastard out and stomp his guts out."

"Don't interfere in my life. I know what I am—"

"—Dammit, don't say it."

"For a short while I thought that I could work here at the clinic, use what I had learned in nursing school, maybe someday pass the exam and get my nursing license. It's not going to happen. He told me to give the doctor two weeks' notice."

"He's forcing you to quit?"

"He thinks I should be home with Danny."

"Why don't you stand up to him? Tell him that you'll not quit. You're needed here."

"You don't understand. Why don't you tend to your own business?" Tears of frustration filled Dale's eyes. "Now get away from me. I've got work to do."

"Wait," Pete said quickly when she started to dart into the laundry room. "If you ever need help, call me at Jude's house. I'll be there until I get a place of my own."

"You're staying around here?"

"I'm going to buy some land, start a horse ranch, and raise rodeo horses."

"Good luck," she whispered through trembling lips.

Pete stood in the quiet of the clinic hallway as the door swung gently after Dale passed through it. He didn't understand himself. He just knew that it hurt like hell to think of her being misused by the coward she was married to. The bastard was smart. He had kept her down by eroding her confidence. Pete dug his hands deeply into the pockets of his pants and went to find Johnny.

The reception room was empty when Pete reached it. He continued on out the door and saw Johnny leaning on the car, looking out over a broad expanse of prairie. Pete lit a cigarette and inhaled deeply.

"Come out to smoke?"

"Yeah. Henry Ann took it pretty good," Johnny said, when Pete leaned against the car beside him.

"Isabel was really out of her mind today. That's the worst she's been."

"While she was out at the ranch, she tried to tell me about men she'd been with, and I wouldn't listen. I'd just walk out. It appears to be all that's on her mind."

"She was a little slut at fourteen. I never touched her. I don't know whether Hardy did."

"It must be some bad strain that Dorene passed on to her."

"I never believed in this 'passing on' thing. If it was true, Jude and I would be down on Mud Creek with a dozen kids apiece."

"Some say that people are the products of their environment."

"That's not necessarily true either. I've known strong, brave men, whose folks were pure trash, and the other way around. I knew a preacher once . . . a real nice man, for a preacher." Pete grinned. "He had three sons: one was a preacher, one a teacher, and the other a killer who was executed over at McCalister. Figure that out."

"Did you ever know your mother?" Johnny asked after he lit another cigarette.

"No, she died when I was three or four. Hardy's ma took care of me until I was old enough to take care of myself."

"Was your mother a kin of Hardy's?"

"Hell, I don't know. Could have been a cousin. Dorene was the only sister he had. I think they had the same mother. Everybody on Mud Creek was related one way or the other."

"Blood can be so watered down by years of inbreeding that all that's produced are runts and freaks. I've seen it in cattle and horses."

"That's not the case with me. I'm certainly no runt. Hell, boy, you're not either. Jude may have got my share of brains, but seems like you got your share and so did Henry Ann."

"Years ago I was told that Dorene and Hardy are the kids of a father and daughter. Is that true?"

"I don't know that either. You probably heard that from Fat Perry's ma. That old woman could spin the wildest yarns you ever heard."

"It doesn't worry you that it might be true?"

"I've not given it any thought."

"What about your offspring?" Johnny persisted. "Do you plan on having children someday?"

"I'd like to think that I will. I've seen too many men grow old without anyone to care whether they lived or died."

"I'll never take a chance on bringing something in the world that people would call a freak."

A car drove up and stopped behind them. A man in a black suit and a brown-felt hat tilted forward got out. He passed Pete and Johnny without a glance and went up the walk and into the clinic.

"And good day to you, too," Pete said. "If he's a salesman, I hope Jude don't buy from him."

"He's Harry Cole. His wife was the nurse in the room with Isabel. I've seen him a couple of times."

"So that's him. Dale asked me not to wave at her anymore. He saw me do it and immediately thought we were having an affair."

Johnny grinned. "You work pretty fast."

"Yeah. It's one of my best qualities. I think I'll see what kinda car he drives."

Pete fingered the knife in his pocket as he sauntered around to the other side of Harry Cole's car. He came slowly around the back of it and up the sidewalk to where Johnny stood leaning against a front fender of his own car.

"Nice car," Pete remarked. "The only thing wrong with it is a flat tire on the back left side."

"Like I said, you work pretty fast."

"Mud Creek survival training," Pete explained without cracking a smile. "Shall we go in and sit for a while? Henry Ann will be wanting to go before long."

Harry Cole carefully took off his hat so as not to muss his hair when he went into the clinic. Millie looked up from her typewriter.

"I want to see Dr. Perry." He gave the woman a haughty stare. "Not as a patient, but on a personal matter."

"I'll see if he's free."

Millie did not like Harry Cole, had not liked him since the day he came to Rawlings. She liked him less since she had come to know Dale and to suspect that he abused her physically as well as mentally. The poor woman put on what Millie called her "happy-happy" act to cover her misery.

Millie knocked softly on the office door, then opened it and went inside, closing it behind her. The doctor was seated. Theresa stood beside him. Both heads were bent over a chart that lay on the desk. Millie waited until he looked up. Then she spoke softly.

"You've got a visitor. Harry Cole. He wants to talk to you about a personal matter."

"Uh-oh," Theresa said.

"Exactly." This came from Millie. "Want me to throw him out?"

"No. We'd better see what he has to say. What do you know about him? I've thrown out a few feelers and learned a few things."

"He's a snob. He likes to hobnob with the rich and powerful," Millie said with a sniff. "He loves to feel important and have people think he's a high muckety-muck. And, one more thing—he'd like nothing better than to be mayor or county supervisor."

"How about one of the trustees here at the clinic?" Jude asked.

"That, too." Millie nodded.

"I'm falling in love with you, Millie." Jude smiled.

Millie fluffed her hair. "You and your brother will just have to fight over me. I'll send Mr. Big Shot in."

"I'll leave," Theresa said. "Good luck."

"You're my luck, Theresa." His smile was so beautiful that she wanted to cry.

"And you are mine, Dr. Jude." The words were out before she realized it. She hurried out the side door. "Oh, my gosh! Why in the world did I say that?"

Jude stared at the door. He hadn't time to analyze Theresa's reply because the other door opened, and Harry Cole came in. Jude got to his feet and held out his hand.

"Mr. Cole, this is a coincidence. Mr. Wrenn from the bank was speaking about you yesterday. Please sit down."

Harry sat down and placed his hat on his knee. "Was John saying that I had overdrawn on my account?" he asked in a manner that said he knew that was not the case. His eyes glittered with interest.

Jude laughed. "Nothing like that. We were discussing men we considered highly qualified for county offices. Your name was at the top of the list. I hope you'll keep this conversation confidential. I don't want the others to think I'm spiking their guns, so to speak."

"You can count on it. Mum's the word." Harry leaned back in his chair and crossed his legs.

"Frankly, I kicked up a fuss because soon there will be an opening here at the clinic for a trustee. There are not too many men around who have had supervisory experience."

"I've had that all right. Supervising men is not the easiest job in the world."

"That's what I was telling John and the mayor. John thought you'd make a good mayor. It's something you could do and still keep your present job. Claude isn't sure he can handle the job for another term. Government surpluses will be pouring in next year. He said that we need someone with experience to direct them to the right place."

"It's gratifying to know that Claude has that much confidence in me."

"I'm sorry, Mr. Cole—"

"Harry. Please call me Harry."

"I'm sorry, Harry, I didn't mean to monopolize this meeting. What was it that you wanted to see me about?"

"Well, Doctor—"

"Call me Jude." Jude leaned forward as if he were eager to hear what the man had to say.

"I stopped by to tell you that my wife can help out here

as long as you need her. We had discussed her quitting and staying home, giving her time for the fancy needlework and flower arranging she enjoys."

"I've noticed the bouquets she's brought to the clinic. She has a knack with flowers."

"We're not in need of the money she earns here. I spoke to her about volunteering her services—"

"—That's most generous of you, Harry," Jude exclaimed. "But I can't build a schedule around volunteers. I need to know when my helpers will be here and how long they will say."

"That's something I hadn't thought of, Jude." Harry nodded his head as he spoke. "I can see where that would be a problem for you."

"In the city we had volunteers who came in once in a while from the church groups. They have to be closely supervised. We thought we'd struck a gold mine when we came here and discovered Mrs. Cole. I was told that she was a great help to the doctor who came down two days a week after Dr. Simpson passed on."

Harry smiled. "Yes, she is very capable and very well organized. We've been married for six years and—"

"—I imagine that you had something to do with that."

Harry laughed. "I wasn't going to say so."

"You didn't have to, Harry."

When Dale glanced out the window and saw Harry's car parked in front of the clinic behind Pete Perry's car, fear kept her frozen for the length of a dozen heartbeats. Oh, Lord! What would she do if he raised a fuss? She went to the hall and stood for a moment, and the thought of fleeing came to mind. It was immediately discarded. Harry had come to tell Dr. Perry that she could not work here. He had warned her that that was what he would do if she didn't give notice.

If it wasn't for Danny, I would walk out the back door of the clinic and keep walking across the prairie until I dropped. I can't leave my son to be raised by that man!

Dale went to peer through the small window that allowed the nurses to view the reception area. She could see the back of Millie's gray head. Pete Perry and Johnny Henry were talking quietly in the corner. The rest of the chairs were empty.

Then she heard laughter coming from the doctor's office. *Harry was laughing!* What was he up to now?

"Ohhh . . ." She jumped when she felt a hand on her shoulder, and turned quickly to see Blanche, the clinic cook, standing behind her.

"Didn't mean to scare ya. I called but guess ya didn't hear. The lady back there with Miss Henry is calling ya. She sounds scared."

"Thank you, Blanche. I guess I was daydreaming."

Dale hurried down the hall. The door to Miss Henry's room was open. Her sister was standing beside the raised bed.

"Something . . . is happening—"

Dale looked down at her patient and saw that the corner of Isabel's mouth had drawn down. She lifted a lid and observed that Isabel's eyes had rolled back in her head.

"She's having a stroke. I'll get the doctor."

Dale ran out of the room and down the hall. She threw open the door to the office.

"Come quick, Doctor. Miss Henry is having a stroke."

She hurried back down the hallway without even acknowledging Harry. Jude was behind her when she returned to Isabel's room. Henry Ann moved away from the bedside to make room for the doctor and nurse.

Dale pulled back the sheet and Jude listened to Isabel's heart through the stethoscope in his ears. He spoke to Henry Ann while still listening.

"Her heart is failing. It won't be long. If Johnny is here, he may want to come in."

"He's still here, Doctor. Shall I get him?"

Jude nodded, and Dale hurried from the room.

"She's dying," Henry Ann said sadly.

Jude nodded again and turned back to his patient.

Henry Ann was glad when Johnny and Pete entered behind the nurse. She moved over close to Johnny. He put his arm around her. The room was so terribly quiet. The rasping gasps for breath that had caused Henry Ann to call out had almost ceased.

Pete stood behind Henry Ann, his hand on her shoulder. He watched Dale, calm and efficient. Damn, but she was a fine woman.

Jude took the stethoscope from his ears. "There's nothing I can do. The stroke brought on a heart attack." He moved to the end of the bed to give Henry Ann and Johnny an unobstructed view of their dying sister.

Henry Ann stood with her head bowed, trying not to remember how uncaring Isabel had been the night her father died.

"Ain't my daddy," Isabel had said when asked to turn down the radio.

Now Isabel was dying. Henry Ann cared, not because she was her half sister, but because she was a human being.

Five long minutes passed. Then Jude moved back to the bed and placed the end of the stethoscope on Isabel's chest. When he lifted it, he pulled the sheet up over her face.

"She's gone."

"Do you think that it was my being here that got her so worked up that she had the stroke?" Henry Ann asked.

"No, I don't think that. Her blood pressure was terribly high, and I couldn't get it down to a safe level. Her kidneys were failing, and water was forming in pockets all over her body. That and the cancer that had spread led to the stroke that caused heart failure."

"I'm glad that I came today. Something told me that I should."

"I'm glad you're here. Isabel had her family with her in the end, even if she had rejected them."

Johnny had not uttered a word since he came into the room. He stood with his back to the wall and ran his fingers through his dark straight hair. He had seen enough death to last a lifetime but was never prepared to see life leave a human body.

"Will you call the funeral home, Jude?" Johnny's voice was low with respect for his dead sister. "We'll take Henry Ann back to Kathleen's. Then I'll go make arrangements."

"Sure. If there's anything I can do, let me know."

"Oh, look. That poor man has a flat tire," Henry Ann said on the way to the car.

"Yeah," Pete said. "Seems so."

Harry Cole had driven his car past Pete's before he realized the back tire was flat. Driving on the rim had ruined the tire. Harry had removed his coat, jacked up the car, and was struggling to put on the spare.

"Hey, mister," he called as Pete rounded the front of the car to get in on the driver's side. "Do you have a tire pump?"

"Nope." Pete kept walking, got in the car, and started the motor.

Henry Ann looked questioningly at Pete. "I can't believe you don't have a pump."

He grinned at her, tromped on the gas, and darted around the man squatted beside the car, his wheels stirring up a dust cloud.

"This car's got a lot of pickup," he said as if pleasantly surprised. "It's hard for me to hold it down at times."

As soon as Dale was free, she hurried to the window to see if Harry's car was still there. He had moved it and was fixing a flat tire. How did that happen? He hated getting dirty. He would never do physical work if there was any way to get out of it.

She went to the reception area. "Millie? What's going on?" she asked fearfully.

"I don't know what happened in the office, honey, but I've got reason to think that Doc fixed things. Mr. Big . . . ah . . . well, he came out all smiles and even spoke to me. He said to tell you that he had some business to attend to and that he might be a few minutes late getting home for supper. He didn't want you to worry."

"He said *that*? Millie, are you sure?"

"Honey, I'm sure. Butter would not have melted in his mouth. He and Doc were laughing like old friends."

"I wonder what happened."

"If I find out, I'll tell you. I've got a feeling that things are going to work out. Doc knows how to get around folks."

"I hope you're right."

Chapter Eighteen

W HERE IS YOUR PRIDE?" Kathleen muttered against the cold, wet cloth she held over her face. "He does not want you. Can't you get that through your stupid head?"

She removed the cloth and looked at herself closely in the mirror above the lavatory. Her eyes were swollen from crying and her face was blotchy. She stared into the sky-blue eyes looking back at her. Other women had survived disappointments in the men they loved, and so would she. There really wasn't such a thing as a broken heart—badly bruised maybe, but not broken. Kathleen felt stubbornness rising in her, a will to do what she pleased, to get out from under the depression that had held her down since Mary Rose was born.

She was luckier than most women; she had a career in writing that she could pursue. *I am master of my own fate. I will stop moping around and get on with my life. I may even find a man who really loves me.*

With those thoughts in mind, she changed into a dress with a soft full skirt, put on her hose and high-heeled shoes, and fixed her face, using a little more makeup than usual. She put on her good black coat and picked up her car keys.

"Where am I going?" she asked herself.

Kathleen stood on the porch and looked around. The back of her neck began to tickle. She had an eerie feeling that someone was near, but she didn't see anyone. She shrugged. She'd had the feeling before, and it had gone away.

She drove slowly down the street. *Double Indemnity* with Barbara Stanwyck and Fred MacMurray was showing at the Rialto Theatre. After Henry Ann's visit was over, she decided, she would go see every movie that was shown. She loved movies and had no one to please but herself.

Kathleen came to a decision suddenly. She drove around the block and angle-parked in front of the redbrick building that housed the law firm of Alan Fairbanks and Son. She had to take the first step. It was what Johnny wanted her to do.

The time had come to break the tie, but Father in Heaven, it was hard to do. She forced herself to put one foot in front of the other until she reached the office and was standing in front of the woman at the desk.

"Is Mr. Fairbanks in?"

"Yes, he is. Your name is—"

"Kathleen Henry."

"Just a moment."

"Send her in, Janet," a male voice boomed from the back office.

The woman lifted her brows and shrugged, then sat back down. Kathleen walked around the partition and into the office behind it. The portly man behind the desk stood and held out his hand.

"Well, well, well. I haven't seen you since you came back."

"Nice to see you, Mr. Fairbanks," Kathleen said, shaking his hand. Seven years ago, he had been supportive of the effort she, Adelaide, and Paul had made to rid the town of Dr. Herman and his influence.

"Sit down, Kathleen. You're lookin' pretty. Doesn't seem like the years have changed you much."

"Oh, but they have. The war years have changed all of us."

"I was glad that Johnny came home all right. So many of our boys here in Tillison County didn't come home, and some of them who did are crippled for life." He shook his head. "War is a sorry business."

"It is that, Mr. Fairbanks. But we were forced into it."

"You're right, my dear. Now what brings you to my office?"

Now was the time. Could she do it?

"Mr. Fairbanks, I . . . don't know if you are aware of it, but Johnny and I have been separated for quite a while."

"Of course, you have. How long was he over there?"

"Four and a half years. I . . . ah . . . don't mean that kind of separation." She rushed on before she lost her nerve. "Before he left, Johnny told me to get a divorce."

The lawyer leaned back in his chair and twisted the pencil he held between his fingers. He pursed his lips before he spoke.

"Did you?" he asked.

"No. I thought he might change his mind when he came back."

"He is the one wanting the divorce? Not you?"

"I guess I want it, too. I don't want to be married to someone who doesn't . . . want me." Kathleen swallowed the lump in her throat and lifted her chin.

"Does he have another woman?"

"No. I don't think he's been seeing anyone else."

"How about you?"

"No, of course not. I worked at an aircraft plant in Oklahoma City while he was gone. When the plant closed, I came back here. I still have an interest in the *Gazette*."

"Humm . . . What grounds do you plan to use to get the divorce? You can't claim that he deserted you when he went to war."

"I'd never claim that. Why do there have to be grounds?"

"That's the way it works. The judge would ask you why you want a divorce. You have to give a reason. Has he refused to support you? Has he threatened you with bodily harm? Has he refused to live with you as husband and wife?"

"No to the first two and yes to the last one."

"That could be the one we could use. In that case, we can go for alimony—"

"No. I don't want anything from him." Kathleen stood. "I've got to think about this."

"Good idea. Do you want me to talk to Johnny?"

"It wouldn't do any good. He's made up his mind."

"But you haven't made up yours."

"Yes, I have, Mr. Fairbanks. I don't have a choice."

"Think about it for a day or two. We'll come up with grounds of some kind."

"Thank you."

She was at the door when he said, "You don't have any children, do you, Kathleen?"

"No," she said, over her shoulder because she was afraid that she was going to cry. "No children."

She got into the car and drove away as if she really had someplace to go. She stopped in front of the library, turned off the motor, and stared at the steering wheel. Minutes passed while her thoughts tumbled one on top of the other. What should she do? She didn't want people to know that Johnny refused to sleep with her— that's what living as *man and wife* meant, didn't it?

She had no idea how long she sat there when a tapping on the window drew her attention. A man with a stupid looking billed cap and big glasses was looking at her. He wore a gray, foreign-looking mustache. She rolled down the window.

"Do ye be all right, miss?" he asked.

"Oh, yes, I'm fine. I was just thinking."

"'Tis sure ye be deep in thought. Is it trouble ye be havin'?"

"No. I'm a writer and I was thinking about the plot of my story. Thank you for your concern. I'm going now." Kathleen quickly rolled up the window and started the car.

The prickly feeling was at the back of her neck again. She wanted to turn and see if someone was hiding in the backseat of the car. She watched the man walk leisurely down the street and around the corner. His accent was Irish or Scottish. She was sure that she'd never seen him before. She wouldn't do this again. It was obvious even to a stranger that she was troubled.

Kathleen reached her house and was surprised to see Pete's car parked in front. When she entered, Pete and Henry Ann were sitting on the couch in the living room.

"Hey, sugar, you're all dressed up." Pete stood and helped her off with her coat.

"Not really. How is Isabel?"

"She's gone," Henry Ann said. "I was with her for only a couple of hours when she passed away."

"Oh, I'm sorry."

"Johnny and Pete are going to make the arrangements."

Johnny came from the kitchen with a glass of ice water and handed it to Henry Ann. *He was making himself at home in her kitchen.* If he looked at her she never knew it because she kept her eyes turned away from him.

"You sure do look pretty, sugar," Pete was saying. "How come you're all dressed up?"

"I had some business to take care of."

"When we get back, let's all go down to the Golden Pheasant for supper."

"Thank you, but count me out. I'll have a sandwich and work for a while. Now if you'll excuse me, I'll get out of these high heels."

Kathleen closed the bedroom door, leaned against it, and closed her eyes. *I will not mope around like a puppy with its tail between its legs any longer!* Her eyes popped open and she jerked open a bureau drawer and pulled out a pair of faded, baggy slacks. They were blue with white dots. Ugly. The top was equally ugly—white with blue dots, some of which had bled onto the white. After washing her face, she examined herself closely in the mirror, then pulled the hair on the top of her head back and secured it with one of her precious, prewar, rubber bands.

She stared at the stranger looking back at her from the mirror over the lavatory. She stood there trembling, accepting that sooner or later she would tell Johnny that she had been to see Mr. Fairbanks.

"Lord, help me," she muttered, and looked away from the pale face and vacant eyes.

Just as she was getting ready to leave the bedroom, she heard the front door open, then close. She looked out the window to see Johnny and Pete going out to Pete's car. She sighed with relief and went into the living room, where

Henry Ann was reading the latest *Rawlings Gazette*. She looked up.

"This is a much better paper than the one we have in Red Rock."

"Paul Leahy, Adelaide's husband, is responsible. He worked for a big paper in Texas before he came here. The *Gazette* is one of the best small-town papers in the state."

Henry Ann folded the newspaper and placed it on the table beside the chair.

"I feel kind of guilty leaving the funeral arrangements to Pete and Johnny."

"I'm sure they don't mind."

"We decided to have a graveside service tomorrow afternoon. Isabel didn't know anyone here except Jude and Pete, Johnny and me."

"A few of Johnny's friends will be there out of respect for him."

"He doesn't expect anyone."

Kathleen shrugged. "People in small towns are very good about things like going to funerals."

"I was so shocked when I saw her. Oh, my. She looked so old and was so . . . hard."

"Barker Fleming, Johnny's father, tracked her down in Oklahoma City seven years ago. She was working in the toughest part of the city. She told him that Johnny had a ranch near Rawlings. That's how he found him. Barker told me, back then, that Isabel was quite ah . . . shameless."

"Jude said the sickness had damaged her brain. I hope that was the reason for the filth that spewed from her mouth." Henry Ann was quiet for a while, then said, "I'll go home the day after tomorrow. I miss Tom."

"I was hoping you would stay longer."

"I have to go back before Thanksgiving. I couldn't be away from home at that time."

"That's understandable. When I was going to school in Des Moines, I traveled through a snowstorm to get home for Thanksgiving. I couldn't stand the thought of not being with my grandparents."

"Our daughter will be in the school play next Tuesday. I made Tom promise to help her with her lines."

"I envy you. Husband and children. It's what I always wanted." Kathleen immediately regretted saying the words, but once said words cannot be taken back.

"They are my life. I hoped for the same for Johnny. He is as dear to me as my children."

"We all want different things from life. Can I get you some more tea?"

"No, thanks." Henry Ann sighed and leaned back on the couch. "I feel like I've been through a wringer."

The phone rang, and Kathleen excused herself to answer it. It was Marie.

"Kathleen, we heard that Johnny's sister died."

"Yes, he's making funeral arrangements now. The plans are for it to be tomorrow afternoon at the gravesite."

"Daddy wants to know if there is anything we can do."

"I wouldn't know, Marie, but I'll pass the message along to Johnny when he gets back."

"Tell Johnny that we'll be there."

"I will, Marie. 'Bye." Kathleen hung up the phone. "That was Marie Fleming, Johnny's half sister. You'll meet her and Johnny's father tomorrow. They will be at the funeral."

"It's nice of them to come."

"They are nice people."

When Pete returned, he was alone. "After we finished up at the funeral parlor, I took Johnny out to the ranch to do chores. He'll be back in to take you to supper, Henry Ann."

"I forgot to mention to him that Isabel would need a burial dress."

"It's taken care of. Mr. Klein asked about it. We went to the dry goods store, bought a gown and a lacy bed-jacket thing to go over it." Then to Kathleen, "How about going out tonight and cuttin' a rug, sugar?"

"I don't think so." Kathleen laughed in spite of her dark mood. "But thanks for the invitation."

"Come with Johnny and me, Kathleen." Henry Ann's face showed concern.

"No, but thanks. You and Johnny should have some time alone together. Tonight is the night I like to listen to the Andrews Sisters and the Riders of the Purple Sage. They're on that *Eight-to-the-Bar* show."

"Jay is a Bob Wills fan," Henry Ann said with a smile. "He likes Eldon Shamblin, the guitar player." Jay was Tom's son from a former marriage. He was four years old when his father married Henry Ann and would graduate from high school this year. Henry Ann was intensely proud of him.

"I'm losing my charm. I struck out all around," Pete said. "I wonder what Millie is doing tonight."

Pete left after a while, and Henry Ann went to freshen up before going out with Johnny. Kathleen sat on the couch and allowed her face to relax. Was this to be her life? Always on the edge? Always hoping? She really should move away from here. She didn't have to stay in Tillison County while getting the divorce.

When Johnny stopped in front of the house, Kathleen went to the small kitchen and busied herself at the counter putting away the dishes she had allowed to dry in the

drainer, leaving Henry Ann to open the door. She heard
their voices, then Henry Ann came to the kitchen door.

"Are you sure you won't go with us, Kathleen?"

"Oh, yes, I'm sure. I have things to do."

She turned to see Johnny staring at her over Henry
Ann's shoulder. He was freshly shaved, his dark hair
brushed back from his forehead. He had on a string tie and
a new suede jacket. He'd dressed up for the occasion. She
looked back at him without visibly flinching. She was glad
that she looked tacky. That would show him that she didn't
care a whit what he thought about her.

"See you later," Henry Ann was saying. "I'm early to bed
tonight. This has been a trying day."

The days were short this time of year. The lights were on
in Dale's house and the car was parked out front when Pete
drove slowly past. He had not had a chance to find out
from Jude why Harry Cole had come to the clinic.
Whatever it was, it apparently was handled cordially.
When he came from Jude's office, the bastard was all
smiles. Thinking about the flat tire that had awaited Cole,
Pete chuckled. It was Mud Creek justice, pure and simple.

Since meeting Dale Cole, Pete had found himself thinking about her at the oddest times. At first it had been her
perky personality and sharp comebacks that had caught
his attention. He had observed her obvious dedication to
nursing and her calm in the face of Isabel's insults. He had
seen women who had been knocked around. But the cruel
evidence Dale bore had made him want to hurt whoever
had done that to her.

He didn't remember ever being so interested in a
woman that he wasn't trying to get in bed, and he was puzzled by it. He had known prettier women, more shapely

women, but when he looked into the big sad eyes of this woman, he wanted to take care of her. What the hell was wrong with him?

Inside the house, Dale was equally puzzled, but about something altogether different. Harry hadn't mentioned his visit to the clinic or where he had gone when he left there. He had been in a good mood during supper, talking to Danny about school, and even telling her that the chrysanthemums in the backyard were especially nice this year.

"We've not had a hard frost."

"Maybe you should pick a bouquet and take it to the clinic before the frost gets them."

It was fortunate for Dale that he didn't expect an answer because she was so dumbfounded that she couldn't have given one that made any sense at all. She discovered the reason for his good humor after Danny had gone to bed.

"I had a long talk with Jude today."

"Dr. Perry?" Dale was wiping dishes, and Harry lingered in the doorway of the kitchen.

"I told him that you could help out at the clinic for as long as he needed you. I want your best effort, hear? What you do reflects on me."

"I always do the best I can."

"Jude is thinking about proposing me as a trustee at the clinic. When that happens, I'll make some changes out there. They need organization. I didn't tell him that I'd even consider it because I've also been approached about running for mayor, maybe even county supervisor." He took in Dale's surprised reaction, then said, "Jude is behind me a hundred percent."

"Why, Harry, that's wonderful."

"It's about time someone in this hick town recognized

my abilities. I could have gone anyplace. Oklahoma Gas asked where I wanted to go. I chose this place or they'd have got that half-ass supervisor from over at Ardmore. I put this place in order in no time. It's the best run Gas and Electric in the state."

"You're a good organizer, Harry."

"Damn right. Don't you do anything out there to embarrass me."

"I won't."

"Don't be swishing your fat ass at anyone around there either. I heard that big-muscled goof-off that hangs around is the doctor's brother. Stay away from him. He's a womanizer. I can tell one a mile away."

"I don't know him, Harry. I've only seen him a time or two at the clinic."

"He waved at you that day. I saw it with my own eyes. Jesus, Dale, you ought to know that he's making up to you for a reason. He's probably goin' to hit me up for a job. It'll be a cold day in hell when I give him one."

Harry had been seething since the brush off he'd been given when he asked for a tire pump. He'd had to go to the station on a tire that badly needed air. He was surprised the tube hadn't been cut to ribbons by the time he got there.

Eddie had looked at his ruined tire and said that he must have run over a really sharp object to put such a hole in the tire and tube. He'd told him that he could put a boot in the tire, and with a new tube he could use the tire for a spare.

"By the way, Dale, clean the knees of the pants I wore today and press them. My coat needs a good brushing, too." Harry yawned without covering his mouth. "I'm going to bed."

Chapter Nineteen

CURIOUS EYES FOLLOWED Henry Ann and Johnny to a table at the restaurant. In a town where everyone knew or had heard of everyone else, Henry Ann was someone new to wonder about. All that was known about her was that she had come in on the bus and had been met by Kathleen Henry. It was hot gossip in town that Kathleen had left Johnny and was living in town. Hell of a note, some said. A man goes to war, comes home, and his wife won't live with him.

If Johnny was aware of the curious glances following him and Henry Ann, he didn't show it. After they were seated, Henry Ann looked around, then plucked the printed menu from between the salt and pepper shakers and the sugar bowl. She glanced at it and handed it to Johnny.

"See anything you want?" he asked.

"The special. Roast beef, mashed potatoes, and gravy."

"Sounds good to me, too."

"If Rawlings is anything like Red Rock, people are wondering who I am."

"Shall I get up and make an announcement?"

"What would you say?"

"I'd say, 'Folks, I would like to present Mrs. Tom Dolan from Red Rock. This lady, who is only five years older than I, took in a mean fourteen-year-old city kid and changed my life. If not for her, I would probably be serving time in McCalister Penitentiary. She's my sister and my best friend. I think the world of her.' That's what I would say."

"Oh, Johnny. I may disgrace myself and cry."

"You will never disgrace yourself in my eyes, Hen Ann."

"I wish Aunt Dozie had lived to know that you came home from the war and that you turned out to be such a fine man."

"She probably knows I came home from the war." His dark eyes, usually so somber, laughed at her.

After the waitress took their order, Henry Ann said, "It's strange, and I feel guilty, but it doesn't seem like a member of the family died today."

"She was sicker than I thought when I took her out to the ranch. She complained about everything. I don't know what I would have done with her if Pete hadn't come when he did."

"You stood by her when she had no place else to go. You couldn't have done more for her. She lived the kind of life she wanted to live," Henry Ann said sadly.

"After I bought the ranch, I saw her in Oklahoma City. I told her that if she wanted to, she could come stay with me. She laughed and said it would be a cold day in hell when she moved to the sticks. I never heard from her again until Sheriff Carroll called and said she had asked him to get in touch with me and tell me to meet the bus."

"Tom and I will help with the burial expense."

"No need for you to do that. Pete gave the undertaker fifty dollars. I put in another fifty. That takes care of the burial, the plot, and a small stone."

"It wasn't Pete's obligation."

"Tell that to Pete. He's stubborn as a mule at times."

Henry Ann glanced at the diners in the booths that lined the sidewall. One man sat hunched over his meal. He looked up. His eyes slid over her and Johnny and then back to his plate. He had a chart of some kind lying on the table and he looked at it from time to time.

"Tom and the children are wondering when you're coming to see us."

"I'd better wait until I can get some decent tires."

"You could take the bus. Come and bring Kathleen. Tom would like to see her, too."

"I don't know about that, sis."

"Oh, dear. I told myself I'd not bring this up, but I've got to say it. I just hate it that you and Kathleen are not together." Henry Ann's expression was troubled.

"It isn't something you need to worry about."

"Why not? I love you both. Do you want to talk about it?"

"I'd rather not. Kathleen and I want different things out of life."

"What things?"

"She wants children. I do not."

"Johnny Henry! You'd make a wonderful father. I remember how you were with Jay—"

"Here's our food." Johnny smiled with relief.

The waitress, thinking that the smile was for her, giggled happily. Johnny didn't remember her, but she remembered him. All the high school girls back before the war had a crush on the best *All-Around Cowboy* of Tillison County. Then he had to up and marry the redhead from the newspaper. It was rumored that they had separated.

"If you need anything else, Johnny, just give me a whistle," she said brightly.

"I'll do that, thank you."

"You're welcome, I'm sure."

"She was flirting with you," Henry Ann said. "Doesn't she know that you're married?"

"She's just being friendly."

The food was delicious, and Henry Ann was hungrier than she thought. Hot beef sliced, heaped on bread, and covered with gravy was one of her favorites.

"Pete has suggested, and I'm giving it some thought," Johnny said halfway through the meal, "that he and I form a company and put on rodeos. I'm not sure how much money it would take to start. It's just in the talking stage now."

"That's a great idea." She smiled into his eyes. "Pete is a talker. He could promote and you could manage behind the scenes."

Johnny looked at her with surprise. "It's just what I thought. We're both interested in raising rodeo horses."

"Do it, if you feel it's right. Henry & Perry Rodeos. I like the sound of it. Rodeos are just bound to get more popular now that the war is over."

"Folks like to see someone thrown on his rear. I always got the biggest hand when I hit the dirt." He grinned, remembering. "I doubt that I can get the money through the GI Bill to finance something like that."

"You could mortgage your ranch."

"I can't do that. Part of it belongs to Kathleen." He looked away, veiling his expression. "I wouldn't ask her to take the risk."

It was completely dark when they left the restaurant and walked down the street to Johnny's car.

"Days are getting shorter," Henry Ann remarked.

"And cooler. On Guadalcanal I wished for a cool night like this."

When they reached the house, Johnny walked with Henry Ann to the porch. The lights were on in the front room and in Kathleen's bedroom.

"Are you coming in?"

"No. I'd better get back. You'll have a trying day tomorrow. I'll be here to take you to the burial. Pete and Jude will be there. Good night, sis. I'm glad you're here."

"I'm glad I'm here, too."

Theodore Nuding rubbed his face with his hands and pressed his fingers to his temples. He had eaten his supper at the restaurant, a treat he allowed himself occasionally. Now he sat at the table in the room he was preparing for Kathleen. His notebook was spread out in front of him. His had been a busy day. He picked up his pen and began to write.

9:30 P.M. *Mother, I am tired tonight. I don't like to admit it, but I've not felt the best lately. I've been working hard. So much to do and so little time. A lot happened today. My darling Kathleen went to see a lawyer. She looked so desolate, so lonely afterward, that I risked talking to her when she parked in front of the library and sat in her car. She is so beautiful. I wanted to stay and look at her, but I didn't dare. She will be happy here in her room, where she will have everything she needs. I'm making out a list and over Thanksgiving, I'll go to Dallas and place an order.*

Johnny Henry's slutty sister died today. I knew that someone had died when the undertaker went to the clinic. Johnny Henry and the doctor's brother went to the funeral parlor, then to the cemetery to pick out a plot. He was at the cafe tonight with a woman. She is the one

*who came in on the bus today from Red Rock. It must be his other
sister.*

*I've been having splitting headaches lately, Mother. At times they
are so bad I can hardly see. I wish Kathleen was here. I would lay
my head in her lap and she would rub the hurt away.*

Henry Ann, Johnny, Pete, and Jude were four of the eleven
people who stood at Isabel's gravesite that knew her. The
others were Barker Fleming, his two daughters and son,
Adelaide and Paul Leahy, and Kathleen.

Lucas Fleming, in a dark suit, with his hat in his hand,
fidgeted beside his father until Barker gave him a quelling
glance. Marie and Janna, who towered over her older sister, both wore dark coats and hats.

Early this morning Marie had come to the house with a
baked ham, potato salad, and a couple of loaves of Mrs.
Fisher's freshly made bread. Kathleen had introduced her to
Henry Ann.

"I'm glad to know you, Mrs. Dolan," Marie said.

"And I'm glad to know you. It was nice of you to bring
food."

"Daddy insisted we start preparing right away as soon as
we heard that Johnny's sister had died."

"I hope I get the chance to thank him."

"You will. All of us will be at the funeral."

Kathleen had avoided Johnny when he came to the
house. She left it to Henry Ann to tell him about the food
Barker had sent over. When she came out of the bedroom,
wearing her dark coat and hat, Pete and Jude were there.
And when they left the house, she had ridden in Pete's car
to the cemetery.

Now it was over. The minister, whom the undertaker
had engaged to read a simple service, had finished. The

casket sat lonely beside the heap of red Oklahoma soil that would cover it. As the group began to move away, Kathleen invited Adelaide and Paul as well as Barker and his family to come to the house.

"You furnished the food, Barker, and besides, you should get to know Henry Ann, Johnny's sister."

"I would like that if it wouldn't be an imposition." Barker nudged his youngest daughter, who groaned at the thought of spending more time with the adults.

"I'll have Pete drop me off at the clinic." Jude took Henry Ann's hand in both of his. "Will I see you again before you go?"

"I'm going back in the morning. This is the first time I've been away from Tom and the kids. I'm homesick for them."

"Lucky Tom and the kids. Take care of yourself. Tell Tom hello."

"Take care of yourself, too. Seeing you has renewed my faith in human nature. Find a nice girl and start a family. That's where true happiness lies."

Jude kissed her on the cheek, lifted his hand to the others, and went to where Pete waited beside the car.

"I'll ride with Adelaide and Paul, Pete," Kathleen called. "Come to the house after you deliver Jude." Ignoring Johnny, she took Adelaide's arm.

At the house, Kathleen insisted that Henry Ann visit with Johnny, Barker, and the Leahys while she and Marie prepared the food. She sliced the ham, and Marie set out plates and silverware.

"There's a cake in the lower cupboard, Marie. I baked it last night."

"What can I do?" Janna asked.

"Cut the cake," Kathleen said.

"Are you sure you want her to?" This came from a smiling Marie.

"I can do it," Janna insisted, and stuck her tongue out at her sister.

"She'll do just fine."

"Now here's a roomful of pretty women." Pete crowded into the small kitchen. "Better let me do that," he said, taking the slicing knife from Kathleen's hand.

"Gladly. I'll slice the bread."

"This knife is dull as dishwater, sugar. Don't you have a whetstone?"

"Sorry. You'll just have to make do. Janna, let's move the kitchen chairs to the other room. There isn't room in here for everyone to sit down."

After the meal, the men went to the porch to smoke.

"If you're looking for land," Barker said to Pete, "You may want to look at the Clifton ranch. I understand that it sold recently, but the owner isn't going to run cattle. It's good pastureland."

"Any of it tillable?"

"Might get a hay crop. It wasn't tilled during the dust storms. It's got good topsoil."

"The man who bought it is a famous writer, so John Wrenn said. It didn't sound like he'd do much ranching himself. He will lease out grazing rights." Paul and Pete had hit it off. Paul liked a gutsy man who had had a few hard knocks and survived them.

"Is anyone living out there?" Pete asked.

"The writer hasn't moved in yet. A fellow from the weather bureau is staying out there looking after the place. Sheriff Carroll says he sits out west of town watching the clouds and making notes on a chart."

"Now that's a job that would grow mold on the brain."

Pete's laughter was sudden and spontaneous. Lucas joined in, causing Pete to look down at him sitting on the edge of the porch. "You a cowboy?"

"Yeah." Lucas glanced at his father, then said, "Yes, sir."

"You like rodeos?"

"Yes . . . *sir!*"

"I'm trying to get Johnny to go in with me and put on a rodeo in the spring."

Lucas's eyes went to Johnny. "You goin' to?"

"I'm thinking about it."

"Could I have a job?"

"If you can cut the mustard."

"Ya . . . hoo!" Lucas jumped to his feet, and threw his hat in the air. The Stetson came down in the yard, and he ran to get it.

"We'll need someone to pick up horse turds, won't we, Pete?" Johnny teased, his dark eyes dancing with amusement.

"I'll do that, Johnny," Lucas said quickly. "You'll let me ride sometimes, won't you? Wait till I tell Janna. She's been practicing barrel racing. She's not very good," he scoffed.

"She'll get better." With his booted foot on the edge of the porch, the other on the ground, Johnny spoke to Barker.

"Sherm, the man living out at my place, found two of your steers in my back lot not fifty feet from the barn."

"How did they get there? Two steers don't usually wander off by themselves. A dozen maybe, but not two."

"Hell, I don't know. Sherm drove them down that dry gulley and back onto your land. One of them had an ear tag."

"I'll look into it."

"How is Bobby Harper doin'?" Paul Leahy asked.

"Dr. Perry said that he'd be off his leg for a while even after the cast is off."

"I'd keep my eye on Mack Boone if I were you."

"He's not the man his father is. I keep him on because of Victor."

"Watch him around Marie and Janna."

"Have you heard something?" Barker was instantly alert.

"A few brags is all."

"I don't like him," Lucas said.

"Any special reason?" Barker's dark gaze honed in on his son.

"Just don't." Lucas wondered if he should tell about seeing Mack with a slingshot the day Bobby Harper was bucked off and broke his leg. He decided that he'd wait and tell Johnny. "You'll not let Mack work at the rodeo, will you, Johnny?"

"The rodeo is just in the talk stage. Don't count on it just yet. We may not be able to swing the deal at all."

"I hope you do it, Johnny."

"We'd better get back home, son. You've got chores before dark. Go in and see if your sisters are ready to go."

"Yes, sir." Lucas bounded up on the porch, and Paul watched him.

"That's a dandy boy, Barker. He's full of beans and vinegar, just like he's supposed to be at that age."

"Not too bad yet. The time will come when he'll want to sow his wild oats. The hard part for me will be turning him loose."

Kathleen said good-bye to Paul and Adelaide and to the Flemings. She stood on the front porch and waved, dreading to go back into the house where only Johnny, Henry Ann, and Pete remained. She had managed to avoid Johnny all day, but now with just the four of them, it would be more difficult.

He spoke to her as soon as she entered.

"I'm taking Henry Ann out to my place. Do you want to come along?"

She swallowed once, hard, and avoided looking at him when she answered.

"No, thank you. I've got some cleaning up to do."

"Come, go with us," Henry Ann urged.

"No. This is your time together. You don't need me butting in."

"Come on, Henry Ann." Johnny took his sister's arm. "She doesn't want to come. Coming, Pete?"

"I'll stay here and give Kathleen a hand," Pete said.

Johnny slapped his hat down on his head as he went out the door and never looked back.

Pete followed Kathleen to the kitchen. "What do you have to do?"

"Well . . ." She looked around. "Nothing, really."

"I didn't think so. Let's go down to the drugstore, get a Coke, then go to the picture show."

"Do you know what's on?"

"*The Outlaw*, with Jane Russell."

"It must have changed today. Yesterday it was *Double Indemnity* with Barbara Stanwyck."

"I could go for that Jane Russell," he said with an exaggerated leer.

Kathleen laughed at his antics. "The show doesn't start until seven."

Pete looked at his watch. "We'll get a Coke, sit on Main Street, and watch the people go by, then go to the show."

"Sounds good. I haven't had a cherry Coke in ages."

Pete ordered the Cokes to be put in paper cups and brought them out to the car.

"I remember when Cokes were a nickel," he grumbled as he got into the car and handed her the cup.

"Thanks. Cokes went up to ten cents during the war."

"I was land-based in the Pacific for one stretch. We looked forward to when the Salvation Army people came. They never charged us for cigarettes or candy bars."

"I've heard other servicemen say that." Kathleen sucked on the straw. "This is good, but not as fizzy as in the bottle."

"You and Johnny have a set-to?" Pete changed the topic of the conversation so smoothly that she wasn't prepared for the question.

"Ah . . . no. Why do you ask?" Her eyes were unwilling to meet his.

"You didn't look at him all day."

"Was it that obvious?"

"Probably not to anyone but me."

"Thank goodness for that." She sucked up the remainder of her Coke, then said, "Were you surprised when you met Johnny's father?"

"Yeah, I guess I was. Jude likes him."

"And you?"

"I like what I've seen so far. He doesn't seem to throw his weight around like you'd expect a man of his means to do."

"I like him very much. I like all the family. Johnny keeps them at arm's length."

"Johnny still has a chip on his shoulder."

"He has a right to have one. Look at what he's had to overcome." Kathleen jumped quickly to Johnny's defense. "He'll get over it one of these days—in his own time."

"Are you two ever going to get back together?"

"I don't think so. I saw a lawyer yesterday. I waited for

Johnny to come home from the war and hoped that he'd want me back. He's made it clear that he does not want to live with me as man and wife." She couldn't keep the tears from her voice and swallowed repeatedly. "I need to make a clean break and . . . and start over."

"He wants you. It's eating him up."

"You're wrong. But stand by him. He needs friends like you and Jude." She looked at her watch. "If we're going to the show, we'd better get on down there."

Chapter Twenty

I HAD A REALLY GOOD TIME," Kathleen said, as Pete stopped his car behind Johnny's. "I love movies. I guess that's the storyteller in me. I'd see a movie every night of the week if I had the chance. Movies were all the entertainment I had during the war." Kathleen knew that she was rambling. Realizing that Johnny was in the house unnerved her.

"I like movies, too. *Casablanca* will be on next week. How about going with me?"

"Can I decide later?"

"Sure."

"Come in and say good-bye to Henry Ann. She's leaving on the eight-thirty bus in the morning."

On the way to the porch Kathleen stumbled on the rough ground. Pete caught hold of her arm and they were laughing as they stepped up onto the porch, still laughing as Kathleen opened the door. Johnny was sitting in her armchair, and Henry Ann was on the couch. He had a bland look on his face, but Kathleen knew him well enough to know that for some reason he was furious. *Too bad, Bud. I'm not waiting around for you any longer.*

"We've been to the show," she said cheerfully, and

slipped out of her coat. "Now Pete's got a crush on Jane Russell."

"Who wouldn't? She's built like a brick outhouse," Pete declared. "That Hughes fellow knows how to pick 'em. I read that he gave her part of the profit to get her to take the role."

"Then she's set for life."

"I also read that he designed the . . . you know . . . the bra she wore to make her look more . . . buxom."

"Well, for goodness sake." Henry Ann laughed. "You must read a lot."

"I do when I find good stuff like that. Where shall I put the coat, sugar?"

"In on my bed. There's still ham left if anyone wants a sandwich."

"You don't have to ask me twice." Pete came out of the bedroom. "How about it, Johnny?"

"None for me."

"Have a seat, Pete, and visit with Henry Ann. I'll make some sandwiches and a pot of coffee."

"Thanks, sugar." He sat down on the couch. "It isn't often I have a pretty woman waiting on me. I'm going to take full advantage of it. You're leaving in the morning, Henry Ann?"

"I'm anxious to get back to the family. I'm glad I came. It was a sad occasion, but I got to see Johnny, Kathleen, and Jude."

"And me, Hen Ann?" Pete teased.

"I saw you a couple of weeks ago when you came to Red Rock looking for Jude. I've wondered about Isabel over the years. When Johnny called, he said that she was sick. I never thought she would go so quickly."

"She and Jude got along like a cat and dog when she

was young, and in the end it was Jude that eased her passing. Ironic, isn't it?"

"Thank you for helping with the burial expense." Henry Ann reached over and placed her hand on Pete's. "It wasn't your responsibility."

"I wanted to do it. I may have helped contribute to her wayward ways. I wasn't too smart myself back then."

"We were all doing the best we could to get along."

"I'm glad you've got a good man, Henry Ann."

"He is a good man. You need to find someone and settle down, raise a family. Tom says that reformed rogues make good husbands." Her eyes smiled at him.

"If that's the case, I ought to be a jim-dandy."

"I always suspected that you were not quite as bad as you wanted folks to think you were."

Johnny got up suddenly and went to the kitchen. Pete's eyes followed him.

"Kathleen is going to get tired of waiting for him to decide what he wants to do. I'd hate like hell for him to lose her."

"I would, too. But they'll have to work it out. He won't talk to me about it."

Kathleen moved the coffeepot to the stove and turned to see Johnny's tall body blocking the doorway. He stood with one shoulder hunched against the doorjamb. With her movements going on automatic, she lowered the flame under the pot, then reached under the counter to bring out a cloth-covered platter that held what was left of the ham. She looked at him then, full in the face, and was proud that she could do it.

"Have you changed your mind about wanting a sandwich?"

"No."

"Cake?"

"No."

"Coffee then?"

"Maybe."

"It will be ready in ten minutes or so." Kathleen squatted in front of the small icebox and came up with a covered dish of butter.

"I'll be here in the morning to take Henry Ann to the bus."

"I figured you would." Kathleen spoke with her back to him.

"I appreciate your letting her stay here."

"It was my pleasure to have her."

"What's got your butt over the line?" Johnny snarled suddenly. "You've hardly looked at me for the past few days, much less spoken to me. Did I impose on your private life by asking if Henry Ann could stay here?"

Kathleen didn't answer. She began to butter the slices of bread she had laid out on a plate.

"That's it, isn't it? You didn't want my sister to stay here."

"I just told you that it was my pleasure to have her. Don't be a bigger ass than you already are!" Kathleen swung around, her eyes bright with anger. "Henry Ann is one of the nicest people I know. Far nicer than you are."

"I'll not dispute that. I never claimed to be an angel, but I'm not a devil either."

"No. You're a stubborn jackass with a one-track mind. You think that you are always right about everything."

"Not quite everything. I don't know you anymore."

"And you don't want to. I'm tired of waiting around for you to make up your mind about whether or not you want to be married to me. I went to see Mr. Fairbanks yester-day."

"And—?" His voice lowered to a mere whisper.

"—And as soon as we can decide on the *grounds* for the divorce, he'll file it."

"What do you mean . . . grounds?"

"We have to give the judge a reason why we want a divorce."

"A *reason*?"

"Yes, a reason. He'll want to know if you beat me? No. Did you refuse to support me? No, even though I don't need your support. Have you been unfaithful? I don't know. Did you refuse to live with me. *Yes!*"

"Why do there have to be grounds?"

"How the hell do I know." Kathleen was snarling now. "I've never been divorced before. Do you think that I'm proud that everyone in town knows that my husband refuses to live with me? I have endured that embarrassment as long as I'm going to."

"Still can't hold your temper."

"Why should I? You've treated me like a doormat ever since you came back. Damn, damn, dammit to hell! I'll lose my temper. I'll swear and even throw things if I want to. This is my house, and if you don't like it, you can get your sorry butt out of it."

"You've really worked up a full head of steam, haven't you?"

"I've got my pride, too."

"Have you got something going with Pete? Is that the reason you went to see a lawyer?"

"Maybe," she said just to irritate him. "I've got my eye on several eligible men."

"Including Barker."

"Barker is your father, for Christ sake!" She was almost yelling.

"He could give you everything you want!"

"How do you know what I want? Have you ever asked me? No, it's only about what you want, or don't want."

"I don't want to go through what we went through before. You know that."

"You're too thickheaded to go find out for sure why Mary Rose was born the way she was. You think that you have all the answers. Well, maybe you've got it into that pea-size brain of yours that it was something I did that caused it."

"You know damn good and well I don't think that!" Johnny turned his head quickly to look in the living room when he heard the front door close.

"Henry Ann has gone out onto the porch so she doesn't have to listen to your ranting."

"If you didn't want your sister to hear me calling you a horse's ass, you shouldn't have come in here and started it."

The coffeepot began to boil over. One step took Johnny to the stove, where he shut off the gas cutting off the flame beneath it. He went back to the doorway.

"Let me know when you want me to sign the papers."

"Oh, you'll know. I'll make damn sure you know," she snarled, and slapped a slice of bread down onto the plate.

"I'll be here in the morning."

"I can hardly wait. As you leave, tell Pete his sandwich is ready."

During the rest of the evening, Kathleen managed to hide to some degree her feelings of smoldering anger. She sat with her guests at the kitchen table. Pete squeezed her shoulder reassuringly when he came in, then proceeded to be amusing. He told stories about things that had happened while he was in the navy, funny things usually at his expense. After that, he and Henry Ann reminisced about their younger days in Red Rock until it was time for him to leave.

When they were alone, the two women silently prepared for bed. Kathleen was grateful when Henry Ann didn't mention Johnny or the overheard words that had passed between them. Heartsick and frightened, she turned out the lights and got into bed.

The years ahead would be long and lonely.

Kathleen told Henry Ann good-bye on the front porch while Johnny waited in the car. He had nodded good morning when he came to the porch for her suitcase, and she had nodded coolly in return.

"Regardless of what happens between you and Johnny, I want us to stay in touch. Besides being Tom's niece, his only connection to Duncan, his brother, you are very dear to us. Write and let me know how you are doing. I pray that things will work out between you and Johnny."

"A lot of time has gone by. Every day that passes we get farther apart. Tell Uncle Tom that as soon as I get a better car, I'll be over to see you-all. Just listen to me, I've been down South so long, I'm even saying *you-all*," Kathleen said lightly. She had to keep things light or she'd cry.

"I'll tell him. Take care of yourself."

"You too."

Kathleen waved, then went back into the house as soon as the car began to move.

What would she do with the rest of the day? She wasn't in the mood to write for her book or to read, which was her favorite pastime. She sat down in the big chair where

Johnny had sat the night before, reached over and turned on the radio.

"Jack Roosevelt Robinson, a Georgia-born son of a share-cropper and grandson of a slave will join the Montreal club, a Brooklyn Dodgers affiliate of the International League. A spokesman said that the signing was not to be interpreted merely as a gesture toward solving the racial unrest. Robinson, who has been playing in the Negro League—"

Kathleen turned the dial and discovered that news was on almost every station this time of morning.

"Today the first refrigerator plane crossed the country with a full load. It is the beginning of a new era. The president of the airline has predicted that within a few months fish will reach the consumer within hours after it leaves the sea.

On another note: Shoe rationing will end November 23. Meat and butter rationing ends December 20 just in time for Christmas."

Kathleen switched off the radio when the phone rang. It was Marie.

"Has your company left?"

"She left this morning."

"Would you mind riding with me over to Frederick this morning? I need to see the dentist, and Daddy says I can't go alone. He would go with me, but he can't leave the plant until late afternoon. I had counted on Thelma, but she isn't well today."

"I'm at loose ends today. I'll be glad for something to do."

"Oh, good. I'll be by in about thirty minutes. Is that too soon?"

"Not at all. I'll be ready."

*   *   *

Johnny and Henry Ann sat in his car as they waited for the bus that would take her back to Red Rock.

"When will I see you again, Johnny?"

"I don't know, sis. I'm trying to get some things sorted out."

"Have you applied for your GI benefits? You're entitled to twenty dollars a week for a year."

"I haven't applied. That's for men who can't find a job. I could get one operating heavy machinery, but it would mean leaving here. I don't want to give up on my ranch."

"The ranch or Kathleen?" Henry Ann reached for his hand and clasped it tightly. "I'm sorry. I promised myself I'd stay out of your private affairs."

"I have no private affairs where you are concerned, sis." He watched the big Greyhound bus come lumbering down Main Street and stop in front of the *Gazette* Building.

"She loves you."

"She did at one time. That may be coming to an end."

"Women don't fall out of love easily."

"You saw how happy she was with Pete."

"Being happy and having a good time with someone doesn't necessarily mean falling in love with them."

"You know how he is. If she should fall for him, it would be like jumping out of the frying pan and into the fire. He'll never be faithful to any woman."

"You could be wrong, Johnny. Pete puts on a good show because he's not sure of himself or where he stands with people. I believe now that was why he was so obnoxious when he was young. If he ever meets a woman who believes in him and loves him, he'll be faithful."

"Time will tell, won't it? We'd better go. They're loading up."

Johnny set her suitcase down beside the bus. The driver opened a side door and shoved it into the compartment.

"Get aboard, folks."

"I want to see Tom and the kids, but I hate to leave you when you're so troubled." Henry Ann clung to Johnny's hand. "Talk to Kathleen."

"I will. Tell Tom and the kids hello."

" 'Bye, Johnny." Henry Ann had tears in her eyes when she kissed him on the cheek.

" 'Bye, sis. I'll be over sometime soon."

Johnny stood on the sidewalk and waited for the bus to leave. Henry Ann waved and he waved back. When the bus turned the corner and was out of sight, he went back to his car. He didn't think that he had ever felt more lonely in his life.

Talk to Kathleen, she'd said. What could he say to her? *I know what you want? I can't give it to you, but I don't want to lose you? How can I live with you as my wife and not make love to you? We would have to be so careful that you didn't get pregnant. The constant worry could, in time, drive us apart. I'm sure there isn't a protection that is a hundred percent safe.*

Last night he had intended to talk to her calmly, to tell her that he and Pete had talked about promoting rodeos and to ask her if she would be willing for them to refinance the ranch. But she had gone out with Pete when she had refused to go with him and Henry Ann. He had said things that he wished he could take back. It was stupid of him to throw Barker up at her. He knew deep down that she would never marry his father.

Johnny started the car. He had told Henry Ann that he would talk to her, and he would. He would explain to her once again that it had taken the heart right out of him when he saw the pitifully deformed body of their baby. He had seriously considered blowing his brains out. At the time he had thought, what the hell good was he to humanity?

The answer had come when he saw the poster of Uncle Sam pointing a finger. *We want you.*

He had enlisted. But not a day had gone by that he hadn't thought of her. Not a night that he didn't ache for her.

Johnny pulled his car into the driveway behind Kathleen's Nash. She should have another car, he thought as he got out and walked up onto the porch. That thing wasn't going to last much longer.

He rapped on the door, waited, then rapped again. Her car was here. He had not seen her walking to town. Had she seen him and was refusing to come to the door? He opened the screen and tried the doorknob. Locked. Then it occurred to him that she had gone somewhere with Pete. He stomped off the porch, got back in his car, and headed out of town.

Chapter Twenty-one

THE WEATHER TURNED BAD two days before Thanksgiving. A cold rain kept Kathleen indoors. It proved to be a good time to work on her book. She forced herself to concentrate on it . . . then she became interested again, and it became easier to immerse herself in the story.

She had not seen Johnny since the morning Henry Ann left. Pete had come by from time to time. He told her that he, Barker, and Lucas had helped Johnny drive his horses up from Keith McCabe's ranch.

Theresa called to let Kathleen know what she was taking to Jude's for the Thanksgiving dinner.

"I wanted to make sure that both of us didn't make pumpkin pie."

"Any pie that I made would be tough enough to dance on. I'll bring the cranberry sauce, sweet potatoes, and apple salad."

"Pete is cooking the turkey. I'll bring the corn bread dressing and the pie. I'm looking forward to it. I hope we don't have an emergency at the clinic."

"I'm wondering how many turkeys Pete has cooked in the past. Maybe I should make a meat loaf."

Theresa laughed. "He says that he can do it. I hope he remembers to take the insides out."

Thanksgiving morning Kathleen was up early. After preparing the food she was going to take to the dinner, she took a bath. Looking at herself in the mirror after she got out of the tub, she was surprised that her face was so pale. She examined herself closely.

Her hair was shoulder length now. She picked up the scissors and snipped until she had short curls across her forehead and from the corners of her eyes to her jawbone. Satisfied that her face didn't look so *bald*, she applied light makeup.

The dress she had chosen to wear was forest green jersey with a gathered skirt and full sleeves caught at the wrist with a wide cuff. It was a soft dress, the color was good, and it made her feel feminine.

The day was bright and sunny, not at all like the Thanksgivings she remembered in Iowa, where, if snow hadn't already fallen, there was the promise of it in the air. Telling herself that she hadn't mashed the sweet potatoes and added butter and cinnamon because that was the way Johnny liked them, but because it was the only way she knew how, she packed the food in a box and set it in the backseat of the Nash.

Only Pete's car was parked in front of Jude's house. He saw her drive up and came out to help her with the box.

"Am I the first one here?"

"Theresa is here. Jude had me go get her while he went to the clinic. Someone over there had a pain or something." Before they stepped up onto the porch Pete stopped. "Kathleen . . . Johnny isn't coming. He went down to Vernon to the McCabes."

For some reason Kathleen was not surprised and swallowed her disappointment.

"That means all the more turkey for us," she said brightly.

"I hope it's fit to eat. I never cooked one before."

"You . . . never cooked one?" She held the door open for him.

"No, but if anyone else can do it, I can. I went right by the instructions Dale gave me. I had her write them down."

"Dale Cole?"

"Yeah."

"I hope she told you to take off the feathers."

"She did. Hey, you've got to meet Theresa's boy. He's a ringed-tail tooter." He set her box down on the kitchen table. "Let me take your coat."

Theresa came from the pantry. "Hello, Kathleen. Do you have anything that should go in the refrigerator?"

"The salad and the cranberry sauce. Oh, my, isn't it a beauty." Kathleen ran her hand over the door of Jude's new refrigerator. "I'm going to have one of these one day."

"The sweet potatoes will stay warm on the back of the stove."

Pete came back to the kitchen with a small, pixie-faced boy riding on his shoulders.

"Know where I found this little peanut? Hiding in the closet. When he grabbed my leg, I was sure that a Jap was about to cut my toes off."

The child giggled happily and held on to Pete's head.

"Kathleen, this is my son, Ryan. Say hello to Mrs. Henry, Ryan."

"How-dee-do, pretty lady," he said in a deep voice, then giggled uncontrollably.

"Ryan," his mother said. "Where did you learn to talk like that?"

Still giggling, Ryan patted the top of Pete's head. Pete swung him down off his shoulders and set him on the floor.

"All right," he said gruffly. "You gonna rat on me ya got to pay." He grabbed him around the middle and, with him dangling from under one arm, left the kitchen.

"What ya gonna do, Pete? What ya gonna do?"

"I'm going to make me some peanut butter."

Sounds of laughter and thumps came from the living room. Theresa rolled her eyes.

"I hope they don't break anything. I don't know which one is the biggest kid. Honestly. Ryan adores Pete, and Jude, too."

"Obviously Pete likes him."

"It's been wonderful for Ryan. He's not had men in his life except his grandfather on his father's side. Believe me, he was nothing like Pete and Jude."

"I don't think there's anyone like Pete."

Jude returned after stitching a man's split lips and a bad cut over his eye.

"Too much whiskey and not enough brains. He'll not be eating turkey for a while."

It became obvious to Kathleen that Theresa and her son had been frequent visitors to Jude's house. She wondered if it was at Jude's invitation or Pete's. Theresa seemed to know what Jude had in the way of china and silver, bowls and pots.

After he proudly brought a golden brown turkey to the table, Pete handed the carving knife to Jude.

"Have at it, brother. You need the practice," Pete said, and sat down beside Ryan. "He might need to take off a leg or two in the next few days or do a little slicing here and there," he explained in a loud whisper.

"Pete, that's awful!" Kathleen's hand went to her mouth.

"Mom, what's awful?" Ryan asked.

"I'll tell you after dinner."

Kathleen enjoyed herself even though she didn't have much of an appetite. Johnny had not been mentioned since Pete's announcement that he wasn't coming. It was Kathleen's fifth Thanksgiving without him, so it wasn't anything new.

During the meal Kathleen noticed Jude's eyes straying often to Theresa. She wore a blue dress with tiny darker blue flowers. Her cheeks were flushed, her eyes shining. Before sitting down, she had whipped off a frilly apron.

After the meal Theresa carefully wrapped the leftover food and put it in the refrigerator.

"Now if Pete's gone tomorrow, the doctor will have a meal."

"Is Pete going somewhere?"

"I heard him tell the doctor that he was going to the city to see about buying some land."

"In the city?"

"Here, but whoever it is he has to see is in the city."

While Ryan napped, the two couples played cards. Pete called the game Pitch; Kathleen called it High, Low, Jack, and the Game. Despite the argument over the name of the game, Kathleen and Pete played well together and skunked Jude and Theresa. After two hours, Jude threw up his hands and protested that they had cheated.

As Kathleen prepared to leave, she told Pete to tell Dale that the turkey was cooked perfectly.

"The dinner was wonderful, the company outstanding. I enjoyed myself immensely," she told Jude.

"Come again, Kathleen."

"Hey, sugar," Pete called as she went toward her car. She paused and he caught up with her. "Shall we see the movie tonight?"

"Ah, Pete, why don't you take Theresa?"

"And have Jude serve my head up on a platter? No, sir, my head's too important to me."

"Is . . . he? They?"

"I think he likes her a lot. I'm not sure if she has gotten to that stage. I'm working on it."

"Why . . . you matchmaker, you!"

"Pretty smart of me, don't you think?"

"You want to get out of the house tonight and give them some time to be alone, is that it?"

"You've hit the nail on the head, sugar."

"Come over and we'll listen to the radio and play two-handed solitaire."

"You got a date."

During the week that followed, Kathleen worked with Adelaide on the Christmas carnival to be held on Saturday. They were raising funds to pay for the remodeling of the room at the clinic to accommodate the iron lung that had already arrived and was set up in a storage room in case of need.

Posters were up all over town, and flyers had been sent to surrounding towns. Because it was an affair that would benefit not only Tillison County, but surrounding counties, announcements had been made on the Frederick radio broadcasts.

Adelaide confided to Kathleen that Paul was working on getting a license to operate a radio station in Rawlings.

"It's something he has always wanted to do. I hope he is able to swing it. He already has a backer."

"Backer? Oh, and I bet I can guess who that is."

"You'd be guessing right, of course. Sometimes I think that Johnny Henry is dumb as a doorknob. He has no idea what a remarkable man his father is."

"Only a few people know what Barker does for this town. The rest of them see him as an Indian and resent what he has. His father made a lot of money, but he taught his children how to use it. Most people, if they had Barker's money, would be sitting around doing nothing. He works."

"Well." Adelaide sniffed. "I didn't mean for you to get on a soapbox. And, by the way, Barker approached Paul with the idea. Not the other way around as you would expect."

"It hadn't occurred to me to expect anything. Paul has a wonderful speaking voice for the radio."

"Everything about Paul is wonderful."

"Oh, Lord. I've started the ball rolling. She'll go on for hours."

"No, I won't," Adelaide said pertly. "I've got to get down to the schoolhouse."

On the day of the carnival, Kathleen worked on decorations all day. She tied up balloons the high-school boys had inflated with an air hose at Eddie's station. She hung strips of crepe paper and made signs on big sheets of butcher paper donated by Miller's grocery.

She was so busy that she hadn't had time for a passing thought of Johnny until, on a trip to the *Gazette* office, she saw his car parked in front of the drugstore. Then, fearing that she would run into him, she grabbed up the newsprint Paul had rolled off. It was to serve as a backdrop on the small stage that had been set up in the gymnasium where the dance would be held. She flung it into the car and hurried back to the school.

The five-member band was not of Bob Wills's class, but they were up-and-coming local musicians and were donating their services. For the carnival they were calling themselves Willie and the Chicken Pluckers. They showed up in hillbilly costumes: straw hats, ragged overalls, oversized shoes with the toes cut out. Just looking at them put Kathleen in the mood for a good time.

People were beginning to arrive when Kathleen dashed home to change clothes. As she dressed, it occurred to her that she had not had her monthly period. The date had come and gone and she had not noticed because occasionally she would go for as long as five or six days beyond her due date.

With one stocking on and one off she went to find a calendar. It had been over five weeks. Now that she was thinking about it, she had only flowed a part of a day during her last period, which in itself was not unusual; three days was her limit. It would just be her luck to start tonight. For safety's sake she put a couple of tampons in her purse.

She was amazed at the number of cars parked around the school when she reached it and had to park half a block away. It was a warm evening for the first week in December, and she didn't mind the walk.

The booths had opened in the classrooms. People, some in costume, were wandering up and down the hallway. Criers were standing in the doorways enticing them to enter. Kathleen made her way to the gymnasium and through the crowd that milled behind the area roped off for dancing.

Pete had been pressed into service to act as announcer

at the dance. The band, playing to liven up the crowd, was putting on a show. The fiddler jigged as he played his violin; one of the guitar players plucked wildly while trying to stomp on the toes of the band members who were not wearing shoes. The drummer, wearing a helmet, kept hitting himself on the head, and the piano player, his overalls on backward, wore an oversize tattered straw hat that covered his ears. The crowd was enjoying their antics.

Kathleen made her way to the stage to join the dime-a-dance girls. Four of the five chairs were filled. She recognized one girl who worked in the Golden Pheasant and another who worked part time at the library. The other two were high-school girls. All four women were pretty. Kathleen was sure they would all have paying partners before she did. As soon as she took her seat, Pete picked up the microphone and began to talk.

"Folks, we are about to get this little shindig under way. It's only going to cost you ten pennies to dance with your lady love. Willie here tells me they will be long dances, so you'll get your money's worth. The band members have donated their time and talent so that every dime that you spend here tonight will go toward that polio room in the clinic.

"For you gents who chained your wives to the washtub so you could come here tonight"—Pete paused for the laughter—"there are five pretty girls sitting up here on the stage who will dance with you, if . . . a big if . . . you've got a ticket. Kathleen, that pretty redhead on the end, is a knockout, don't you agree? The little blonde next to her is just as cute as a button. The brunette will dance your legs off as will that one with the pretty brown hair next to her. The little 'un on the other end was made for a slow, cuddlin' waltz. Sugar, I'm goin' to dance with you before this night is over.

"Willie's going to start the evening off with our own Bob Wills's 'San Antonio Rose.' If you haven't got a ticket, gents, go get one, get two or three dozen. You'll use them before the night's over. Remember just ten cents. That's two packs of chewing gum. Wouldn't you rather dance with your sweetheart or one of these pretty girls than chew gum or smoke a ten-cent cigar?

"One more thing, folks. If you don't dance, that's all right. You can drop a donation in the jar right over there on the ticket table. It could be your kids or your neighbor's kids who come down with polio. They'll have a better chance if we have that iron lung set up and running." Pete drew a string of tickets out of his pocket. "I'll start it off with the beautiful redhead."

He came to the stage and held his hand out to Kathleen. By the time they got to the middle of the dance floor, men were coming through the gate with a partner or hurrying to choose one of the four girls on the stage.

"You've missed your calling." Kathleen matched her steps to Pete's. "You should have been a ringmaster at a circus."

"Think so?" Pete laughed and whirled her around. "Honey, I'm just now gettin' warmed up."

Willie had a surprisingly good voice. Following "San Antonio Rose," the band played "Tumbling Tumbleweeds," a slow waltz.

"Looks like a good crowd."

"Each dance will last a little over ten minutes. Think your feet will hold out?"

"I'll not dance every dance."

"Wanna bet? We'll have to limit the number of consecutive dances or one of these gents will hog you all evening."

Kathleen laughed. "Wanna bet?"

She would have lost the bet. The five girls never had a chance to sit down. Men stood in line to dance with them. Kathleen danced with men she had never seen before. Some of them danced really well, while others merely swayed back and forth, which was fine with her.

The band was playing "When I Grow Too Old to Dream" when Kathleen stepped into the arms of a well-dressed man with dark hair, graying at the temples. His coat was an expensive tweed.

"Good evening, Kathleen." The words were said softly in her ear as they moved across the floor.

"Good evening."

He held her firmly to him, making it easy to follow his steps. She wondered vaguely at the familiarity of his using her first name, then dismissed the thought.

Theodore Nuding was sure that she could feel the pounding of his heart. After seeing her name listed as one of the ladies who would be available for dancing, he had taken great pains with his disguise. He had darkened his hair, put in the false gray, colored his eyebrows, and even darkened the skin on his face. He was better at making himself look old, but tonight he had wanted to look attractive.

He turned his head until his nose touched her hair and breathed in the scent of her. She was so lovely, so graceful. He spread the fingers of the hand on her back in order to feel more of her. They danced slowly. He knew that he danced well. His mother had taught him.

The dance was over all too quickly for Nuding, but he was a patient man. He released her and stepped back. She had not said a word after the initial greeting, but it had not been necessary to hear her voice. He knew it as well as he knew his own.

"Thank you, my dear," he said, and quickly walked

away before she could examine his face too closely. By the time Nuding reached the back of the crowd where he could watch her unobserved, she had another partner and was dancing.

Kathleen was a little puzzled. Something about the man she had just danced with was familiar. Her mind, accustomed to ferreting out details for her stories, searched her memory and came up with nothing.

To her utter surprise, when it came time to change partners again, she found herself in Johnny's arms.

"Where did you come from? I didn't see you here."

"You've been too busy to look."

When Willie began to sing, "Thanks for the Memory," Johnny's arms tightened around her just a fraction. They didn't talk. Kathleen couldn't have carried on a coherent conversation because she was flooded with conflicting feelings: resentment that he had stayed away for so long and gratitude that he was here and holding her. She closed her eyes and enjoyed the wonderful feel of him, his breath in her hair, the warmth of his hand on her back and his heart beating against hers.

The dance was over before Kathleen realized it. They stood together in the crowd waiting for the next song.

"How are your feet holding out?" Johnny asked. "You've danced every dance. We can sit this one out."

"They're still all right."

"If you don't want to polka, we'd better move over to the side." The song was the "Beer Barrel Polka," and some of the dancers were showing off. He took her hand, and she followed him to the side of the dance floor.

"I'll use a couple of my tickets and you can sit out if you're tired."

"I'm not that tired."

Words dried up between them, and they watched the dancers. Dale Cole was dancing with her husband. Theresa was dancing with Doug Klein from the funeral home. Millie was there and didn't lack for partners. Kathleen saw Judy taking pictures of the band for the *Gazette*. Later she was dancing with a cowboy with sandy hair and sideburns. After one dance with Theresa, Jude mingled with the crowd, explaining about the iron lung.

"We're going to have a tag dance, folks. This is the way it works." Pete's voice came over the microphone. "All you men without a partner give your ticket to the gate keeper and come on in. For the next twenty minutes you can tap a gent on the shoulder and take his partner. After you've been tagged, you can tag another gent. Now this is going to be fun. Turn the lights down, boys. Everyone enjoy the dance."

Pete watched, thinking that Harry Cole might lead Dale off the floor and was relieved when they started dancing. Cole was playing the big dog. He had swallowed hook, line, and sinker Jude's line about his run for public office the day he had come to the clinic to give notice that Dale was going to quit. Pretty clever of Jude. If it had been left up to Pete, he'd have just rearranged the bastard's face. Pete waited until a dozen couples had exchanged partners before he tapped Harry on the shoulder.

"You're tagged. My turn with this pretty woman," Pete said cheerfully.

Harry looked at him first with surprise, then as if he'd like to run him through with a rapier. Pete paid him not the slightest attention, just elbowed him aside and took Dale in his arms. They moved away from the stunned man.

"Why? Why, did you . . . do that?" Dale gasped.

"Because I wanted to dance with you." Deep in the

crowd, he tightened his arm around her. Pete was a strong dancer and she followed him easily. "Is it so wrong to want to dance with you?"

"He'll be furious." The distress was notable in her voice.

"I gave him the chance to get off the floor if he didn't want to be tagged." Pete moved his cheek against her hair.

"He . . . never thought anyone would want to dance with me."

"He was wrong! I've been waiting for the chance."

"You'll be stuck with me."

"I hope so. Are things going all right?"

"I guess so."

Johnny tapped him on the shoulder. "Go away."

"Not on your life. Give up, man, or I'll deck you."

"I'll be back, Dale."

Pete looked for Kathleen, knowing that they would dance for only a minute or two before someone cut in. He tapped her partner on the shoulder and took her in his arms.

"How ya doin', sugar?"

"Good. Johnny saw you dancing with Mrs. Cole. Her husband is giving you dirty looks. He looks mad enough to chew nails."

"Is that why Johnny cut in?"

"I don't know. Someone cut in on him."

"That bastard beats her. Did you know that?"

"I'd . . . heard—"

Pete was tapped on the shoulder by the man in the tweed coat. When he took Kathleen's hand she noticed he had a deep white scar across the back of his hand. A man she knew at the plant in the city had one like it. She turned to look up into his face, but they were too close.

"Hello, again." His voice was a mere whisper in her ear.

"Do I know you?"

"Name's Robert Brooks."

"Kathleen Henry, but you knew my name."

"The announcer said, 'Kathleen, the pretty redhead.' He was right about you being pretty."

"Thank you."

Johnny tapped the man on the shoulder. His arms dropped reluctantly from around Kathleen, and he moved away.

"Who is that guy?"

"He said he was Robert Brooks."

"He's been watching you like a hawk."

"Maybe I remind him of someone."

Johnny had to give Kathleen over to another partner. He looked for Pete and found him dancing again with the nurse from the clinic.

"I wish you . . . hadn't—" Dale was saying.

"Why hasn't he cut back in?"

"He's too . . . angry."

"Godamighty, Dale. As bad as I wanted to dance with you, I'd not do anything to get you hurt. What's the matter with that son of a bitch?"

"He's always been like that." Her voice quivered.

It was the last few minutes of the dance before intermission. The lights were turned down even more. Pete pressed his cheek tightly against hers.

"You don't love him, do you?"

"I've forgotten what love is."

"Leave him. Dale, honey. I'll take care of you and the boy." They were barely moving now.

She stirred in his arms and looked up at him. "You don't know what you're saying."

"Yes, I do. I'm in love with you. Don't ask me why. I just

am. I've given this a lot of thought. I've been looking for a woman like you all my life."

"You can't be!"

"I am! He's made you feel that a man wouldn't find you desirable. Godamighty! I should beat the hockey out of him just for that. I damn sure will if he hurts you again."

"Please. I'm married to him. He'll take Danny."

The music ended, and seconds later the lights came on.

"Thank you, Mrs. Cole," Pete said loudly enough for those nearby to hear.

"Intermission," Willie was saying. "We need time to smoke and wet our whistles. We'll be back in fifteen minutes."

Pete turned away when he saw Harry walking across the floor toward his wife.

Chapter Twenty-two

THERE'S A FELLOW OUT THERE slappin' the shit out of his woman."

The piano player, a veteran, leaning heavily on his cane, came in from outside where he had gone to smoke.

"What did you say?" Pete jumped to his feet.

"Some no-good fart-knocker is out there beatin' up on a woman. Somebody's got to do somethin'. Hell, I can't do nothin' with this bum leg," he added, as Pete shot out the door.

In a shadowed corner away from the door Harry was holding Dale against the wall with his forearm against her throat. His other hand was fastened in her hair.

"You're a worthless slut. You're a goddamned trashy whore. You've been carryin' on with that mouthy son of a bitch. You've disgraced me—" He slapped her, his hand against her cheek making a loud clapping sound.

"Get away from her!" Fury tore through Pete, shutting off his breath. He started to speak again, choked, and gulped down spittle and air. He grabbed Harry by the back of the neck.

"Bast . . . ard! I . . . ought to kill you!"

Harry was snatched back so suddenly that he stumbled

and never had a chance to regain his balance. Pete's fist slammed into his mouth, knocking him off his feet. Blood splattered over his white shirt.

"Get up, you shithead. You're goin' to know what it's like to get some of what you've been givin' her."

"No! Please . . ." Dale caught Pete's arm.

Pete was too angry to hear her pleading. He shrugged her arm away, reached down, and grabbed Harry by his coat and hauled him to his feet. He backed him against the building and slapped him first on one side of the face and then the other, rocking his head back and forth. Blood from Harry's nose ran freely down over his mouth and onto his shirt. Pete continued to slap him, cursing him with every blow. Harry hung almost limp against the building.

"You sorry, rotten piece of horseshit. You're not fit to lick her shoes. Try picking on someone who'll fight back, you low-down, stinkin' coward!"

"Hey, fellow, that's enough." Willie put a hand on Pete's arm. "Leave enough of him for the sheriff."

Pete stepped back, and Harry slumped to the ground.

"What's going on here?" Sheriff Carroll, his flashlight illuminating the area, came out the door of the school. Johnny was behind him.

Pete went to where Dale leaned against the building, her face hidden in the crook of her arm. He put his hands on her shoulders and turned her toward him.

"I'm sorry. I'm so damn sorry. I caused this by dancing with you, didn't I?"

Dale stood with her head bowed. "He would have found another excuse."

It was some time before the men watching Dale realized that she was crying. There was no contortion of her features, no quivering lips, only a soundless outpouring of grief as tears crept down her cheeks.

"He'll kill me now, and Danny will be alone with him," she said hoarsely.

"What happened here, Mrs. Cole?" Sheriff Carroll asked.

"He was . . . angry with me."

"Did he hurt you?"

"He slapped me."

"This isn't the first time," Pete said. "I've seen bruises on her, around her neck, where he's choked her. He's a yellow coward. A man who beats a woman is as low a son of a bitch as there is."

"Looks like you taught him a lesson. Mr. Cole, can you get on your feet?"

Pete didn't wait for Harry to move. He reached down, hauled him up, and leaned him against the wall.

"Put the yellow-backed, belly-crawling shithead in jail. He's not man enough to fight anybody but a woman."

"I can't arrest him because he slapped his wife. There's no law against it."

"Now that's a hell of a note!"

"Can't help it, son, that's the way it is."

Harry came out of his daze and away from the wall. He pulled a handkerchief from his pocket, held it to his nose, and pointed a shaky finger at Pete.

"He attacked me."

"You're lucky he got to you first," Willie said. "I'd of broke your damn neck. Wife beaters are at the bottom on my list of human beings."

"Who are you to judge?" Harry sneered.

"Take over for me in there, Willie." Pete put his arm around Dale.

"Yeah. It stinks out here."

"If you even think about doing this again, I'll strip the hide off you and feed it to the buzzards." Pete shoved Harry back up against the wall.

Harry stiffened his legs and with a show of defiance moved from the wall. "Let's go home, Dale."

"She's not going."

"She's my wife."

"Dale?" Pete held her arms and looked into her face. "I'll find a place for you. You don't have to go with him."

"I've got to. Danny." The look of hopelessness in her eyes tore at Pete's heart.

"You and Danny. Make the break, Dale," Pete pleaded. "I promise you that he'll not hurt you or Danny ever again."

"Come on, Dale. You're only making things worse for yourself." Harry turned to the sheriff. "I have a standing in this town. You arrest this ruffian, or I'll have your job."

"You can have it anytime you want, Harry," Sheriff Carroll said calmly.

"Mr. Cole to you. I'll be down Monday morning to file charges."

"I'll be out of town all next week, *Harry*."

"Come on, Dale." Harry moved away, fully expecting Dale to follow. When she didn't, he turned. "Come with me now or you'll be on your fat ass out in the street to-morrow morning . . . without Danny. Don't expect to see him again. I'll not have him corrupted by trash like you're hanging around with."

Pete looked at Dale, waiting for her answer. She was staring at Harry as if she had never seen him before. Slowly she shook her head.

"I'm through with you, Harry. You've hit me, shamed

me and Danny for the last time. I wish I never had to see your mean face again." There was a fearful tremor in her voice.

"That does it! You been screwin' this—"

"Say it, and you'll be swallowing teeth," Pete threatened. The men standing around, even Johnny and the sheriff, grinned.

"Well, it seems you've made your choice," Harry sneered. "I'll get my son and take him home."

"The boy belongs with his mother," Pete said, with his fist drawn back. "Stay away from him."

"I'm taking my son. The law will back me. Isn't that right, Sheriff?"

Sheriff Carroll looked steadily back at Harry. "The boy stays with his mother."

Harry exploded in a rage. "You'll be sorry for this." He pointed his finger at the sheriff. "I'll ruin you! I've got influence in this town."

"We'll see how much influence you have after folks find out how you treat your wife."

Harry was too angry to comprehend the sheriff's words. He pointed a finger at Pete.

"As for you, you'll wish you'd never come to this town, this county or this state."

"Go home, Harry," Sheriff Carroll said firmly. "You've caused enough trouble here tonight."

Almost choking on his fury, Harry stumbled off into the darkness.

"Sheriff, will you go with me and Mrs. Cole to get some things for her and the boy?" Pete asked when Harry had left.

"Why sure. Be glad to."

"Where is the boy, Dale?" Pete asked gently.

"In the playroom."

"Do you know him, Johnny?"

"No, but I'll find him."

Pete came close, and whispered. "Take him to Jude's. We'll be along."

Kathleen was dancing with the man in the tweed coat again. Johnny waited for the dance to end, then beckoned for her to come to the side of the dance floor.

"What's going on? Where's Pete?" Kathleen asked him. "Someone came in and said he was in a fight."

"It wasn't much of a fight. Dale Cole's husband was slapping her around, and Pete lit into him like a tornado." Johnny chuckled. "Pete's a caution when he's riled up."

"Good for Pete."

"Mrs. Cole is leaving her husband. Pete asked me to find her boy and take him to Jude's. Do you know him?"

"I've seen him, but from a distance. He goes to Emily's grandmother's house after school. Emily is right over here." Kathleen tilted her head toward a pretty blonde girl. "She'll help you find him."

"That fellow in the fancy coat is still watching you." Johnny had started to walk away, but turned back. "How many times has he danced with you?"

"I haven't counted them." Kathleen felt a little thrill that Johnny might be jealous. "He's kind of good-looking and real nice. He hardly says a word."

"He's a stranger around here. I wouldn't get too friendly with him. I'll get Emily and find the boy."

After Johnny left, Kathleen sat down and slipped off her shoes, a hint that her feet were tired. Paul came and sat down beside her.

"Tired, huh?"

"My feet feel like they weigh a hundred pounds each."

"Addie said you've danced every dance."

"She got me into this. I'm thinking seriously about putting a wicked spell on her."

Paul chuckled. "I just bet she'd handle it."

"People turned out, didn't they? They know how important the clinic is to the town."

"We've made a tidy sum for the clinic tonight. The donation jar over there is stuffed. Someone put a couple of hundred-dollar bills in it."

"No kiddin'? That's great. Usually when someone donates that much they want credit for it."

"The booths did well, but the dance took in the most money."

"It's a good band. Is Willie and the Chicken Pluckers really their name?"

"It was Will Hartman and the Boys. They've got a good gimmick going with the hillbilly outfits. If I were them, I'd capitalize on it and keep the theme and the name permanently."

"Even with a gimmick, the music was good."

"Someone said Pete got into a fight outside. I'd hate to tangle with that bruiser. Being in the navy for sixteen years, he's probably fought his way out of a hundred bars."

"Johnny said it was because Mr. Cole was slapping his wife. I hope the sheriff files a report, then we could put it in the paper. Maybe the Gas and Electric Company will transfer him out of here or, better yet, fire him."

Paul's homely face lit up in a smile. "I'll talk to Sheriff Carroll."

Emily and Johnny came by. Emily held the hand of a small blond boy.

"Emily is going with me," Johnny said as they passed.

"Danny is more comfortable with her. He doesn't know me."

"Anything changed between you and Johnny?" Paul asked after Johnny left.

"Nothing has changed. I intended to see Mr. Fairbanks again this week, but he's away for a few days working in the city. I don't want to talk to Junior."

"Going to make it final?"

"It's what Johnny wants." She slipped her feet back into her shoes. "Do you think I'll be deserting the ship if I leave now? The crowd has thinned down, and I am tired. Your wife worked my tail off today."

Paul chuckled. "She's good at that. She can get more work out of people with her sweet ways than an overseer can with a whip. Go on home. You've done your duty."

There was more traffic than usual because of the carnival. Kathleen didn't notice the car that followed her at a distance, stopped with lights off and sat there until she was in her house and the lights were on.

Theodore Nuding lingered for several long minutes in his dark car and stared at the lighted bedroom window. After a while he drove slowly out to the Clifton place, parked his car in the shed, and went into the house.

The front hall was jammed with boxes and crates that had been delivered the night before. He had given strict orders that the truck arrive at twelve o'clock midnight, not a minute earlier or later. A bonus of fifty dollars to each of the two men would be the reward. The cargo was unloaded quickly and silently. After the men were paid, they had left quickly and silently.

Nuding went to the small room where he kept his personal belongings. After removing his good clothes, he dressed again for work and went up the stairs to Kathleen's room. This was where he spent most of the time while he was in the house. He loved to be here, where she would be. He settled in the comfortable chair at the table and opened his observation diary.

11 P.M. *Mother, dear Mother. This has been the most wonderful evening of my life since I lost you. I danced with Kathleen five times. I wanted to dance every dance with her, but I had to be careful and not be too conspicuous. I held her in my arms, Mother. I actually held her. She is slender as a reed and moves like an angel. I pressed her against me—her breasts and her belly. She is perfect. Her skin is like smooth silk, and on her nose are tiny little freckles. I wanted to fall at her feet and worship. I had so wanted her here for Christmas, but I fear I will not be ready. It is taking me a little longer because I tire so quickly. I've already decided how I will take her. A man in Dallas advised me and arranged for me to have what I need. It is wonderful what money can do. For a while I thought I might have to eliminate Johnny Henry. Now I don't think it will be necessary. They are drifting away from each other. Doing away with him would not be difficult, but the death of a war hero would bring attention to Rawlings. Any number of officers would be poking about, and I don't want that. I am still not feeling well, Mother. I tire easily. I was so excited tonight that I forgot to be tired until I was on the way home. Tonight I will go to bed early so that I can work in her room all day tomorrow. The sheriff wouldn't expect the "weatherman" to be out on Sunday.*

Nuding closed the journal on his rambling entry, leaned back, closed his eyes, and relived the time he had spent with Kathleen.

*   *   *

By Monday noon the town was buzzing, not only about
the success of the carnival, but about the supervisor at the
Gas and Electric beating his wife. At Paul's urging, Sheriff
Carroll had filed a disturbance report which could be legally
used as a news item in the paper. Paul wrote the story,
which would appear in the Tuesday edition of the *Gazette*.

> The success of Saturday night's carnival to raise
> funds for the polio ward at the clinic was slightly
> marred by an altercation that required Sheriff
> Carroll's attention.
>
> Harry Cole, manager of the branch of
> Oklahoma Gas and Electric, became enraged at
> his wife for dancing with another man during
> the tag dance. The sheriff was called by a con-
> cerned citizen who discovered Mr. Cole abusing
> his wife outside the school. The lady suffered
> bruises on her face, a cut lip, and a black eye
> which were attended to by Dr. Jude Perry.
> Charges are pending.

Pete hired Junior Fairbanks to appear with Dale in front of
a judge to get a restraining order against Harry Cole,
which was granted after the judge saw Dale's face. She and
Danny had spent the night at Jude's, with Millie Criswell
acting as chaperone. The humiliation of the town's knowing Harry had been beating her was making Dale physically ill. She had walked the floor most of the night.
Concerned, Pete asked Theresa and Jude to talk with her.

"He is the one who should feel humiliated," Jude
counseled Dale. "You've done nothing to be ashamed of.
The higher you hold your head, the less people will think
of him. You are an excellent nurse. We value you here at

the clinic. If you choose to, you can work toward getting your RN."

"I love nursing, but can I make a living for myself and my son?"

"You can work full-time here," Jude said gently.

"Thank you, Doctor. Now I'm wondering why I put up with him for so long. The final straw was when I realized the influence he would have on Danny."

"You put up with it because he was 'the devil you knew'. You were afraid of going into the unknown. We all are."

Jude was amazed at the depth of Pete's feelings for Dale Cole. Although a very nice person, she was far different from any woman he had thought Pete would be interested in. She was mature, had a child, and was rather plump. None of this seemed to matter to Pete. He had fallen in love.

Later that day Pete moved Dale's and Danny's things into the room at Mrs. Ramsey's, where Kathleen had stayed when she first came to Rawlings. It had been Theresa's idea for them to rent the room; she felt that Dale should not be alone at night because that was when Harry would most likely try to harm her.

"I'm glad to have you here." Mrs. Ramsey put her arms around Dale. "I suspected what was going on at your house from the things Danny would say. You poor dear. You have put up with a lot."

Harry, of course, put out his version of what happened on Saturday night. The four employees at the Gas and Electric listened politely and didn't believe a word of it.

"I tried to get her to come home with me. She may have had a drink of something. She never acts the way she did unless she's been drinking. She fought me like a wild woman. Look at the marks on my face. What was I to do?"

To Harry's way of thinking, the stink in the town would die down. He was worried about word getting back to his bosses in the city. Tuesday, when the *Gazette* came out, he became so angry he put his fist through the partition in his office.

The "weatherman" read the *Gazette* at the Frontier Cafe while he was eating his lunch. The article in the box on the front page caught his interest, and he read it through twice.

On the one occasion that he had been to the utility office to have electricity turned on at the Clifton place, he had witnessed Harry Cole's treatment of an employee. The man had not understood his instructions. Harry Cole had berated him, calling him a stupid lout. Nuding had wanted to put his fist in Cole's face. The employee, needing the job, had stood quietly and taken the insults. At that moment Nuding had formed an instant dislike for Harry Cole.

An idea was beginning to form in his mind. Most men were animals, in Nuding's opinion, and a man who abused a woman, God's most perfect creature, was the lowest form of animal life. Nuding folded the paper and sipped his coffee.

With his weatherman props in his hand, Nuding rose, paid his bill, and left the restaurant. He drove to his place on the hill. The sky was cloudless, giving him no excuse for being there. He took a roundabout route back to the Clifton place, left his car in the shed, and went to his secret room.

From a locked box he took out a sheaf of handwritten

notes, a carefully labeled vial of clear liquid, and a syringe with a needle attached. For the next half hour he studied the notes. One part stood out from the rest. *An injection of more than one cc is fatal. (Destroy syringe and needle after use.)* Nuding had purchased it for his own use should something go wrong with his plans to keep Kathleen with him. He could never endure the consequences of an arrest and had made plans to join his mother should that happen.

At the restaurant it had occurred to him that he should test the potency of the liquid to be sure it would work if he needed to use it on himself. A man who would beat a woman was the ideal guinea pig for him to try it on. He filled the syringe with one and one half cc's of the liquid, placed it in a small metal case, and slipped it in his pocket.

He knew what he was going to do. He just had to plan carefully when he was going to do it.

Chapter Twenty-three

IN THE DAYS THAT FOLLOWED, Kathleen found herself thinking about the man in the tweed coat. Something about him made her uneasy. She couldn't put her finger on what it was. He had been a perfect gentleman and a very good dancer. During a rather fast fox trot, his breathing had become labored as if he was tiring; but he didn't hesitate and murmured a rather breathless "thank-you" when the dance was ended.

Kathleen described him to Adelaide, but her friend didn't know him. They explored the possibility that he was a salesman passing through town who had come to the carnival because there wasn't much else to do.

The only news she had of Johnny came from Pete.

"We were having a beer last night at the Silver Spur and Mack Boone came in. His daddy is Barker's foreman, but he's been laid up for a while and Boone has been taking over."

"I know who he is." Kathleen poured herself more tea and refilled Pete's coffee cup. "He used to compete at the rodeo and seemed to be a sore loser. It was always someone else's fault if he didn't place. The animal didn't perform or he wasn't given the mount he drew. Johnny called him a whiner even then."

"Sounds like him. He's got his claws out for Johnny. Threw out a few remarks about Fleming cattle wandering over to the Circle H. Johnny ignored him for a while. Then Mack said something to one of the cowboys about Marie Fleming having the hots for him and following him around until it was hard for him to get his work done. Faster than you could spit, Johnny had him by the throat and shoved up against the wall."

"Marie can't stand Mack Boone. She's in love with Bobby Harper; she told me so the day we went to Frederick."

"Johnny's got a short fuse these days. He would've strangled Boone, if I hadn't interfered. He thinks more of the Flemings than he lets on, especially the kids."

"Lucas has always looked up to Johnny as a kind of hero. I wish Johnny would pay more attention to him."

"He did a pretty good job of it when we drove the horses up from McCabes'. They were thicker than thieves. Barker kept his distance, probably so the boy could be with Johnny. Lord, I wish I'd had a daddy like Barker when I was growing up."

"Barker should be told that Mack is making remarks about Marie."

"Johnny warned Mack that if he ever heard of him even mentioning either of the Fleming girls, he'd be walking spraddle-legged for the rest of his life. Then he added that he had a witness who saw him driving Fleming cattle onto Henry land, hoping Johnny would be accused of stealing them. Johnny told him that if it happened again, he would go to the sheriff and swear he had tried to sell them; that is, after he had strung him up by the thumbs and left him hanging all night.

"The way he said it would have put the fear of God in me. Johnny can be a mean son of a gun when something doesn't set right with him. Must be his Cherokee blood."

"The last time I saw him was at the carnival."

Pete reached over and squeezed her hand. "If you'd ask me, I'd say he's missing the boat. Once in a man's life he has a chance to catch the brass ring. If he misses it, he's out of luck."

"Have you caught your brass ring, Pete?" she asked softly.

"Yes, and I'm going to hold on to it. Dale is filing for divorce. She hasn't said that she would marry me. It's too much to ask her to make a decision like that right now. I don't want her to come to me because she thinks she can't make it on her own. I want her to want me as much as I want her."

"You're a good man, Pete Perry. Dale is lucky you fell in love with her."

"Lordy, sugar." Pete laughed, and his blue eyes gleamed. "No one's ever called me a *good* man! I've been a horse's patoot most of my life."

"I don't believe it."

"Johnny could tell you things about me that would curl your hair."

"Pete Perry, have you looked at me lately? If there's anything I don't need, it's more curls in my hair."

The end of the week marked the seventh week since Kathleen's last menstrual period. She didn't dare to hope that Johnny had made her pregnant six weeks ago when they made love. She had been heartbroken when she came out of the bathroom and found him gone. She had curled up in the bed and sobbed. Maybe it was then that one of his sperm had made its way into one of the eggs her body had released. *God, please let it be true.*

The doctor who delivered Mary Rose had said that he had no idea what had been responsible for her deformity. All these years Kathleen had wondered if something she had done during pregnancy had caused it.

Johnny, however, had been certain that his heredity was to blame and had left her. When she had needed him the most, he had let her down. Why was she still madly, crazily in love with him?

On the spur of the moment, Kathleen decided that she would go to the clinic and talk to Jude, not as her friend, but as Dr. Perry, MD. She called Millie and made an appointment, fearing that if she thought longer about it, she would change her mind.

The morning of the appointment she was so nervous she couldn't drink her tea. She considered canceling. Then strengthening her resolve, she bathed, dressed, and walked to the clinic so that on the way she could plan what she was going to say.

"Good morning." Millie's was a cheerful greeting when she entered the reception room at the clinic. "Have a seat. Doctor will be with you in a minute."

Before she could sit down, Jude opened the door of his inner office. "Morning, Kathleen. Come in."

"Oops. Short minute," Millie exclaimed with a good-natured smile.

Kathleen's legs felt like stiff sticks as she walked into Jude's office. He went behind his desk and motioned for her to sit down.

"I never got to thank you for your part in making the carnival such a success. Enough money was raised to outfit the polio ward. Now let's hope we don't have any patients. The medical journals indicate that researchers are close to a polio vaccine, but it could still be years away."

"Working toward a good cause usually brings a community together. A lot of people had a hand in making the carnival a success."

Kathleen chose to get right to the point of her visit before she lost her nerve. She swallowed hard before she began.

"I realize that you're busy. But there are a few things of a personal nature that I'd like to discuss with you . . . confidentially, of course."

"Of course, and take as much time as you want." He leaned forward and studied her pale face.

"You may have heard that Johnny and I had a baby in 1942 before he went to war." She paused to take a deep breath. "Mary Rose lived only forty-eight hours. She was . . . she was—"

"I have the medical records," he said kindly, and reached for a folder on his desk. "Theresa and I have gone over them carefully. Do you want to know what we think about the birth?" Kathleen nodded and he continued. "Your baby was born without a cap on her skull. It's a condition called anencephaly and is not compatible with life. It was a miracle she lived as long as she did out of the womb."

"What caused it? Johnny thinks he . . . that his mother—"

"Let me help you," Jude said, seeing her struggle for words. "Johnny thinks that his mother is the product of an incestuous coupling. He had convinced himself that her resultant defects were passed along to him and to Isabel, each in a different way. It made Isabel wild and uncaring for anything except her sexual pleasure, and it made him unable to sire normal children. He has no explanation as to why the *blight*, as he referred to it, skipped over his other sister, Henry Ann."

Jude went to the bookcase, pulled out a large volume, brought it back to the desk, and opened it to a place he had marked with a scrap of paper.

"I don't know if Dorene was the product of incest. If she was, so was my father, Hardy. They were brother and sister. No one disputed that or the fact that the folks on Mud Creek were a lusty clan that took their pleasure whenever and wherever it was convenient." He sighed in disgust.

"It's a medical fact that continuous incest within a family for generations will produce people of an inferior intellect, stunted stature, and deformity. Not one thing points to this being the case with your baby."

Kathleen sat in frozen silence, her eyes riveted to his face.

"I believe that a natural but rare failure to develop properly in the womb is what happened to your baby." His palm was covering a picture on the page of the book. "This may be difficult for you to view, but I think you should at least glance at this, if only to convince yourself that such birth defects have been recorded in other pregnancies and were no fault of yours or Johnny's."

Jude removed his hand. Kathleen looked down at the sketch of a baby, then quickly away. Her eyes filled rapidly with tears.

"Is that comparable to the way Mary Rose looked?" Jude asked gently.

Kathleen nodded, her face crumbling. While she composed herself, he returned the book to the bookcase, then waited for her to wipe her eyes.

"I must tell you that I've not had much experience in pediatrics. Theresa worked for a year in that department at St. Anthony in the city. We discussed this case after Isabel died and Johnny mentioned 'watered-down blood.' Of the hundreds of babies born during the time she was there, Theresa can recall only one case similar to your baby's condition. It was definitely not the fault of the parents. They had already had four perfectly normal beautiful children."

"Thank you," Kathleen whispered. She allowed the tears to roll down her cheeks unchecked. "I wish I had known this . . . back then."

"Is this what's keeping you and Johnny apart?"

Kathleen gulped and looked away from the kindest eyes she had ever seen.

"He may have fallen out of love with me and used the baby's birth as an excuse to leave me."

"That doesn't sound like the Johnny I used to know. That Johnny would have said plainly why he was going."

"He did. Later."

"Had he been looking forward to the baby?"

"He could hardly wait. We had names picked out for a boy, and a girl, but we just knew it would be a boy. The last few weeks he wouldn't go any farther away than the barn for fear that I would need him. We talked about a little girl with red curls, or a boy with dark hair like his.

"On the morning my water broke, he was so excited. Then when it was over, they brought Mary Rose to me and let Johnny come into the room. They had given me the bad news and told me how she would look, but they hadn't told Johnny. I'll never forget the look on his face. Nothing has been the same between us since. He became more and more distant. Then he enlisted—not to beat the draft; his number was not that high on the list. He just wanted to get away from me."

"Did he talk about the baby at all?"

"No. All he said was that he couldn't give me the family I wanted. He told me to get a divorce while he was gone and find someone that would." Kathleen twisted the handkerchief in her hands and blurted, "I may be pregnant."

Jude sat back in his chair, showing not a trace of the surprise he was feeling.

"I still had on my nightgown the morning he came to tell me that Gabe Thomas had been killed. It just happened. I know he was sorry because he got right up and left the house."

"You've missed your period?"

"Yes, but sometimes I'm late."

"How do you feel about the possibility of being pregnant?"

"I don't dare hope—"

He pushed a calendar toward her. "Show me when you had your last period and when you made love with Johnny."

Kathleen's finger traced along the dates then stopped. "Here. I seldom go more than three days." Her finger moved to another date. "And this is when we . . . were together."

Jude turned the calendar toward him. "At that time you were in your most fertile period, Kathleen."

"But . . . one time? After so long?"

"Oh, yes. Many women conceive after long periods of abstinence."

Kathleen began to smile. "Jude . . . ah, Doctor, I'll

thank God every day for the rest of my life if he lets me have this baby."

Jude frowned. "Don't get your hopes up . . . yet."

Kathleen didn't listen. "I can't help but hope. If there is the slightest chance . . . I'll hope. I don't want Johnny to know. Please. You won't tell him?"

"If you're pregnant, it isn't my place to tell him; but I think he should know." His voice was grave, his eyes somber.

"No. He'll be angry and think that I tricked him into my bed. I don't want him to know. He doesn't want to chance having another child. I don't want him putting a damper on my happiness." Kathleen's voice was almost shrill. Her blood was pounding.

"We may be getting the cart before the horse here."

"When will we know? I'll not be able to stand the suspense."

"If your dates are right, you are six weeks into your pregnancy. Have you experienced any morning sickness?"

"Not really. I haven't been drinking my tea or eating my toast for the past few mornings, but I chalked that up to a case of the nerves."

"If you want an examination, I'll call Theresa to prepare you. She'll stay with you. She's very good at this."

"Will you be able to tell with any degree of certainty?"

"I believe so. While you're being prepared, I want to refer to some of my medical books. I've not gotten to the place yet where I think I know everything." His smile was beautiful. *The woman who gets you, Doctor Jude Perry, will be a lucky girl.*

*   *   *

Kathleen walked home from the clinic with a smile on her face.

Her heart was celebrating.

At first she had been horribly embarrassed about Jude looking at her private parts. A sheet had been hung so that she couldn't see the doctor or the nurse during the examination. With Theresa being there and acting very professional, as if this was something they did every hour of every day, it had been easier than she expected.

When the examination was over, Jude came around the curtain and smiled down at her.

"I can say, and Theresa agrees, that seven and a half months from now, you may expect a permanent addition to your family."

Kathleen had burst into tears. No way on earth could she have stopped them.

Before she left she asked again that the visit be confidential, and was assured word would not leave the examination room.

At home, she sat down in the big chair, leaned her head against the back, and allowed her mind to absorb the wonderful news. Next August she would have Johnny's baby. It would be all right. God wouldn't be so cruel as to give her this happiness, then take it away.

She placed her hand on her stomach.

"Oh, baby, I'm so glad you're here. There may only be you and me; your daddy may not want you, but I want you so much, and I'll love you so much—"

Theodore Nuding watched Kathleen when she left the house and walked to the clinic. She would be doing some volunteer work, he presumed. If she had been sick, she would have driven the car. When she returned a couple of hours later, she was waltzing along, swinging her purse as if she didn't have a care in the world.

When she was safely in the house, Nuding checked his watch, started his car, and drove to the Gas and Electric office. He had been carefully studying the schedule of the employees. This was the time that he could catch Harry Cole alone in his office.

Harry Cole was looking through the mail left on his desk, searching for a letter from the head office in Oklahoma City. Two days after Dale left him, he had written asking for a transfer to another office. He was having difficulty here, he explained, because of his wife's indiscretions. He had put up with it as long as he could; now he wanted out of the marriage and out of Rawlings.

He rocked back and forth in his swivel chair thinking that he wouldn't have to put up with the stupid cow. She had served her purpose; getting her pregnant right away as he had planned, hoping to stay out of the war.

Harry was sure now that he would not be asked to run for public office nor be offered the position of trustee at the clinic. The *bitch* had seen to that. He had been humiliated when he was served the order restraining him from going near her and Danny. But anger, resentment, and knowing that he was right overrode the humiliation.

This was best for him after all, he decided. He was tired of living with a wife who acted like a whipped puppy. He wouldn't have any trouble getting another woman. This time he would be more choosy. He leaned back in his chair and visualized a young blonde with a slim waist and high, pointed breasts urging him to come to bed.

He'd not marry again. He was certain that he could get what he wanted without tying himself down. There were other advantages as well. The money he earned could be spent entirely on himself. His daydreams were interrupted when he heard someone come into the outer office.

"Office is closed until one o'clock," he called. "Didn't you see the sign on the door?"

He listened for the door to close; when it did not, he got up from his chair and went to the counter where customers paid their bills. A shabby-looking man in an old brown hat stood there.

"Didn't you hear what I said? The office is closed until one o'clock."

"I heard you and I saw the sign. I want to report that one of your electric poles is down and wires are on the ground."

"Where? Did you run into it?"

"I'll show you on the map."

"All right, but make it snappy." Harry went back into his office. A large map of the area was under a glass on his desk. He sank down in his chair.

"I thought it important that I report the wires down."

"The road crew will be in soon, and they'll know about it; but show me if it'll make you happy, then leave. I'm busy," he said harshly.

Nuding moved around behind him to look at the map over his shoulder.

"Humm . . . It was along here somewhere near where the two main roads meet." He made a few humming sounds, and a grunt or two as if studying the map while he took the syringe from the metal box.

"This is the place. Right here," he said, and jabbed the needle just above the hairline in the back of Harry's neck.

"What the hell?" Harry jumped.

"I'm sorry about that. I must have had a pin in my tie." Nuding returned the syringe to the metal box and moved around to the front of the desk. "I lied about a pole being down."

"Get . . . out—"

Nuding looked at his watch. "In about fifteen seconds."

Harry's face began to sag. His hand fell from the edge of the desk onto his lap.

"What . . . Why—" Then the slack mouth opened and closed without making another sound, reminding Nuding of a fish.

"Why did I do it? Because you deserved it. I did you a kindness and injected you above the heart, so that it wouldn't take long. Good-bye, Mr. Cole."

Harry's eyes glazed over and his head fell to the side.

Nuding nodded with satisfaction, walked calmly out of the office and back to his car. *It was good to know that the poison developed by the Nazis during the war was as deadly as the seller said it was.*

Harry Cole's sudden death of a heart attack was a shock to all who knew him. An employee had found him sitting at his desk when he returned after his noon meal. Dr. Perry, acting as coroner, could not find a mark on him and had to assume, without an autopsy, the cause of death to be heart failure. Sheriff Carroll agreed, and an autopsy was not ordered.

Dale learned the news when Doctor Perry returned from the Gas and Electric office. She was stunned. Harry was not a good man, but she hadn't wanted him dead.

"Could my leaving him and the humiliation he suffered have brought on the heart attack?"

"He appeared to me," Jude explained, "to be a man who was constantly under stress. I can't say that a little more pushed him over the edge. From what I learned while talking to the people who worked with him, he seemed during the past few days to have accepted your leaving and was looking forward to a transfer and a new life somewhere else."

"He was always angry at something or someone. If it wasn't me, it was Danny, the men at the Gas and Electric, or someone that he imagined had slighted him in some way. It's strange, but Harry was only happy when he was angry."

"The stress finally caught up with him."

"I've got to tell Danny."

"Pete has gone to the school to get him."

"Thank goodness for that. I should leave now, Doctor. I'll have to make funeral arrangements."

"You'll have all the help you need. I'll take you to Mrs. Ramsey's. That's where Pete is taking Danny."

Later that day Dale was given a letter marked *personal* that had arrived at the office. The message inside came from the main office in Oklahoma City and was a dismissal.

Numerous complaints about conduct unseemly in a manager of one of our substations have been made over the past year. We have no choice but to dismiss you immediately.

Dale ripped the letter to shreds and flushed it down the toilet. Harry was dead. Danny need never know that his father was fired from his job on the day he died.

After the funeral, Dale and Danny moved back into the house. Life had suddenly opened up for Dale. The fear she had lived with for so long was no longer there. She tried to feel sorry about Harry's death, but she felt only relief.

*   *   *

Pete had been very discreet about the help he had given Dale, knowing that it would be easy for tongues to start wagging. Now that he knew what he wanted, he was satisfied to wait.

Instead of leasing or buying land for his horse ranch, Pete decided to put all his assets into the rodeo promotion plan. He spent time talking to Keith McCabe in Vernon, whom he had met when he helped Johnny with his horses. Keith was crusty, a fount of information about the rodeo business and willing to share his knowledge. He had contacts who could supply the information he didn't have.

Johnny had become as irritable as a cow with its teat caught in the fence, and Pete told him so . . . often. Finally one morning, Johnny told him to find another partner for his rodeo scheme because he would be unable to raise the money for his part without mortgaging the ranch, and he would not do that because Kathleen owned part of it.

"Why the hell don't you go see her?"

"I don't want to intrude," Johnny retorted sarcastically. "She seems to have plenty of company."

"What do you mean by that?"

"Every time you come out here you've got something to say about her. She's had her hair cut. She's making progress on her book or Barker came and fixed her sink. She baked a peach pie or some other bit of news."

"I like going there. She's good company."

"It's a free country."

"Dammit, Johnny. You're going to mess around and lose that woman. She'll pack up someday and hightail it out of here and you'll never see her again."

Johnny turned and leaned over the motor he was

working on. Not with a flicker of an eyelash did it show that his heart had jumped up into this throat.

"Is she leaving?"

"No, but for some reason she seems to smile and laugh a lot more than she did. She's happy about something."

"Maybe she filed for the divorce."

"Have you been notified?"

"No, but—"

"Then she hasn't filed."

"I suppose you've been divorced and know all about it."

"I've not been divorced, and I will never be if I can help it. When I marry, it'll be for as long as I live."

"Good luck," Johnny said, and walked away.

It no longer worried him that Pete would make a play for Kathleen now that he was so enamored with Dale Cole. It was a relief in a way that Pete was keeping an eye on Kathleen. It shook him when Pete said something about her moving away. He hadn't thought of that prospect.

He hadn't seen Kathleen since the night of the carnival two weeks before. If he went to see her now, just six days until Christmas, he'd have to have a reason. He couldn't just walk in and tell her that he was so hungry for the sight of her that he couldn't eat or sleep, or that wanting to make love to her was causing his guts to boil just thinking about it.

The only rational thing he could say was that he wanted her to have the gifts he had made for her that first year he was away. The year when he really didn't care if he lived or died.

He would wait, he decided, until a couple days before Christmas, then go see her and take the chance that she wouldn't slam the door in his face.

Chapter Twenty-four

KATHLEEN WAS BOTH HAPPY AND FEARFUL. She was happy because of her pregnancy and fearful each time she went to the bathroom that she would see color, which would mean that she was aborting. She didn't even mind the morning sickness that usually lasted not more than an hour. It was unpleasant, but she endured it gladly because it meant that she was really pregnant.

She longed to tell someone about this wonderful thing that had happened. If she told Adelaide, she would argue that Johnny should be told. So would Marie and Pete. They all loved Johnny. She loved him too; but when he found out, he would hate her. She couldn't bear having him think that she tricked him into making love with her so she could have this baby when she knew he had sworn never to father another child.

The days passed one after the other without as much as a call from Johnny, not that she expected one. The book was half-finished. She wrote to her editor and promised the complete manuscript by April. At night she would read one of the books she brought home from the library. Her favorite authors were Zane Grey and Bess

Streeter Aldrich. She read *A Lantern in Her Hand* twice, something she almost never did.

Mrs. Frisbee, the librarian, told her about a new book by another Kathleen, Kathleen Winsor. *Forever Amber*, a rather racy historical novel, was one of the year's best-sellers. It was enjoyable reading, but Kathleen was not particularly interested in English history.

Her other pleasure was the movies. She went on Sunday nights when fewer people were there. The big nights were Friday and Saturday. Some of the Rialto movies were old. She didn't mind. She went to see an old W. C. Fields picture even though she didn't like slapstick comedy.

As Christmas approached, she got into the spirit and decorated her living room with red paper bells, and silver 'icicles' hung on the green ropes she looped across the window. She mailed Christmas cards to Tom and Henry Ann in Red Rock, Hod and Molly in Kansas, and to the McCabes's.

Pete had been by to tell her that she was invited to spend Christmas at Jude's. In addition to Theresa and her boy, Dale and Danny would be there.

"I don't think I can come, Pete, but thank Jude for inviting me. Barker asked me several days ago. Invite Johnny. If he knows that I won't be there, he'll probably come. I hate to think of his spending Christmas alone."

"I'll ask him. Hey, you look awfully chipper. Did some-one die and leave you a million dollars?"

Kathleen laughed. "I'd look a lot more chipper than this if that happened."

"I'll have to bring you some mistletoe. There are big clumps of it in the trees along the road. I'll hang it in the doorway so I can kiss you every time I come over."

"You don't have to go to all that trouble." She reached up and kissed him on the cheek. "You are a dear, dear friend, Pete. I want you to know that."

Pete was to remember those words in the days ahead.

Nuding was exhausted. He sat in the chair in *her* room and looked around at what he had accomplished during the past two weeks: the plump high bed, satin coverlet and fancy pillows, the Persian carpet on the floor, the armoire filled with clothes from Neiman Marcus, lamps, the desk and typewriter, the dressing table with drawers filled with creams and perfumes. He even had a selection of books for her to read.

He had gone to her house Sunday night while she was at the movies. It had been easy to come across the back field and let himself into the back door with a special key he had. For half an hour he had moved through her rooms, touching her things and wondering why he had not given himself this pleasure before.

She was neat. He knew she would be. Her clothes were aligned in the closet: dresses, skirts, blouses. He buried his face in them, breathing in the scent of her. Before he left, he treated himself to a handkerchief from the drawer of her dresser.

Nuding's main purpose in going there had been to type a note on her typewriter saying that she was leaving. He didn't want anyone looking for her right away and hoped to convince her friends that she was leaving Rawlings to start a new life. He seriously considered burning down the house, but he didn't want to leave Kathleen, once he had her, to come back and do it.

The next day he had gone to Frederick to buy Christmas bells for her room and paper to wrap the gifts he had for her. Now all he had to do was wait until Sunday.

> 10:20 P.M. *Mother, I worked day and night to get the room ready for Christmas. It's in shades of green, her favorite color. What isn't green is ivory. It is somewhat like your room, Mother, except your room was in two shades of blue. After she has been here a while and has become content, she will let me know if she wants a different color. I wish I wasn't so tired. By Sunday I will feel better because then Kathleen and I will be together forever.*

Nuding closed the journal, took the handkerchief from his pocket, and held it to his face. This time next week he would be sitting here with his darling Kathleen, his princess, his angel. She would be his, all his.

Christmas had come to Rawlings and with it cold weather. The temperature went down to freezing. Kathleen put a sweater on under her coat, a scarf on her head, and walked to town. She remembered that her landlady's daughter had been told to walk some every day while she was pregnant.

The downtown was decorated with ribbons, lights, and artificial swags of greens. Kathleen prowled the stores, bought a scarf for Mrs. Ramsey and perfume for Emily, aftershave lotion for Pete and Jude and Paul. A week ago she had bought gifts for the Flemings. They were wrapped and ready to take when she went there on Christmas Day.

At the ten-cent store she bought a small toy for Theresa's son, Ryan, and one for Danny Cole. Then, remembering that she had nothing for Theresa and Dale, she went to the drugstore and chose a fancy box of bath powder for each of them. She walked along the street looking in the stores' gaily decorated windows. When she reached the men's store, she stopped. She had gifts now for everyone except Johnny.

Leroy Grandon had owned the store when she first came to Rawlings. He had wanted to date her, but she'd had eyes only for Johnny Henry. During the war Leroy had sold the store, married a war widow, and moved to Ardmore. The store was more up-to-date now.

An attractive display in the window caught her eye. A light blue cowboy shirt with dark blue piping and buttons was draped over a brown-leather saddle. A wide leather belt lay coiled beside it. The enterprising merchant was playing Christmas music. The song grabbed at her emotions and made her want to cry. *I'll be home for Christmas, if only in my dreams—*

On an impulse, Kathleen went in, bought the shirt and the belt and asked for them to be gift-wrapped.

Leaving the store, she continued on down the street. At the corner a gust of wind hit her. It was so cold that it almost took her breath away. She turned her back to it and didn't see Johnny coming toward her. Holding her scarf under her chin to keep it from blowing off, her shopping bag in her other hand, she started across the street. When she stepped up onto the curb, he was there in his old sheepskin coat, his hat pulled low on his forehead and the leather straps of a horse halter looped over his shoulder.

"Don't you look before you cross the street?"

"Hello, Johnny. I looked." Her cheeks were rosy from the cold. Her breath came out in small white puffs.

"Where's your car?" *Dear Lord! He had dreamed about Christmas at home with her.*

"At home. I walked."

"Won't it run?" *He was home now, and it was Christmas, but they were miles apart.*

"It did yesterday. I walked because I wanted to. How have you been?"

"Fine. Working."

"Pete said you got your horses up from Keith's. How's Ruth?"

"All right. They miss Granny. She died a year ago."

"I'm sorry to hear it."

"Ruth asked about you and said to tell you to come down."

"There's not much of a chance of that. I'm pretty busy."

"I'm pretty busy myself. I came in to the leather shop to get this halter sewed. If you've finished your shopping, I'll give you a ride home."

"I'm not through, but thank you anyway."

"I can wait. I'll get a haircut."

"Thanks, but I'll walk." *I need the exercise because I'm carrying MY child, you uncaring dolt!*

"Suit yourself."

Feeling as if he had been slapped in the face with a wet towel, Johnny walked on down the street. She had changed. She had looked him steadily in the eye and declined his offer of a ride. She had passed the time of day with him as if he were a neighbor she met on a street corner instead of a man with whom she had lived, loved, and had a baby. At one time they had been so close that each had known what the other was thinking.

Was she seeing someone else? The lawyer's son, Junior Fairbanks? Had she fallen in love with Jude? The idea of the job in Central America was becoming more tempting all the time.

Johnny was so absorbed in his thoughts that he forgot to stop in at the barbershop and went on down to where he had left his car. Just as he was getting in, Barker stopped across the street and called out to him.

"Hold on a minute, Johnny." After he parked, his father came across the street. Johnny threw the halter in the back of his car and waited. "It's cold. We might get a norther out of this. You got plenty of hay?"

"Yeah. I got a load from McCabe. What's on your mind?"

"Quite a bit. Let's get in the car out of the wind. I'm getting so damned old my bones creak."

Johnny almost smiled. "Guess I've got eighteen years before I get old and my bones creak." He went around and got under the wheel. Barker slid into the seat beside him.

"I heard what happened between you and Mack Boone. Not from Mack, but from another one of my men who was there."

"Yeah. What about it?"

"Thanks. What he said about Marie wasn't true. She and Bobby Harper have something going. I don't know how serious it is yet."

"Bobby's a good man. I've not heard anything about him that would change my mind."

"I've no objections to Bobby. Mack turned his attention to Janna. It was a mistake. Janna is not Marie."

"She's half his age for chrissake!"

"He put his hand on her, and she hit him across the face with a rope." Barker's face, usually stoic as the head on the nickel, creased in a smile.

"Good for Janna."

"He won't force himself on her. He knows that if I didn't kill him, you would."

Johnny sat quietly and watched Kathleen going into the *Gazette* building.

"I warned him."

"I had a talk with Victor and told him I had to let Mack go. He understood. Mack had a few words to say about you before he left. He's out for trouble. Be on the lookout for him."

"He's a two-bit crook. He drove your cattle onto my land, planning to call the sheriff and say that I'd stolen them. If he'd been smart, he'd have put them in the barn."

"He can't take credit for having many brains, that's sure." Barker opened the car door and stepped out. "By the way, we'd like for you to come out for Christmas. Kathleen will be there."

Johnny chewed the side of his jaw, then said, "Okay."

"See you then." Barker shut the door and backed away, not wanting to press his luck by saying more. By the time he reached his car and started the motor, Johnny was headed out of town.

From the window of the *Gazette* office, Kathleen saw him drive past. She placed her shopping bag on the floor beside the coat rack and pulled the scarf from her head.

"You've had your hair cut," Adelaide said, coming in from the back room. "I like it."

"And hello to you too."

"Your cheeks are rosy and your nose is red, Santa Claus."

"Ho, ho, ho. Have you been a good little girl?"

"Have you?" Paul leaned in the doorway. "We've not seen much of you lately."

"I'm working on my book. I promised to have it finished by April."

"Do you need any help researching the kissing scenes?"

"With you? Your wife would cut my throat."

"It might be worth it." Paul leered and twisted the end of an imaginary mustache.

"All right, Tyrone, just simmer down." Adelaide gazed with mock anger at her husband.

"Tyrone Power?" Dramatically, Kathleen placed the back of her hand to her forehead. "Tyrone Power, right here in Rawlings."

"Well for crying out loud," Adelaide exclaimed. "You're sure in a feisty mood."

"It's Christmas, Addie." Kathleen sat down in the swivel chair. "Anything earthshaking to write about?"

"Paul's working on a couple of stories that came in on the radio. General George Patton died from the injuries he received in that car accident in Germany a few weeks ago. And Cordell Hull won the Nobel Peace Prize."

"It's a shame that a man like General Patton, who goes all through the war, is killed in an accident when it's over."

"What are you doing Christmas? Judy and Sheriff Carroll are coming over. Want to come?"

"I would, but Barker asked me to come for dinner."

"Will Johnny be there?"

"I doubt it. More than likely he'll go to the McCabes'."

"Have you seen much of him?"

"Not since his sister's funeral." She didn't think it necessary to mention that she had seen him just now on the street corner.

"Have you given up on him?"

"Yes." The answer was quick and blunt.

"Well, I guess that takes care of that."

Kathleen slipped into her coat. "I better get along. I want to stop at the library, and I fear that it's getting colder by the minute."

"Paul and I will come by Christmas night if you're going to be home."

"I'll be there."

The wind was so cold that Kathleen decided against walking the extra blocks to the library. By the time she reached home she was out of breath. Leaving her packages and her coat on the couch, she went to the kitchen and lit a fire under the kettle to heat water for tea.

She felt good about her encounter with Johnny. She was pleased that seeing him didn't hurt quite so much. *It's because of you, baby. I know now that I'll always have a part of him with me.*

The following day was Saturday. Pete stopped by.

"Hello, sugar. Is the coffeepot on?"

"I can put it on in a hurry. Leave your coat there on the couch and come to the kitchen. What's in the sack?"

"Donuts. Fresh. With sugar on 'em."

"Well, now, you're the kind of company I like to have."

"I need your expert advice."

"Bribing me with the donuts?"

"Yeah. Pretty smart, huh?"

"I'm glad you came by. I have a sack of presents for you to deliver."

Pete took a package from the pocket of his coat and carefully unwrapped it. He lifted the lid on a pink box. Inside was a gold-colored oval vanity that held face powder and a bottle of Coty perfume.

"It's beautiful," Kathleen exclaimed.

"Do you think Dale will like it?"

"Of course, she'll like it. Any woman would."

"I want to give her something that a woman would like, but wouldn't buy for herself. I don't think she's had many things like this."

"That's sweet, Pete."

"I wondered if I could get you to wrap it kinda fancy."

"Of course. I have some pretty Christmas paper and green ribbon."

"I bought some toys for Danny. Dale says he still believes in Santa Claus, so we'll have Santa leave them."

"You're happy, aren't you, Pete?"

"Does it show that much?" He grinned nervously. "I've not had anyone to do things for for so long that I forgot what Christmas was about. It makes all the difference when you have someone you care about."

"Yes, it does."

"You're a great gal, Kath. I hate seeing that sad look in your eyes."

"I'm not sad! I'm happier than I've been in years. I've become reconciled to the fact that Johnny doesn't want me. I've decided to go on and make the best life that I can for me and . . . for me."

"Are you staying here in Rawlings?"

"No. I can't stay here. After the first of the year, I'll decide where I'm going. My book is due in April. I'd like to get settled somewhere by the end of January."

"That's just a month away. Is there anything I can do to help?"

"I would hate leaving my furniture. I may call on you to help me with that. Barker is such a good friend. He'll help me find a place." Using both hands she gestured widely. "One thing about my kind of work. I can do it anywhere."

Pete watched the expressions flicker across her face. He could have fallen in love with her if he hadn't met Dale. Dammit. Johnny could have the world right here in his hand and he was letting it slip away.

Chapter Twenty-five

By Sunday, the wind had gone down, but it was still cold. Kathleen had planned to go to church services, but her morning sickness had lasted a little longer than usual. She sat in her big chair, nibbled on toast, and listened to the radio.

In the middle of the afternoon, while she was making Christmas cookies to take to the Fleming's, Marie called.

"Are you going to the Christmas Eve service at the church tomorrow night? If you are, I'll stop by and pick you up."

"I'm not sure, but if I decide to go, I'll meet you there."

"We're looking forward to having you here Christmas."

"I'm looking forward to it, too. I'm making cookies to bring. See you then if not before."

Kathleen was not sure that her cookies would compare with Mrs. Fisher's, but she enjoyed cutting out the bells and the stars and sprinkling them with colored sugar. After they baked she placed them on a cloth on the counter. By the time she returned from the movie, they would be cool enough to pack in a tight tin.

She arrived at the theater only minutes before the movie, *Going My Way* with Bing Crosby, started. She liked

Bing Crosby in anything and had been looking forward to this movie. She settled down happily in the middle of the theater to watch.

When the show was over Kathleen stopped in the lobby to wish Mrs. Lansing, who had been selling tickets at the theater for years, a merry Christmas. Then humming "White Christmas," she drove home and parked the Nash in the driveway.

Kathleen unlocked the door, pushed it open, reached and flipped the light switch. Nothing. The room remained in total darkness. *The bulb had burned out.* She closed the door and groped her way toward the bedroom and the switch just inside the doorway.

When a hand was pressed to the back of her head and a cloth to her nose, she hardly had time to struggle before she went limp, and a blanket of darkness settled over her mind.

"Good morning."

Kathleen's eyes were open, but her mind was fuzzy. She squinted against the bright sunlight that blazed through a high window.

"Are you hungry?"

Hungry? The thought of food was revolting. Her stomach lurched. She gagged. Her hand found something soft and held it to her mouth. She tried to lift her head and focus her eyes. Her vision cleared enough to make out a man sitting beside the bed.

"I'm . . . going to . . . puke—" she gasped.

"Oh, my goodness."

He moved quickly and placed a bowl on the bed beside her face. She bent over it, gagged and gagged, but very little came up.

"I'm sorry you're sick. I gave you a very small amount of chloroform. Just enough to get you here."

"You gave me . . . chlor—" She gagged again.

"What do you need?"

"Cracker. Piece of . . . bread."

The man left her sight. Kathleen's head fell back against the pillow. Her mind was clearing enough for her to know that she had to get food into her stomach. She felt something pressed into her hand and lifted her lids enough to see that it was a soda cracker. She chewed it and swallowed, then waited a minute before she attempted to open her eyes again.

When her stomach had settled enough so that she could think, she realized that she was in a strange, very comfortable bed and a man had held a basin for her to throw up. He had also brought her a couple of crackers and placed a wet cloth on her forehead. Carefully she opened her eyes. He was sitting there looking at her. His shirt was white, his tie dark. His face was a blur.

Alarmed, she lifted her head, made an effort to focus, and looked around. *What place is this? What am I doing here?*

"Where am I?" she demanded. "Did you say something about chloroform?" She tried to sit up. He gently pushed her down.

"You're not strong enough to get up."

She looked wildly about, then beneath the covers. She was wearing something made of heavy cream satin.

"Where are my clothes?" Panic made her voice shrill. "Who took off my clothes?"

"You'll not need those old things anymore. You've a wardrobe of new things. The very best."

"Who are you? Where am I?" She tried to get up again.

"No, don't get up yet." He was strong and held her down. "I don't want to use the constraints."

"Am I in a hospital?"

"Goodness, no. You're at home."

"No. I'm not at home."

"You are. This is your home now. You will learn to love it here and never want to leave."

"This isn't my home!" she insisted and peered intently at him. "Oh, my Lord, you're Ted Newman!"

"You remembered," he chuckled delightedly as he moved off the bed and onto the chair. "Yes, I'm Ted Newman, who worked a few feet away from you in the personnel department at Douglas Aircraft. I thought you were the most beautiful thing I'd ever seen. I took care of you then, too. I followed you home every night to see that you got there safely."

"Why, Ted, why?"

He smiled at the puzzled look on her face. "When I first saw you standing beside the water cooler, I knew that someday you would be mine, and I wanted to protect you until I could make a safe and beautiful place for you."

"What in the world are you talking about?" she gasped.

"I know it's hard for you to understand now, but you will. You see I took care of my mother for thirty years. The last twenty of them in a room much like this. She depended on me for everything. When she died I had to give her up."

"I'm sorry she died, but what has that to do with me? Did you follow me to Rawlings? I haven't seen you around town."

He smiled again. "I have many faces. Remember the man who came to your door the day that garage man confronted you in your house? I was guarding you. I would have killed him then if he had touched you."

"It was an . . . old man who came to the door."

"Yes." He looked pleased. "I can be old, young, a Scottish immigrant, or a businessman who likes to dance with a pretty woman with red curly hair at the school carnival."

Kathleen's mouth opened and closed without saying a word. She was stunned and terrified and weak all in one. She feared that if her eyes left him, he would pounce on her.

"You . . . You were nice . . . then." The words came in a hoarse whisper.

He leaned forward. "You needn't worry that I'll hurt you, Kathleen. I would die before I harmed a hair on that beautiful head."

"You . . . undressed me!"

"I had to get you out of those awful clothes. I never touched you in a lewd way. I never will."

"Yeah? You perverted son of a bitch! You try to rape me, and I'll scratch your eyes out."

"I swear on my mother's grave that will never happen. That aspect of life doesn't interest me."

"Then why in the hell am I here?"

"Hush! I won't put up with swear words coming from your mouth. It is coarse and unladylike. There are a few rules that I insist must be obeyed. No swearing is one of them."

"That's just too bad." She threw back the covers. "I'm leaving."

She swung her legs off the bed and felt something drag. She looked down in shocked horror. A cuff circled her ankle, and attached to it was a small chain. When realization struck, she stood and lashed out at him with her fist. He took the blow without flinching and grabbed her wrist.

"I had to do that, Kathleen. When you get used to being here, I will take it off." He released her wrist and stepped back out of her reach.

"I'll never get used to being here!" Sobs rose in her throat.

"You will, my darling girl. I promise you will. It will take a little time. I'll take care of you, be so good to you that you won't want to leave me. I've arranged all this just for you." He waved his hand around the room. "We will sit together in this lovely room in the evenings. During the day while I'm away, you can read or write a book. You can't know how I've dreamed of seeing you here."

"Why?" she managed to say over the sobs in her throat.

"Why you? I understand your wanting to know that," he said kindly. "You are everything that is lovely, virginal—"

"I'm not a virgin. I'm married!"

"I know, but that doesn't matter. You have not been with a man other than your husband. I admire you for that. To me you are virginal—"

"I'm pregnant! You stupid fool. You could've killed my baby with that chloroform!"

When he heard her words, his face seemed to freeze; then his nostrils flared. Ice-blue eyes bored into hers, and she felt cold chills run down her spine.

"Whose?" he asked, the calm voice belied by the cold look on his face.

"My husband's," she retorted sharply, her anger overriding her fear. "I'm not a slut!"

The cold mask dropped from his face in an instant. He smiled, his eyes shining with pure pleasure.

"This is wonderful, Kathleen! Oh, my dear, beautiful, darling girl. We will have our own little princess."

Kathleen looked at him in astonishment then said softly, "You are out of your mind."

"Not at all, my angel." He laughed; and when he did, she had to admit that he was quite handsome. "We will make plans. You can have anything you want for little Kathleen."

"Little Kathleen?"

"Of course. My mother was Kathleen, my angel is Kathleen, and our little princess will be Kathleen."

She sank down onto the bed, her mind groping for an explanation. He was crazy, but in a way that she hadn't ever heard of before.

"It could be a boy," she said dully.

"No! It will be a princess. I will not tolerate a male. Is that understood?"

She leaned forward and put her face in her hands. She had to think. He had said that he wasn't going to rape her, but she couldn't be sure. He had undressed her. At the thought of having lain naked in this strange bed with his eyes on her, her face grew hot beneath her hands. If he raped her, she would lose the baby. She had to think . . . to plan, and she needed time.

"Don't be afraid of me, my angel. I'll not hurt you." His voice was as soft as that of a lover.

"I will hurt *you*, if I can." She spoke forcefully with her face still in her hands.

"I know, and I can't blame you for that. You don't know me yet or understand the depth of my feelings for you."

"I don't want to know you. I want to go home."

"Are you hungry yet? I'm going to have to leave and fix

you something. This is Christmas Eve. You can open your gifts tonight. That will cheer you up."

"I've got to use the bathroom."

"Of course." He opened a door opposite the bed. "I'm embarrassed that this closet is so crude. I didn't have time to prepare it as I wanted. Everything you need is here: toothbrush and paste, soaps, shampoo, and a supply of sanitary napkins, which you will not be needing." He picked up the box and set it beside the door to take out when he left.

"How do I get in there? I'm chained like an animal."

"The chain reaches to any corner of the room, my Kathleen. I'm sorry I had to go to such extremes. I'll take it off in a month or two—"

"Month or two?" Despair gave way to tears, and she began to cry. "I want to go home! Please take the chain off and let me go home. It's . . . Christmas—"

"Don't cry, darling girl. I'd take the chain off if I dared. Look. You have a new typewriter, the very best, and reams and reams of paper. You can write all the stories you want. I have a collection of your stories.

"Wouldn't you like to see the clothes I bought for you at Neiman Marcus? I went down to Dallas and asked for a model with red hair to try on the clothes. She wasn't nearly as pretty as you, my angel, but she was about your size. I showed the salespeople your pictures. Oh, yes, I have many pictures of you. Someday I'll show them to you, if you like."

If Kathleen had not been so confused, she would have noticed the beads of perspiration on the man's forehead and how his hands shook as he brushed back a strand of his brown hair.

"Do you like this?" He opened the wardrobe and

brought out a lovely green dress of pure silk. "Look at the lounging robes at this end. All the shades of green. You are especially lovely in green."

"What shall I call you?" Kathleen scarcely looked at the clothes he was showing her.

"Ted or Teddy. Mother called me Teddy. She hated it when someone called me Theo."

"Teddy, I need to use the . . . closet."

"Oh, I'm sorry." He went to the other side of the bed, knelt, and removed a padlock he had fastened through several links to shorten the chain. "Now you can go to the closet, or to any part of the room. Is the ankle bracelet comfortable?"

"I hardly know it's there," she replied sarcastically.

The ankle-length garment she had on was made of heavy satin, high at the neck and with long sleeves. It was modest for a nightgown.

"Excuse me," she said pointedly.

He tucked the box of sanitary napkins under his arm. "Push the button here at the side of the door if you want me. I'll be back with your breakfast."

Teddy unlocked the door, went out, and closed it. Kathleen heard a heavy bolt slam in place. He had wanted her to hear the clang, to know that she was locked in.

The chain on her ankle was amazingly light. She lifted the nightgown and sat down on the toilet. Her bladder was full. She couldn't believe that she was here, locked in a luxurious room, at the mercy of some kind of psychopath. He must be totally mad if he thought that she would ever be content to stay here and let him "take care" of her, as he put it.

She went back to the bedroom and looked around. She knew instinctively that he would hurt her before he would

let her leave despite his denials. He had gone to too much
trouble to get her here. With the baby to consider, her options were limited, and she must plan carefully. First she
had to find out where she was. Was she still in Rawlings,
or had he taken her to some other place?

Logic told her that she was near Rawlings. He had been
watching her . . . guarding her, he claimed. He had been
spying on her. How else would he have acted so quickly
when Gabe Thomas came into her house?

Look at this! She read the titles of books on the shelves
inside the glass door of a tall, ornate secretary. A shelf of
Zane Grey, works by Hemingway and Daphne du Maurier,
including *Rebecca, Frenchman's Creek*, and *Jamaica Inn*.
How did he find out that these were some of her favorite
books? A stack of Western magazines lay on the bottom
shelf. They were from the company that published her stories.

The slanting lid on the secretary opened to provide a
writing desk. Inside the pigeonholes were fancy notepaper
and envelopes. Several good fountain pens rested in a
holder alongside a bottle of ink.

Kathleen moved past the small gas heater that made the
room toasty warm to the dressing table. Hardly noticing
the expensive creams and perfumes, she sat down and
gawked at herself in the mirror for a full minute. She felt
as if she were living a nightmare. Nothing seemed to make
sense.

A rap sounded on the door. "Kathleen, may I come in?"

"How can I keep you out? You've got the key."

He unlocked the door, swung it open, and picked up a
tray from the table beside the door. Kathleen could see out
into a hall to what looked like the railing of a stairway.
Teddy stood hesitantly in the doorway.

"I brought toast, jam, and a pot of tea. But there is something I forgot to tell you. The other end of the chain around your ankle goes through the floor to the room below. You can't leave this room even if you should knock me senseless. If anything should happen to me, my precious girl, you would stay in this room and starve to death. I wanted you to know that so that you'll not be tempted to do something foolish."

"I would yell and scream and make enough noise to raise the dead."

"There is no one to hear you. No one." He smiled. "You're a spunky woman, my angel. Your mind is working right now on ways to get away from me. Save yourself the effort."

"My husband will be looking for me. He'll tear you apart."

"He won't find you. If I had thought he'd be a threat, I would have eliminated him. Here, I found some green tea in Dallas. It's your favorite, isn't it?"

"What . . . do you mean . . . eliminate him? Would you have killed him?"

"Let's not be crude, my darling. Killing is not a subject ladies should be concerned with. Would you like to have your tray there on the dressing table?"

"I want to know. Would you have killed Johnny if he had gotten in the way?"

"Maybe we should clear the air on this subject and be done with it. I would have killed him if it had become necessary. Johnny Henry or any other man means no more to me than a fly on the wall. Now may we drop the subject?"

Kathleen stood slowly. "He wouldn't have been easy to kill."

Teddy laughed. "There are a hundred ways to kill a man without his knowing he is about to die. I know them all."

"You tell me this and expect me to be content to stay here?"

"I told you because you insisted on knowing. Drink your tea and eat the toast. The jam is strawberry and comes from Canada. It is very good."

"Ted Newman couldn't have afforded all this. Who are you . . . really?"

"Theodore Nuding, my precious heart. I had reasons for using the Newman name in the city. Now be a good girl, eat your breakfast, and change into something pretty. This is Christmas Eve, and you are my Christmas gift."

Chapter Twenty-six

JOHNNY SAT AT THE KITCHEN TABLE hunched over a plate of pork and beans and a helping of cottage cheese. He was tired. Today he had pulled the old tractor into the barn to work on it out of the wind. In the process he had smashed his finger and cut the back of his hand. To top it off, he found he had only a sliver of the Lava soap he needed to wash the grease off his hands. He was not in a very good mood.

His thoughts returned to Christmas Eves he had enjoyed on the farm in Red Rock. Aunt Dozie had bustled about, cooking pies, baking bread, and scolding him for being underfoot. Henry Ann had sneaked around wrapping presents and hiding her gifts. She always insisted that he hang a stocking and on Christmas morning, childish though it all was, he'd find a gift as well as an orange, an apple, and stick candy tucked inside.

After he and Kathleen married, she always cooked a special dinner on Christmas Eve just for the two of them. She decorated the table with candles and wore a sprig of mistletoe in her hair. On Christmas Day they would go to the McCabes' or to Paul and Adelaide's. One time she had persuaded him to go to Barker's with her.

Johnny finished his meal. Sherm had gone to spend Christmas at his sister's. Pete, no doubt, was with Dale Cole and her boy, and Jude would be with Theresa and Ryan. Johnny had thought about Kathleen all day, especially after he had dug down in his duffel bag to find the bracelet and necklace he had made for her the first Christmas he was in the Pacific.

While washing the dishes, he began to think about going into town, stopping by her house, and giving her the presents. What the hell could he say?

I made these on Guadalcanal the first Christmas I was there and forgot to send them to you.

I just discovered these in my duffel bag.

All the guys made this stuff when they didn't have anything else to do.

Hell, he'd not say any of those things. If he intended to give the presents to her, he should go in tonight and knock on her door, give her the package, and get the hell off her porch. While he was in town, he'd give Barker a call and tell him that something had come up, and he couldn't make it to dinner tomorrow, and that would be that. Christmas Day would be like any other day. He'd spend it working on the tractor.

Now that he had a plan of action, Johnny put on his sheepskin coat, picked up the tissue-wrapped package, and went out to his car.

The stars always seemed brighter on Christmas Eve. Tonight the sky was studded with millions of them. He thought back to the night in '38 when he and Kathleen had driven back from visiting the McCabes. It was a night like this, but not so cold. She had snuggled close to his side with her hand resting on his thigh. They stopped at the ranch and made love for the first time. She was everything he had ever dreamed about. He had never been so close to heaven in his life.

Deep in thought, he reached town before he realized he had arrived. Twilight Gardens was closed when he passed, as were most of the businesses along Main Street. Lights were on in houses all over town. Families had gathered for Christmas Eve behind closed doors. Pete's car was parked a block from Dale Cole's house. He was being careful to avoid gossip, which told Johnny that Pete must really care for the woman.

Johnny's car was the only one moving on the streets. He drove to the edge of town where Kathleen lived. Along the way lights shone from every house. When he reached hers, it was dark. He stopped in front of the house, disappointment weighing heavily on him. The Nash was there. Had she gone to Adelaide's or to Jude's? He doubted that she would go to Jude's. She'd not wanted to intrude on him and Theresa.

Maybe he should just drop by Paul and Adelaide's place and be surprised that she was there. He moved the car on down the street, turned around, and went back up Main Street. There were no lights in the back room at the *Gazette* office and none in the apartment upstairs.

Johnny looked at his watch. It was only a little after seven. It seemed later because the days were short at this time of year. Would Kathleen have gone to bed? Maybe she was sick. He turned the car around again, went back, and parked behind the Nash. He knocked on the door and shook the doorknob. She had taken his advice and locked it. After knocking several times, he went back to his car, sat for a minute, then headed back to the ranch.

*   *   *

After a sleepless night, Johnny was up at daylight. He drank warmed-up coffee and went out to do chores in the crisp cold air. He couldn't decide if he wanted to go to Barker's for Christmas dinner. He might feel like a fish out of water. He debated the pros and cons in his mind.

What if Kathleen completely ignored him? What if she gave him a present and he didn't have one for her? He had already decided he wasn't going to give her the gifts he had made during the war in front of the Flemings.

By damn, he'd forgotten to get anything for Lucas and the girls. The drugstore was usually open for a few hours. If not, he could get Stan to open for him. He could get something for the girls there . . . but Lucas was another matter.

An idea hit. He went through his navy duffel bag and found a knife he'd taken off a dead Jap on Ondonga, a small island in the Pacific, where unexploded Japanese shells and buried mines were more of a danger than the nightly air raids. Even now he could smell the mud and rotting vegetation on that hellhole. That was all behind him, thank God.

He worked on the blade, polishing it with steel wool, then sharpened it. It was a wicked weapon. The grip had a notched bow called iron knuckles. Barker would make sure that Lucas understood that the knife was a memento from the war and not a plaything.

Dressed in his good tan twill pants and a blue shirt, Johnny left the ranch. He reached town just as Stan was locking the door of the drugstore. Fifteen minutes later he was back in the car with Blue Waltz perfume and Tangee lipstick for the girls, fancy soap for Mrs. Fisher, and a cigarette lighter for Barker.

At Kathleen's he parked behind the Nash. With her gift

in hand, he knocked on her door. After a minute or two he decided she wasn't there, that one of the Flemings must have come for her. Disappointed again, he went back to the car and drove slowly out to Barker's ranch.

Marie, followed by Janna and Lucas, answered the door.

"I'm so glad you came. Merry Christmas, Johnny."

"Merry Christmas to you."

"Hang your coat there on the hall tree, Johnny, and come on over by the fire," Barker called from his easy chair beside the fireplace.

A Christmas tree stood in one corner of the room with presents on the floor beneath its branches.

"Here are a few things to add to the tree. I didn't put names on the packages, but I know what goes to who." Johnny handed the sack of gifts to Marie.

"We thought you might go by and bring Kathleen. We were waiting for the two of you before we opened the presents."

"I stopped by, but she wasn't home." Johnny hung his hat above his coat. "Her car was there, so I thought you'd picked her up."

"I offered, but she said she'd drive out." Marie set Johnny's gifts beside the tree. "We saw Adelaide at church last night, and she was surprised that Kathleen wasn't there. Janna and I and Mrs. Fisher went by the house after the service, and she wasn't at home then, either. She doesn't usually go out at night except to the movies, and then she drives the car."

"She'll be along." Barker was pleased that Johnny was there. It was the first time since he came home from the war. "How are things going out at your place, Johnny?"

"Pretty good, I guess." Johnny backed up to the fire-place. The heat felt good on the hands clasped behind him, but he continued to worry. "When did you last speak to Kathleen, Marie?"

"It was Sunday, I think. She was baking cookies, then she was going to the movie. She usually goes to the show on Sunday night. I asked her to go with us to church Christmas Eve. She said she'd meet us there. That's why we went by her house last night."

"She said that she'd be here at a certain time; it's not polite to be this late and especially at Christmas." Mrs. Fisher, concerned about the meal she had prepared, spoke bluntly.

"Kathleen is never inconsiderate." Marie jumped to Kathleen's defense.

"No, she isn't," Barker said. "And she is one of the most punctual people I know."

"Maybe she's sick and can't get out of bed to answer the door." Janna voiced what had suddenly occurred to the others.

Johnny immediately started putting on his coat. "Do you have a key to the house?"

Barker reached for the sheepskin hanging on a hook beside the door. "Yes. I have a master key."

"Why don't you wait a little longer?" Mrs. Fisher said. "You may pass each other, then we'd have to wait for you."

"She's almost an hour late. I think they should go." Marie had a worried look on her face. "Will you call, Daddy, if . . . she's sick or something?"

Barker nodded. "Why don't you go ahead and open a few presents."

Janna and Marie shook their heads. "We'll wait." Lucas scowled.

Barker followed Johnny to his car. Johnny didn't speak until he had parked behind the Nash and they had walked up onto the porch.

"The window shades are still down."

He rapped on the door several times, then stepped back to let Barker insert the key. The door opened easily and Johnny went inside.

"Kathleen," he called.

Hearing no answer, Johnny walked quickly to the bedroom. The bed was still made. With his heart in his throat, he passed through the bathroom to the other small room and then into the kitchen. Barker was behind him.

"Sunday she told Marie she was baking cookies. They're still here on the counter." Barker opened the back door and looked out, then closed it.

"It's cold in here." Johnny touched the small gas heater in the corner of the living room. It was cold.

In the bedroom once again, he opened the wardrobe. Her clothes were there. The pages of her manuscript were neatly stacked beside her typewriter. A sheet of paper was in the machine. He glanced at it and back when a word or two caught his eye. His heart was thudding in his ears when he jerked the paper from the roller.

After thinking about it for a long while I have decided to leave Rawlings. I don't want anyone looking for me, and I don't want anything in this house that would remind me of the past.

I AM STARTING A NEW LIFE

Johnny read the note twice and handed it to Barker. Sick with fear, he watched as Barker read the note.

"She didn't write it," Johnny declared when Barker handed him back the note.

"How do you know?"

"Because if she had made a decision to go, she wouldn't have baked cookies and she wouldn't have left her purse."

Johnny reached down beside the bed, picked up a brown-leather handbag and opened it. Kathleen's driver's license was inside, as well as six one-dollar bills. In another compartment, he found her wedding ring.

"She wouldn't have left without this. She was taken by force and during the night because the shades are still down."

"Who would do such a thing?"

"Call the sheriff. I'm going outside to look around."

After Barker made the call, he phoned Adelaide to see if Kathleen was there.

"The last time I saw her was on Friday. Paul and I were planning to go over to her place tonight. You can't find her? Oh, my Lord. Is there anything we can do?"

"The sheriff is on his way. We'll let you know."

Johnny didn't wait for the sheriff. He went directly to Dale Cole's house, where he knew he would find Pete.

"Is Kathleen here?" he asked as soon as Dale opened the door.

"What's up?" Pete appeared in the door behind her.

"We can't find Kathleen. When did you see her last?"

"Saturday. She said she was going to the Flemings' today for dinner."

Johnny told them about finding the note and Kathleen's purse. "She wouldn't walk away and leave her purse, even if she didn't want the rest of her things."

"She's not at Jude's. I was by there before I came here to get Dale and Danny. We were getting ready to leave. I'll take them to Jude's and help you look for her."

Four hours later Johnny had to face the fact that

Kathleen had vanished without a trace. He went back to her house for the fourth or fifth time to see if there was any news. Marie was there by the telephone. Bobby Harper, on his crutches, was with her. Adelaide and Paul were there, too. Barker met Johnny on the porch.

"Anything?"

Johnny shook his head. "We need men on horseback to look into every building or vacant shack. Some sick bastard may have taken her to an out-of-the-way place like that and left her there." Johnny's eyes were bleak with worry. "Barker, I've not asked you for anything, but—"

"You don't have to ask, son. Kathleen is family. I'll call out the men at the ranch, the tannery, and some people I know on the reservation. We'll organize a search in the country. You handle the one in town."

"Thanks."

"Johnny, Dr. Perry wants you to come by there when you can," Marie said from the doorway.

"Does he have news?"

"No. He asked if we had any."

"I'll go over there."

Johnny had to keep moving. The thought that he might never see Kathleen again was tearing him to shreds. He drove automatically and stopped automatically in front of Jude's house and got out. Jude came to meet him. Johnny shook his head when he saw the question in the doctor's eyes. Jude turned to Theresa, who stood in the doorway, and relayed the "no news" message.

"Let's sit in the car," Jude suggested. "You look worn out," he said after they were seated. "Have you had any dinner?"

"No, but Marie brought some food to Kathleen's." There was a world of misery in Johnny's eyes. "She wouldn't have just walked away leaving her purse, her money, her clothes. Her picture album is there and her grandmother's crocheted dresser scarf. She wouldn't have left the manuscript she's been working on. Someone else wrote that note or made her write it."

"I've not known her long, but I can't see her just up and leaving on Christmas and not telling anyone. She sent over a sack of presents with Pete. He asked her to join us for dinner, but she said she was going to the Flemings' today."

"What did you want to see me about, Jude? I need to go check out a few things."

"I've been struggling with my conscience. Yes, before you ask, I do have one."

"I've not given it a thought one way or the other," Johnny said tiredly.

"That was a little play on words because I'm nervous about breaking a promise in telling you this. But under the circumstances, I think you have a right to know that Kathleen came to see me right after the school carnival."

Johnny's head jerked around. "Was she sick?"

"No. She was pregnant."

"What?" Johnny leaned forward as if he had been struck in the back of the head. His hand reached out, then fell back. "What?" he said again more softly as breath returned to him.

"She came to talk to me about the baby you had that died. She wondered if something she had done could have caused its congenital defect. I explained to her that the baby had failed to develop in her womb which occurs without any apparent reason to one fetus out of several thousand."

"Whose is it?" Johnny turned his head and looked blindly out the window when he asked.

Jude was quiet for so long that Johnny turned to face him. "Whose, dammit?"

"She's your wife. Do you need to ask?" Jude answered quietly, but his words were laced with anger. "I guess I understand now why she didn't want you to know."

"I've been with her only one time in five years."

"Once is enough."

"But . . . it took a long time before."

"Kathleen is pregnant. She's about two months along now. If you have any doubt that it's your child, take it up with her."

"I have no doubt." Johnny rubbed his hand over his face.

"She made me promise not to tell you. She said you swore you'd not have another child, and she didn't want you putting a damper on her happiness." Jude regretted that his words were so cutting.

"She knows why I didn't want another child," Johnny said harshly. "I let her go because her top priority was having a family. She wanted a dozen kids if she could get them because she was an only child and never had any family except her grandparents."

"She was smiling from ear to ear when she left the clinic that day. She kept asking me if I was sure."

"Would being pregnant make her . . . do something like run away?"

"Not Kathleen. She'd not do anything that could cause her to miscarry."

"God, Jude! What am I going to do if I can't find her?"

"I don't know, Johnny. I'm here to do anything I can."

"Thanks. Tell Dale that Pete has gone out with one of the deputies. He said that he'd come by for her later."

"I'll tell her." Jude got out of the car. "Would you take a sandwich or something with you?"

"No, thanks. I've got to get on back."

Johnny drove down the street and stopped. He needed to think. He had sensed something different about Kathleen when they met on the street. Now he knew what it was. She was leaving! She was going to go off some place, have his baby, and never let him know. Godalmighty! What a mess he had made of his life and hers.

Unaware of the tears in his eyes until his vision blurred, Johnny started the car moving again, then braked. Something Jude had said suddenly came to his mind. *Undeveloped in the womb . . . one in several thousand births.* Dear God! Had he been wrong all this time thinking that their deformed child was his fault? He had been so sure! He had deprived himself of being with the woman he loved because he was so sure. And Kathleen. What had he done to her?

She had come into his arms willingly, eagerly that morning. She had been as loving as a woman could be. He had touched a little bit of Heaven again; but feeling undeserving of her and angry at himself for having been carried away by the moment, he had rushed off. He hadn't considered how she felt then. Now that his child was growing within her, what was her attitude toward him? Would he ever know?

Kathleen might have come to the end of her patience with him. Even if that were true and she was going to leave, she would not have done it in this manner. She wouldn't have wanted to cause pain to Adelaide and the Flemings . . . especially not on Christmas.

God, let her be all right! He had to tell her that he had never stopped loving her; that was why he never stopped wearing his wedding ring. He wanted to be with her when she had his baby. He wanted them both, even if this baby was like Mary Rose.

Why would she even consider taking him back? He put his head on the arm folded across the steering wheel and cried the harsh, dry sobs of a man who was a stranger to tears.

Chapter Twenty-seven

FIRST DAY OF CAPTIVITY.

WHEN EVENING CAME, Teddy, as he wanted to be called, rolled in a serving cart with a tray of food and a pot of tea. On the lower shelf were several fancily wrapped packages. Kathleen was served noodles in a sauce, green peas, bread, and a sliced orange. The food was good, and she was surprised that she could eat.

Wearing a white shirt and tie and the tweed coat, he silently watched her while she ate. When she finished, he removed the tray to the hallway and placed the packages in her lap.

"Are you giving these to me?" When he nodded, she asked, "Why?"

"Because it makes me happy to give you pretty things."

"I have nothing for you."

"I told you, my Christmas gift is you." He handed her an oblong package. "Open this one first."

Kathleen removed the paper and lifted the lid from the box. She gasped. Lying on dark velvet padding was a large emerald suspended on a silver chain. Her eyes flew to his face. He looked like a child on Christmas morning.

"I can't accept this."

"Don't you like it?"

"That isn't the point. I can't accept something like this from someone I hardly know. It cost too much money."

"I have plenty. Open the other packages."

In the other boxes were a set of earrings and a ring. All were set with large perfectly matched green emeralds.

"I don't know what to say."

" 'Thank you, Teddy,' would be nice."

"I can't accept them, but thank you for the kind thought."

"Put them away. We won't talk about it now." He didn't seem to be offended by her refusal. "This is your first day here. You may want to go to bed now. Play the radio if you like. Sometimes music is soothing. I'll see you in the morning."

"Is there a lock on the door?"

"Yes, but I won't lock it. You have the chain."

"I mean on the inside."

"Why would you want one?"

"So that I can undress in privacy," she shouted.

"No need to yell, my precious. I will never come into this room without knocking first."

"I would rather you didn't call me endearing names. I am your prisoner, not your precious."

He laughed. "My darling, beautiful Kathleen. You are far more wonderful, more precious, to me than I dreamed. Everything about you is perfect from the top of that glorious red hair to the tip of your lovely toes. I would worship at your feet, but"—he paused—"you might kick me," he said, chuckling.

"And you would be right, Mr. Know-it-all!"

He went out the door laughing.

SECOND DAY — CHRISTMAS DAY.

By the end of this day, Kathleen was acutely aware that she was at the mercy of a man who was highly intelligent, terribly kind to her, but mentally deranged. All her wit and courage would be needed to escape from him.

She began to form a plan, make some rules for herself to follow. She could not afford to irritate him, yet she would not be docile. She would eat the food he brought her, not only because she would be needing her strength, but because of her baby. If she could make him think that she had accepted her captivity, he might grow more lax and maybe even remove the chain.

He had measured carefully. The chain allowed her to go anyplace in the room, but not out the door and into the hallway. Slipping the chain from her ankle was out of the question. She had tried it. It was a snug fit within the cushioned pad.

How did the idiot think she could put on the underwear he had supplied with the chain on her ankle?

She decided not to mention it to him. In a dress without panties, she felt naked. So she wore two of the nightgowns and a robe and, because she didn't want to anger him, the emerald necklace, the earrings, and the ring.

THIRD DAY.

Kathleen cried most of the day. The dam that had held back the tears for the last couple of days had burst. The sobs surged out of the depths of her misery. She wanted to go home. She longed for the safety of Johnny's arms.

Did Marie or Adelaide wonder why she wasn't at church service on Christmas Eve? Had Barker come to see why she hadn't come to dinner Christmas day? Adelaide and Paul had planned to stop by in the evening. Surely they were wondering what had happened to her.

Kathleen continued to cry. She wanted Johnny! Would she ever see him again? *Johnny, I love you. Please don't forget me. Remember that I love you.*

"Why are you crying, my darling?" Teddy asked when he came in and found her sobbing on the bed.

"I guess . . . I'm just lonesome." It was the first thing that came to mind.

"Why don't you put on one of the pretty dresses I bought for you? That should cheer you up."

"I can't put on stockings."

"I'm sorry about that, my angel. You understand, don't you, that I can't take the chain off. I can't lose you, my precious girl, now that I finally have you."

Kathleen wanted to hit him. She wanted to scream for him to get out of her sight and stop groveling at her feet as if she were a goddess. His constant, cloyingly syrupy endearments grated on her nerves and made her want to scratch his eyes out.

FOURTH DAY.

Kathleen no longer feared that Teddy intended to rape her. Her plans, should he try, were to grab his testicles with one hand, squeeze and twist, and shove stiff fingers in his eyes with the other. A girl at the aircraft plant had told her that was how she had warded off a rapist.

Teddy knocked each time before he came into the room. Usually he sat in one of the chairs and watched her. Once he brought a notebook and wrote several pages. He was very open about it when she asked him what he was writing.

"A journal. A man never knows where he's going if he can't recall where he's been."

"You're terribly smart, Teddy. Where did you go to college?"

"My dear, you flatter me. I didn't go to college. Mother taught me at home. She was brilliant."

"You must have loved her very much."

"Yes. She was the most magnificent creature I had ever known until I met you."

"Teddy, I could in no way be like your mother."

"Precious girl, you outmatch Mother in sweetness and in beauty. She knows that and understands it."

Kathleen searched for another topic of conversation, not knowing how to respond when he spoke of communicating with his dead mother.

"Read me what you are writing."

"Would you like to hear it? Really?" His eyes smiled into hers when she nodded.

"*Three-thirty-five.* I put down the time because feelings are sometimes different at different times of the day."

"I hadn't thought of that."

"*Three-thirty-five P.M.*" He read from the journal. "*Mother, this is my fourth day with my darling Kathleen. I am so happy. She is everything I told you that she would be: beautiful, intelligent, kind, and understanding. It is amazing that God could make such a vile creature as a man and such a perfect creation as my Kathleen. She has been so—*"

"—Teddy, please don't read any more. I'm not any of the things you say I am, and it's embarrassing to hear you say so. I can be mean, quarrelsome, and I have a terrible temper. My grandma said it went with red hair."

"You couldn't be mean, my heart. You're modest. It's part of your charm, your goodness."

"Do you mind if I lie down and rest for a while?"

"No, my sweet. I'll just sit quietly and watch over you."

"You don't need to do that. I'm sure you have things you want to do. I'll be all right." *Please go! Pl . . . ease go!*

Kathleen lay down on the bed and turned her back to him.

"I do have a few things to do. Rest, my wonderful one. I'll be back soon."

When she heard the door close, she turned her head to be sure that she was alone, then heaved a sigh of relief and let the tears roll down her cheeks. How much longer would she be able to endure this without having a screaming fit?

FIFTH DAY.

Kathleen suspected that Teddy wasn't well. He hadn't touched her since the morning she awakened in this room. He had been strong then, holding her down on the bed. And it had taken strength to carry her out of her house and up the stairs.

Long ago she had dismissed the notion of trying to overpower him, not only because of the chain on her ankle. She couldn't let herself be hurt in any way that would harm the baby.

Kathleen began to notice that at times Teddy winced at some apparent pain, and his face became wet with perspiration. Something was wrong with him. Dear Lord, don't let him have a fatal heart attack. The thought of being chained in this room until she died of starvation was so horrible it made her stomach heave.

SIXTH DAY.

Teddy's face was pale and his hands trembled when he brought her breakfast.

"Are you sick, Teddy?" Kathleen asked with concern.

"Only a headache, sweet girl. It will go away. I'll lie down for a while and be good as new."

"Teddy, don't leave me chained. Please. If you got sick, I'd die up here." She had promised herself she wouldn't beg, but suddenly she was terribly frightened.

"My precious girl." He cupped her cheek with his palm, the first time he had touched her since the first day. "I'll not leave you. When I depart from this world, you and the little princess will be with me."

His words were not comforting. They implied a deadly intent that frightened her more than ever.

He didn't come back until evening. He brought bread and cheese, an apple, and a pot of tea. He sat in the corner of the room and watched her. When she finished eating, he took the tray and left with only a few of the sugary words she had come to detest.

SEVENTH DAY.

Theodore Nuding, also known as Robert Brooks, sat beside the oven in the kitchen of the large Clifton house hugging a blanket around his shoulders.

This was supposed to be the happiest time in his life, the fulfillment of his dreams. It was not fair, Teddy thought, that the curse had chosen this time to rear its ugly head.

"It runs in the family, my dear Teddy," his mother had said. "It has dogged my Greek ancestors down through the ages. I can't avoid it and neither can you. You must constantly keep your affairs in order."

He had heeded his mother's advice, even to the filing of his will. The means of his escape from a painful, lingering death had been tested. Unlike his mother he had prepared for the inevitable. She had left it up to him, and even if he did say so, he had performed his duty admirably.

When he went to meet her in Heaven, he would take his darling Kathleen and the little princess with him. He couldn't bear to think of going without them.

A random thought struck him and brought a smile to his face. What was the date? The thirtieth of December. Tomorrow would be the last day of the year 1945—the perfect time for him to take his darling little family to meet his mother.

Johnny and Tom Dolan waited in front of the *Gazette* office for the Greyhound bus that was bringing Hod Dolan down from Kansas. Tom had arrived on the fourth day of Kathleen's disappearance and this was the seventh. The whole town had turned out to look for her, yet not a single clue had turned up.

Johnny was near exhaustion. He couldn't sleep, had hardly eaten anything. His whiskered cheeks were sunken. The eyes he turned to Tom were flat and bleak.

"I hope Hod will have some new suggestions for us. Unless Kathleen has shelter, she can't last much longer."

"I hate to say this, but she could be out of the state, out of the country by now."

"She's near. I just feel that she's around here somewhere. Someone took her who wanted to get back at me, or at Barker. Maybe something was printed in the paper that hit someone the wrong way. She's part-owner of the *Gazette*."

"You've not been home long enough to make many enemies," Tom said.

"I made one. He worked at the Fleming ranch until Barker fired him. Pete got to him before I did. He said he didn't know anything about Kathleen. Guess he smarted off at first, and Pete mopped the floor with him. Here's the bus." Johnny and Tom moved out away from the building and waited for the door of the bus to open.

United States Marshal Hod Dolan stepped down. He was a tall, impressive man in a black suit and a dark hat. Except for the streaks of gray in his black hair, he looked enough like Tom Dolan to be his twin.

"Hod! God, it's good to see you." The two men clasped hands and shoulders.

"How'er ya doin', Tom. It's been a hell of a long time."

"Too bad it takes something like this to get us together."

"Johnny. Lord, man. You're no longer that skinny kid who helped me track the Barrow gang." Hod grasped Johnny's hand.

"A lot of water has gone under the bridge since then, Hod."

"Dammit, Johnny, I don't know what to say. Kathleen is not only our brother's daughter, she's special."

"Thanks for coming, Hod. We're about at the end of the rope. We need someone to show us a new direction."

"Molly said to say hello. She would have come down, but she's got her hands full with the kids."

"The car's over here. We'll go on out to the house, and Tom and I will fill you in. Barker has a crew out on horseback and so does Pete Perry. They may be back by now."

"What's this? Kathleen's old Nash? This old heap still runnin'?"

"Yeah. My old car doesn't have but one seat. I kind of rearranged the inside so I could haul stuff."

It was almost dark by the time Johnny parked the Nash alongside Kathleen's house. Three other cars were parked along the street: Pete's, Barker's, and Bobby Harper's.

"Nice little house," Hod said when they stopped.

"Kathleen has been living here since she came back from the city. Come on in. There should be some food in there if you're hungry. Folks have been good about bringing it in."

Bobby Harper met them at the door. He flung it open, then stepped back on his crutches to let them in.

"Bobby, this is Hod Dolan. Kathleen's other uncle."

"Howdy." Bobby stuck out his hand.

"Johnny?" Marie came from the kitchen and put her arm around Johnny's waist. "Any word?"

Johnny shook his head. "My sister, Marie Fleming, Hod. She's been coming every day. We didn't think it a good idea for her to be here alone, so Bobby took on the job of staying with her."

"Hello, little lady. I bet Bobby didn't mind takin' on the job a'tall."

"No, sir. I sure didn't." Bobby grinned broadly.

"Put your things in the bedroom. I'll have supper on the table soon if Bobby will help me. Have you seen Daddy, Johnny?"

"Not since morning. Has anyone called?"

"A lot of people have called wanting to know if there was any news." She reached up and put her hand on his rough cheek. "You've got to eat something. You'll be sick and not able to help Kathleen if she needs you."

"All right, little sister. I need to go wash off some of this road dirt."

Johnny and Tom had filled Hod in on everything from day one to the present by the time Pete and Barker came back to the house. Johnny introduced them to Hod, and the four continued the discussion at the supper table.

"Paul, down at the *Gazette*, made posters with Kathleen's picture and the offer of a five-hundred-dollar reward for information. Every town within fifty miles has been saturated with them. Paul saw to it that every paper in the state of Oklahoma and some in Texas received a news release."

"No bites?"

"Nothing."

"News coverage and a reward of that size will usually get you something if there's anything to be got." Hod was sorry he had been so blunt when he saw the look of despair cross Johnny's face.

"We've gone over the whole county by car and by horseback. We've looked into every nook and cranny." This came from Pete, who had put in almost as many hours as Johnny looking for Kathleen.

"Maybe we should go back over the area, slowly, starting at the edge of town and fanning out to search every foot of ground. You're reasonably sure she's not in town?"

"Folks in town have known about the reward for five days. I believe that if anyone had noticed anything slightly suspicious, we would have heard about it by now."

"Fifty men from the reservation will be here at daylight. Some will be on horseback and some afoot," Barker said quietly. "Some speak very little English; but they are good trackers, and I'll be with them."

Hod studied Barker. If he had not been told that the man was Johnny's father, he would have guessed it. Johnny had his father's classic Indian features.

"The volunteers will meet in front of the *Gazette* in the morning at seven." Pete helped himself to a piece of corn bread. "Mayor White is in charge of them. We'll have to decide what we want them to do."

"Hod, Keith McCabe will be back here the day after tomorrow. He'd been here since the first of the week and had to go home today to tend to some business." Johnny had eaten to satisfy Marie, but the food was sticking in his throat.

"It'll be good to see that son of a gun. By the way, what was Kathleen wearing when she was last seen?"

Johnny answered. "She went to the show on Sunday night. The ticket seller said that she was wearing a green dress and a black coat."

"Her coat had a round collar and big gold buttons down the front," Marie said while filling Johnny's coffee cup.

Pete got up to leave. "See you in the morning, old hoss," he said, and clasped Johnny's shoulder.

"I'll be going, too. Are you bringing Marie, Bobby?" Barker asked.

"Yes, sir. I'm learning to drive pretty good with one foot."

Marie put on her coat. "I'll be here tomorrow, Johnny."

"Tomorrow is New Year's Eve," Tom said. "Maybe it will bring us some good news."

Chapter Twenty-eight

EIGHTH DAY.

KATHLEEN KNEW IMMEDIATELY that there was something different about Teddy, aside from the fact that he was pale and not quite steady on his feet when he came to her room with her breakfast.

His eyes shone as if he were terribly excited, and his face was damp with perspiration. He was freshly shaved, which was not unusual, but he had also trimmed his hair.

"Eat your breakfast, my precious pet. I have things to do downstairs, then I'll be back." He placed the tray with a pot of tea and a piece of toast on the dressing table.

"Teddy, unchain me and let me come down and help you."

"No, no. There's no need for that. You'll be free of the chain soon enough, sweet one. Would you like for me to wash your hair this morning?"

"No, thank you. I washed it last night."

"It's lovely, my darling. You're lovely. Eat your breakfast like a good girl."

"Teddy, do you feel all right? It scares me for you to be sick."

"Because you love me, sweet one?"

"I . . . could learn to care for you," she told the lie easily because it was what he wanted to hear. "What if you get sick? If I'm chained in this room, I can't help you."

"It will not come to that, I promise. Eat your breakfast before your tea gets cold. And, my beautiful Kathleen, put on the emeralds: the necklace, the earrings, and the ring. I want to see you decked out like the goddess you are. Humm?"

He went to the wardrobe and pulled out a foam green peignoir with a gown to match.

"You haven't worn this. Wear it for me, angel girl. It will make me happy. I'll be back soon."

Kathleen was trembling with fear by the time he left the room, his feet spread apart in an effort to keep his balance. As soon as the door closed, she went to the place where the chain disappeared in the hole in the floor and tugged on it for the hundredth time.

Eat your breakfast. How many times had he said that today? Enough times so that it seemed to be more important than usual.

She lifted the top from the teapot and sniffed. It smelled the same but had he put something in the tea? She held the strainer over the cup, poured the tea through and carried it to the toilet. She emptied the second cup, then crumbled the toast in the toilet before she flushed it.

Fear ran rampant through her.

You'll be free of the chain soon. What had he meant by that? If he wasn't going to turn her loose, the only way she would be free of the chain was if she were . . . dead?

He is going to . . . kill me!

Since that first day, she hadn't considered that he would do that. He had said that she would come to love it here. She took that to mean he planned to keep her here for a long time. Did he think that he was going to die and wanted to take her with him?

The thought sank into her mind like a chunk of lead.

She told herself that she wouldn't panic. She had to plan what to do if she was going to live to have her baby. If he put something in the tea, it was to put her to sleep or to make her drowsy and easy to handle.

She had to suppress the anger that made her want to scream and throw things. She couldn't afford to allow rage to cloud her mind when she was going to need every bit of courage she possessed in order to be ready when he came back to the room.

Kathleen hurriedly dressed in the green gown and peignoir, fastened the necklace around her neck, and attached the earrings to her earlobes. With the ring on her finger, she lay down on the side of the bed nearest the door. Hugging a pillow close to her, should she need it to protect her baby, she tilted her head so that she could see the door through the slightest lifting of her eyelids.

With her heart beating like a tom-tom in her breast, she waited.

Johnny, will you ever learn that I've never stopped loving you? Will Jude tell you that I was going to have your baby?

Time went slowly, and her mind raced. She wondered how she would be remembered if she didn't make it through the day. Would Johnny grieve for her? He had loved her fiercely at one time, and she had been sure he loved her the morning she conceived the baby. She wondered if her body would ever be found, or if Teddy would bury her in some dark hole somewhere.

During the hour that followed, she moved from time to time so that her arms and legs would respond when she needed them. She began to think that he wasn't coming back, that his plan was for her to stay here in this room until she died. Then she heard his footsteps on the stairs and repositioned herself so that she could see him when he came in.

He rapped softly on the door.

She didn't answer.

He rapped again louder. After a few seconds of silence he opened the door. It took all the control that Kathleen possessed to lie still when he entered the room. He paused just inside to look at her.

"Are you asleep, my angel?" His words were slurred.

He was in formal attire. His black suit had satin lapels. His shirt was startling white, his bow tie black. On his feet were black patent-leather shoes.

"Did you drink your tea, darling girl?" He glanced at the tray, where the tea strainer was filled with leaves. "I see that you did, my heart. You are my good sweet girl."

He brought his hand out from behind him. In it was a hypodermic syringe with a needle attached.

Kathleen felt a gigantic surge of fear and with it a fierce determination to fight him to the last breath! Not sure what she was going to do, she watched him as he watched her.

"Queen of my heart," he murmured. "My darling Kathleen. You and I and our little princess will soon be together forever. I have adored you since I first set eyes on you. I have guarded you and killed your enemies while I waited for this day. It's all written in the journal, dear one.

"Remember the supervisor at Douglas who wanted to take you out and called you a bitch when you refused? He is no more. Nor is the garage man who went into your house uninvited." He held up the surgical syringe. "I tested this lovely product on that detestable creature who beat his wife. It worked beautifully."

Teddy rocked back on his heels, almost lost his balance, and grabbed onto the doorjamb with his free hand.

"You are so beautiful in the green gown. The emeralds are lovely only because it is you who wear them, my precious girl. You drank your tea, humm? I didn't want you to be frightened. I had not planned to do this now, but the curse is on me as it was on Mother."

He stopped his rambling and began to cry.

"There is no one to help me, so I must do it myself. I had hoped for more time so that I could see our little princess. But this is the way it must be. You will feel no pain, my lovely one. Within fifteen seconds, I will be with you."

Kathleen hugged the pillow. It was hard to wait for him to approach the bed. Adrenaline was pumping through her veins. She thought of nothing but keeping him from injecting her with the needle.

"It's time to go, darling," he crooned, and came to the side of the bed.

When he bent over her with the needle poised, Kathleen's eyes flew open. She reared up with the pillow in front of her and, with the strength of desperation, she rammed it against him. Her feet hit the floor, found purchase, and she shoved again. He toppled back, staggered, and fell, his head hitting the floor. He tried to rise but fell back.

Dragging the chain, Kathleen went around him to the dressing table and grabbed the heavy crockery teapot. She was ready to bring it down on his head when he opened his eyes, looked up, and smiled.

"I'm dying, my precious. I pierced my hand with the . . . needle. It will take a minute. Let me look at you. You will join me, for no one knows that you are here. If you wish to do it without suffering, use . . . the needle—" His mouth remained open when breath left him. Ice-blue eyes continued to stare up at her.

When Kathleen's numbed mind came to realize that he was dead, she dropped the teapot, backed away as far as the chain would allow, and screamed and screamed.

The air was so cold that their breaths were visible when more than a hundred men and boys spread out over the countryside in search of a clue to Kathleen's where-abouts. In ten groups of ten or more, they moved across the prairie searching every wooded area, every shack and shed.

Barker and his Cherokee worked the land south of Rawlings on horseback and on foot. Johnny covered the western area with a dozen volunteers. His horse zig-zagged through a small forest, with Johnny leaning from the saddle searching the ground for anything that would be foreign to the area. It was warmer in the woods out of the wind. He dreaded finding evidence that would tell him that she was dead. *God, please don't let it happen.*

He met up with his crew on the other side of the woods. The plan was for all the crews to meet at the crossroads directly south of town at noon to exchange information. Volunteers, organized by Adelaide, would join them, bringing a noon meal.

A dozen cars were lined up at the crossroads. The women had built fires in the ditch along the road, and coffeepots were sending plumes of steam into the air. Blankets, on the ground, were spread with sandwiches, pies, and cakes.

Johnny dismounted and removed the saddle from his horse. After slipping a halter on the animal, he attached a long lead rope to the bumper of the end car. The tired horse began cropping the short dry grass.

Pete came in with his crew, then Barker and a group of Cherokee. The Indians put hobbles on their horses and turned them loose. Another group galloped toward them from across the prairie. The quiet, subdued circle of men took sandwiches, then squatted down on their haunches to eat and to drink the hot coffee.

Johnny made the rounds to talk to the leaders of the crews. Barker stood with a man Johnny didn't know. He was a Cherokee, wearing a leather tunic. His hair hung past his shoulders in two braids.

"Anything, Barker?"

"Nothing. Johnny, meet Jacob Rides Fast. Jacob, this is my son, Johnny Henry."

"Howdy." Johnny stuck out his hand.

"I'm glad to meet you and sorry to be doing it under these circumstances." To Johnny's surprise Jacob Rides Fast spoke with an accent similar to that of the men he had met during the war who were from the eastern states.

"Jacob brought the men down from the reservation, Johnny. He's a member of the Cherokee Nation Council."

"I appreciate the help," Johnny said.

"We will come back if you need us."

One of the Indians spoke to Jacob in Cherokee.

Understanding the language, Barker said. "I'll go with them."

"They are hesitant about going to the fire for coffee and food," Jacob explained to Johnny after Barker left.

Barker returned with two cups of coffee. He handed one to Jacob.

"Tom and Hod rode in," Barker said.

"Maybe they've found something."

As Johnny moved away to find Kathleen's uncles, his eyes moved over a group of young Indian boys scuffling and tossing a ball. He looked away and then back. One of the boys was wearing a black coat, and he had seen a flash of a gold button. His heart thudded, then sank with disappointment when he realized the coat was mid-thigh on the boy. Kathleen's coat had been long.

When the boy, running to catch a ball that had been thrown, ran toward Johnny, he noticed that the coat was ragged along the bottom and that the lining hung down. It had been cut off. Johnny ran across the field toward the boy.

The boy peered up at Johnny with fright when he grabbed him and swung him around. Johnny had eyes only for the coat. It had a round collar and gold buttons down the front to where it had been cut off.

"Where did you get this coat?" Holding the frightened boy by the shoulders, Johnny yelled again, "Where did you get this coat?"

The boy said something in Cherokee, then repeated the words over and over.

"Johnny, Johnny." Barker repeated his name, and shook his arm to get his attention.

"It's her coat!"

"He doesn't speak English. Let me talk to him."

"What's he saying?"

"He's saying that he didn't steal it."

"It's Kathleen's coat. Where's Pete? He'll know it's her coat."

Barker pulled the frightened boy aside. He was not much older than Lucas. He and Jacob talked to him for several minutes. The boy pointed as he spoke to them. Johnny waited, his heart filled with hope, his head telling him that this could be the dreaded end of the search.

"He found the coat yesterday while we were looking around the old Clifton place. He was out with me and the men from the ranch. His father works for me. He said he found it in a place filled with boxes. He thought the coat had been thrown away. He cut it off with his knife. He wanted to wear it because he was cold."

"Hasn't anyone searched the Clifton place?"

"We went there the first day and back again yesterday. The house is boarded-up and locked. Two sheds on the place are padlocked. Wind said that he climbed in a little window and found the coat in a box. He didn't tell me because he thought I'd make him put it back."

Hod and Tom arrived to hear what Barker had to say. The boy stood trembling and looking up at the tall, angry-faced men.

"Where is this place?" Hod asked.

"Four, maybe five miles." Johnny headed for the cars. "You and Jacob coming, Barker?"

Barker spoke to Jacob, then said, "Jacob will wait here and look after the horses."

Two cars left the crossroads, Johnny driving the Nash,

Tom, Hod, and Barker with him. Pete had flagged down Sheriff Carroll and hopped in the car with him, telling him the news as they followed the Nash.

"Tell me what you know about this place, Johnny," Hod said.

"Not much. Do you know anything about it, Barker?"

Barker leaned forward to rest his arms on the back of the front seat so he could be heard.

"It's been for sale for a couple of years. It sold recently to a man who hasn't moved in yet according to Wrenn at the bank. I looked up the deed because I was interested in buying some of the land. The deed was made out to Hidendall, Incorporated. All the stock in the corporation is owned by a man named Theodore Nuding."

"Hell and damnation, Johnny. Slow down," Tom cautioned, as the back wheels on the Nash skidded at a corner.

"The Clifton ranch is a big one," Barker continued. "I leased some of the land before Mrs. Clifton died. No cattle were run on it during the war."

"How many acres?"

"I'd say maybe a couple thousand or more. It goes into the county east of here."

"That's it ahead," Johnny said.

"Don't go into the driveway just yet."

Johnny slowed, then pulled up onto the grass off the drive. The sheriff parked behind, and he and Pete got out. Pete reached into the car for a crowbar.

The big old house with a porch on two sides was boarded-up. Not a sound was to be heard except for the wind sweeping the dry leaves on the front lawn.

"Let's go in."

"Wait a minute." Hod stood on the edge of the driveway.

"A car has been going in and out of here. It's the same car, according to the width of the tires. A heavy truck has been here since the last rain."

Sheriff Carroll seemed content to let the U.S. Marshal take the lead. The men followed Hod up onto the porch. The door was locked. The drive led around the side of the house to a shed with doors wide enough to let a car drive through.

It was padlocked, but that did not deter Pete. He slipped the crowbar under the hasp and with one yank pulled it free of the wood. The rest was easy. The doors were pulled back.

"Laws!" Sheriff Carroll exclaimed. "That looks like the car that belonged to the weatherman. He was here for a couple of months checking clouds, but he's been gone now for several weeks."

Pete and Tom searched the shed, Hod and Johnny the car. Across the front seat of the car lay charts, several small instruments, and a pair of powerful binoculars. Nothing pointed to Kathleen's having been in the car.

"Goddammit!" Johnny backed away from the car and wiped his face with his hands.

Pete popped the lock from the shed close to the house. It had one small window that only a skinny kid like Wind could have squeezed through. And as he had said, it was full of boxes. The men went through them, throwing them out the door after they were checked. Some of the boxes contained scraps of wallpaper; empty food cans or were filled with wrapping paper and smaller boxes.

"Johnny," Tom said in a hushed voice, and pulled a green dress from a small box.

"It's hers." Johnny had to steel himself before he asked, "Anything else?"

"Underwear, shoes."

"Oh, God!"

Pete stood in the yard and cursed silently, then headed for the house with the crowbar.

Hod looked at Tom and shook his head. The signs were not good. If Kathleen's body was not in the house, he was almost certain that it would never be found. Not much is worse for a family than not knowing what happened to a loved one.

The wood splintered when Pete yanked the screws from the lock. Then without the slightest hesitation, he rammed his foot against the door. It flew open with a force that banged it against the wall.

In the attic room at the top of the house, Kathleen heard the sound, but was afraid to hope. She stood as close to the open door of the room as the chain would allow and listened. No other sound reached her. Disappointment brought tears.

"Damn you, you old son of a bitch," she said to the body on the floor. "I hate you, despise you, I'm glad you're dead!"

She was still crying when she heard male voices. She grabbed the teapot and threw it out the door of the room. It bounced against the wall and broke. She threw the hand mirror, the brush, and finally a jar of face cream. Anything to make noise.

"Help me!" she yelled. "Help me . . . please. I'm up here. Somebody help me!" She thought she heard sounds but didn't know what they were or where they came from. "Help me! Please . . . I'm up here, and I can't get out! Please come up here!"

Dorothy Garlock

From down below came a shout that rolled up the stairway.

"Kath . . . leen."

A door opened. "Kath . . . leen!" Johnny's voice.

"Johnny! Johnny! I'm up here!"

"Kathleen!"

There was more shouting downstairs, then the sound of boots on the stairs. Kathleen was crying uncontrollably when Johnny reached the top and rounded the corner so that she could see him. Her arms reached out to him. He grabbed her to him, lifting her off her feet, kissing her wet face.

"I love you, love you," he murmured over and over. "Are you all right? Honey, are you all right?"

"I'm all right. I'm all right, now. Don't leave me, Johnny." She clung to him as if she would never let him go.

"I'll not leave you . . . ever. Sweetheart . . . are you sure you're all right? It's been so long—" He looked down into her face. "I've been out of my mind."

Men crowded the hallway outside the room. Johnny's smile spread all over his face as he turned to tell them she was all right. From the shelter of her husband's arms, Kathleen saw first her uncle Hod, then her uncle Tom. Tears flowed as she kissed each of them. Barker, Pete, and then the sheriff filed in. They looked around the luxurious room at the top of the old house with amazement.

"I've a lot to tell you," Kathleen said, seeing the astonished looks on their faces. "The man on the floor is Theodore Nuding. Be careful when you lift the pillow and don't prick yourself with the needle. I shoved it back at him before he could stick me with it. Whatever's in it killed him."

"He doesn't look like anyone I've seen before," the sheriff said.

"He was the man in the tweed coat, Johnny." Kathleen snuggled closer after Johnny opened his coat and folded it and his arms around her. "He said he killed Gabe Thomas and Mr. Cole. I'll tell you everything, but . . . please take off the chain so we can go home."

Chapter Twenty-nine

Pete drove away from the Clifton house with Tom and Barker crowded in beside him. Johnny and Kathleen, with their arms around each other, sat in the backseat of the Nash. Hod and the sheriff stayed at the Clifton house to wait for the undertaker.

"There are some valuable things here," Hod said, picking up the emerald necklace Kathleen had thrown down on the dressing table. "All this stuff should be loaded up in some of the boxes we found in the shed and taken away for safekeeping until it's decided what to do with it. Folks will be coming to look the place over."

"I told your brother to send out my deputy. No use telling Johnny to do anything. His head was in the clouds." Sheriff Carroll shook his gray head. "Can't blame him a doggone bit. That boy was half out of his mind."

"This is one of the strangest cases I've ever come across. Kathleen said he never hurt her and that he didn't as much as hint of anything sexual with her. He bought all this in her size and in colors to suit her."

"He did all this work here. If he'd hired anyone from town, word would have got out. How in the hell did he do it?" Sheriff Carroll looked down into the still face on the floor.

"It's odd that he seemed to worship her as an idol. Maybe after we read his journal we'll understand it."

"He sure had me fooled. I never thought that he was anything but what he said he was, a weather observer."

Pete began to honk the horn as he approached the crossroads. The men who waited there and the women who had not yet left after serving the noon meal lined up alongside the road to cheer. Pete slowed the car to a crawl as they passed. Kathleen waved with tears streaming down her face. The car stopped only long enough to let Barker come out to thank the men who had donated their time to search for Kathleen.

The excitement was just as great in town. Pete honked the horn, and soon a dozen cars fell in behind with horns blasting. The procession went slowly up Main Street. Smiling people came out onto the sidewalks and waved.

At her house, Kathleen left Johnny long enough to go into her room and put on old familiar slacks and a flannel shirt. She tossed the green gown and peignoir and the other robe she had worn over it in the corner.

Teddy had not purchased a coat. He had not intended for her ever to leave the room.

It was dark by the time people stopped coming by. Marie, preparing to leave, hugged Kathleen.

"Daddy and I decided we'll have Christmas next Sunday. Will you come?"

Kathleen looked at Johnny. He smiled and nodded.

"We'll be there."

Marie, blinking back tears, and with Bobby Harper beside her, escaped out the door Barker held open for her.

Kathleen went to him and put her arms around him. He patted her on the shoulder.

"I'm so glad I'm a member of the Barker Fleming family. Tell that little boy who found my coat that I'm going to buy him the best sheepskin coat I can find."

"I'm glad you're home, daughter."

Johnny stepped forward and held out his hand. "Thanks, Barker. I never knew what having a family was like . . . till now."

"You are part of us, Johnny."

His face showed no emotion, but Kathleen was aware of the turmoil churning inside this wonderful, kind man who was Johnny's father.

When all who remained were Pete, Tom, and Hod, Pete rose and put on his coat.

"I'm taking Tom and Hod over to Jude's to spend the night. We were thinking it might be a little crowded here."

"That's the best thought you've had in a month of Sundays." Johnny handed him his hat, and they all laughed.

"You'll be back in the morning?" Kathleen asked her uncles.

"I'm going back to Red Rock on the noon bus. Hod is staying on a while, then coming over to my house before he goes back to Kansas. I want him to see my boys and my pretty little girl."

"I have to see them before they sprout wings and fly away," Hod said. "He's done nothin' but brag about them for the past hour."

"You're staying a while, Uncle Hod?"

"For a while. Kidnapping is a federal offense. I'll stay until the case is assigned. The sheriff feels that he may be in over his head here."

"Come on, Mr. U.S. Marshal," Tom said. "Let's get out of here and leave these two alone. Are you so darned old you can't remember when you wanted to be alone with Molly?"

"Remember? I still want to be alone with her." Hod hit Tom with his hat. "What about you and Henry Ann?"

"She was gone four days when Isabel died. That's the last of that monkey business. My wife sleeps in my bed every night from now on."

"Then you understand how I feel." Johnny opened the door and waved them out. "Good night, gentlemen. I'll thank you tomorrow."

Pete had a parting shot as he went out the door. "We'll be back about midnight with a shivaree."

"You do and you'll get a load of buckshot in the rear." Johnny closed the door and opened his arms. "Come here to me, Mrs. Henry. I don't know how I'm going to do it, but I'm going to make up for five years of lost time."

When he kissed her, she returned his kisses fervently. She was afraid that after she told him about the baby, this wonderful loving man would feel that she had betrayed him.

"I've something to tell you." She closed her eyes and buried her face against his collarbone.

"I have a lot of things to tell you. Let's go to bed so I can hold you while I tell you how much I love you." He brushed her hair back from her face and looked into it earnestly. "Honey, this has been the worst week of my life. Worse than the week in the New Georgia Islands when eight thousand Japs were less than a mile away, bombing us at all hours of the day and night."

"I've always loved you. I want you to know that."

"I do. And I was a fool to put distance between us." He reached behind him and turned off the light.

In the bedroom, Johnny turned back the covers, took off his clothes, and got into bed. Kathleen came from the bathroom, leaving the light on and the door ajar.

"Do you mind if I leave the light on?"

"Leave it on, sweetheart. Just come here." He folded back the covers and held out his arms.

She slipped in beside him, closed her eyes when his arms went around her, and pressed her full length against him. *God*, she prayed. *Please don't let him turn from me when I tell him.*

"Oh, Lord! You feel so good." He sighed. "I've missed you so much."

"I've got to tell you—"

"Let me tell you." Johnny kissed her, then whispered, "I went to see Jude, and he told me that about next August we are going to have a baby."

Kathleen went still and waited.

"Is that what you were going to tell me?"

"Yes, but I was afraid—"

"He explained what had happened to Mary Rose. One baby out of several thousand is born like that. It wasn't my fault or yours. I was an ignorant, prideful fool who was too stiff-necked to go to someone who could explain it to me. Jude thinks that I'm a damn fool and don't deserve you. I knew that even before I thought I'd lost you."

"You want the baby?"

"I want the baby, sweetheart. I want all the babies you want to give me. Don't cry, honey. I love you so much. I didn't know how I was going to get through the rest of my life without you."

She kissed his neck, his chin, his rough cheeks until he

desperately sought her lips with his. The kiss lasted a long time and was full of sweetness.

She whispered that she loved him and she had been afraid he would think she had tricked him that morning.

"I was so hungry for you that a team of mules couldn't have stopped me from making love to you."

"I bought you a Christmas present."

"Yeah. What?"

"I'll give it to you Sunday when we go to Barker's."

"I was there Christmas. When you didn't show up for dinner, Barker and I went looking for you. He pulled every string he could trying to find you. Somehow I've got to make things up to him, too."

"He's been a good friend to me, Johnny. I think a lot of him and all the Flemings."

"I guess I've been jealous of all he could give you that I couldn't."

"I just wanted you, Johnny. From the first, it was you, only you."

"The first Christmas I was overseas, I made some things for you, but I was afraid to send them."

"I wish you had. I was so lonesome for you."

"You won't be lonesome anymore. Kiss me again and tell me you love me."

He pressed her hand to his chest. She could feel the powerful beating of his heart. Her fingers stroked the short hair curling from his brown skin. Leaning over him, her lips drifted down his chest, the taste of his warm, moist skin on her tongue. His body quivered, and she became aware of the movement against her thigh.

"You'd better stop, or I'll not be able to," he whispered.

"I don't want to stop."

"You've been through a lot today."

"But I'm here now . . . with you. You'll never get away from me again. I'll nag you, chase you, hang on to you." She nipped his chin.

"I want you. I'm about to burst wanting you."

"I know," she said happily. "I can feel it."

"Maybe you should rest for this little cowboy's sake." His big hand covered her belly.

"He won't care. He's in there snug as a bug." She slipped her arms around his neck. "I want you to love me."

His lips crushed hers hungrily. "Then I'll love you— that is, if you think he won't mind." He punctuated his words with soft, but firm kisses.

Epilogue

August 23, 1946

MOTHER AND CHILD FINE

FATHER A NERVOUS WRECK

Mr. and Mrs. Johnny Henry are the proud parents of a dark-haired seven-pound boy who was promptly named John Barker Henry. Dr. Jude Perry, assisted by his wife, Nurse Theresa Perry, was forced to eject the father from the delivery room for causing a commotion.

The story ran in a black box on the front page of the *Rawlings Gazette*. Paul and Adelaide jokingly considered putting an extra out on the street.

The morning after the birth, a spotted pony was tied up in front of the clinic with a gift tag that read: To little Johnny from Uncle Pete and Aunt Dale. Johnny swore to get even when at noon, he had to leave Kathleen and the baby, carry a bucket of water to the pony, and clean up a pile of manure.

*   *   *

It had been a year like no other.

For months Kathleen's kidnapping and what occurred afterward had been the talk of the town, county, and state. Much had been learned about Theodore Nuding. To sum it up, he was wealthy, very intelligent, cunning, and insane.

When the autopsy was performed on his body investigators found no evidence that he was ill. The doctors theorized that he believed so strongly that a curse had been passed down to him from his mother that when he started having severe migraine headaches, he was convinced that he was about to die. It was the poison that had killed him, as it had Harry Cole.

His attorney came forward to claim the body, and Nuding was buried in a corner of the Rawlings cemetery with only the attorney present.

The only explanation of Theodore Nuding's obsession with Kathleen seemed to stem from the fact that her name was Kathleen and her hair was red. Pictures of his mother, whose name was also Kathleen, had shown that she, too, had red hair. According to his journals, for more than twenty years he had kept his mother in a room similar to the one he had prepared for Kathleen.

The story of Theodore Nuding was so amazing that the University of Oklahoma Medical School asked permission from his estate to study his journals.

A few days after the burial, Kathleen and Johnny received the startling news that Kathleen was the sole heir to the Nuding estate, which included the stock in Hidendall corporation, property in Oklahoma City, the Clifton ranch, thousands in savings bonds, and almost a hundred thousand dollars in cash in a lockbox at the bank in Oklahoma City.

The will had been signed and dated a month before the

war ended and while Kathleen was working at the aircraft plant. It was unclear why Theodore was working there. He was financially secure and was not in danger of being drafted into service. He was registered as 4-F, because he had a major heart murmur.

The first words out of Kathleen's mouth when told of the inheritance were, "I don't want it."

"There is a provision made for that," the lawyer said. "If you should refuse to accept the inheritance, the entire estate will go to Iva Togori."

"Let her have it."

"Iva Togori is the woman known as Tokyo Rose. Mr. Nuding believed you to be a patriot who would not want a traitor who had broadcast propaganda to our men in the Pacific Theater to take money back to the Japanese who had killed so many of our men."

"What shall I do, Johnny?"

"The decision is yours, honey."

"I don't want her to have it."

"Mr. Nuding was counting on that," the lawyer said. "Do you have a lawyer in the city?"

"Johnny, would Mr. Gifford be our lawyer? You've known him for a long time."

"Grant Gifford?" the lawyer asked. "I know him well. He's out of public office now. If you wish, I'll work with him on this."

Grant Gifford took over as financial advisor and manager of the estate. At first, Kathleen feared Johnny would be stiff-necked about the inheritance. She immediately had it transferred to both names, meaning that his signature was required on all documents.

As soon as the money was available, a large portion of

it was given to the clinic so that a wing could be built and a surgeon added to the staff.

The Rawlings library was enlarged to include a children's section, and funds to support a reading program and extended evening hours were provided.

A sum was set aside for Emily Ramsey's college education. She was the little girl whose mother was killed by Marty Conroy.

The Henry/Fleming scholarship fund for children of the Cherokee Nation who wanted to continue their education after high school was established, with Barker Fleming and Jacob Runs Fast as the trustees.

Johnny and Kathleen decided together that they would keep the Clifton ranch, but they would never live in the ranch house.

In the spring a full page ad was placed in the *Gazette* announcing that the Clifton house was being demolished. Anyone who in any way had helped search for Kathleen Henry when she was kidnapped and taken there was welcome to come and take whatever they wanted: windows, doors, stair railings, flooring, plumbing and electric fixtures, or lumber.

After two days, there was hardly enough left to make a good-sized bonfire.

Kathleen gave the wardrobe full of clothes to the church for their bazaar. Johnny suggested that she keep the emeralds and put them in a lockbox at the bank.

"They will be your security, honey, if we should have another Great Depression. The man owes you that for what he put you through."

In July the first Henry/Perry rodeo was held at the Rawlings fairgrounds. Willie and the Chicken Pluckers put on a warm-up show and were such a success that Pete booked them for rodeos in Ardmore, Duncan, and Elk City.

In August the remodeling was completed on the Circle H ranch house in time for Johnny to bring his wife and son home.

CHRISTMAS, 1946

The old Nash, sporting new tires and a fresh paint job, stopped in front of the Fleming ranch house. The Henrys were reluctant to give up the old car even though a new Dodge sat in the garage at home.

Johnny, carrying his son, followed Kathleen with a basket of gifts, to the door. Barker opened it immediately.

"Merry Christmas," sang the chorus behind him.

"Merry Christmas to you," came the cheerful reply.

"John Barker, go to grandpa while I take off my coat," Johnny said after he had stepped inside the door.

Barker took the child to the rocking chair beside the fireplace.

"You'll never guess what Daddy got John Barker for Christmas," Janna said from behind her hand.

"Don't tell me it's a tomahawk." Johnny, now totally at ease at the Flemings', liked to tease his youngest sister.

"How did you know?" Janna retorted, and flounced away.

"Surely not!" Kathleen grabbed Johnny's hand and held on to it tightly.

"If his grandpa gave him a tomahawk, we'll hang it on the wall until he's old enough to use it."

"Johnny!"

He pulled her to him. "Lord, honey. No one could have

made me believe last Christmas that I could be so happy this Christmas."

"You always have been too stubborn for your own good, Johnny Henry, but I love you . . . mightily!"

"But not as much as I love you, Kathleen Henry."

"All right, you two, stop necking." Marie was sitting with Bobby on the couch. "This year we're going to open the presents on Christmas Day. Last year we didn't open them until New Year's Day."

"That's not a bad idea. Let's do it this year." Johnny held Kathleen close to him.

"It's a rotten idea," Lucas snorted.

"What do you know about it? You're just a skinny, ugly kid." Johnny roughed Lucas's hair.

"Soon I'll be big enough to whop your . . . ass—er . . . hind." Lucas darted a quick glance at his father.

"All right, boys." Barker held John Barker firmly against his shoulder and gently patted his back. "Settle down or I'll have to get up and whop both your hinds."

"We'd better watch it, Lucas," Johnny said in a loud whisper. "The chief is about to go on the warpath."

The girls giggled.

Lucas snickered.

Johnny laughed.

Kathleen stood back and watched the horseplay between her husband and his young brother and could almost thank Theodore Nuding for the despicable act that had brought them all together as a family.

PETE PERRY'S CORN BREAD

½ cup flour
2 cups yellow cornmeal
1 egg, slightly beaten
1 teaspoon salt
3 teaspoons baking
  powder
2 tablespoons sugar
1 small can cream-style
  corn
½ cup milk
Mix and Beat Vigorously

Add:
½ cup finely chopped
  green onions
¼ cup chopped bell
  pepper or green
  chilies

In a 9 X 13-inch cake pan, or 12-inch heavy iron skillet (preferred) melt a large tablespoon of lard, Crisco, or meat drippings in a 375° oven. Pour melted grease into the cornmeal batter, mix well. Bake in the skillet or pan until golden brown 35 to 45 minutes.

DOROTHY GARLOCK is one of America's—and the world's—favorite novelists. Her work consistently appears on national bestseller lists, including the *New York Times* extended list, and there are over fifteen million copies of her books in print translated into eighteen languages. She has won more than twenty writing awards, including five Silver Pen Awards from *Affaire de Coeur* and three Silver Certificate Awards, and in 1998 she was selected as a finalist for the National Writer's Club Best Long Historical Book Award.

After retiring as a news reporter and bookkeeper in 1978, she began her career as a novelist with the publication of *Love and Cherish*. She lives in Clear Lake, Iowa. You can visit her Web site at www.dorothygarlock.com.